Worldwide Praise for the Riveting, Revelatory Erotica of John Patrick and STARbooks!

"If you're an avid reader of all-male erotica and haven't yet discovered editor John Patrick's series of torrid anthologies, you're in for a treat. ...These books will provide hours of cost-effective entertainment."
— *Lance Sterling, Beau magazine*

"John Patrick is a modern master of the genre! ...This writing is what being brave is all about. It brings up the kinds of things that are usually kept so private that you think you're the only one who experiences them."
— *Gay Times, London*

"'Barely Legal' is a great potpourri ... and the coverboy is gorgeous!"
— *Ian Young, Torso magazine*

"A huge collection of highly erotic, short and steamy one-handed tales. Perfect bedtime reading, though you probably won't get much sleep! Prepare to be shocked! Highly recommended!"
— *Vulcan magazine*

"Tantalizing tales of porn stars, hustlers, and other lost boys...John Patrick set the pace with 'Angel'!"
— *The Weekly News, Miami*

"... Some readers may find some of the scenes too explicit; others will enjoy the sudden, graphic sensations each page brings. ...A strange, often poetic vision of sexual obsession. I recommend it to you."
— *Nouveau Midwest*

"'Dreamboys' is so hot I had to put extra baby oil on my fingers, just to turn the pages! ... Those blue eyes on the cover are gonna reach out and touch you ..."
— *Bookazine's Hot Flashes*

"I just got 'Intimate Strangers' and by the end of the week I had read it all. Great stories! Love it!"
— *L.C., Oregon*

"'Superstars' is a fast read...if you'd like a nice round of fireworks before the Fourth, read this aloud at your next church picnic ..."
— *Welcomat, Philadelphia*

"Yes, it's another of those bumper collections of steamy tales from STARbooks. The rate at which John Patrick turns out these compilations you'd be forgiven for thinking it's not exactly quality prose. Wrong. These stories are well-crafted, but not over-written, and have a profound effect in the pants department."
— *Vulcan magazine, London*

"For those who share Mr. Patrick's appreciation for cute young men, 'Legends' is a delightfully readable book...I am a fan of John Patrick's ... His writing is clear and straight forward and should be better known in the gay community."

— Ian Young, Torso Magazine

"... Touching and gallant in its concern for the sexually addicted, 'Angel' becomes a wonderfully seductive investigation of the mysterious disparity between lust and passion, obsession and desire."

— Lambda Book Report

"John Patrick has one of the best jobs a gay male writer could have. In his fiction, he tells tales of rampant sexuality. His nonfiction involves first person explorations of adult male video stars. Talk about choice assignments!"

— Southern Exposure

"The title for 'Boys of Spring' is taken from a poem by Dylan Thomas, so you can count on high caliber imagery throughout."

— Walter Vatter, Editor, A Different Light Review

Book of the Month Selections in Europe and the U.K. Featured by A Different Light, Oscar Wilde Bookshop, Lambda Rising and GR, Australia and available at fine booksellers everywhere

They play hard, they get hard, they fuck hard ...

Play Hard,
Score BIG

A Collection of Erotic Tales
Edited By
JOHN PATRICK

STARbooks Press

Books by John Patrick

A Charmed Life: Vince Cobretti
Lowe Down: Tim Lowe
The Best of the Superstars 1990
The Best of the Superstars 1991
The Best of the Superstars 1992
The Best of the Superstars 1993
The Best of the Superstars 1994
The Best of the Superstars 1995
The Best of the Superstars 1996
The Best of the Superstars 1997
The Best of the Superstars 1998
The Best of the Superstars 1999
What Went Wrong?
When Boys Are Bad
& Sex Goes Wrong
Legends: The World's Sexiest
Men, Vols. 1 & 2
Legends (Third Edition)
Tarnished Angels (Ed.)
Billy & David: A Deadly Minuet
The Bigger They Are...
The Younger They Are...
The Harder They Are...
Angel: The Complete Trilogy
Angel II: Stacy's Story
Angel: The Complete Quintet
A Natural Beauty (Editor)
The Kid (with Joe Leslie)
HUGE (Editor)
Strip: He Danced Alone
The Boys of Spring
Big Boys/Little Lies (Editor)
Boy Toy
Seduced (Editor)
Insatiable/Unforgettable (Editor)
Heartthrobs
Runaways/Kid Stuff (Editor)
Dangerous Boys/Rent Boys (Editor)
Barely Legal (Editor)
Country Boys/City Boys (Editor)
My Three Boys (Editor)
Mad About the Boys (Editor)
Lover Boys (Editor)
In the BOY ZONE (Editor)
Boys of the Night (Editor)
Secret Passions (Editor)
Beautiful Boys (Editor)
Juniors (Editor)
Come Again (Editor)
Smooth 'N' Sassy (Editor)
Intimate Strangers (Editor)
Naughty By Nature (Editor)
Dreamboys (Editor)
Raw Recruits (Editor)
Play Hard, Score Big (Editor)

Contents

Editor's Note

Most of the stories appearing in this book take place prior to the years of The Plague; the editor and each of the authors represented herein advocate the practice of safe sex at all times. And, because these stories trespass the boundaries of fiction and non-fiction, to respect the privacy of those involved, we've changed all of the names and other identifying details.

INTRODUCTION: PLAYING HARD, SCORING BIG
by John Patrick

If you want to play hard, it helps to go outdoors. At least, that's the advice of Philip Gambone in *Frontiers*. "The phrase '*nei giardini, di sera*' (in the gardens, at night), which appears so often in my Italian gay guide, may sound like a stage direction from *The Marriage of Figaro*, but it's indicative, especially in the South, of how gay men meet in Italy. For example, the *Guida Gay* offers many of listings for outdoor cruising areas in Naples piazzas, the railroad stations, public toilets, parks, market areas and beaches. In contrast, there are only two gay bars listed for the entire city, which is almost twice as large as Boston."

Of course, in Italy, you can find sex *indoors* as well. Lots of it. "The farther north you go," Gambone writes, "the more gay bathhouses, called *saune* in Italian, you'll find. Rome has two. Milan, five. On my trip through Tuscany two years ago, I checked out the Florence Baths, a fairly clean and attractive facility that also serves as a kind of health club, snack bar and general meeting place. There I met several Italian men, including Luciano, a guy from outside Florence who lives on a farm with his sister. Luciano seemed typical of many of the Italians who were there that Saturday afternoon. Hard-working and modestly prosperous, he would come to the Florence Baths every so often to enjoy some 'gay space' and perhaps find a sexual partner.

"The activity at the baths seemed about evenly divided between sex and conversation, some of it between friends who had met there, some between strangers newly acquainted. I wrote in my journal: 'A gross generalization but here goesCthe Italians want to talk. The foreigners want to have sex.' Like all generalizations, this one was challenged by other men I met who offered different opinions.

"Simone, a blond, 28-year-old Danish-Italian I talked to at the gay beach near Torre del Lago two summers ago, told me that the only thing Italian gay men wanted to do was have sex. Abel, an Egyptian with a university degree who was working as a cook in Siena told me, in broken Italian, that he found Italian gay men to be the weirdest people in all of Europe. Sex with Italian men was just about impossible, he said. Still, he seemed to think that there was quite a bit of sex available in Florence. He had tried to hang there for a few months but didn't like it because, in fact, there was too much sex available morning, afternoon, evening which made it impossible to concentrate on anything else!"

One of those hot Italian men plays hard in Jim Hillman's delightful story, "Angel" (in the anthology *Hard* from Black Wattle Press), at, of all places, a peepshow: "Even with the door to the cubicle almost closed I could still keep my eye on the entrance through the crack next to the door jamb. I could already gauge the Italian man's curiosity from the one thing he said in the auditorium. With both the old man and me in here I was certain he would follow. He did. He stood in the doorway and checked out the room. He could not see me but I watched through the crack as the expression on his face changed when he caught

Edited by John Patrick

sight of what the old queen was doing in the open cubicle next door. His expression began with a grimace, then changed into a look of curiosity as he eyed my dick.

"From my vantage point I could see that he was fascinated by the way my cock went from flaccid to rigid while the mouth beyond the hole licked around the head and shaft. A bottle of amyl was passed between my legs, which I accepted and drew on heavily. As I got the full rush I imagined the warm, slimy mouth pumping the length of my shaft belonged to the man outside. As the fumes subsided, I realized that my cock was no longer being sucked; instead, a hand fumbled with my equipment. The stranger was no longer visible through the crack.

"The hand tugged once on my cock and the same voice said, 'You've got a big cock, mate.' He then made a clumsy attempt at sucking me and scraped my shaft painfully with his teeth. My reflexes drew me away. I pulled my jeans up and stepped outside. The old queen was offering the man amyl, which he bluntly pushed away. This time it was me taking my chances so I dropped my jeans to my ankles and said, 'You like it, huh? Then kneel down and suck it properly.'

"I was surprised that a straight man would want to suck cock when I thought they were so frightened of catching AIDS. I thought of the words of a friend, 'All men are sluts.' Maybe this guy proved it. Although he gagged on my cock several times he kept sucking me and I could tell he wanted to see me come. He wasn't good enough at giving head to keep me hard so I pulled out and made him stand up.

"Just to complete the whole fantasy his smallish but very handsome dick came with foreskin intact. I sucked the tip of his prick and licked inside; his whole body lurched. I couldn't stop wondering what this man thought of me; did he despise me or did he desire me? I reached up under his shirt for his nipples, but he pulled my hands away. I took that as a sign that this was to be just a blowjob. I supposed that he viewed that type of arousal as taboo, too easily identified as homosexual. His swollen cock drooped slightly to the right.

"In the red incandescent glow it was hard to see him clearly, but his pent-up sex oozed through the darkness. The only bodily contact he allowed were my two hands gripped firmly on the back of his thighs just below (but not on) the cheeks of his bum. I could have been anyone, man or woman. Was that what turned me on? His dick was covered by a perfect sheath of skin darker than the rest of him.

"I looked up at him to see what was in his eyes. He was not even looking at me; his eyes were closed. He looked so fucking beautiful although I wasn't even seeing him totally naked. I wanted to stroke the rest of him so badly but feared that he would balk and leave. I swallowed him and bore up and down on his shaft using my lips and tongue. He groaned and put his hand on the back of my head, coaxing me on and off him. It seemed, from his reaction, that no one had ever pleasured him this way before.

- 2 -

"At that moment I felt I had some power over him and could read exactly what was going on in his mind via the distended muscle in his groin. His knees bent, his back arched, and he blew down the back of my throat, his entire body writhed with convulsion. This brought on my own orgasm and I shot a stream of cum between his legs, all over the pants that were now around his ankles. We both took a long time to recover. Eventually I got to my feet, spat his cum out and looked right into his eyes."

In his novel *Milkman's On His Way*, David Rees tells about how the narrator Ewan went to play at the beach and scored big: "I thought nothing so marvelous would ever happen to me again; indeed, I wondered if I had just dreamed it all.... The cloudless September weather held hot, still. We lay on the beach and walked along country lanes, and in the evenings we went to the cottage, then, later, to a pub.... All the clichés: walking on air, strolling hand in hand into the sunset.

"It was not, now, two boys masturbating, one of them imagining the other was a girl. Screwing. At first I was frightened; it would be painful, I thought. Did I really feel an urge for this? It was, perhaps, a denial of my maleness? I should penetrate: that was what it was for. Wasn't it? Everybody said so. Into Paul? The idea was ridiculous. I wanted him inside me; I wanted to be fucked. Only that would give me absolute satisfaction, emotionally.

"'If it hurts,' he said, kissing me, stroking me with his fingers, 'I won't do it. I promise. This will make it easier'.

"'What?'

"'KY. A lubricant.'

"Pain, yes, quite severe he wasn't small but only for a moment as he entered: after that, though it still hurt a bit (I would get used to that in time; indeed soon there was never any discomfort), it was the most natural, normal and utterly beautiful experience. His hand, still slippery with KY, on my cock, a sensation more superb than any I had ever felt, then orgasm so perfect I thought I was changed from a body into pure dazzling light. And he, coming, the spurt and gasp of him inside me: oh, yes; this is what life is for, Ewan: for this I was made."

Unfortunately, some of us don't start playing hard until very late. In his book *Life Outside*, Michelangelo Signorile talks about Lonely Old Queens, specifically Arthur, a seventy-three-year-old retiree who has spent much of his life picking up younger men on the streets, in bars, and in other locales. As he sits with the writer in his comfortable condominium apartment, he laments about the gay world and his own relationship to it.

"I just want to surround myself with these young guys," he says. "I love watching them, and I love their bodies. But then, even if they do want me to give them a blowjob, I think that's kind of freakish and weird because I can't believe someone would be attracted to men my own age. I think I'm, well, quite honestly, *grotesque*. I think all older men are. I'm in no way even remotely

attracted to men my own age, and I don't like to hang around people my age."

Signorile reports: "Though he had been having furtive gay sex since his teen years, Arthur didn't come out to family, friends, and colleagues until he was sixty-seven. For most of his life he played the role of a heterosexual, dating women but picking up men on the side. He says that for many years he'd have sex every night with men he'd meet on the street or in bars and believes in fact that his compulsiveness was spurred by his having to remain so secretive."

"When I was living in L.A. many years ago, I was picking up guys on Hollywood Boulevard every night," Arthur says. "Then New York, on Forty-second Street, in dirty movies, in bars. It is the only intimacy I knew, the only way I could be close to a man. I couldn't have a relationship, but I wanted to be close to men. And I hated gays, hated myself. So I went out of my way never to pick up another gay person no, I was grossly homophobic, hated myself for doing this, and hated men who acted gay or said they were gay. I only picked on people who I perceived as straight men, men who wanted a blowjob. It wasn't until the instant I came out at the age of sixty-seven that I suddenly found gay men attractive beautiful, even."

Well, better late than never, we always say.

Speaking of playing hard, our favorite sportswatcher Jim Provenzano in the *Bay Area Reporter* made note that the following story was nestled discreetly in a corner of the *SF Examiner/Chronicle* Sports section: "New Hockey Sex Scandal. Another sex abuse scandal is jolting the jockey world of Canada involving allegations that staff at Maple Leaf Gardens lured boys into sex with offers of free tickets and player autographs.

"One alleged victim says he was part of a sex ring from 1975 to 1982 in which group sex took place in the back rooms of the building, sometimes during the Toronto Maple Leafs games.

"A former maintenance worker at the arena, Gordon Stuckless, appeared in court... on charges of indecent assault and gross indecency....

"At least two other arena employees, one of them deceased, allegedly were involved in a sex ring."

This was followed by another story about 54-year-old John Robey who worked at the Gardens for 25 years. He turned himself in after being exposed as the one who "allegedly lured boys into sex with free tickets and other enticements."

Mainstream newspapers, Provenzano asserts, have been shocking readers for some time with this "sex ring" business. "I have had sex in possibly every position known to man, and a few not. I've boinked less than your average Casanova, but more than a Benedictine monk. I've done it in, on, and around locker rooms, in groups, and alone. But I have never, for the life of me, recognized, categorized, or consummated anything that has consciously been called a SEX RING. What the hell is a sex ring? The 'ring' connotation has deep, dark Dante-esque implications, rituals in the woods, that sort of stuff. A

bit of it also has a morbid allure of grotesquery, like ringworm. Then there's that group sex ambiance, daisy chains performed by Julian Beck's Open Theater behind a rest stop on I-90. Now, this may not be your cup of jizz, and these days it ain't mine either. But are you 'jolted?' Are you 'shocked?'

"The implication behind the term, and the rhetoric, is sexphobic, and heterosexist, and bullshit. A sex ring, the mainstream media implies, is disgusting! They cannot imagine anything more than two people having sex in a married, monogamous, missionary position. Beyond that, anything is more of an alien mutation of breeding, something foreign, perverted, nefariously concocted and deserving of eradication, and not what it really is, which is the normal sexual behavior of human creatures.

"Besides, the concept of trading sexual favors for goods is the foundation on which our economy is founded.

"Sex Ring could also have certain Wagnerian implications, too, but this is not the arts section, and there's more than enough opera writing over there. The *Chronicles* articles and the subsequent shuffled-away court case (they're just Canadians, after all) will not shed light on the real facts of this case, i.e., how old were the 'boys' who were 'assaulted' by these crotchety old men. How often did they return for more 'autographs,' and, of course, to get down to the rank odiferous details, *what really happened?* Boyd McDonald would have gone to town on this one, particularly with the juicy tidbit of knowing that the sex took place in the stadium. Now, isn't that every boy's dream to get balled in the ballpark, to score on the field, to get the goal, by luck or by puck? Who wouldn't want to get holed by Hull?

"I'd let any 54-year-old groundskeeper, usher, or even hot dog vendor salaciate me, so long as I could get a free whiff of the locker room, or even catch a glimpse of Steve Vickers *apres la douche.*

"...And what forces compelled them to turn in their compatriots in sin? Didn't they like the free tickets and 'other enticements'? And how exactly do you define sexual 'assault' when a young man says, 'Okay?'

"And what is it that prevented these young men from just not returning to the Maple Leaf Gardens over and over again from 1975 to 1982? Did they suffer from that common affliction of being possessed by the hockey sex demon? Or was it the magnetic power of *The Sex Ring*? That must have been it!"

So now, dear reader, you are about to join a "sex ring" of our own, featuring several of our favorite authors, and where the playing is always hard and never dull!

SLOW DANCE AT DAWN
by John Patrick

"New account!" my manager hollered when I walked into work at the bakery where I was holding down a summer job. "Bread and rolls. Take the trays on the early run."

I made my regular deliveries first. Nell's Diner opened for breakfast at five-thirty; I was at the delivery door by five with an otherwise empty truck and no need to rush. I carried the bread into the kitchen and tried to look nonchalant when I gave the cook the invoice to sign. He initialed it with a flourish. I separated his copy and met his eyes. He was a little taller than me, about 25, and rather handsome in a blunt sort of way.

"You look familiar," he said, his curly dark hair falling seductively over his forehead.

"I guess I look like a lot of guys," I responded.

"Yeah, like maybe that cute little Gibb brother." Andy Gibb had a number-one single at the time. I was flattered. I smiled, but I didn't know what else to say so I clipped the delivery slip to my board and muttered, "I'll be back tomorrow."

"Wait a minute." He looked at the wall clock. "Grab a seat at the counter." The clock showed five-ten. I could spare five minutes. I left him in the kitchen and pushed through the swinging doors into the diner. I sat at the counter and looked around. A row of booths divided the windows. Blinds had not yet been raised and a sign reading "Closed" still hung in the front door. The counter stretched neatly around a gleaming grill. He came out of the kitchen with a plate of food. He pushed it in front of me and my mouth began to water.

"Here." He set a fork next to the plate. "It's my own recipe. Tell me what you think."

I dug in a forkful. Steam swirled over the plate. I blew on the omelet, then chewed. I looked up in surprise. "It's good." I tried another forkful. "Very good."

I studied the plate as I ate. It was probably the biggest omelet I'd ever seen. It was also the best omelet I'd ever eaten. Bart sure knew how to throw eggs together.

He smiled. "It's the fresh tomatoes. The crisp bacon."

I cleaned the plate and licked the fork. "Thanks."

He said, "See you tomorrow?"

"For sure."

I began to plan my morning deliveries a little earlier, arriving at the diner with time to spare for breakfast. At the quiet counter before opening time, Bart fed me his specialty omelets and toast and hash browns. We got into the habit of conversation with a cup of coffee.

"I miss the juke box," he said one morning, out of the blue.

"I was in a diner once," I offered. "They had jukes on every table. It was

really neat."

"Seen those in a catalogue. The owner, old Nell, says music is a nighttime thing." He gestured to the TV above the counter. "She says folks want news in the morning, talk shows at break time and more news at noon."

"Not the same as music," I agreed.

Bart pushed his coffee cup aside and leaned over the counter. "Just once," he confided, "I'd like to have a jukebox in here and someone to drop a quarter and say, 'Hey, Bart, how about a slow dance.'" He looked at me closely and my fork rattled against my plate. He stood back, laughing. "That would be something. A slow dance and a side of hash browns." His strong fingers tapped a tune on the counter.

I finished my coffee and slid off the counter stool. "See you tomorrow, Bart."

He said, "Hey, son, I'll be here."

A week went by before I got up the nerve to take my portable tape player into the diner. That day, after I had unloaded the delivery, I said, "Hold on a sec, Bart. I've got something in the van."

He frowned at the receipt. "That's everything, isn't it?"

"Almost."

I walked through the kitchen and set the player on the counter. Bart followed me through the swinging doors.

"How 'bout a dance?" I croaked. I cleared my throat. "I'd like a slow dance, please, and a side of hash browns."

He shook his head, turned away and walked toward the front door. I stood with my hand frozen on the tape player, my feet immobile beside the counter. He pulled the shade.

When he turned back, a smile was brightening his face. "What are you waitin' for? Start the music, pretty boy."

I watched as he lifted his apron over his head.

The Carpenters began to sing "Close to You."

"I thought it should be old-fashioned, like an old diner juke box."

He lifted my hand and placed it on his hip.

I took the hint and put his hands on my shoulders. I linked my fingers and pulled him a little closer.

We kept on swaying gently, even when the song had ended. Then, before I could step away and stop the tape, he slid his hands across my shoulders. I felt his fingers on my scalp and my head bent up to his.

And that was how I shared my first kiss with Bart at the diner before opening time, after the day's deliveries and a slow dance, our crotches rubbing together sensuously.

Suddenly, he let go of me. He appeared a bit flustered, and said, "Now, how about that side of hash browns?" He disappeared into the kitchen. I sat at the counter, trying to catch my breath. I wasn't sure I could eat breakfast if I couldn't breathe. Bart's kiss had literally taken my breath away.

Bart came back with two plates, which was also a new thing. Usually he just had coffee while I ate.

But this time he came around the counter and sat next to me, and when the tape was through, I flipped it over and pushed the play button again.

"I didn't mean to do that," he said.

"What?"

"Kiss you. I don't know what came over me."

"I wanted you to" I reached over and placed my hand on the obvious bulge in his jeans.

"You sure you?"

I answered by kissing him this time, but he soon took over, wrapping me in his arms, drawing me over on top of him. If I had thought our first kiss was incredible, this one was even better.

I came into Bart's arms and we kissed and my heart leapt with desire and hope as my lips parted. Bart's hands couldn't stop moving. He frantically sought and released the buttons and zippers binding my clothing. I lay back against the counter, my shirt open, my pants open, my cock ready. He began by running his tongue underneath my erection, making it throb and pulse. Wanting release and begging him for it, I pumped my hips up and down. I ran my fingers through his long black curls and moaned as his tongue licked and caressed my swollen cock, then tongue-washed my balls. I couldn't remember when my cock stood so hard and erect, begging, begging until at last Bart's practiced mouth closed over it. Feeling my fullness, knowing I was close, Bart took my cock in both hands, the tip of his tongue flicking over and over the head. Then he sucked it in and out. I arched my body, my hands pressing his face closer. The spasms began, shaking my body. I came, and, gasping and panting, I begged him to stop. The cock dropped from his mouth but over and over he kissed it, refusing to let go.

"You are perfect," he murmured. He lifted his head, hair streaming, face wet like someone rising from the sea. He narrowed his eyes as I leaned back. "This is a perfect cock. I love this cock."

I moaned, feeling free now to let him know I would reciprocate if he asked. I swallowed hard, asked, "Is there anything I can do for you, Bart?"

"No," he said, wiping some of my cum from his mouth. "Not now. It's late. I have to be openin' soon."

- - -

I made it a habit after that to bring the tape player with the bakery delivery. Sometimes Bart had coffee on the other side of the counter; sometimes he sat with me and we ate together.

And sometimes, when the deliveries could wait, and the first waitress had not yet arrived on shift, Bart would lock the delivery door and pull the front shade. In that early half-hour of the morning, I'd start the music and say, confidently, "A slow dance, please, and a side of hash browns." Then Bart would come into my arms and we'd dance around the diner, usually to Andy Gibb singing "I Just

Want to be Your Everything," which Bart said was "our song."

Then, before breakfast, he'd suck me off.

I also got into the habit of stopping by the diner on my way home from work. Those afternoons found me cleaning grease vents and scrubbing grills, side by side with Bart. It was then I discovered that the reason Bart had not invited me to his home was because that he was married to "old Nell," that she was in fact his "old lady," and he enjoyed having a little on the side. Nell would come in, do some bookwork and leave. She paid no mind to me.

One morning Bart surprised me by saying that his wife worked the morning shift on the weekends and he wondered if I'd like to stop by his house for a "slow dance."

"No hash browns?"

"Oh," he snickered, "I think we can work something up."

What he worked up was a boner, the first time I'd seen it. But before we got to that, we danced. It was strange at first, dancing with Bart in the bedroom he obviously shared with Nell. I was a starry-eyed teenager, hardly believing this was happening.

He gripped my firm ass, pulling me closer. I smiled when I felt his erection pressing into mine. We swayed together, gliding across the floor, caressing each other. When Bart led me closer to the bed and started kissing me, I thought how wonderful it would be to feel his tongue dancing elsewhere. As if reading my thoughts, he pushed me to the bed and soon his fingers were fluttering across my erection. Teasing me with his fingers, setting me on fire with his mouth. I moaned as he pressed tightly against me.

I felt my orgasm building, my breath quickening. Bart, as usual, took it all; he swallowed every drop of my cum.

But instead of kissing my cock and licking it after I shot, he felt me panting on the bed and he stripped.

My eyes were wide when he turned and stood beside the bed. He was huge, easily the biggest cock I'd ever seen to that point in my young life. I guessed it was twice as thick as mine, and a good three inches longer. I knelt on the bed and did my best, although I was quite the neophyte in those days.

"Do it, baby! Do it now!" he ordered me.

Opening my mouth wide to accommodate his huge organ, I finally took Bart into my mouth. Tears stung my eyes as I tried to get it all down my throat. I gagged, and the cock slipped out. I coughed.

Bart stepped closer, stabbing his cock deep into my throat. He began fucking my mouth, thrusting his organ in and out, plunging deeper and deeper into my throat. Soon he was moaning with pleasure as he enjoyed the warmth of my mouth around his prick. In and out, the voltage seeming to grow stronger with each climactic moment. But he didn't come. He pulled out and lay on his back, his legs bent and spread open to accommodate my head. Bart's cock was so hot and swollen with his excitement, and I sucked it hungrily into my mouth. My

fingers played with the tuft of pubic hair.

Unable to control himself, he feverishly pushed his legs in, encircling my head, pressing closer. Soon he was cooing and purring as he thrust his hips forward, encouraging me to suck harder. As the spasms rocked his hairy, wiry body, I pulled the cock from my mouth and began kissing it. I didn't stop as the orgasm burst from his hot, swollen prick. The cum was soon dripping off my cheeks. Then I sighed, my fingers resting over the throbbing organ.

We lay quietly then, surrounded by Andy Gibb's music, ever so sweet and sensual.

- - -

A couple of weeks later, I went off to college, but whenever I went back home, I always stopped in before dawn at Nell's for a slow dance with a side of hash browns.

THE ALTAR OF THE BOY
by John Patrick

"Ben is always talking about boys. He never stops talking about boys. He also sometimes refers to an imaginary creature called the Boy. The Boy is a mysterious reference to a generic totem to all boys in all lands that Ben worships on the altar of the Boy."
— *Gus Van Sant, "Pink"*

A month before I was to graduate, I was being sucked off by my history teacher, Dr. Ingmar. He was doing this just to help me out. I needed a B or better in his class to keep my scholarship and the course was very strange to me, so now I was going to get the grade I needed.

I would never have dreamt of letting myself be sucked off by someone as strange as this guy, but at one point during the grunting and groping I smelled his hair, his stiff, white-yellow shock of old Swedish ancestral hair, and it brought back memories of Jason, and a haystack that we played around in back on our farm, when we owned one, a memory that I love.

My orgasm with this man I had otherwise no attraction for at all was so intense I nearly passed out. Dr. Ingmar held me tight around my middle as he deep-throated me and took all my cum. I decided he was a pretty damn good cocksucker after all.

My father always said you can find some good in everyone, one of many homilies he lived by. He was a jerk and a loser, a total failure, but he was right about that. But only when it came to sex. The rest was all bullshit.

It all started when Dr. Ingmar said, "Let's go for a drive." I smiled. He added, "So we can talk it all over."

He drove us to the Marina and across the Golden Gate Bridge into Marin County. The fog was heavy and wet.

"Right after I moved here, I had a dream," he told me. "I dream I was lying on a beach. The sun was so bright and the sand was like a giant, breathing body. In the dream it was like, finally, I was getting to do the stuff that everybody else did. I was lying on the beach with a boy!"

He took the first Mill Valley exit. Without the light from the freeway traffic, it was suddenly very dark.

"Why're we going to Mill Valley?" I asked.

"No reason. Just driving. Anyway, when I woke up I thought at first I'd dreamt about an actual memory, that I had gone to the beach with another boy. Then I realized there weren't any beaches where we grew up; it was just a dream. I felt somehow cheated."

I didn't say anything; I was just too scared. He was driving up a warren of narrow streets which wound around a steep hill. Then he slowed down and I got glimpses of people puttering about behind their windows, which was soothing to me. I missed having a normal home life. After we lost our farm, and came to the city, both my parents had to work and were seldom home.

He finally parked in a desolate place. I knew what was coming. He put his arms around me. "I'm sorry you're having such trouble with my class," he said. His embrace was soft, but muscular underneath. I lay in his arms, feeling safe.

We talked a bit, while he explored my body. He said how nicely put together I was, and got me hard. I can't recall ever being harder.

Then the blowjob began, and to come like that, it was amazing. It felt so good I wanted to make it go on forever.

I didn't need to make a second visit to Mill Valley, but I wanted to. Dr. Ingmar put me off, but finally agreed. On the way, I told Dr. Ingmar about me and Jason in the haystack. While I told my story, Dr. Ingmar stroked my cock.

Jason told me that he had "done it" with his sister, aged twelve. The girl in question was such a quiet little thing that I was really shocked and doubted the truth of his story. He was always making stuff up. To test him, I asked him if he would get her to do it with me, too. He said he would. One day we were playing up in the hay loft and Jason steered the conversation around to sex. She wanted to look at my "thing," I suppose to compare it to her brother's, and I let her. She told Jason to take his out. She sat there, holding both of our by-now stiff pricks. I wasn't ashamed, even though Jason's was about an inch longer than mine and thicker. I told her she had to do it with me. She didn't want to, but Jason made her.

So upon an altar of sweetly scented hay, under the dusty rafters of the barn, Jason's obedient sister offered up her hairless cunt. While her older brother looked on complacently, I shoved it in her. I came almost instantly. Then, Jason took my place and, without any embarrassment at my presence, shoved his cock in her and gave her a much longer, much better fuck than I had managed. Watching him do it turned me on uncontrollably and I jacked off into the hay before he even finished.

A week or so later, other boys were recruited and we all took turns fucking her. Jason, I noticed, remained the champ, with the biggest cock and the ability to sustain the longest fuck.

From that day on, I began to fantasize about Jason. I longed for the next time we would be together so I could watch his cock go into his sister. I didn't fuck her ever again, just watched as Jason did the deed, always shooting a load within minutes.

Then one day in the dead of winter, his sister disappeared. My folks said she "suffered a breakdown" and had to be locked up. I was horrified to think that our taking liberties with her may have caused her this trouble. Jason went with me to the hayloft and we talked about his sister. He said he didn't have any idea what was wrong with her, but he missed her terribly. "My cock sure misses her," he said, stroking the enormous bulge in his jeans.

Soon Jason was pressing hard against me. I reached around and grabbed his basket. I got a little carried away at this point, and I pulled his zipper down, pulled out his hot cock and kissed it with enthusiasm. He moaned in approval. I

sucked harder, then licked my way up his belly, then returned to the cock. I breathed warmly over it, inhaling deeply of the scent of his sweat. I began to lick around the head, then began to suck it in earnest. He ran his fingers through my hair as I sucked his cock head into my mouth and swirled my tongue around the underside. Then I began to lick down the shaft, and I couldn't believe how much pleasure this gave me. I began to tease his balls, too, kneading them very gently with my fingers as I licked up and down his shaft. I tried to swallow its whole length. I felt the head of his cock touching the back of my throat, still wrapped around perhaps four inches of Jason's meat and I took a deep breath and held it. Hungrily, I swallowed him all the way, pushing his cock down my throat until the shaft filled me. Jason was turned on so much he started to come. I pulled it out just in time, and his heavy load spurted out on the hay.

I could hardly wait to meet Jason in the haystack again, but he kept me waiting for nearly a week.

It was a sunny Sunday and everyone was at the church social. I talked Jason into leaving early.

I got nude right away and lay back waiting for him. He took a few moments to tantalize me with the sight of his huge prick, then he flung himself on the hay.

He was soon lying between my thighs while his fingers stroked my cock.

"I wanna fuck your pussy."

"I haven't got a pussy."

"Yes, you do. It's a boy-pussy."

"You're crazy."

"No, horny. Horny as hell."

He licked his way between my legs, my cock, my balls, between my buttocks, and then his fingers played with my ass. Before I could start thinking whether it was too much even in darkness, with a precise thrust of the fingers, coated with spit, he penetrated me. Then in and out, with slow, deliberate movements at first, then faster and faster. "Okay, you're ready."

He lifted up, spit on his cock.

"I want to watch it," I begged.

"Open your thighs," he told me firmly. "Spread your legs as wide as you can." Shaking, I forced myself to open my thighs wider. I was as open as possible, and ready to receive his big dick. I lay there nude, spreading my legs, exposed, anticipating with terror and dread, yet with a passionate hunger for the cock. I gasped as the pain flowed through me. Soon I was writhing in mixed pleasure and pain. I cried out and found myself trying to force my thighs together again, resisting. Jason was not pleased. "C'mon," he growled.

I breathed deeply, loving the sound of his threat. I felt him pushing my thighs open even wider as he forced himself in me. I watched in horror as his cock disappeared completely inside me. I spasmed in pain as he began. As the pain mounted, I felt myself giving my body over completely. He paused when he pulled all the way back, making me look at the swollen, gleaming cock, hard

with arousal. As he stroked himself, I could feel the throbbing in my own cock that told me I was going to come soon. He bent down and kissed my cock, biting and sucking at it as he leaned against me.

"Oh, God," I moaned as he chewed and suckled on my ball sac. Jason sensed that I was very close and he went back to shoving his cock back in me. Now he used just the right rhythm.

I was so close, and for the first time I begged him to fuck me. He smiled faintly. How could he refuse to heed so heart-rending an appeal for assistance? Particularly from one who wanted nothing better than the opportunity of worshipping his big cock, his beautiful body? Enthusiastic as he was to oblige me, he teased me by backing off. He was, I found out now, quite the exhibitionist, and as he knelt over me stroking his cock, my excitement was soaring, savoring the sight of the biggest dick I'd ever seen so close to orgasm. He was delighting in my writhing on the hay, desperate for release. Jason touched the tip of his prick against the entrance to my boy-pussy. With a whimper of surrender, I opened up for him again. He pushed the cock into me, and I whispered, "Oh, yes...oh, yes...." as I felt inch after inch going in. He worked his prick in and out of my ass, fucking me with it as I rocked my hips.

He was not ready, even yet. Instead, he drew the filthy prick from me and placed it against my lips. "Worship it," said he. "Worship the prick that was giving you such pleasure."

"Oh, yes," I heard myself whispering. I accepted the slimy cock into my mouth. I licked it obediently. When Jason drew it away, I tried to relax into the pain I knew was coming.

"Oh, god," was all I could say as Jason paused, torturing me with that moment of anticipation. Then he shoved it in me, sending a surge of pain through my ass and my whole body. I let my breath out as a moan as the pain flowed through my body. I squirmed until Jason commanded me to hold still while he fucked me. My moans grew louder, and I whispered, "Fuck me, please!"

The strokes increased in frequency, the pain rising until I was overwhelmed with the agony. It was unbelievable. I was still on the edge of orgasm, ready to climax. My breath came in great shuddering gasps. Then I felt his mouth on mine, felt his tongue thrusting in. Then Jason settled down on top of me as his cock went into me all the way. And as he plunged into my boy-pussy, I came, moaning wildly and shuddering underneath the thrusting weight of Jason's sweating body. My orgasm was intense and quick, overwhelming me. As I finished my climax, I felt Jason's thrusts slowing, as he began to fuck me with all the tenderness he could muster. He now took his time and made love to me slowly, his thrusts perfectly controlled. I savored every entrance into me, my gasps and moans growing as Jason continued. After many long minutes of thrusting, I felt Jason getting closer, and I lost myself in the ecstasy of the moment.

I felt him easing his cock out of me, felt him crawling on top of me and again guiding his cock up to my face. Now it was coated with his cum. I parted my lips and accepted the head of his cock into my mouth, worshiping it once more with my tongue and lifting my head to thrust as much of his shaft into my mouth as I could. I licked all around his head and the underside of his shaft, working very hard to pleasure him even though in this position I could hardly move my head. I did manage to get it hard again, however.

Satisfied, Jason slid down my body, positioning himself over me again, and put his renewed cock up against my boy-pussy. With one thrust, he entered me again and started to fuck me fast and furious. The tempo of his fucking was increasing, going deeper than before as he kissed me passionately. Then he was coming again, and I felt the spasms of his cock deep inside me. I felt desperate, trying now to keep it in me. Jason lay on top of me, kissing and nuzzling me for many long minutes.

While I had been telling my story, Dr. Ingmar brought me close to orgasm. Once we had parked, he went down on me immediately, and I came.

My sopping-wet, cum-coated cock lay against my thigh. He kissed it one last time, then lay there humming. My head was cradled in his shoulder. I said to him, "You sound happy."

"I've never been happier."

"What are you humming?"

He took the opportunity to lift himself up on an elbow and begin to sing to me in a low tenor, "In short, there's simply not, a more congenial spot, for happy-ever-aftering...."

He paused suddenly, his eyes locked on my smiling face. "We can't ever do this again, you know," he said. His eyes were suddenly wistful.

"I know, but thank you for the lessons, doctor," I said softly.

"Lessons?"

"On how to suck dick."

"From what you've told me, Jason taught you everything you need to know."

With that, he leaned down to kiss my cock, and I gave up the last of my worries, leaned back and rested my head on the seat. Then he started humming softly as he took my cock back in his mouth, while his fingers began to probe my ass.

I co-operated, lifting my ass from the seat.

One finger, then two sank into me. "Would you like an 'A' this semester?" he asked.

I didn't answer that question. Instead, I repeated what Jason had said, "Worship it."

And, of course, Dr. Ingmar did.

HARD BARGAIN
by John Patrick

"How long is it, *really*?" Matthew asked.

The salesman was responding to a classified ad offering sex-by-the-hour. Forever a size queen, Matthew was so intrigued by the tempting copy that he finally made a date. The cost was to be $100. He was not a rich man, but he thought he could swing it; after all, he was in Manhattan on an expense account.

As he talked to the advertiser, he was actually enjoying playing the role of the experienced client.

Matthew felt his dick pulse at the soft sound of, "I'm just a boy trying to pay his way through college."

Matthew nodded. He was almost unbearably horny now.

"I think you'll do," he said. He gave the boy directions to the hotel and hung up. Already, his mind was creating fantasies of the college boy's appearance to say nothing of that "ten-inch piece of prime meat."

He got up, used the toilet again, sprayed cologne throughout the small room and brushed his teeth.

When he heard the knock on the door, he didn't immediately get up out of the room's well-worn easy chair. He put out his third cigarette of the hour in the ashtray, checked his reflection in the mirror, and brushed his thinning brown hair away from his forehead. But then he got cold feet. He thought if he didn't answer the knock, he hadn't committed any sin. Just go away, he willed the boy on the other side of the door.

But when the knocking became more persistent, he was afraid the neighboring guests would be disturbed, so he went to the door and peeked through the peephole. The fish-eye lens made it impossible to tell whether this was the student stud with the long dick so he unlocked the door and let him in, eyeing his shape and admiring his smell as he strode past him into the room. He shut and locked the door and smiled as he regarded the student.

The student, who said his name was Paul, stood with his hands on his hips. The stone-washed jeans looked well-worn and they were displaying the biggest basket Matthew had seen in ages. Hell, he displayed the best *everything* Matthew had seen in ages, from a perky nose, to Cupid's-bow lips, and bouncy, shoulder-length blond hair.

"Well?" Paul asked. "Any complaints?"

"Yeah, you're wearing too many clothes."

"Well, take 'em off me, then," Paul teased.

Matthew's eyes narrowed a bit. This was almost too easy, he thought. What if he was a vice cop, trying to entrap him? He'd seen set-ups like this before on TV.

"You a cop?" he asked.

Paul laughed. "They wish!" He sat on the edge of the bed, spread his legs wide apart.

Matthew's eyes bulged. Paul rubbed the magnificent bulge and, like an obedient dog, Matthew stepped forward.

"Actually," Paul continued, "the cops in the city hate call boys. The services especially. That's why I left the service." Matthew, his mind totally befuddled by the youth's beauty, ignored his patter and pulled money out of his wallet. "As we agreed on the phone," he mumbled as he shoved cash into Paul's palm. Paul smiled sweetly at him, counting the money, then putting it in his sneaker.

"Let me just call my roommate and let him know I got here safely."

Matthew started to complain, but he put a sweet-smelling finger to his lips and shook his head. "It's something I have to do."

Paul made a quick call, then turned back to Matt, offering him his bulging crotch. "I am in safe hands, aren't I?" he cooed in his ear.

Matthew grunted in response and started to unzip Paul's fly. He shimmied the jeans down a bit until the cock was standing proudly at attention.

Matthew gasped, shaking his head. "My God," he muttered, "you are incredible."

"Told you, man," Paul said.

Matthew dropped to his knees and started licking the thick, long, clipped cock. He doubted it was really ten inches long, but now it didn't matter. It really was one of the longest he'd ever seen, and it was at least six inches 'round. Oh, he thought, if this was the Big Sin, he was ready to go to hell.

He pushed Paul's pants down to his knees, and Paul did the rest of the work of pulling them off altogether. The incredible penis dripped pre-cum on Matthew's cheek as he thrust his member in Matthew's face. Matthew grabbed the dick with both hands and slowly slid it into his mouth.

Paul grunted in appreciation. "Now that's talent," he complimented, but Matthew didn't answer. He was too busy licking the shaft of the dick, then the soft spot just under the head of his penis. Here he paid particular attention, giving it quick, short licks until he thought Paul would surely explode.

Paul pushed him away and said, "I like it doggy style."

Blinking, Matthew got up and took off his pants. He got on the bed while Paul produced a lubed condom from the pocket of his jeans, unwrapped it, and put it on the cock. Now Paul mounted him. He slid into him until his balls slapped Matthew's inner thighs. He pushed in and out, out and in.

This was perfection, Matthew thought. He could scarcely believe what he was doing and what was being done to him. He looked behind him to see Paul, head back, eyes shut, fucking away. Matthew felt like he was watching himself in an X-rated play from a front-row seat. Here he thought he would just be allowed to suck it for $100 and now he was actually getting fucked by the biggest cock he'd ever seen.

The phone rang. He groaned, looking at the clock. It was after midnight. When he was out of town, he always called his wife at 11:45, and he'd forgotten tonight. Well, no wonder.

He struggled to reach the phone. Paul kept fucking him.

"Hello, honey."

Just then, the stud pulled out, then slammed back in. Matthew gasped into the phone and then coughed, trying to mask his response. He was furious with Paul for nearly blowing it for him, but simultaneously, the thought of being fucked while talking to his wife filled him with such an emotional charge that he grabbed his cock with his free hand and jerked it while he continued his conversation with Sue.

"Yeah, well, I had trouble catching a cab after the meeting. You know how it is."

He listened for a moment while Paul pushed himself harder and deeper into his ass.

"Yeah, I miss you too."

Paul pushed Matthew over so that he almost dropped the phone. Paul was slamming into his trick with such ferocity that Matthew could scarcely breathe, let alone carry on a conversation with his wife.

Suddenly, he felt Paul coming. "Oh Jesus, oh God," Paul moaned in ecstasy.

"Oh, nothing dear I just uh I just dropped my cigarette. Filthy habit."

Paul brought his hands around Matthew's body and began jacking his dick for him. Paul grinned at him and pushed against him again and again. Matthew got closer and closer and finally hung up.

"Jesus," he shouted as he came, his cum soaking the sheets beneath him.

A sly grin was on Paul's face as he continued to move in and out of Matthew's wet ass and the hustler fingered Matthew's penis. "You like it rough, don't you?" Matthew asked.

"Takes one to know one," he answered with a wink

Matthew suddenly felt his age, thoughts of his wife making him lose most of what was left of his erection. "Hey," he complained, "Stop it. I'm beat." He tried to pull away, but Paul held him tight.

"What about me? I'm hard again."

"I paid you for getting *me* off," he answered with some disgust at Paul's brazenness, but Paul kept fucking him, harder and faster.

"Jesus," Matthew muttered as Paul slammed into him, eyes shut tight, moaning and then screaming, in pain or pleasure, Matthew didn't know which and didn't care.

The fucking lasted for several more minutes until finally, the hustler shuddered and was still.

"Jesus, you fucked me so hard my ass is raw."

"You got more than you bargained for then."

Totally spent, Paul pulled out, and it was then that Matthew saw that the rubber had broken sometime during sex, and they could both see his cum dripping from its end.

"What kind of crappy rubbers do you use, anyway, you shit?"

"They've always worked fine," he said.

"Damn! Are you safe? Have you been checked?"

He laughed ruefully. "Yeah, I have been have you? How often do you do this, anyway?"

"Never. I mean, it's been a long time."

"Yeah, right," he said as he strode quickly into the bathroom to take a shower.

Matthew lit a cigarette and stared out the window while Paul showered, then quickly dressed. Matthew turned in time to get a glimpse of Paul leaving the room without another word.

Matthew showered himself. He toweled off, already starting to feel foolish for freaking out.

What were the chances he'd get AIDS from this stud? Hell, he was so young, he reasoned, he couldn't be infected already. And besides, he always wore a condom, and he had been tested.

Then another thought struck him. What about other sexually transmitted diseases? Sue would kill him if he came home with something more than the flowers he usually brought her after his trips. He never forgot the time he caught the crabs. What a mess that was to explain.

He took a deep breath. *Steady. Steady.* Nothing had really happened. Sue would never know. He prayed to God for forgiveness as he lay in the darkness, waiting for sleep. Suddenly the phone rang on the night table next to his bed.

"Yes?"

"This is Paul's roommate. Is he still with you?"

"Of course not."

"That's strange he usually calls me before he leaves a john." "Well, that's your problem."

He hung up the phone and tried to fall back asleep, but he couldn't. He smoked another cigarette.

There was a knock on his door, hard and insistent.

Matthew sat bolt upright in bed. "God, what now?" he complained loudly.

He got up, threw his robe around his skinny body, and approached the door. He squinted through the peephole. It was Paul.

"What is it?" he asked the student as he opened the door.

"I couldn't leave it that way."

"Come in," Matthew said.

The youth had obviously been drinking. In fact, he was nearly drunk. Matthew regarded him a new light. This was not a bad kid; this was a hugely hung "college student" who liked to fuck doggy-style and who had fucked him so hard that the lousy rubber broke. Matthew had never been fucked so long or so well in his entire life, and it had been by this for-hire student!

Paul fell onto the bed, mumbled something, and rolled over.

Matthew stood beside the bed trying to get a grip on what was happening.

The best sex partner he had ever had in his life had passed out on his bed in this cheap hotel and he had a six a.m. plane to catch back to Omaha. It was already three a.m.

Matthew couldn't sleep if he wanted to. He sat on the bed and watched Paul sleep. He rolled Paul over onto his back and carefully unzipped him. He again shimmied down the jeans until the cock was fully revealed. The sex organ was simply magnificent even when limp! He examined it as he had never examined a penis before in his life. The heavy veining, the large purple head, the soft blond pubic hairs. Then he went to the balls. They were large, befitting a cock so huge, lightly furred.

God, Matthew thought, nobody this gorgeous could ever be sick. He bathed the balls with his tongue. They still tasted a bit of the soap Paul had used earlier. Matthew tugged Paul's sneakers off, then the jeans. The stud was now gloriously splayed on the bed. Matthew went back between the thighs and continued making love to the cock and balls.

While he sucked, he remembered that this guy had come twice up his ass. Another first. The whole scene was turning Matthew on. He stroked his erection while he kissed and licked the cock, and came again himself. Then he laid his head on Paul's thigh and continued kissing the cock head, until he finally dozed off.

A WANTON CRAVING
by Rick Jackson

When my adventure began, I was walking along the broad sweep of Copacabana Beach, admiring the blue of the bay and, especially, the wildly erotic bodies that littered the sand. The men wore next to nothing as they lay or chatted or ambled about the golden sand and showed all the world incontrovertible proof that the gods of creation must be gay else they could never have formed such heart-stopping beautiful creatures.

There may be a man in Rio with mediocre looks, but I certainly hadn't been able to find him. The ones who crossed my path were all poster boys for what people like Jesse Helms used to rail against as miscegenation. The blending of Portuguese and African with perhaps some stray Spaniard or Arawakan thrown in for flavoring over the course of four centuries bred so beautiful a people that a man can't swing a dick without hitting four or five young studs so fine and savory he would pay money to fuck them in his mama's parlor. Their muscles are hard and many, their coloring runs the gamut from one savory brown to another and back again, and they universally have tight asses and cute faces enough to satisfy any wanton craving.

I was lost in horny thought contemplating the studly masses so I didn't pick up right off that Paulo was talking to me especially since it was in Portuguese. I know about six words of Spanish, but they weren't close enough to help me a lick. Paulo jabbered at me for a while, but even if I had been better at the lingo than Deus Ramos, I still wouldn't have heard a word. Even among the vast sun-drenched herds of nearly naked Brazilian beeves, Paulo was the kind of guy a man had to stop and look at and study up close before he worried about words.

I maneuvered us over to a bench, half afraid he would wander off before I had finished memorizing his dimples and brilliant smile, his chocolate brown pecs and firm belly, and, especially, the improbably green eyes that seemed at once so exotic and surprising. Paulo appeared content to chat with me in Portuguese in return for an occasional English encouragement. He was positively vibrant with the rawest, most joyously masculine energy; I just wish I knew what the hell he was chattering on about.

After twenty minutes or so, I decided to cut through the inter-cultural confusion and make my move. I reached over and put my hand onto Paulo's thigh, but it didn't stay there. He moved it up to his cotton-clad crotch and traced my palm along his thick dick. His eyes and moist lips told me everything else I needed to know. I snatched him to his feet and dragged him down the beach towards my hotel.

The only reason I didn't do him up the ass in the elevator was that the priggish bastards had put in a security camera probably what I deserve for staying in an expensive hotel. By the time we got to my room, I was long past ready to move beyond talk. I reached down and locked a hand behind Paulo's neck and pulled his face against mine. His lips tasted of some local spice or

Edited by John Patrick

other, but his tongue had a positive hunger for sloppy Yanqui lovin.'

As our tongues grew first fluent and then frenzied, my hands moved south, slipping salaciously along Paulo's broad back and down his spine to linger in the small of his back, where they forced Paulo's pelvis forward to grind his stiff dick into my own. He wriggled and thrust hard against me even as I moved on, sliding my hands beneath the thin cotton of his shorts and pushing them down until all my hands felt were his firm, full glutes grinding away towards man's ultimate glory.

When I let up on his mouth and moved my lips slowly along his neck, Paulo jabbered for a moment and then started making a noise that was half whimper, half moan, and all man. I pulled away from him just long enough to lose my own shorts and then fucked back against his firm belly, dueling with his dick as my tongue licked the sweat from his neck and then ripped roughly down his touchy ear canal. The racket he was making changed to a high-pitched wail that sounded for all the world like a soprano vervet with his tail caught in the escalator.

My tongue was having a good time, but that was nothing compared with the party my hands were having spreading Paulo's perfect glutes wide and reaching deep into his sweaty ass-crack. Those twin sugar loaves of Brazilian power bucked and ground and clenched together, but they couldn't get enough of my hands. The harder Paulo's dick slid up my belly, the faster and farther his ass arched outwards on the down-stroke, practically begging me to hand him a very good time. The way our dicks were pounding together, I was half afraid I would embarrass myself by nutting too fast.

When I unhanded his ass and pulled away, Paulo's green eyes glinted hard, daring me to disappoint him and see what he would do. I answered his challenge by pushing his ass backwards onto the bed and shoving my face into his crotch. He was sweaty and musky and tasted more like man than any mortal has a right to. Heavy nuts hung low and hairless between his thighs, but they tasted even better. The harder I sucked and licked and pulled those Brazilian nuts with my teeth, the more Paulo's hips humped upwards against my face.

I felt something wet in my own crotch and distantly realized that he was returning the favor, but I was too busy to care. I kept at him until his nuts and thighs were licked clean and chewed ready. Then I eased away and wrapped my hand around his dick. I suppose I should have realized Brazilians don't cut their babies, but the huge wrinkled foreskin I found trying to kiss me was at once the best thing I had seen all day and a real challenge.

I needed to move this thing along, to show Paulo the good time we both needed. Everything about the wild, throbbing creature I held in my hands, though, demanded study. I put my nose to his wrinkled lips and inhaled the unique fragrance only a man's natural skin can produce. Born of sweat and musk and aged rich through a tropical day, that scent is man's oldest and finest wake-up call. When I eased his `skin down and saw the purple knob that soft,

- 26 -

dark cowl was hiding from the world, I needed every ounce of willpower I had to keep from slamming my mouth down and draining him dry.

Paulo's hips bucked upwards, fucking my fist and sliding his sinfully sexy `skin down off his glistening head to leave him standing tall and hard and defenseless before me. I let his hips fall back onto the bed and held tight as his `skin reclaimed its treasure for a moment. Then up he bucked again and soon he was fucking my hand and grinning at my naive wonder. He moaned something deep and low that sounded like "Shashlik porks Maria!" but probably wasn't.

I kept my hand busy as my tongue licked its way up his flanks and across his hard, sweat-salted pecs. His tits were swollen stiff with the need I took time to satisfy as my lips and tongue and teeth used him and then moved on. His pits were even better wantonly musky and deliciously rank as any stray llama's butt hole. When I finally pulled my mouth away from his pits and looked into his face, the vision I saw staring back at me was one I will never forget.

He was incredibly beautiful, of course; but he was more than that. Even through the strong lines of his jaw and brow and the raw sensuality of his lips, those green eyes carried so timeless an innocence that I was suddenly possessed by an uncontrollable and immensely wicked urge to fuck him senseless.

Before he could even flinch, I struck. In one swift, savage move, I rubbered up, lifted his legs, and slammed my thick Yanqui dick up through Paulo's tight ass. I'm six-two and Paulo is about five-seven. His gorgeous dick is just fine for a man his age, but when the gods passed out asshole, they must have been feeling stingy. He obviously wasn't acting like a virgin, but a man sure as shit couldn't prove that from his hole. Granted, everything about Paulo had me so turned on that my dick was swollen to a personal best, but I had never felt anything as tight and hard and unyielding as Paulo's tender butt hole.

If I had tried to ease the fucker in, I might have popped his shithole straight across the room. As it was, before his reflexes could begin to register the grief rolling his way, I was buried deep and grinding my stiff, rust-colored pubes into what had been his hole a moment before. Paulo took what I had like a man, but it cost him. His gorgeous face twisted like a gargoyle's reflected nightmare, his heels and hands jerked tight around me, and a desperate keening echoed unawares from the very depths of his tormented soul.

I waited for a moment, watching one horror after another march across Paulo's face until he looked more like an El Greco crucifixion than a young peasant boy. After an age, his green eyes opened enough to gleam through and I tore his ass up.

I didn't jerk my dick all the way out of his butt, but I came close. Only the impossible swell of my meat and the incredible limitations of Paulo's hole kept me anchored deep. The slick, hot feel of his guts collapsing across my head promised there was more tight, hungry ass to plow and that particular bottomland had lain fallow far too long. I ripped forward again into Paulo's tight furrow and through his guts. Even stricken with agony past understanding, my

little buddy kept his heels pressing hard against my ass, urging me ever forward.

Long before Paulo's body lost the pain of temporal innocence and found pleasure in every reaming stroke slashing upwards through his shuddering guts, my dick and hips found the cadence that powered them relentlessly forward. As my hands held Paulo's shoulders and the base of his neck, my tongue licked and probed wherever it was jolted by the frenzied bucking of our savage loins. Almost at once, I slipped into that timeless trancelike state between waking and ecstasy where I couldn't say my name, yet I heard our animal noises and felt the slick sweat and raw textures of man sliding across my flesh and folding tight around my bone.

I could not tell who screamed what or why we fucked our way onto the floor. I only know that we did just as I know that Paulo's body learned to love love as I made loving it my truest calling. I think we tried several positions because I remember slamming his ass against the wall and knocking down a cheap hotel lithograph of Christ atop Corcovado and thinking how really delicious sin could be when two men put all four of their heads together.

The harder and deeper I reamed Paulo's ass, the more I thrust myself into him. Usually when I fuck some gorgeous young creature up the butt, I don't worry too much about metaphysics or love or honor or justice. I just worry about busting the best nut possible. Paulo's almost otherworldly beauty and obvious sincerity though the gods themselves probably didn't know what he was gibbering about bred a difference within me even as I bred him harder.

I wasn't interested in nutting and then bolting right away. I wanted Paulo to feel the furious frenzy of my love perhaps only the love of our shared moment, but true love nevertheless. As I reamed his ass ever more raw and smothered his face with kisses, some perverted corner of my psyche was drifting along in free association. I shall forever afterwards associate Portugese with Paulo. That led me to think of the Brownings and their sonnets and how I could count the ways I loved him: one, two, three, and into an infinity of building bliss as each cruel, counted thrust of my thick dick did things to Paulo's ass beyond his most sinister imaginings.

My lust fed on itself and made that gluttony its only goal. I was soon drifting along on a magical wave of ever-cresting rapture that roared louder with every mile and pretended to know no horizons. When, at last, I jolted back to life and found my dick blowing one savage load of Yanqui cream after another up into Paulo's glorious guts, I felt almost cheated that my eternity had come to an end and left me, forever afterward, aware of how a man could feel, yet sure that the rabid frenzy of our first rut would never come again.

We came close. After I had spewed everything but my gizzard up Paulo's ass, I did something I almost never do I let him have all he wanted of me. The greedy bastard wanted a fucking buttload of me, but that's what he got. We took turns wearing each other out and feeding off McDonald's protein for the next three days. There may be fancier restaurants in Rio, but the arches were next

door and neither of us wanted to be out of bed too long or, by that time, could walk very far. Then, a lifetime too soon, my time in Rio was over and I had to leave. I hadn't seen much of Rio but the beach and Paulo's ass and dick and smile, but those were enough for me to remember my time in Rio as the vacation of a lifetime.

MY ANTONIO
by Rick Jackson

Damn, I just love Hawaii. What with one thing and another, I've been more places than I can remember, but I have yet to find any place like home. Hong Kong has soaring skyscrapers backed by verdant peaks; Ulithi in the Western Pacific has a shallow atoll with warm, clear water that makes a simple swim an ecstasy; Saudi Arabia has exotic history and friendly people. Hawaii matches them all and within a few square miles.

In addition to all its natural glories, Hawaii also has tourists who come to help us live the experience. We get our share of gawky Japanese honeymooners and fat German dowagers, but on any beach stroll down Kalakaua, a guy can find more fresh beef than in Texas and the Argentine put together.

Antonio Francisco Salazar y Cabeza de Vaca was a perfect case in point. I was minding my own business, munching some McFries and contemplating the sunset, when I passed the bronze, lei-draped statue of the Duke, standing with his long board on Kuhio Beach, as though still ready for action. Tony was giving it to him, flashing away with a disposable camera and a smile that would last the ages.

More than most, I can get wrapped up in the infinite Zen of a Waikiki sunset, but Tony seduced my eye away from that natural display to one even grander. He was quite young, with a flat, bronzed belly and pecs to match showing through his opened shirt a sort of Menudo aged a bit to savory perfection. The thin cotton shorts he wore clung to his ass the way my tongue deserved, but I was even more entranced by the monster basket he had hanging low. Hawaii had bleached his hair until he seemed to belong more to the Banzai Pipeline than the Prado, but his black Iberian eyes gleamed like liquid obsidian: sultry and hard and ready to cut out any young man's heart on a playful whim.

Whether he saw me admiring or just noticed I was near, he handed me the camera and asked, in English accented just enough to be sexy, if I would snap him in front of Duke. I'd willingly have snapped the guy on the live CNN International feed. When we'd clicked off a half dozen different poses, I even let him have a few fries and chatted him up as the back of my hand accidentally slipped across his basket. In its turn, his dick accidentally surged back and we were in my condo and naked more or less in that order before you could say, "Bienvenido."

His body was a living study in contrasts: massive muscles rippled one over the next, yet one thought of Ganymede rather than Herakles; his pits and crotch were awash in musky curls of jet-black down, but, except for a thin trail of promise leading downward from his belly button, the soft skin across his sweeping pecs and belly were hairless and tender and begging desperately for my tongue. Each gloriously defined pectoral was crowned with a chocolate-colored column of tit-flesh swollen like twin prows probing the unknown from a Spanish voyager of an earlier era.

As our naked bodies stood grinding together in my foyer, those demanding nipples dug deep through the harsh, rust-colored carpet that grows across my chest and demanded satisfaction.

I slipped to my knees before him and had my tongue through the buttons of his Spanish fly before my man-handling paws could envelop his ass. Tony wriggled and writhed as I worked my way down to his wrinkled nuts to give them the attention they craved. My hands seethed with the knotted, flexing muscles grinding hard against them through the thin cotton of his shorts. My thumbs hooked around his waistband and had him naked in a second of ecstatic liberation that gave my tongue and lips and teeth undoubted access to the dark, musky pleasure-pouch swinging low between his solid thighs.

First I slurped away at his scent until he was licked raw; then my lips engulfed his swollen stones so my teeth could grate along the hairless skin of his sack, relishing the rippled texture of the furrowed sperm-wells. I was too busy to hear his moans of anguished ecstasy or feel his hands pulling me impossibly harder into his crotch as he danced and writhed and squirmed in sweet torment atop my face.

Tony's ball bag felt so friendly locked away safe inside my mouth I'm surprised my hands had the sense to keep polishing his ass. I suppose the way his muscle-bound glutes were churning away captivated my palms the way his huge balls enthralled my mouth. He certainly did nothing to keep my fingers out of his sweaty ass crack, wriggling and twisting away like the Whore of Babylon in a Ke'eaumoku strip joint.

Soon, though, my teeth and lips were twisting away on autopilot and my fingers led the charge, ignoring grinding mounds of magnificent man-muscle to the left and right, digging straight down the heaving cleft of his hairless fuck-trench until they reached the timeless target of man's truest devotion.

His tender asshole nearly raped my hand, reaching out to snare my fingers on the fly-by and demand a slow, grating ravage before I ransacked his foundations. His torso twisted and bucked away from my face as my rough fingers slid and skidded through his pulsing fuck hole, chafing him into a frenzy that could only find a single remedy. I almost pulled him down to the carpet to give him what he wanted, but until that day, I'd never thought of keeping rubbers in my foyer.

Instead, I let his spit-slicked nuts slide out of my mouth, unhanded his hole, and dragged his swollen uncut, love-leaking lizard into my bedroom. Most guys stop for a moment to admire my view of the Ala Wai and the mountains towering beyond, but there was so much towering closer, tourist Tony didn't give the window so much as a glance. His hands and lips and dick were all over me, pleading for the pounding he needed to make his trip through paradise complete.

I took a brief moment, as I rubbered up, to savor his hard, young body as it lay sprawled across my bed in the most abject panting anticipation. I still felt the pulsing need of his asshole around my fingers and knew how tight and eager his

body would be as I slammed my thick nine inches of aloha deep. For a moment, I even thought of adding some more lube to my log; but the rubber had come with enough to keep it from rupturing before I did. After that brief, charitable moment, I decided to give it to him as rough and raw as Nature intended.

In the few seconds I'd invested in politically correct condomizing, Tony's gorgeous dick had leaked enough crystal-clear love-honey onto his belly to float a new armada and proved he was ready to surrender command of the seas. I couldn't resist reaching down to play with his `skin, sliding it back down his shaft to reveal the purple plum I would squeeze the sap out of before I let him escape.

Tony's skin was soft and hot and wet with expectation. His blue vein throbbed in my hand and, when I jerked the lose cock sock up over his head, his whole body arched high in instinctive answer to my challenge. More love-lube oozed from the wrinkled thrum gathered together in my fist. It gushed down across my fingers and made me merciful or maybe I just didn't want to see it go to waste.

I dropped his dick and shoved that hand back up his ass crack to wipe Nature's own lube across his yearning asshole. The slick, hot stud-sauce made his butt lurch towards my hand, but I was only there for a moment. I let him lick what little was left on my fingers so he could taste how good he was, fore and aft.

Even before he'd finished licking his chops, I had his legs rolled back and his ass in position to pleasure. His eyes shone with a radiant greed completely at odds with his chicken-licken face. My hands locked onto his shoulders as my dick moved between his spreading glutes and found its target. Like a Torquemada, I crashed my way through the tender, feckless tissues guarding his fuckable virtue and kept on smashing forward until the last, straining shreds of his asshole were wrapped tight around the thick base of my bone and the cruel, stiff curlies I kept there were grating him from without while my dick did him deep from within.

As my dick did what came naturally, I had time to watch young Tony's face and memorize every mouth-watering contortion. When my swollen knob rammed up into his body, his eyes slammed shut to keep them from popping out. His jaw locked tight to hold in the agonized shriek of absolute submission that tried to gurgle up from his ravaged depths. Knots of anguished, outraged, overpowered muscle stood out from his temples down the length of his body like a chain of Greek beacons. His mortal body rebelled against the very dick his soul needed to soar about Olympus. With Tony, what I like to think of as the reflex of the rape passed off after a moment, as his choice young body remembered a lesson older even than reflexes: the need to breed. The hard, carnal core of his being tore along my butt-busting bone, clenching and stroking and ripping one sublime sensation after another from my shank as his brain settled down to enjoy the best fucking time a young man can have in paradise.

By the time his huge, dark eyes opened again, his ass was rolling along my rod like a bullet train bound for satisfaction. All I really had to do was hold tight and let him hump up my shank, but when I have a man like Tony impaled below me, nailing the living shit out of him is no trouble at all. His hands tore at my back and flanks as his heels dug into my ass crack doubtless in hopes of getting more shoved that way soon.

His wet lips, still slick with sweet pre-cum and the scent of his own asshole, finally unclenched and parted in a sighful moan of satisfaction that sounded as fine in Spanish as my rhythmic cadence-counting grunts of impact did in English. My mouth sank to his neck and left shoulder and then to his ear to set his rippled flesh crawling with my tongue-fucking technique.

If Tony had been having a good time before, once my wet tongue drilled down towards his brainstem, my nine inches hammering home from the other end lit one serious fire in his thrust chamber and launched his tight little ass into orbit. He jerked and flailed about and howled like a congressman at a tax audit, but I didn't mind. The glow in his eyes and thin trail of spittle trickling down his chin as he jabbered away in wicked Spanish needed no translation.

I lifted him off the bed so I could sink my teeth around his bronze-hard tits while I fucked him. What with his change of angle and the hard lesson I was driving home, his ass stopped cavorting along my cock on its own and learned to let me do all the work for a change to use his heaving body any way I wanted. I crammed up into the magnificent man hanging in my arms, slamming my hips harder into his firm butt until he must have felt his gizzard jiggle loose. Our sweat-racked torsos skidded and pounded together as my pole reared upwards, reaming through his shattered hole and through the man-hungry guts that finally had all they could handle.

Tony was thrashing past all understanding, growling profane prayers with a savagery known only to profound ecstasy. Every nerve in my body was stretched and searing. I had to hold him tight above me, keep him sliding along my slick body, and guide my shank where it belonged even though neither of us was really conscious of anything but the hard, hot, heaving flesh of the other.

Almost before I knew it was happening and eons before I was ready my balls cinched tight and shot the cream rocket of creation off the launch pad. If Newton's Laws had been right, Tony should have zipped up off my shank and landed just south of Saturn. Instead, when my body finally blew its booster and coasted slowly back towards earth, I found Tony still splayed out around my ruins. His guts were still tight as ever, but the load I'd shot up his tight Iberian butt had taken its toll or so I thought.

I had no sooner felt my rubber retro-flushing jism down my shank and onto my poor, sweaty nuts than I realized Tony had been plenty busy, too. The dicking his prostate had taken conspired with the friction of our hard, rutting bellies along his lizard had milked it dry. Great streams of frothy cream cascaded from his pecs and smeared down his belly to join the overflow of my

own load on my nuts.

I dropped his ass onto my dick to give it one more thrill and then rolled us back over onto the bed. Tony's legs and arms held me tight for half past forever while the AC dried our sweat and our seed mingled low and we murmured quietly to each other the way men do when nothing really needs to be said. Our bodies had said it all.

When he finally complained that his leg had gone to sleep, I pried us apart and half carried his ass into my shower for a long, hot, messy recovery before we traded places and I let him have the ride of his young life. We even, somewhat awkwardly, used his throw-away camera to take pictures of the event pictures I'm sure Tony wouldn't even show his own mother. By the next morning, I'd talked the kid into checking out of his hotel and spending the rest of his island holiday in the sun at my place.

We did get out of the apartment a few times to lie naked on the beach just below Diamond Head. Now and again we went out for McFood. Mostly, though, we stayed in, saving Tony a fortune on hotel bills not to mention entertainment. With a kid like my Antonio, I was happy to oblige. After all, that's what the aloha spirit is all about.

A CHEAP THRILL
by Austin Wallace

It was Saturday May 21. Summer was still a month away but the day had been sizzling from the beginning. The sun was setting but the unbearable heat was still lingering around, ready to pervade smoldering air into the oncoming night. My fan is working full tilt; its slow steady hum combining with the thick muggy atmosphere to bring a lazy drowsiness over me. I reach up to open the blinds hoping to entice a wayward breeze through my bedroom window. In the distance a flash of lightening and the gentle roll of thunder give forewarning of an approaching storm. I hold a faint desire that it will also bring a cool and comforting wind.

I switch on the radio hoping it will relax me and take my mind off the oppressive heat. A drop of sweat begins working it's way down my forehead. I brush it away but it is like trying to stop a tidal wave. I remove my t-shirt and lay down on the bed to let sleep overtake me. A mild state of unconsciousness begins, along with thoughts of last nights embarrassing disaster. My actions still hang over me like the dark cloud that is fast approaching the house. To make it short and simple, I had thrown myself, in a somewhat inebriated condition, at a man who was already taken. I had all the subtleties of a drag queen in a new outfit. It was obvious to everyone within earshot what I was up to. After the encounter I truly felt like tired trash. I went directly home and crawled into a corner to pass quietly into the night, with thoughts of him burning paths through my brain. I guess my friend was right when he said I should have known someone that cute is hardly ever unattached.

Sleep was slowly coming and I was ready to welcome it with open arms when amid the patter of beginning rain I hear a persistent tapping that slowly rouses me back to the real world. I finally realize that someone is knocking at my door. I get up knowing it is someone for my roommate who as usual is out of town for the weekend having the time of her life while I remain at home having a time with my life. I descend the steps in my running shorts, since I was not out to impress lesbians tonight. All the lights are off and I slowly caress my way down the wall to the door. I grasp the cool hard knob and flip on the outside light to see who has made me move in this heat. As my eyes focus through the screen door the face and body come into full view and I let out a slight gasp as my mouth drops open. There he was, last night's disastrous party ego deflator standing exceptionally in the flesh on my doorstep, as a squeaky "hi" escapes nervously from my lips. He returns a much throatier version of my greeting and asks if he can come in since he was beginning to get wet. Like the rain it took a few seconds for his words to sink in. "Oh yes, I'm sorry," I say and in my haste to open the door nearly fall over. I manage to regain what little composure I have left and open the door just wide enough for him to enter. He passes precariously close to me and I inhale a scent that sends a tingling sensation through my body. I close my eyes and take a deeper breath. I open my eyes and

he is staring at me. I let out a small laugh then close and somewhat consciously lock the door. The click is clearly audible but I don't know if he hears it or just files it away for future reference.

I suddenly realize what I am wearing and feel exposed to the world. I hold back the urge to run up the stairs and instead reach to turn on the hall lamp nearly knocking it off the table. The light pierces through the darkness spraying us with an illuminating glow. I stare at him and our eyes meet in the way I thought they had last night. My mind races with infinite erotic and bland outcomes to this highly unexpected visit as I think maybe this attraction wasn't all one-sided. Since we have no living room I ask him up to my room and lead the way as my mind works desperately for some shreds to begin a conversation. I flip on the light in my room and reach for a t-shirt to cover my exposed flesh. I point to the chair for him to sit as I plop down on the bed. I turn down the stereo and begin playing gracious host by offering a drink. He surprisingly asks if I have beer and I jump up and make my way half running the short distance to kitchen. I grab two bottles out of the fridge and quickly return. As I hand it to him, I notice he looks amazingly cool for the temperature.

The rain begins to fall steadily now as a light breeze finds its way through the window, rattling the blinds. An eternity seems to pass before I decide to utter words. Since I'm an upfront guy I start with the question that has been running through my mind all day.

"So why didn't you tell me you had a lover?" The question cuts the air like lightening in the night sky. It seems to jolt him to the situation. After blurting it out I suddenly want to pull it back. But then I think, why. I really have nothing to loose since I had pretty much thrown out all my cards for everyone to see last night. I chug some of my beer and lean back on my elbows preparing myself for his response.

"You didn't ask," he says, and that is all he says.

I glare at him and realize how opaquely honest that answer is. I suddenly have the feeling of trash return to my shoulders. I speak again without thinking; my sarcasm coming through full bore.

"Then why are you here? Looking for some cheap thrill to make your own relationship more interesting?" He laughs and I feel he can see right through me. We both seem to know I would gladly give up the cheap thrill at this moment. I change the conversation and ask how he knew where I lived. He says he called someone we both knew from the party. I made a mental note to later thank them or kill later depending on how this evening goes. I ask again more politely why he is really here. He says I disappeared last night before we really had a chance to talk. I explain that after my behavior in full of view of everyone I didn't feel comfortable just hanging around. He laughs again. That's twice now but this time it does not upset me. The breeze and rain pick up and I move to lower the window since I can feel raindrops coming inside. He lowers himself from the chair and sits on the floor directly across from me. I catch his smell again and

begin to feel a spark of sexual electricity in the air. I say nothing this time not knowing whether it is my own long dormant hungry desire for him or a mutual crescendo of sexual frustration waiting to explode in a magnificent display of sexual arousal, or whatever.

He starts the conversation this time. "My lover and I don't exactly have a mutually exclusive relationship. As a matter of fact I know he has been seeing someone else for the last couple of months. It also wouldn't surprise me if he went home with someone last night." I hold my mouth in check and wait for more of his confessions.

"As you may have noticed he was getting pretty drunk and right after you left we had our own little scene. Accusations flew and I left. I assume he stayed and met someone because he didn't come home."

I don't know what to say. All sorts of thoughts run through my mind. Here is my chance to be with him. But do I really want to get in the middle of this? Do I really just want to be a revenge fuck? I pause briefly then reach out my hand to his. I begin to feel all tingly as if there is static electricity in the air, but I cannot judge his reaction or lack there of. I start to take my hand away when he grabs it and pulls it towards his chest, which feels, firm and warm to the touch. He then leans closer to me till we are face to face. Time freezes around us and the lights flicker. The air grows tense with sensuality and I am ready to lose all self-control. I move my face forward greatly anticipating the contact. The storm outside rages on but inside the passion is just beginning to light up. Our lips touch with frenetic energy. Our mouths part and tongues begin with a frantic desire that needs to be quenched. Hands search obsessively over clothed bodies, feeling, grasping, and trying to figure out the unknown. Every touch burns like the sun, sending shivers through my body. With less than tentative care he removes his shirt and pulls mine over my head. I run my hands across his slightly hairy chest with a less than moral interest sweeping through my mind. I suddenly have a compulsive emotion to completely possess him. My hand continues slowly to make its way downward gently touching each spot heading for my final destination. My hand comes to rest between his legs, massaging, stroking his already firm shaft through his jeans. A groan escapes from one of our throats. We both stand and I unbutton and lower his pants. He is wearing no underwear and his erection springs out already wet with precum. He lowers my shorts and I match his hard wetness. He takes me in his arms and smothers my neck and shoulders with kisses as he lowers me onto the bed. Our hands continue exploring each other, endlessly searching the many zones of pleasure that are rising to the surface. We roll effortlessly like the thunder outside, our bodies entwining in a steamy scene of sexual ecstasy. He chews vigorously on my neck, my body shuddering at each bite. I run my hands up and down his back feeling his muscles twitch. I reach down to stroke his round firm ass as he presses his groin into mine, our hard cocks pushing and straining against each other.

He rises above me slightly and begins to make his way down my body. He stops to encircle his wet tongue around each nipple, licking and nibbling sending waves of rapture through my body. He continues downward kissing and licking each crevice and curve with his tongue following the thin hair trail to the prize below. He reaches my hard penis and tantalizes me with the tip of his tongue, moistening my shaft with his up and down motions. He reaches down with his hand to cup my balls slowly massaging them as he takes them into his mouth. The groan this time is all mine. My cock seems to get even harder as he works heartily stroking, licking, upward, downward imploring me steadily toward the nearing edge of pleasures impact. He then takes my entire hard wet shaft in his mouth and my back arches as I run my fingers pleasingly through his hair, my body twisting with desire. The storm reaches its peak and is passing but we have fallen into a hurricane of unstoppable fornification, waiting to hit the beach in a thunderous crash of foam. I pull his head up to mine and kiss him hard and deep then roll on top of him so that I am now the sexual master. My mouth is watering for his cock so I waste no time in going straight for what I want. I take his engorged member in my mouth rolling my tongue up and over and downward. Then I take his balls in with his cock and enjoy the salty taste. I come up for air and see him staring lewdly down at me and I dive in with even more gusto, working furiously at bringing us both closer to what we both need and desperately desire. I come up again and he pulls me to his face covering my mouth with his in wet cum flavored kisses. We grabbed at each other's hard wet cocks, working them up and down with firm even strokes. He reaches one hand around to finger my wet hole, heightening my own sense of pleasure.

Our motions and passions increase. The heat between our bodies soon matches that of the room. Faster our strokes quicken, nearer to the abyss we head, faster, quicker, and harder, our hearts pounding in unison. He works his finger inside of me and I feel I cannot hold back any longer. I fling my head back as cum spurts across his chest and face. Over and over the waves seem to flow out of me. I moan loudly and feel a warm spray on me as I look down to see his cum accompany my own across our sweaty bodies. All of a sudden all my anxieties, tensions, sexual frustrations melt into the night. It is an explosion that makes me weak with joy. I collapse on top of him and we cling to each other regaining our breath. I finally stir to get a towel but he pulls me back down, our wet sticky bodies rubbing against each other as he begins anew to smother me in warm kisses, the tingling sensations returning to me. I take this as a sign he will stay the entire night and our hands start exploring each other again. On into the deepening night we continue until sleep overcomes us both.

Light breaks through the cracks of the blind. A body next to me moves and I awake to look at it. He is still here and this is not a dream. The night comes flooding back, filling me with giant expectations and questions. I fall asleep again and when I awake again he is up and staring at me. I stare back longingly.

No passion was going to exhume itself this morning however as he gets out of bed and begins to get dressed. I pull on my shorts and shirt and head to the kitchen for some coffee.

He follows and I offer him some but he says no. I look at him. "What now?" I ask. He shrugs, "Let's see how it goes." And I feel strangely content with that reply. He grabs the pen off the memo board and scribbles his phone number on it. I then grab him and push him against the wall and kiss him hard and deep and he returns the affection. "I've got to go," he says. He turns and I follow him down the stairs to the door. He gives me a hug and

one of those pecks on the cheek and is out the door making me feel ridiculously giddy. He pops in his car and I watch until he is out of sight and after. I close the door and climb the now long stairs back to the kitchen. I pick up my coffee and look out the window. It is going to be another sizzling day. I lean against the still cool wall and stare at the memo board.

A bead of sweat appears on my forehead and a lewd thought pops into my mind...but that can wait till another time

LUST BEHIND GLASS
by Thomas C. Humphrey

Brian's at it again. I spy through the side door of my tiny darkened bungalow as he moves the Nordic Track to the middle of the rec room and prepares for his exercises. My breath quickens as he inches his tee shirt up his awesome torso and slowly pulls it over his head and off his arms, as if he is stripping before an admiring audience. He glides one hand across his firm pecs, sensually cupping them and lingering to toy with the nipples. He gazes admiringly at his tensed biceps, posing like a competitor in a bodybuilding contest

As he positions himself on the machine and jiggles his buttocks around to get comfortable, I ease out my door into the narrow, unlighted courtyard that separates us. I kneel down and peer directly up his spread legs, where his baggy shorts frame the tight pouch of his jock strap, the elastic bands spreading into a wide, inverted "V" before they retreat into a thick tangle of coarse hair and disappear beneath his dimpled ass cheeks. My cramped erection throbs painfully, and I shift it around until it thrusts straight up toward my navel.

Brian and I have only a casual nodding acquaintance. I rent my tiny apartment from his grandparents, Rose and Tony Fiore, for my first year as a fine arts major at the university. He has moved in with them while he studies veterinary medicine. When we accidentally encounter each other, we have nothing to talk about. I am not remotely interested in his studies, nor in his rigorous exercise routine except voyeuristically and, so far, he has not shown the slightest glimmer of creative instinct that would draw him toward the arts, unless one considers a fixation on overdeveloped pecs and deltoids and abs to be an art.

I watch him doing overhead lifts and leg curls, straining against the resistance of the machine, his body misted with fine droplets of perspiration that cling individually to the dark tangle of hair on his chest and underarms, glittering in the light like tiny diamond chips strewn across black velvet.

Brian is tall and massive, with a face of classic Italian beauty crowned by a mane of jet black hair. Both his prominent nipples sport thick gold rings, his left eyebrow sags slightly from the weight of three heavy studs, a green and black tattooed snake coils around his thick left biceps, a tattooed arc, F-I-O-R-E, canopies his button-like navel. Undoubtedly, he could melt the heart of any one of dozens of admiring women or men. But in three months, I have not seen him in the company of either sex.

Instead, he exercises. He dresses in "comfort-fit" slacks or baggy shorts that camouflage, obscure deny what lies underneath. But always, always, around the house he is shirtless. It is as if his only defining quality is washboard abs, tensed pecs, firm biceps a beautifully disciplined body that ceases to exist just below the waist, a carefully calculated ruse to draw attention to all the relatively insignificant secondary characteristics of masculinity while completely denying the primary attribute of genitalia, the ultimate requisite of maleness.

And I? I, too, have retreated behind a ruse of sexual self-sufficiency. I have known and accepted my orientation almost for as long as I have been conscious of existence. But instead of seeking a companion, I spend hours fast-forwarding and pausing gay porn tapes and fantasizing until excitement and need reach a certain insistent peak before I allow myself solitary release.

We both are children of our times, I think, isolated and self-absorbed, pursuing our own form of virtual life, while his grandparents, probably well into their eighties, are out for a Friday night of dinner and dancing to the Dixieland sounds of a bistro along the waterfront. I do not know what personality quirk or phobia has caused Brian to retreat into his sculpted body, but I know only too well what has driven me to deny human intimacy.

Just before I reached puberty, I watched my favorite uncle waste away from the ravages of AIDS, witnessed his own family turn their backs on him, heard their talk of God visiting a deserved plague on faggots. Just days before the end, defying my parents, I sneaked into his hospital room alone and sat holding his decimated hand, staring through tear-filled eyes at his once-handsome face, now jaundiced and skeletal. Speaking as if he already knew my orientation, in a rasping whisper, he cautioned against repeating his mistakes of pleasure-seeking promiscuity. With mounting terror, I sat crying and taking his warnings to heart until his voice weakened into a piteous nonverbal rale.

A year later, after absorbing dozens of sex education pamphlets and public service admonitions, my best friend, Rusty Mimbs, and I reluctantly agreed to stop our mutual masturbation. Although we both were as pure as newborn lambs, we gravely decided that we might have the virus, which we might spread to the other through a microscopic cut we might have on our hands. From then on, our intimacy consisted of occasional tight embraces while fully clothed. We could not even risk a kiss, afraid that intermingling saliva posed a potentially lethal threat.

Now, Brian's proximity reminds me at what cost Rusty and I reached our fearful adolescent decision. As I watch Brian's chest expanding, his thighs tensing, his muscular arms bulging, every movement adds to my growing excitement. More than usual tonight, I long for human touch, the often-imagined exhilaration of skin against real skin, of shared emotion, of psyche attuned to another's real responses. I creep onto Brian's patio, just a few feet from the closed sliding glass door, drawn ever closer to this greatly desired other, as if by some irresistible force.

My heart catches in my throat as Brian breaks his accustomed routine and absently caresses his bulging crotch as he lies at rest on the padded bench. I ease up against the patio door. His baggy shorts tighten noticeably, and once, when he bunches them, I peer up his hairy thigh and catch a glimpse of the large mushroom head of his cock poking from the side of his jock strap.

As the movement of his massaging fingers becomes more purposeful, I reach into my shorts and squeeze my engorged cock tightly. Brian raises his buttocks

off the bench and quickly slides shorts and jock strap down below his knees and kicks them off onto the floor. He lies completely naked. His thick cock pulses against his abdomen, its tip brushes against the tattoo above his navel. My breathing becomes a series of ragged gasps, and I shove my own shorts down my haunches, freeing my raging hard-on.

Brian pinches and rubs his mushroom cock head between thumb and forefinger. He loops a thumb beneath the base of his cock and thrusts it outward, away from his body. A thick strand of shiny precum follows its movement, finally breaks, and ropes down the long, veined shaft. Brian runs his thumb up the shaft, gathering the viscous liquid, which he rubs all around his cock head. He wraps his hand around his cock and slowly strokes it.

He gets up from the bench and stands in the middle of the room, alternately thrusting his cock straight out with a thumb and steadily stroking it with one, then both hands. Every time he forces the shaft away from his body, it seems longer and thicker as massive as his sculpted physique.

From my squatting position, my body quaking with desire, I strip off my tee shirt and grapple to remove my shorts. In my frenzied haste, I lose my balance and thump against the plate glass. Brian freezes, and his eyes momentarily register wild-animal alarm and preparation for flight. Then he visibly relaxes and steps toward the door, his hand still girdling his cock. I know that he has spotted me.

I desperately want to retreat into the surrounding darkness, but I am unable to move. I crouch on the patio stones like a Rodin bronze fused to its base as Brian draws nearer. Except it no longer is Brian, but the Bel Ami star, Martin Valko, his low-slung bull's balls dangling against my chin as he presses his huge cock against the door, smiling down at me all the while. I shyly raise my hand and tap a faint drumbeat against the glass that insulates his body from my touch. I close my eyes, the glass vanishes, and my fingers caress the living flesh of his ball sac; my hand rotates to cup both heavy orbs in my palm.

I slowly raise my head, and his thick cock traces a pattern of precum down my face until it reaches my open mouth. As I take him in, he sighs contentedly and grasps both handfuls of my hair and pulls me even farther down on his thick rod. I wrap my arms around his loins and squeeze his firm ass cheeks, which flex powerfully every time he drives deep into my mouth.

As his excitement builds, his low moans become a more and more distinct guttural language. I look up, and he no longer is Martin Valco, but super-macho Jeff Stryker, reciting his dominating litany, "Oh, yeah! Yeah! Suck that big cock! Oh, yeah! Yeah!" as he tugs at my hair painfully and tries to shove all his monster cock down my throat. And I am no longer myself, but that quintessential bottom, Kevin Wiles, lips stretched to the maximum, cheeks puffed out like a blowfish, allowing Stryker to plunge full length time after time, relishing the abuse of his cock, only a slight hint of panic in my eyes.

As his thighs begin to tremble and the thick tube on the underside of his cock

swells and pulses with the first throes of orgasm, the door again is between us, and Brian gyrates his pelvis and strokes his cock and rubs its head against the glass. Finally, he spurts his heavy load all over the area where my face is pressed tightly against the other side. I watch the wide slit in the end of his cock head dilate and release burst after burst of semen. I ravenously lap at the glass, frantically trying to taste this long-denied nectar.

When he is spent, Brian rubs his semen around on the door with his cock head. Smiling broadly, he turns his back, leans over, and presses his ass cheeks against the glass. I study the contours of his dimpled buttocks, the dark brown crimped circle guarding his entrance, and the soft rosiness beyond. When he reaches back and spreads his cheeks, I press my face against the glass until my cheekbones ache and jab and parry with my tongue, battling to make contact with the much-desired prize only a fraction of an inch away.

I look across his muscled shoulders, and Dano Sulik, pouty and handsome, leers back, occasionally tossing his unruly shock of blond hair out of his face. He sensually grinds the twin globes of his perfect ass cheeks in my face and licks his already- moist lips, full and inviting. Without saying a word, his entire being pleads, "Fuck me!"

Before penetrating him with my steel-spike cock, I dive between the fleshy orbs of his tight ass cheeks, my tongue circles the perimeter of his hard muscle, parts it, and slips inside. Time after time, I plunge my tongue full length into his soft, musky opening, while he gyrates and presses even tighter into my face, moaning in a fit of ecstasy.

When he is ready for me, I stand, guide my throbbing cock to his opening, and shove inside him with one quick thrust. Sulik's gyrations become frantic. He grasps my ass cheeks and tugs me closer to him, driving my cock even deeper into his eager cavity. I wrap my arms around him, pinch one nipple roughly, and slowly stroke his cock, sliding the foreskin back and forth over his cock head. I hardly move my body, letting this hot porn stud do all the work as he writhes around and tightens his velvety sheath around my cock, rapidly driving me toward explosion.

As I begin to erupt deep inside him, he pulls away and turns to face me. He is once again Brian, the door separates us, and I hunch and rub my cock against the glass, spreading my seed all over as it volleys out in great bursts. Brian reaches forward and mimes cradling my balls until I am spent. He cranes his neck downward, as if to kiss me through the glass.

Just before I close my eyes, it is Johan Paulik tugging my head toward those delectably kissable lips, Johan reaching for my poker-stiff cock. I throw one arm around his back; our torsos meld tightly. I reach for his slightly upturned, marvelously thick cock, and open my mouth to accept his eager, probing tongue. As he drives his tongue deeper and deeper into my mouth, we grind our pelvises together and stroke each other's cock faster and faster.

Another intense climax builds rapidly. As my balls tighten and lift toward

my abdomen, I open my eyes to see Brian with head thrown back and eyes glazed in ecstasy. Instead of retreating back into fantasy, I keep my eyes open. The sight of Brian in the flesh is infinitely more arousing than any porn fantasy. Our eyes locked on each other, we both pound our stiff rods in rhythm. Just as my second load spatters against the glass, Brian groans loudly and spills profusely against the other side of the door. He smiles as he rubs his cock head against the glass, spreading his cum. He reaches up and glides his palm across the glass, as if caressing my chest, and then bends down to kiss my lips through the door.

Abruptly, he pulls back, winks and smiles, and, with a quick movement, throws a switch, plunging the room into darkness, and hurriedly draws the heavy drapes. I gather up my clothes and head back across the courtyard in new-found contentment.

After a few steps, I turn and gaze at the patio door. In the eerie blue light reflected off the drapes, our splotches of semen streak down the door, leaving thin, silvery snails' trails on the glass. Seeing this evidence of our shared passion, I somehow know that the scene will be repeated.

As I turn again toward my lonely bungalow with its stacks of no-longer-essential porn tapes, I wonder whether Brian ever will open the patio door and whether I will go inside, if he does.

THE GREENHORN: DON'T ASK, DON'T TELL
by David Laurents

"What do you think of it?"

Eddie stared up at the tank in transparent awe. "It's...it's *huge*."

Luke grinned. "Wait'll you see what I've got to show you inside."

Eddie blushed, his pale, handsome face turning all rosy as he nervously looked behind him to make sure no one had heard Luke's double entendre. He tried to make the action seem casual by running his hands along the tank's hull, but it was painfully obvious that this was an afterthought. Luke sighed, *What am I doing getting involved with someone so green*, he wondered, *so...so damned young*. But, man, he was cute. Luke worked out as often as possible, but try as he might, he spent far too much time sitting at the controls of the tank to ever manage a body like Eddie's, built from training and hard work out in the sun. But that didn't stop him from wanting to experience a body like that secondhand. Or, more literally, by hand....

"Come in," Luke said, climbing onto the rungs leading to the hatch. "You're never going to believe what's inside."

Eddie took a last nervous look around, then hurried up and into the tank. A smile broke out on Luke's face when Eddie gasped as he descended into the control cabin. It was a common reaction, akin to visiting New York City for the first time. A bank of screens gave a three-sixty view of their surroundings, while AC chased away the wet jungle heat.

Eddie ran his hand along the plush fabric of the seats, then stood in front of the screens, gawking at the view like a tourist.

"Impressive, isn't it?" Luke asked, stepping up behind Eddie and wrapping his arms around him. Eddie stiffened, evidently alarmed, and tried to step out from Luke's grasp. "Shh, it's all right. They're not windows, they're monitors. Did you see any windows on the outside?" Eddie paused in his struggling, letting this new information sink in, then relaxed into Luke's embrace. Luke ran his hands down Eddie's chest, nuzzled at his ear. After a moment, Eddie turned around to face him, to tentatively return his kisses and explorations.

Luke sat on one of the command chairs and pulled Eddie into his lap. They kissed and groped again, Luke slowly guiding Eddie along with gentle direction. Eddie wasn't all that green, Luke discovered, or if he was he faked it well as he met Luke's passion with equal intensity, and grew bolder in his explorations, reaching down to fondle Luke through the fabric of his camouflage pants. Luke tilted his head back, reveling in the feel of Eddie's hand along his cock, the rub of the fabric. He longed for Eddie to unzip him, to pull his cock out from the clinging green fabric and lock his lips around it instead. But there would be time for that. He didn't want to rush Eddie, who idly let his hands wander back up Luke's chest to tweak his nipples.

Luke opened his eyes again and smiled at him. He tugged Eddie's unbuttoned shirt from his pants and ran his tongue up and down Eddie's hard,

chiseled chest, exploring all the planes of its surface, the salt taste of his skin.

"Watch this," Luke said, after a moment, smiling. "Put the chair back, Peter," he called aloud. Slowly, the back of the chair flattened into a bed. "Thanks, Peter," Luke mumbled absently, running his tongue around Eddie's left nipple.

"You're welcome, Luke."

Suddenly, Eddie jerked away from him, rolling onto the floor.

"What?" Luke asked, wondering again why he was getting involved with someone so young. So he doesn't like his nipples bitten, Luke told himself. OK, I can live with that. He could have just told me so, more simply.

"Who the hell was that?" Eddie demanded, and suddenly Luke knew what was the matter.

He smiled as he sat up, facing Eddie where he struggled to put his shirt back on. "It's just the computer." He reached forward for Eddie, to gently interfere with his putting on his shirt again by holding him, caressing him.

But Eddie drew back, still clutching his shirt around him. "It sounded like a person. Is there someone else in here? Is someone watching?"

Luke sighed, and thought of his erection in his pants, realizing he would have to slow down a whole lot if he ever wanted it taken care of. "It's supposed to sound like a person," he explained. "It's an AI, an Artificial Intelligence. It's programmed to think like a person." Eddie looked about to protest again, but Luke didn't give him the chance. "But it isn't. I call him Peter because it's quicker than his code, P1 R25. More personal. I spend a lot of time alone in here, talking to the computer, and it helps me feel like I'm not talking to myself. But he is just a computer, not a person. We're alone in here, just the two of us."

Eddie looked still unconvinced. "Can't it turn us in? I mean, won't it have records of us being in here or something?"

Luke sighed and reminded himself to go slow, gently. "I was going to do this later, but if it'll make you more comfortable we can take care of it now. Peter, you are not to register anything about Edward McDonnell. Erase every trace of him from your records: voice, image, the works. Also, I want you to erase the fact that I ever gave you this order. But, I want you to keep the order in effect, just hidden so that it can't be traced. I have a feeling," Luke said, smiling at Eddie and running his hands through Eddie's short, blond hair, "he's going to be coming here often."

Eddie looked around the tank as if searching for some evidence that the command had taken effect. Luke smiled at him, gentle and reassuring, waiting for Eddie to resume their lovemaking.

"As you ordered, Luke," Peter said.

Eddie relaxed visibly and stopped clutching his shirt around him. It fell to the ground again, revealing his magnificent chest, still wet in places from Luke's tongue. "Happy now?" Luke asked, and Eddie smiled and nodded. "Good, now get back up here."

Eddie laughed out loud, his voice ringing out solidly to fill the cabin. "As

you ordered, Luke," he said, and climbed back into Luke's lap.

- - -

Luke watched from the hatch as Eddie hurried away from the tank, making a beeline for the mess hall before doubling back towards the barracks. He sighed at Eddie's obvious attempts at subterfuge and wished, not for the first time, that he could talk to the AI about this as he climbed back down into the control cabin and lounged, naked, in the command chair. But he knew not to. The AI was programmed with military regulations, which forbade homosexuality. Since Peter had no record of Eddie ever being there, they were safe, but if he spoke openly to Peter, the computer would be forced to turn them in when it filed its next field report.

And anyway, while Peter could respond to questions and directives, even analyze military strategy and learn from its own mistakes, the computer thought too literally to understand human relationships, to understand desire, trust, love, mistakes.

So, Luke kept his thoughts to himself, musing in silence late into the night, and many nights to come. And, for the next three weeks, until he was sent South into combat, he and Eddie conducted their brief but tumultuous affair in secret within the control cabin of the tank.

- - -

Luke glanced at the time-display on the control panel again, then back at the sensor displays showing the tank's surroundings. He had hoped Eddie would come say goodbye to him that night, that they would make love one last time before he went into combat, in case he might never return. But it seemed he was wrong. He cursed himself for being such a sentimental fool, felt angry to find he was blinking back tears as he stared at the barracks, waiting that one last moment, hoping against hope, to see Eddie running towards him and Peter. Eddie's beautiful face swam in front of his vision, the sharp lines of his body, the gentle curve of his cock as it arched towards Eddie's belly when erect.

Luke shook his head, to try and clear the image, but it was no use. He couldn't get the boy out of his mind, and all the scenes of their lovemaking came flooding back to him: the awkward and touching first night, as they explored each other's body and grew used to it, learning what most turned each other on; the quickies they had when Eddie was off duty for half an hour and came to find him in the tank; times they spent just being intimate, touching, holding, kissing; sometimes Eddie came and with hardly a word dropped down on his knees to unzip Luke's pants and take his cock into his mouth, as if he were desperately starving for it; the first time they had anal sex, Eddie's first time ever, and the welcoming way he trusted Luke, lying back on the command chair and spreading his legs wide and inviting.... All these images came back into Luke's mind in a rushing flood, like the way they said a man's life passed suddenly before his eyes in the moments before he knew he was about to die.

Luke had grown hard as a rock thinking of Eddie, and he wished Eddie had

come to *say* goodbye even if they hadn't fucked farewell. There had been more to their relationship than just the sex, damn it.

But he couldn't wait any longer. He had his orders, had to be at the new site by 04:00. "Roll on out," he told Peter, then settled down in his chair to sulk.

- - -

Eddie jerked to his feet when he heard the engines rev. He'd been sitting with his back against the tank's hull, waiting for Luke to return. He had spent half an hour banging on the hull, climbing up to the beach to see if he could slip inside and surprise Luke when he came back, lying naked on the command chair, waiting for him, but the tank was impenetrable.

After a while, Eddie gave up banging lest someone overhear him and wonder why he was attacking the machine. He had settled down out of sight from the barracks to wait for Luke, so they could see each other one last time and say goodbye.

As he was waiting he kept thinking about Luke, wondering what he would do for the three weeks that Luke was in combat. He knew he would worry about him all the time, wondering if he was okay, worrying that something might have happened to him. He knew Peter was the latest in advanced tank design, he could tell just from the brain that computer had, but he worried it might not be enough protection to save Luke, if the combat got bad.

When the tank lurched forward, Eddie realized Luke was already inside, that he had been in there the entire time. Eddie leapt to his feet and dashed in front of it, jumping up and down and waving his hands, trying to get Luke's attention on the sensors. But Luke was ignoring him. He kept driving straight ahead as if Eddie did not exist. Eddie couldn't believe it. He felt a tearing pain inside his chest. Was this the same Luke he'd fallen in love with over these last few weeks? What had happened that Luke could so coldly ignore him like this? Had this all been just a fling to him, using Eddie for his body and caring nothing about him? Eddie recalled their last few weeks together, all the times they had shared, and wondered if they had all been a lie. He thought of how he had trusted Luke enough to let himself fall in love with him, how he had even given up his anal virginity to Luke, because he wanted to, because he cared for him. Had even that been for a lie? He thought back to that moment, lying in Luke's chair, which Peter had lowered into a bed, his legs in the air, and the wondrous feeling of Luke's cock sliding inside of him, the connectedness he felt at that moment, when they were one. It had seemed so genuine, but perhaps it had all been an act, all Luke's intimacy and little gestures just a means to keeping him believing this was real, that they were in love with each other, when Luke was just doing it all for the opportunity to fuck him.

Eddie couldn't bear the thought and decided to let the tank run him over. But at the last moment, he dove to one side, cursing that the AI wasn't programmed to keep from running over their own men. What was the point of having a computer run the tank, if it couldn't tell who was the enemy and who wasn't?

And, suddenly, Eddie realized what had happened: Luke had told Peter not to register him, not by voice, or image, or anything. Luke had no idea he was even there!

"Ha!" Eddie shouted, laughing. He picked up a rock and threw it at the retreating tank. Then, in a whisper, "You're just jealous, Peter, because he loves me." Smiling, Eddie returned to the barracks, dreaming about their reunion, a few weeks from then, when Luke would come back to him.

HOW I MET THE BLOND BOMBSHELL
by Kevin Bantan

It was the last thing that I expected when I was called into my boss's office. "Hal," he began, although when he said my nickname, it always sounded like 'hell'. The connection was appropriate, I would find out straightaway. "Hal, it pains me very much to say what I'm about to say." Yeah, right. Like a hernia feels like a disembowelment. All I heard was that my job was being eliminated as soon as I could clear my cubicle of my personal items. I was being fired, but what I was told was that my job was being 'outsourced'. My usual distaste for jargon turned to loathing as I plodded back to my work space, empty Hammermill copy paper box in my hands. Outsourced. May your soul and the souls of all the faithful departed rest in outsourcing. Amen. "What are you doing, Hal?"

My cubicle neighbor, Jill, had stopped to ask me something and was stunned to see me stashing my stuff in the box. I was carefully placing my autographed, framed photo of Lassie in it at that moment. "Giving a first-hand demonstration of the term 'sent packing'."

"You can't be serious."

"I can be, when given enough motivation. Like now. My job's been vaporized."

"That's awful. How can they eliminate your job? What will we do without you?"

"You're about to find out." After a few more minutes of uncooperative conversation, Jill got the message that I didn't want to talk, hugged me and left. Without a word to anyone else, I carried my box out of the building and out of my former co-workers' lives.

I left the box inside the door in the foyer of my apartment and sat heavily on my plushly padded sofa. At least it was paid for. Cue the wry smile. That was a minor consolation. I wasn't in debt, and I did have several thousand in my 'Fuck You Fund', which I contributed to every week in case just such an unlikely occurrence as what had just happened happened. The phone rang, but I decided to let the answering machine field the call. I wasn't in the mood for chatty conversation, and I certainly didn't want to talk to anybody from work. Well, ex-work. I hadn't turned down the volume on the machine, so I heard my chipper voice saying, "Hi, this is Hal. If it's you calling, Dave, I won't let you unplug me this time, so hang up. Anyone else, please leave your name and number and I'll get back to you." I don't care, I liked the allusion to *2001*. It turned out that it wasn't someone from the office. It was my friend, Ducky. Don't ask, it's a long story. "Hey, Hal. What's goin' on? They said you didn't work there anymore. What's up? Call me." I really didn't want to talk to Ducky at that moment, but maybe it would be a good idea to pour my heart out to somebody, and Ducky was a good listener when his mouth could keep itself shut long enough.

"Before you say anything, skip the platitudes, Ducky. I'm in no mood."

"They fired you?"

"Outsourced me."

"Well, that's a little more comforting. I promise I won't spout drivel. I'll just give you my shoulder to cry on."

"What, that bony thing?"

"I see that you haven't lost your sarcasm in the midst of this crisis, Hal. But I'm strong. I can take it."

"Yeah, trouper that you are. Meet me at Flamingos after work. 5:30?"

"I'll be there, bony shoulder and all."

The place was mostly deserted at that early hour. Frank the bartender asked after my state of health, and I was forced to give him an abbreviated version of my personal disaster. He was suitably sympathetic, in a bartender sort of way.

"Hi. You don't look any different," Ducky said, plopping down on the stool next to mine.

"How am I supposed to look? Like a decaying piece of shit?" I could see a snappy rejoinder forming on his lips, but for once he exercised restraint.

He leaned toward me and said in a voice barely above a whisper, as if conveying a state secret, "I have an idea."

"I don't need ideas, I need a job." He gave me a look of impatience, which told me that he'd discovered the reason for my getting the boot and it was sitting next to him. "Sorry. Go ahead."

"That's better."

"So, what's the idea?"

"It's so appropriate that we're here."

"Ducky, either tell me what little thing is on your mind, or shut up."

He gave me a Joan Crawford *Mommie Dearest* look, but he hadn't plucked enough hairs to get the arch right. I resisted telling him, but it took some doing. "It must be hell to be fired during that time of the month," he said and smiled, pleased with himself.

"How do you know it's not PMS?" He was considering a rejoinder, but Ducky's short-term memory is notoriously fragile, and I could see that the possibility of forgetting THE IDEA was getting the better of him.

"All right, Mister Outsourced, here it is. You can work here."

"Here? As what? A waiter?"

"No, of course not. Something much more important."

"Oh, a valet."

"They don't have valets here."

"I know." I got the metal hanger look again. I was going to have to mention the need for more plucking, lest he make a fool of himself doing that to somebody else. But now wasn't the time.

"I don't know why I bother to help. Anyway, there's an opening here for an exotic dancer."

"What? You've got to be crazy."

"That has nothing to do with it. Look, Hal, you have a dynamite body. Half of the people in the city have seen it and agree."

Well, that was a slight exaggeration, but I decided not to quibble. "But the guys here are nothing more than glorified go-go boys."

"So? They make a hundred dollars a night. More sometimes."

"That much?" I thought of my measly salary at my former place of employment. "But all they wear are tiny gold G-strings and chokers."

"Don't go false modest on me, Hal. I've seen what you wear at the gym." There was that. Okay, I'm a cock tease. Maybe I did have more than enough exhibitionism in me to shake my bare fanny for the adoring masses.

An exotic dancer. Meat on the hoof for the boys to ogle. I pondered the notion over two more drinks, Ducky using his best persuasive tone to convince me how great THE IDEA was. I closed my eyes, trying to shut out his babbling as my mind's eye beheld the dynamite-looking blonde, who was my favorite dancer. I conjured the image of his oversized pouch swaying with each movement, its contents waving the lustrous fabric, making it glint in the spotlight shining from overhead. I was getting an erection to match the one I pictured forming behind the folds of gold caressing his jewels. That could just as easily be me, turning on the hormone taps of the horny gay men gathered around the pedestal on which I gyrated. That made me stiffer inside my jeans. And getting paid well for my lewdness, to boot. Oh, hell. Why not?

"Okay, I'll do it."

"I knew my silver tongue would persuade you." Hardly. It was the golden pouch of the beautiful blond, that had done it. No need to deflate Ducky though. Sometimes our delusions are all we have.

He waved at the barkeep. "Frank, Hal wants to audition for the exotic dancer position."

"No kiddin'! I can't wait to see more of that gorgeous body of yours, Hal. Man. But the owner isn't here yet. I know. David is backstage." He called somewhere in the building and hung up. "Go through that door over there to the second door on the right."

"I'll probably never forgive you for this, Ducky," I whispered before I got off the stool, wanting to make it seem that I was less interested than I was. But the fact that I was going to go through that door meant that my mind was made up. Besides, if I got the job, I'd get to meet the blond bombshell.

The door was next to the stage, where traveling male meat would occasionally put on a lewd enough show. The corridor, into which the door opened, was surprisingly long. The first door I figured was the entrance to the back stage area. The second was a ways beyond that. I took a breath and knocked. It was opened by a beautiful, tanned blond with a contrastingly white smile. He was short and his build compact and hard. I recognized him immediately. He was the stud who had occupied my daydream minutes earlier. I

couldn't believe my good fortune. He introduced himself as David and ushered me into the room. He was wearing jeans and white high tops, untied. His bare chest and upper abdominal muscles were gym perfect. "So, Frank says you're interested in auditioning for the dancing position." Then, suddenly, he smiled. "Hey, I recognize you."

"Yeah, I come to the club every now and then. My name's Hal, by the way. And I'm not sure I'm cut out for the job, but I just had my position at work taken out from under me, so I could use the money."

"Sorry to hear that, but there's a lot of that going around. In fact, its often done under that guise to get rid of gay employees."

"Really?"

"Really. If I were you, I'd check with a former co-worker you can trust to see if there's someone new in your office."

"Cubicle."

"Whatever. But find out."

"Thanks, I will."

"Okay," he said, going to a chest of drawers and opening the top one, "This is the outfit, as I'm sure you know." Yes, I had seen that roomy pouch on David, cut to allow the equipment to jiggle around in it. And if I had to guess, there was a lot to jiggle. "You can change in here or through that door's the back of the stage."

"Well, if I'm going to be naked, for all practical purposes, it would be stupid to feign modesty."

"That's true. I'll get into my costume, too, to help set the mood." Good. He pulled out another G-string, which glinted in the overhead light and started stripping off his clothes. I did the same, trying not to watch his total unveiling. I'd seen everything he had before, except for his cock and balls. A touch of mystery fuels the imagination. When I was disrobed, I pulled up the pouch by its narrow metallic strings and arranged myself in it. The lining of the string felt great against my equipment. I could imagine what it would do to my sensitive nerves, when they brushed against it as I shook my booty. That was the idea, probably. The choker was elasticized. I slipped it over my head and positioned the center of it over my Adam's apple. I eyed myself in the adjacent wall mirror and had to admit that I looked sexy as hell. I turned around to see that David was dressed for work, too. "Well, Hal, I have to tell you that you are one gorgeous number in your costume."

"Uh, thanks." I noticed that he seemed to be adjusting himself, too. At least at first. When he kept doing it, I began to get other ideas. I walked over to him as he continued to look at me and play with himself. I leaned down and kissed him. He kissed back. I felt his other hand on my crotch, as his tongue found the inside of my mouth. He rubbed the silky lining against my sensitive organ, producing the effect he desired. Then the hand disappeared. It took hold of my right wrist and guided it to his shiny pouch. I played with him in like manner,

making him hard in no time. "You want that, don't you?"

"Yes," I replied, honestly. I sank to my knees and kissed the gleaming material. My lips felt the bulge my hand had created. I pulled down the string and hooked it under his scrotum. A nicely formed, long, narrow, erect penis greeted my eyes. I needed no encouragement to lean forward and take it into my mouth. I worked my way down the shaft, pulling back and going farther, with each foray. I wondered if this was my audition, like the notorious casting couch, and figured, if it was, I'd better get to his pubic hair, whether the thing choked me or not. As he hardened completely in me, I was able to take all of him. The modest circumference helped slightly but it sure made up for it in length, I realized, when I retreated to his head. I started moving on him in earnest, determined to show David how talented I was without even moving the rest of my body. I fondled his sac, which responded by going into motion. I was really into it, happily impaled on David, when I heard the door behind me open. Not knowing what to do about being caught red-handed and -mouthed, I froze.

"Well, I can see I'm going to enjoy dancing in this club," a friendly voice said. I relinquished David to see what was attached to the voice. I blinked a couple of times to make sure that my mind wasn't playing games on me. He was about six- three or -four. His features were dark, in a sexy, Mediterranean way, his face was gorgeous and his hair came well past his shoulders. He looked familiar, for some reason. Had I seen him somewhere before? He was wearing black leather pants and cowboy boots. "Sorry to interrupt you guys. I'm Paris," he said, holding out his hand. David and I took it in turn and muttered embarrassed greetings. It's never easy being caught in the act, although this was my first time. It had also been my first time getting fired earlier in the day. Then David started to re-pouch his jewels, but Paris stopped him. "That's too beautiful to hide, David. May I?" With that I got up and let the tall, dark stranger put his hand on the shaft and plant a kiss on his mouth. Why he looked familiar to me bothered me. I studied the body. It was powerfully muscled and darkly tanned.

When he'd had his fill of David's mouth, he said, "And how about you?" He turned to me and put his mouth on mine. His hand reached inside the material covering me and groped me. It was a fine grope. After a few minutes, he withdrew. "You guys have me all horny. Anyone interested in a three-way?" At first the question didn't make sense, because we both had to be interested for it to be a trifecta, but that turned out not to be a problem. As sparsely furnished as the dressing room was, it had a couple of chairs and a large mirror on one wall. Paris sat to take off his cowboy boots. Long, narrow feet appeared. Then he stood and unzipped his jeans, pushing them downward. As he pulled at one leg and then the next, he was in profile to me. He had a beautiful butt and a rather large, thick endowment. He saw me looking and said, "I guess the three of us are pretty evenly matched." In truth, we were. David was not as broad, but that was irrelevant. I wondered what he had in mind for the three-way. "So, what do you

guys like to do? Obviously you like to suck, Hal."

"Well, that was Hal's initiation, Paris. All of the new guys suck me, when they get hired. Actually, I'm a first-class cocksucker."

The tall hunk looked at me. "Well, I usually like to screw."

"Great. David can suck me and you can fuck me." I couldn't believe my ears. I was going to have at that high, round ass? I was going to get to fuck this Adonis? "Well, shall we?"

He kissed us both for good luck. David dropped to his knees, his eyes betraying his delight. He wasted no time trying to devour the dark cock whole. "What about lube," I asked. "Already done. Let me warm you up." He took me in his hand and started stroking me. It didn't take more than five good jerks to get me up and raring to go. I positioned myself behind him and eased my way in. He was prepared all right. I wondered if he were perpetually greased in case he might get lucky on the subway or in a plane. If he was a slut, the tightness of his hole was giving away no secrets. It felt great. As I moved in him, I let my hands rove over the hard mounds that were his pectoral muscles. I strummed his abs, playing no particular tune. His body was a real turn-on. Paris was caressing David's head and offering encouragement to me, as if I needed it. But it was nice to hear what a stud I was and how good I was making him feel. It was mutual.

At one point, I turned my head toward the mirror, which showed us in profile, and realized that he was watching himself being sucked and fucked. He smiled widely, and I returned the gesture. Then I turned away, so that he could enjoy the scene in private. He alerted David that he was going to come about two seconds before I felt his sphincter tighten around me. I heard David moan. Then I heard myself moan, as I shot my seed into the stud I was riding. Man, what a workout, and I hadn't even started to work yet. "That was fucking great, guys," he said sincerely and kissed us again. We retrieved our G-strings and put them on. "Now I'm glad I interrupted. Uh, where do I change?" David took him out and down the hall and returned in less than a minute.

"Oh, man, Hal. Do you know who that is?"

"No, but he looked familiar."

"Paris is a big model. He was *Playgirl* magazine's Man of the Year last year."

"You're kidding!"

"Nope. You just screwed the stud millions of women fantasize about going to bed with every night."

My debut at the club was overshadowed by Paris's appearance, but what the hell. I had gotten to know him intimately, and I was quite satisfied with the results. I wasn't even that self-conscious about wearing only two thin strips of gold material on my body. I got some very nice comments from the clientele, as a matter of fact. The ego stroking was welcome, and I was making more money than before.

After I had been working at the club for a couple of weeks, I took David's advice and called Jill on the pretext of not having talked to her since I had been let go. And what do you know? A perky young thing named Mindy was not only ensconced in my former cubicle, but she was also doing the same job that I'd done. Well, well, well. Can you say lawsuit? My attorney could and filed one. He thinks we have an excellent chance to win it, too. I was so grateful to David that I took him out to dinner that night and back to my apartment to show him my gratitude. I finished what I'd started in the dressing room and was richly rewarded for the perseverance. David, in turn, showed me how talented his mouth was and offered up his high hard ones for me to pierce. It was quite a night. I won't say that we've exactly become an item since then, but I have changed the message on my answering machine, if that tells you anything.

HOT REUNION
by Kevin Bantan

The invitation arrived, as it did every year. I opened it without enthusiasm, but I admit that I was a bit curious about which city would host the annual get-together of the Bantan clan. The annual notice never failed to rekindle my shame. It wasn't that I had African-American relatives that caused me guilt, it was how they had come to family: My ancestors had been slaveholders.

I did a double take when I looked at the embossed card. As bad luck would have it, the reunion was going to be held in the city where I was living. That meant a double whammy. My parents would come visiting, and I couldn't use the hardship of driving to another time zone as an excuse not to attend.

The thought crossed my mind that my mother had engineered the plot to bring the event to me, and I wouldn't put it past her. On the other hand, there were surprisingly numerous listings for Bantan in the phone book, and I knew that many of them had to be black, given the parts of town where they lived in this largely segregated city.

The inevitable phone call came that evening. "Kevin, dear, did you get your invitation?" I was never Kev to them, as I was to my friends. I was always Kevin, which earned my parents an 'A' for annoying. Unfortunately, I was named after my great-great-great-great grandfather, the slave owner, who had fathered children, whose posterity lived here in town and looked nothing like me. And yet we shared a common ancestor.

"Yes, Mom. It came today."

"Isn't it wonderful that the reunion will be held there?"

"Yeah, great."

"Kevin, I know you aren't crazy about getting together with your relatives, but why don't you reconsider, just this once?" Because I'm filled with self-loathing for what great-great-great-great granddaddy's prick did to his female house servants, that's why. However, given the location of the reunion, I knew that I had an uphill battle to try to find an excuse not to go. So I shouldn't have been surprised that I lost the argument and agreed to attend. My anger at having caved in kept rising the longer she kept me on the phone.

Once I cut the connection, I let loose, hurling the pink Princess phone into the wallboard across the room. That wasn't very productive, but it did feel good. For a moment. At least I had several weeks to make the repair before the appearance of ma-ma and pa-pa.

And there was the minor consolation, if you could call it that, that I wouldn't have to hide the boyfriend *du jour* from them, there being none to hide. Small favors.

It was a lovely, warm day and Mother was in rare form, as my father told me she always was for these things. Father seemed not to have a strong opinion one way or the other, but he agreed with her that at the very least it was a way to bring the family together for healing, forgiveness and kinship. Why didn't they

just have a big revival, hold hands, exorcise the demon and be done with it? Why did they have to heal, forgive and rub noses every year? And how many darkies do you have on your staff, father, I wanted to ask.

The big deal was being held at a picnic ground just outside the city. It was a place where the local American Indian group held its annual powwows. But today it would no doubt be overrun with people sporting skin colors ranging from nearly albino to ebony and everything in between. Family. What a bogus concept.

The picnic grounds were set on rolling hills, which were punctuated with pavilions and copses of bushes and buffered on three sides by woods.

We were barely out of the car when my mother grabbed me by the arm and yoo-hooed to a black woman, whom she told me was my Aunt Flora. Oh, joy. Of course, Rita and Flora hugged and fussed as if it were old home week. I guess it was. Then the heated kinetic behavior spilled over onto me, and I was helpless to resist Aunt Flora's excellent impersonation of a boa constrictor. Well it was better than being punched for the excesses of the guy who long ago had fucked this odd family into existence, I guess.

After my aunt ceased her rolfing session, we were greeted by other people along the route to the food tables. Everybody knew my mother. Father was taking it all in stride, but my unease remained at a high level. If I could just procure about five paper plates full of food, I could keep my mouth stuffed all afternoon and perhaps be able to fend off high-spirited relations' invasive queries about my health and welfare, both of which had seen better picnics.

The food choices reflected the diverse cultural tastes of race and geography. But no matter how guilty I felt toward my dark-skinned relations, there was no way in hell that I was going to eat chitterlings. I settled for a couple of hamburgers, which two uncles I'd never met, Harvey and Jim, were serving up. Harvey was pepper, Jim, salt. From their incessant bantering, it was evident that they were old friends. That made me feel a wee bit better but still not ready to party. I glopped some potato salad onto the plate, speared a deviled egg, scooped up some of Aunt Marnie's special corn relish (according to my mother) and some vinegar slaw.

Then I left my parents and retreated to the perceived safety of a picnic table well away from the madding crowd. To hell with togetherness. Mother could berate me all she wanted to later for my antisocial behavior, but I knew that if I hung around her and father, I'd end up getting introduced to every person in attendance, none of whom I would be interested in meeting.

Two bites into the first burger, I realized that I hadn't gotten myself anything to drink. To slake my thirst would mean a return to the tumult. I decided to tough it out.

Just then a voice behind me made me jump. "Come here often?" it asked. I turned to see a smiling, handsome, medium brown-skinned young man about my age, who was somehow managing to balance a plate and two large Styrofoam

cups in his hands. I grinned at the silliness of the question but played along. "My first time. You?"

"My twenty-something. Mind if I join you?" It was foregone, as far away as we were from the rest of the family, but I was willing to indulge him, as good-looking as he was.

"No. Please," I said, half-rising to help relieve him of part of his burden; his plate. He thanked me and settled in across the table, put one of the cups at the top of my plate, and said, "Leo," flashing a smile, which I knew would live in my memory for years to come, it was so engaging.

"Pleased to meet you, Leo. I'm Kevin," I said holding out my hand. He laughed, revealing the dazzling teeth again. "No, I'm sorry, Kevin. My name's John. I just wanted to get the astronomical sign out of the way. People still do that to try to start conversations in the bars. Can you believe it?"

"I don't have to. I experience it all the time. Usually I just say Zorro."

"Pardon me?"

"The sign of the 'Z'," I said, demonstrating with my finger. He got it and laughed. He had great teeth. "Usually they think I'm crazy and leave me alone. Anyone who can't come up with a better opening line, I know I won't be interested in, no matter how cute."

"Me, neither. But what can you expect? It's not as if you go to the bars for quality conversation."

He gave me a sly smile, which made me wonder what his meaning was. What kind of bars was he talking about?

"Tell me about it. It would get in the way of pheromone sniffing, I suppose."

"It would. So where in this great land of ours did you hike in from, Kevin?"

"Please call me Kev, John. Actually, I live here."

"Really?! So do I. And you can call me JoJo."

"Thanks for the drink, JoJo. How did you know I was still thirsty?"

"Oh, I happened to see you leave the food area without any refreshment. So, I figured I'd bring one to you. Besides, you'll be glad for it when you taste the vinegar slaw. Very spicy."

"That was awfully nice of you. You're pretty observant."

"I hope so," he said and took a bite of his ham sandwich, averting his eyes.

What the hell did that response mean? He was intent on the plate now, scooping up some fermented beans, from the looks of them. It gave me a chance to look at JoJo without the distraction of his neon smile, and I realized that he was way beyond handsome. He was absolutely gorgeous. When his dancing black eyes, which were surrounded by feathered, arcing lashes, looked up to lock onto mine again, he smiled shyly. The last thing I would have predicted happening at this event, was exactly what was occurring.

I was suddenly in unbridled lust for the man sitting across from me, a man, who was my cousin however many times removed. Kissing cousins, I mused. Doubtful. If the latest speculations about the prevalence of homosexuality were

to be believed, there was, at best, a two percent chance that the adonis facing me was gay. Not groping odds, for sure, because the probability of becoming an in-the-kisser cousin were pretty certain, if I tried it. I sighed. God, JoJo was beautiful!

"So, are you enjoying the company of our special interracial family?" I asked, with enough sarcasm to dare him to take exception.

"Actually, I find it interesting. We Bantans resemble the melting pot America professes that it is. Your body language back there and what you just said seems to indicate that you're uncomfortable being here, Kev. Is it the race thing?"

"Yeah. Guilt. Shame. Choose any other suitable synonym."

"Why?"

"I'm the namesake of the man who owned your ancestors, JoJo. Shouldn't I be ashamed of that?"

"No. *That* Kevin Bantan did, not the one sitting across from me. I don't hold what happened a hundred fifty years ago against you. Or any of my other white relatives, for that matter. It happened, and now here we are having our annual picnic, trying to be one happy family. Frankly, I find that very encouraging. And Aunt Rita's a hoot. She and mom have always been the catalysts in bringing us together. They feed off each other."

"Your Aunt Rita is my mother," I said, glad that she was out of my sight and thankful for the drink JoJo had brought me, having sampled the slaw. "Catalyst is a kind term to describe enthusiasm run amok." He chuckled, showing the white enamels that my tongue ached to lick. "And your Aunt Flora is my mom."

"No kidding? She should be a sumo wrestler, as good as she is at hugging." He showed more mirth and whites. *Please don't do that, JoJo. Assault and sexual battery charges are in my near future, if you keep it up.*

"We call her the python, surprisingly." We laughed.

He looked at my plate. It still had one uneaten hamburger and plenty of the side dishes left. My hormones had neutralized my appetite. I didn't need to eat anymore anyway, because I was going to die from testosterone overload shortly.

Then JoJo said, "Hey, if you're finished, why don't we go for a walk in yonder woods, Kev. It'll be, uh, less crowded."

Than what? It was only the two us now.

"Sounds good." It sounded terrible, actually, but maybe they wouldn't hear his screams when the crazed homosexual attacked his body. Maybe they wouldn't find mine for days after he'd beaten me to death in justifiable moral outrage for the unwanted advances.

The woods were much deeper than I had imagined. The farther we got into them, the quieter it became. The sounds of humans were extinguished. An occasional bird would call to its mate. Poor word selection, because that was exactly what I wanted to do with JoJo's body. We made small talk, telling each other about our jobs and where we lived.

JoJo lived and worked on the east side of town. I did both up north. So it was no surprise in a city as large as ours that our paths hadn't crossed. And certainly not in the bars, because we were looking for two different sexes.

My angst returned at that thought. The really frustrating thing about it was that the more I determined that he was unattainable, the more I wanted JoJo's beauty. It's probably some kind of masochistic tendency in my severely flawed psychological makeup. "Doctor Freud will see you now, Mr. Bantan, but don't get your hopes up."

We came to a wide, shallow stream which cut through the trees. "Well, this is a pleasant surprise. Do you think it's Meander Creek?"

"Could very well be," I said. We both picked up stones and skipped them across the surface of the water. "Great minds," I said.

"That, too," he said. I looked at him, and he returned my stare, his onyx eyes twinkling. "Or has my gaydar failed me for the first time in years?" I could not believe my ears. My mouth dropped open.

"Are you serious, JoJo? You mean...you're...."

"As a three dollar bill."

"I don't believe it. I mean that's great, but I couldn't tell. How did you know?"

"I saw you, when you arrived. My heart actually skipped a beat, by the way. Several times, to be truthful. So, I watched for any gesture, any sign, anything at all that might give you away."

"And?"

"Nothing. But I saw my opening, when you forgot to take something to drink with you. I decided that a cousin as beautiful as you couldn't possibly be straight. I also decided that I'd drop a hint here and there. You picked up on them, I could tell by your eyes. At least you were considering what the meanings were. They would have gone completely over the head of a straight guy. And you mentioned 'cute' in terms of the bars. That's an adjective for boys on my street. So, my next move was to get you away from civilization and hope for the best."

He looked back to where we had come from. Then he looked up and down the stream and smiled. He closed the gap between us and put his lips on mine and I felt the stirring below almost immediately. "Even more delicious than I expected these ripe cherries to be," he said, as we held each other. His body felt wonderful against mine. "It looks as if there's a ford in the creek a little ways down. Maybe we can find a clearing on the other side. It should give us some added privacy, on the assumption that our rug-rat relatives aren't adventuresome enough to chance crossing it."

"Let's do it," I said, before kissing him again. He took my hand and we walked happily toward the jutting stones.

On the other side, about a couple hundred feet farther on, there was a grassy clearing, as if it had appeared magically, courtesy of the love gods. The space

was roughly a twenty-foot irregular circle into which dappled light descended. After more feasting on each other's full lips, we undressed. It being summer, the disrobing was easy. I shed my polo shirt, walking shorts and briefs, kicking off my Topsiders as I did so. JoJo needed to lose a short-sleeved rugby shirt, long denim shorts and sports sandals.

Then, in the oasis of light, we were naked to each other. And what a nakedness JoJo was. His shiny brown skin highlighted every ripple of his developed muscles from his calves to his neck. Like mine, his long cock hung out and down leisurely from his body. Both it and his sac were markedly darker than the rest of his body. We seemed to be about evenly matched in that department. I wondered, briefly, if we had inherited our granddaddy's organ.

We took some time admiring, caressing and complimenting each other over the results of the other's strenuous workouts and natural assets. Then it was time to get serious. We pressed our bodies together. We wrapped our arms around each other as our tongues and lips sought out similar pleasure. I managed to disengage from JoJo's mouth to flick my tongue over his teeth. The ivories of a piano would never produce a sweeter tune. I kissed and licked his face as he returned the favor. I inhaled his scent and lapped his neck and kissed his shoulder. His hands worried my back and round cheeks.

Then I disengaged to get another look at the thing that had started to press insistently against my sac and perineum. It was even more lovely erect. I put my hand around it, savoring the silky feel of the skin. The slit was large, like mine. JoJo remarked about our similar endowments, as he squeezed my head, making the eye-like opening wink.

We leaned into each other's face as we continued to grip the erections tightly. Should someone have stumbled onto us at that moment, he probably would have thought that he was witnessing some secret homosexual marriage rite. JoJo came off my lips and whispered, "I know where I want what I'm holding." Then he licked my ear, causing me to shiver. Usually I'm a bottom, but the thought of being inside that body was irresistible.

Slowly we sank to the ground, with JoJo ending up on top of me. When he left my lips, he kissed and sucked down my body. My dark nipples stood at attention from the glorious suction used on them. I moaned as my innie threatened to become an outie when he inhaled it after reaming it.

My cock, which had been engorging from his body play, made him forget my navel as it grew upwards past it. Amazingly, he took the better part of my erection into his mouth and began to prepare me with his saliva. His mouth was mutely eloquent in its communication with my manhood.

I had to pull him off, because he was sending me toward orgasm fast. He dropped a couple of liquid bombs onto me and spread the wet stuff over my head and upper shaft.

"You look so comfortable, Kev. Why don't I just go ahead and help myself to this beauty?"

"Be my guest, cuz." He did, slowly sliding me into him until he was impaled on me.

"Mmm. Feels great." He leaned over and kissed me.

"It does."

Then he massaged the hardness inside him; the feeling was incredible. I played with his dark nipples, making them rigid in my fingers. The nubs shone and stood in high relief.

I turned my attention to his long, dusky cock. I played my fingers lightly over the shaft and head as he slowly fucked himself with the lighter-colored model of the one I was stroking. I fingered his opening with my other hand. He closed his eyes and bent his head back, savoring the double pleasure he was receiving.

Here we were, two cousins of different colors, joined in the most intimate celebration of maleness.

My hands left his bobbing hardness so that they could delight in the feel of his hard muscles. I played them over his chest and abdomen. I stroked his big thighs.

Then I caressed his sides. "Oh, god, that feels so arousing, Kev." I kept it up.

His movements became more animated as his prick moved higher in the air, and I went over the edge, unable to resist the smooth friction of his inner muscle. When he was sure that he had claimed every last bit of my come, he slid off me, causing my body to shudder from the final pleasure to my sensitive nerves.

Then he moved up my body and offered himself to me, a gift I was eager to accept. I stuck my tongue into his wide opening and teased it, making his shaft twitch and him giggle. The lilt of his voice was music to my ears.

I felt intoxicated by the warm feelings I had for him already. I took his head into my mouth and nursed on it, as if it were an all-day sucker. I gripped his solid hemispheres and slowly guided more and more of him into me, manufacturing saliva at a dizzying rate. He got to the point where he, too, was receiving too much of a good thing.

He held my head and said, "Stop, Kev. I've mooned over your granite cheeks since I first glimpsed them in the parking lot, and I don't want to be disappointed now that you have me more than ready."

What could I say to a compliment like that? I opened wide and let him slide out, reluctantly. He glistened darkly in the filtered afternoon sun, and that exquisite sight was all the encouragement I needed to retract my legs and beg for it. He moistened his first two fingers and coated my passage with his spit. Then he nudged against the opening, and I swallowed his crown again. "You okay, Kev?"

"Close to nirvana."

"I know what you mean. Me, too, cuz."

Gently, he pushed in all the way. I wrapped my ankles around JoJo's sleek

back as he began to fuck me. It felt wonderful having his cock in me, and I told him so. I was rewarded with another kiss and a chance to lick those pearls of his. My tongue snaked behind his lips and he moaned from the stimulation of his gums. He rewarded my effort with his own tongue in my mouth.

"Oh, man, Kev. You feel so great this way, too."

As he fucked me, I drank in the beauty of the flawless body and strikingly pretty face looming over me, lost in the pleasure of the fuck.

"I'm yours, JoJo," I said, stroking his sides again.

"I accept the offer."

Balanced on his hands, he was deliberate in his lovemaking until the stimulation of his sides and his gathering urge took over and propelled him into a more rapid thrusting in my gut.

"Oh, god, you are so beautiful, Kev."

I closed my eyes and moaned at the pleasure he was giving me. He moaned back. His big slit shot his come deep within me. I managed to open my eyes to see the ecstasy on his face and smiled. My awesome lover. My cousin. JoJo.

We lay together in the clearing, murmuring sweet nothings to each other, playing lazily with our wannabe erections and nuzzling and kissing as the sun rode high in the sky. That is, until we fell asleep. When we awoke, the sun had mostly deserted us, the clearing markedly diminished of light.

"Man, we need to get back, Kev."

"Yeah. They'll be sending out a posse for us, and they won't like what they find."

We scrambled to get dressed, hugged and kissed deeply one last time and headed back toward the partiers. We held hands until we came into the open ground. The number of relatives had thinned somewhat. Even the human perpetual motion machines, our mothers, were at least seated, if not at rest.

"Where in the world have you two been," my mother asked, with a note of "I told you so" in it. Bad guess, mother.

"We decided to walk off the food we'd eaten, and when we sat down at the stream, it was so peaceful that we just dozed off."

"Good answer," I heard JoJo whisper behind me. I could sense his arms wanting to go around my waist and draw me into him, but they behaved, sad to say. Under the circumstances, it was prudent.

"Well, I'm glad you two boys got to get to know each other," Aunt Flora said. Yes, you could put it that way.

"Not nearly as glad as we are," JoJo whispered.

I chuckled at the remark.

"What is so funny, Kev?"

"Well, you really had to be there."

Soon the sky was inky and the throng had thinned to a skeleton of the huge family. We left last, when Flora and Rita were satisfied that the campground was in suitable repair to return it to its owner. JoJo and I had committed our

respective phone numbers to memory, reciting them to each other in hushed tones, along with a heartfelt phrase, before we got into our parents' cars.

"Well, you certainly seemed to hit it off with John," my father said.

That was comparing a snail to an elephant, but all I said was, "Well, yeah, he's a nice guy."

"Aren't you glad you went now?"

I didn't answer. I just let the shit-eating grin spread across my face. Mother could look into the back seat for the answer, if she really wanted it.

JoJo has been great, although he insists that we attend all the family reunions. I don't care anymore, because he's helped me to get over my guilt about my namesake.

DON'T SAY ANYTHING
by John Patrick

Davey had left me again. He said he wasn't coming back but he didn't pack his suitcase.

I finished at work about five. I went home and took a shower. When Davey hadn't returned by seven, I walked down to Christopher's and ate nachos, had a few beers. There was a rerun of *Psycho* on the big screen over the bar; and when Anthony Perkins approached the shower curtain with his knife, the bartender rang a bell so no one would miss watching Janet Leigh die. I was glad to be absorbed in anything. I watched the black blood disappear down the drain and drank another beer. When I'd finished, I called my apartment; there was no answer, and there were no messages. I had another beer. I went home around nine. I tried to watch television, but the weight of a weekend without Davey hit me. I went into his room. The room smelled of him, a kind of delicate sweatiness that made me think of his cock, his balls, his sturdy young legs, his asshole. Mostly his asshole.

I stood over the bed he occupied when he didn't sleep with me, whenever he was mad at me. I thought about that first day, meeting him at the pool. How beautiful he was: radiant really. And then how quickly I found out how maliciously innocent he was.

But I loved him. I could not lose him, not now. Give me another month, I asked the powers that be. When I thought I was going to cry, I left the room, Davey's room.

I went into the bathroom, stood there. Where was Davey? I kept asking myself. I knew the answer, of course. Davey was with a stranger, getting fucked senseless. He needed that, I knew. Yet I needed him. I needed him to tell me it was just sex. That what we had was the good stuff. I needed him to tell me everything was fine. To get in bed and spread his legs, prove how much he loved me, missed me, wanted me.

As I got ready for bed, I figured if he came home now and said it was fine, it would be fine. I washed my face, stripped.

Davey didn't come.

I told myself this was dumb. There were reasons why he wasn't there that had nothing to do with me. A boy's gotta do what he's gotta do. He has never been unfaithful to me, that I know of, not once in the whole eight months. It's just when I complain about it that he gets mad.

I got up to take a sleeping pill. I looked at myself in the mirror. Under the bright light in the bathroom, my face looked haggard, old. I saw tears welling in my eyes. This kid was getting to me. I'd never fucked anyone before like I fucked Davey. Never, ever. I became mildly aroused just thinking about it, how good he made it. I went and lay down, finally fell asleep.

When Davey came, I was deeply asleep. He smelled of sex, of cool air, of everything but me. He started kissing me, and his breath, his saliva tasted of

beer. It was all I could think of. I wanted to drink him in. His hands were cool on me as he tore away the sheet and went down on me.

My cock throbbed under his spell; he was claiming my cock as his, his own personal fuck-toy.

All the hatred of the night before fell away as he climbed over me and I felt him slide down on my erection. It was like a dream I was having of how it could always be like this. Hell, it was always like this! He'd go away, but come back again, and then we'd have it like this, with me barely awake. We pushed against each other. I reached to touch him, but he wasn't hard. No, he had probably come several times since last night; it was as if this was just for me.

"Ahhh," he said, and held his ass high over me, with just the head of my cock in him. I pushed a little. His face above me was startled, foolish with unbelieving eagerness, like a schoolboy's. He was still. He let me fuck it now. I know it hurt, nearly too much, and I thought about stopping, of not giving him this pleasure, but I could not deny my own. God, he loved to get fucked! Through the drug and my fatigue, I could feel some deeper consciousness, some other pain, returning. But I eased against it, against him, shoved it in him, and then I knew I wasn't hurting him anymore, and he wasn't hurting me anymore. Now it was easier, and he pushed too, but gently. I wanted this, just this. He wanted it, too. And, God help me, I wanted it to last forever.

Then he tilted back into the dim light and I couldn't see his face any more. He began to thrust faster, harder. I looked down to see he was jacking off; at last he was hard, ready. When he began to cry out, I felt myself shake. I wanted only him. It was the same old thing, really, but it was always a bit different. He came, but there wasn't much of a load. What there was just oozed over his hand. It was probably like his third, maybe fourth orgasm since he left.

He bent gently towards me, lay on me and kissed my neck. I continued to slam into his ass. He groaned when I finally let loose inside him, my load of cum filling him.

Then his fingers reached towards my face, felt my wet hair, my open mouth. "Please, don't say anything," he begged.

My cock slipped from his ass with a resounding pop. "There's nothing to say," I said. "Nothing at all."

IN DEEP
by John Patrick

I come home from work and I want it. If I'm very good, Blake lets me have it. If I'm very bad, he lets me have it, only harder, rougher. Blake and I have an unusual relationship, by some standards. We are equals he craves my ass as much as I crave his cock. We are not top and bottom, master and submissive, it's just that we give each other what the other one craves.

I love to have my ass fucked, to have him deep in, and hold out as long as I can before the pain finally makes me cry and come.

Seeing Blake's cock hard makes my ass twitch so much that I can't stand it. Then Blake falls down on top of me, eats my ass out while I suck him.

I would never say no to Blake, his cock is so beautiful, nine inches long, very thick; it's the most luscious one I had ever encountered until the other night.

Blake's face was stony when I walked into the apartment after a hard day bussing tables at the Hilton. As usual, he was wearing his plaid Western shirt and jeans and his hair ran straight back from his forehead in a waxy sheen. "Over here," he said.

I approached him cautiously, seeing he was sitting on the sofa with someone I did not know. "I want you to be the animal you are," he said, his bittersweet blackberry eyes flashing. "I want you to show Kurt what I left him for."

Kurt? I had never seen him, but I knew all about him. He was the great love of Blake's life, at least until he met me. Kurt had taken a job in Miami and Blake couldn't go with him. The separation meant the end of the relationship, not Blake's meeting me.

I smiled at the big blond sitting next to Blake. He was older than Blake, not particularly attractive. Blake had always said that Kurt had not aged well. He looked pretty good to me, although it was obvious from his creased, wrinkled skin he was spending way too much time in the sun.

"Prove to Kurt you're worth your weight in gold, my golden boy," Blake said, dropping his empty beer bottle on the floor, next to what looked to be about a dozen other empties. I assumed Kurt had showed up some time before and the two had been boozing.

Kurt watched, enthralled, as I squirmed when Blake grabbed a clump of my hair and tugged it back. "Go on, show him," he ordered.

Kurt's face flushed. Blake's drunken behavior was embarrassing even him. I pressed my lips against his bulging crotch. Drunk or sober, Blake could always get it up.

In a blaze of desire, I tugged off my boots, then my shorts, without interrupting the feeding frenzy of my ravenous mouth at Blake's crotch. Blake unzipped his jeans while I pulled my shirt up over my head and removed it; I was naked now. Quickly I was back between Blake's widely parted legs. Kurt's breathing was excited now, matching Blake's. With a strong hand and a firm thrust of his hips, Blake positioned his long tool, playing the tip at my lips for a

fleeting moment, teasing me, teasing himself, teasing Kurt. His cock seemed to grow straight out of his fist. Overcome with the hunger, with a groan of satisfaction, Blake penetrated my mouth. Kurt assisted him, moving his body into the best position for me taking him as well. I obliged them willingly.

Before long, Blake was ripping me apart with his mouth, lifting me up higher to thrust his tongue into my hole. I rocked my tight little ass into him as he prepared me.

When I could take no more, Blake shoved his erection inside me, plunging in and out, deeper every time, making my body yield to him a bit more with every thrust.

"Take all of it, boy. Show Kurt you're worth all my efforts. Open to me, and let me come inside you," Blake whispered in my ear.

He wrapped both hands around my waist now, holding on tight as he fucked me. Our bodies moved together, his eyes shut tight in concentration. I rode him with a passion, making sure to press my ass in tight against his beefy body. This motion drove him crazy and he fucked me hard and fast, giving it to me as I cried out my pleasure, my voice filling the room.

Kurt's rapid breathing and impassioned voice urged his ex-lover on. "Yes, oh yeah, that's my Daddy. Show me how you want me to do it," Kurt said in a voice heavy with desire and sensation. Blake increased his speed then, as if challenged, and I was riding him back as hard and fast as he was giving it to me, sucking him in, body pounding, close to the edge.

"Like this, you mean. Like this?" Blake continued as our pace increased, both of us sweating and shining from our efforts.

Kurt had his face right down at the action. "You got all of it inside him. God that's gorgeous!"

This was the kind of thing I had expected would come from Blake someday. I had hated him when I heard about what he did to his boys, and then the hatred had slowly twisted and transformed into a fascination. An obsession. And then a raging fury of hunger for his cock. I smiled, feeling my body pounding with the oncoming wave of an orgasm that threatened to blow my body apart. I took everything Blake had to give and was stronger than Kurt had imagined. He stroked my cock as his ex fucked me and I came with a vengeance then, my ass muscles pulling and manipulating Blake's dick as his orgasm ripped through his body, all sensation shooting out into my ass.

Blake's voice was urgent, insistent. "C'mon, don't be shy, Kurt. Fuck him now."

Kurt pulled back and reached down then, and I saw his body was pulsing, pounding with sensation. As his fingers touched the sensitive tip of his swollen cock, I saw pre-cum seep from the head. I took him in all at once, my heels digging into the floor, and I rubbed his big, beautiful cock all over my face.

And as Blake continued to fuck me, I felt his aftershocks. The sweat between us had become a slippery second skin that bound us together as one. Pinching

myself was unnecessary I knew I was in heaven. There have been times when he had accused me of never living life for the moment. He could never say that again.

- - -

"Are you gonna be good to me, baby?" he asked, almost pleading. He looked at me vacantly, reclining on our lovers' bed. Blake had passed out in the living room. Kurt had taken a shower while I cleaned up the mess he and Blake had made in the living room.

Kurt was still wet from his shower, but his smell was too good to wash away. Grinding his hips, his buttocks pushing into the mattress, his fingerings preparing the way for me, he asked, again, "Well, you gonna?"

"You want me to fuck you, Kurt?" I asked, a reverence in my voice. "Real hard, like you gave it to me?"

Standing naked, I caressed the lube all over my cock. He wanted to beg me; I could see it in the tension of his mouth, the way he bit his lip, holding back the demand.

It was my time now. I had now been allowed to make the moves, after I had obeyed Blake's sexual demands, as he had for the two years he had been Blake's lover.

Kurt remained on his back, which surprised me. I was unsure if he might change his mind. Relinquishing sexual power must have been hard for him, but then I remember that he was once like me, being trained for life by Blake. Now he was testing how much I had learned, or maybe the fact he was here at all was to test me, to see if I could do it.

Now here he was, on his back, legs wide, his hole is taut and taunting, nakedly exposed.

I decided I would be his benefactor and give him the fuck he craved on my terms. I climbed on top of him like I had watched people do a thousand times before in the porn Blake and I watch. I immediately started driving into him. I stare down at him as he sank into another place, felt the electricity of his power and my own. Sweat from my face dropped onto his lips, and he drew my head down as I thrust, lunged heavily into him, and he kissed me. I fed his voracious hole, slamming him now, on a collision course to coming, as his legs wrapped around me, clasping for deeper penetration. Gasps and grunts greeted my ears as he urged me to erupt within him.

"Okay," I raggedly breathed out as I came. "Okay, just for you."

"Oh, what a wonderful boy you've been," he whispered in my ear.

And we stayed that way for a few minutes while I calmed down. Finally he pulled away.

I gripped his erection. "Please, Kurt," I begged.

He let me guide his big cock between my splayed legs. Rubbing the head against my ass-lips I taunted him again. Then in one movement he pushed his way in until he was buried deep inside my boy-cunt. Grasping my hips, he began

to stroke in and out, building tempo until he was pounding, slamming into me, and my body was rising and pushing into each incredible stroke.

After he himself had been fucked, he was now of a mind to really make me suffer.

"Does Blake take good care of you, honey?"

"When he's sober," I grunted each word between strokes. I had become erect again, and I began rubbing it, deliberate and hard. Kurt slowed to match my pace, his huge cock grinding inside me purposefully, until it became too much for him and there could only be one conclusion. For a long moment he ceased his movement and my breath caught in my throat as we seemed to hover over the notion that maybe he could hold off his orgasm, keep on some more. Then he gave me another stroke, his cock burning into my ass, and then another and another, until he was moaning and crying out, filling me with his cum.

As I let his post-orgasmic body slide down my torso, he looked at me with a bit of embarrassment. "This wasn't my idea, you know. He *insisted* I stay."

"I'm so glad you did. I've been wanting to meet you for a long, long time."

And now I looked at his face, seeing him really for the first time. He was a good-looking guy. The eyes were blue, like mine, but not wild, as they had been when we were in the room with Blake. He was only a couple of years older than me, but his eyes belonged to a much older man, and I feared for myself for the first time.

And when he wrapped his arms around me and whispered, "Come back to Miami with me, baby," I kissed him.

FANTASYLAND: (Hard Sex in the Big Easy)
by David Patrick Beavers

Doug unpacked slowly, stowing shirts and pants away in the chest-of-drawers in the bedroom of the cottage he'd rented for the week. Always the same cottage. He liked the familiarity of surroundings whenever he was away from home. Even though New Orleans was simply his vacation place of choice, he refused to try a hotel or a guest house. His friends, whom he often met with during these respites from real life, always chose to try new places to stay each year. Doug found what he liked the first time he explored the Big Easy and wasn't about to part with it.

None of his friends were joining him this year, though. Their work schedules and social schedules were too full. Besides, they preferred coming during the more festive weeks of Halloween or Mardi Gras, when absolute fun-filled anarchy reigned supreme in the Quarter. He preferred the late weeks of September or the early weeks of October. The weather was usually cooler, sometimes raining even. Humidity was still a factor, but it was nowhere near as brutal as it was in the summer months. He could stroll around comfortably in the day or the evening. Leave the cottage and step out onto the corner of Barracks and Bourbon Streets, almost in the middle of the normal chaos.

But the first order of business was getting some groceries nominal supplies to stock the refrigerator in the kitchen. While New Orleans was certainly a town known for its cuisine and libations, there were times when a simple apple, a slice of cheese or a couple of cookies would fill him, rather than a platter load of delicious and heavy Cajun grub. He turned out the light, threw on his worn leather jacket and scooted out the front door.

Twilight. The low, enticing sound of jazz ebbed toward him like a slow, incoming tide. Just a couple of blocks down Bourbon, he could see the beginnings of the night's revelers meandering with aimless intent in the street, along the sidewalks, lingering below and atop galleries. The air was redolent of beer, of spicy dishes, of incense and oils, reminding him of all the good times he'd had in the city over the years.

As he walked, he crossed over and cut down Dumaine Street to Royal. Just a block south of Bourbon Street, Royal Street lay claim to those less focused on partying and more focused on spending. Art galleries, poster shops, antique emporiums, clothes and jewelry were most all housed here on Royal. This was more his speed. A little shopping, coffee at the coffee house and the good old A&P.

The tiny market was situated on a corner, its white front doors of scuff-marked wood creaked as people went in and out. The claustrophobic aisles reminded him of the markets in Manhattan. Enough room for two normal-size people to pass shoulder to shoulder and not an inch more. Still, for such a small market, the shelves were well stocked and the assortment of fruits and vegetables was good. Doug filled a hand basket with odds and ends bottled

- 79 -

water, a six-pack of diet cola, coffee, non-fat milk, some red apples and bananas, chips, a brick of cheddar cheese and some cookies. Odds and ends to snack on in the middle of the night if he so chose.

As he waited in line for the only cashier to check him out, he caught sight of a short youth entering the store. Even though he was from Los Angeles where striking youths abound, there was something subtle in this youth's look. A lean form in clothes that would be considered too unhip to most city kids. A flannel shirt of navy and red that fit him, and Levi's that were normal, like 501's or 505's, and boots of some sort that were practical laborer's boots, not the faux gazillion-dollar trendy name brands of the day. Even more than his uncomplicated style, his face was intriguing. A very squared, powerful jaw and full lips. And eyes that stood out. Large and almost almond shaped, the brilliance of the blue of his irises couldn't but be noticed. Dark brows were furrowed in a sort of frown that was softened somewhat by shaggy, reddish-brown hair that was in need of a cut.

While he was preoccupied with his thought, the checker adroitly blasted through the goods in his basket, ringing up his total and having it all bagged before he could finish digging his wallet out of his pocket. He paid for his groceries, picked up the bag, then with some reluctance, headed out of the A&P. Back to Royal Street, back to the cottage.

He could have lingered outside the market, waiting for the young man to emerge, but such folly was no more than a waste of time. He'd tried ploys like that in the past and they never amounted to much.

Night fell quickly. With the darkness, the living came to elaborate life, filling the bars and restaurants of the Quarter. Doug wasn't a drinker. Had never really been one. He preferred to be in control of his mind, as best as possible, when he was out and about.

Still, he did enjoy gambling now and then. He decided that first night there would be spent on the riverboat, playing the one-armed bandits in the casino. So, after putting away his meager rations and after having a quick shower, he put on his jeans, his tennis shoes, a green T-shirt and his jacket and set out for Riverwalk where the casino was moored.

The night air was damp, but cool and refreshing. The simple frenetic energy from the people milling about in the streets gave him the extra lift that he needed. He wound his way down Dumaine to Chartres, then cut through Pirates Alley, coming into Jackson Square. The usual musicians played their personal favorites, the fortune tellers and sidewalk artists had their tables all set up all around the Pontalba Apartments, the Cabildo and the square itself with its lush green lawns and imposing statue of Jackson upon his rearing horse. He decided to pass through the park to Decatur Street.

As he went around the statue, he happened upon the young man he'd seen in the market. Parked on a bench, he was absorbed in a sketch he was doing. Doug assumed it was a sketch of the statue. He slowed his pace a little, debating

whether to strike up a conversation or not with the young man. But to make small talk seemed both trite and obvious. The young man seemed to be concentrating with almost blind focus on his task. Doug let a slight sigh slip from his lips as he pressed on.

Even with all the superfluous sounds of music and chatter and the clopping of hooves from the horses and donkeys drawing hansom cabs, his little breath of an utterance broke the young man's concentration. He looked up at Doug, with what Doug perceived to be a scowl, then his face softened, almost expressionless, as he leaned back against the bench. He set the pad aside and dropped his pencil into a teak box by his side. His fingers were covered with the gray-black of soft lead.

"It's getting too dark to finish," the young man said.

"It's been dark for quite some time now."

The young man looked up into the night sky and grinned. "Yeah, yer right there."

"Well...." Doug's mind shut down. "I suppose...."

The youth waited for the rest of the thought. But it didn't come. "You suppose it's dark?"

Doug grinned an embarrassed grin. "You can always go back to it in the morning."

The boy nodded. "You going to the river boat?" he asked, suddenly.

Doug shifted uneasily, thinking he should just move on. "It's a possibility."

The young man nodded again. "I'm Jason."

"Doug."

"Where're ya from? California?"

"Is it that obvious?" Doug asked.

Jason shrugged. "You've an accent."

"Californians don't have an accent."

"Yeah they do. Elongated O's. Syllabant S's. Things like that," Jason said. "Nothin' hard or real distinct, but noticeable just the same."

"Where're you from?" It was Doug's turn to inquire.

"Oregon," he said. "Tilahook. It's where they make the cheese." Jason let out a cackle. "An' God does it stink."

"You visiting, too?" Doug asked.

"Naw. I moved here a year ago when I got out of high school."

"Going to Tulane or LSU?"

Jason leaned forward, pulling a cigarette out of an unseen pack in his shirt pocket. He lit a wood match, took a long drag, then blew out the flame with a plume of smoke. "Nope. Came to work on a krewe."

"Crew?"

"K-r-e-w-e," he spelled. "For Mardi Gras."

Doug studied the young man's face. The hint of a beard line from the day made his pale olive skin almost blue in the moonlight. A man's beard on a boy's

face. A broad bridged, rounded nose seemed neither big nor small, yet it softened the sharp angles of his cheeks and jaw and intensified the shadowy darkness around those brilliant blue eyes. Rolled-up sleeves bared slender, yet muscular forearms that led to hands that were thick and long fingered. A laborer's palm with a pianist's fingers.

"The floats," Doug said.

"Yeah, like that." Jason stacked his teak box atop his sketch pad, then leaned back against the bench again, his arms stretched out and relaxed along its top. He stretched out his legs stiffly as he yawned. Lean legs. 501's, Doug thought. Denim that fit. Denim that allowed some shapely form to be seen.

Doug felt his cock strain just a bit. An impulse reaction. A twitch of awareness. He wanted to slip his hand down his jeans to adjust himself, but there was no discreet way of doing that, so he took a few steps back, toward Jason. "What are you drawing?"

Jason looked at his sketch pad a second, then handed it to Doug. "Nothin' special."

Doug gently flipped through the pages. Nudes. Male nudes. Some full renderings, some just partial sketches of parts of the body. A hand, a torso, eyes, feet... a study in anatomy. Young men, old men, men in between. A study in aging anatomy.

Doug was no art expert, but he'd studied it quite a bit over the years, more as a hobby than anything else. Still, he could tell from what he knew that Jason had an instinctual talent geared toward the classical.

"How come you're not in an art school?" he asked.

"What for?"

"Well, you've obviously got talent...."

"I just like to draw. Art school's expensive. The degree I could get isn't worth dick-squat out on the open market."

"You could always *adapt* your talent for other venues," Doug said as he handed back the sketch pad.

"Other *venues?*" he asked absently as he squashed his cigarette butt under his boot.

"Art director. Scene design. Architecture. Murals."

Jason picked up his stuff and stood. "May as well play the lottery, too, or hit the Black Jack table."

"That's pretty pessimistic."

"What can I say? I'm a realist." He extended his hand to Doug. "Thanks, though, for the encouragement."

Doug hesitated a brief second, then shook the young man's lead-stained hand. A firm grip the youth had. Rough palms. "Well, it's still something to think about."

Jason drew back his hand, cupping the pad and teak box like school books in the other. "Good luck at the casino." Doug's expectancy was halted. This was a

very polite dismissal. The young man had to be on his way. "Thanks...."

Jason raised an awkward hand a weak good-bye. An even more awkward and shy tight smile strained his lips, then he nodded and padded off, back toward Pirates' Alley. Doug tossed out a feeble "Bye" as an afterthought. Just move on, he thought. But he couldn't. He watched the young man disappear into the darkness. Now the casino seemed less appealing. He wanted to follow Jason. See where he went. What house or apartment he disappeared into. A place to focus on while he was here. A person to focus on. His feet found motion. Not toward Decatur Street, but back the way he'd come. His path mirroring the one just taken by Jason. He was feeling the slight flush of adrenaline excitement. Feeling the strain in his crotch even more. Cold trickles of sweat bled down his sides as his feet picked up their pace.

- - -

Doug's face stuck in Jason's mind. The man must be in his late thirties or early forties, but he was, in his opinion, a handsome man. A younger Peter O'Toole look. Thick medium blond hair that was silvering, a forelock hanging boyishly across his forehead. Slight wrinkles around beautiful gray eyes. Gray like Oregon skies in autumn. Buttery brown skin set off by the green of his T-shirt. Even in the darkness, beneath the open jacket, he could see the broad expanse of a muscular chest beneath the cotton. Nothing contrived about the man. No pretty boy veneer, no costume Daddy striving for a look. He just seemed to be a man. A simple man. Like the men he'd grown up around in Oregon, who wore jeans and flannel, who had burly arms and broad shoulders from day-to-day labor. Men who smelled of the timber line or diesel or Old Spice cologne. Men he liked. Men that made his body tingle and his cock strain hard.

He'd found some men like this on occasion in New Orleans. Mostly visitors from Texas or New Mexico or Iowa. Most of the men were married to wives, who willfully hid the other side of their lives. The others, well, almost all, were involved in long, term relationships with other men who were visiting the Big Easy with them. Only a few were single. Still, even though he was young, he didn't seem to fit some ideal of youth these men sought. He had to pursue them, even if only for an hour or an evening. They always pursued those short-haired, shaved- down, tall, lean, muscled Junior Adonises that floated in from Miami, or San Francisco, or New York. These men had magazine fantasies, his friend Larry would say. That's why he didn't want to stick around talking to Doug. Doug was probably just like the others. He just had time to kill.

It was early evening. The river boat would eat up a few hours of his time, then he'd hit the bars or the bath house on Toulouse seeking a score for the evening. Bah. He might as well have set up Doug with Larry. Larry, his long-haired, hard-bodied, well-endowed roommate. Larry, who stripped on a bar top in a gay bar in the Quarter, getting down to an amply filled G-string and his black cowboy boots. Larry from New York with a Puerto Rican mother and a

blond German father. Well, he thought, time to get back home.

He had to work in the morning his other real job, a short order cook at a diner. He was almost to his block on Burgundy, when he felt the presence of someone behind him. Night time strollers in the residential part of the Quarter were not all that common. He casually glanced behind him, but saw no one. Still, he shoved his free hand into his pocket and fished out his house keys. While New Orleans was fun, it did have more than its fair share of crime. A corner house on Burgundy and St. Ann. A small affair that he and Larry rented, it was all charm on the outside and in dire need of an overhaul on the inside. That's the way it was with many of the rentals. The wrapper was the eye catcher. The inside, well, one always thinks *I can fix it up*. He bounded up the steps and hurried inside.

- - -

Doug felt like some sort of stalker, sure that everyone in every house around was peering out through curtains at him lurking in the shadows. He wasn't sure what to do now that he'd come this far. All he knew was that his heart was racing, he was clammy with nervous sweat and his prick was a rigid pipe about to burst. He decided it best to move along casually, like any other tourist. He could head up St. Ann to Rampart then perhaps double back around blocks. Too bad he didn't have his camera with him, he thought. He could pretend to take pictures. But who'd believe that? It was night. He rounded the corner of Jason's house, noting the number, walking slowly with his head downcast and his eyes surreptitiously on the windows. A light was on in a rear room. The window was right there, flush with the sidewalk. An easy peek. But the blinds were closed. Good blinds, too, that overlapped well, blocking out all viewing.

He sighed. Continued on to Rampart. As he walked, he passed a small store. Nothing as glamorous as the A&P, though. He ducked inside, scanning the small, cluttered interior. He then asked the nonplused clerk if he had pens, tablets, index cards something he could use to write on. The clerk had Bics and tiny, spiral note pads. Doug paid for them, then went out. He needed to sit for a minute. He jaywalked across Rampart and ducked into the park. An open bench worked well enough, but the light was poor. He scribbled a note to Jason on the note pad, leaving him the address of his cottage and the telephone number.

He sat a while longer, trying to muster up the courage to actually leave the note. A blinding buzz filled his head, he rose to his feet, then headed back the way he'd come, almost getting himself clocked by a speeding car as he jaywalked again.

As he came down St. Ann Street, his pace slowed. He noticed brighter light streaming from the window.

As he neared, he could see that the blinds had been opened slightly. An icy blue blast of nervous fear ripped through his spine. He cautiously glanced around, hunting the telltale signs of light coming from other homes. Most he could discern were coming from the rears of the houses. People tucked away in

their private spaces. He stopped just to the side of the window and peered inside. Through narrow slits, he saw Jason just snapping the elastic waist of a pair of navy boxers. He'd just missed the change, he realized. The young man was digging through a tiny, stuffed closet for a T-shirt. His lean, smooth back was flawless. Shoulder blades, sharp and angular, were clearly displayed, accentuating very broad, squared shoulders. His waist seemed tiny. The boy was actually thin. Almost skinny.

By comparison, Doug suddenly felt his own middle-aged thickness.

Jason tossed a black T-shirt aside, then pulled out a red one. As bright as Christmas it was. As he turned toward the window, he slipped the T-shirt over his head. Doug's mouth went wet with wanting as he saw the young man's smooth torso, with its ruddy brown aureoles, small and oval shaped, nipples barely pinched by cold. Ribs delicately displayed beneath taut, smooth flesh. A concave, stomach and just the hint of jutting hip bones, a hair line above the boxers. Clean fingers pulled a red curtain down on the show of skin.

Doug ducked back just as he saw Jason raising his head. He was sure the eyes of the world were upon him just then. The light went out in the room. Doug quickly bowed his head and hurried past. As he got to the corner, he realized that the young man would never be interested in him. He looked at the sweaty, folded-up note he'd been clutching in his hand. He looked at the front door of the house. He wadded up the note and let it fall from his hand as he hurried away.

He walked in a blind funk all the way back to Bourbon Street. The sudden sight of people and lights, the wonderful sounds of music wafting through the air, somewhat quickly resuscitated him. He could still continue on his way to the riverboat. Gambling might keep his mind focused on something other than Jason.

- - -

Try as he might, he couldn't sleep. He kicked the covers back, turned on the light and slipped out of bed. The hot shower hadn't worked, the warm milk hadn't worked, even the over-the-counter sleeping tablets hadn't worked. His body was tired, but his mind was wide awake. The red digital display on the clock read 11:23. Which meant to the rest of New Orleans, it was only 10:58. He stepped into his jeans, pulled on socks and shoes and ran a comb through his hair, then threw on his flannel shirt over his T-shirt and headed out of his room. Larry still gone down bumping and grinding for the singles, fives and tens that were being stuffed into the pouch of his G-string by all manner of men.

He locked the door, then skipped down the steps. The night air was damp, almost wet. As he came down the walk, he spotted a crumpled wad of paper on the sidewalk. He playfully kicked it with the toe of his shoe, but it was damp and stuck to the leather rather than rolling along. He bent over and peeled it off. As he did so, he noticed that it had been folded up neatly before it was crumpled. The faint traces of blue ink bled through. Curious, he peeled open the folds. The

lettering was neat, all block capitals. He read the note from Doug.

A slight panic overcame him. And excitement. There was an address and a telephone number. Still, he felt a surge of caution well up inside him. The man had followed him home. It was a little disconcerting. He pocketed the note, then lit a cigarette and trucked down the street. He would spy on this man as this man had spied on him.

Barracks Street was pretty barren. Other than lights from a few windows, the street was devoid of human activity. He found the cottage, there on the corner, all dark and locked up. Maybe Doug was asleep. He hesitated a moment, then one foot after the other stepped up the stoop to the door. He could ring the bell, or he could knock. Everyone outside the house could hear him knocking, he thought. Sound travels well along narrow streets. He pushed the door bell. Inside he heard the tonal *bing-bong* of the simple door chime. No jarring buzzer. A hollow, almost haunting sound it was to him.

He waited. And waited. No answer. He pulled the worn scrap of folded paper from his pocket. He'd found it discarded. The man had had second thoughts. Jason didn't know whether to leave or to wait. He stepped back down to the sidewalk. Walked around to the other side of the cottage. The shutters were closed. He thought for a moment, then quickly beat a path back to his house.

Once inside his secure bedroom, he shut his door, locked it, then closed his blinds. He quickly stripped down to his boxers then stared at himself in his small dresser mirror. A framed snapshot of his slender form reflected back at him. His eyes had dark circles. His whiskers were just ready for a blade. His hair seemed limp and fly-away. Long fingers ran an exploratory path across his chest, down his stomach, to the waist band of his underwear. His member swelled quickly, slipping through the fly of the navy cloth. He reached in and pulled his scrotum out as well, the dark of the fabric making all the more light the flesh that now wanted to be touched.

He skinned away the boxers and kicked them aside. Bony hips protruded beneath his skin. Fine pubic hair haloed his cock. His ball sac was as smooth as white velvet. He disliked his body. It was boyish. Not manly. He'd always wished he'd been built more like his father, stocky with a furry chest and legs. But he'd inherited more of the genes from his mother's side of the family. His uncles were all thin and as smooth as salamanders. Still, the thinness of his form made his cock and balls seem large larger than they actually were. His scrotum hung low, his testicles the size of small walnuts. He felt their looseness. He could wrap three fingers around their top. His erect penis stretched just over seven inches. The head was perfectly shaped, though the shaft was slender like his whole form. It curved just slightly to the left. A very slight curve indeed. He pulled its length slowly. A drop of precum oozed from the slit. He let go of his cock and turned. A small ass he had. Not enough padding to make sitting for any length of time comfortable. Would Doug want him if he saw him like this? A skinny guy with nothing outstanding? He felt a flush of embarrassment at the

imagined thought of Doug, naked there with him. He had to find out, though. Had to.

- - -

Doug crossed the street, then fished out his keys. The night had been a wash. He'd dumped fifty bucks into the one-armed bandit and lost it all. His stop-off at one of the bars only resulted in another ten bucks spent on faux beer and moderate chatter with a couple of guys from Biloxi. A couple they were Elliot and Jack a little older than he was and quite a bit drunk. They tried to entice him into a three-way. While it might have been fun if they'd been sober, he wasn't in the mood for a quick exchange of orgasms, then to have them fall asleep. He'd been there, done that, too many times before.

He stepped up quickly to his door, cursing himself for not leaving the porch light on. He fumbled with the keys, then finally succeeded in getting the door open. As he stepped inside, he flicked on the light. Closing the door behind him, he noticed an envelope on the floor. Picking it up, he glanced at the mail slot in the door. Something from the owners, perhaps? He flopped down on the couch and opened it. The Polaroids caught his eye. He pulled out the photos and stared at them.

Jason.

Sitting up in bed, his long fingers squeezing the base of his very hard cock and bulging ball sac as if they were some fleshy bouquet in his lap. Doug's penis sprang to life. He instinctively unfastened his belt and unzipped the fly of his jeans. Jason on his stomach, his face demurely turned to the camera, his lovely rear end peeking out from beneath the sheets. Jason, still on his stomach, his ass hiked high in the air, one hand pulling his cheeks apart, exposing his most private opening.

Doug immediately kicked off his shoes as his hand found his rigid prick. He could've shot a load right then and there. He withdrew his hand quickly, then leaned forward and laid the three pictures out on the coffee table. He picked up the envelope again. A folded-up piece of typing paper was inside. He pulled out the note and read it: *If you're interested, I'd like to get together. Just leave your door unlocked. Jason*

Unlocked? When? Doug got up and went to the door. He opened it and peered out to the street. Nowhere could he see anyone nearby. Still, he could feel eyes on him. Eyes hidden by the night. A boldness came over him. He reached into his opened jeans and grabbed hold of his thick, meaty dick, massaging himself beneath exposed cotton briefs. He wanted to flash his prick, his balls, but he restrained himself. After a few moments, he retreated back into the cottage, quietly closing the door behind him.

He turned out the light, then went to the kitchen to turn on that low, 15 watt bulb in the hood over the stove. More than a night light, but not as bright as any other, it gently basked the kitchen and part of the living room with its almost surreal glow. He stripped down right there by the door, leaving his clothes in a

heap. He quickly went into the bathroom and brushed his hair into place and the foulness of fake beer from his breath. He figured the young man wouldn't rush in so quickly, if he found the courage to come in at all.

Returning back to the living room, he shoved his pile of clothes behind one of the chairs, then returned to the couch, where he gathered up the photos and lay back on the soft cushions. His cock was straining hard against his belly, the dripping head of his prick just poking through the fleshy opening of his ample foreskin. He studied the pictures by the dim light. The boy was handsome, yet beautiful. His mouth ran wet just imagining his lips pressed against Jason's puckered hole.

His cock twitched eagerly in response to his fantasy. Doug set the pictures down and squeezed hard at the base of his shaft, so hard that the dull pain helped his head clear and his dick slacken. He heard the ticking of his wristwatch. As he removed it, he glanced at the time. 1:37 a.m.. He set the watch on the end table, then closed his eyes.

Minutes passed. Then more came and went. Doug fought against sleep, but the longer he waited, the more tired he became. He pulled himself up off of the couch. A half hour had passed. Jason wasn't coming. He rubbed his eyes, then gathered up his watch, his clothes and the photos and went through the kitchen, past the small bathroom, then into the bedroom. Dumping the clothing aside, he set the watch on the dresser, then slipped into bed. He propped the photos up on the night stand against the lamp and the clock. Something to fantasize about in the morning. Maybe he would stop by the young man's house in the morning and see.

- - -

Jason remained huddled up in the tiny alcove between two houses. A spot for someone's garbage cans on collection day. He'd seen Doug step out onto the porch, his hand down his pants. He'd almost bolted out from hiding and up those steps right then and there, but he'd been paralyzed, fearful of it all being a tease, or worse.

He hadn't thought that the man was a complete stranger. Someone who might want to hurt him. He didn't believe that, but the mere hint of that thought kept him locked into his place in the shadows. From his vantage point, he could tell there was some small light on still in the cottage. A very faint light. He'd been hiding there for over an hour and a half and the damp night air was chilling him to the bone. Even cold, though, his crotch and cock were still hot and sweaty with want.

He could feel his heart beating fast. An adrenaline rush. He took his first step out onto the sidewalk, exposing himself under the halo of street lamps. He wondered if Doug was still up. If he was waiting. He just wanted to creep in unnoticed and find the handsome man there. Adrenaline took over and his feet flew over the blacktop and up the steps. A shaking hand gripped the knob and turned. It opened. Quiet hinges attested to the maintenance of the home. After

slipping inside, he eased the door shut behind him and surveyed the interior. The light came from the kitchen. He saw his letter and the envelope there on the coffee table. No pictures though. He moved to the chair and sat quietly. He removed his shoes, his socks, his jacket, his pants. No boxers this time. No T-shirt. Just the plaid of the flannel covered him. His cock thrust out between the tails of his shirt. He slowly unbuttoned each button as he gingerly walked through the living room, then kitchen, then the bathroom. The bedroom door was open wide. He could see the dresser and its mirror and in that mirror he saw reflected back in the faint moonlight, the sleeping form of the man.

He stood there, paralyzed again. Just staring. His heart pounded fiercely. The man shifted in the bed, his body turning over, facing the doorway in which he stood. A lazy hand slid up to the covers. Jason opened his shirt completely, letting it slip from his shoulders and slide down his arms and back into a heap at his feet.

Doug shifted again in the bed, turning over, his hand and body catching the bedclothes and pulling them down a bit. Jason tiptoed to the edge of the bed, a nervous hand pushing the covers down farther. He eased himself down onto the mattress, sliding first one leg, then the other beneath the sheet. A thick, rough hand spidered over to his thigh, caressing its length. Jason scooted down into the bed as Doug rolled over to face him.

"I thought you wouldn't come," Doug said with a smile.

"I was scared to," Jason admitted.

Doug's arm slipped over Jason and drew him closer as his feet gently kicked down the covers, exposing them both. Jason's hands pressed against Doug's chest. He could feel the meaty, furry muscles of the man's chest. His right hand continued on, slipping around to his back, then his buttocks, hairy and warm and pliant, then over his hip to his groin. Thick, fleshy hardness. He pulled lazily on Doug's cock as Doug pressed his lips to his own mouth. The man's thick, long tongue snaked between his lips. His own slithered across the man's, feeling its hunger. Jason released his grip on Doug's prick, then pressed the man back against the mattress as he slipped on top of him. Jason's smooth legs brushed up and down against Doug's furry thighs and calves as he ground his cock and balls against Doug's. He could feel his shaft massaging Doug's thick, spongy member. Doug started to pant down his throat then eased his mouth from Jason's.

"Whoa!" he laughed. "You've got me so fucking hot I'm ready to come."

Jason grinned, licking the tip of Doug's nose. "So? Shoot a wad, then we'll have you shoot again."

"Not yet," Doug said quietly as he rolled Jason over onto his back. He kneeled between the youth's splayed legs, his fingers tracing a slow trail down the young man's torso. He sighed a contented sigh, then hovered over the lad, bringing his mouth down onto a nipple. His lips wrapped over the aureole, delicately sucking it while the tip of his tongue ran lazy circles around the nipple

tip. Jason shuddered with pleasure, his fingers combing through his man's thick hair, massaging his scalp as a wet, hot tongue painted across his chest to his other nipple. Lips and tongue suckled greedily and Jason squirmed with delight. He shuddered again as he watched the silver blond fox steal down his stomach, making his muscles contract with ecstasy, to the soft down of his groin. Whiskers dusted the shaft of his dick, making it twitch and slap Doug's cheek. Slick, warm wetness engulfed the head, then the entire shaft. Jason's hands came down easily on Doug's head as Doug pressed his nose and chin into his groin. Being deep down this man's silky hot throat felt so very, very good and so very, very right.

Doug's mouth ran wet as he bobbed up and down with quickening pace on his young man's rigid cock, his tongue sweeping its delicate underside, feeling it, feeling him, completely connected to him, in him. His hands ran up and down Jason's velvety hard thighs, over his stomach, over his groin, caressing the sensual flesh. He felt the weight of the young man's legs wrap around his shoulders, his heels digging in, massaging his back, encouraging him to suck the length of cock jammed down his throat.

Jason felt his balls contract sharply as his body tensed. He let his hands flop back to the bed as he closed his eyes and surrendered. Jizz spurted over the back of Doug's tongue and down his throat. He sucked harder, his tongue squeezing Jason's prick. More spastic spurts splattered the back of his throat again and again until the lad winced with exhaustion. Gripping the base of Jason's cock, Doug took one last, slow draw from the softening dick, extracting the last few gloppy drops of thick cum. He let the young man's prick slip from between his lips, then swallowed the creamy, abundant load stored in his mouth. He stared at the beautiful penis in his grasp. Gingerly he pressed his lips against the tip of the head and brushed his tongue over the piss slit. He heard Jason groan.

He drew himself up beside his young friend and kissed him again. A long, sloppy kiss they shared. His own cock was straining now as Jason's excited breaths slipped down his throat as well. He felt the pressure of the young man's hands against his shoulders, pushing him flat against the mattress, then felt him straddle his midsection. Jason pulled his lips away, his tongue skiing down his man's neck to his torso, across his chest and nipples to his side.

Jason slid his hand under Doug's arm and eased it up, exposing the thick, dark blond hair of his arm pit. He buried his nose into the bush, inhaling deeply the scent of this man, a musky, almost spicy scent. His tongue washed all over Doug's pit, lapping up sweat while drenching it all further with his own saliva.

He felt his man's body tense sharply as an audible groan whispered in his ear. He pressed his smooth torso against the warm fur blanketing Doug's form, then sat up and pressed his ass against Doug's thick, big dick, letting the fleshy rod nest in his crack. "Oh geez...!" Doug moaned. "That's gonna make me shoot."

Jason grinned. "It's been a long time since any guy's been inside of me."

"Well, I'm in no rush."

Jason smiled coyly, then turned himself around and displayed his cherry ass to Doug as he grabbed hold of Doug's thick prick and full, hairy balls. He nuzzled his face into the sweaty, thick growth of Doug's groin, inhaling the faintly acrid and musky smell. His lips wrapped around one of his man's testicles, sucking the egg-sized orb into his mouth. His tongue stroked it gently as he felt Doug's beefy hands massaging his ass cheeks.

He let loose his mouthful of scrotum, then ran his tongue over the exposed tip of Doug's glans. Jason loved foreskin and Doug had plenty. The tip of his tongue snaked beneath the prepuce, swirling around the big head of Doug's cock. He then gently but firmly gripped the thick shaft beneath the head and pulled down, drawing the thick foreskin back down the shaft, exposing the shiny pink knob beneath. Doug shuddered beneath him. Jason's lips wrapped around the monster cock head. He slowly inched his way down the shaft, his effort oiled by saliva that ran out of his watering mouth.

Doug pushed himself up a bit and slammed his face in his boy's ass crack, his lips and tongue hitting a bulls-eye on the puckered rosette that was his lad's fuck hole. Lips sucked hard on the tight orifice, drawing it up slightly as his tongue pushed inside. Jason moaned through his mouthful of cock-meat and he almost choked as he took the rest of Doug's length down his throat. The man's piece seemed massive, but his throat relaxed the more Doug tongue-fucked him and he sucked harder and harder, drawing up folds of foreskin onto the back of his tongue each time. All of a sudden, Jason felt Doug's strong arms wrap around his waist and yank him back. His butt landed squarely atop Doug's face, as Jason watched Doug's cock twitch then spew wildly, white, hot semen. It splattered on him, on the bed, on Doug's stomach and thighs. He grabbed the meaty rod, gripping it hard, and pumped up the last remaining drops while Doug's tongue snaked up into his ass. Jason writhed and bent back down to suck up the cum-filled prepuce into his mouth. His tongue swirled beneath the thick fold of skin, slicking the large head. He pulled the skin back down the shaft as he felt his asshole, laden with warm spit, loosening up. He let go of Doug's cock and pulled his ass from Doug's mouth. Rolling back on top of him, Jason planted his lips on his man's, feeling their fullness, smelling himself on his man's chin and whiskers.

Jason wanted this man to fuck him. Wanted to feel the massive rod deep within him. But he also didn't want it to simply be a one-night stand. "I have to go," he whispered.

"Go?" Doug was shocked, disappointed.

"Gotta work the early shift tomorrow."

Doug groaned a sorrowful sound. "So, this is it? Just one night?"

Jason lay his head on his man's chest, his finger drawing a lazy spiral around the furry nipple. "Well, you're from out of town, aren't you...?"

"I'm here for six more days," he said. "I know it's not a lifetime, but

beginnings don't always mean endings."

"You're such a handsome man, Doug. The kind of man I might get to like too much."

"And you, my young man," he sighed, wrapping his arms around Jason and squeezing him hard, "you are perhaps even more than that to me. So, you see, you're not the only one risking the intoxicant of emotion here."

Jason reluctantly peeled himself off of Doug. "I'll be home tomorrow at three."

"Three o'clock," Doug repeated. "You like the Garden District?"

"It's a fantasyland, but yeah...."

"I know a place...."

Jason leaned over and gave him a quick kiss, then stood up. He scooped a fingerful of Doug's spent cum from Doug's thigh and smeared it on the shaft of his penis. "Then I'm marked with your scent," he said with a smile.

"Please...." Doug started as he began to get out of bed.

Jason stopped him. Pushed him gently back down. "Sleep well tonight. Think of me." Doug watched Jason leave his room. Listened to the young man slip into his clothes then creep out the front door. When he heard the click of the latch, his heart sank a bit, yet he held out his hope for tomorrow and for the rest of the week. New Orleans had always been his favorite town. Now, it seemed to hold the possibility of being a new home. There would always be logistics to work out work and what-not then again, there was always the possibility of courting something long distance for a time, with trips out here and Jason to him. Time will out, as the expression goes. In the meanwhile, enjoy the day, the moment, this time and see what might develop.

CHERRY NO MORE
by Jason Carpenter

The Beatles made my cock hard well, all but the drummer, Ringo. Nice name, but not sexy at all. I often sprawled on my bed with my boxer shorts pulled down and watched them on TV, stroking my erection. That's all I seemed to do back then: jerk off. All around me the '60s were in full swing. Flower power, love-ins and free love dominated the media. But not for me. As a teenager, I felt I was the only virgin left in the universe outside a convent, and secretly suspected the priests and nuns were getting more than me.

I learned which way I swung early in life. I got my first woody watching James Dean in *Rebel Without a Cause*. My cock nearly burst through my jeans at the sight of him in that leather jacket, a cigarette dangling from those magnificent lips. And he was so nice to that cute Sal Mineo! Knowing my preference for guys didn't help much, however. The closets of independence were still firmly closed and locked by society. No one openly admitted being "queer." So I had no idea where to find others like me or what to expect when I did. Hence, I regularly milked my own snake to keep my sanity.

As I was poised to blow my load, the telephone in the hall jangled, interrupting my efforts. I waddled, shorts around my ankles, and snatched up the receiver. "Hello?"

"Hey, Jason. What'cha doing?" my long-time friend and running buddy, Clayton, asked.

"Nothing," I sighed, watching my cock shrink between my fingers.

"Got any money?"

"Of course not," I answered.

"Me neither. Want to go to the park and watch some softball? Maybe one of the girls' teams will be playing."

Clayton had as much luck finding girls as I had finding guys. "Might as well. Give me half an hour to get ready."

"Okay. I'll honk when I get there."

I hung up, took a quick shower, and dressed to impress: Purple bell-bottomed slacks and a black shirt. Then I brushed my shoulder-length blond hair until it fell perfectly. Cool.

I heard the muffler of Clayton's ragged Plymouth Valiant before I heard him honk. Janis Joplin was screaming her lungs out to *Piece of My Heart* from the radio when I slid into the front seat. Clayton drove to the park and cruised the four playing fields. "No women," he said glumly, parking by a field where a game was in progress. The score board told us the home team was down by one run going into the bottom of the last inning, with one out.

The first guy came to bat. Easy out a pop fly to center field. The next batter got to first on a ground ball the shortstop mishandled. Then the third batter came to the plate amidst cheers from the bleachers and his teammates. "Come on, Matt!"

"You're the man!"

"Send it sailing, Matt!"

I guessed him to be in his early 20s. He wore shorts and a T-shirt, showing off legs and arms rippling with muscle. His rounded ass wiggled enticingly as he took his batting stance. "Belt it, Matt!" I called out.

He turned at the sound of my voice and our eyes met. I waved timidly, embarrassed, and felt him give me the once- over. When he smiled it was like a neon sign flashing, "I like what I see." And I knew I'd found a soulmate. A shiver radiated through me.

He knocked the hell out of the first pitch, sending it flying over the left fielder's head, and narrowly missing clearing the fence. No matter. Matt ran like a rabbit, crossing home plate on the heels of the runner in front of him for an in-the-park home run, winning the game for his team.

"Damn, he's good," Clayton said.

"Yes, very," I agreed.

"Well, I guess that's that. Now what can we do?" Clayton asked.

"You go on. I'm going to hang here. Walk around for a while. I'll walk home."

Clayton shrugged. "Okay. See ya," he said, suspecting nothing, since I often walked the three blocks to my house.

After Clayton and most of the players and fans left, Matt strolled to where I sat. No words were exchanged. He simply nodded toward his car and walked away. I followed, my heart racing. We got into his car and he drove away. "What's your name," he asked.

"Jason," I answered, as his hand rubbed my thigh.

"Eat me, Jason," he said.

"How? I mean, now?"

"Jeez! A cherry? Just take my cock out and improvise," he instructed. "There isn't any wrong way."

My God, I thought breathlessly, *I'm about to taste my first cock!*

With trembling fingers I unzipped his shorts, watching in awe as ten solid inches of meat blossomed forth manna to a starving man. I encircled the girth of rock-hard tube with my fingers as though I were touching hot coals. It pulsed and throbbed in my hand but not as fast as my heart was thudding in my chest. I bent toward him tentatively and lowered my lips over his purple dickhead, feeling a rush like no other in my life. I gobbled as much of him as I could, dizzy from the taste and smell and texture of him. My cock stretched long and hard in my pants.

Matt ran his fingers through my hair. "Slow down ... you'll make me come. I just want an appetizer until I get to my place."

I slowed down then, electing to lick his meat from top to bottom instead of gorging myself. Moments later the car stopped and Matt killed the engine. "We're here." I sat up and, with some difficulty, he stuffed his cock back in his

shorts.

His apartment was Spartan, a stereo and king-sized waterbed accounting for most of the furnishings. Posters of Arlo Guthrie and Jimi Hendrix adorned the walls. Matt sat on the undulating bed and pulled me between his thighs. He undressed me slowly, planting hot kisses on each new section of my flesh to appear. When he tugged my underwear down around my knees my cock stood tall and proud, pre-cum oozing from the tip. When he took my cock in his hot mouth I went weak in the knees, so turned on I could not hold back. A flood of cream gushed up from within me, tightening my balls. I grasped his shoulders and poured my jizz down his gulping throat. He swallowed every drop and tongued me clean.

Embarrassed, I collapsed to the bed beside him. "I'm sorry. I didn't mean to...."

"Hey, no problem. I remember my first time. I never got my cock out of my pants before I shot off. Now that I've taken the edge off, we can have some fun." He undressed quickly and spread out beside me. Our mouths locked in a hungry kiss as he rolled my balls between his fingers. "Roll over," he said.

I obeyed, spreading my legs wide. Matt snagged a container of petroleum jelly from the night table, dug out a gob with his fingers, and slicked it up and down my ass crack gently. When his finger prodded my bulging anal bud then eased past my ass-ring, investigating my insides, I swallowed hard, shaking like laundry flapping on a clothesline in a stiff breeze.

Matt withdrew his finger and inched up between my legs. His cock head slipped up me, followed by about six inches of bone-hard meat. I squirmed beneath him, lifting my hips for more. In one smooth thrust he rammed forward, filling me with cock until colored lights blinked before my eyes. In and out he moved, fucking up me, his big balls brushing my own. Already my cock flowered up against my belly.

Matt put his hands under my arms, grasped my collarbones and commenced to pound up my deflowered hole, rutting for the sweetest part. My body ebbed and flowed with the liquid motion of the bed, as Matt fucked me hard and fast. "Jeeezuss!" he cried, straining forward in one gut-filling thrust.

My insides burned and clenched as I pushed back toward him, feeling the hot river of his cum bath my guts. The smell of fresh-fucked asshole and pungent spunk filled the air. I floated on a sensory cloud as Matt continued to gore up me until he was sated. The nerves in my anus tingled magnificently as his cock dwindled and receded from me.

"How was I?" I asked.

His breath came in labored puffs. "Tight ... sweet ... wonderful."

We snuggled, kissing and touching until he recovered. My cock pressed hard between us. Matt fisted me lackadaisically. "Can ... can I," I stammered, eager to experience even more.

He smiled, blue eyes twinkling. "Want some ass meat, huh?"

I nodded, feeling a wide grin split my face.

"Go for it, man," he said agreeably, stuffing a pillow beneath his stomach, raising his rounded ass globes.

Wanting to learn, I took my time with him, pressing my face against his butt cheeks and parting them with my hands.

I drew my tongue down the dark line of his crack. His puckered flower clenched, but I wriggled the tip of my tongue up him, tasting his sweetness. He rotated his hips, anxious to be speared. My cock slapped my belly in agreement.

Taking a dab of the same lubricant Matt used on me onto my finger, I painted his asshole then held my throbbing cock in one hand and screwed it up him until my wiry pubes met his white globes. The feeling was so intense I feared pulling back for the first stroke, afraid I'd again blow my load too quickly. Just the tight, hot caress of his bowels surrounding my meat gave me pleasures I had only dreamed of before that day.

"Don't tease," Matt moaned. "Fuck me."

Ever so slowly I began to stroke in and out of him, watching my shaft appear and disappear into his body. The bed took up my rocking motion, moving him back to meet my forward thrusts. Gripping his hipbones, I fell into an easy rhythm, fucking his ass like I knew what I was doing. Judging by his groans, I did.

I increased my speed, ramming deeper and deeper into his slick innards, my dangling balls slapping his. I recognized the orgasm building in me. So different than when I jerked off. To actually have my meat buried up the ass of a great-looking guy so far over-shadowed masturbation as to make it obsolete. My whole gut clenched and tightened as white-hot cream sprang from my balls, coursed a delicious path through my shaft and, with heart-stopping release, exploded out my dick-slit, splashing and anointing Matt's guts.

Animal-like, I fucked into him relentlessly, teeth clenched hard, eyes shut tight, staggered by the feelings washing through me. Another short, sharp climax followed the first, emptying my balls and making my crown so sensitive it ached. All my man-juice now occupied Matt's clutching depths. His asshole sucked air and spit cum as I slipped my rod out of him.

"Well," he asked. "Everything you thought it would be?"

Speechless, all I could do was kiss his reddened globes, his spine, and his broad shoulders.

He struggled up from the waterbed and took my hand. "Shower?" he said, dragging me to my feet.

The water beat down on us, hot and refreshing as we washed each other. The residue of our sex swirled down the drain. Matt's body, hardened by athletics, made me glad he was my first. His large cock, blue-veined and bulging, looked ready for action again. And my lesson was incomplete.

I knelt before him, stroking his cock with long strokes while ducking my head and catching his drooping ball sac between my lips. I sucked his balls,

wanting the juice that gathered in them. His hands pressed against the sides of my head, moving me upward to his cock. I licked the cut corona until he could stand it no longer, running my tongue back and forth between the crease of his dick-slit, then engulfed his rigid pole, taking his satin slab down my throat.

His buttocks pumped, fucking my face with long, deep thrusts while I tugged his ball-sac, rolling it in my fingers. Even with his hands over my ears I heard him cry out: "Suck me!"

I sucked, hollowing my cheeks and applying all the pressure I could. My reward was a long, stringy spurt of cum. My mouth filled with Matt's essence, slippery and salty. I swallowed my very first load of jizz and sucked for more as it burned down my throat. Matt pulled his cock from mouth and milked the last precious drops of his cum onto my lips. I ran my tongue around my lips, savoring each tangy gobbet.

Matt hung from the shower head with one hand to keep from falling. "Man, you're a natural-born cocksucker!" he praised.

I guess he was right; I've never had a complaint.

After Matt came into my life everything changed. He knew many men like us, and the places to look for fresh meat. He was a master cherry-picker, and taught me well.

Thanks to him, had I painted a small cherry on my cock for each virgin I've popped over the years, I'd need a thirty-six-inch cock!

DRILLING CREW
by Corbin Chezner

By midnight it was still so hot someone had left the doors of the beer joint open to the dusty street. Inside the musty, dimly-lit tavern, Tejano music blared from the jukebox. The Mexican-American natives of the small South Texas town kept their distance from the white strangers. Because their work was nomadic, the burly, sunburned crew from Zandex Drilling Rig had grown accustomed to feeling like outsiders. If they were lucky and made a well they might be at a site six weeks. A dry hole and they moved the rig even sooner. During their off hours, the drilling crew stuck close to each other.

Tonight, the roughnecks took up three tables in the center of the bar. Wynona, a big-bosomed, bleached-blonde barmaid, took their orders. Four Chicanos played pool in a corner opposite the street.

Ramon, the mustachioed bartender, was tight-lipped, eyes trained warily on the clientele. In South Texas, smart bartenders kept a weapon hidden in case of trouble. The oppressive heat and the choking dust and the clash of cultures could turn streets mean quick as the flash of a switchblade. No one knew it, but Ramon had his eye on one roughneck in particular. He needed some gringo butt tonight. He needed it bad.

As Wynona handed out another round of longnecks, Jeffrey Lee Daniels, a blond Zandex roughneck, buzzed now from six beers, blurted out, "Hell, Wynona. You're about the only damn woman we've seen in this town. Where are the others?"

Without missing a beat, the barmaid shot back, "We keep 'em locked up when wild-ass roughnecks is in town."

The Zandex crew hooted with laughter but the Chicanos remained silent, eyeing the table menacingly.

Dan Steele, operations manager of the Zandex rig, tried to ignore the hostile looks; he wanted no part of a brawl. Not tonight. Although over the years he'd been in more fights than he could remember, at 42 he'd begun to slow down. Now, more often than not he'd let a fight pass him by when he could help it.

Steele peered across the table at Jay Zike, his crew chief. The toughs in the little burgs always wanted to challenge Zike; why, Steele wasn't sure. Envy maybe. Zike was tall and tough looking with a lean physique and riveting hazel eyes that turned the heads of men and women alike. But Steele knew there was more to it. The way Zike carried himself, for one. He'd swagger into a room like he owned the place. Mr. Cool, he'd stand surveying his surroundings, broad shoulders arrow straight, one narrow hip slung lower than the other. Zike kept his light brown hair cropped in a burr. When a tough got in his face, no big deal. He'd curl his lips into a mean grin. He'd snigger and his hazel eyes would flash and his olive skin would glow. When he was in the mood, trouble energized Zike. He never backed down, no matter the size of the adversary. Steele liked a man with balls.

Steele decided he'd best get his subordinate out of the joint before the fight started. He leaned across the table and said quietly, "Ready?"

"Suits me." Zike shrugged his broad shoulders. "I'm about ready to hit the sack."

At least Zike had the sense to know when to call it quits, Steele thought. He nodded in agreement and both men got up from the table.

"You boys pussyin' out on us?" one of the crew called out from the adjoining table.

Steele decided to let the crack slide. Instead, he just looked over at the men and grinned, his blue eyes shining with merriment. If they got in a brawl and stayed out too late, tomorrow their asses would be dragging.

As Steele and Zike walked toward the exit, Daniels elbowed his rooming buddy, Barry Medders, another roughneck. "Wha'd I tell you?"

"That don't mean nothin'."

"To hell it don't. They're doin' it, Medders."

Medders shook his head. "You're crazy."

When the two men got back to the motel room, Jay switched on the TV for noise and both men undressed for bed.

"That damn Wynona had some fine tits," Jay muttered as he struggled out of his Levis.

"Women like that don't make it easy on a man," Dan put in, "being away from his ole lady two weeks at a stretch."

"Tell me about it! If I couldn't pull my damn pud I'd go nuts, I reckon." Jay stepped out of his Jockey shorts. He picked the pile of clothes off the floor and threw it on the chair next to his bed. He looked over at Dan. "Beer joint sure was a dive."

"No more than the others," Dan said. He thought about all the towns the crew passed through, the taverns they drank in, when they were on the road in search of oil. Right off, a list of his favorite watering holes sprang to mind: The Half Moon, the Zarape, the Bluebonnet, Rod's Derrick, Bottoms-Up. Maybe he'd write a book someday.

"Damn, I'm beat. You worked my damn tail off today, boss," Jay said. He sighed and collapsed onto the bed.

"And there's more where that came from," Dan teased. He peeled off his underwear and flung the pile of clothes on the other chair. Then as he turned toward the bed Dan caught his own image in the dresser mirror and his dick pulsed. Dan Steele still had a damn fine physique. In the mirror, he admired his black, curly hair; he still had a good hairline, unusual for a man his age. Norma, his wife, told him once that his sea blue eyes could even lure another nut to the sack. Over the years, he'd learned to use them to his advantage. But only in a pinch. He sucked in his stomach, admiring the breadth and squareness of his shoulders and the mat of dark hair across his chest. It pleased him that below his chest the hair narrowed to a line that plunged to his belly button. His dick pulsed

again.

"We made good progress today?" Jay finally asked.

Jay's words startled Steele from his narcissistic reverie. Steele gazed over at the other man, finally, and said, "100 feet, probably." Then he padded to the door to turn off the lamp and the TV. "We could hit pay dirt tomorrow."

"Yeah? I hear the company's really been bearin' down."

Dan sighed. "The brass in Houston, they ride my ass, for sure"

"Why? We work our buns off. What you make of it?"

"Ain't easy tryin' to compete with the damn Arabs."

"I guess you're right." Jay flipped over on his stomach and Dan turned off the TV and the lamp and padded back to his own bed.

"Dan?"

"Yeah?"

"You ever wish you'd done somethin' else?"

"Like?"

"I don't know. Anything."

"Oil drillin's all I know. It does get old, though," Dan finally admitted. "Bein' away from home so much. You?"

"What?"

"You ever wish you'd done somethin' else?"

"Yeah, sometimes. The wife, she don't like it much. 'Cept when I bring the paycheck home."

"The pay *is* pretty good, considerin'...."

Jay finished the thought: "Considerin' there ain't hardly any other jobs."

The men grew settled then, and Dan lay staring at the blue and lavender light that flickered through the threadbare curtains, bathing Jay's backside in surreal imagery. The sounds from outside loomed large in his mind, like the ticking of a clock. The sounds bleep, sizzle, bleep came from neon that pulsed though the giant flashing Bel Air Motel sign that fronted the highway. Sleep eluded him, and before he realized it his mind was in sync with the sounds from the sign: bleep, sizzle, bleep. Bleep, sizzle, bleep, akin to a faucet dripping. As the sounds from the sign continued, a mantra surfaced from the depths of his mind. Bleep, sizzle, bleep. Fuck Jay's butt. Bleep, sizzle, bleep. Fuck Jay's butt.

Dan didn't know where the words came from. Suddenly, he felt uneasy; he didn't like losing control of his thoughts. His heart raced and his dick pulsed again. Fuck Jay's butt? No way. But the mantra continued, still in sync with the sign. Bleep, sizzle, bleep. Fuck Jay's butt. Bleep, sizzle, bleep. As seconds ticked by, Steele felt empowered and energized by the words, and his cock grew so hard it felt like a 20-pound weight between his legs. He sensed he was outside himself observing as he rose from bed. Moments later, he found himself at the foot of Jay's bed, ogling the fleshy mounds of the younger man's butt, his cock primed for action.

Suddenly, Steele heard himself blurt the unthinkable: "I want to fuck your

butt, Zike."

Jay flinched and raised off the pillow. He peered back at the other man, a perplexed look on his face. "Huh?"

"You heard right, dude."

"You gone queer on me, Steele?" But the protest, if that's what it was, sounded hollow, and Zike lay silently for a moment, as if considering Steele's offer. Finally, Zike took a deep breath, splaying open his legs and raising his butt off the bed like a cat in heat.

Chuckling to himself, Steele lowered himself onto the bed and crawled to the other man. His dick pulsed again as he eyed Zike's young, hard buttocks; he spat and began kneading the moisture along the shaft and into the head of his throbbing dick. He spat again and inserted his finger in Zike's fuck hole.

Zike hissed and moaned and thrust his butt up so Steele could better probe his hole. Finally, breathless from desire, he blurted, "Give it to me. I want your big cock in my butt."

Zike was so hot now Dan thought he smelled cum. As if in a dream, Dan's heart pounded and it took both his hands to guide his big cock to Jay's fuck hole. He watched enthralled as the engorged vein in the center of his thick meat inched inside the other man.

Suddenly, Jay clamped his hole tight and he reached around to slow Steele's entry. "I don't know. Maybe I can't "

"You'll be beggin' for it," Dan kept on, inching his throbbing pole deeper.

Jay gasped and dug his fingers into the pillow, his hole still clamped tight on Dan's cock.

Dan leaned down and throttled the other man's ear with his tongue. "Loosen up, dude. Give me all your hole."

Jay gasped again, and suddenly Dan's big dick slipped in all the way, past Jay's sphincter.

Dan hesitated for a moment so Jay could adjust to him. Then he began fucking in earnest, slow at first, then faster. He'd retract slowly and then he inched back in; out, in; faster now, harder. As Dan's thrusts grew even faster, the younger man joined in, thrusting his butt higher yet so Dan could have all of him.

"Oh, man, do it! Give me all your cock."

Dan gave Jay what he wanted, fucking all the way to the base of his cock. Then he pulled nearly all the way out, like he was about to stop.

"Please, do it! Give me your dick." Jay moaned and thrashed his head and dug his fingers into the pillow again. "Shit, fuck, do it!"

Steele arched his head to the ceiling and laughed. Then, mercifully, he resumed fucking, harder and faster. Moments later, in a final ball-busting thrust, Dan arched his head to the ceiling again and let loose, spewing his full load deep into Jay's butt. An instant later, Zike pulsed and blasted his own load of thick, white cum onto the sheets.

Half an hour later, in Room 118, just across the parking lot of the U-shaped motel, Jeffrey Lee Daniels, a hunky blonde with a pouting mouth, and Barry Medders, a brunette with the look of a choirboy, lay naked next to each other on the queen-size bed.

"Don't you want to do it?" Jeffrey Lee urged, eyeing the brunette hunk. "What, you afraid it's queer or somethin'?"

Medders shrugged. "Well, ain't it?"

"Hell, there ain't no damn women here. You're horny, ain't you?"

"Sure, but "

"All the other guys is doin' it."

"You're shittin' me."

"Honest to God truth."

Minutes later, Medders and Daniels finally uncoiled from the 69 position, each struggling to swallow the other's load as Medders' mind swirled with confusion. Jesus! He was a married man, for God's sake, not a damn queer! So was Daniels! Maybe the other man could make sense of it. He gazed over at Daniels and tried to ask but the cum had made his tongue too thick to speak.

Meanwhile, in the bedroom off the motel office, Coy Hobbs let loose his load, at last. He jerked wildly and the thick white cream gushed out the end of his dick and plopped against the bed sheets. He lay in silence for a few moments, recovering. Then he reached in the nightstand and switched off the video monitoring device to room 118. He plucked a tissue to wipe himself and smiled at his good fortune. These oil field workers made damn fine guests. Fine, indeed!

The gringo drilling crew had made Ramon Gonzales realize he had to have gringo butt tonight. He had to. After closing the bar for the night, the handsome Chicano jumped in his Chevy Camaro and drove to the Bel Air Motel. He circled the perimeter of the motel, his brown eyes scanning for prey. Finally, he spotted a rig parked next to the cement block fence that shielded the motel from the liquor store parking lot next door. Then he saw a room with its door open; he slowed the car and eased it into a vacant parking space. Ramon's heart raced as he got out of the car and ambled to the open door. The trucker lay on the bed. He returned Ramon's gaze and smiled. He pulled back the sheets to show a 10-inch hard-on. Ramon nodded and smiled as he entered the room, closing the door behind him.

On the front side of the motel, Dan Steele slept contentedly with Jay Zike's dick buried in his ass; the Bel Air Motel sign flashed until dawn.

THE LITTLE DEVIL
by James Lincoln

"Mie love ys dedde,
Gone to hys death-bedde,
Al under the wyllowe-tree."
Thomas Chatterton (1752-1770)

10:08 p.m., May 17th

Late night in Louisiana, the time when moonflowers open their buds in quiet explosions of white to attract the night moths and the sweet scent of jasmine hangs in the humidity. I had come up from sleep in degrees, a painful, uneasy extraction into wakefulness. Listening to the vibrato of the oscillating fan, feeling its breath lightly across my bare skin beaded with perspiration, I lay there wondering why I was awake. The covers had been kicked off again and were lying in a bundle at the foot of my bed like a faithful dog. I was stretched out, naked save my boxers, which clung to my sweaty body like cellophane. The room was decidedly, tragically, empty; I could feel its unequivocal vacancy the same way you can comprehend someone's presence without seeing them.

In the semi-darkness I fumbled for my cigarettes. Yes smoking again. I quit two years ago. Then, about three weeks back, I looked down and there was a cigarette burning in my fingers, plumes of bluish smoke coming out my nostrils. I don't even know where I got the pack. I'll quit again. Soon.

I found the cigs on the nightstand, shook one up from the soft-pack, took it between my lips, lit up. I inhaled deeply, held it, let it out in one long sigh. I reached over and moved the ashtray nearer and flicked a bit of gray ash into it.

His funeral card was on the nightstand.

Oh Christ. How could I have forgotten, if even but for a moment?

10:12 p.m.

I remembered the first time I saw him. I was at Ellen Waverly's home discussing something work-related, sitting in the living room sipping iced-tea, when the front door burst open and this gawky youth bounded inside. He had a ragged backpack slung over one shoulder and was holding a piece of notebook paper in his hand with an A+ on it. He was skinny as a rail and wore a shirt with sleeves too long for him and faded jeans with rips in both knees. His hair was chestnut brown and thin and wispy and long, like a girl's, parted in the middle but with errant strands falling into his brilliant eyes which were a grayish-green, the color of Spanish moss.

"Mom," he said excitedly. "I just "

"Not now Brien," she said. "I have company."

I smiled at the youth and he averted those gorgeous green eyes shyly.

"Go have your snack. I'll talk to you later," she ordered. My eyes fell down his back to the tight-fitting jeans he wore as he left the room. I suddenly became afraid his mother may have noticed my lingering gaze so I quickly cleared my throat and pretended to be bothered by the interruption. "Kids," I probably said,

shaking my head and rolling my eyes.

"He's at that age," she apologized and I wanted to strangle her. Instead I nodded knowingly and tipped my iced-tea her direction before taking a bitter sip.

As we talked I could hear Brien in the kitchen. Footfalls across the linoleum, an unmistakable gait. The unsealing sound of a refrigerator being pulled opened. I could picture him peering inside it, hands on knees, turning this way and that as he considered the cold contents. Rattling noises, the closing of the fridge door. Cabinet opening and closing. A glass being set down with delicate fingers. Pouring juice, perhaps. Jar lid opened, closed. I heard all this and visualized it like some guy listening to an old radio play, and all the while I kept up the appearance I was in the living room with Ellen Waverly sipping iced-tea.

Ellen finally finished with me and we both walked to the front door. Not so fast; she remembered more to talk about. I looked over and saw Brien appear in the kitchen doorway, glass of milk in one hand, a huge molasses cookie in the other. He leaned against the doorframe and was quiet as a mouse, nibbling on the cookie, beautiful hair falling in his face. His mother looked his way and scrunched up her face in annoyance but she didn't tell him to leave. Every now and then I would look his way but he would self-consciously cast his eyes down. However, when I returned to Ellen (she was still talking away), I could feel Brien's eyes return to me.

We played eye-tag like that for a while. It wasn't long before he knew I was playing and it was difficult for him to keep a grin back. Then I caught him with a double-take. His grin let loose what a gorgeous smile! and he blushed.

His mother was oblivious to all this, just as I was oblivious to the mundane Adult Conversation I was apparently engaged in; it is a wonder I didn't commit so egregious *lapsus linguae* which would have found me out.

Ellen snapped her fingers and it was like a hypnotist ending the session. "Let me get that for you," she said. Yeah, whatever. I watched her leave the room, her heels clacking on the floor, then looked over to Brien. "Congrats," I said.

He raised his dark eyebrows in question.

"The A-plus. Congratulations. That's pretty impressive."

A huge, beaming smile. You'd think he'd never been complimented before. Then his mother was back, handing me something, showing me out.

That was the first time I saw Brien Waverly. The second time was a few weeks later. I'd been over at Ellen's a number of times afterwards but I never saw him there. Just a pair of dirty sneakers left at the foot of the stairs, or another essay (Percy Shelley, B-) held to the refrigerator by a magnet pretending to be miniature fruit. I wanted to ask where he was or how he was doing but I was afraid to; adults and young men just aren't supposed to recognize each other's existence.

A few weeks later I was in my front yard just finishing the exhausting chore of laying down fresh cement in my driveway to replace a frost-heaved section. It

was a Saturday afternoon and I had just smoothed it out with the trowel when a shadow fell draped over me. I looked up.

"Hey," he said.

I almost fell into the cement while standing up. "Hi. Brien, isn't it?" Cool, like the cucumber.

He nodded and then smiled mischievously. Suddenly he bent down and pressed his hand into the cement and held it there a moment before unsticking himself carefully. Brien wiped his hand on his jeans, admired his own work, and then took off. "Later," he said over his shoulder with a flip of long hair. And he was gone. I stood there, dumbfounded.

That was the second time I saw Brien Waverly. Here is the last: *He is lying supine in a dark cherry-wood casket, eyes closed, mouth a colorless, lipless line, face highlighted wrongly with an unnatural mortuary orchid pigment, hair combed neatly and cut short, hands folded over his chest and looking out of focus in the soft lighting, small frame clad in something he would never wear, surrounded by a horde of flowers he would not have appreciated.*

10:38 p.m.

I stamped out my cigarette and leaned back against the damp pillows. The fan continued its systolic breath across my body, shaking its head reprovingly. I tried not to think of the tragedy, that strange concatenation of helpless events, but it is as difficult not to think of some circumscribed matter as it is to prove a negative.

That may have been the worst of it that there was no one to blame. It was times like these you want to believe in an all-powerful Being with some master plan just so you have someone to fault. I peeled myself off the mattress and padded into the bathroom and clicked on the light-switch. The florescent bulbs flickered to life and I turned the faucet on and then splashed cool water on my face. I found myself involuntarily looking at the mirror. I didn't like what I saw. A bad likeness. Muscle-tone gone I'd stopped working out my skin a sickly ashen color. I'd lost a lot of weight, too, and people were starting to worry about me. Something wrong? they'd ask. I couldn't tell them.

I stumbled back to bed. Turned on the lamp on the nightstand. Then I reached over and picked up the funeral card which had printed a poem Brien had written and would have been embarrassed about had he known his mother found it, let alone distributed it to friends and family. "Take Me to Elysium," was the title. It was naturally touching, but for all the wrong reasons. Everyone put some sort of presentiment into it, shoveled religious hooey on top of it, and no one saw it for what it was -- a love poem to me.

Then there was the picture of him I had taken and given an extra print of to his mother. A radiant boy with that long, silken brown hair hanging in his face, a look of surprise on him. Thin, dark eyebrows, long lashes. Tight lips with that wry grin. The cute urchin nose. He was leaning back on the couch and wearing shorts and his legs seemed to go on forever and his right hand was absently

scratching his flat stomach under his shirt.

I put the card carefully back on the table and closed my eyes and tried to remember that day. Instead exactly what I was afraid of happened. I thought about the accident.

It was a freak thing.

An elderly man in a late-model Ford hydroplaned through a stop just after a summer shower slicked the roads down. The car plowed like a galleon right into a Minivan driven by an Asian woman who had just picked up her young daughter from recital practice at the local elementary school. Thankfully, everyone was okay. Everyone, except for Brien.

He was half a block away, coming home from my house.

A hubcap. The impact sent it flying. Some say they heard it whistling like a teakettle, screaming in the air; others say there was no noise at all. It had struck him from behind in the nape of the neck with such power he received a contusion on the part of his spinal chord that controls all motor function including brain activity. He was on a respirator for about a day but there was no point; he was dead the second the hubcap thudded into his neck.

What was that Aristotle said? Luck was when the guy next to you gets hit with an arrow.

I turned off the light and tried to think about better times.

11:12 p.m.

It was the day I took the pictures of Brien that the sex part began to unfold. I had just loaded my camera with a roll of film I'd found crammed in the back of a junk drawer in the kitchen when Brien dropped over. "Hey," he said, throwing himself on the couch. (How graceful his awkwardness ... how awkward his gracefulness). He pointed the remote at the TV and clicked it on and the tube sprung to life.

This had become our routine: after school he'd hang around watching television for a couple of hours as I worked. We talked little; he just wanted to be near me. Sometimes I'd fix him a sandwich, other times he'd raid my cabinets. (Once he consumed an entire tin of salted cashew halves.) Then, after his shows were over, he'd click off the set and take off. "Later," he'd say, tossing the word back over his shoulder.

That was how it commonly went. This particular day deviated from that, all because I'd found that unused roll of film. He was sitting on the couch, absently scratching his abdomen under his shirt, grinning at something funny on the tube, and I called out his name quickly so he'd look over fast. He did and I clicked off the first shot on my new roll. "Thanks," I said, expecting him to protest, to get huffy, maybe even chase me around the room and snatch at the camera. But instead of being mock-angry with me a broad smile appeared, a gushing grin that was a little pathetic.

I think I understand now. I gave no instructions, put him through no ordeal. I didn't tell him to comb his hair or stand up straight or put on Sunday clothes.

There wasn't that underlying sense he wasn't good enough, that he wasn't who the photographer wanted him to be. I accepted *him*, not wanting a Perfect Son or a Perfect Student. I took *his* picture, Brien Waverly's, and he was quite simply flattered I did.

Sensing his enjoyment of being photographed I asked if he wanted me to take one more. He nodded and I clicked off another shot. "How's this?" Brien asked next, pulling his sleeve back and flexing his biceps for me. It was comical because he had no muscle to speak of and he knew it. I raised the camera and put my finger on the button.

Click.

"All right, that's enough Hercules," I said. "I'm going to use up all my film."

"One more," he begged. Then he moved apart his knees and exposed his crotch to me.

My heart skipped a beat. Does he know what he's doing? I asked myself. Of course, you idiot; he's a teenager. He wasn't some sexless innocent; he'd been jerking off for at least five years now and he may well have gone all the way with a peer.

"Well?" He asked.

No harm, I figured. I mean, he was posing like that and I was looking right at him and that image would be engraved in my memory forever; if I could see it and remember it then surely I could photograph it, for what was a photograph but a frozen memory?

Click.

"Okay, that's enough," I said.

"Hey," he whined impetuously, making the word into two syllables. "Take another." And then he drew his legs up and pushed them far apart and sunk back into the couch and gave me a come-hither look with those sumptuous green eyes that made my dick swell up and strain painfully against my pants. I had to bend over to keep the erection from hurting, and to keep him from seeing it. I sat next to him and put down the camera, remembering when I was a boy having a boner in class and being called to clear the blackboard, simply refusing to get up, even when Miss Hansen said I had to march right down to principal Bartlett's office for being insolent.

"Awww," Brien said when he saw the camera go down.

"Come on. Sit right," I said.

His legs dropped to the floor peevishly and he pushed himself back up into a sitting position, brooding now, lower lip poking out, arms folded across his chest.

"Listen Bri ..." But I couldn't find the words. Or rather, I could, but they weren't my own and I didn't want to use them. All I could do was sigh and slouch back in the sofa next to him, defeated.

And then an amazing thing happened.

"My birthday is the eighteenth of next month," Brien said. "That's in like six

weeks."

"And?"

"It'll be okay then," he said, still looking straight ahead.

I whetted my dry lips. "You mean taking pictures?"

He turned to me and laid a hand on my thigh. I felt my dick gain weight even further. His hand was soft and warm. "Forget the camera," he said, then lifted his eyebrows up and down like Groucho.

I turned crimson. "You little devil ..."

"That's me. A regular demon." He removed his hand and went back to watching television. I stared at him in awe. The intensity with which he was suddenly focused on the program belied what just transpired. It was as if he had been sitting there glued to the tube for hours and I had just made the whole thing up.

11:41 p.m.

I thought now, in my bed, of how implacable time became for me then. The date of May 18th was like one of those puddles of water you see laid out across a long stretch of highway in the distance, seeming to evaporate as you near, laying themselves out again further ahead. It was the torment of Tantalus. Indeed, it seemed almost as if some days repeated.

I had seen Brien several times in those weeks after his seductive suggestion, of course, and I enjoyed the time he hung around me, but everything took on the quality of a preface. How I rue that I viewed those last few weeks in such a half-real, anticipatory way, not lapping it up fully, imbibing myself on his company. And I felt ashamed that all throughout that countdown I was afraid he'd get a peculiar haircut, or grow a mustache, or get a face full of piercing, or put on an inordinate amount of weight. I was also afraid something might happen to him. I thought he might get sick or have to go out of town or he might break one of his gorgeous legs.

At night when the day was its most relentless, refusing to let go and yield to the next I'd lay awake and fantasize about Brien and my cock would become turgid and my hand would absently stroke it to a hardness that could not be denied. Then I would free it from my shorts and pump it up and down, trying to imagine my hand was his. Then I'd stop suddenly, wanting to save as much come for him as possible, but that killer smile and those beautiful green eyes would appear before me and the come would well up and I would have to either jerk myself to eruption or let the unstoppable come ooze out without fanfare.

It was about four weeks ago, around the time I was questioning whether Brien had forgotten his offer, when he revealed to me his continued eagerness. Rain was coming down in freshets, beating an angry tattoo on the roof. It was that time in Louisiana in the spring when the humidity would build and build and then thunderheads would mass and let loose with a cleansing afternoon shower and cool everything down. They'd only last about a half hour, but in that time a lot of rain would fall and the streets would be scrubbed clean and there'd

be a new day on the other side of it. Brien arrived in the middle of the storm and he was soaked through and through. His clothes clung to his ectomorphic body, nipples two dark spots seen through the wet material of his T-shirt, his blue jeans soaked black, shoes squeaking, hair completely sodden and much darker than it should have been. No matter what he did he couldn't keep those errant locks of hair from falling in front of his face. I gave him a beach towel but that clearly wasn't enough. "Want me to throw your clothes in the dryer?" I asked.

He grabbed his shirt in two hands and squeezed rainwater onto the floor. "You think?" He asked sarcastically but with a grin on his beautiful, seraphic face.

I gave him one of my T-shirts and a pair of white boxers and told him to go in the laundry room and wrench as much water out of his clothes in the sink, then toss the load into the dryer. A few moments later he came into the living room in my clothes. My shirt was too big on him and the neck came down far. The shorts were big on him, too, and he pulled the extra fabric away from his legs and made flaps out of them and laughed. His feet were bare for the first time around me cute, small feet, and his toes wiggled self-consciously as he made his way to the couch, grabbed the remote, tossed himself into the cushions and zapped the television on.

Brien watched his shows as the storm played through. The cable threatened to go out a few times, bursting into static but clearing right up, and the lights dimmed once. Thunder pealed, mostly in the distance, but one strike was close enough and loud enough to make Brien jolt. Rain was thrown slantwise at the window by an angry wind and the sky was almost as dark as night. All this, over the racket of the dryer, jeans and socks and shirt and underwear falling all over themselves, a cloth orgy.

Finally his clothes were ready and I told him so but Brien didn't care, comfortable the way he was, bare feet up on the coffee table. Then a commercial came on and Brien hit the mute. The rain seemed to grow louder to take up the slack in noise. "I've got it all planned out."

"Come again?" I asked, turning from some mundane task. Lighting flashed and thunder pealed the way it might had I said something augury.

Brien drew his legs up onto the couch, hugging his knees. The oversized leg-openings of my boxers allowed me a glorious vision of the underside of his smooth legs. I could also make out a surprisingly large bulge between his legs. He was indeed a beautiful creature, and there was something maddeningly sylphlike about him. He reminded me of a ceramic elf I used to put on the mantle come Christmas, a little pixie who sat much like Brien was now. This youth didn't belong in my living room, he belonged dancing in a forest glade, frolicking with satyrs and sileni.

"Got it all figured," he said. "I'll sneak out the night before my birthday, come here. At midnight, well, it'll be my birthday and I'll be ... you know, fair game. What do you think?"

"Okay," I said, cool as the cucumber.

"It's a plan, Stan," Brien said and grinned his killer grin and his toes, gripping the edge of the cushion, did a little wave, and again I thought he belonged with fauns and nymphs. "I'll be here, I promise. Midnight. "

"The witching hour," I said. Thunder should have clapped *then* but it didn't.

"You got a beer?" Brien asked, once again changing gears on me so fast it seemed to nullify what just occurred.

"Too young," I said.

"Too young to buy, not to drink."

"Yeah, but I'd get in trouble for serving."

"Really? My mom lets me drink wine on special occasions."

"I really don't know how it goes," I said. "Just forget it. Besides, I don't think I have any."

"Funny," Brien said. "It's like with driving. I can drive have been for a couple of years which means I'm taking responsibility not only for my own life but the lives of everyone else out there. Yet apparently I'm not able to take responsibility for my own body."

"Yes, well ..." I trailed off. Too complex. I noticed the storm seemed to be passing away now; the sky was nowhere near as dark, now the color of wet gravestones, and the rain had tapered to a light drizzle.

"I wrote you a poem."

"You did?"

"Actually it's not for you, it's about you. What I want you to do to me. It's not very good, but I got the idea to write one after I did a paper on a British poet."

"Can I see it?"

"Nah," he said.

"You little devil."

He winked. "Regular demon."

That's when I realized the storm had pretty much stopped. It was also late; Brien should have been home already. "I guess you can go now," I said with sadness.

"Yeah." He got up and went off to the laundry room and changed. When he came back in he was in his own clothes and he tossed me my T-shirt and boxers. "Thanks. But I would have just worn nothing."

I gulped audibly at that.

"Later," he said on the way out.

That night I wore the T-shirt and boxers that Brien had on, smelling him against me, having no idea he had been lying in a hospital brain-dead for hours.

11:52 p.m.

My mind turned back to it: the accident. I must have heard the sirens it was only a few blocks away but I don't remember. And I didn't check the papers the next day, either, catching instead the national news. It was over a day later when

a friend of mine called to tell me about the terrible tragedy that had just befallen poor Ellen Waverly. The tragedy was that Ellen had lost a son.

I thought it over now and came to a revised conclusion. The worst part was not that there was no one to blame, but that I couldn't tell anyone just how devastating it was to me. When Brien's mom thanked me for coming to the wake, I almost burst out crying. I wasn't there for her, I was the decedent's lover, and if anyone doubted that they could read the poem Brien wrote about me ... only I couldn't say that's what it was about.

But I didn't cry. The tears could not be found. Only a numbness.

I tried to move on. Get out, do things. There'd been a guy on the Internet I'd been talking to who wanted to get into my pants. I'd been putting him off. Impetuously I wrote him, said okay, only now he and his old boyfriend had gotten back together and he put me off. That made me feel even worse than I already felt so I just up and went out to a gay bar and went home with a guy who claimed to have a nine-inch uncut dick. I really don't know how long his penis was, though; when I started to unzip him I noticed the knees of his jeans were worn and close to ripping and I thought about Brien coming home that day with the A+. Then I thought about how his mother treated him that afternoon, like a nuisance, and I got mad as hell.

"What fuckin' gives?" The bar guy said, looking down at me. I stood up and told him to forget the whole thing, my mistake. For a few seconds there was a sense of real danger, that he might get violent, and there was a part of me that wanted just that so I could be beaten and feel some physical pain to match my internal one, and so that I could inflict some serious damage on someone else to release my anger. But I managed to leave without incident.

Then there were those little things. Flipping channels, seeing something Brien would laugh at, knowing he never would. The weight of that would crush me, make me feel sick, but again I could not cry.

One night I ended up out at the edge of the driveway in my shorts. I just suddenly had to see that handprint and make sure it wasn't gone. Like that made sense.

It reminded me of the negative handprints found in caves where Upper Paleolithics would hold their hands up to the stone walls and blow pigment around the edges. And it reminded me of the tracings I and every other elementary school kid made of their hands come November, turning the shape into a turkey. Brien placing his hand there seemed as distant as those two things. It seemed as if he never did it, yet here was the substantiation, literally engraved in stone.

I crouched down at his palm print and placed my hand over it, tried to match up the fingers as best they could. Then I realized I was feeling the exact opposite of Brien's hand. He was so not there it was killing me.

But still, no tears.

11:58 p.m.

Now, late night in Louisiana, the time when moonflowers put out more fragrance to attract the night moths in the same devious way the carrion lily emits the odor of rotting meat to attract flies. I rolled over on to my stomach, felt the fan blow across me, pause, breathe back the other way, pause, breathe again, pause...

Something was wrong. The fan continued running I could hear it moving dumbly side to side but I felt no air touch my perspiring body. Something was in between me and the fan, blocking the flow of air.

That's when I heard his dulcet voice.

"Hey."

I turned and looked to the foot of the bed where a slight form separated itself from the shadows and moved into the moonlight coming through the window. It was Brien. He was completely naked, smiling obliquely, hands relaxed at his sides, hair falling in his face. His cock was longish, hanging down between his milky legs beneath a neat, small thatch of light brown pubic hair. Otherwise his body was completely hairless and smooth, his porcelain skin radiant, almost phosphorescent.

No. He wasn't there, I thought rationally. He was gone. This Brien-thing was a mirage, a waking-dream, a hallucination created by stress. "I'm dreaming you," I told it. "You aren't here."

It shrugged. "Then pretend."

Why not? I nodded and swung my legs over the edge of the bed and sat up. Then I opened my arms for him to come to me and he did. I took his shoulders, cool and soft, and pulled him down to me and my lips touched his. Lightly touching, then firmer. He turned his head slightly to the side and closed his eyes. My tongue licked at him and he opened his mouth and let it in. I was exploring his teen-mouth and now he was exploring mine. It overwhelmed me. I had to pull back.

"Brien, I "

I noticed movement directly behind him. Something like a snake rising up over his right shoulder. It was thin and the same color as his flesh and instead of a snake's head there was a pointed, almost triangular tip, resembling something like a caudal fin on a cephalopod. My face must have registered my surprise and confusion for the Brien-thing narrowed his eyes and then turned behind him to see what held my confused gaze. "Oh, that," he said and giggled mellifluously. "It's mine."

I didn't understand until he turned around and showed me his bottom and revealed the slender, slinking thingthat was a chimerical tail emerging from his coccyx. He reached out for it, took it in his hands and draped it over his arm and stroked it like a pet. "Yes, I know," he said. "It's new. So are these." He ducked his head and I saw two curved horns poking up.

"I don't get it," I said. "You're like some mythical woodland creature. You should be playing a flute."

"Yours, maybe," he said and lifted his eyebrows up and down seductively. My cock stiffened.

"It's simple, really," he explained. "I'm a little devil. That's what you called me, right? I'm one of those -- what do you call it? - an incubus. Come to rape you."

"Incubi rape females," I said, not believing I was having this conversation. "Succubus?"

"They *are* female. Steal semen from men."

The Brien-thing frowned and let go of his tail. I expected it to succumb to gravity but instead it slowly lowered on its own and hovered around the floor. He scratched at one of his horns. Then he smiled. "A gay incubus!"

"I'm partial to male succubus," I said. "Has a certain *je ne sais* what."

We both grinned at each other. Then he held up a slender finger and said, "Watch this. It's like a, uh, a magic trick." He stepped backward from me and his tail came around and fit into his outstretched hand. He brought the head of his tail up to his mouth, stuck his tongue out, and licked it. My cock pulsated with each swipe. Then he sucked on it, feeding it into his mouth, hollow-cheeked. He bobbed it in and out, then licked some more, polishing it. Now he brought some saliva up from the back of his throat and spit onto it. The spit oozed out of his pursed lips and touched the head of his tail and slid down. He took his tongue and smeared it all over good. My dick was heavier and more engorged than I could remember.

Brien let go of the tail, its moistened end gleaming. The tail held itself up as he turned sideways and bent down and put his hands on his knees like he was looking inside the fridge for some milk. The tail stretched up high and then curved down in a fast swoop and headed straight for his asshole. It made contact and Brien moaned and was almost pushed forward off his feet as it pressed itself against his star and squeezed inside until the head was completely buried in him. He closed his eyes and moaned again and flexed at the knees, squirming his ass around the shaft violating him.

I was rock-hard, watching his tail ass-fuck him. Brien bounced now on his haunches in rhythm to the caudal appendage's motion. He picked up speed as it disappeared up his butt, retreated, dipped back up into him with such force it almost picked him up off the floor. My hand grabbed my cock through my shorts and held it tightly to keep it from exploding.

That tail was strange. Beyond prehensile, it seemed to have some mind of its own. Then, other times, Brien seemed in perfect control of it. The way I figured, it was more or less operating on conscious and unconscious impulses. The point is, he was fucking himself, but it had the spontaneity and surprise of someone else fucking him, and he was obviously loving it.

Finally Brien stopped, caught his breath. The tail slid backward out of him, at first slowly retracting, then toward the end being squeezed out quickly until the head came out with a slight, moist pop. It dangled inactively now behind him as

Brien stood up and came to me. "What did you think?"

"Can't you tell?" I asked and nodded to my dick. It had all but ripped through the come-sodden cotton of my boxers.

"Wow! For me?" Brien knelt down and he put his hands on my legs. His slender fingers crawled over me and worked into the waistband of my boxers and then gently pulled them down, up and over my cock, the material peeling off stickily. Freed, my dick seemed to greaten even more. I leaned back on my elbows and raised my hips up so Brien could get my shorts under me and down my legs and off. He climbed on top of me now, grinning. We fell backwards together on the mattress. Our mouths met again and our tongues found one another quicker and more passionately than before. I slid my hands down Brien's smooth back and cupped his beautiful ass.

"Oh Bri," I whispered. "Why are you here?"

"I promised," he said.

"Promised?"

"It's my birthday, silly," he said. Then he put a finger on my lips and shook his head, warning me not to destroy the magic. "Shhh," he said, eyes flicking toward the digital clock across the room. Then he began moving up over me, sliding his semi-hard dick up across my stomach and chest. He scooted up me and grabbed my head in his hands and pushed his hips forward until his dick came up into my face. It wasn't nearly as fat as mine but it was long. I seized it in both hands. Brien gasped, pushing my head closer to his manhood. Then I took it in my mouth and sucked on it. I made a tight "O" out of my mouth and he began to slowly rock himself in and out of my lips. His pre-ejaculate tasted like sugar. Then he removed himself and climbed over and lay across the bed. "That was awesome," he said. "No; you're awesome."

"Didn't you want to come?" I asked.

"There's time."

He was flaked out on his back, arms up over his head. My hand went across his chest, felt his nipples, his nascent pecs and incipient six-pack, then slid down through his soft pubic hair. I grabbed his dick and gave it a playful tug, keeping it stiff. It throbbed in my hand and he closed his eyes and took a deep breath.

"I can't believe you're dead," I said to him. I felt my eyes water up.

"All of us die into adults."

I thought about that. It was true. How many people have I been since childhood? How many ghosts had I left behind?

I let go of his cock and crawled up and kissed his nose. Then I moved back down, kissing his left chest, flicking my tongue over his nipples. "Mmm," he said, putting his hand on my head and shoving me gently lower. I licked down across his flat stomach, in and around his navel, lower still, all the while running my hands across his smooth body. His toes curled, his tail flapped lazily on the mattress. Now I was back at his penis. I drew my tongue up it and it quivered, kissed the bulb-shaped head, licked pre-come out of his hole and sucked on his

nectar. Then I decided I wanted him to come right then and there and quickly I began to jerk him off into my mouth. His body began to go into a paroxysm of carnal appetite. "Oh no, here it ... oh shit!" He bucked up, jamming his dick in me, rising up off the bed, and Brien squeezed off several rounds of his sweet confection into my mouth.

"Oh my God, that was great," Brien said. "Okay. Your turn. Want me to suck you off?"

I shook my head. "Turn over."

He looked at me, narrowing his eyes, his dark eyebrows lowering. Then he shrugged, moved some tresses of hair from his face, and got onto his stomach. He looked back at me, unsure of what I was going to do, a little hesitant. I caressed his back and then slid my hands down to his butt and then took his tail lifted and it gently out of the way. I bent down and kissed his rear, then licked at it.

"Like my ass?" He asked.

"Want me to show you how much?"

"Oh, yes, show me."

I pulled aside his cheeks and put my face down at his cute puckered hole. It was the most exquisite, indefectible, inviting asshole I had seen. I licked all around it, him moving his hips in response to each lick, and then I sucked hard on the ring of muscle.

"Okay, okay," he said in surrender. "That's enough!"

"Hmmm?"

"I want your dick in me. I want to sit on it."

I pulled back and wiped my mouth with the back of my hand. He rolled over and then pushed me down on my back and straddled me quickly. Brien's hair was in tangles, but he didn't care. There was something feral about him that turned me on. He squatted on me and his tail came underneath eelike and wrapped around my cock. It pulled it upward and positioned me against Brien's hole. He lowered, winced, then smiled knowingly; a split-second later I burst inside and he dropped several inches. The tail slithered off, unneeded. Then he squeezed down further on me, gobbling up my length with his asshole. He stopped, slowly raised up, then came back down. Now he was squeezing and flexing his chute. It was heaven.

"Feel good?" He asked.

"Very. You?"

He didn't answer, instead rocking up and down on me, crouching on my dick, looking quizzical. "Good, yes. But I want to be on my back when you come inside me."

"Okay." I raised up on my elbows, looking at him squatting there on my dick casually. His hair fell in front of his face again. I actually seemed to grow even harder. Then he tried to pull off me, tugging me up with his ass at first, as if we were tied. Then I was spit out and he climbed off. We scrambled, taking up new

positions quickly. Brien worked up under me and bent his knees and grabbed them and pulled them back to his chest, his ass open and waiting. I got on top and worked my knob up against his star and pushed. He gasped. His feet were by shing against my chest. He squeezed his eyes shut in ecstasy and thrashed his head from side to side, his face beneath tangles of hair, as I slid in and out of him. This position was terrific; I was getting further inside than before.

"Fast now," Brien ordered. "There's not much time left."

I did push-ups into him, dipping in and out of his luscious asshole which gripped me tightly, not really paying attention to his warning. And then suddenly I froze up, feeling something touch my own hindquarters. He had brought his tail up under me and it was poking against my own hole.

"Oh no," I said, "you aren't going to "

"What?" He asked coyly, pressing further. It made me stiffen and try to get away, sliding deeper into Brien's ass, almost up to the hilt. He bit his lower lip. His sinuous tail squeezed hard, unable to get in me, coiling, trying to burrow into too small a place. There was a sharp pain. I was about to tell Brien to stop, that I was too tight, when that sublime moment of entry occurred, that beautiful moment when you open up and accept the trespasser and it fills you up.

"Oh God, that's so damn good," I cried, savored the fullness in me, then managed to return to my own fucking. It took us a moment to get it together. I'd got too fast, then slow, and he'd go too fast. Finally we were synchronous and when we hit this groove it was something phenomenal. My gliding strokes lengthened and I humped his eager ass with abandon. In and out I pounded, going all the way up inside him so that my thighs pressed against his ass cheeks.

"Oh yes," he said, flicked his green eyes to the clock, and said "hurry." He gyrated his hips, doing everything he could to get me all in him. It got savage but he urged me on. "Please, do it," he said. He bucked uncontrollably and I held him down and fucked him hard and fast until I had built to an unstoppable orgasm. My come burst inside him first in one amazing volcanic blast and then in a succession of massive, drawn-out spurts, one after another, and I could feel his ass gulp it all down as he squealed with pleasure and came himself all over us.

Finally, when I was completely enervated, his tail slid out of me and I collapsed next to him and stroked his silken hair, pulling strands out of his face, running my fingers up over his horns. "This is unreal," I said, my dick growing comfortably flaccid. "I don't understand it."

"Shhh," he said.

"I mean, this has got to be an hallucination."

"What?" He asked. "I'm a gay succubus. I came to steal your semen. Got it." He patted his rump.

"I think you got it *all*," I said, still amazed at how much I'd let loose. I yawned, feeling very sleepy. He curled up against me and I held him tightly against my body. "So, maybe I have created you somehow, made you up in my

head. I may well be crazy. But it doesn't really matter. I mean, you can't take this away from me."

"That's the spirit," Brien whispered. He sounded sleepy too. Or maybe it was resignation?

"I guess this puts me in the same category as alien abductees and other 'experiencers,' like those who claim some loved one came back and hovered over their bed and told them everything was okay." He pulled back from me and smiled, parting his hair one last time. "It is, you know."

My eyes watered and I looked at him through a prism of welling tears. "Is it?" I asked, voice breaking.

"Absolutely." He looked over to the clock. It was 12:59 a.m. I understood, but I didn't like it. "No," I said, "don't. Please."

But it was too late. He'd climbed off the bed, turned to face me. "Later," he said.

The clock flashed to one. And he was gone.

That's when the tears finally came.

STREET TOUGH'S BALL
by Bert McKenzie

I stood in the park, shooting baskets, just trying to perfect my shot. It was late and I was bored. I dribbled the ball a bit, pivoted and hooked it back over my shoulder, missing the hoop by a mile.

"You throw like a girl," a voice called out from the dark. I froze. I had been warned by my landlady not to go out at night and particularly to stay away from the park. The neighborhood wasn't safe. But I put that down to the paranoid rambling of a little old lady. I wasn't afraid. I could take care of myself. At least that's what I thought till that moment. Just beyond the cone of light stood three shadowy shapes. I didn't really know what to do, so I scooped up my ball and tossed it back at the basket again.

One of the three figures moved quickly, darted in under the basket, snagging my ball. He turned and jumped, putting the ball neatly into the hoop. He caught it again as it fell through the chains hanging from the metal ring, then turned to confront me. "That's how a man shoots baskets, faggot."

Man! He was not what I would term a man, hardly more than a boy, maybe in his late teens. The kid stood looking at me defiantly, challenging me, waiting to see what I would make of his insult. He was short and wiry, about five feet, four inches, with a thin physique. Dressed in cut-off jeans and a low- cut muscle shirt, his tight arms and smooth chest gleamed bronze under the street light that illuminated the basketball goal. He was Hispanic, with dark, curly hair and thick lashes. There was just a hint of darkness, the beginnings of a mustache over his full, sensual lips. He stood waiting for a response.

"You think you can beat me at a little one-on-one?" I asked. I had to show some bravado, and besides, how could the kid know I had played all-star in college?

"Fuck, man, no problem. But what's in it for me? Why would I want to shoot hoops with a faggot?" Again the term, faggot. I knew he was just trying to insult and goad me. He had no clue to my sexual orientation. But I decided to play along and call his bluff.

"You think I'm a faggot? How about if I win, I get to fuck your ass."

His eyes widened a bit at that. Did I see fear, excitement, desire? Then he puffed up his chest and thrust his chin forward in a false sense of bravura. "Yeah, sure faggot. Only if we win we get to fuck your lily white ass, all of us." He moved his head and the two other shapes stepped out of the shadows to join him. One was a tall, gangly looking boy, at least six foot, two. He had a shaved head and dark, ebony skin. He was dressed in baggy jeans with the crotch down to his knees and a dirty t-shirt. The other boy was around six foot tall, but built more like a linebacker, thick arms, a barrel chest and tree trunks for legs. He was light skinned with shaggy, red hair and a face full of freckles. This boy was dressed in shorts, sneakers and a sleeveless shirt.

"I said one-on-one."

"The faggot's afraid he's gonna lose," the redhead jibed as he pulled a knife out of a pocket in his shorts. "Afraid he's gonna lose his ass."

"That right, faggot?" the Hispanic boy asked. "You chickening out? We don't like chicken-shit faggots. We might just have to fuck you anyway and then carve you up."

"Give me the ball," I said in my most authoritarian voice.

"Come get it," the boy said and held it out. I stepped forward, reaching for it, but at the last second he tossed it in the air. His tall, black friend jumped for it, catching it and darting out of my way, bouncing it on the asphalt.

"Yeah, come get it, faggot," the black kid taunted, dancing back and forth with the basketball. I made a grab but he was half a second faster, passing it to the chunky redhead. "Shoot, Donny, shoot!" The redhead threw the ball wide, over the basket and right into the Hispanic kid's hands. He tossed it expertly into the hoop.

"That's two," he called as I grabbed the ball. "We're only going to twenty-one, faggot."

I bounced the ball twice and easily lobbed it into the basket before any of the three boys could react. We were even. The Latin kid grabbed the ball and passed it to Donny while he jockeyed for position. I moved in on the redhead, but he backed up and over me like a steamroller, knocking me to the pavement. There was no referee to call a foul and the game didn't stop just because I was down. The black kid scored another basket and passed the ball on to the Hispanic kid.

"Go, Joey," the redhead called as I made a grab for the ball. Despite his quickness, Joey didn't stand a chance against my superior experience. I snagged the ball and turned to shoot. But as I did, I felt the wind knocked out of me. The black kid had elbowed me in the gut, taking the ball and expertly firing it into the hoop. "Way to go, Ace!" Donny called, high-fiving the black kid. This was definitely not going to be a sportsman-like game.

Now I was pissed. I grabbed for the ball, snatched it and made another basket. Reaching in to get it again I was knocked to the ground by the big kid while Joey scored. I was beginning to wonder if this was basketball or soccer. Obviously my skills at the sport did little good. I might have been easily able to out-perform these three punks if it was a fair game. But I didn't stand a chance against the three working together with their street tough tactics. To save my ass I was going to have to cheat as much as I could.

The game continued, only I did my best to even the score. Joey grabbed for the ball and took my elbow in his face. But a bloody nose only made him play that much harder. My foot tripped Ace as he ran with the ball, sending him sprawling on the asphalt. Donny was the hardest one to foul. Built like a brick wall, he didn't seem to have any weak spots. As the game was nearing ten points, even on both sides, I decided to hit below the belt. A knee in his groin sent the big redhead rolling on the ground and another basket for me.

Soon we were tied at fifteen points. The three street thugs were glistening

with sweat and breathing hard, but no more so than I was. I reached down and peeled off my wet shirt. Joey suddenly looked a bit more intensely. "Hey guys," he called. "The faggot's getting ready for us, starting to strip. Come on, let's finish this so we can pork his ass."

"I'm getting ready too," Donny said, pulling his shirt over his head and exposing a solid chest with the hint of red fur dividing his nipples.

"Me too," Joey said and pulled off his muscle shirt.

"Well, I can't fucking play in these," Ace whined and unzipped his baggy jeans. He stripped down to boxer shorts, taking off his t-shirt as well. Then the game started again, but now it was charged with a new electricity. No matter how it ended, there was going to be sex. You could smell it in the air, that hot aroma of musk and male sweat, and something more.

We played on, but now that we were close to the end of the game things seemed to change. It was almost as if we were playing in slow motion. No one was able to score. The ball just kept rebounding off the backboard. The violence of before seemed curbed as well. It was almost a gentle, seductive game, shiny bodies moving and gliding in a dance of hot lust. Trying to block a shot, I came up against Joey, our torsos touching, sliding against each other. My nipples suddenly became erect and I felt a stirring in my groin. I was really beginning to enjoy this.

Then Ace jumped for the ball. I meant to block him, but lost my balance and made a grab. My hand connected with his boxers and there was a ripping sound. In seconds the tall black boy stood there, his shorts gone and his long, black, uncut dick exposed to the air. "Go ahead and shoot!" Donny called and Ace began to move. But my eyes were riveted to that dark penis bouncing over low hanging balls.

He took the shot and I instinctively jumped to block it, tipping the ball away from the basket. But at the same moment I felt the cool air on my nuts and dick. As I jumped, Joey grabbed the waistband of my shorts, jerking them down to my knees. I lost my balance and toppled to the ground and Joey yanked, stripping the shorts completely off. Then Joey pulled off his denim shorts as well, exposing his short, thick Hispanic prick to my view. "Come on, Donny. Strip. We're gonna play skins vs. skins." The stocky redhead slowly slipped off his shorts too, revealing a long, slim cock already half hard and slightly distended over full balls nestled in a bright red nest of pubic fur. "Now, let's play," Joey shouted and threw the ball to Ace.

As we continued our game with a new intensity, I began to grow more excited. Four hot, sweaty, naked bodies playing round ball in a public park; anyone who drove by, or even looked out their windows on Fifth Street would see us. It was a real turn-on, but I didn't have time to think about it. We were already tied at eighteen points and now battling for the finish.

I scored again, twenty points and one basket from victory. Then Donny blocked me, threw the ball to Ace who easily sank it. Tied at twenty all. I caught

the rebound and pivoted, only to collide with Joey who made a grab at the ball. I ducked and charged, more like football than basketball, but Donny blocked me again, knocking the ball from my hands. Joey grabbed it and threw. It sailed up for the basket, hit the rim and almost went in, but started to bounce back. Then Ace jumped up, and tipped the ball, sinking it. Twenty two. My ass was theirs.

Just then we heard sirens and red flashing lights appeared down the street. Someone must have seen us and called the cops on the naked perverts playing in the park. The three boys grabbed their clothes and took off running. I reached for mine and realized they were gone. The three punks must have taken my shorts as well, with my wallet still in the pocket. I took off after them. There was a stream that cut through the park and a big cement culvert that allowed it to pass under the street and into a drainage ditch. The boys jumped a chain link fence and ran down into the culvert. I followed.

I plunged down into the darkness under the street and ran headlong into a firm body. Donny and I toppled together to the damp ground. I struggled to my feet and was about to say something when Joey grabbed me from behind, clamping a hand over my mouth. "Shut up!" he hissed in a hoarse whisper. "You want us all to land our naked asses in jail?"

"We're trapped, Joey," one of the other boys whined. "They put bars on the other end of this."

"Just shut up," their leader argued. "They won't come down here. They're afraid of rats."

"Rats?" another voice echoed nervously.

We were all breathing hard. I could feel Joey's chest rising and falling as he held me against him. Then I felt something more, a firmness pushing against one of my buns. My own dick instantly responded, growing with excitement. I moved slightly and Joey's cock slipped into the crack of my ass. He relaxed his grip on my mouth and slid one hand across my chest to twist my nipples.

A light played down into the culvert outside. We could hear the cops talking, shining their bright flashlights all around. "Joey?" Donny whispered, but Joey was too busy to reply. He slid his firm cock up against my sphincter and pushed hard. The head slipped inside, causing a searing pain. I bit my tongue, trying not to cry out.

Slowly he fed me more, sliding his dick into me inch by inch, fucking me dry. The pain began to subside, replaced by that full feeling of having a hard piece of boy dick up my ass. I groaned softly with pleasure, all the while the flashlight beams were slicing down into the culvert just inches from where we were humping. It felt incredibly good, although exhilarating because of the sense of danger. This must have really heightened the fun for Joey too, because he reached down to grab my hips as he shifted into high gear, fucking my ass hard and rough.

The lights and voices disappeared as the cops lost interest. "What the hell are you doing, man?" Ace whispered.

"We fucking won, didn't we?" Joey hissed through clenched teeth. "Get over here." I could feel my hot Hispanic stud tense up, then he began to blow, shooting his load deep into my ass. With a groan of pleasure, he fell back against the concrete, his spent dick popping free. "Next," he said.

"Give me that white ass," Ace growled and quickly took Joey's place, positioning his uncut dick against my abused hole. Joey's cum provided a natural lube, greasing my butt and allowing the black kid to slide in easily. "Oh, fuck, this is hot!" he groaned as he began to slam into me from behind.

I suddenly felt an incredible sensation around my dick. In the darkness I could just make out the shaggy red hair as Donny swallowed me, taking my cock down his throat. With the hot fucking I was getting, it didn't take me any time to reach orgasm. In a matter of seconds, Donny's hot wet mouth was bringing me to the edge of infinity. I began to shoot down his throat. At the same time, Ace began to unload in my guts.

We pulled apart and I collapsed to the wet floor of the culvert, covered in grime and sweat. "Come on, guys," Joey ordered, and the three boys headed back out into the night still naked, carrying their clothes.

"Hey," I called. Joey stopped and looked back at me. "Thanks for the game."

"You ain't gonna get that kind of workout at the Y," he replied, and then climbed back up the chain link fence to disappear into the night.

ONLY SOME ARE DANGEROUS
by James Hosier

Looking back on it, what I did to Dr. Murdstone seems cruel. What I did to Andy Bradford was worse. He was stupid but I was mean and Andy didn't deserve it.

Dr. Murdstone was our Biology and Health Science teacher and he loved boys. Nothing against that I've made a lot of money out of people like him it was just that Dr. Murdstone made his preferences so obvious. The girls had to sit at the back of the room. "To avoid any possible embarrassment when delicate matters were being taught," he said. Ha! It might have fooled the principal but it didn't fool us.

He started to take a real interest when you reached the ninth grade. This is not to say that he wasn't already on the prowl earlier. Seventh grade boys would get a friendly pat on the butt for a nice drawing of a flower bud or a seed pod.

As far as Dr. Murdstone was concerned, the buds blossomed and the seeds ripened in the ninth and tenth grades, helped along by his incessant double-meaning comments.

"Mine is much bigger than Ken's, Dr. Murdstone." The speaker was referring to a walnut.

"Is it now? You'll have to show me some time."

"Mean soil temperature is measured at a minimum depth of one foot...." he dictated, and then added with a lecherous wink to the boys in the front row, "The first few inches don't count." Peals of girlish laughter came from the back of the room.

When, in the ninth grade, he came to sex, there was no stopping him. Female anatomy was covered in just three lessons and was soon disposed of. After that we spent week after week drawing diagrams of the male sexual organs. A question from one of the girls received a very terse answer. If one of the boys asked him about seminal vesicles or the prostate gland, he'd go on for the rest of the lesson.

Andy Bradford was in ninth grade and a year younger than me. I only really knew him through the swimming club and through our mutual interest in bikes. Now don't get me wrong when I tell you that Andy Bradford was a good looking kid. He was blond-haired and blue-eyed. I recall some guy at a contest saying he looked like an angel. In many respects he was right. Andy was the most innocent person I'd ever met. Andy just gazed at anybody who told a dirty joke as if the guy had been speaking Mandarin Chinese. I recall once that someone had a double-page spread torn from some magazine of a nude model draped over a Harley Davidson and showing everything and I mean everything. "That's one of the first Electroglides. They had a lot of trouble with the starter motor," said Andy.

A better name for him would be a 'dumb blond'. It wasn't, I think, that he was really stupid. He was just so trusting that he fell for every trick in the book.

He spent so much time going on false errands that none of his school assignments was ever done on time. They were always last-minute efforts. A lot of the teachers tried to have him pulled out of the swimming team so he could concentrate on school work more, but our coach fought to keep him and Andy stayed on the team.

We were changing one day after a practice. "James, when you were in ninth grade did you have to do an essay on reproduction in rabbits for old Murdstone?" he asked.

"Yeah. He does the same things year after year."

"Do you still have it?"

"I must have."

"Can I borrow it to copy? I have to hand mine in tomorrow morning at the latest. If I don't, the principal will be sending for my mom again."

"It won't do you any good," I said. "As far as I recall, I got a grade of D for it."

"No matter. I just need to write it."

"Okay. You'd better come home with me and I'll dig it out for you."

In fact, when I managed to unearth it, I found that I'd gotten a D-minus. "A scrappy, untidy account," was written on the top of the first page and "Your work *must* improve!" at the end. My diagram of a male rabbit gave the animal a cock that wouldn't have been out of place on Tarzan. I pointed that out to Andy. We laughed about that. Andy took it and returned it the next day and I thought nothing about it for some weeks until we were again in the changing room.

"What did Murdstone say about your essay?" I enquired.

"Ha! You did me a real favor there! I got an A."

"You what?"

"I got an A!"

I didn't believe it until he brought it into school and showed it to me. Not only had he copied my mistakes but there were others of his own. My poor diagrams were even worse in his version. But he had told the truth. Written on the top of the first page were the words, "A thoughtful and well-constructed account. Well done!"

"What did he say?" I asked.

"He said I had a talent for biology."

"I suspect he thinks you might have a talent for something else," I said.

"What?"

"Oh come off it, Andy. The guy's queer. You must know that."

"He's a bit strange, yeah," he said. You see what I mean about the dumb blond? We left it at that.

My suspicions mounted when Dr. Murdstone started attending our practices. He had been responsible for our First Aid training for some time but rarely came to watch us. Soon he was a regular fixture, sitting alone in the spectator area and clapping wildly whenever Andy did anything spectacular. When he offered to

drive Andy home one evening, I knew I was right. I don't know where Dr. Murdstone lived but I was pretty sure it wasn't near where Andy lived. Andy lived a few blocks from our house and I'd never seen Murdstone in the area. I was left to walk home. As the rear lights of Murdstone's car vanished, I determined to get rid of him. It wasn't just that he'd given Andy a lift and not me. I'd had one or two confrontations with Dr. Murdstone in the past few days. It was time he left.

All that was necessary, I thought, was for Murdstone actually to do something to a boy instead of hinting at it and in the presence of a witness. Then it would be a question of putting the facts in front of the Principal and "Goodbye Dr. Murdstone!"

The more I thought about the plan, the better it looked. Andy was ideal for the bait and I would be the witness. Not a proper witness unfortunately. I'd only be able to hear what went on.

In the old days, before Dr. Murdstone came to the school, there was an oxygen cylinder fixed to the demonstration bench in the Biology lab. He got so mad about people turning the tap on, trying to get a high from the oxygen that he moved the cylinder into the store room and bashed a hole in the dividing wall to take the rubber pipe. The hole was really crude and he'd made no attempt to fill it in neatly with plaster. He'd also set up the storeroom as an office. He marked essays and conducted his private interviews in there.

I did a bit of research on the timetable to find the best time. As luck would have it, the ninth grade boys were in the gymnasium in the fifth lesson on Tuesday mornings and we were scheduled for biology. I hung around in the biology lab until last.

"Did you wish to speak to me, James?" Murdstone asked.

"Oh. Not really, sir. I was just thinking about something."

"Well, you'd better hurry to your next lesson." He vanished into his office. I dashed downstairs and was just in time to catch Andy before he went into the showers.

"Dr. Murdstone wants to see you." I said.

"When?"

"Now."

"What does he want?"

"Search me. He said it was urgent."

"I'll have a quick shower and get dressed."

"I wouldn't. You know what he's like. Have your shower afterwards."

I followed him up the stairs congratulating myself. Andy had a nice little ninth grade butt, long legs and seemed to be pretty well equipped up front too; just the sort of boy to get Murdstone worked up.

I opened the lab door. "After you," I said. Andy knocked on the store room door. I hung around near the hole in the wall.

"Come in." I heard it more clearly through the hole than Andy.

"Come in!" Louder that time. Andy entered and closed the door behind him.

"Ah! Andrew. What can I do for you?"

"I was told you wanted to see me urgently, Dr. Murdstone."

I pressed my ear against the hole. This was the critical moment.

"Yes I did. How's the swimming?"

"Pretty good."

"Good. Er...how's that essay on asexual reproduction coming along?"

"You said it doesn't have to be handed in until the end of next week."

"I know. I just wondered how it was coming along."

"Well, er...okay," said Andy. I'd have bet my bottom dollar that he hadn't started it.

"Good, good. Let me know if there's anything you don't quite understand."

"I will."

"Good. Very good. Err ... but there was one other thing. You see how untidy this room is."

"I guess it is a bit."

"I don't have time to do it. I was wondering if you'd like to be my sort of biology store keeper. Come in a couple of times a week and straighten things a bit. You're someone I know I can trust. Some of the chemicals here are dangerous. The other boys don't have your common sense or your interest in biology."

"I guess I could."

"The only thing is that I'm not sure you're tall enough. See if you can reach that shelf with the specimens on it."

"This one? It'd be easier if I stood on a chair or something."

"Try this. Oh yes! You're taller than I thought. Strong, too. See if you can lift this."

"This?" I heard Andy grunt.

"My word, you really are strong. Excellent biceps development! I chose well."

"I ought to be going down now," said Andy. "I need to take a shower and the other guys play tricks with my clothes and stuff."

"What sort of tricks?"

"Nothing much. They hide my clothes and if I leave anything in the pockets, they take it."

"That's easily remedied. Leave your things here in the office. Here's a spare key in case I'm not here. You could change here too if you wish."

"That's real decent of you, Dr. Murdstone," said Andy. "Thanks a lot! When shall I come and do your office?"

"Any time. But Wednesdays and Thursdays would be best. I have very few classes then."

"I could manage after school on Wednesdays and we have a study lesson on Thursday mornings in the library."

"That would be admirable. And I have a coffee machine here as you see. Help yourself."

"Thanks, Dr. Murdstone. I'd better go or I'll get hassled by Mrs. Leeds for being late for her lesson."

"No problem. I'll write you a note to say I kept you. Don't forget. Tomorrow after school."

"I won't. Thanks again."

I just had time to get out of the lab. Andy might not have gotten hassled. I did. I found the principal teaching our class. My usual excuse, "Sorry I'm late. I had to see the principal," just wouldn't work.

I muttered something about looking for Mrs. Schneider, who should have been teaching us.

"She is delayed at the dentist's," said Dr. Goodchild. "Hence I am attempting to fill in for her. It is I, Hosier, who arrange the timetable here, not you. I am more aware of the staff situation in this school than you. Now sit down."

Aware of the staff situation? I thought as I took my place. Was he aware, I wondered, of the pederast who taught biology? If he wasn't, he soon would be!

I spent thirty-five valuable minutes after school on Wednesday with my ear against the hole. Thirty-five wasted minutes. All I heard was the clink of glass and a very ordinary conversation about swimming and football.

Thursday was more interesting. "Who are your really close friends, Andrew?" asked Dr. Murdstone. They seemed to be drinking coffee together.

"The guys in the swimming club mostly. James Hosier is a good guy. I get on well with him."

"A nice lad," said Dr. Murdstone. "He lives near you, doesn't he?"

"Yes."

"And do you visit with each other?"

"Only once. I went round to his place to ... err ... to borrow something."

"And I'll bet you were there for ages listening to music and doing all sorts of other things eh?"

"No. What sort of other things?"

"Two boys together. I'll bet you talked about sex."

"Well, yes we did to some extent."

"What does 'some extent' mean?"

"It doesn't matter. It's not important."

"You don't need to tell me. I know boys. James is a year older than you. I guess it was all about penis sizes, eh? Aha! You're blushing, young Andrew. An instant give-away. We'll say no more. Next time, though, do come and ask me if you're uncertain about something. James is not qualified, though I'm sure he is, well, very well equipped."

"Yeah. He's got a microscope. I remember noticing that," said Andy.

"I don't imagine a microscope would be needed for what you were examining," said Dr. Murdstone. Andy said nothing. I heard them sipping, then

Andy said something about dusting the skeleton and I slunk away.

Dr. Murdstone caught up with me in the corridor on the following day. "Ah, James," he said, "you're friendly with Andrew Bradford aren't you?"

"Yes, we're buddies," I lied.

"I thought so. Tell me, does he confide in you?"

"Quite a lot, yes."

"What can you tell me about him? In the strictest confidence of course."

"Well... his parents are divorced. He lives with his mother." That much I had heard from my Mom who had met Mrs. Bradford once or twice. "He seems to miss his dad a lot," I continued, making up the story as I went along. "He seems to want to relate to a man somehow. I can't really explain that."

"Quite normal," said Dr. Murdstone, as if he knew the meaning of the word. "Does he ask you questions about sex?"

I managed to look suitably embarrassed. A long glance at the floor and a bit of foot shuffling. I'm quite good at that.

"Don't be ashamed. It's quite normal. What sort of things does he ask you about?"

"Well, sir, in complete confidence...."

"Yes, yes. Go on."

"Mostly about gay sex. Why the hell he thinks I should know about it beats me. I'm a hundred per cent hetero but he wants to know what gays do and if it hurts. Questions like that. He came round to see me once and I thought once he was trying to seduce me. He was on about penis sizes and wanted me to show him mine. I didn't of course. I guess it's just a stage he's going through."

"Possibly. Thanks a lot James. Now I know how to help the boy."

"You won't say anything to him? About this conversation I mean?"

"Certainly not. It's entirely professional. Thank you for being so honest."

Everything went wrong on the following Wednesday. Mrs Leeds chose to go though one of my essays after school. I was ten minutes late on my listening station and I had a busy evening ahead of me. I had a lot of homework to do and a client waiting for a fifty-dollar mouthful of my spunk.

"I've got several friends who are that way," Dr. Murdstone was saying. "Really nice guys. Intelligent too. Perhaps I'm a bit of a rebel, but I think there's something really nice in a deep friendship between a man and a boy."

"Oh yeah?"

"Yes. Some boys need a man to help them through adolescence and some men need the companionship of a boy."

"Why?"

"That's a good question. There's something about a boy. A zest for life, I suppose you'd call it, and boys are attractive...."

"I wouldn't say so."

"Oh but they are. Look at yourself for example. Slim and yet so muscular...."

"Shouldn't the formic acid be locked in the poisons case?"

"Eh? Oh yes, it should. That was my fault. As I was saying...."

"There's sodium bicarbonate in here. That's not a poison, is it?"

"No, it's just as well you're around. Some of those boys in the swimming club now. I'll bet you've had thoughts about them at times."

"Only that they swim better than me. I think I'll finish this shelf tomorrow if that's all right with you. I ought to be getting home."

"Visiting with James tonight?" asked Dr. Murdstone.

"No."

"What does James do in the evenings?"

"I don't know. I've never asked. Swimming probably."

I nearly laughed out loud. I suppose you could call it swimming. I make a point of leaving it alone on Tuesdays so the client gets a full load on Wednesday evenings. I heard Andy putting his coat on. I made my silent exit.

Something had to be done to bring things to a head. It seemed obvious that Andy really didn't understand what Murdstone was after.

It was a fine evening. I finished my homework more quickly than I'd thought so I walked round to Michael's house and took a diversion through the park. It's not my regular route. True, there are plenty of potential clients lurking there. Unfortunately they are usually pretty elderly; an instant turn-off and they don't spend much an even greater deterrent.

The last time I'd walked that way, one of them sidled out of the bushes on to the footpath. "Five dollars if you let me suck your cock," he said. I told him where he could put his five dollars.

Thus I avoided the footpath and set off through the trees to the gate nearest Michael's place. It was fortunate that I was looking where I was going. I nearly stepped on them. At the foot of one of the trees was a clump of the strangest plants I had ever seen. I'd seen plenty of things exactly like them but the ones I had seen were animal; not vegetable. Five penises, each about seven inches high, grew out of the leaf mould! The shiny purple heads lacked a slit. Otherwise they were identical with the genuine article. I looked round. There were still several people in the park, including one man who seemed to have been shadowing me since I walked through the gate. I left them and went to Michael's.

An hour later, and fifty dollars richer, I returned to the spot and picked one. I wrapped it in my handkerchief, still slightly damp from thigh wiping. Michael always provides a towel but, because he prefers to dry me off himself, there's always somewhere he's missed. It would give the fungus an authentic smell, I thought.

On the following morning I waited for Andy, pretending to be looking at the video recorders in Hawkins' shop window.

"Hi, James! Thinking of buying one?"

"Gosh, I wish I could afford to," I said. I could have afforded to buy three and still have something left over but he wasn't to know that.

"Me too."

For a moment I wondered whether to come clean with him. To stop the Murdstone business and tell him that there were at least three guys in our town, three really nice guys who would be glad to supplement his allowance. I didn't. I wish to hell I had. Instead I produced the fungus.

"When you next see old Murdstone, show him this," I said.

"Why don't you show him yourself?" he asked. There wasn't a trace of amused recognition on his face.

"He doesn't like me that much. Besides which, I'm going to be tied up all day. By the time I get to see him, it'll have started to rot."

"What shall I say?"

"That's up to you. I found it in the park but don't mention me. There's a bunch of them by a tree near the Montpelier memorial. I guess he'd like to see it. It might be rare."

"I'll show him. I'll see him this morning. I help him in his office."

"I didn't know that. He must think highly of you to let you in there with all those dangerous chemicals lying about."

"Yeah. I guess he must. Can't think why."

I got to the lab that morning so quickly that it was lucky Andy didn't see me. My ear was against the wall as he closed the store room door behind him.

"Hi, Andy. How are you?"

"Fine thanks, Dr. Murdstone. You?"

"Oh, mustn't grumble. All the better for seeing you."

"I have something for you," said Andy.

"For me?"

"Yeah. I thought you'd like to see this."

"Aha! A phallic toadstool. They're not that common. Where did you find it?"

"There's a few of them near the Montpelier memorial."

"Amazing things aren't they? People in the old days had lots of superstitious beliefs about them. You can see why. They really do look like a phallus."

"Oh yeah. I guess it does!" said Andy. He sounded amazed.

"The size is right. The color is right and it would have felt stiffer when you picked it."

"Err ... yeah."

"Stiff as a poker, eh?"

"Well, actually...."

"They go limp pretty quickly after they've been plucked. That's plucked with a 'p' if you get my meaning." He laughed. Andy laughed as well.

"And are they edible?" he asked.

"I wondered if you'd ask that. We're on the same track. I thought we were. It depends on the specimen of course. Yours would be very edible. Very edible indeed. Juicy too. Shall we try...."

I wondered whether to fetch the principal. It took me about ten minutes to

come for Michael. Taking into account the fact that Andy was a year younger, there might be time for Dr. Goodchild to catch them at it. I opened the door and found myself face to face with the man himself!

"Ah Hosier. Dr. Murdstone in his store room, is he?"

"Yes sir. I was just coming to see...."

He pushed past me, went into the lab, knocked on Dr. Murdstone's door and went in. I put my ear to the wall again.

"Glad to find you here," said the principal. "Morning, Bradford."

"Good morning, sir."

"Hope I'm not intruding," said Dr. Goodchild.

"Not in the least," replied Dr. Murdstone who must, I guessed, have been pretty mad.

"I just came to talk about your list of prize winners. Perhaps Bradford would excuse us?"

"Oh! Sure," said Andy. I just had time to make myself scarce before he emerged.

I heard the siren that night but never gave it much thought. Neither did I pay much attention to the fact that Dr. Murdstone was with the principal for much of the next day. I guessed it must be something to do with the prize list. I was just furious that I'd have to wait another week and find something apart from a toadstool. I tried to find Andy that day but couldn't. Again, I didn't think anything of it. Searching for one individual in our school is like looking for a moving needle in a big hay stack.

I heard the full story at the swimming club. "Have you heard about Bradford?" someone asked.

"No."

"Tried to kill himself last night. Found a poisonous fungus and ate it. They reckon he'll be in the hospital for weeks. Coach is going to sling him out of the swimming club."

"Why, for Christ's sake?" I asked.

"Mentally unstable. Too much of a risk to have around a pool."

"Maybe it was accidental," I said.

"How the hell can eating poison be accidental?"

"Maybe someone told him it was edible."

"Far from it. Old Man Murdstone told him it was poisonous. Apparently the principal was there at the time. It was on the desk and they were talking about it when the principal went in. No... he tried to do away with himself. I agree with coach. He was a good swimmer, but we can do without weirdos on the team."

I never went to see Andy in the hospital. I know I should have; just couldn't bring myself to do it. Even when he came back to school I avoided him. I met him some weeks later in the street.

"Oh, hi! How are you?" I asked.

"I'm okay."

"I was real sorry about you being dropped from the team," I said.

"It's okay. It wasn't your fault."

I don't think I have ever seen anyone as miserable as he looked as he said that. He brightened.

"Hey, you know those toadstools?" he said.

"Yeah."

"I found the clump of them you mentioned and I met this guy there. He's an expert on that sort of thing. He's taking me away for a weekend, to some valley or other where there are loads of different types of fungi.

"A weekend of mushroom plucking eh?" I said, "With a 'p'."

"Yeah. It'll be different anyway. Get me away from here."

Something inside me snapped. I was about to make some sort of joke about having a pee before the 'f' but I didn't.

"You're not to go, Andy," I said.

"Why not? What's gotten into you?"

"Don't ask me why. Just don't go. You want to get back on the team, don't you?"

"No chance. Mom's had a letter from the principal. They've even arranged for me to see a shrink."

"You, dear old Andy, will be back in the team tomorrow. Don't ask me how but you will. It's possible that you might not see me there again but you'll be back. That much I promise."

"But.. er... how?"

"Just don't ask me. But I'll be with the principal tomorrow. It won't be very pleasant but you'll be back on the team. But no mushroom-plucking weekends. Okay?"

"If you say so. He's a real nice guy though."

It felt odd, some two weeks later, to be sitting in the spectator seats next to Dr. Murdstone. I was off of the team for six weeks "on health grounds." We were both cheering for Andy and when he won I felt better than I had felt for years!

SUSSEX COLLEGE
by James Hosier

"But you can't do it for nothing," I said.

"Why not?" Luke replied.

There were a good many answers to that question. Number one was that people like Luke could ruin my very profitable sideline business. I'd never met anybody quite so naive. You'd think that a kid whose father was a diplomat would have a bit more common sense.

"For the simple reason that, if it weren't for you, he'd have to go and find a hustler in town and that would cost him," I said.

"But I like it," he said.

"Do you boys want anything?" Mom called up the stairs.

I opened the door. "No, thanks Mom. We're okay."

"I'm just going shopping. Help yourselves if you're hungry."

I closed the door again. She'd never, ever, said that when any of my other friends called. More often than not she'd say "Not another one, surely?" when the doorbell rang and my buddies would get the sort of welcome they'd expect if they had leprosy. Luke was different. Luke went to Sussex College.

In the years I've been alive, Sussex College has been a drying-out center for alcoholics, not popular in our middle class neighborhood, though I could point out one or two prominent residents who could have profited by staying there. Then it was empty for about a year. As little kids we played there. There was a big glass conservatory at the back of the building. I recall we broke every single pane of glass and then built a camp fire on the tiled floor.

The news that it was to be a very exclusive private school pleased everybody. In a remarkably short time, extra wings had been added to the main building and a huge sign, "SUSSEX COLLEGE", stood by the newly painted gates. At first, my buddies and I tormented the students unmercifully. Quite a lot of them were foreign. The genuine home-grown Americans spoke to you as if you were some sort of idiot. The boys had identical very short haircuts and smart clothes. The girls just treated us like dirt. We soon left them alone and renewed our assaults on the sign-board with a well-aimed air rifle, or by painting out the first three letters of the school's name. Little did we know....

I met Luke on the Tuesday of Easter week, in a sports store. He was after running shoes and I wanted a new pair of goggles for swimming. We both ended up at the counter together. He produced an American Express card. The assistant was none to happy about it. He explained that it was his card but on his dad's account. The assistant called the manager, who took the card into the back office to call American Express. I went to pay for the goggles and found I was a dollar and seventy five cents short. I offered to ride home and get the rest.

"That's ridiculous," said Luke in exactly the same high-handed tone he'd used with the assistant. "Here!" He reached into his pocket, produced his wallet and extracted two dollar bills. I couldn't help noticing that there was enough

there to pay for several pairs of running shoes.

Naturally I said I wouldn't hear of it. He said he wouldn't take the money back. I asked for his name so that I could repay it, at which point the manager re-emerged and fawned all over him, from which I gathered American Express had given him an earful and that my new benefactor wouldn't miss two dollars for a few hours. We left the shop together.

"You from Sussex College?" I asked.

"Yes."

"I thought you all had a long Easter vacation."

"We do. My dad's a diplomat in West Africa. I was going out to join the parents, but they're having another of their revolutions so I'm having to stay here."

"All alone?"

"Not exactly. You see, my folks asked Dr. Gotham to find a family I could stay with, but he decided I'd be better off staying with him."

I'd seen Dr. Gotham's name on the sign-board: "R. GOTHAM (Principal)". It had more letters after it than our doctor has.

"So, what are you going to do now?" I asked, feeling a bit sorry for him.

"I don't know. Get a cab and take these back to college, I guess. There's nothing else I need for the moment. I guess we could get a burger first."

"No bread," I said.

"You don't need to have a bun."

"I mean, no money. I already owe you two bucks."

"Oh, forget it. Come on. My treat."

"Only if you'll come back to my place afterwards so I can pay you. It's not that far."

He said there was no need. I stuck my heels in so he agreed. I rang my mom from the Burger Bar and explained that I had met a boy from Sussex College, etc. etc. She wanted me to bring him round there and then.

We chatted about swimming and running, about school, about motor bikes, and about girls. The usual thing. The table was littered with paper plates, cups and plastic cutlery.

"Have they repainted your school sign yet?" I asked.

"Several times," said Luke. "Sussex College turns into Sex College about once a month. Dr. Gotham must be thinking that someone knows his secret."

"What secret?"

"Oh, nothing."

"Come on. What secret?"

"Well, you know." He was blushing slightly. "They're all the same. The guy who ran my prep school was."

"Was what?"

He didn't answer but just shrugged his shoulders. "I guess we'd better get this lot cleared away and go and meet your folks," he said.

"Just Mom. Dad's at work," I replied. He paid the bill in cash and we left.

Needless to say, Mom approved highly of my new acquaintance and slogged off all my real buddies to him. They were all ill-mannered oafs according to her. When he said he wasn't keen on pop or rock or rap but preferred Mozart, he went even higher in her estimation.

"We wanted to get James into Sussex College," she said, "but there was such a waiting list!"

It was the first time I'd heard of it. It was probably the fees that put them off.

I took Luke up to my room and paid him what I owed him. Now, unknown to my parents, I have a bottle of Jim Beam hidden in a ski boot in the bottom of the wardrobe. It was a present from Charlie, who runs the Jim Beam Bar.

"Care for one?" I asked, getting it out. Jim Beam has several remarkable effects. It loosens tongues and inhibitions. I wanted to satisfy my curiosity about Dr. Gotham.

"Sure," he said. I poured out a generous slug. He wanted water with it. I got that from the bathroom. He didn't seem to mind.

"I'll bet you don't often get whisky at Sussex College," I said.

"Oh, sometimes."

I made out like I was writing on the palm of my left hand. "Dear - Doctor - Gotham," I said. "I - feel - it - is - my - duty - to inform you - that - one - of your - students...."

"He dishes it out!" said Luke, laughing. "He reckons it makes it better."

"What?"

He blushed again. "Sex," he said.

"Are you trying to tell me that this Dr. Gotham, your school principal, has it off with you and gives you whisky?"

"Of course. Like I said, all school principals are the same."

"They're certainly not! Ours isn't for a start." The thought of having sex with Dr. Goodchild was quite funny. "Ah! James. I have, err, sent for you to, err, insert my, err...."

"Why don't you tell your parents or the police or the Federal Bureau of Investigation? Have him taken away and locked up."

"Why should I?"

"Because it's wrong and immoral. That's why." That was me, James Hosier, speaking. James Hosier, who had his ass fucked at least three times a week and whose cock was in great demand. I didn't feel too much of a hypocrite. At least I did what I did of my own free will and got well paid for my services.

"But I like it. We all do."

"You can't really like it," I said. "You might not mind it but it's not something a person can like. So I've heard anyway."

It was true that there had been one or two moments when I had felt ecstatically happy and forgotten my nakedness and hairy-chested partner. More often than not I tried to keep my eyes shut and get it over with as soon as

possible.

"Can I have another drink?" Luke asked.

"Sure." I filled his glass. He didn't want any water that time. He was about halfway through it when Mom went to the shops.

"I don't see why he should pay somebody for giving them pleasure," he said. He put down his glass and lay backwards on the bed.

"How many of the boys are involved?" I asked.

"All of us to some extent. He only does it properly when you're sixteen though."

"Properly?"

"In your ass."

"And you're the only student there for the Easter vacation?"

"Right. Thank God for revolutionaries!"

"And you actually like it?"

"So right! Somebody holding you tight. A great big cock sliding into you; feeling him shoot his cum into you. You don't know what you're missing."

I didn't know whether to believe him or not. In the Burger Bar he'd told me about the girls at Sussex College. According to him, they lived in a separate building, guarded by some ferocious old cow of a house-mistress. That tied up exactly with what some of the swimming club guys had told me. Several of them claimed to have it off with Sussex College girls pretty regularly. However, their tales of rich, sex-hungry girls who had their own television sets, CD players, luxurious furniture in one case a gigantic water bed, which had been well and truly used did not tally with Luke's account of one small radio/cassette recorder being allowed or of ex-Government military furniture. To be fair he had never been in the girls' block. He reckoned it would be easier to get into Fort Knox. Tommy Askwith in the swimming club reckoned he got into his girl's room through the window. We hadn't believed him at the time. In the days when it was a clinic, all the windows had been barred. Tommy said the bars had been removed. Luke said the bars were still there.

I sipped my drink and let him carry on talking.

"He starts when you're about thirteen," he said. "He dishes out tape measures and asks the boys to measure their cocks limp and erect. You have to write down the dimensions and put the paper in his private box. Of course, some exaggerate...."

Not half as much as you are, I thought but I said nothing.

".... and then they get sent for," he continued.

"Alone?" I asked, wondering how Dr. Gotham could possibly find time to run his school.

"In twos and threes mostly. I think he sorts them by size. He gets you to wank another boy and get him stiff. Then he measures them and checks against the papers. If the figures don't tally exactly, you have to stay behind after it's all over."

"What?"

"Well, then you have to carry on as fast as possible. The first boy who shoots his load is the winner. He gets a dollar."

"And what about the ones who got their dimensions wrong? They had to stay behind if you remember."

"They get wanked by Dr. Gotham personally and keep coming back every evening at eight o'clock. He calls it his eight o'clock club."

"And what then?" I asked.

"What do you think?" he asked in that superior Sussex College tone. "Fourteen, all clothes off and 'I'm sure you're going to taste nice'. Fifteen and 'I'm just going to put my finger in there. I won't hurt you', and by the time your sixteenth birthday comes round, your ass is itching for it. If your birthday happens in school time, he throws a party for you afterwards. It was just my luck to have been born at the end of July. I had to wait till September."

"Worth waiting for?" I asked.

"Gee! Was it! I'll never forget that evening. Me kneeling on the bed. Him putting the grease in and sort of spreading it round inside with his finger and then boy oh boy! A real live cock to work on. Just feeling it pushing in and then that great jerk you get when it rubs over your button."

He could have got it all from book learning. I was beginning to doubt it. There was only one way to find out.

"Are you actually telling me that you like getting screwed?" I asked.

"Sure, you ought to try it some time."

It was on the tip of my tongue to tell him that I'd had a cock in my ass more times than he'd had hot dinners but that revelation could wait. "Prove it," I said.

"How?"

"You've got an ass. You say you like being screwed. I've got a cock."

"But you're not that way."

"Of course not but there's a first time for everything." That was true. Not being gay myself, I was quite happy for other guys to do things to me but I'd always drawn the line at actually screwing. I'd often wondered what it felt like. The nearest I'd come to anything like that was the night when I got my rocks off between Walter Eames' legs on the night round at Greg's place. I only did that to get him ready for Greg. Actually to screw somebody, especially a toffee-nosed Sussex College student, would be some achievement. Not one to boast about at school but an achievement nonetheless.

"When's your mom due home?" he asked.

I laughed. "Not for ages," I said. "Her idea of shopping is to meet as many people as possible and compare notes about teenage sons."

"I suppose we could," he said, doubtfully. He looked at his watch.

"But unfortunately you haven't enough time," I suggested. I was about to mark him down as one of this world's great liars.

"I've got all the time in the world. It's just that I'm due with Dr. Gotham

tonight. Do you reckon he'd know?"

"What does it matter if he does?" I asked. "He can hardly moan at you for doing what he's taught you to do."

"I don't think he'd like it much, but I guess you're right."

He got off the bed and started to undress.

I'd never really looked at a teenager undressing before. Sure I'd seen them peeling off their clothes at the swimming club but that's different. In the first place, most of them are skinny and have more zits than a leopard's got spots. Secondly, not one of them is in the slightest degree anxious to have my cock in his ass. Watching Luke peel of his expensive looking gear was quite a revelation. No zits and pretty powerful torso and arms. He undid the buckle of his pants and pulled them down to reveal a really good pair of legs; not too hairy but just enough to promise a lot more elsewhere. I couldn't help thinking that if I were the principal of a private school and saw Luke in shorts, I might be tempted to invite him into the office. From that moment I stopped despising Michael. I'd been sixteen when he first had it off with me. I had actually turned up on his doorstep in shorts, and I don't think I was as good-looking as Luke.

"What about you?" he said with a grin. "Looks like you might come in your jeans if you don't get them off pretty soon."

"Oh! Sorry," I said, jumping out of my daydream. I started to undress but couldn't take my eyes off him. He stepped out of his shorts and just stood there grinning and watching me. I think it was the slimness of his waist that registered first. Every line of his body seemed to point to one thing: a really nice- looking cock.

In the past, as you know, I've tended to laugh at guys who go on about the beauty of cocks (mine especially), but I had to admit that Luke's steel-hard tool was superb. I'd guess it was about six inches long and possibly a little more than an inch in diameter. It was uncut, but rounded at the tip rather than pointed. It was surrounded by a bush of hair so black that it seemed to shine.

"Hey, you've got a good body," he observed as I dropped my boxers.

"So have you."

"Nice cock, too." He reached out and took it in his hand. His fingers felt very soft and smooth.

"Got the necessary stuff?" he asked.

"Oh shit!" I replied. I've always got a fresh condom in my wallet, but I don't keep anything else in the house. I provide the engine. It's the client's job to keep it well oiled.

"We should have got something in town," he said.

"We didn't know we'd need it, did we? Hang on. I'll find something. I went to the bathroom. There was nothing suitable in the medicine cabinet. In the end I found a jar of hand cream on Mom's dressing table. "There's not a lot left," I said, unscrewing the cap. "I guess it's on her shopping list."

"More than enough," said Luke. "You won't need a lot."

He clambered up onto the bed and got down on all fours. I'll say one thing for Dr. Gotham. The guy was a connoisseur of asses. Luke's was as white and as smooth as a peeled egg; a perfect hemisphere and, despite his position it felt rubbery, soft. I parted the cheeks. There were just two stray hairs growing at the edge of his little puckered opening. I ran my finger round the inside of the jar, got it covered and pressed against it, praying that I was doing it right.

To my amazement, the finger just slid in, almost as if it had been sucked in. Luke had been telling the truth.

"Man, that feels good," he said.

"It'll feel even better soon," I replied. I tried to rotate the finger in alternate directions as Michael had done to me. It felt warm and moist in there; feeling not unlike sticking your finger into a mousse a thing I used to do when I was a kid save that the base of the finger was held so tight that I wondered if I'd be able to get it out again.

Slowly, though, the grip seemed to relax and I gave the finger a half turn. "Oh, Jeez!" he gasped. Another turn in the opposite direction. He didn't say anything that time but the way he sort of quivered told me enough.

I guess I must have spent about ten minutes massaging inside him. I'd like to have done it a bit longer. He was wriggling about on my finger like a caterpillar on a pin. Unfortunately, I was all too aware that I was getting dangerously close. A drop fell from my cock head onto the bed cover. Slowly, and hard carefully, I pulled out, bringing greasy knuckles back into the daylight, and slipped the rubber on, mostly, I confess, to protect the bed.

"Do it!" Luke gasped. I shuffled up behind him, grasped that incredibly slim waist and put my cock between his ass cheeks. They felt cool and smooth. I'm ashamed to say that I had to fumble around a bit. Greg never has to with me; nor for that matter does Michael but then Greg's a doctor so he knows all about these things, and by the time he actually got round to fucking me, Michael had explored the territory pretty well before he entered.

Finally, I found it. Maybe he helped. I think he must have. I held on to his hips and pushed forward. I've never experienced anything like that moment. First, the initial tightness and then the feeling that my cock was sliding into a warm, silk sheath that had been custom-made to accommodate it. The muscular ring rolled down the length until it was gripping somewhere near the base. I could feel his pulse.

He said nothing. Remembering the night in a Florida hotel when Michael first took my cherry, I was surprised. Michael had to shove a hand over my mouth to stop me from waking up the entire hotel. Since then I guess I've gotten used to it but it still makes me yelp. All I got out of Luke was a kind of gasp and an encouraging wriggle.

If you're asking me to remember every split second I'm afraid you're going to be disappointed. I know that several emotions went through my brain one after another. First there was the thought that an upper class kid from Sussex

College was on the end of my cock. I remember hammering into him, proving, I hoped, that an expensive education didn't protect anyone from being fucked. Our bodies smacked together. My balls jiggled between his ass cheeks. His hands slid forward and he collapsed onto his front, dragging me down with him. We lay there for a second or two and then I pushed into him again. He wasn't a bad sort, I thought. In fact, he was a really nice guy, a loving kid, and it was hardly his fault if he'd been sent to Sussex College. I remember kissing the back of his neck. I don't remember biting his ear but it was certainly bleeding slightly when we finished.

I came first. I couldn't help it. I tried hard to hold back and make it last but I couldn't. I felt it flooding out of me and back over my cock head. He kept squirming for a few seconds and then, still silently, he came. We lay there. I was panting for breath. He seemed half asleep.

"Thanks a lot, Dr. Gotham," I said.

"Why thank him?"

"Because he's a damn good teacher," I replied.

"I'm a good student."

"I grant that. I'd go so far as to say you're top of the class."

He laughed. "I'm afraid I made a hell of a mess on your bed," he said.

I drew out of him. That was a nice feeling. He rolled over onto one side. He wasn't kidding! There was a soup plate-sized wet patch on the coverlet. We took it with us into the bathroom and put it in the bathtub to soak while we showered together. That was great. We soaped each other, twining soapy fingers in each other's pubic hair, pushing hands between each other's ass cheeks, then down the legs. Next, as the water cascaded down on to us, we held on to each other, lips against lips and with tongues pushing into each other's mouth. I don't think I have ever felt so happy. I didn't even care about the bedcover.

Clean, dry and clothed again, we lay together on the bed. I wondered if he would like to spend the rest of the vacation with us. Mom would have been delighted, but he said it was out of the question. Dr. Gotham would never allow it. Perhaps next time there was a revolution, he said.

"I could always visit on Sundays," he said. "We're free every Sunday. It would be nice to have something to do, if you know what I mean."

I squeezed his hand and started a bit of very fast thinking. Sunday, as you know, is my Greg day. You could truthfully say that, by Sunday evening, I am both spent and shagged out. Now, my birthday was due in May, just a few weeks away....

"What do you think?" asked Luke.

"This coming Sunday I'm tied up, but yeah, after that let's make it regular. My folks visit with my grandparents Sundays so the house will be empty." I said and fell to thinking again. It should work.

"What are you thinking?" Luke asked.

"Several things. How many other boys in your school would do this sort of

thing?"

"Most. Why? Thinking of having an orgy?"

"Maybe. I've just decided something."

"Oh yeah? What?"

"That I am retiring from passive life," I said, and I leaned over and kissed his forehead.

THE ERECTION CREW
by Peter Eros

Our topping-out ceremony was very special. I was suspended in our improvised sling on the upper platform of a two-thousand-foot tower, being serviced by each of the other five members of our team. Erection specialists is what they call us. We're the nearest living thing to sailors of the windjammer era. We talk of going "aloft," we work in all weathers, and we need to understand rigging and knots as well as any bosun. Like sailors, we stay out from home for long tours of duty.

Mostly we travel from state to state in company trucks, and so usually have no wheels of our own for cruising at night or to steer back home for a weekend break. Our only regular source of recreation and enjoyment is each other. But with a hunky, libido-obsessed crew like ours, that's no hardship. In fact, it's a positive testosterone-packed gratuity, a sexual jackpot.

When I interviewed for this job with the foreman, Clint, I didn't wait for him to come into Rapid City. I rode out on my Harley Sportster to the site, a desolate and remote area of shale and limestone, with little vegetation or apparent animal life, in the South Dakota Badlands.

All I could see in Clint's slightly lop-sided face were his two very bright eyes, which were examining me closely without betraying any definable emotion. His close-cropped steel-gray hair and mustache were matched by the dense mat of hair on his massive pecs, spreading and straining the checked-flannel of his shirt, which was open to the midriff. His neck was burned by sun and wind to the consistency of a leather harness. His cut-off sleeves revealed massive biceps and strong, hairy forearms.

Clint sat opposite me with his legs splayed wide, his left hand unselfconsciously fingering the massive, unrestrained sausage extending down the left leg of his frayed and faded jeans. The fat mushroom head, clearly outlined, seeped a flattering damp patch, which I saw as a silent homage and an assurance of enjoyable employment, as he steadily regarded my deeply tanned, handsome and wholesome face and body.

I was dressed in a gray tank top that emphasized my impressive musculature and gave tantalizing glimpses of my large, pumped nipples, pierced with steel rings. My 501s were tight, worn and faded: the inseam of the right leg split from crotch to mid-thigh. The bottom button was undone. I'd shampooed and blow-dried my chestnut hair and flashed him with my baby blues. I learned early in life that sex is a visual art. I'd been pumping iron for a week in preparation for this meeting. I really wanted the job and was all seduction and guile as Clint questioned me about my work history in the trailer-cum-office that also served as his home on the road. The rumpled, unmade bed behind him seemed to me a positive incentive, and an invitation.

"We can get the equipment we need" he said, "but we can't always find guys that are *equipped* for the job. Not just anybody can be a tower hand. Fear of

heights may be the only universal fear. Are you an adrenaline junky?

"Yep, I sure am, Sir," I said, as I stretched my legs and caressed my own ample bulge. His eyes flickered.

"Well, some new hires, otherwise as tough as hickory, find that climbing up the outside of these digital TV towers, and leaning backward into space, with nothing but death below in case of a mishap, is so terrifying that they can't tolerate even one full day of the work. We don't have any of the safety nets used in other types of high-up construction."

"Sir, I've crewed on a tanker, been a bull-rider in rodeo, a roustabout with the circus, worked on oil rigs and on 500 foot radio and cell phone towers. My first few weeks on towers I hung on tight. The insides of my arms were bruised from hugging the steel framework. But I've gotten over that, and I heard a hint that your particular crew might be more to my liking. I guess, apart from anything else, I just want the challenge of goin' higher. I enjoy danger."

"There's a certain thrill to it, if you're willing to put up with the risks. There's plenty of fresh air and the vistas are second to none. At the top you're a third of a mile high. On a calm day it's a really beautiful sensation. But if you stop being scared, you're in trouble. We're a bit like cowboys on a trail drive combined with the kind of reliance on each other of roped- together mountain-climbers. We stay out in the field a long time. One of our 2000 foot cloud-scrapers can take more'n six months to complete, with just six men to erect more'n a thousand tons of steel. It can make a tower hand feel that life is passing him by. Have you got a woman at home?

"Nope."

"Good. Some of our guys have had a wife and kids - the whole catastrophe. But crews without women problems have next to no problems a'tall, and that's the way we like to keep it. This crew is all single or divorced. We really depend on *each other*, for *everything,* if you get my meaning. Some guys I've interviewed haven't been sufficiently liberated. They felt disconcerted, discouraged."

"Well, I've got references, Sir, and I'll be happy to demonstrate my skill and adaptability if I get the chance," I said, popping the second button on my jeans and licking my lips, as I pushed the sheaf of papers, topped by my week-old HIV negative report, into his free hand.

"Glad to see you match our safety standards, boy. Seems like you're a natural, Steel. How'd you get that name, by the way?"

"My Daddy was a steel worker in Pittsburgh when I was born. He wanted for me to be big and strong and named me accordingly. It ain't done me no harm."

Clint rose and stood in front of me. He gripped my shoulder firmly with his right hand, and turned my face up to him with his left.

"I guess it's time for that demo of why your ability might be in demand."

As I slid forward from my chair, I ripped his buttons apart and released his monster engorged cock and ample, low-slung, hairy balls, which almost

concealed a black rubber cock-ring. Kneeling in front of him I reverenced his spunky salute with lips and tongue, breathing in his sweet aroma of man-juice and sweat. He sighed as I probed his seeping slit with my tongue, then tantalized the glans with tongue and lips before sucking him deep into my gullet. At the same time I massaged and pulled on the meaty balls in his bulging scrotum. With the other hand I probed up under his shirt to tweak a teat. He gripped my head in his huge hands and groaned as he thrust deep, massaging my Adam's apple.

"Oh yeah, boy! Oh yeah! You're gonna give me steady joy!"

"Mmmm! Mmffff!" His rich discharge filled my throat and mouth as I gulped and slurped my appreciation, savoring the tangy load of jism that had built up in his hot testicles through a busy week that allowed little time for recreation.

The first time I saw Clint's crew in action, the men were sprinting across the pasture in front of my bike as I drove into the construction area that Friday afternoon. Perhaps a foot race, I speculated, or an impromptu football game. Then the men pulled up at a guide-wire anchor, grabbed a set of tools and got to work adjusting tension on a cable.

Link, svelte and wiry, leapfrogged onto Clay's massive shoulders and used the extra height to adjust a cable clamp, as Clint and Dekimbe installed grounding wire near the giide-wire anchor. While the tower hands don't usually sprint from task to task, moderate weather makes them hustle, especially when work has been delayed by high winds and icing.

Josh was away. He was driving the transmitter and copper antenna from the East Coast. He arrived that evening having driven eight straight days there and back in a rental truck. Dekimbe, a shaved-head Nigerian, our token black, prepared dinner, which I was invited to share, Clint being satisfied with me and all. Having confirmed my hire on his cell-phone with the company headquarters in Texas, and me having no commitments anywhere else, and my entire wardrobe and worldly goods packed in a duffel bag on the back of my bike, I stayed. I was to bunk in the same trailer as Josh and Dekimbe.

I could tell from Dekimbe's lingering handshake that he had worked and fought with his hands. The flash from his eyes, coal black and darkly expressive, was like a spark off a flint. His sculpted body was mouth-watering. Wearing only denim cutoffs, he walked tall but didn't appear to know the splendor of his bearing. The shorts did nothing to hide his ample genital proportion.

We made small talk as he cooked, his orotund voice, with its quaint phrasing, rich and soothing, as we waited for the others to finish work and join us. My half-closed eyes lingered on the glistening mahogany giant as the gentle breeze mussed my hair and sexual reverie overwhelmed my imagination.

Clay joined us first. He has a Genghis Khan ponytail and Charlie Manson eyes. Shirtless, sweaty and heavily tattooed, wearing black fatigue pants and combat boots, he perched atop a stool, a cigarette drooping from his lips, and

glowered like a gargoyle, squinting through the smoke. But once his face relaxed I realized that, despite the shaved head and pigtail, he was ruggedly handsome. His tattoos were all geometric, tracing and accentuating his attractive natural contours.

Link is nick-named *The Pussy*, not just because of his feline slimness, green eyes, almost feminine prettiness, and avid anal appetite, but because he's survived unscathed several alarming falls that could have ended his career. As I soon learned, his willowy appearance is belied by the tremendous strength his wiry muscles exhibit on the job, and by his full-sized cock, which would do credit to an adult porn star. He's sleek, spare and diamond hard, with a tattoo of a rampant panther on his right bicep. Blond and just twenty-one: tight jeans emphasize his inviting basket and bubble butt.

"We got us some sky today, boys!" Clint said with satisfaction as the men gathered up their tools at sunset. As darkness fell and obliterated the vast contours of the surrounding countryside, we sat around a campfire in the lee of the chuck wagon to eat, swapping stories and chit-chat between bites. I was able to study my new companions, their faces bronzed, their limbs burnished, their hair bleached until they were uniformly the color of rock. Nomads by choice, they had become part of the environment.

Josh arrived late, his hair looking like Rogaine treatments gone haywire. Eight days of stubble blurred the normally neat lines of his mustache. Red, strained eyes and gaunt exhaustion didn't add to his sociability. But, even slouched and weary, his thick-set boxer's build was impressive. He stumbled to the trailer, fell into bed fully clothed, and was instantly asleep.

Not long after the sun's departure, a penetrating chill rapidly replaced the warmth of the day, causing us all to shiver. Our paper plates and disposable cutlery discarded in the fire, we headed for bed. Clay and Link, arm in arm, loped to their caravan. Clint, with a loud yawn, slouched toward his trailer, and Dekimbe and I followed Josh's still detectable scent. Snoring loudly, the exhausted driver didn't stir when Dekimbe turned on the light.

As the Nigerian closed the door behind him he smoothly enfolded me in his arms and ate my mouth. His huge tongue prodded my own into an enthusiastic response. We sucked each other's life breath as our bodies crushed together and our hands explored. He lifted me bodily onto his cot and began to undress me, having discarded his own shorts in a maneuver I didn't even see, his huge wang proving what they say about Negroes. It bounced intimidatingly.

I guessed correctly that it was over twelve inches long, but it was the girth, in excess of nine inches around at the base, that really frightened me, despite my excitement. Something of my concern must have registered on my face and Dekimbe laughed darkly.

"Don't worry, pretty white boy. Break you in gradually, we will. Tonight I try a sample of what you've brought me. Skin a rabbit!"

As I raised my arms he pulled the tank top over my head and set to snacking

on my protuberant tits, tugging on the rings with the tip of his tongue. Tentacles of joy snaked through my body to set off fireworks in my cerebral cortex. A hand scrambled at my waist, tugging my buttons apart to release my swollen, dripping cock. The huge lips sucked their way down my midriff as I writhed and groaned my delight and surrender.

The huge tongue enfolded and titillated my upright prick, probing delicately under the glans, as I sighed and wriggled and kicked off my jeans. The huge callused hands caressed and squeezed my ripe balls and probed my dilating ass pucker. A spit-slicked finger tickled my prostate.

Then Dekimbe really surprised me. In one swift move he knelt, straddling my hips, grabbed my unshielded prick and sat back on it. It was like being sucked into a vacuum. He was tight, warm, moist and elastic: his anal muscles actively engaged in his sliding, squeezing assault on my primed shaft.

"You like my gateway to paradise?"

"Yeah, man!"

He threw his head back and sang melodiously in Hausa, his native tongue, as he bounced his conduit, his melon buttocks slapping on my upper thighs, his huge prick bouncing on my belly, his balls mashing against my pubes, knees squeezing my ribs. His fat fingers pinched and tweaked my nipples. Sweat rolled off his brow and splashed on my midriff, pooling with my own in my bullet-hole navel. An indescribable expression of fire and force pervaded his whole being.

I grabbed his hips for leverage and thrust back, power-fucking my hard-bodied server with a special delivery up his hot, juicy rump. I moved my spit-slicked right hand to his bobbing, wrist-thick prick, massaging the fat mushroom head with vigorous strokes.

"Oh, yesss!" he murmured, "Oh, that feels so good!" Dekimbe plunged his fuck-hungry hole up and down, pile-driving my quaking member up his butt as I tugged on his balls and applied more spit and polish to his humongous cock shaft, until the two of us erupted. It felt like my whole body was straining to empty through my cock as Dekimbe's sphincter sucked on me like a milking machine. I pounded into him, my legs nearly numb, as my sperm jetted into his depths, and his mighty discharge splattered in huge globs the length of my torso. One landed on my upper lip and I hungrily licked it clean.

He scooped his pungent and deliciously savory cum from my chest and fed it to me, as he gazed gravely into my eyes. Then he fell, gasping but gleeful, into my embrace. He brought his lips to mine, his tongue to my tongue, and we shared a long, slow taste of life. He licked my temples and my throat as, still embedded, I arched against him, exulting in the warmth and strength of his embrace, and the warm, velvety suction that still held me. Reluctantly he released my deflated probe and nestled beside me, tracing my eyebrows, my nose and my sharply defined lips with his rough, cum-sticky fingers. I sucked them into my mouth and he grinned. "You're somethin', Steel." He chuckled. "For a white boy, you a real find!"

I was loathe to leave his comforting embrace, but the bunks were too narrow to sleep comfortably abreast. I slid into my cot at the end of the trailer and was soon contentedly asleep. I awoke as a gust of fresh air swept through the trailer, making me shiver with its sharp breath. I was lying face down, my arms above my head, my chin resting on my left bicep. I felt the side of the bed depress and opened my eyes. Josh's face lay next to mine, his gray eyes intent but friendly, gazing at me in the dim early morning light. He'd evidently showered before stretching alongside me, his swollen member prodding my hip. He inhaled deeply the smell of me, still gamey from my nocturnal romp. He licked my armpits, my nape. He did a slide along the dimpled hollow of my back and planted kisses at the delta, before pulling my butt cheeks apart to probe my prominent pucker with his insistent tongue.

A rosy glow permeated my whole being. I stretched luxuriantly and undulated my hips in invitation. He vigorously tongued and nibbled, and my well exercised anal lips spread encouragingly as I murmured, "Oh yeah! Eat my ass!"

He licked and lapped, thrusting his tongue deeply, priming my hole. He cupped my muscular butt in his hands and pulled me onto his face as he slurped my manhole. I reached back and ran my fingers up and down his engorged shaft.

"Saddle up if you wanna fuck," I said.

He nestled his precum and spit-slicked cock into the crease of my ass, working it back and forth. I grabbed it and buried the head in my hole.

"C'mon, fuck me, man."

He grunted and slid in with one smooth, continuous shove. Buried to the hilt, he remained still for a time, as I massaged him with my colon walls. Then he started to pump. I was quick to pick up his pace, rocking back and forth as he humped. We rolled onto our sides and as he plowed my ass he sucked and nibbled the back of my neck and chewed on my shoulders.

My ass was steamy and hot as Josh rewarded me with a jolt, a spasm of delight.

"Oh, Christ, yes! Fuck my ass, Josh, fuck it!"

As he pounded into me my head fell back against him and I jacked my pod. His last jolts rammed into me as Dekimbe pushed my hands away and sucked my dick into his mouth, at the same time pulling and teasing my tingling nipples. My pearlescent progeny squirted into the appreciative, lip-smacking maw, as I rocked my hips and clenched my teeth, coming silently in several more hard spurts.

There was no time for lingering embraces. The sun would soon crest the horizon and there was work to do. We showered together quickly in the portable bathroom, economically wetting ourselves then turning off the faucet to soap up before a quick rinse-off. By the time we got dressed Clay and Link were halfway up the tower. They returned to the ground a few minutes later, shaking their heads.

"It's howlin' up there," Clay reported. Clint nodded.

"I seen how it was," he agreed. "No problem, Clay. Don't worry about it."

"It's not worth dying over," Clay added.

We had a bacon and egg breakfast, then Clint kept us occupied assembling clamps to attach cable to the tower. We were sheltered from the cold wind in the back of the rental truck, swapping stories about our exploits and our conquests, getting hornier by the minute, as the tumbleweeds rolled by and the wind never let up. By the time we'd finished the required clamps we were in real need of release.

"Okay," Clint said, "we can't do no more work today. Let's get us some pleasurable relaxation. I reckon Steel needs a proper introduction to our ways."

Everyone whooped and hollered and headed for the trailer where Dekimbe and Josh whipped the mattresses off the cots and abutted them together on the floor. Clay and Link produced a roll of rubber sheeting and spread it over the top. Then we stripped and went at it, exploring each other's body with lips and hands. Before long Clint was turning down the thermostat on the heater. The air was charged with animal electricity.

Clay and Link lay together and Clay reached up a hand to pull me down.

"I think you need an intro to some real man-pussy, babe." Happiness shone in Link's eager eyes and on his voluptuous lips. Health glowed in his rich coloring and lurked in the luxuriant curled locks, which clustered in glossy rings to the shapely shoulders of the ravishing boy. He basked in my gaze with a natural ease and elegance, proudly conscious of his youth, health, and comeliness. His was a unique kind of beauty in flesh and blood, prepared to demonstrate an insatiable talent.

Together Clay and Link pushed me onto my back and jointly licked and nibbled my bobbing prick until, satisfied, Link straddled me and encased me in his well-lubed and eager flesh. I couldn't see Clint, who lay above my head, his legs holding down my arms, as Josh knelt astride my chest and thrust his cock into my unresisting lips. I soon became aware that Josh was simultaneously sucking on Clint as I slurped and gobbled on his handsome, heavily veined prick. Dekimbe stood astride my body, between Link and Josh, as Link hungrily gulped on his massive skin-shaft, attempting to deep throat it.

Unable to see Clay, I quickly became aware of him. He spread my legs and knelt to insert his cock along with mine into the accommodating, voracious orifice of the bouncing blond. Link emitted feral growls as he slurped on Dekimbe and responded to the dual ass packing. I'd never known such intense pleasure as Clay's prick slid in and out of Link's spasming hole in tandem with my engorged joystick, the incredibly hot and tight orifice squeezing us together.

I can't tell you who came first. It all seemed to happen at once. As Josh climaxed against my soft palate Link came in thick, gooey globs all over my belly and Clay and I shot simultaneous loads up Link's twitching hole. Josh was drinking Clint's jism which filled his mouth in great hot spurts.

Link, unflagging despite his own eruption, continued to suck Dekimbe, rhythmically up and down, pausing on the upstroke and moving his head around in a circle. One hand played gently with the ebony balls as the other slid between the massive legs and inserted three fingers up his ass. With a mighty preliminary breath, Link sucked down toward the root of the black cock and tickled the Negro's prostate. Dekimbe let out a mighty cry and let fly. Link gasped and gobbled, trying to consume the spunk as it pumped out, but the discharge was impossible to contain. It bubbled out the side of his mouth and dribbled down his chin. The smell of spent sperm was all pervasive.

This was only my introduction to the kind of orgy that kept them going. But as the days warmed and the tumbleweeds stayed put, we managed to keep our libidos in check long enough to successfully complete the tower. Midafternoon of the final day, Clay found Clint in the transmitter building, put on a long face and told him, "Somethin's gone wrong!"

"What?"

"We've run out of tower!" and Clay slapped him on the back.

Though several days of electronics work remained, the most weather-sensitive part was over, well ahead of deadline. Which brings us to the topping-out ceremony. Can you imagine the euphoric sense of liberation, totally naked with a group of hunky guys you've come to love a third of a mile high? Being the new guy I was hoist in the improvised sling, expertly roped in swaying suspension, as they took turns reaming my voracious ass, according to an increasing size scale. First Josh, then Clay, followed by Link, then Clint. Dekimbe naturally was last.

Lubricated with four loads of cum, my ass had never been so exercised as I contemplated the thick dark cock, throbbing tautly. Gently Dekimbe inserted the fat, circumcised mushroom. I'd never been so stretched, but despite a slight ache the sphincter slowly accommodated itself to the huge intruder. Dekimbe allowed me to take my own time as he pressed in, aware of my contorted face and gasps of pained pleasure as he forced more and more of it inside the fiery sponginess of my slowly relaxing rectum. Despite four previous copious eruptions, my own cock was stabbing upward, dribbling precum over my belly.

The others who had already experienced the Dekimbe challenge made gentle, encouraging sounds. Every dick was hard around the circle, their balls up tight and ready for explosion as the tension mounted to the final circle jerk countdown.

I felt soft lips on one nipple; it was Josh. His bristly mustache brushing my hairless pec. Clint sucked on the other, his under-nose brush and two-day stubble doing a similar job. Shock-waves of pleasure were spreading through me in all directions, as Clay sucked on an ear and caressed my sweat-slicked head, and Link sucked my bouncing prick deep into his practiced throat.

"Oh, yeah, Steel," the giant husked. "I's got you now. I's way up inside you!"

My head sagged forward, like a new mother trying to see the birth, and then

snapped back to loll in Clay's embrace, my whole body swaying loosely in total surrender to a warm and throbbing fullness I had never known before and a sense of anguished joy.

Dekimbe's ebony face shone with sweat as he thrust, setting up a steady, deep motion, as the others cradled my hanging body, rocking me back and forth to the black man's increasing tempo.

Link encircled my rigid prick and ball sac with finger and thumb as he launched into a paroxysm of sucking, sensing my fresh cum boiling near the surface, as Dekimbe cried out with a mighty bellow and squirted his huge load into my already overloaded ass.

His discharge backed up and overflowed my conduit, dripping down my ass crack onto the platform, as I filled Link's mouth with an unrestrained load of boiling cum in spurt after spurt, and the others wanked out jetting streams that criss-crossed my body with lacy tendrils; a salute of semen, high in the thin, cold air.

As you turn off your television, think about our obscure, vertigo-inducing profession. Somewhere a tower hand is climbing a ladder to go to work, or just maybe, to fuck in the wild blue yonder.

I'LL DO ANYTHING
by James Wilton

Joey owed me, the asshole. A while back he'd sold me two cords of fire wood. He cashed the check I had been stupid enough to give him and never delivered the wood. Sure, he had plenty of reasons but that is what he was so good at; he was a con artist through and through. Before long Joey had some trouble with the law so he went to jail. Then I heard from my friends that he was periodically showing up in town when things were tough, trading sex for a warm bed, food, and, he hoped, some pocket money. At least he had the sense to keep away from here until one cold, rainy afternoon I heard a knock on my door and there was Joey, soaked to the skin. He'd hitched into town to find that Len, his most reliable benefactor, was not home. For some reason he thought that he might be able to wait at my house until Len returned. I slammed the door in his face.

He knocked again. And kept knocking. I opened the door and took a good look at him. The cold had gotten to him and he sniveled about the rain. Once he was one hot little kid with a hairless, well-defined body, but the years of mischief had taken their toll. He still looked hot but with a little more flesh and some deep age lines. Still, the sight of him made my crotch stir.

Joey again begged to come in. I asked him why I should do him any favors when he still owed me $250. He struck a cutesy pose and said he'd make me happy if I did. I told him I could take care of making myself happy. This brought on the line I was waiting for: "Please, I'll do anything. It's so cold out and I'm freezin'."

"Anything?"

"Anything."

He stood hunched and shivering inside my door. I sent him down to the basement to put his clothes in the dryer. He asked what he should wear and I told him that we'd worry about that later. He came up blue with the cold. I smiled to myself as I looked at him and planned my revenge. His hair was plastered down with rain water. He was bent over and hugging himself but I could see that his cock and balls were shriveled up like raisins. Not being a monster, I handed him a towel and had him get into the shower he both wanted and needed.

Meanwhile, I changed into a jockstrap and bathrobe and dug out my old paddleball racket.

Joey came back into the living room wrapped in the towel and I checked him out from head to foot. He was clearly warmed up and his basket bulged out under the terrycloth. His chest and arms still showed some definition and his square jaw was held up high. He had sprouted some hairs on his chest. He was not altogether bad looking.

But having been with so many men in the past, he seemed to sense my thoughts and gave a smug look as if to say that he was doing me a favor by

- 157 -

being there. Not right! Looking him right in the eye, I said, "You were a shit once and you're still a shit."

Immediately his eyes dropped and he apologized. He didn't know what for but the bullshitter in him told him that was the part to play.

"I can never forgive you for what you did, you little bastard!" I reached out and pulled his towel off.

He looked at me and then down at his crotch. Both of us watched his cock stir and begin to rise. I was tempted to grab it but decided against giving him any kind of thrill.

I had him bend over my lap for the spanking he deserved. I ran my hand over his firm, hairy ass. It was like two velvet-covered melons. I raised up the paddle and let him have a sharp thwack on both cheeks. He stiffened and moaned in pain and surprise. I came down again and again, letting my anger get control. After about ten good ones I stopped and rubbed my hand over his red buns. They were nicely warmed. As I rubbed his buttocks, I felt a slight humping motion from Joey's hips. I rearranged my position and spread my legs a little farther apart. Suddenly a hard cock slipped off my left thigh and into the space between my legs.

I was spurred on to a renewed attack. As I raised the paddle for another several whacks, I closed my legs together around his hard dick. Every time the wood slapped on Joey's ass he humped his tool between my thighs. Every time he humped me I mocked him for liking the spanking. "Why you little pervert, you're getting off on this abuse. You deserve to be whipped!"

After this round was over I again rubbed his beet-red buns and this time ran my hand down his thigh so that my fingers slid down his crack and onto the root of his cock. It was swollen and hard. As I manipulated the base of his balls Joey moaned with pleasure and humped my legs. By this time he was dripping precum and my legs were well lubricated.

Enough! This was not supposed to be a turn-on for Joey. Besides, I had a throbbing erection of my own and was afraid that I might pop if we kept this up. I kicked him off my lap.

"What the fuck you doin', boy?"

He stood there with an enormous hard-on.

"Are you a masochist? Is that what you are?

He blushed. "No."

"Then why do you have an erection if you aren't into abuse?"

"I don't know. It just happened."

"Well, would you like it more if I hurt you some more? I can get a belt and really lace your behind."

"Oh, no! Please! The paddle was bad enough. I don't think I'll be able to sit down for a week."

As he said this, his eyes became riveted on my cock. I was so hard the elastic tented out in front of me. "Do you see anything that interests you, you little

pervert?"

He nodded.

"Okay, drop to your knees and lick my balls inside the jock and don't use your hands."

He worked his tongue into the "tent" and did an admirable job of keeping me excited. Then I had him work the balls out of the pouch and take them both into his mouth. He did so well I thought my cock would rip through the fabric.

"Pull this jock down with your teeth and work on my cock, asshole. And, keep your hands away from your own cock, too. You're here to service me, not have a good time." I pushed his hand off his hard-on with my foot and gave him a kick in the balls. He howled with surprise and pain and hunched over but didn't miss a beat on my tool.

It didn't take long before I was ready to shoot. I pulled out of his sucking mouth and gave my dick a few jerks. The cum shot out with surprising force. He tried to back away but I grabbed the hair on the back of his head and held him there. "Oh, no, you little shit. Your pretty face is gonna be my cum rag." My cum splattered all over his face and dripped off his chin and nose. I grabbed a fistful of hair and dragged him into the bathroom and had him kneel down in front of me. I moistened a face cloth and ordered him, "Wash your filthy spit off my cock."

As my dick softened, I began to feel the urge to piss. I hadn't planned it but this was a perfect chance to continue my humiliation. When he held my dick up to wipe my balls, I let out a stream of piss that hit him in the face. Again, I grabbed the back of his head and held him there to suffer this new indignity. My urine washed the cum off his face and rinsed it on down his chest and crotch. I looked down to see he had another erection.

"So, you like to be pissed on, do yah? Is there no end to your degeneracy?"

He had no answer.

As my stream slowed, I pulled back on his hair, opening his mouth so the last few spurts flowed down his tongue.

"I thought you'd like something to drink."

His face screwed up into a look of disgust at what he had just swallowed. But in spite of his revulsion at the thought of swallowing piss, the whole scene obviously excited him. I stepped back to view the kid as he knelt before me with my piss running down his body and dripping off his throbbing dick into a puddle on the floor.

"Well, well. What a sight. I had no idea you were so depraved. Look at you. Now I'll have to wash you off before you're fit to leave this room."

With that I dragged him into the shower with me. I soaped him down, front and back, enjoying the feel of his body as I went. He still had an erection. He'd been up for so long I figured that he was getting pretty uncomfortable. That was fine with me. As I soaped his crotch he tried to hump my hand for relief but I wouldn't let him. Every time he reached for his cock I pulled his hand away and

gave him a hard slap. As I washed his crack I worked a finger into his hole. He bolted upright. Once he was used to the feeling he groaned with pleasure and backed down onto my finger to get more into his ass.

"So, we like something hard up our asshole, do we?" This time he wasn't too embarrassed to answer and whimpered a yes.

Since the one finger was clearly not filling him I worked in a second, a third, and, finally, a fourth. He was writhing and sobbing. I was afraid he would slide away from me and fall in the tub, but he kept pressing down onto my hand, trying to get more.

I'd never fisted anyone but this looked like the way we were headed. Sure enough, with the soap for a lubricant I massaged that tightly stretched ring until it relaxed enough to ease the tip of my thumb in. Joey shrieked as he was widened even more. But he quickly settled down to his chants of "Oh yeah! More! Oh yeah, man."

With one arm around Joey's heaving chest I worked the other up the chute bit by bit. My cock was hard again and I humped his thigh as I worked on his ass. Suddenly I had passed the wide part of my fist and his anal ring closed down toward my wrist, pushing my hand all the way in.

Joey sucked in a long hiss of air as I fully entered his rectum. I could feel his pulse all around my fist. My hand was in a tight, warm, moist sack. Slowly I pulled back until the ball of my fist was against the ring again, then I eased back up the canal until I hit the top. Joey was panting and hanging on my other arm.

As I gave him another plunging, he straightened up and began to shoot without even touching his cock. Amid his gasps of ecstasy my arm felt what only my cock had felt before: a climax from the inside. His whole rectum contracted with the ejaculations. Against the side of my hand I felt his prostate pulsing and the muscles at the base of his cock contracting. It was such a turn-on that my humping dick shot out its own jism on his side.

Joey was so exhausted, I had to hold him up as I eased my hand out of his ass. He was gasping and shuddering as I leaned him against the side of the stall, then I washed off my arm and left him to clean himself as I dried off.

While Joey was in the basement getting his clothes out of the dryer, I called Len. The phone rang several times until he finally answered. After telling him Joey had showed up on my porch, I said, "Please, come get him before I do anything to him I'll regret later."

While we were waiting for Len to arrive, true to form, Joey tried to hit me up for some cash.

"You little shit!"

"Hey, don't you think I earned at least something for all the abuse I took? You couldn't get a hustler to do that for less than a hundred bucks."

"Maybe, but you obviously enjoyed yourself so I figure you owe me something for your pleasure. Let's say you knock fifty bucks off what you already owe me?"

"Fifty?"

"Yeah, that leaves four more sessions just like that and then we'll be even."

"Four more like *that*?"

I was firm. "Four."

He looked down at the floor, shook his head and softly asked, "When do we start?"

A few days later, Len and I went out to dinner together and returned to Len's house to watch a new video. Once inside, I took a piss and afterward, passing the bedroom, I noticed the door closed. Suspecting trouble, I mentioned it to my host. Len didn't remember shutting the door.

Len decided to investigate. To our great surprise, we found Joey sound asleep on Len's bed. I wouldn't let Len wake the sleeping beauty. Instead, I signaled him out of the room. He got us each a beer and, as we drank them, I reminded him of the undelivered wood and told him all about my recent session with Joey.

"I didn't know that boy had it in him," Len laughed. I suggested that he join me in giving the boy another installment in his payback. Len smiled; he agreed that the boy badly needed discipline. He fetched some lengths of rope and we went back to the bedroom. Joey protested, but while we tied him down, spread-eagled, his throbbing erection showed that he was not too upset with the situation.

Len was amazed. He had always had vanilla sex with the kid and never suspected his masochism. Len pulled off his belt and laid a few light welts across Joey's ass while shouting at him about breaking and entering. He reminded the kid that he had enough of a record with the local police that he would be up the creek if we called in a complaint. Joey grunted at the thwacks and, between blows, begged for an end.

After about ten swipes, Len stopped and we looked down at the rounded hairy buns with their fresh, red stripes. At the top of Joey's legs, between his balls and his asshole, we saw the telltale bulge: during the whipping the little twerp had kept his hard-on. To assuage his disbelief, Len reached beyond the balls and felt Joey's raging pole.

"He's dripping like a whore!" reacted Len. Meanwhile, Joey began to hump Len's hand. "I can't believe it. When you told me the story of that day with Joey I thought you were exaggerating. I never thought he'd really get into S & M."

The sight was a real turn-on. This humpy kid was lying naked on the bed, his arms and legs tied to the four corners, his muscular back tapering down to the reddened melons of his ass. His tight thighs and arms pulled on his restraints as he wildly humped Len's hand. Before he could come, he pulled him back. "This isn't supposed to be a massage for the burglar, yah know." The sight, the new feeling of dominance, and the feel of Joey's erection throbbing in his hand had Len really turned on, and without a moment's hesitation he opened his jeans to release his erection.

Not being shy, I followed suit. What a relief. Once we were both naked, we returned our attention to our captive. His red buns looked inviting. They were warm to the touch and my hand must have felt cool because Joey let out a sigh as my hand ran across the furry, warm flesh. I could feel his muscles move under my palm as he gently humped the bed. Knowing it would be a tease, I continued feeling the mound but let my thumb run down the length of his ass crack. As it passed over Joey's pucker, he gasped and tried to lurch backward. Both Len and I laughed at the sight and commented that this pig was ready to poke.

Len wet his middle finger with a minimum of spit and obliged the kid with a little more intensity than was expected. He rammed his digit all the way up the boy's chute in one jab. Joey let out a howl and tried to thrash against his restraints. But, in short order, Len said he could feel the muscles constricting around his finger as the writhing stopped. Joey was enjoying having that intrusion.

This gave me an idea and I led Len out of earshot and explained my plan. Since Joey was known to skirt the law and cheat even his so-called "friends", I thought of a way to keep him in line. We'd accommodate his love of anal stimulation with a variety of objects and photograph the proceedings with the threat to expose Joey to his straight friends if he ever gave us a hard time again. Len loved the idea and we scoured the house for suitable toys. A carrot and beer bottle were the obvious first choices. Then came the handles of a hedge trimmer and toilet plunger. A candle added a nice touch.

As we approached Joey, he had no idea what we were up to. Since we didn't want to do any real harm, I got to lubricate his ass. It was obvious that I was doing the kid a good turn as he moaned and backed onto my finger. I enjoyed the feel of twisting around in the opening and seeing the result as this little toughie twitched in ecstasy. Len reminded me of our plot and had to pull my hand away from the target. He replaced it with the carrot, which had Joey squealing since it was so cold.

When he heard the click of the camera, he froze and immediately caught on to his predicament. At first he pleaded, saying that he was only kidding and wasn't really enjoying this. When he saw that he wasn't making any headway, he tried warnings. At this, Len picked up his belt again and reminded the boy that he was not in a position to threaten and that any more misbehavior would result in the distribution of these pictures. The drop that appeared on the end of Len's erection showed how much he was enjoying the scene.

The other objects made interesting photos and, in every case, Joey's body belied his anger as he writhed back against the intruding objects. The lighted candle was a festive end to our photo session.

As Len was taking the last picture, a drop of wax fell on the inside of Joey's thigh causing him to shriek, more from shock than pain. Aha, another idea was hatched. We pulled the candle out of its "holder" and held it over Joey's ass. As

the hot wax fell, he cried out and jumped. Len and I found this so erotic that our cocks jumped back to full erection. Len began a trail of drips that led up one side of Joey's muscular back and down the other. All the while, our victim was pleading and trying to move out of the way of the next drop he anticipated. Out of curiosity, I thought to check the results of this "torture" on the boy's penis. As expected, he was at full erection and tried to hump the hand that grasped his tool.

Since we were assured that we weren't hurting the boy, we decided to turn him over and wax him on some more tender flesh. We knew that Joey was wiry and strong so we were especially careful not to lose control as we rolled him onto his back. We were right and he did try to break away but Len and I prevailed and managed to get him tied down at the ankles and wrists.

As we stepped back and looked down on the bed, we were presented with one really hot sight. Here was a taut, slim twenty-five-year-old spread out wide for our enjoyment. The hair on his head and body was sandy blond. His blue eyes were glazed over with lust. His cleft chin was stuck out in an attempt at defiance. His pectorals, covered in a dusting of hair, were rising and falling as he caught his breath after the vain struggle. The hair ran down his tight stomach and widened out at his bush. Two decent-sized balls nearly touched the sheet below as they hung in their loose, generous sack. Above this stood a perfect cock: it curved slightly up toward his navel and became a bit thicker at midshaft. The head was bright red-purple with a defined rim, making it slightly wider than the rest of the member. The slit was surrounded with dried pre-cum as a testament to the arousal he had experienced. Below these genitals stretched two muscularly defined legs with ample hair covering the thighs.

Len and I both needed to grab some pleasure from this package before we continued our torment. I had to have that dick. First, I hefted those balls. The scrotum was soft as fine kid and smooth as silk. The balls were loose in the sack and slid around easily. At this contact with his tender area, Joey's cock gave a jolt and seemed to stiffen even more. I was drawn to that column. I grabbed the shaft loosely and felt another jolt pass through it as the boy's hips rose and he humped into my hand. Each time I squeezed the dick, it stiffened and then the precum began oozing down from the slit. I couldn't avoid bending over and partaking of that clear cum. My taste treat resulted in a tactile treat for the boy as my tongue cleaned off the head and slit of his cock. His upward lunge and loud moan made me fear that I might have pushed him into an orgasm. I didn't want that to be happening so soon and immediately backed off to savor this sight before me and the feeling of that viscous fluid on my tongue.

Meanwhile, Len decided to go for more direct pleasure. He climbed up on Joey's chest and stuck his engorged dick right into the kid's mouth. As I looked up from the crotch I was enjoying, I watched my friend's ass humping his cock well into the open maw below him. Joey might have protested that he didn't want to be used but he certainly took to servicing the dick in his mouth. By the

time I had backed off from playing with the dick, I heard Len grunting that familiar call of ejaculation. I stepped around to see him bury his dick to the root and mash his balls into Joey's lips as he came down the boy's throat. He rolled off Joey's chest and lay beside him, both of them catching their breath.

Since I was still horny and not at all slowed down, I took the chance to explore this boy with both my hands and eyes. His chest was nicely defined, the product of physical labor, not gym time. The surface was thinly coated with hair but I could clearly feel the heat rising from the skin. The nipples were erect and Joey's chest muscles spasmed as I ran a finger over them. Seeing that I had a powerful erogenous button here, I subjected him to a little tit torture. As I tightly squeezed and twisted them, my victim came to life and whimpered in response. His dick, which remained stiff but had deflated enough to be resting on his belly after his encounter with Len, jumped back to attention. When I worked on both at once, Joey's gasping reaction let me know he was enjoying this.

Next, I ran my hand over the moist armpits and felt the definition in his upper and then lower arms. From there I felt his corded neck and strong jaw. His cleft chin led to sensuous lips, which I traced with my finger. At the mouth crack, I forced the lips open and followed the path Len's cock had just enjoyed. The boy was so sex-crazed that he began sucking my finger like a calf. He raised his head to get more in and sucked harder and harder, wanting to draw some fluid from my digits.

All this action had caught Len's attention and he got off the bed to rejoin the action. Relighting the candle, he tormented Joey with the thought of where the wax might drop and how it might feel. He raised the flame high so that the first drippings were cool but Joey still jumped from the contact. The first target was the belly, a tender place, indeed. Next, he lowered the height to turn up the heat and aimed for the nipples. The shriek of pain was undermined by the drop of precum that slowly fell from the erect dick into the pubes below. That dick looked like a fun target and we focused our attention there. When the first drop of wax hit the shaft we got quite a different reaction from what we had expected. Rather than call out and writhe in pain, our target exploded in a no-hands orgasm. Cum shot all the way up Joey's chest and over his shoulder.

Realizing that the candle game was over, I used my fingers to squeegee up the jism from Joey's chest and returned to feeding him my fingers. This time he did have some cum to taste and swallow. Between the powerfully erotic sight of this boy shooting and feeling him tongue my fingers, I was ready for my own climax. Len helped me untie Joey's ankles and I used his own saliva to moisten my dick as I raised his knees and mounted him. The lube from our makeshift dildos made entrance easy but the anus was still nice and tight. I pushed all the way in in one smooth glide and then looked down at the body below me. Joey had been limp when we untied him but the anal assault was arousing him. With his hands tied above his head he looked totally vulnerable. He rocked his head back and forth as he moaned his pleasure. I withdrew most of the way and

rammed in, full force, to the hilt again. Back and forth I drove as he became more and more excited. In a very short time, I reached that point and ground my pubes into his ass as I filled him with my semen. I collapsed onto his chest and felt his erect cock jabbing my belly. Once I had deflated and involuntarily withdrawn, I climbed back and made way for a waiting Len.

All this action had brought him back to arousal. He quickly replaced me and sliced his way into Joey's body. They both moaned in unison and Len pressed in fully. His fucking took a little longer than mine since it was his second orgasm. Joey didn't seem to mind as he writhed under the pleasure. I added to his stimulation by playing with those nipples. As Len increased speed and seemed ready to pop, I reached down between them and grabbed Joey's erection. Without much jacking, I brought him over the edge. His anus's reaction to the orgasm must have felt good to Len since he quickly followed with a bellowing climax of his own. Panting, he, too, dropped down close to his roommate.

I helped myself to a shower, leaving the two of them on the bed. When I came out, Len got up and took his turn. Afterward, we untied the wrists on our sleeping boytoy and went in to watch the video we had rented.

After an hour or so, we heard the shower running. Soon, Joey came in and sat down to watch with us. Nothing was said, but we knew that the undeveloped films were an assurance that nothing was ever going to be said, and, for a time anyway, Joey was going to behave.

The first portion of this adventure originally appeared in the collection *Dangerous Boys/Rent Boys.*

THE COCK WORSHIPPERS

A Series of Tales About the Adoration of the Male Sex Organ
Few cocks have been worshipped as much as that of Ken Ryker's, shown on
the preceding page in a scene from *The Ryker Files*, courtesy of Vivid Video.

HUMONGOUS
by John Patrick

The Adventures of the Awesome Dick Bliss, Seven Tales of Playing Hard,
Coming Hard

I. SPELLBOUND

Dick Bliss had a hard-on the minute he tugged off his jeans. He stood beside
the bed with his monster cock throbbing in Ross's face. Ross was rendered
speechless. Spellbound. He just sat there, dumbfounded. The cock he had
fantasized about so often was right here, in his room at the guest house in Fort
Lauderdale and he had only been in town a few hours. Earlier, when he was
checking in, he picked up the local bar rag in the lobby and saw this ad right
away: "Dick Bliss, star of *Big Boys*, in town doing 'private parties' for a 'limited
time'." Ross called the number; Dick called right back. He asked Ross what he
was into. Ross told him all he really wanted to do was to see it. Dick chuckled.
"That'll be two hundred."

So now Ross was looking at it, all nine and one-half, thick, cut inches of it. It
was, Ross thought, quite probably the most splendid penis he had ever laid eyes
on. The rest of Dick wasn't bad either, but it was obvious he'd been spending
too many nights at the disco and not enough days in the gym. He needed a shave
besides. Yet that cock could not be denied. There it was. Now he could examine
it, to learn it, to make it his own. It was a raging red thing two and a half inches
thick, with the flaring head a good three inches wide. When he grabbed it, pre-
cum oozed from the head, and the shaft pounded and grew even harder in Ross's
hand. With his other hand, Ross felt Dick's balls. They were huge and actually
seemed to quiver under his touch.

Dick leered at Ross. "Well? All you gonna do is look at it?" Ross felt like
saying that for two hundred, Ross could do whatever he wanted with it, but
before Ross had the chance, Dick leaned over a bit so the massive cock head
was only a couple of inches away from Ross's mouth. Ross had admired it
enough, goodness knows, when it was out of reach, to find the prospect of
paying it homage very enticing. He could no longer just be satisfied with
looking at it. Ross opened his mouth, and Dick just slid it in. Dick grunted softly
as Ross began to deep-throat him.

"You like that?" Dick barked after a bit.

Ross nodded.

"I bet you want it up your ass, don't you?"

Ross shook his head; he really didn't think he could take such a member up

his ass. He hadn't been fucked in a couple of years at least, and then it was by someone who was quite ordinary. This was extraordinary, and he had all he could do to get it down his throat. Sucking was his greatest pleasure, and he thought he was doing pretty good with this one when Dick suddenly pulled back and his cock slipped from Ross's mouth. Dick went on talking dirty, but his voice weaved in and out of Ross's mind, igniting the fantasy long held secret inside him.

"Oh, what the hell," Dick said, and ordered Ross to stand up. He scooted Ross around so his hands were braced on the air conditioner mounted in the window. He pushed up Ross's bathrobe and exposed his ass. Dick began kissing Ross's neck, rubbing his stubble against the tender skin under his jaw and driving him wild with desire. As Dick sucked and nibbled on Ross's skin, Ross's body went limp, his arms and legs slightly bent. He was getting ready to be fucked. Dick was rubbing his stubble against his shoulders, massaging him with his tongue. Then Dick speared his hard tongue into Ross's asshole. "AAAaagghhh!" Ross cried. Ross could never resist a rim-job, and his legs trembled in excitement. As he continued the tongue-fuck, Ross's body jerked.

Almost sobbing, Ross begged, "Oh, God, please, fuck it!"

He grunted, spit on his cock, and plunged the enormous cock into Ross. He began with short, slow motions, then used longer ones that accelerated into the rapid jackhammer thrusts he was famous for. Ross's face was almost forced into the windowpane, through which Ross could hear cars going by on the highway. The street noises, the hum of the air conditioner, the slap of Dick's balls on Ross's ass, and Ross's groans and grunts blended into a weird, steamy song of sex. Dick responded, clearly loving this moment of ecstasy; he sped up his thrusts, grabbing Ross's long blond hair like reins as he rode his ass. "God, I love to fuck," he shouted.

"I know, I know," Ross muttered, remembering *Big Boys* and *Hot Rods*, and all his other videos. Ross had collected them, gotten off countless times on the sight of him fucking some pliant youth, usually a skinny blond boy. Dark-haired Dick was a double for Tom Selleck, hairy chest, moustache, studly build. He was Ross's ideal truck driver, landscape crewman, cop. But he wasn't any of those things. He was a porn star. And before that big break, Ross read somewhere, he had waited on tables. Maybe he had unloaded the trucks for the restaurant; maybe that's where he got those naturally hard, power-packed muscles. Whatever the truth, he had found his calling: fucking.

"Oh, you got a fuckin' tight ass," he screamed as he shot a load into Ross.

Pre-cum oozed from Ross's cock but he was too enraptured with the idea that he'd just been fucked by Dick Bliss to come. He just hung on to the air conditioner as Dick finished and pulled out. He squeezed his sore butt. "Yeah, that's one nice ass."

Satisfied he had given another stellar performance, Dick left Ross there and went into the bathroom. Ross heard the shower running as he slowly made his

way back to the bed and collapsed. Ross knew he would be sore for days but he didn't care, he had just realized a dream.

Dick showered quickly and was drying off by the window. He seemed to take unusual interest in the scene by the pool, noticing some of the guests were naked. Ross responded that it was a "clothing optional" resort. Intrigued, Dick tossed his wet towel on the bed and wandered, naked, out onto the patio, which had puddles all around the edges of the pool from the heavy rain the night before. He was splashing water with his toes as he moved away from Ross, and Ross gazed lovingly at his ass, a tight, firm ass, nearly as splendid as his front.

Ross followed Dick, telling him he was going to relax in the Jacuzzi. Dick said he was going to look around, take a dip in the pool.

Ross edged himself into the Jacuzzi and felt the water swirl around him. It was Saturday afternoon, and there were hunks galore around the pool. The whole scene at the guest house was blowing Ross away, what with the landscaping of the walking paths, the row of green coconut palms in the turf around the pool, and Jimmy Buffett playing on somebody's tape deck. He was getting into this vacation after all.

Ross noticed a couple of guys in Speedos at the hibachi were getting high. Friends of theirs were lying on chaises near them, rubbing their bodies down with cocoa butter and tropical oils. And across from him, the airline stewards he'd seen registering earlier were dipping their toes in the steaming water, talking about their hectic flight schedules. Soon they were laughing about the bubbles and climbing in. As soon as they were sitting, one reached into his gym bag and pulled out a cold bottle of pink champagne. "We've got to celebrate, Greg," he said.

Behind Ross, in the rush of the water jets, he could feel Dick slide in, the pulse from his body streaming under Ross's legs. He felt the grip of thighs, the press of pecs to his back.

Oblivious, the stewards raised a toast. They clicked their cups as if they were about to sail off on a cruise.

Dick moved over, beside Ross.

"How was the water?" Ross asked.

He squeezed Ross's ass. "Oh, real nice, but this is nicer."

On the other side of the tub, Greg, the dark-haired steward, was pinching himself about how they had two whole days to "Par-ty," they said together, sneaking peeks at Dick.

Dick wasn't saying anything, moving in closer like nobody was watching. Ross was barely breathing. He felt his hand touch Ross's penis, and he seemed reassured that Ross was still swollen with want. Ross hadn't come, and Dick told Ross he'd stick around for a while and then he'd let him suck it while Ross jacked off. "No extra charge," he had said.

Now Dick moved away from Ross, got out of the Jacuzzi and approached the guys smoking the pot. His cock was now semi-hard and bobbed sensuously

between his thighs. The guys looked down at it, smiled.

Dick was friendly toward the pot smokers, and they gave him what was left of their joint. Ross could read Dick's lips, telling the boys he would see them later, and then he sat across the way smoking the roach, his legs sprawled across the arm of the deck chair. The legs sticking out were firm and tan in the rich early afternoon light. A stream of bright sun lit his incredible crotch. He settled farther into the chair, shifting his legs to better show off his cock to whoever happened to be watching. Ross knew what he was up to, and he blushed. One of the stewards, the cuter, blond one, whose name was Frankie, was watching Dick intently now and smiled, raised an eyebrow, and picked up his drink. Ross looked at his friend and he saw their eyes lock as they made what appeared to be a devious toast. Ross envied their friendship.

Ross's stomach felt heavy as he watched Frankie climb out of the Jacuzzi and approach Dick.

"That's him, isn't it?" Greg asked.

"Who ... ?" Ross muttered

"Dick Bliss, the porno star."

"Perhaps you're mistaken."

"Oh, please," Greg interrupted. "There's only one cock like that."

"I'm not certain "

"Oh, I see. You want him all to yourself, that's it."

"No, not really."

"You just want to play dumb, huh? C'mon, no need. See, it's all being arranged. There, he's nodding. He said yes."

Ross's heart started thumping.

"Don't worry. We don't want to steal him away. We just want to watch him fuck you," Greg said.

His words crashed in between thunderous heartbeats, and Ross peered at the clock on the wall over a stack of towels. Two-thirty.

The other stewart returned. "Your big buddy has agreed to the party."

"I don't know " Ross hesitated.

"You like the way that sounds, your *big* buddy?"

Ross was caught off guard; he spiraled in a vortex of desire and anxiety. "Yeah," Ross breathed. He took a moment to calm the spinning sensation. "Yeah," Ross said carefully. "I wouldn't call him a buddy exactly "

"But God, he sure is *big*." Greg interrupted.

Ross felt weak inside.

Dick came over, smiled. "We're havin' a little party."

Back home in Cincinnati, Ross enjoyed a reputation as being a rough boss at the electronics firm he worked for. A player, yes. A fuck, yes. Ross knew that a long time ago. So it was time for him to speak up. "But three's a crowd," he said.

"But four is a par-tee," Dick corrected him with a conspiratorial wink.

Ross opened the door to his room, without even thinking about what he would do once he was in there with them. At the same moment, he suddenly seemed to go cool on the whole idea, his illusions and enthusiasm dwindling away. It was clear that in situations like this you could rely on only the law of desire, a law that was obviously unfathomable, unpredictable, constantly changing. Forget the stewards ... Ross wanted only Dick.

Ross closed the shades, turned up the air conditioner. Dick stood beside the bed. The stewards set their champagne and some cups on the table and stood close together, stroking their meaty pricks.

Ross sat on the edge of the bed and ran his hands down Dick's naked hips. He began caressing the inside of his thighs, watching the cock twitch before him. He started stroking the length of him, teasing, moving against him until Dick stood excited and fully erect again. And just as Ross was about to take the cock into his mouth, he remembered that they were not alone.

Ross pulled away from him, leaving him hanging as he glanced quickly around the room, behind him, feeling suddenly guilty, dirty, on display. The stewards had seated themselves in the two chairs by the window, watching, still stroking their pricks. Their eyes met Ross's: their eyes were excited but calm, intense. They nodded for Ross to continue. Ross paused for a moment, his body still close to Dick's, shining with sweat, excited. Everything inside Ross's head told him to stop. *Good boys didn't do it in public, in front of others.* But Ross was beginning to understand: those rules did not apply here. This was different. *Dick Bliss* was different. Ross took a long breath and turned back to Dick, pulled by the heat, the pulse between his legs overpowering the voices in his head. *Go ahead, let them watch. Make it good.*

Dick took Ross's silence as his cue, and from then on silence reigned, broken only by Dick's softly moaned encouragement, and the startled sighs of the stewards watching Ross do his best to deep-throat Dick's huge cock.

After a few moments, Ross opened his eyes. The earlier tension he had seen in Dick's face had softened into a beautiful smile. "Oh, man," he said as Ross stroked him. He touched Ross's face, then ran his finger along Ross's jaw to his neck and forced his mouth back down in his crotch. It was as if Ross were on a porn set, as he was near to everything and far away at the same time. He waited for a while before sucking it, but without feeling as if he were waiting, rather as if he were suspended in time, just holding the massive prick and admiring it. Ross held Dick, caressed him, pulling gently, teasing, running his hands over the fabled length of him, playing at the tip. His tongue moved along the cock's length before, finally, he took him back inside his mouth.

Dick was watching Ross, his hips now moving under him, his torso a strong, smooth curve of desire and energy. Dick's breathing quickened, and he let out a soft groan of pleasure as he felt the warm wetness of Ross's mouth surround him. He let his head hang back for a moment as Ross pleasured him. Ross's body was pink and shining with the pulse of desire. Ross wanted him, here, this

minute, regardless of who was watching. Dick got onto the bed, told Ross to climb over him and stick the erection up his ass.

Ross did as he was told, and everything melted into a dream-like state, somehow connecting but not connected. Ross straddled Dick and took him in his hand and guided Dick's monster inside him, a soft moan of pleasure escaping Ross's lips as inch after inch slid in. Dick lifted and moved inside Ross, deeper, filling him, until their bodies were snug together. It was too much, too soon, and Ross pulled up, teasing Dick at his opening, then started again, letting him in a little, a little more, a little more, until he thrust the cock hard into his ass. Unexpectedly, the cock slipped in easily. Ross began bouncing gently, and he cried out in pleasure, surprised at the intense pleasure of this. They moved together, both breathing like athletes in a race, excited, fueled by unbridled passion.

Then Dick pulled Ross over with him, rolling him onto his back, and Ross was quickly guiding him back in his ass after the turn. Ross pulled Dick's body down on top of him, wanting to feel his weight, embracing him as he would a lover. Dick left his embrace and lifted Ross's hips, fucking him hard for a bit, then slower, then lifting his cock out part way, making Ross want him back in again fully. Ross's muscles contracted around Dick as he pulled out, only the tip teasing at Ross's entrance, Ross's body wild with the moment between having and not having.

For Ross, the stewards had disappeared. All he could see, hear, or feel was Dick. His muscular body was tight against him, then rising up to slide back in, moving on him furiously, gaining speed, both of them moving together, in one ecstatic rhythm.

Ross could hardly catch his breath; he was gasping for air, his words coming out in pieces, "Oh, fuck me. Fuck me!" in and out with Dick's quick thrusting. Ross's sweat was mixing with Dick's, and he was rocking with him, hips pushing up to meet him, taking him and barely letting him go before moving back up for more, taking more, needing more.

Ross's fingers dug into Dick's back and Dick cried out in a throaty voice full of pain and pleasure, concentrating, working his body, moving his hips against Ross, glancing across the room now to see how his act was playing over there. The stewards, Dick saw, were standing now, and the energy was flowing to them as well. Dick was soon throbbing on the edge of release. His body responded to the need to put on a show, and Ross moved with him, sucking and teasing with his muscles, pulling and coaxing him. But Dick held back, wanting Ross to release him. Ross saw Dick was looking at him with an aching question. Dick was asking his permission to stop now, to let the others in. Ross smiled back and nodded a yes. Slowly Dick pulled from Ross's ass, and things started to happen around Ross. Dick moved away and Greg slid between Ross's thighs. Greg began rubbing gently against Ross's hard-on as his hips moved forward to meet Ross's. Greg and Frankie were all over Ross now, and Ross remembered a

dream, the one about having two cocks at once, two cocks inside him and the terrible, but wonderful, pain.

Dick knelt near Ross's head and drew Ross's head toward him; Ross began sucking him again.

Frankie lifted Ross up and slid behind him. His cock pressed against Ross's asshole, insistent, demanding. He began pushing forward, and Ross could not tell how long it took to make its way inside. Fingers teased Ross's nipples, his hard-on, raked fiercely along his back and sides and always the cock in his ass was sliding farther and farther, until it was lodged inside him.

Greg began to wedge his cock in alongside Frankie's, and soon Ross was almost weeping as Greg began to slide into him, his smooth chest pressing his pecs, and he was crushed between Greg and Frankie, and the stewards were kissing Ross everywhere, their cocks sliding in and out, slowly at first, alternating then synchronous and back again. Greg's legs wrapped around them both as he began to thrust harder and harder, as Ross's moans got louder and louder and the stewards were whispering words of encouragement, and the world once again began to dissolve, to slow, to freeze with that particular, peculiar stillness that came when Ross was lost in a world of sin and perversion. Their bodies dripping wet and panting, the stewards slammed Ross's body between them for a considerable time, and then the two cocks erupted, one after another, and Ross could not tell which was first. As they climaxed, Dick shoved his cock back into Ross's gaping mouth, groaning with approval as Ross devoured him. "Oh, yeah, swallow that cock!"

The stewards pulled out of Ross and Ross was soon on his back again, Dick over him. The stewards stood alongside the bed and watched as Dick entered Ross again. He barely had the head in before he started to come. He hugged Ross's body tight in response, his orgasm exploding inside of Ross, his moans and the encouragement of the stewards filling the air.

Finished, Dick stayed in Ross, caressing him, rocking him gently. The stewards eased down beside them, began cuddling them. An exhilarating feeling of freedom and satisfaction washed over Ross. He rocked with Dick, breathing in sync with him, caressing his back, the back of his neck. As Ross came, finally, he kissed Dick's forehead gently, and forgave him for making him part of his act.

"Hey, I gotta go," Dick said a few minutes later. But he wasn't making much progress toward the door. He sat on the bed, smiling. They were finally alone; the stewards gladly paid Dick two hundred for the right to watch him fuck Ross. They invited Ross to dinner tomorrow night. Dick took their two hundred and Ross's and shoved the bills into one of his boots.

"For you, Dick," Ross said, pouring the last of the pink champagne in a cup for him.

The clouds had taken over the sky and it was threatening to rain again. There were sea-grape leaves and hibiscus bushes outside shaking from the long,

whistling gusts of wind and brushing against the windows. Ross had locked his door on the other guests and the rest of the world, and he fell upon Dick once more, devouring the cock again.

As Dick sipped the cheap wine, Ross filled his mouth with the fabled cock one last time, the cock that was everything he had dreamed of, yet he was awake. Wide awake.

II. SWEET RELIEF

Gary hadn't been this drunk since the Fourth of July, when he'd called Dick Bliss and tried to get him to meet him at Hunter's bar. Dick had just returned from a week of turning tricks in Florida and he didn't sound too happy to hear from Gary, but he didn't hang up on him either. There was a lot of noise in the background and Dick kept telling Gary he couldn't hear what he was saying. Finally Dick said he had to go. He had company and they were ready to shoot off the fireworks. Gary understood; he probably had a hot young number there and was about to fuck the daylights out of him. Yeah, there'd be fireworks all right. Dick had the biggest cock Hollywood had ever seen, and he knew how to use it. There were a hundred videos to prove it.

Gary didn't know why he kept calling Dick. He could just pop *Big Boys* into the VCR and get off, but it was the idea of it, he guessed, that he was right in Hollywood, so close yet so far away. Into a dead phone, Gary told Dick he'd call him again sometime.

Now here Gary was again, getting drunk and calling Dick. But this time, Dick was friendly and made a date with him. Dick said he would meet Gary at the bar in an hour. Gary raced to the bar; he needed a drink or two to get ready to take that cock up his ass. He met his buddy Baker, who bought him a drink and proceeded to tell him all about the boy he had met at the A & W a couple of months ago. His wife had left him over the youth.

Oh shit, here comes Dick, Gary thought, looking towards the entrance, *and he's got some kid with him. The kid looks fifteen. Dick's "companions" keep getting younger.*

Baker smiled when he saw Dick, but then he saw the kid he's with. Gary could tell Baker had met the kid before. Turned out he was the kid from the A & W. "Small world," Gary said.

Baker was obviously shaken, said he was going. Baker paid the bar tab. Dick insisted that Baker stay, that they should all have a drink. Baker calmed down when the kid started to rub his back, cajoling him into staying. They all had a drink. Gary didn't need another drink, but Dick said he was paying. Dick had never bought Gary a drink. Never, ever. Gary smiled, and thought things were getting interesting.

They finished their drinks and Gary went to take a piss. When he came out of the bar, the guys were already in the car. Baker was behind the wheel cranking the motor, and Gary climbed in, sitting next to the kid, whose name was Billy. Dick was upfront with Baker. Billy had said little and said even less on the short

trip to Dick's little apartment, which he called "the fuck pad."

They arrived at Dick's.

"I'm drunk," Gary said. He had trouble getting out of the car. "I'm sorry."

"It's okay," Dick said, propping Gary up. "Come on in."

"Is it okay? I'm really drunk. I better just stay here."

"It's okay. Come on in."

"I'm sorry. I can leave. Catch a cab."

"No, no. Just come in. Sit on the bed. Take your shoes off. Lie down. It's all right. It's okay."

By the time Gary got to the bedroom, he felt the need to pee again. But he did more than that. He made a terrible mess in the bowl and, suddenly sober, he frantically cleaned it up.

It's the cheap whiskey, Gary said to himself. He remembered the first time he was here he got sick. Dick's toilet had backed up and he asked Gary to fix it. Dick started drinking and kept filling Gary's glass and saying, "You're not drinking enough." Gary knew it'd be easier for him to take Dick's cock if he were drunk. Gary fixed the toilet and Dick said he'd fuck him for free.

Now Dick came in, asked Gary if he was okay.

No, I'm snookered again, you asshole, Gary thought.

Dick didn't seem drunk at all. He took Gary into the bedroom, made him lie down. Gary didn't want to lie down; he wanted to leave. Dick started talking to him about this kid he picked up the other night. The kid said he wanted to see Dick's prick, but he'd never paid for sex before. Dick told the kid, "If you haven't paid for it yet, you will."

"He only had twenty bucks, which he'd made off a trick the hour before. I said twenty bucks was enough, just to see it."

Then the kid said, "Well, I guess twenty bucks doesn't seem like much. Doesn't seem like paying for it at all."

"Hell, it's a bargain. I spent twenty-five taking that queeny kid Jeffrey out to eat and to a movie and I didn't even get his clothes off."

This was crazy, Gary thought now. Here they were in Dick Bliss's bedroom talking about other boys when, right in the other room, Baker was with that cute kid, fucking him, but Dick doesn't seem to care. With Dick's reputation, Gary knew he had boys all over town. Dick then told Gary about a kid named Phillip who lived over in the Valley. He came over to Dick's last week. Now he was one of his steadies. He was only going to talk to him but the kid kept rubbing his crotch while he was sitting in his truck so he took the kid home, fucked him for three days.

Dick took off Gary's clothes, began giving him a massage. He kept asking if Gary felt better. Gary kept telling him all he wanted to do was die.

"Billy's kind of rough," Dick said of the boy with Baker in the other room. "I screwed him in my truck the first time. He asked me to take him out to dinner. I said, 'All I've got is seven dollars.' He said, 'That's enough.' So I took him for

burgers. When we came out, I just had to have it so I laid it to him right in the parking lot. But I don't think he liked it much. He just laid there chewing gum and fiddling with the knobs on the radio."

Gary blinked. He couldn't believe Dick was telling him this. How could anybody play with the radio while Dick was fucking them? But Billy must have liked something because he was back again. Still, he was in the other room with Baker, and Dick was massaging Gary's ass. *Go figure*, Gary thought.

Suddenly, Billy and Baker came in. They got naked and began embracing and kissing like long-lost lovers while stroking each other's prick. Gary looked behind him to see Dick fondling his throbbing cock. Gary moaned when he saw it, realized how much he'd missed it.

Billy left Baker and dropped to the bed next to Gary, began kissing him all over. His average-size, cut cock dangled in Gary's face. Gary inhaled his pungent, boyish scent.

God, he's cute, Gary thought. The boy tensed as Gary's tongue touched the tip of his cock, licking the precum from his piss slit, then lapping at the shaft contentedly.

Dick and Baker were all over Billy, caressing, pinching, kissing his flesh while Gary sucked him. Baker reached out and began fondling Billy's bloated ball sac while Gary sucked. Baker juggled them like golf balls before sucking each testicle. It seemed he was going to swallow Billy's scrotum whole. Gary ran his hands through Baker's long dark hair as he continued his oral assault on Billy's balls. Meanwhile, Gary greased Billy's delicious cock with liberal amounts of saliva. Up and down on it he plummeted, forcing his prick deeper into the back of Gary's throat.

The air simmered with raw lust. Gary began to jack himself, and he was stunned to find he could actually get it up despite the booze.

Billy's body stiffened as he neared his orgasm. His cum started spurting down Gary's throat, but Gary didn't gag; he simply swilled down one shot after another.

As the last blast of cum filled Gary's mouth, Billy pulled away.

Dick moved over to take Billy's place before Gary, but Gary didn't start to suck him right away. Instead, he kissed his hairy chest, taking each nipple into his mouth, playfully biting on them as he felt them growing harder. Gary worked on his upper body until his hair was soaked with Gary's spittle. Then Gary eased down to Dick's sex, sucking him deep into his mouth, tasting his gritty texture, rolling the flesh around on his tongue. Dick was so horny by this time it was merely a matter of seconds before he was ready to explode. Gary sensed this and squeezed the base of his cock firmly to suppress his orgasm.

"Hey, whatcha doin'?"

"Please, fuck me." Gary was desperate to be fucked by porn's biggest stud again.

Billy had moved to the edge of the bed and was blowing Baker. He halted his

blowjob to watch as Dick got into position and lifted Gary's ass into the air. Billy decided he wanted Baker up his ass so he lied down next to Gary. Gary and Billy kissed as Baker got into position next to Dick. Both studs began by rubbing spit on their stiff pricks. Dick kissed Gary's ass all over, even plowing his tongue into Gary's tight hole and rimming him without hesitation. This was a new wrinkle; Dick had never, ever rimmed Gary. Baker kissed Billy's ass cheeks but didn't stick his tongue in.

Dick was very methodical, scouring Gary's asshole. At one point, Gary clamped down on his tongue as he kept up the frantic pace.

Meanwhile, Baker was already in Billy, fucking away.

"Please, Dick," Gary begged. "Fuck it!"

Dick nodded, and Gary waited excitedly as Dick slathered some lotion on his prick. In moments, Dick was shoving the cock head into Gary. The pain, despite Gary's drunkenness, made him dizzy. He screamed. Dick pulled it out, rested, watching as Baker was having fun over Billy.

"Okay," Gary said, breathing hard, and the stud started playing with his ass cheeks, gently sliding his cock in and out and around, going deeper and deeper each moment.

Soon Dick was poking Gary with his trademarked quick and precise thrusts. Gary quickly grew accustomed to the thickness of it and Dick finally had it all in him. His jackhammering was so smooth it almost took Gary's breath away. Once again, Gary realized, he was getting the fuck of his young life, this time with an audience.

Billy and Gary could barely contain their excitement at this tandem fucking. They kissed each other and began moaning in unison. Seeing Dick's cock sliding in and out of Gary, as well as seeing Billy and Gary kissing, turned Baker on incredibly and he stepped up his attack on Billy's asshole.

Gary cried out; the pain returned suddenly. Dick was close to orgasm again and his cock swelled a bit. Gary's ass muscles were no match for Dick's huge, rampaging cock. His hairy nutsac swung wildly, hitting Gary's own nuts with jarring blows as he picked up the pace.

Gary looked up to see Baker had pulled out of Billy and was jerking his cock, eager to follow Dick. But Dick was reluctant to leave Gary; he took his sweet time. Finally he did pull out, then moved out of the way as Baker got on his knees and slowly sunk his prick into Gary. After Dick, it was a sweet relief. Baker had only fucked Gary once before, but Gary had been so drunk he didn't remember much about it. Now, as Baker pushed all the way in and started banging his butt, Gary realized he may have been missing something. Baker was good.

Dick now got behind Billy and lifted his ass. They kissed each other as they watched Baker begin fucking Gary. Dick entered Billy and Billy started to groan. Gary knew what he was going through, the pain, the sheer ecstasy of having that much cock in him. That turned Gary on and he maneuvered his hand

so he could stroke his nearly-erect cock as Baker thrusted his prick into him.

Soon they were all roaring together, and Billy's eyes filled with tears. He was close to hysterical as the tenseness tumbled out of him, and he jerked himself to orgasm, with Dick and Baker close behind, filling the two asses with their cum.

As they wound down, eventually, Billy struggled to sit up on the bed.

"Wow," he said, shaking his head, amazed by all the dramatics. Gary looked at Dick. *So beautiful,* Gary thought, *so free, so loose with his favors, his smiles.* Gary reached out and touched Dick's now semi-hard cock. The moment was breathless: no sound, no room, no anything except eyes and mouths and each other's presence. Smiles faded into serious faces for a moment. Gary leaned in, just a subtle move toward the man. Billy leaned in, too, ever so slightly toward the tempting cock.

"God," Baker said quietly, his eyes smiling up at Dick warmly. Dick smiled, aware of his effect on the others, of his sexual power.

There was a moment's pause. Dick's body seemed to glow; his body was one big tease, and they began to eat it up, their eyes full of passion. They each took their turn sucking, licking, and kissing Dick's humongous cock goodbye. For now.

III. COME WITH ME

The stud in the photographs in *Torso* seemed to look back at Jimmy. Every night Jimmy was lost in the beauty of the photographs of the stud. Jimmy began panting as his imagination raced in a fantasy begun many nights before and then enhanced when he actually saw the stud live, at the restaurant where Jimmy bussed tables. Jimmy did not dare to speak to the stud, but the memory of seeing him fueled his nightly fantasies. In his lonely room, Jimmy was glistening, naked in the moonlight, his cock exposed, hard. Jimmy stroked himself recalling the stud's eyes, the need he saw in those eyes. Jimmy's body moved now in a rhythm that began the same way each night, over and over ... a thin veil of sweat forming between the tight, firm ass cheeks, along his firm belly, his body pulsating as he slipped his fingers down to his raging cock ... desire that flowed now, slippery and wanting as he arched, thrusting, and building ... building... until he finally came.

Since he had seen the stud in person, all he had been able to focus on every night was this secret aching for him. Never before had Jimmy fantasized about a real person, someone he had actually seen. And now that he had seen him, this stud had something wicked about him that captured Jimmy completely.

In truth, Jimmy had almost begun to like the single life. After his disastrous affair with David, a man twice his age, he had regained his pride and his strength, or so he thought. He'd been seeing older men again: gentle men with money, who wooed him with gifts. They desired him; Jimmy liked them, although he couldn't really talk to any of them. Still, he thought it was enough, that nice was okay for a while. It eased the stress of daily living. It was easy,

noncommittal. After a time, he began to forget about the stud. He'd put away his picture. He told himself it had just been a phase; just a chance that it had happened at all.

Then one of his older friends bought Jimmy a VCR. Now Jimmy had to have tapes. He went to the video store and there he found box after box with the stud's picture on it. The magazine had simply called him "The Dick," but now Jimmy knew the stud's name was Dick Bliss. Jimmy rented two of the videos the first night, and each night thereafter two more until he had seen every Dick Bliss video the store had. The clerk chuckled on the fifth night, saying something to the effect that Jimmy "sure must like Dick."

"Got that right," Jimmy muttered, grabbing the plastic boxes off the counter, and racing out of the store.

He had spent all his money and seen all Dick Bliss's videos when, suddenly, he saw him on the street, accidentally almost plowing right into him. The stud had smiled, not sweetly or warmly, and yet not exactly in a snide or rude way, either. Later that day, Jimmy saw him again at the cafe, where Jimmy had been promoted to waiter, and the only words exchanged were about the stud's order.

Again that night Dick Bliss's presence began to fill Jimmy's dreams, night and day, making concentration at work a virtually impossible task. He kept waiting for the stud to re-appear, either on the street or in the cafe.

Jimmy's patience was rewarded late one night. The cafe was about to close. In fact, Jimmy had already checked out and was counting his tips. The stud sat at a table in front and ordered apple pie and coffee. Jimmy went to the restroom and when he returned to the dining room, the stud was tossing a five dollar bill on the table. The stud looked up, directly into Jimmy's eyes, and smiled. Then he turned and left the cafe.

Jimmy followed, at a distance. The stud was taking his time, ambling down the boulevard, and although the traffic was heavy on this Saturday night, Jimmy could have been walking alone down some silent tunnel. Figures and colors bent and twisted before his eyes, flashes of light making him blink as he followed the stud.

The stud turned on a side street and started walking up the hill. Jimmy's breath quickened. As Dick turned yet another corner, Jimmy thought he had lost the stud. Then Jimmy felt a hand on his shoulder.

"Come with me," Dick said, taking Jimmy by the hand, his husky voice filled with purpose.

They went between two buildings, climbed up a slight incline to a stand of trees. It was quiet, dark. Jimmy had not let go of Dick's hand, and now the stud yanked Jimmy to the ground, making him kneel before him. Jimmy's logical, safe side raged at him to stop this, to stand up, run. But his other side, his midnight self, was blossoming now, ravenous from the long wait, the unfulfilled nights past, begging him to continue.

It seemed to be more than just wanting the man. It seemed a test of his entire

self, of all his actions up to now. He thought about the many nights of dreams, the desire for the edge, the yearning for the pleasure and the pain.

Jimmy ran his hands over the snug black pants, felt the tight, round ass and muscular thighs. The bulges and strength and sexuality that mesmerized Jimmy in the photographs in the magazine and on video came back to him now. With his cheek pressed to the stud's groin, he could almost taste him on his tongue. He was suddenly aware of his desire in a real and tangible way, wanting to feel the stud's prick harden in his hand, wanting to search and explore the muscular body. He began unbuttoning the stud's jeans. Dick did not stop him. Jimmy left Dick's jeans loose and moved his hands up along the stud's hard belly, over the cotton of the white shirt, unbuttoning the tiny buttons one by one. Jimmy ran the palms of his large hands over the pink, hard tips of the stud's nipples and they stood at attention in the moonlight. With a quick glance down the hill, Dick instinctively reached into his pants and suddenly exposed his cock. Jimmy gently pried the stud's hands away.

"Beautiful," Jimmy whispered. "You are so beautiful."

Dick stood still, quietly surrendering to a worship that always got him off. Jimmy slipped the black jeans over the curve of the stud's hips, his eyes devouring the tease of the half-hard prick. Then, looking up into the stud's eyes, he ran one long finger over the pulsing flesh.

The stud sucked in his breath, suppressing a moan of pleasure. Jimmy, dizzy from the contact, his face hot with embarrassment, his excitement building about having sex with this man of whom he'd only dreamed. He was quickly forgetting David, forgetting the many nights alone, waiting and wondering. He licked the head of the prick, then took it in both hands. It *was* huge, far more imposing than he ever would have imagined, and the fact that he now had it in his hands made him think that this was all just a continuation of his fantasy, a dream, unreal not actually happening at all.

But Dick moved his hips forward and took Jimmy's head in his hands, shocking Jimmy back into the reality of his situation. Jimmy was living his fantasy; the famous cock of Dick Bliss was being pushed into his mouth. In and out it went, pushing and pulling, stroking, guiding, teasing at Jimmy's wet lips, then plunging in deeply as Jimmy groaned in pleasure. They moved together, Dick giving it to Jimmy as one who lives to please. He gave him what he'd been wanting, what he'd been waiting for; gave it to him gently at first, then rough, banging in and out, endlessly.

Dick's groans of pleasure excited Jimmy, his mouth working fast and deep, sucking and circling and teasing until Dick let out his breath, close to an explosion of pent-up desire and need. Jimmy's mouth lightened its touch: just in and out, gently now, but still not stopping.

Dick ran his fingers through Jimmy's hair and groaned, "Oh, yeah, suck it," over and over. But soon his voice trailed off. With one hand Jimmy kneaded and caressed the stud's body, teasing his balls as the giant cock responded to his

touch. Beads of sweat shone on the fine fur that graced Dick's body. "You feel so good, mmmm...." Jimmy's face was bright, flushed with passion and pleasure, eyes closed in concentration, as his tongue danced over the head of the cock, then he took it deep again.

Suddenly, Dick yanked Jimmy up, forced him to turn around. Dick's hands, once cruel and diligent, were now smooth and soft, wandering gently over Jimmy's body. Jimmy felt the stud's hands rubbing his back, down over his ass, wandering to his inner thighs, up and over again onto his back, over his strong shoulders and down again to Jimmy's crotch. Seeing how much Jimmy wanted it, Dick unbuttoned Jimmy's jeans and released the boy's cock. He pushed the jeans down to expose the buttocks.

Jimmy raised his hips up and backed toward Dick's erection.

Dick spit on his cock, slid the head inside. As he began working the fullness inside, Dick held Jimmy's ass cheeks in his hands. Jimmy, bending low, hung on to the trunk of the tree. Their bodies were heated and sweaty and glowing in the moonlight as Dick began shoving his cock into Jimmy.

As Dick's cock entered him more fully, Jimmy was amused by the fact that he no longer felt embarrassed by his nakedness in the wild. It was somehow liberating a strange sense of safety in this world of surprises, unknowns. The fucking started in earnest, soon sending waves of unbearable desire through Jimmy. Eyes closed, he whispered, "Please, come in ... come inside... come inside me." He went on, begging for Dick to fuck him, whispering his need, his voice filled with hunger, and they became lost in the storm of their passion.

Dick groaned as he guided the cock between Jimmy's ass-lips. The long shaft disappeared slowly, inch by inch, into Jimmy, then more ... more ... until Jimmy's body met Dick's, the shaft deep inside him now. Dick thrust gently into him, feeling the snugness of the boy's body as he tried to pull out, then slipped back in. Jimmy moaned, tilting his head back under the wave of gratification that rolled over him as Dick filled him at long last, moving in and out gently, moving in tight, up against the top of his ass. He opened his eyes to watch as cum spurted from his cock in a rush of pleasure, then his eyes fell shut again, and he lost himself in the force Dick's practiced fuck.

Dick's eyes were ravenous, taking in each stroke, fiery with passion as he pulled out, thrust gently in, out; he never got bored with the sight of his organ disappearing each time, then reappearing. His face was red with excitement and effort, pumping into the boy who had so wanted him. He gripped Jimmy's ass, focused on the sensation. Jimmy was building toward another orgasm as he moved his hips against Dick. Dick's erection slid smoothly in and out of Jimmy, shining now in the moonlight, and Dick began talking for the first time, praising Jimmy's tightness, his boyish beauty.

Dick moaned, hands pulling Jimmy's hips in against his crotch, Jimmy's legs growing weak with passion, the smell of sex mixing between them, their breath hot and quick and excited. Then, in one quick motion, Dick lifted him up, and

began to come. "Mmmm, oh, yes, oooh that's good...." Dick's voice filled Jimmy's ears with words and sounds of pleasure Jimmy had only dreamed of hearing for so many nights, and Jimmy came again.

- - -

The room was warm and comfortable as Dick laid Jimmy gently onto the bed, Jimmy's arms around Dick's neck. They held each other for a moment before Dick pulled back, sitting up on the edge of the bed and brushing Jimmy's hair away from the clear blue eyes, which seemed to be filled with something more intense than passion. Silently Dick wondered what Jimmy was feeling; he was surprised he was feeling so much emotion toward this boy. Such emotions made him nervous. He rose from the bedside, looking down at Jimmy, his hair wild and shining on the pillow, eyes glazed, body young, trim, hairless and, most of all, eager.

Jimmy looked up at Dick through a veil of sensation, his body throbbing, ready to resume their sex, to come again.

Dick kissed down the boy's smooth neck, sucking and biting playfully, cupping Jimmy's ass cheeks in his hands and lowering his mouth to first one nipple and then the other, gently sucking and teasing them as Jimmy sighed and moaned with pleasure.

"Come on, kid, let's take a little soak."

Jimmy found himself in a beautiful black-and-cream marbled room. Small hollows in the walls housed thick, brightly burning candles. Ferns in pots were hung from the ceiling by black chains. Steam curled up from a large, round bath sunk deep into the floor. A small stone waterfall brought water out of the wall, down over stones in sensual patterns and into the tub. It seemed that the water was constantly renewed because it wasn't overflowing or changing its level. "Wow," Jimmy gushed.

His body relaxing already, Jimmy lowered himself into the sumptuous bath.

Dick turned a knob and soft music started playing.

Over the roar of the water and the music, and Dick lifted Jimmy's hips up out of the water, holding his body in his arms, and their cocks bumped together. Jimmy closed his eyes. "Oh, yes," he sighed. "Mmmmm, yes...."

Jimmy stroked the stud with his tongue, feeling the hardness of Dick's swelling cock against his mouth, his face aglow with passion and desire once more, smiling his thanks. Jimmy bent at the waist and took the cock head in his mouth.

"Ooohh, yeah...." Dick moaned in pleasure as Jimmy's fingers were busy along with his mouth. Dick began moaning, stroking Jimmy with his words of praise and desire, his breathing quickening. "Mmmmm, oh yes, so good. Ooohhhhh, take it, take it all."

The cock was in Jimmy's mouth, as deep as he could go, then out again. Dick's body was alive with the pulse of blood, rushing and pounding through him, and he became harder than he had in months.

Dick held his breath for a moment as Jimmy worked him furiously, concentrating, then suddenly let out his breath in a wave of sound. "Aaaaaaahhhhhh!" Dick arched desperately into Jimmy's mouth, tensing and expanding with orgasmic pleasure, pumping in spasms of pleasure over and over again. His groans filled the room. Jimmy stayed against him.

Their eyes met for a moment as they sat on the bed together, loose and relaxed, if not a little disheveled. Dick seemed to enjoy reliving the fuck they had just enjoyed. He talked about it as if he were reviewing it for publication.

But Dick's voice weaved in and out of Jimmy's mind. He was exhausted now, and had given up wondering who this stud was, how he lived, and he had given up completely his practical mind's concerns and let himself go. He had spent some time deep into the territory known only in his dreams until now, deep into the fantasy the stud offered him. Now, inexplicably, the stud looked at Jimmy and for an instant Jimmy could have sworn he saw a glint of something he'd never seen before in the eyes of anyone who had fucked him.

Dick squeezed the boy's ass and said, "I thought you might stay tonight, since Larry's gone and it's Saturday night and you don't have to work tomorrow. I mean, unless you have a date?"

Jimmy raised his eyebrows. "Nooo, no date." He thought a second, then asked, "Who's Larry?"

IV. TOO MUCH

Mark had been directed to the house behind the Boylesk theater. It was used to house the dancers and to provide a place for them to meet clients. Officially, it was a massage parlor, or so the sign on the door said.

Mark entered a reception area where an overweight bearded gent dressed only in a towel took his money and checked him off in his spiral-bound appointment book. He stared at Mark blankly for a moment. What kind of expression was Mark expecting anyway? Maybe the man had already gotten so used to escorting men in and out that he simply could not respond at all. But even so, even if he was completely used to it by now, there would still be a special look on his face, Mark thought.

Finally came a half smile, and the attendant pointed across the room to a long hallway. "Room seven," he said, and, with a quick slap on Mark's ass, Mark was sent stumbling down the hall. "Have fun," the attendant said.

The door to room one was half open, and Mark could hear moans of pleasure mixed with slurping and sucking noises. Mark couldn't resist peering into the doorway. A young blond man was naked on a massage table and was receiving a blowjob from another young blond man. When the sucker saw Mark he gently eased the door shut. Mark continued on. All of the other doors were closed.

Mark got to room seven and knocked.

"Come on in," a deep voice called out.

Mark opened the door and there he was, Chad Carpenter, star of over 100 videos. Chad had done everything, and he had fascinated Mark as no other porn

star had for nearly three years. When Mark heard Chad was dancing for a week's engagement over the Thanksgiving holiday, he tried to book a flight but everything was filled. Mark decided to drive, see some relatives along the way.

Chad's show was disappointing to Mark because there are state laws that prohibit totally nude dancing, but the boy was charming and a terrible tease. Chad wore his blond hair considerably longer than in the videos and he appeared to be much smaller and more delicate. But Chad's ass was even more splendid than Mark had remembered it, and Chad delighted in bending over and opening it up a bit for his adoring fans. Mark sat way in the back for the first show, and then moved up front for the second. It was after that show Mark saw Chad in the lounge and Mark agreed to meet Chad "next door" the next afternoon.

Chad apparently had the star's quarters. There was a huge bed, covered only with a messy sheet, a small refrigerator, tables, chairs, and an adjoining bathroom.

They sat across from each other for a few minutes, chatting pleasantly, and then Chad jumped up and served champagne in cheap glasses.

Mark didn't know what he had expected, but it wasn't this. Champagne in the middle of the afternoon with Chad Carpenter! A fully-clothed Chad besides! He guzzled his wine, while Mark sipped it. Chad re-filled his glass several times. He appeared to be a nervous sort, and Mark confronted him: "Is there something wrong?"

"What?"

"I just wondered if I'd done something wrong."

"Oh, no, nothing's wrong," Chad said, getting up to fill his glass again. "You're just a very attractive man, you know. People who visit here, well, you know, it's like my job, that's all."

Mark was terribly flattered. Maybe, he chuckled to himself, he could have some of his hard-earned money back? "Actually, this is a first," Mark said. "I mean, the first time I've ever been with anyone, well, famous."

Chad blushed, and suddenly lost his balance, plopping down on the bed. He quickly regained his composure, sat up, and the contents of his champagne glass spilled as he drew it to his lips.

He finished the wine, and told Mark to come over to him. Chad blinked as Mark sat down next to him and began stroking his stomach, his armpits, then his crotch. Mark simply couldn't hold back; he at least had to fondle the merchandise. This was suddenly too much for Chad, apparently. He dropped his glass on the floor and grabbed Mark's wrists and pushed him backwards across the wide bed. He fell forward against Mark, pinning his body beneath him, using his weight to full advantage to quiet the now-wriggling mass beneath him.

Suddenly Chad rolled heavily sideways, landing on his back with Mark above him. Mark held his arms crucified away from his body.

Chad smiled an oddly wistful smile. "Fuck me," he begged.

With that Mark tilted his head down and kissed him. And like so many

before him, Mark lost himself in the joy of kissing those well-kissed lips. If there was one thing Chad had learned in all those hours before the cameras, with cold women and men under hot lights, it was kissing.

In all Mark's life, he had never experienced such passion hitting him full force. The room was burning with Chad's kisses. And Mark was writhing against him, and finally Chad let his hands go, uncertain what else to do. Mark seized the opportunity, and quickly reached down to his waist, and pulled off his T-shirt. The sight of him nearly naked was too much, somehow. Mark was speechless. Having this universally beloved, and beautiful, porn star in bed with him took Mark's breath away. Chad reached out suddenly and turned off the bedside lamp, as if he sensed asking Mark to fuck him in bright light was just too much.

Before Mark could start thinking whether it was too much even in darkness, Chad was pulling off Mark's shirt as well. Soon he had their jeans removed. Chad wore no underwear and, Mark thought, his cock was every bit as gorgeous as it appeared in video after video, sliding in and out of innumerable mouths, cunts, and asses.

Chad gently directed Mark now because Mark seemed lost, and Mark took his direction flawlessly. As Mark removed his briefs, Chad slapped a palm against his ass, then fingered his tits. He seemed to be surveying Mark, as if he were casting him for one of his videos. "Tight little ass," he noted, "Smooth chest, juicy cock." He ran a finger through the tuft of dark hair at Mark's crotch. He sighed then, and leaned back on his elbows, offering himself to Mark. Mark took Chad's raging hard-on in his mouth and sucked on it, lost in long-suppressed desire. He had wanted this for a long, long time.

Mark straddled Chad's torso, and ran his hands over his chest, lightly flicking his nipples. Chad's body stirred slightly under Mark. Mark bent down and they kissed again.

In a matter of seconds Mark was stretched out full length on top of Chad, clasping his head with his hands and kissing him as if his life depended on it. Mark began pumping his hips, grinding his stiff prick against Chad's sweat-slicked belly. Chad's hands slid down his back and cupped his ass, squeezing the cheeks with every thrust of Mark's body. Chad's fingertips dug into Mark's crack. Mark's mouth worked its way on down, kissing Chad's throat, his shoulders. Mark's head swung lower and he gently took Chad's left nipple between his teeth, flicking it with his tongue. Chad groaned, and his body squirmed gratefully, blissfully beneath Mark. Mark's tongue made a wet trail across the incredibly hard ridges of Chad's belly to the first fringe of his blond pubes. His fat cock had stiffened to full hardness now. Mark took it in his hand and gazed at it, the cock he had seen being sucked and adored and glorified by so many gals and guys. He traced the veins along the meaty, white, cut shaft. "Oh, it's beautiful," he sighed.

Mark rolled his tongue around the cock head, gently, teasingly, and then

suddenly descended, taking the entire shaft down his eager throat. Chad cried out. Chad seized Mark's head with both hands and began pumping his hips, cramming his luscious cock deep into Mark's mouth. After a couple of seconds, Mark found his stride, matching each upward thrust of his with a downward plunge of Mark's own. Mark reached up, gripping each of Chad's hard nipples between thumb and forefinger, and squeezed. Chad's groans of delight at Mark's technique took on an added intensity. Chad wrapped his legs around Mark tightly and rolled them over. In this position Chad could easily ram his dick down Mark's throat.

After a few minutes of the most marvelous face-fucking Mark had ever enjoyed, Chad pulled out, and Mark was able to bathe his nearly hairless balls with his tongue. Mark looked up to see Chad was staring back down at him, his eyes bright and feverish. Chad took his cock in his hand and slapped Mark's face with it, rubbing it over Mark's nose, eyes, cheeks. Pre-cum coated Mark's skin.

Mark's hands wandered up and down the length of Chad's hard, muscled torso, kneading the sweaty flesh, then again pinching his nipples. Chad took his balls out of Mark's mouth and went back to fucking his face. He reached behind him and grasped Mark's dick, pulling on it with short, quick strokes. Finally, he got some lube and coated Mark's cock.

"I want you to fuck me as hard as you can," he said.

"Sure," Mark smiled.

Chad took a big dollop of the lube and worked it into his asshole, then sat on Mark's erection. The cock slid right in. Soon Chad was gasping, arching his back. Mark plowed into him as energetically as he could. Sometimes he pushed all the way in and stayed there, as Chad began to grind his hips into Mark. Gradually, Chad picked up the tempo, and Mark's cock was plunging in and out with a hard, fast rhythm. Chad jacked off while he fucked Mark's cock. Cum was soon spewing out of Chad's dick, in one ropy loop after another, splattering across Mark's chest, and Mark's cum was soon filling Chad. Mark reached up to pull him down, and kiss him as he finished.

A few minutes later, Mark held Chad close. Chad seemed in no hurry for Mark to leave. Chad lay there humming, his head on Mark's shoulder. Mark said to him, "Well, you sound happy."

He twisted his head to look up at Mark's face. "You fucked me good, mister."

"No, *you* fucked *me*."

"Whatever. It was good." Then Chad paused suddenly, his eyes locked on Mark's smiling face. He put up a hand to caress Mark's face. With that, Mark leaned down to kiss him goodbye.

- - -

Mark arrived just in time for the midnight show. He was lucky and got a seat in the front row.

Chad danced last and was joined on stage at the end of his act by the five other dancers. Here he just held his own, blending indistinguishably into the crowd as he pressed his way forward among the men standing there, sexy, well-built men just like him, to step over to Mark and bend down and kiss him.

The crowd roared. A star was what he was and now, and in one of the defining, unforgettable moments in Mark's young life Chad whispered in Mark's ear, "Why don't you come next door and fuck me?"

This time, the fat man at the door smiled the moment he saw Mark and told him to go right back, that Chad was expecting him. Mark felt as if he was being given a second chance when none was needed really, and it wasn't costing him a cent.

Chad was naked, fresh from a shower. No words were spoken; he just took Mark in his arms and kissed him. Then he said, "That was great, mister. Just how I like it. You did that really good."

Mark dropped to his knees before him. It was party time. Chad's cock was only partially hard. Mark leaned forward and kissed the knobby, circumcised head. The sleek crown twitched and spasmed a moment. Mark gave it a couple of licks and kissed it again. Then the warm knob was in his mouth, pulsing and throbbing between his lips, stretching and hardening as he sucked.

Mark lathed the bulbous head and pre-cum oozed from it. Chad's right hand dropped down to the back of Mark's head. The cock was now rigid in his hand. He pumped him steadily, his lips working the crown, sucking and licking the knob. Suddenly, Chad shuddered. His cock twitched and spasmed. His cum filled Mark's mouth.

"Shit!" Chad cried, pulling Mark's head into his groin, his hips jerking and quivering. Chad's cock jabbed at Mark's mouth, then the rhythm slowed. Soon, the famous cock lay peacefully on Mark's tongue, the pubic hair tickling his nose.

"I'm sorry," Chad said. "I haven't come all day. I usually come two or three times and" He paused, stroked the back of Mark's head. "Damn, you're good, mister."

Mark released his cock and got to his feet. The penis he had fantasized about so often glistened lewdly between his legs. Mark stroked it as Chad started removing Mark's clothes. Again Mark saw the delicateness of him, the fragileness despite the taut muscles. Chad had just come and there was that hint of vulnerability in his eyes, when for a moment the walls were down. Now there was a part of Mark that wanted to make love to him, slowly and sweetly. But there was another part that knew Chad wanted to be fucked until it hurt.

Soon Chad was on his knees on the bed, his ass high in the air. Mark covered his ass with little kisses. His tongue probed his asshole and Chad flinched. Mark steadied him with a gentle hand as he licked his crack up and down, over and over, until he cried out, desperate for cock. Mark smeared the lube all over his erection. He entered him slowly, and it was too good. Mark became dizzy,

thought he was going to pass out, it was that good. Chad collapsed to the bed, letting Mark drill his ass harder and harder until everything went black around Mark, and Mark came harder than he had ever come before. It was all too much. Much too much.

V. NEW FACES

"You'll be fine. He'll love you. You're such a pretty boy," Chad's agent, Bernard, told him before hanging up the phone. Chad smiled. He never grew tired of hearing it. His line of work was built on being pretty, and by contrasting skin color and big dicks, that and new faces. Once upon a time, Chad had been a new face, but now he was a familiar face, some said perhaps too familiar. He had, some said, become a transcendent star who could sell a video with the image he had built over dozens, maybe hundreds, of features and magazine layouts. Now it paid to keep doing something new on camera. The options were few, after fifty videos, so now his fortune depended on his partner.

All the way to the shoot he thought about his partner, who had been christened Dick Bliss, with the emphasis on the dick part. It was said he had the biggest one in Tinseltown, which was really amazing considering that Gavin Jones, Chad's last partner, said his was the biggest and it measured eleven inches when it was fully hard, which was seldom possible.

Chad was driving up to the shoot alone. He had been to this particular location before, a really nice house that belonged to some minor actress and her husband. The husband, Howard, who, it was said, was bisexual, liked porn and got off on watching videos being made in his own house. Besides, he got paid. What wouldn't people do for money?

Chad hoped Dick would consider him pretty, pretty enough to get it up for him. Chad checked his make-up in the rearview mirror. He looked good today, he thought, but he had never considered himself as pretty, not even when people told him so. He tended to look at himself with his mother's reproving eyes. In his mother's eyes, whatever anybody had was all that they had, and it was neither enough nor so good that it didn't need improvement. Moreover, flesh was weak. In his mother's mouth the word "flesh" had a creepy sound that made Chad want to pull the sheet over his head, and darkness to make him invisible. To Chad, the plesures of the flesh were all that was good in life.

Chad had worked for Robert, the director, several times, and he knew this was his usual patter. He tried to make his bottoms comfortable because it could get intimidating at times, all those big-dicked tops Robert seemed to find. Today, Robert was saying, "It'll be so easy it'll be like stealing money. No, really, it's easier than that, easier than stealing. It's like sitting back and having money fall on you, hundreds and hundreds of dollars float out of the air and fall on you like spring rain. It's an easy shoot. Easy. Easy."

Chad just nodded his head. Robert was Mister Porn Biz, meaning that he was Mister Bullshit. He knew just the thing to say, just the anecdote to tell to get a boy laughing, and forgetting about the hard work to come. Bernard always said

that Robert could sell sin to Jesus. When he first heard that, Chad laughed. Maybe he could sell sin to their Jesus, he had thought, but certainly he couldn't sell anything at all to the Jesus of his mother and of his youth. Listening to Robert in his head as he closed the door of the bathroom, never really believing anything that he said, but going along with it anyway, and he started giving himself his ritual enema. While he prepared himself, he looked in the mirror.

God, Chad thought, *I really am pretty, even when grimacing in pain.* That was it, he had decided long ago, he could look good while he was suffering, and that was his secret. He never tired of looking at himself being fucked. It really was more fun watching it than it was actually doing it. He cleaned himself completely, then took some deep breaths before going into the bedroom where the action would be filmed.

Chad walked into the bedroom and there, sitting on the edge of the bed, was Dick. Dick looked away, and Chad wondered if he'd done something to offend him. Then he looked back. Now what Chad saw looked like desire right there in his eyes. Pools of it. Deep blue swirling currents of it that threatened to suck Chad down.

Chad had never felt such an immediate reaction. He stood there, staring at Dick while the crew got ready.

Robert picked up on the fact that Dick seemed to be responding to Chad and told them to just go into it. One of the cameras on him to catch the close-up, Chad ran his tongue over his lips, looking at Dick's erection and moaning. He opened his mouth, imagining Dick's huge meat between his teeth. As the fantasy unfolded, his hands sought his own cock. It was hard, just as he had known it would be. The flesh ached and throbbed, begging to be sucked and licked and squeezed. He started panting and pulling on his cock.

Dick was watching, but Chad couldn't really believe it. Surely, this stud was teasing him. "Probably straight as a board," Chad mumbled to himself. Yet he could not help but imagine all wild and wonderful things happening when he was with Dick. Chad could smell sex, and he knew it wasn't just his. He looked down at Dick's incredibly long prick, hard, mouth-watering. Chad looked around the room, seeking direction, wondering what Robert wanted him to do next. He looked over and saw Dick was still watching him. His eyes were inviting Chad to take over. But Chad only went so far. He turned and stood with his ass in Dick's face. With two fingers joined together, Dick searched for the opening. And when he found it, he shoved his fingers in, deep inside Chad. Then he started finger-fucking him real good. He added another finger and smiled at the tightness. Chad made the walls tighten as Dick continued, and he found himself getting ready to climax. Chad slowed down; he couldn't come now.

Suddenly, Dick removed his fingers and stood behind Chad. Soon bolt after bolt of red-hot sex shot through him. But Chad couldn't come because all he could think about was how big Dick really was. He nearly swooned; he was beside himself, wanting Dick to fuck him harder.

"Oh, keep fucking me, stud. Fuck me real good!"

"Oh, yeah," Robert crooned, making his first pronouncement on the electric scene he was capturing on film.

As a rule, Dick was not a very imaginative lover; he just kept doing what he knew would drive a gay boy crazy. But Chad was turning him on uncontrollably. Growling like a tomcat on the prowl, Dick bent down and started kissing Chad's shoulders and neck. His cock moving in and out so fast, he knew Chad could feel the friction.

When Chad heard Dick crying and cooing above his head, he began to moan, shaking his head back and forth real hard. Dick clutched Chad's head, began kissing his cheek, then his mouth. Dick got really worked up and started fucking Chad much, much harder.

Robert was overjoyed. He'd never seen Dick carry on this way with a bottom. He shouted to the boys to keep on.

Chad was soon aching and throbbing, not knowing pain from pleasure any longer, then deciding they were the same. Dick let go of Chad's head and held onto his sides. He shoved Chad to the floor and spread his legs wide. The next thing Chad knew, Dick's cock was back inside him. He could swear his ass was now on fire. Dick hauled him up so Chad was on his hands and knees. Chad smiled and swayed his hips back and forth seductively. Dick slapped the buttocks, then held Chad's hips steady and parted the lips of his ass and eased his way gently back inside.

Now Dick took it very slowly, going a little bit deeper each time. Slowly, gently. Chad squealed when he felt Dick plunge it all the way inside of him.

No cock had ever been in him this far, Chad thought. Dick gripped the bottom's ass on either side, letting him know he was getting ready to fuck him to orgasm. Chad tried to keep from screaming, but Dick's orgasm made his legs tremble.

He'd never had a cock that big before. But oh, it felt so good! When Dick pulled out of him, Chad whimpered like a baby.

Dick came across Chad's back, the cameras catching the close-up from different angles. Then what happened next was unlike anything Chad had ever felt. Dick pushed his cock right back up the bottom's ass so hard and so deep that Chad could not stifle his scream. Then Chad began rocking back and forth as Dick continued the fuck.

For the first time, Chad became aware of the cameras. Both were recording him now, and he heard Robert urging him to come.

Riding the wave, so close, so close. Chad felt it coming and it was so hot. Dick was fucking him so hard and so fast, he knew he'd be walking crooked for a week. The orgasm rushing through him and through his cock was the biggest he'd had in ages. The actors rocked and swayed and bucked for at least two minutes. Panting, Dick rested his head against Chad's back.

"That's a wrap!" Robert yelled.

It was over. Chad needed Dick to help him get dressed. Dick had fucked him so hard, he was sore and aching and burning all over. The lights went off two seconds after he was dressed. Dick and Chad just sat there smiling at each other as the crowd shuffled out of the bedroom.

For the first time, Chad noticed a tall, gaunt man who now entered the bedroom and came over to them. He offered Chad his hand. "I'm Howard. This is my house, and you two were unbelievable."

"Thanks," Dick said, beaming.

Howard sat down on the bed next to them and began talking. Chad wasn't paying any attention. He wanted nothing more than to leave, to rest. But he didn't want to leave without Dick. Suddenly, he felt the need to pee. He excused himself and went to the bathroom. When he returned to the bedroom, Dick had taken off his pants and was bending over Howard, fucking him.

Chad was hardly surprised; awed would be more like it. Dick's boundless energy amazed him. He knew that Howard must have made the stud a very nice offer. Still humping, Dick turned his head. Chad looked far from happy but there was something else in his eyes. Dick knew the look; it was a look of passion, that a whore like Chad was always ready for more sex.

Dick said, "Come on over here." Grabbing Howard by the hips, Dick continued fucking him while Chad climbed to the top of the bed and put his limp cock into Howard's pouty mouth.

Howard had finally stopped talking, and he was definitely enjoying himself, sucking Chad to hardness while being fucked by Dick.

Chad was getting off on watching Dick; the stud really seemed to be having a good time doing what he did best. Still fucking, Dick moved his hand around to wrap his fist around Howard's cock and started jerking. Yanking his meat added to the pleasure of fucking his tight, skinny ass. So did watching his head bobbing up and down on Chad's luscious young cock. He pounded Howard's ass harder when the man seemed close to coming. Just as he felt Howard's cock swell in his hand, he looked up into Chad's emerald eyes.

He remembered how Chad had loved being fucked, and as if he was showing off, he started plugging Howard hard and fast.

"Ah, yeah," Howard groaned, "fuck me good."

Chad saw Dick was enjoying it, even though there was no love in it, the way there seemed to be when he was fucking Chad. This was just raw sex, just hammering his stiff cock in and out of this hot, tight fuck hole. "Oh, Dick, fuck him good," Chad moaned as Howard went back down on his cock.

Just then shot after shot of Howard's jism fired out of his cock.

The trio ended up in a heap, Dick's softening dick still up Howard's ass, and Chad's semi-hard cock in his mouth. They relaxed like that for a couple of minutes, then Chad and Dick rolled away. Howard promptly fell asleep, satisfied.

As Chad and Dick pulled their pants back on, they kissed each other and

Dick said, "We make quite a team, don't we?"

Chad smiled. "Somehow, I think this is just the beginning...."

VI. THE SPECTACLE

Decidedly, there was no man in the world quite like Dick Bliss. He was a Don Juan, an exhibitionist, a sodomist and he had the biggest dick the porn industry had seen up to that time.

By the age of twenty, he had made dozens of straight porn films and had had all the experiences that might be expected of a whore who had spent many years in a brothel. And yet, to many minds, there was no more seductive, fresh, sexier stud in all of America.

Early in his career, when he wasn't fornicating for the cameras, he could be found taking it off, and showing it off, for clients around the world willing to pay hundreds of dollars an hour for the pleasure of seeing his cock rise to the occasion. When not otherwise engaged, Dick became notorious for a stage show wherein he screwed a different girl on stage every Wednesday, or at least it appeared he screwed them, for, eventually, he had developed an aversion for sticking his cock into a cunt. This was rumored to have been a reaction to having caught some terrible malady from a female rock star who took him on tour with her, got him coked up, and had her way with him for several days.

When he came out of his drug-induced stupor, he was broke and was talked into making gay porn. He was an immediate sensation, and soon he became an attraction at certain showplaces attracting that specialized crowd. The making of a spectacle in public certainly became one of Dick's trademarks. He told a reporter once that he envied dogs because they fuck on the street, and about how he used to stop to watch them, shamelessly, with such an amused curiosity that people would stand around him and watch him watching them.

Even when Dick took a lover, the famous, bearded writer Larry Lincoln, the desire for creating a spectacle remained. There was no equal to his pleasure in being watched by his lovers or strangers while he engaged in sex.

His lover's large house in Holmby Hills became the scene where Dick presented himself to anyone who wished to watch. For his part, Larry found great excitement in watching Dick entertain clients, engage in masturbation, and Larry often participated in the escapades.

One day in early spring, Larry returned home from a business trip to find a young blond named Chad in residence. Chad, Dick explained to his lover by phone the night before, had been his recent co-star in a porn film and Dick told Larry he had never been with so provocative a bottom. Larry was greeted by Chad, and was delighted with such a graceful welcome and seductive smile. He agreed with Dick that Chad was the epitome of blond and boyish sexuality.

In a twinkling of an eye, they were naked. Chad first began to kiss Dick's body passionately all over, while Dick was stretched on the bed. Chad attacked the hidden recesses of Dick's armpits, his asshole, then sucked the tips of his nipples. Then kneeling, he pressed Dick's prick into his mouth.

Seeing Larry standing next to the bed, Chad straightened up on his knees, offered his mouth to his prick. Larry's was a rather short but robust and well-formed prick.

Larry took the lovely head of the effeminate young man in his hands, and plunged his prick between the lips he offered him. He mouth-fucked him for several moments, then could stand it no longer. The boy raised his ass, and Larry knelt behind him. He opened the furrow of Chad's bottom. Chad begged, "Put your tongue in it, lick me all around inside."

Larry was amazed that Chad seemed to act with such natural grace, squirming and wriggling sensuously as his tongue darted to and fro in his ass. "Well," Dick called to him, "what's keeping you from stickin' your prick in? Don't you see that he wants it? Fuck him, open him up for me."

Chad took Larry's cock between two fingers and applied it to his asshole.

"Push," Chad said. "Oh, yes, there you are...a little more...yes, yes. That's it. Oh, shit."

Dick was right, Larry quickly discovered. Never before had he enjoyed such an asshole, which responded with the most delicious contractions to the spasmodic reactions of his prick. Chad's ass was engulfing it, and Larry became immobilized on his knees, his hands clamped to Chad's hips, his eyes glazed and fixed on that luscious bottom. When he felt Chad's asshole clench against his prick, he seized his buttocks, and fucked with such a vigor that Chad had to let up on Dick's cock and cry out. Larry plunged in with little thrusts until he was in to his balls. It was too delightful, and he wished to prolong the delight. He withdrew his prick and slapped the buttocks gently, then kissed them, over and over. He drew the lovely young reddened ass toward him and, after drawing his prick back along the ass crack, letting Dick see how excited he was, with a single massive stroke he plunged in to the balls again.

As he thrust into him, he heard Chad sob and groan and then suddenly Chad was crying out in a different tone. He had allowed Dick's cock to slip from his mouth and Dick was coming. Chad's face was crushed against Dick's spurting prick. Delivering himself up to his own orgasm, Larry made two or three more thrusts, and discharged into Chad. Drawing himself back on his knees, clinging to the boy's bottom, he savored the spasmodic contractions with which the walls of Chad's ass squeezed the head of his prick.

Chad, squeezing Dick's cock between his thumb and index finger, milked out of it a thick drop of spunk and collected it on the tip of his tongue. Then, greedily staring at the biggest cock in porn, he fondled it, caressed it with his mouth and nose, rolled his cheeks against the organ.

Then he held the prick by the root, while he caressed the balls. Then, as if seized by an erotic madness, he arched, whinnied, and rolled his body over him in frenzied contortions, rubbing against him, and soon the sublime, shattering peak of orgasm seized Chad.

They took a little respite, then began a new bout of fucking. Both of them

had to go to work to give Dick back his vigor. Dick was on all fours over Chad's face. Chad's tongue flecked and darted, slipping up the shaft, titillating the tip, his lips rubbing against the pubic hairs, sucking the prick gluttonously.

Larry bent his head to see closely, delighting in Chad's talent. Chad, who by now knew all the artifices well, was aware of one whose effect upon Dick would be immediate. As the young lad sucked Dick, he rubbed his finger into Dick's asshole, and Dick's prick suddenly swelled, while Larry attacked Dick's anus with little flicks of his tongue.

Once Dick was fully hard, Chad then squatted down in reverse over Dick. Chad groped between his thighs and seized with his hand Dick's member, then sank down and buried it into his ass. Dick clutched Chad's shoulders, and plunged his prick into the blond. Larry leaned over to see. Chad cried out, arching and squirming as he adjusted to the pain. Larry stood back a bit to witness the passionate coupling of two magnificent specimens of manhood. Shuddering at the spectacle, he began jerking his prick.

Chad could now embrace both bodies. He took Larry's erection into his hand and started sucking it, making it jerk, contract, and throb. In his piston-like movement, Dick made Chad's body shudder, and he quickened the lunges of his stabbing tool. Doubly used, Chad was soon swooning under the penetration of his ass by Dick and his mouth by Larry. He fucked the prick violently now, and amid the groans and sobs and gasps. As Larry came in Chad's mouth, he told him that he had brought him the greatest pleasure that he had ever experienced in all his life. Larry thanked him and showed his gratitude by a thousand little kisses.

VII. SOLITARY PLEASURES

Noah was the first to admit he masturbated often during his adolescence. At that time it was a curiosity, something new to do, and there was no risk of ever getting tired of it. And Noah still did it today, a lot. Noah would do it before he went out looking for sex, to take the edge off. The whole secret, the whole attraction of this pleasure was that it was *solitary*. Even in a crowd, it was a solitary pleasure. One of Noah's favorite things to do was to go to the Go-Go Lounge and watch the dancers.

Noah was at the Go-Go one night when his life changed forever. He was sitting at one of the tables way in the back, smoking quietly. It was then that he saw the stud he'd seen dance with one of the girls on Wednesdays, when they stage a "live sex show" and bring in a male to "do it" with the girls. The stud's name was Dick Bliss, and Noah had tipped him generously, so generously that Dick apparently remembered him. He came towards Noah, shook his hand and asked if he could sit down beside him. Noah considered himself bisexual, and if he ever got it on with a man, it would be with one like Dick: virile, sexy, a laborer type. Besides, Dick was billed as having "the biggest dick in the West," and Noah saw Dick had the longest member he'd ever seen, although the night he saw his act with the star dancer, Pussy, he never got it fully erect.

The waitress brought them beers and after she left, Dick looked at Noah for a few seconds, then said: "You lookin' for some action tonight?"

It was a bold move Noah admired his straight-forwardness but Noah wasn't sure what he had in mind. Noah's heart raced. He was normally shy, and found it hard to pick people up. Noah nodded, and in a half-embarrassed, half-amused way, asked, "But aren't you dancing tonight?"

"No. I just came in to get my check from last week. Then I saw you...." Dick lifted the beer bottle and moved his tongue suggestively over the rim. Taking a sip, he closed his eyes and leaned his head back a little, moved his chair closer to Noah, their legs now touching under the table.

Noah welcomed the night closing around him, the potential of sex with this stud. He hadn't had sex with anyone for weeks. The music in the background became faint. The voices of many conversations merged around him. He thought only of the need deep inside of him. And wanting to give way to this pressing desire, a desire becoming more urgent as he thought about Dick's show last week. An unforgettable show. An incredible cock, fully hard or not. Knowing that this moment might never come again, Noah pressed his hand into Dick's crotch. As Noah stroked him, the excitement became unbearable, especially once he let Noah undo his trousers, exposing himself fully. Knowing he was in a public place, but not caring Noah only wanted to touch the stud's equipment.

He remembered again the sex show, how much Dick loved showing it off, this huge meat. How all eyes watched the dancers with envy and longing. Noah thought about how it would be to lose himself in an explosion of passion. Noah felt the world around them receding, his vision blurring. He saw only the stud, heard only his moans. Nothing else mattered. As he stroked Dick's cock contentedly, Pussy started dancing.

Dick pushed Noah's hand away and zipped up his pants. "Come on," he said. "We've got fifteen minutes."

Stunned, Noah obeyed, without any idea what this would cost him, or really what was involved. Dick took Noah by the arm and led him backstage and to Pussy's dressing room. It was a narrow room, just big enough to contain a dressing table mounted with a mirror surrounded by lights and a swivel chair, a sink, a screen with G-strings draped over it, and a small iron bed on which lay a large fluffy bear.

Dick pushed Noah to the bed and stood before him, a colossus to Noah's mind, everything a man should be.

As if sensing Noah's desire, Dick clasped his hand behind his head, pulling him toward him. Noah was shy and tentative at first, pausing for a moment, looking up into Dick's steely eyes. Dick smiled, placed his hands around Noah's face and drew it tight into his crotch. The bulge against his flushed cheek, Noah could tell Dick was swelling with desire.

It seemed they were both filled with so much longing, for different reasons, but wanting the same thing. There had been no mention of payment, which

surprised Noah. Cautiously, Noah unzipped Dick's pants, knowing of the treasure he would find underneath. It seemed Dick was waiting for him, even *longing* for Noah's mouth.

Now his voice took on a cruel edge: "Show me, man, show me how only a man can give another man head, show me how you do it!"

Dick responded to Noah's movements as Noah caressed him at the very heart and soul of his being. Dick moaned, and Noah began panting with excitement. Noah kneaded the swollen flesh, smiled as it became hard and erect. Noah continued caressing it with warmth and passion.

"Suck it," Dick demanded.

Noah parted his lips slowly, and kissed the head of it, tasted the salty, sweet treasure at the piss-slit.

"Ooh," Dick murmured.

Noah sucked the head into his mouth, breathed the musky scent of Dick's crotch. He moved his hand up the shaft. The cock throbbed, as if it was simply aching for release.

Certain Dick would explode at any moment, Noah closed his lips around the cock, sucking him. His mouth opened wider, pulling inch after inch into his mouth. Hot and wet, sucking him deeper and deeper inside of him. Noah went on sucking it contentedly, like a baby with a bottle after the initial hunger has passed. Dick moaned, began moving his hips in time with the jerking of Noah's own cock. Soon Dick was urging Noah to lose himself in a frenzy of orgasm. Noah wanted him so badly. Wanted to come for him, if that was way he wanted it. But he also wanted to fill his mouth with his salty-sweet cum. Noah couldn't contain himself; he came, the jism spurting onto the floor. Although he had let the cock flop from his mouth, he continued lavishing it with kisses.

Still panting, Noah gazed up into Dick's eyes. Now the look on his face was of amusement, and in that smooth, firm voice he said, "You need more. Much more."

A shiver of desire ran through Noah. "Come home with me then."

Dick smiled. "No, you come home with me."

As they drove down Wilshire Boulevard in Noah's Mustang, on the way to Holmby Hills, Dick explained that he had a wealthy lover, Larry, and he also had a visitor named Chad. Noah, Dick stressed, would enjoy them. Enjoy them *all.*

Noah had never had a three-way, let alone a four-way. The prospect excited him beyond his wildest imagination.

"You're beautiful," Dick told him. It was a line that had worked many times before, perhaps because Dick meant it every time. The line worked this time too, it seemed. Noah's body softened, lips tilting up to smile at Dick, to beg for a kiss.

It seemed to Noah that all Dick wanted was to treat him gently, to kiss away those lines on his forehead. He seemed to want to taste the sweat at the back of

his neck while he was fucking him, to give him pleasure he had never known. Yes, Noah felt, this stud wanted to fuck him until he screamed for mercy.

Noah was Dick's type: a small, slightly effeminate young man, reserved, and perhaps sexually confused. Dick also liked blonds, and he fingered Noah's hair as they drove along, admiring the sheen of it, the color, the cut. Noah revealed that he was a hairdresser, and would love to cut Dick's hair sometime. Noah kept wondering what this "date" with Dick was going to cost him. He wanted to offer Dick something, to see where that might lead.

Dick laughed. "I've never been with a hairdresser before. At least, that I know of." He took Noah's hand in his and brought it to his dark, curly hair. "What do you think you could do with it?"

"I'll have to give it some thought. I really like it the way it is." Noah withdrew his hand, put it back on the wheel. What Noah was thinking about as they drove along was not Dick's hair. Having just sucked the stud's prick, he wondered just what might be in store for him when they got to wherever it was they were going.

Larry's house was nestled back from the road, deep in a forest of trees, and you couldn't really tell how large a place it was. One thing, Noah had lived in Los Angeles long enough to know he was in rarefied territory here, and that Larry could easily afford to keep someone like Dick in residence to cater to his every whim.

Larry and Chad were in the master bedroom, in the gigantic bed covered with soft pillows and silks, watching television. Dick introduced Noah, and told them he was taking Noah to the bath for a "little soak."

Dick tore off his sweatshirt and Noah's body beat once more with a deep hunger for this man. He kissed and licked a path down his belly to his pubic hair. He unzipped Dick's pants and let them drop to the floor.

Noah could not hold back a moment longer, and he ran his hands up over the stud's naked body, over his thighs, hips and waist. On his knees, his face level with the stud's beautiful cock, Noah licked Dick's upper thighs, his balls, then moved his tongue quickly to the swelling shaft, then down in long strokes along the heavy veins, fingers brushing and caressing Dick's balls. His tongue danced over Dick's cock teasingly. Dick moaned and cried out, his body tense with concentration, hips moving beneath Noah's mouth as Noah licked and sucked and coaxed the pleasure through the stud's body. Noah's hands caressed him, then clutched Dick's buttocks, lifting him up to his mouth. Feeling Dick tighten his ass and pump gently, carefully into Noah's mouth, Noah worked the swelling cock.

Suddenly, Dick pulled Noah up and tore his clothes from his body. Dick turned him around.

Chad and Larry appeared at the door of the sumptuous bathroom. They observed the skillful way Dick opened Noah up to his cock. As both men gazed at the inviting ass, their cocks stood erect, and being the proper host, Larry

offered Chad first entry. But Chad said he'd rather watch Dick fuck Noah first, placing a hand on his distended organ. With a pant and a sigh, he suggested to Larry, "Play with it while we watch the show."

They left it to Dick to spread open the ass cheeks, and he pressed a finger in there to test the tightness. "Hmmmm," he moaned. As he finger-fucked Noah, he decided he needed his cock caressed and toyed with. He motioned to Larry to bring his mouth to it. Larry was always happy to take Dick's aching prick into his mouth. Dick leaned back and put his hand on the silken hair, forcing Larry's head to bob up and down on his swollen prick. As he was pressed into a sudden frenzy of excitement, he almost wanted to shoot his load into his mouth right there and then, but looking up and seeing that Noah was anxious to be fucked, he positioned the butt up in the air, whereupon Chad moved forward and began licking and rimming the ass. "Now it's your turn," Chad said, as he wiped his mouth. Larry felt Dick's now fully hard cock and lapped and stroked Noah's ass, then backed away to make room for Dick to do his thing.

Carefully Dick insinuated the cock head into Noah, then, pressing it back and forth, moved on him, up and down, up slowly, teasing, then down hard. Finally, Noah was taking him deep inside his body, head back, sucking him in, body arched and sweating, closing tightly on him as Dick rode him, wanting him harder and deeper, desperately wanting it.

Chad's mind was spinning at the undaunted sexual energy of Dick as he watched the stud over Noah. Dick fucked him with all his might, and then, as Noah's orgasm approached, Chad seized his prick and sucked it into his mouth. This broke Noah's concentration, and he held back, enjoying the suck.

Chad let Noah's cock free a few moments later and stood with Larry beside the fucking men, licking and caressing their skin. No parts of their rutting bodies escaped their kisses, their sucking bites, the arousing touches of their expert tongues. At last Chad could no longer play the voyeur and flung himself into the fray. He got in front of Noah and pushed his ass toward him.

"Yeah," Dick said to Noah, "if you want to come as you've never come before, fuck him."

Noah took Chad by his buttocks and pressed his prick straight inside. A groan of happiness broke the silence. As he pumped his throbbing member into the younger blond, Dick stepped up his attack on Noah's anus. Meanwhile, Larry brought his fingers to Dick's asshole.

Suddenly, a wave of pleasure overcame Dick as Larry's swift tongue began to flick over and around his exposed anus. One finger was plunged into Dick's asshole, while the fingers of his other hand stroked Dick's balls. There was such sensuality overloading Dick that soon his cum was spurting in explosive blasts inside Noah's ass. This set Noah off, and then Chad came, but not before Larry went to his cock in order to take the blond's delicious load in his mouth. For several moments, their bodies were wriggling and twisting and writhing in a fleshy knot.

After a light meal to give them back their strength, Chad and Dick put on a show. They were insatiable, those two performers, possessed of a passion that seemed to take new vigor from its own excesses.

At the end, Noah and Chad knelt, doggie-fashion, on the huge bed, ready to be fucked. Dick and Larry stood behind them. As the two older men began fingering the assholes of the younger ones, Larry kissed Dick, and congratulated him on finding a gem like Noah. It seemed that now, at last, their ménage was complete.

NATURE BOY
by Frank Brooks

Between church and Sunday dinner, Buddy named after his pa's favorite pro wrestler in the olden days, Nature-Boy Buddy Rogers, slunk out behind the pigpen to sun himself and stay out of sight of the house. His father couldn't abide the sight of an idle boy and would sure as hell, if he caught him, put him to work slaving at some unnecessary chore until the dinner bell rang if he didn't drag him into the woodshed first for a bare-assed whipping "for good measure." Pa was big on discipline, and Buddy felt the crack of a switch across his bare butt at least once a day, and usually more.

It was a blistering-hot August morning, and Buddy was glad to be shed of his strait-jacket church clothes and viselike leather shoes, which felt three sizes too small. Since he'd been a barefoot boy in these hills all his life, all shoes felt like torture instruments to him. Now he was dressed in his favorite outfit, a pair of tight jean cutoffs so short that they hardly contained his oversized cock and balls. A little rag around his middle was all the clothing Buddy needed or cared for.

He'd intended to laze in the sun behind the woodpile back of the pigpen one of his favorite hiding and jack-off places, but as he was rounding the corner of the pigpen he heard whispers, giggles, and other sounds that put him on alert. It didn't take him but a few seconds to figure out what was happening and stealthily he climbed the pile of stacked firewood so he could lie on his belly on top of it and peer down behind it. His heart was pounding and his entire body throbbed with anticipation and excitement.

Just as he suspected, there they were! Standing in the grass not more than ten feet from Buddy's woodpile perch, his older brother, Teddy-Ray, was mounted on the bare behind of Jenny-Sue, Teddy-Ray's betrothed. They were both still in their church clothes. Teddy-Ray had his hard cock sticking out of the unzipped fly of his suit pants and into Jenny-Sue, who was bending over in front of him, her dress up around her waist, her panties down around her ankles. Teddy-Ray gripped her bare, upturned girl-ass as he fucked his gleaming cock into her pussy hole again and again. Jenny-Sue gasped and giggled and moaned like a cow with each in-out motion, and Teddy-Ray grunted like a bull. Buddy could hear the squishy noises of their fucking organs and could smell their sex scents. As he watched them, he worked his swollen cock, which was nearly busting out of his cutoffs, against a round slab of firewood.

"Oh Teddy-Ray, I feel it!" Jenny-Sue crooned.

"Are you gonna cum, darlin'?" panted Teddy-Ray.

"Oh Teddy-Ray, yes, yes!"

"Me too!"

The fucking pair went into moaning, jerking spasms and Buddy swore he could hear his brother's cum splashing inside Jenny-Sue's body. He got so excited, squirming atop the woodpile, that he dislodged a loose slab of firewood

and instantly found himself crashing, along with several wood chunks, onto the ground not five feet from Teddy-Ray and Jenny-Sue.

"Filthy little pervert!" Teddy-Ray gasped, cum still spurting from his cock as it popped prematurely out of Jenny-Sue's pussy. He was panting as if he'd just escaped being hit by a freight train.

Jenny-Sue, still spasming and disoriented, fell over as Teddy-Ray let go of her ass. "What?" she blathered. "What?"

Buddy, shaking his head to clear it, scrambled to his feet as Teddy-Ray lunged towards him. Then he darted away, sprinting across the pasture, and soon dove into the woods. He thought he was safe, but before he could turn around to see for sure, Teddy-Ray tackled him, pinned him down on his back, and sat on his bare chest. Teddy-Ray's big cock, still slick with pussy and cum, throbbed in Buddy's face, and Teddy-Ray banged him across the cheeks and nose with it.

"You gull-darned little runt! Is this what you wanna see, sissy-boy? Take a good look! Is this what you want?" Teddy-Ray shoved his cock into Buddy's mouth. "Choke on it!" He forced all eight inches down Buddy's throat, scouring Buddy's freckled nose with his groin-hair. "Suck it, whore-boy!"

Buddy took every inch without choking and did as his brother ordered, sucking like a calf, smacking his lips around the hard, veiny tusk of fuckmeat, twirling and wiggling his young but experienced tongue at the most sensitive parts of his older brother's cock. Teddy-Ray's loins worked almost involuntarily, grinding his cock in Buddy's face.

"Oh fuck!" Teddy-Ray moaned. "Oh shit!" His eyes rolled back and he grabbed Buddy's blond head, fucking Buddy's mouth, pumping hot jets of cum down Buddy's throat. When he'd finished, he rolled off.

Buddy lay there panting, licking his lips, still savoring the taste of his brother's sweaty, pussy-flavored cock. He swore he could feel his brother's hot load pooled in his stomach.

Teddy-Ray stood up and tried to tuck his half-hard cock back into his suitpants. "I got grass stains on my church clothes now, you little shit! Ma's gonna kill me. I oughta break your arm!"

In the distance, the dinner bell started clanging.

Teddy-Ray fixed Buddy with a glare. "You say a word to Pa about me and Jenny-Sue humping behind the woodpile and I'll give him the lowdown about you sneaking off down to the wayside all the time when you're supposed to be doing chores. Pa would love to hear about that."

"I ain't saying nothing," Buddy said. "I ain't no snitch."

...

"What's the world coming to?" Pa said. "Ma, more potatoes. The reverend says there's sodomites in our very own midst. What next! We already got pinko commie hippies living just about on our very doorstep, and now sodomites. Lord help us! Ma, I asked for more potatoes."

When Buddy tried to take more potatoes for himself as he was passing them

from his ma to his pa, his pa yanked the potato bowl out of his hand.

"You've had your share, boy," Pa said. "I swear, you're part hog. Eat us out of house and home, you would, if we didn't watch you." Pa piled the remaining potatoes onto his own plate.

"Nature-Boy needs a haircut," Ma said.

"That he does," Pa said. "Looks like a sheepdog, or one of them blasphemous hippies. I'll get out the sheep shears tonight."

"I don't need no haircut," Buddy said.

"No back-talk!" said Pa.

"I think he looks kinda cute with the hair in his eyes," Jenny-Sue said, nudging Buddy's bare toes under the table with her own. She'd kicked off a shoe and was trying to play footsie with him.

Buddy pulled his foot away, blushing. He didn't dare look up from his plate at Jenny-Sue. Although he had no serious interest in Jenny-Sue, or in any other girl for that matter, he sometimes wondered what it would be like to fuck her just once. And Jenny-Sue was willing — too willing! Ever since she'd caught him jacking off out back, she'd been trying to get him alone with her. His cock apparently had impressed her because it was bigger than Teddy-Ray's eight inches.

"He's starting to look like a heathen hippie," Pa said, "and I'm going to shear him like a sheep. And boy, I'm warning you, if you take your shoes off once more during church service, I'll drag you outa there in front of the whole congregation and tan your hide on the church steps. That I will."

"I don't know what gets into him," Ma said, shaking her head. "Bare feet in church! I never!"

"Bad influences, that's what," Pa said. "Like the reverend preached: sodomites in our very midst. And heathen hippies. Bad, sinful influences all around us. I thought I'd never see the day when God-fearing hill folk like the Johnsons would be drove off the land by foreclosures and then have a tribe of heathen hippies move in, almost on our very own doorstep."

"I thought you had a feud going with the Johnsons," Jenny-Sue said. "I thought you were glad to see 'em go."

"Just a thirty-year feud," Teddy-Ray said under his breath.

"Never you mind," said Pa, giving Teddy-Ray a warning scowl. "At least they weren't heathen hippies. If I look out my front window and see one of them long-haired heathens strutting by, by heaven, I'll blast their behinds with buckshot, I will."

"Amen!" Ma said. "Send 'em back where they belong."

"Ain't the old Johnson homestead all of three miles away?" asked Jenny-Sue. "I doubt we'll see any hippies strutting by here."

"And sodomites," Pa said, ignoring her. "I wish I know'd who. They say you can't even tell with some of 'em. In our very own midst, says the reverend. I wish sometimes the reverend would be more particular with his words and do

some specifying. In our very own midst, he says. I wonder who."

Teddy-Ray smirked at Buddy, who kicked him under the table. Teddy-Ray kicked him back and the table jerked.

"What's going on?" Pa said.

"Nature-Boy's kicking me again under the table," Teddy-Ray said.

"That's it, I've had it with you, boy!" Pa pushed back his chair and got up. "First he disgraces the very house of the Lord, baring his filthy feet during a church service, and now he's being disrespectful at the Lord's table. Outside, boy! Get movin'!" He caught Buddy by the ear and dragged him, squirming, out of the kitchen and to the woodshed. There he pushed Buddy down over a hay bale, yanked his shorts down enough to bare his ass, and laid into him with a recently cut willow switch.

Buddy jerked with each crack of the switch across his bare ass, but he didn't cry out. It had been years since his Pa had managed to get so much as a whimper out of him. In fact, he seemed now to half enjoy the warm, tingling glow he felt in his ass cheeks for hours after a whupping. Sometimes the feeling even made him horny enough to jack off.

"Had enough?" Pa said, wheezing from the exertion of the whipping. "You keep misbehaving and there's a lot more willow waiting for that skinny behind of yours. Now, this afternoon I want you to go out with the scythe and cut down every last thistle on the property, and I don't want you coming back here till it's done."

"It'll take me ten years!" Buddy whined, pulling up his cutoffs and turning around. "There's ten zillion thistles out there."

"No back-talk, just do as you're told. You comb all hundred and eighty acres for thistles and don't come back here till you've scythed down every last one of 'em. If it takes you fifty years, so be it."

"Maybe I won't never ever come back."

"Suit yourself," Pa said. "Don't expect me to come looking for you."

...

Buddy went to the edge of the property, out as far from the house as he could get. After a half hour of scything down thistles and getting a heap of thistle thorns in his soles, he'd had enough. It had to be over 100 degrees and he was not only drowning in sweat, but was so thirsty he could hardly swallow. He slipped into the woods and soon was refreshing himself beside a spring. After drinking like a camel, he shucked off his shorts and flopped down on the mossy spring-bank in the sunshine and slowly worked the foreskin on his rigid cock, thinking about Teddy-Ray fucking Jenny-Sue.

As he jacked himself, he sensuously worked his over-sized bare feet and toes and squirmed against the soft, sun-warmed moss. It seemed he was always horny these days, always in need of getting off. If he didn't get off five times a day he went crazy.

"Hot damnnn!" he moaned, squeezing his smooth legs together and pointing

his toes as the jism squirted out across his flat brown stomach and he felt hot, throbbing sensations in every part of his body. He humped his tight loins until he'd jacked out every drop, then scooped up the warm cum-gobs with his fingertips and sucked them up. He never wasted cum. He liked to eat it.

Back in the field, he scythed for about five more minutes before he'd again had enough — enough forever, as far as he was concerned. It felt like he'd been working ten years already and he'd hardly even begun to cut down all the thistles on the property. Fuck it! He thought. Besides, he was hornier now than before he'd jacked off. His cock was still fully hard and the taste of his own cum had made him hungry for more.

Leaving the scythe lying where he'd dropped it, he set off through the woods and a half hour later emerged onto the county highway. After a short walk, he arrived at the old wooden outhouses. There wasn't a car in sight, but he knew that wouldn't be the case for long.

In the men's outhouse, with its two stalls and piss trough outside them, he took off his shorts in the stall closest to the piss trough and sat down on the wooden bench that served as a toilet. There was a saucer-sized hole in both side-walls of his stall, so he could look into the stall to his right and out at the piss trough to his left. As soon as he sat down, he started working his throbbing boy-meat. He loved this place. In fact, he often fantasized leaving home for good and moving in here permanently.

The walls of the outhouse, both inside and outside the stalls, were a mess of graffiti, both words and pictures, some of them Buddy's own. Anybody who entered the shed-like building knew instantly that this was a veritable den of iniquity and had been one since the olden days. Arrows pointing at the glory holes told how to use them: STICK IT IN HERE FOR A GOOD TIME!

As expected, Buddy didn't have long to wait for some company. Soon he heard a car with a defective muffler squeal into the wayside. Car doors slammed. Giggles and shrieks. The voices of a teenager and his girlfriend. She went into the women's outhouse, he into Buddy's.

The new arrival stood at the urinal trough and pulled a big floppy cock out of a pair of white shorts. Buddy, his freckled nose in the glory hole and hardly a foot from the pissing cock, inhaled the heady aroma of fresh piss and licked his lips. The teenager had hardly finished pissing when he turned to the side and shoved his dripping, stiffening cock into Buddy's mouth.

"Suck it, man! The fuckin' bitch won't put out today. I got blue balls. Oh man, eat that hog!"

As Buddy sucked, the teenager hung from the top of the partition, fucking Buddy's mouth through the glory hole and sighing contentedly as Buddy pleasured him.

Soon the boy's girlfriend was whining outside. "Jimmy-Boy, come on, what're you doing in there, I wanna go!"

"Bitch!" the boy whispered, humping faster, fucking Buddy's throat.

"Jimmy-Boy, come on!"

"Fuck you, bitch!" The boy trembled and his bucking cock sent a torrent of spunk down Buddy's gullet. "Ohh fuck!"

Buddy was still sucking as the boy withdrew his cock. Buddy saw tanned, sinewy hands pack away a big cock and watched the boy knock open the screen door, which then slammed shut behind him. The hot rod roared to life and squealed out onto the highway. Buddy relaxed back against the wall, stroking his cock and savoring the taste of the youth's cum as he waited for the next sweaty cock to come sliding through the glory hole.

...

Buddy felt high. It was like all the cocks that had slid between his lips and shot cum down his throat this afternoon had shot energy into him. He felt like he was floating, his whole body extra-alive and a-tingle.

He'd lost count of how many cocks he'd sucked. This had to be a record afternoon. He figured that in three hours he'd sucked at least a dozen cocks, and maybe more. When cocks came sliding through the glory hole they always looked big in fact, huge even though some of them actually weren't. He burped up the taste of jizz shot from those big, sweaty, beautiful cocks he'd sucked off.

It seemed that men and boys were always extra horny on Sunday afternoons, maybe because of the dreary church service with its depressing sermon they'd had to sit through in the morning. Or maybe the sermon, with all its raving about licentiousness and debauchery preachers always seemed to have one-track minds actually set the loins of the men and boys on fire. Maybe he should be thanking the reverend for preaching those "sodomite" sermons of his lately. The reverend was drumming up business for him without intending to.

All joshing aside, Buddy wondered how much the reverend knew. Sometimes when the preacher shouted the word "sodomite" his bulging red eyes caught Buddy's for a moment as they swept over the hushed and aghast congregation. At least Buddy thought the man's wild eyes had caught his own. But maybe he was just imagining it. The reverend might be bluffing with all his shouting about "sodomites in our very midst." He might not know anything at all. Still, it wouldn't be unlikely for the reverend to know about this wayside and what went on here and even who came here. Buddy had sucked off so many cocks here that it seemed impossible that by now word about him hadn't spread all over the state. The fact that Teddy-Ray knew about his wayside cock-sucking troubled him. Teddy-Ray never came around here, so how had he found out?

Buddy was sitting there brooding over these things and wondering if he should jack off now and leave for the day or wait around for a few more cocks to suck. When he did leave, he didn't know where he was going to go, but it wouldn't be home. He had hardly even begun to accomplish the scything chore his pa had assigned him, and he didn't dare go home. The man would beat him to a pulp. In fact, if he never went home again, it would suit him just fine. As he often fantasized, he now imagined himself getting out on the road, putting up his

thumb, and hitchhiking away forever, going somewhere, anywhere, and never coming back. As he was daydreaming, he heard vehicles approaching cars and trucks a whole caravan, it sounded like. That was strange, since it was rare that more than one or two vehicles at a time ever came down this stretch of road, so the sound of so many got him curious and he slipped out of his stall and peeked out the outhouse door.

Three cars and two pickups came squealing off the highway and into the wayside parking lot. A gang of teenaged boys were riding in the backs of both pickups. Buddy recognized some of them bullies and trouble-makers, the kind of boys it was always better to avoid and he knew instinctively that it was time to hightail it out of there. He shimmied into his cutoffs, slipped out the door, and headed straight for the woods.

"There's one," a voice shouted. "Hey you, cocksucker, come back here!"

"Sodomite!" another voice shouted. "Get him!"

Buddy dove into the trees and ran like a deer. He wasn't running from his angry brother now, he was running from merciless bullies who'd probably kill him if they got hold of him. He was running for his life.

...

Drenched with sweat like he'd just climbed dripping out of a stream after a swim, Buddy stumbled out of the woods into the late-afternoon sunshine. He'd escaped, at least for the time being, but in his panic he'd got lost and didn't know where he was until he spotted the farm buildings across the field before him and recognized the old Johnson homestead. Lucky for him, the Johnsons didn't live here anymore or they'd have shot him on sight due to their life-long feud with his pa.

"Hey man, what's happening?" A man sitting in front of one of the farm buildings shouted at him from across the field and waved. He was a tall, bearded man with dark hair that hung past his shoulders in back, and he was naked except for a pair of ragged cutoffs that didn't cover much more of his loins than Buddy's own cutoffs covered his.

Hippie, Buddy thought. He'd seen hippies on TV, but this was the first one he'd ever seen in the for-real and he felt both excitement and nervousness and eyed the man with curiosity and suspicion. He was a muscular man, tanned all over and wearing a beaded headband across his forehead like an Indian. Buddy moved across the field warily as the man called out again, and again motioned him over.

"Whatcha doing?" Buddy asked when he got close enough.

The man was perched on a stool in front of a small round spinning table, playing with a pile of gleaming gray mud that had been piled on it. The small motor that made the table-top spin was humming, and from inside the nearby shed came the loud sound of phonograph music.

"Throwing pots," the man said.

Buddy tensed, ready to dodge if the man threw any pots at him. The hippie

was maybe a little nuts, crazy on LSD or something.

"Watch." The man dug his fingers down into the mess of spinning mud, which soon rose up between his fingers and thumbs and started to resemble a bowl. "Now we bake it and we got ourselves a vase. I'm Steve, by the way." He reached out, but Buddy declined to shake his muddy hand.

Buddy introduced himself, as usual explaining his name: "Nature-Boy Buddy, after Nature-Boy Buddy Rogers, the pro wrestler, heavyweight champion of the world."

"Far out, man! Hey, Kurt!" He shouted towards the open door of the shed. "Hey Kurt, come and see what stepped out of the woods!"

The music kept blasting and Steve shrugged and stopped yelling.

"Can I make a pot?" Buddy asked. Playing with that slippery mud looked like fun.

"You think you can?"

"Sure I can. It looks easy."

Steve chuckled. "Yeah, it *looks* easy. Sit down here in front of me and I'll help you." Steve spread his long legs and patted the stool between his thighs.

After a moment's hesitation, Buddy perched himself at the edge of the stool and felt Steve's muscular arms reach around him to heap more mud onto the spinning disk. He then guided Buddy's hands to the mud and helped him to begin shaping a pot. The man's hands and forearms were huge, bulging with sinews and veins, and his muscular abdomen and chest pressed smack up against Buddy's bare back. His legs pressed against Buddy's legs as he leaned forward and Buddy could feel something hard pressing against his butt. He shivered when he realized that Steve had a hard-on.

"That's it," Steve said. "Use your fingers and thumbs. That's it: firm but gentle. You're getting it." He let go of Buddy's hands and let Buddy take over. "You're all sweaty," he said into Buddy's ear, breathing on his neck and giving him chills. "What have you been doing?"

"Running in the woods," Buddy said. He felt something pulse against his ass as Steve pressed harder against him. The man's cock felt as big as a hammer handle. Buddy shivered again and the wet pot under his fingers collapsed. "Darn it!"

"It's harder to do than it looks, isn't it?" Steve said.

"Let me try again."

"Later, I've got a dozen pieces to get done this afternoon." He turned towards the door and shouted. "Kurt! Kurt, get your ass out here!" When there was no response, he put his fingers to his lips and gave a piercing whistle.

The music stopped and there was the sound of bare feet on wooden floor-boards. A man poked his head out the door of the shed.

"What's happening?"

"Come out here and meet our guest," Steve said.

The man in the doorway smiled when he saw Buddy and he stepped out. He

was a long-haired blond man, as tall as Steve and dressed identically. "Who's this?"

"This is Buddy, and he just came out of the woods."

"Came out of the woods?"

"Like a faun," Steve said. "And his nickname is Nature-Boy."

"After the heavy-weight wrestling champion of the world, Nature-Boy Buddy Rogers," Buddy explained.

"Far out!" the blond man said, shaking Buddy's muddy hand. "You can call me Kurt. Just plain Kurt."

"I was thinking you might want to show Buddy your studio while I finish these pots?" Steve said.

"You read my mind," Kurt said. "Come on, Nature-Boy." He led Buddy to a pail of water to wash up, then took him into the shed.

Buddy looked around the single large room with its tall windows built into one wall and its paintings and photographs hanging all over the others. Most of the pictures showed one or more naked boys, and he stared wide-eyed. "Are you an artist?"

"Painter and photographer," Kurt said. "Do you like my work?"

"Yeah. Who are these guys?" Buddy couldn't take his eyes off the pictures. They gave him a hard-on. Although he'd seen lots of naked boys, he'd never seen a *picture* of one, and for some reason the pictures made his cock so hard that he thought it would bust out of his shorts.

"Boys I've known here and there," Kurt said. "Steve and I have been around: New York, California, Florida, even Europe, and now here in these hills. Coming here was Steve's idea. He wanted to get away from the rat-race. Do you like my models?"

"I guess so," Buddy said, shaking with excitement. He noticed that several of the boys in the photographs had hard-ons shiny, as if they'd just been sucked on. Most of the boys were long-haired hippies.

"I'm working on this painting now," Kurt said, pointing to a picture on an easel. The picture showed two naked boys sitting side by side on a log in the woods, their arms around each other as they kissed. Each boy had a hard-on that pointed at his belly-button.

Buddy flushed. He'd never seen two boys kiss before. His blood felt like it was boiling.

"Do you like it?" Kurt asked.

"Who are they?"

"Some young friends of mine in California. I took photographs of them to work from although I'd rather have them sitting here posing for me in the flesh, of course. I always like it better when I can work from a live model. Do you think you might like to model for me?"

"I might," Buddy said.

"Great! As I always say, there's no time like the present, so why don't we try

a pose. Let me help you off with your shorts so I can have a look at you."

Buddy felt weak in the knees as Kurt undid his cutoffs. He wouldn't have had the strength to resist if he'd wanted to, and he didn't want to. He hadn't felt so excited since the first time he'd sucked cock. As Kurt pulled his cut-offs off, he felt more naked than naked and his boner pointed at the ceiling.

Kurt's mouth dropped open. "Where did you get *this*!" He stared at Buddy's hard-on and twanged it with a finger. "Is this *real*?" He felt Buddy's cock with his fingertips. "Incredible!" He grabbed a yardstick and pressed the end of it to Buddy's groin. "Nine and a half inches! Steve will shit when he sees this!" He trailed his fingers up and down Buddy's chest and stomach. "Baby, you're too much!"

Buddy was shaking. He'd never had anybody moon over him like this, except maybe Jenny-Sue when she caught him alone. He stood there helplessly as Kurt lifted his arms one by one and sniffed his armpits, then licked them, then sniffed them again, rolling his eyes as if Buddy's scent got him high.

"You're a nature-boy, all right," Kurt said. "I haven't had a whiff of real boy in a month. In fact, I was wondering if I'd ever get my hands on one again." He nuzzled Buddy's nipples and sucked them.

Excited, Buddy stroked his cock, easing his foreskin up and down as Kurt licked his chest and stomach and belly button, then his fat pink balls. Nobody had ever done these things to him and he was as fascinated as he was turned on. Kneeling, Kurt took Buddy's hand off his cock and pulled the tight foreskin completely down. The huge purplish-pink cock head gleamed and Kurt sniffed it, then licked the moisture off it. Buddy's toes curled against the wood floor and he almost hit the ceiling as Kurt kissed and licked his super-sensitive knob.

"You like that?"

"Yeah!" Buddy said, rolling his eyes and rocking his loins.

Kurt's mouth opened wide and he swallowed Buddy's knob and a third of his cock-shaft, looking as if he had an arm stuffed in his face. Buddy grabbed the man's blond head and started to fuck. Kurt choked, but Buddy couldn't stop. He had to fuck. He had to ram his arm-like cock down the man's throat. He hugged Kurt's head and humped. He was in heaven. Too soon he felt the searing, itching, surging sensations not only in his cock but throughout his body. He grunted, his body jerking as he fucked his spunk down Kurt's throat. Kurt, choking, clung to him, sucking and swallowing.

Buddy pulled out and stumbled towards the nearby couch and collapsed on it. He felt as if a cyclone had hit him.

"I've never sucked a piece of meat that big in my life," Kurt said, sitting back on his heels and wiping his mouth, "and I've sucked a lot of dick. Are all the boys in these hills hung like donkeys?"

"Not all of 'em," Buddy said.

"You're cute," Kurt said. He stood up, pulled off his shorts, and started jacking his stiff cock. It was big, but nowhere near as big as Buddy's. "You turn

foreskin had pulled back and his naked cock head felt like a baked apple sizzling against Buddy's pucker.

"Yeahhh!" Buddy sighed, thinking, *Cornhole me!* He'd never been cornholed before, but he knew all about it. His schoolmates had been making jokes about cornholing for years and some of them claimed to have cornholed their younger brothers. Teddy-Ray had many times threatened to cornhole Buddy, but he'd never yet done it. Buddy bent forward, bracing his hands on his knees and turning up his ass to give Steve the best shot at his asshole.

"Look at that, he's dying for it," Kurt said. "Give it to him!"

Tightening his hold on Buddy's hips, Steve leaned into Buddy and suddenly Buddy's cherry gave way. The tiny pucker gaped wide-open and Steve's cock head stuffed it like a fist. The rest of Steve's cock followed, stretching Buddy's asshole to the limit. Steve and Buddy moaned in unison.

"Baby!" Steve sighed. "Fucking tight!"

Buddy thought he was going to shoot off without touching his cock. He'd never dreamed getting cornholed would feel this good. It would be exciting, he'd guessed, but he'd also thought it would hurt like hell. But instead, except for the few seconds of pain he'd felt at first, it now felt like heaven, and he couldn't help but squirm and gasp as Steve slid his cock in and out. "Aw fuck!"

"Yeah baby, I'll fuck you!" Steve said, working his cock in and out faster. "I'll fuck you, you little satyr."

Kurt leaned close to watch Steve's gleaming cock slide in and out. "He's taking every inch, man. Give it to him, man, fuck him good!" He was pounding his cock as he watched.

"Damn!" Buddy gasped, wiggling his fucked boy-ass. "Hot damn!" His cock flexed and dripped, daggers of fuck sensation shooting through it even though he wasn't touching it. He knew it would shoot off at the touch of his hand.

"He's a natural fuck-boy," Steve said. "Is he a suck-boy too?"

"Let's find out," Kurt said. He moved in front of Buddy and pressed the tip of his dripping cock to Buddy's nose.

Buddy opened his mouth and Kurt sank his cock to the hilt into Buddy's face. It felt incredible, being stuffed from both ends at once. Buddy sucked, smacking his lips, twirling his tongue. At the same time, he tightened his asshole, sucking Steve's cock with it as greedily as he was sucking Kurt's with his mouth.

"Oh fuck!" Steve grunted, ramming to the hilt up Buddy's asshole. "Oh wow!" His big hands encircling Buddy's waist, he fucked rapidly, smacking his loins against Buddy's ass. His cock flexed and he grunted as his cum exploded into Buddy's guts. "Oh baby!" He hunched over Buddy, humping and grunting as he fucked bullets of spunk into Buddy's asshole.

Buddy shivered. The feel of a man's cock suddenly coming inside his loins sent him over the brink. Fuck sensations ripped through his untouched cock and spunk exploded from his gaping piss hole. He felt orgasmic throbbings not only

in his cock and balls, but in his asshole as well. He grabbed his cock to help squeeze out the thrills, and in his excitement he sucked so hard at Kurt's sliding cock that, as his own cum was still splashing onto Kurt's feet, Kurt began pumping jets of spunk down Buddy's throat.

"Drink it!" Kurt gasped. "Aw fuck, Nature-Boy! Aw baby!"

...

Buddy sprawled on the couch in Kurt's studio, playing with his cock as Kurt sketched him. Steve was back outside throwing pots. Buddy enjoyed being looked at and admired, and enjoyed being able to lie here and play with himself so freely in front of a man. His body still throbbed after the fucking Steve had given him and he hoped that before long Steve would come back inside and fuck him again, or that Kurt would. He really dug getting cornholed. He'd never imagined it would feel that good. "How long can you pose for me today?" Kurt asked.

"For as long as you want," Buddy said.

"You don't have to get home, like for dinner or something?" "I ain't got no home," Buddy said, stretching. "I'm a free man."

Kurt eyed him suspiciously. "You're a runaway, huh?"

"Fuck no! I didn't run away, I was kicked out. Now I'm a free man, just out wandering around."

"With just that little rag around your hips."

"It's all I need," Buddy said.

Kurt drew for a minute, then said: "You can stay here with us for as long as you want, you know. We can't pay you, but we can feed you."

"So what do I gotta do?" Buddy knew that they wouldn't feed him for free.

"Exactly what you're doing now lie around naked so I can draw and paint you. Steve will probably want to sculpt you."

And fuck me, Buddy thought. He could dig that. He could dig living around this place, lying around naked, sucking cock and getting cornholed. "So, when do we eat?" he asked.

IN THE MIX
by Dan Veen

Funny, how life can change in just one night.

Things weren't going well between my boyfriend and me. At home Sean was sullen and non-communicative. When we went out he was usually insulting.

Then came the company mixer at my office. It was the party where office boys network with the CEOs. Families and friends of the employees come to relax and have a good time.

Of course Sean was in a worse mood than ever.

At the party I noticed Sean dancing and paying a lot of attention to a certain co-worker of mine.

This guy is named James and seems to have some special power over guys. He's good-looking, as good-looking as you could possibly want. James is six-foot-four of solid black muscle and bone. He has big hands with long fingers, and his shoulders are wide and his waist is smooth and his butt is tight-curved, like a dancer's. Nice box, too. The kind you always give a second look just to be sure you saw what you saw. You can tell James packs a lot of power down there.

Yeah, James is good-looking, but I could never figure out exactly what it was he did to get all of that attention.

Well the three of us ended up pretty drunk. We decided to go to our apartment complex, which was near the party. Why I agreed to do this, I'm not sure. Maybe I knew what was coming and secretly wanted it.

We got there, lit a fire, and had more drinks.

I went to take a piss. While pissing I left the door open. I heard James and Sean laughing. I could see them in the living room out of the corner of my eye.

I watched James reach over and place his hand on my boyfriend's crotch and squeeze. He then leaned over and gave my Sean a deep, lascivious tongue kiss.

I couldn't believe my eyes. Sean had never (to my knowledge) done anything like this before!

I was furious, but something kept me from busting them up.

I looked down and realized that I had a tremendous hard-on. James continued to kiss and squeeze my boyfriend's box. With his other hand James unbuttoned Sean's shirt. He started rubbing Sean's chest.

I didn't know whether to stay in the bathroom and watch (I was more turned on than ever!) or go back in the room.

James's hand starting snaking down into Sean's pants.

Just then James looked up at me and told me: "We're going up to the bedroom."

They wanted to be alone for a while, James told me.

James said that I should come up ... LATER.

I listened as our bed creaked and moaned. I heard my boyfriend saying stuff and talking dirty. Really egging James on to fuck him.

I had never heard Sean talk that nasty with me. I was confused shocked

- 215 -

excited. My hard-on raged. Dripped.

Sean, my own boyfriend, was upstairs in bed with another man, screaming in pleasure to get fucked!

The floor really started pounding. I pictured them fucking, pictured James plugging Sean's hole. I heard them laughing and shouting. How could they treat me like this? My own boyfriend and another guy just start brazenly fucking each other in our own apartment! In our own bed!

The sounds from the bedroom above teased me. I'd never heard Sean yelling like that when I fucked him.

I was furious.

But hornier than ever.

My hard-on got the best of me. I wanted to see them now. Needed to see what was going on.

Finally I couldn't take it any more and took off my clothes and went up to join them.

"Ung!" Sean was on all fours in the middle of the bed.

"Uhm!" James was humping Sean, humping my boyfriend slowly, thrusting deliberately into his behind.

"Dammit! Fuck my hole!" Sean spat.

They were both naked and covered in sweat.

"I'm fucking your hole, bitch!"

My eyes adjusted to the soft bedroom light as I watched James fucking my boyfriend.

James humped Sean, humped him like an animal, a dark hulking animal fucking doggie-style.

Sean is a svelte, ivory-skinned redhead, so watching James fuck Sean's hole was like watching a huge mastiff dog raping a slender greyhound pup.

"Take that dick! Open up that ass!" James was vicious in his dicking, but I'd never seen my boyfriend as turned-on and horny as this. Getting James's dick up his hole transformed Sean into ferocious fuckpup.

Over the next hour I watched.

I watched as James turned my boyfriend every which way to fuck him. I watched Sean do everything that James wanted and then some.

Sean was a total mindless slut for cock now. A complete cock hole. Sean eagerly complied with every nudge of James's dick. My boyfriend was anxious to do anything to get that huge cock of James as far up into his hole as he could. It seemed to fit in there snug, too. James's huge black member seemed to stretch my boyfriend's baby-pink ass-slit to the max. That cock pounded Sean's ass-lips with ferocious smacks. I watched James slamming into Sean's hole, his balls bouncing like twin wrecking balls.

The sounds of my boyfriend getting fucked drove me crazier. That smacking socketing sound, like a foot stuck in a mud hole; messy wet slurps of massive dick thwacking into the suctioning pocket of my boyfriend's tight ass.

James slid out of my boyfriend's ass. It was when James had Sean suck him off for a while that I realized that James's cock was well over ten inches long. I swear, I couldn't believe that Sean had got that huge thing up his tight ass-pussy!

Sean could only suck about half of James's black-steel cock, it was so long and thick.

Sean really got into sucking too. I'd never seen Sean so wild with lust, so eager to suck cock. But something about this fat black log made Sean cum-hungry. Sean loved raking his pink tongue over James's slick ebony balls and cock shaft. He loved getting James's thick black knobber porked down his throat.

James put my boyfriend's ankles over his shoulders and stuck his dick back up in him and pounded Sean's reddened, slippery ass savagely for about fifteen minutes non-stop.

All the time Sean ran his hands through James's hair, tongue-kissed him and fondled James's huge low hanging balls, and yelled out for James to fuck him harder, harder. Sean's eyes would glaze over with spasms of total fuck lust. His prong would drool out big dollops of cream.

When James finally came, that prick hammered on for what seemed like ten minutes. He really nailed Sean's hole. My boyfriend kicked and screamed for more cum, more dick, more fucking. I watched James's pumping fucker unload in Sean's asshole.

They remained coupled, James plugged deep into Sean's hole, and they kissed for a long time....

Then, when James finally pulled out, his cum dribbled in gobs from his cock all over Sean's balls and butt and all over the bed and floor.

My boyfriend's asshole was matted and distended from the incredibly rough fuck. It glistened with James's lube and sperm.

James then looked down at me and said, "You'd better clean that up. I'm going in there again as soon as I catch my breath."

I'd never done anything like this before, but the next thing I knew I was kissing and licking my boyfriend's used and abused hole while he and James continued to kiss. I smeared my face in it.

My boyfriend's hole actually steamed from the hot fuck James had given it. The funk of Sean's ass juices clotted my nostrils. I stuck my tongue where James's dick had just fucked. I reamed out the ravaged folds of my boyfriend's hole. James had shot massive curds of very thick white cum it was hard to swallow all of the drippings but I managed to get my boyfriend all clean and ready.

Then Sean looked down at my cum-smeared face. He laughed at me. I guess it was kind of funny, like my face was hit with a custard cream pie while I licked my lips.

Sean gave me his balls to suck too. I tongued them off, taking each one in my

mouth.

Sean said, "That was great why don't you clean him up now too?"

James said, "Yeah man, suck my cock. Make it good and hard for your little boyfriend's ass!"

I smacked my lips and started sucking like I was told.

It was the first time I had a look at James's really huge dick. His dick was as black and as hard as the rest of him and shone like some spit-polished nightstick. Except for the head of it. His cock head was furled with brown velvet foreskin. The pulpy skin folds were gummy from James's steady ooze of dick paste and my boyfriend's ass juices.

"Suck it, fuck-face." The black rod prodded my lips. My tongue obediently slurped the smell of James's cum-cheese and Sean's ass. "Let me feel you blowing my meat."

It probed into my mouth. The long ebony wedge reamed out my cheeks. The chocolate jumbo marshmallow of his cock head plugged my windpipe. My throat was filled up with big black dick!

"Yeah, get your mouth down on that dick. Give it some neck. Neck it! Neck the whole fucking thing!"

I deep-sucked his dick. I really wanted to make James's dick feel good.

He got hard again fast. James's stiff pole practically gagged me.

Then I watched as James withdrew his long dick from my lips and started to fuck my boyfriend's already-upturned ass.

He did this again and again for most of the night, making me clean his dick off between fucks of my boyfriend's ass.

Towards morning I was begging for some release, and Sean allowed me to climb on his ass to get my nads off before they went to sleep.

All the time I mounted him, my boyfriend and James were laughing and petting like I wasn't even there.

Sean's asshole was so stretched and so sloppy after all that dicking that I felt like I was in a giant pussy. But I just needed to cum, I needed to cum bad, fucking blind, fucking furious, ramming my meat up Sean's hot hole.

Then James nonchalantly stuck his finger up into my humping ass and made me cream off. And boy did I shoot! It was wild.

Funny how life can change in just one night. You think you know who you are and where you are going, and in just one night all bets are off. All reality gets rearranged. There's a new game-plan.

Life sure has a way of spinning around a hundred-and-eighty degrees on top of one special dick.

That morning, James fucked my boyfriend again before James had to leave. They made me watch the whole fuck. They even made me slick up James's cock for him, and ream out Sean, so the huge cock would get into Sean's ass easier.

Since that occasion, I know Sean has seen James many times although I was not there. I can tell by the condition of my boyfriend's asshole when he comes

home. In fact Sean gets a kick out of making me taste his asshole with my tongue after he comes back from getting fucked by James.

Just imagining how James fucks my boyfriend gets me all hot again. It makes me want to go screw that slutty fuck hole of Sean's good and hard right now.

Sean has had the most mischievous smile on his face lately, like he's planning a surprise. What I've found out is that Sean is making arrangements to move me out to the garage. Well, after that night I guess I don't have any dignity any more, because I just don't care how they humiliate me as long as they let me in on their fucks as long as I get sloppy seconds in my boyfriend's ass or on James's big cock.

The mix of both these men just turns me on.

Lately I've even had fantasies.

Fantasies about getting James's magic cock up my own ass.

Or Sean's cock.

Or both their cocks.

At once.

FUN & GAMES
by John Patrick

Karl opened another bottle of wine and filled up Andy's tall, fluted wine glass. The Chardonnay was a particularly good one, but the way Andy was knocking it back, Karl was sure it was just another excuse to unwind with the aid of alcohol. Andy seemed to be drinking more than he had when they were lovers. Something was bothering him, Karl knew, but he wasn't about to ask what it was until, or, rather, after, he'd fucked him.

Despite Andy's fatigue, the wine was making him feel very sexual. He might have to go for another week until his lover, Greg, came back to town, so he thought that he might as well get his fill now. Besides, he'd missed Karl's thick eight inches.

"Okay, Karl, I've got an idea," Andy said, sounding tipsy. "Why don't we play a game where we each ask the other person to help act out a fantasy? Do you understand what I mean?"

Karl nodded.

"Good. Then explain it to me. 'Cause I don't know what the fuck I'm talkin' about." Andy started to laugh loudly at his own silliness, then attempted to compose himself. "Okay, Karl. Since I suggested it, I'll let you go first."

Karl rubbed his chin for a moment, trying to think what he'd like to get Andy to do first. Ever since Andy had left him for Greg, he'd been sorry he'd been such a slut. Andy deserved better, Karl realized. All he could think of, it seemed, was how good it had been with Andy. Now that he'd managed to get Andy back, for only one night, he was going to take advantage of it. "Okay. See that empty wine bottle on the table? I want you to use it to play with your ass, then push it up there."

"I don't know." Andy realized he was more than a little drunk when he got up from the sofa and promptly fell back down again. His second attempt was met with greater success, and, laughing, he quickly stripped off his sneakers and jeans. He wore no underwear and Karl sighed when he saw the ass he had been missing in the flesh.

Andy teased the lips of his smooth ass with the slim neck of the bottle. Karl got some lotion from the bedroom and handed it to Andy.

Slowly Andy began inserting a bit of the bottle into his hole. As he relaxed, it became easier to insert more of the neck into his now-sloppy asshole. He moved it in and out of himself like it was a glass dildo, stopping only to use the fingers of his right hand to hold back his ass lips so Karl could get a better view.

Karl was playing it cool, but from the way he wiggled uncomfortably on the sofa it was clear to Andy that his erection was causing him discomfort in his jeans.

When Andy had done enough to satisfy the requirements of his dare, he rested the bottle back on the table and contemplated what he wanted from Karl.

Inspiration struck, and he disappeared into the kitchen. Shortly he was back,

grinning broadly. He held a can of whipped cream. "I want you to squeeze this stuff slowly over the head of that big dick of yours and let it run over your balls."

Karl laughed. "Are you serious?"

Andy nodded. "And then I'll lick it off."

"Oh, okay," Karl agreed. Standing up, he started putting on a show for his ex-lover. Slowly, and in an exaggerated manner, he undid his belt before going to work on the buttons of his 501s. He slid his jeans seductively down his legs before stepping out of them. Then he pulled his white T-shirt up to reveal his tight stomach muscles. His smooth, sun-tanned skin contrasted sexily against the white of the shirt and his matching briefs.

Andy gasped at how beautiful his ex-lover still was. In fact, he looked even more buffed now than he had seven months ago when they parted. And it was always a turn-on to see that big, stiff cock of his straining the seams of the briefs.

Andy licked his lips in eager anticipation of the show to come. He began jerking his own erect cock wildly. "Get 'em off," he told Karl, growing impatient.

Karl obliged, slipping off his underpants and letting his stiff penis spring back with a resounding slap against his abdomen. Pulling back his foreskin to reveal his head in all its throbbing glory, Karl held his penis while his right hand began spraying on the cream. The coldness made his cock jerk, which gave Andy an extra quiver of pleasure as he watched.

A mound of whipped cream sat on Karl's knob before making its sensual journey down the length of his shaft, then continued its journey on to his balls before slipping down his inner thighs. "Yummy! That sure looks mighty tasty," Andy said, in the fake Deep-South accent that had always caused Karl to laugh out loud.

Karl stepped over to the sofa and stood before his ex. He sprayed some more cream on his cock and then put the can down.

"Oh, Karl," Andy moaned. He had jerked himself to near orgasm.

"Don't come yet. You always came too soon."

Being reminded of one of the reasons they had parted stopped Andy momentarily, but he was too drunk, and too excited, to let the appetizing feast before him go to waste. Soon he was greedily licking the head of Karl's dick with his warm tongue. Cock never tasted this good, he thought to himself as he licked every drop off the head of Karl's penis, which disappeared into his mouth.

After he had sucked the prick clean, he concentrated his sweet tooth on his balls, licking them of the last vestiges of Redi-Whip.

Andy had left his own cock alone during this process, but now he returned to it, leaning back to stare at the fully erect member throbbing before his eyes. "Enough fantasies," he told him. "I need to be fucked."

Karl knew how Andy liked it best and he lay outstretched on the bed while Andy carefully positioned myself over his penis. With Andy's right hand firmly gripping Karl's shaft and his left opening the lips of his ass, he carefully guided the prick into him. It had been a long time since he had experienced Karl's large meat and it was with some difficulty that he took it. Soon he was moving himself up and down on it hard.

Andy loved the feeling of being in control, even as a bottom-boy, and he couldn't remember it being so exciting. Here he was fucking the big dick of his ex-lover, while his current lover was a thousand miles away. It was not something he had done before, and the sensation was one of total decadence and deviance. It was like the feeling he had as a child when he was doing something he knew, morally, he shouldn't. That was how Andy felt now. He was being terribly naughty and loving every minute of it.

As Andy focused on the sensation of having this huge prick in him again at last, the urge was too strong. He firmly gripped his own erection. It felt incredibly firm and sizeable, and he stroked it feverishly, savoring every moment.

But suddenly he realized that Karl was the one who was about to come. It was so unexpected, yet it was most welcome. An almighty rush came to Andy's head as he felt the powerful orgasm grip Karl. He held on tightly to Karl's cock as it slammed into him, and the pulsating waves of ecstasy flowed through him. His own jerking was fast and frenetic, and in what seemed like a mere moment, a torrent of spunk was shooting from his cock.

Andy pulled himself off and lay down next to his ex. From the tone of his slow, heavy breathing, it was clear that Karl was finished for the night. But Andy was restless and thirsty. It hadn't been bad sex; it's just that he could have done with more of it, much more of it! Still, it had been fun. The only problem was that Andy was excited about what might be ahead for them. He rolled on to his side in the bed and stared at his ex, who had dozed off. God, he was gorgeous, Andy thought. Why had he let Karl's casual affairs bother him so much? Why hadn't he simply made a game of it?

Andy got up and went to the kitchen to get something to drink. When he opened the refrigerator, he found there was a bowl of fresh strawberries just begging to be eaten. He sat at the little table in the kitchen and nibbled on a strawberry. He thought about what had just happened. While Karl was fucking him, Andy realized anew what he had been missing. With Greg, he had begun to really know how a prostitute must feel. He had so often lain there and pretended that the thrusting and groaning was exciting him, while in his mind all he could do was hope it would be over quickly. Sex with Karl was so much different....

Suddenly Karl was in front of him. Andy shifted in the chair uncomfortably.

"Can't sleep?" Karl asked, brushing his long blond hair away from his eyes.

"Nope. I had a hunch you were hiding fresh strawberries in the refrigerator."

"They're for breakfast." Karl sat down next to his ex. Andy knew Karl could

be a regular Captain Queeg when it came to his strawberries; he could sense the possibility of an impending argument, and that was not somewhere he wanted to go right now. Swiftly he fed Karl a strawberry as a way of distracting him. As Karl swallowed, Andy had another strawberry ready. This time he held it in his mouth and brought it close to Karl's. Karl bit softly into the ripe berry as Andy held it in his mouth. Slowly he nibbled away until their lips were touching, and then he felt Karl's tongue exploring his mouth. He reciprocated, and felt the warmth of his tongue against his own. Gradually the slow and sensual exchange grew in passionate intensity until they were both frantically kissing, long and hard.

Andy could hear his breath becoming harder, and sensed his growing arousal.

"I don't remember you ever being this much fun," Karl said. Before he could think of a good response, Andy found himself pushing Karl down onto the floor on his back before lying on top of him.

He ran his fingers over Karl's firm chest. "Well, stud, I don't remember you being this hard...." His hand traveled down to Karl's cock. "Everywhere."

He pushed his tongue deep into his ex's mouth. Yes, the renewed lovemaking had thrilled Karl to a semi-hard state. Before long, Andy had kissed his way down Karl's body to begin sucking gently on the cock, softly pulling it into his mouth.

Karl exhaled deeply, took his ex's head in his hands, and pushed his cock deep down Andy's eager mouth. Andy sucked for a few moments, then pulled back and began teasing Karl. Starting at the ball sac, Andy began nibbling, kissing Karl's skin. Inch by inch his lips moved upwards, teasing him unmercifully. Oh, how Andy's ass ached desperately for the cock he had so missed.

"Oh, fuck, that feels so good," Karl sighed.

Andy's tongue was now working at a faster rate, slapping backwards and forwards, thoroughly wetting the boner. Finally it was too much too bear. Karl had to fuck his ex again. He rolled him over and lifted up his legs and let them hang over on to his back. Now, as he buried his head into his crotch and kissed Andy's erection, Andy's legs gripped his back, pushing his groin upwards, hard against his mouth. Andy writhed as Karl licked Andy's throbbing prick.

Any doubts that Karl was really the man for him were all but gone now, as he reveled in the pleasure his prick was receiving. He couldn't concentrate on the pleasure, though, for fear he would come too soon. But Karl kept sucking and licking until he thought it would explode. He was at the very pinnacle when Karl stopped. It was as if he knew the exact moment that he was going to orgasm and decided his ex should wait.

"Ohhh!" A loud moan of pleasure came forth from Andy as Karl pushed the head of his penis into his ass. Even the copious amounts of lubrication left over from the previous fuck didn't make the entry any easier. But as Karl slowly

worked his cock in and out of Andy, it glided more easily.

Andy spread his legs wider and reached down to stroke Karl's cock as it slid in and out. He could feel the veins standing up along his shaft. As Karl permitted this interruption, he asked, "You miss it, don't you?"

"Oh, yes. You don't know how much."

"Oh, Andy," Karl gasped, taking his ex in his arms and sending his cock in to the hilt.

"Fuck me harder. Oh, that big dick feels so good in my ass." "Yeah, yeah." His voice was deep and breathless with excitement. He happily obliged the request and fucked Andy's ass with greater vigor.

"Oh, yes! Yes! Fuck me! Fuck me! Oh!"

Andy's hand had moved to his own cock and he had reached the point of no return. He groaned loud, then let out a resonating scream as he climaxed. At Andy's moment of orgasmic release, he could feel Karl's pelvis start to shake, then felt his penis pulled from inside him. Karl wanted his spunk to mingle with his ex's on Andy's stomach. "Oh, yeah," Karl sighed as he watched Karl's cum join his.

Karl slumped down next to Andy, catching his breath. He drew a long, slow, deliberate breath and groaned in pleasure.

Andy lay still, his eyes closed. Content at last, he would have slept there if Karl had let him.

The next morning, as Andy was preparing to leave, Karl invited him back for more "fun and games."

"Okay," Andy said. Andy was under no illusions about a renewal of their relationship at some level. It had been like this before, when Andy met Karl, near the end of Andy's relationship with Tom. Andy was always involved in "relationships," while Karl took passing moments of pleasure where he could find them. Andy could never live with that day after day. No, Karl made a far better clandestine lover than a real one.

Now they were together again. They would part, of course, but they would come back to each other again, sooner or later, for more "fun and games."

SECRET LUSTING
by Leo Cardini

Strange feeling, this walking into the stately, midtown Manhattan office building where I work dressed in a black leather vest and cowboy boots, a tight, white T-shirt and tighter, faded blue 501s. With every step I can feel my Levis inching up my ass crack in back while straining against the bulge of my jockstrap-enclosed cock and balls in front, the crotch worn dangerously thin to a surrender-flag white.

To be honest, I only dropped by the office this late Saturday afternoon because I had an audition down the street earlier. Yeah, I know; it sounds like a cliché, an aspiring actor working as a secretary. And to top it with another cliché a secretary secretly lusting after his boss.

Ah, yes, Mr. Colin Slater, the inspiration of so many of my bedtime jack off sessions: he of the broad-shouldered, narrow-waisted physique, and of the clean-shaven, square-jawed good looks; a man I'd only ever seen dressed in impeccably tailored suits and stunning ties knotted just right, as if he'd just stepped out of a men's fashion magazine, complete with thick, black, combed-back hair never out of place, manicure-perfect nails, and dark, quietly expressive eyes.

But I guess I'm getting off the subject. Auditions were being held nearby for an off-off-Broadway stage version of that classic of gay erotica, *Mineshaft Nights*. Now, I'm too young to ever have gone to the Mineshaft myself, but I must've re-read that book a dozen times, memorizing the lay of the land and picturing myself in the Shaft during its down-and-dirty heyday, where I'm sure I would have fit right in.

I figured I'd audition for the part of Little Ricky, since I look like him: five-ninish, blond and blue-eyed, pretty well-built and (fuck, why *shouldn't* I admit it?) blessed with a big dick. And he's always been my favorite character, since he was always getting into hot-tempered, quick-fisted trouble, and then getting punished, tied up ass-vulnerable to take dick up his ass, or forced down on his knees, his face shoved into some stud's crotch, his mouth impaled on the guy's dick until explosions of hot cum scalded their way down his throat. Which is why, I guess, he always got into so much trouble in the first place.

Anyhow, though I hoped to gain an edge on the competition by dressing the part, I got the usual "Don't call us we'll call you," and I figured I'd drop by the office, since I was passing by, dash in, pick up my glasses that I'd left there the day before and be on my way.

Well, I can't find my glasses anywhere. Then I realized I'd probably left them in Mr. Slater's office. Yeah, sometimes I take them off when I'm with him because I think I look sexier that way.

I pull out my key to his office and unlock the door, looking in on the familiar, tastefully decorated room. At the far end, in front of the wall-length window with a view of Manhattan to die for, his enormous walnut desk faced

into the plush-carpeted room. On my left a wall of bookcases and his computer workspace, and on my right an off-white sofa and easy chair and a coffee table completed the decor.

Now, that's strange. His computer's on, and his gym bag, that familiar black-canvas, red-trim repository of Mr. Slater's athletic gear that would never know how much I envied them their intimacy with him, rests on the carpet beside his desk.

I step in. And then I nearly jump out of my fucking skin when I hear the sudden whirr of his printer as it slides out a page of print. So he must be in the building, stepping out of his office, as he often does, after giving the command to print out a document. Just think, this very moment he might be barely yards away, down the hall in the men's room, absentmindedly grasping his dick to direct the forceful stream of his warm, yellow piss into the bottom of the urinal, totally oblivious to the fact there's someone in his office who'd sell his soul just to witness him, cock in hand, engaged in such a routine, manly act.

I see my glasses on the coffee table. I scoop them up, go to exit...and then stop.

That gym bag. Unattended. Irresistible in the allure of its hidden contents.

With squirming cock and my heart beating out of control, I reason Mr. Slater won't be back for a good minute or so, and step over to his bag, lowering myself onto my haunches and unzipping it.

As I pull it open, the smell of Slater-sweaty gym clothes greets my nose with all the appeal of a taboo aphrodisiac, the prized distillation of the stretch and strain of his early morning workout.

I reach in and rummage about through the limp dampness of his clothes until my fingers feel that familiar, rough-textured blend of cotton and elastic. Yes, his jockstrap! I pull it out and hold it up for examination: a white Bike, medium, swim-style strap. Where the pouch meets the back straps it's still sweaty. And on the inside of the pouch piss stains! Mr. Slater's piss stains, the possible product of a mid-workout whiz.

I press the inner pouch against my nose and inhale. Dammit, is there any odor in the world that can compete with funky, aromatic crotch-smell? My body comes alive and sensitive, my nipples sting, and my free hand can't help itself when it's drawn into my crotch to examine the dimensions of my tortured hard-on as it rebels against the double constraint of my own jockstrap and my tight Levis.

With the pouch still pressed against my nose, I stand up, the better to rub my dick through my 501s. I close my eyes and sniff again, drawing the jockstrap across my face like a washcloth, suffused with the heady sensations of crotch odor, pouch press and dick rub. I feel so lightheaded and horny, all thought of caution evaporates and I let this moment of perfect sensuality transport me heavenwards.

And then I hear the click of the office door closing!

I plummet back into reality, open my eyes and freeze on the spot.

Yes, it's Mr. Slater.

As he locks the door behind him, I tear the jockstrap from my face and pull my hand out of my crotch.

I realize I've never seen him out of business clothes before and for a moment I think maybe I'm dreaming this up, so perfect is the image of him standing there: black cowboy boots (unlike mine, they're square-toed), a wide black leather belt, and a black Western-style shirt with white snaps, the sleeves rolled up, stretched taut against the rock hard muscles of his upper arms, and the front unsnapped halfway down to his waist, revealing the spread of fine black hair that covers his chiseled chest. And dark-blue, tight-fitting Levis that highlight his trim waist and oh my God! a pronounced, decidedly remarkable bulge on the left side of his crotch forcing its way down his pants leg.

"I was just...uh...." I said, dropping the incriminating piece of evidence into his bag, "...sniffing my jockstrap."

"No!"

"Oh, I think you were," he says, sauntering towards me. "That and rubbing your crotch."

An odd moment for my hand to return to just that spot.

I pull it out again with, "I came in to get my glasses...and...."

"And whatever. Well, it's good to see you," he says stepping behind his desk and sitting down, checking me out, head to toe. "And since you're here, you might as well make yourself useful."

"Oh?"

Pointing at the printer, which was now once more at rest, he says, "I was just about to do some editing. Would you mind?"

I take the pile of printout sheets, tamp them into a neat stack and step over to hand them to Mr. Slater. But before I do, my eyes happen to fall on the top page. In fourteen-point boldface it bears the title: "COACH DOUGLAS!"

Now where have I heard that name before? But before I can drag it out of my mind, I read the next line: "by Leo Cardini"

What the...? My mouth falls open as I look over at my boss.

The smile on his face makes clear he's pleased with my reaction.

"You know what that is?" he asks, pointing at the manuscript.

I scan down the first page, catching the familiar names of Norm and Tony, and then look up at him again.

"Does this mean you're Leo Cardini?"

His smile broadens. Christ, he's handsome. He should be on a billboard, advertising something.

"I mean, your pen name's Leo Cardini?"

He nods yes.

"Well, I'm one of your biggest fans! Especially those stories in *Freshmen*. The ones about those guys from Jamaica Plain Norm, Tony, Mike. To which, I

guess, this is a sequel?"

Another nod.

"Oh, if you only knew how much of a fan of yours I am."

"Well, if all my fans were like you, I could make a killing in used jockstraps."

"Yeah, well, uh...anyhow, I guess I never really thought much about who the real Cardini could possibly be, except for some real hot dude." I think, but don't dare say, I guess I was right. "I surely never imagined he'd be my boss's alter ego."

"Hmm. Well, now you know. It doesn't bother you, does it?"

"Me? No!"

Bother's not the word. Horny, yes. And anxious, on the verge of...daring something drastic, like getting down on my knees and licking his boots.

And as I stand there, trying to push myself into action, the pause between us is so full of possibilities, it's almost unbearable.

Finally, he leans back into his chair, looking me up and down again, and says, "I'm just about to do the final edit before sending it off to *Freshmen*. Would you like to help?"

Well, this isn't exactly what I hoped for. However....

"Help? Sure! What do you want me to do?"

"I'll make my edits on hard copy, and you transfer them to my computer file."

Well, in a matter of minutes we're busy at work; Mr. Slater at his desk with red pen in hand, and me at his computer terminal, recording the changes as he slides each completed page over to the side of his desk nearest me.

The first page, since it's the title page and the text begins half way down, takes no time. While recording the two minor changes he has made, I read about Norm and Tony running into their high school football coach just outside Chaps, this gay bar in Boston.

Pages two through five go quickly enough as their super-stud of a friend Mike joins them and they all go over to Coach Douglas's apartment and get stoned out of their minds.

Then page six. Just as Mike appears in the doorway after taking a shower, dressed in nothing but a worn-out jockstrap, and it is time to move on to page seven, I read what Mr. Slater's written all in caps at the bottom of the page:

WOULDN'T YOU BE MORE COMFORTABLE WORKING WITH YOUR SHIRT OFF?

I turn to him. He looks up at me with raised eyebrows: questioning, inviting, challenging.

Smiling back at him, I pull my tee shirt up over my head and drop it onto the floor. The palpable thrill of his assessing gaze as his eyes travel across the gym-sculpted features of my nearly hairless chest stings the nubs of my nipples, stiffening them into hard, sensitive prongs that ache for his touch.

Just as I think I've got the guts to get up and approach him, he goes back to his text! Shit!

But two pages later, at the bottom of the page, just as Tony reaches into Coach Douglas's crotch to fondle his balls while Mike's busy sucking away on their gym coach's oversized dick, Mr. Slater's written: BOOTS LIKE THOSE DON'T BELONG IN AN OFFICE LIKE THIS.

Now, I could've pointed out that he was wearing boots also. But since he's the boss, I simply acquiesce, the brief breeze of sock-smell hitting my nostrils heightening my increasing horniness.

Two pages later, when Coach Douglas liberates Norm's big fat Polish sausage and deep-throats it, a new comments reads: WHITE SOCKS?

Off come the socks.

Just one page later, on page eleven, off comes my belt. Oh, that it would find its way across my butt!

At this point, I can hardly wait for page twelve!

Which lives up to my expectations. Just after Coach Douglas slides a finger up Norm's ass, I get up to take off my Levis. Drawing inspiration from the text, I manage to bend over and expose my own back-strapped butt to Mr. Slater as I slowly slide off my Levis, taking much longer than I need so as to show off my own little pink, puckered butt hole.

I crane my neck towards Mr. Slater and see with cock-hardening satisfaction he's found my butt worthy of his interest. Then, as if he's drawn inspiration from contemplating my butt hole, I see him hurriedly scrawl something on top of the next page and slide it towards me.

DOES THIS SOUND PLAUSIBLE?

"What do you mean?" I ask.

"I mean the guy's a virgin."

"You mean Norm?"

"Exactly. Sure he's been rimmed, but there's a world of difference between a flexible tongue and a rigid digit, or to be more exact, three of them. Does it make sense he could take three fingers up his ass, even greased up the way they are, and actually like it?"

"I don't know. Wanna try me and find out?"

"I'm talking virgin territory."

"How do you know I'm not?"

"Hmm," is all he says, making it clear he doesn't know whether or not to believe me.

But as if to accept me at my word, he opens his lower left desk drawer, reaches deep into the back of it and pulls out a large plastic jar of Vaseline and a white hand towel. And then, moving over to his sofa, he pulls the coffee table off to one side, and sits down sofa center.

Placing the Vaseline and towel on the floor, he says to me, "Okay. You're on."

I rise to my feet, naked except for my jockstrap, acutely aware of the waistband inching down the flat terrain of my lower abdomen as the pouch stretches and swells with my growing erection.

I approach Mr. Slater. With every step, I feel the unbearably pleasant ache of the reposition of my cock and balls within the stretched-to-the-max confines of my jock-pouch.

Standing in front of him, I look down at my swollen package barely inches from his face. He stares at it with an interest that makes me feel privileged, and I can't resist twitching my cock against the cotton and elastic pouch in grateful acknowledgment of his attention.

With one hand, he fondles my equipment through the straining material. I go crazy at the feel of his fingers and my cock responds with a fresh infusion of blood, forcing my dickhead to nuzzle its way out above the waistband, an inquisitive show-off glistening with a bead of pre-cum lodged in its piss slit.

Mr. Slater doesn't say anything, but he gives a slight nod, as if in appreciation.

"Now turn around and bend over. Yeah. And pull your ass cheeks apart."

I'm probably imagining it, but I swear I can feel the warmth of his gaze as he surveys the territory between my ass cheeks and then stares deep into my hole, which I repeatedly clench in a bid for his continued interest.

"So this is what a virgin butt hole looks like."

"Yes, sir."

He lightly brushes the tip of his fingers against its rim. The flutter of sensations networks through my body like tiny electric shocks, and I can't resist letting out a moan.

Eventually, he abandons my butt and I hear him busy with the jar of Vaseline.

Then I feel his fingers again as he greases the rim of my hole, setting off a whole new array of sensations. And just when I feel it doesn't get any better than this, he slips a finger in.

"Oh!"

"You okay?"

"Yeah!" I say breathlessly.

I'd contracted, but now I loosen my butt hole again, and he works his finger in and out several times, each time probing deeper. Then he pulls out and re-enters with two fingers, carefully stretching my hole with expert patience and precision.

Once he's able to maneuver the two of them in and out with ease, he inserts a third, which I must admit I don't think I'll be able to take at first. But I will myself to accept it and in no time the determined willing turns to desperate wanting.

And as he works his fingers in and out of my hole, I reach into my jock-pouch and grab my dick. The sensations of butt-probe and cock-stroke flood my

bent-over body like an irresistible undertow of sensuality.

Then I feel him withdraw from me. He wipes off his fingers and slaps me on the ass, emphatically ending the scene.

"Well, I guess you've assured me Norm can take three fingers up his butt hole ... and like it."

He rises, heading back to his desk.

"But...."

"Fifteen, twenty minutes, we'll be done with the story," he says, all business again.

He can't abandon me like this! Not the way I feel! But he's already seated at his desk again, pen in hand. The agony of this sudden desertion, while I can still feel the stretch of his fingers inside me, is absolutely, diabolically...wonderful!

So, with greasy hole and aching hard-on, I go back to his computer. The toolbar on the lower screen tells me there's only four pages to go. These four pages are going to be an eternity, I think.

And they are. But it's an exquisite eternity of almost unbearable anticipation. The few minutes it takes to conclude this assignment are like nothing I've ever experienced. I feel all the more aroused for the prison-like constraint of having to sit at Mr. Slater's computer, my punishment to word-process a porn story about four hot studs, a story that never lets me forget how horny I am myself, the length of my sentence measured in...well, sentences. Sentences that meander into paragraphs that drag slowly down the pages, while the squirmy sensation of my cock pressing against my jock-pouch and the itch of recent invasion in my butt hole suffuses me with a heightened sensuality made all the greater by the awareness that once we're done, well, I have no idea what'll happen next, if anything at all, except for a quick trip to the men's room to secretly shoot my load.

Never have the words "The End" been a more welcomed sight. As I give the print command, my cock and balls ache with the need to blast a load of cum.

Though I know it's going to take forever for the damn thing to print out, I rise from my chair and stand by the printer, completely uncaring that my hard-on won't go away, as I wonder, "Now what?"

Mr. Slater neatly puts away his editing tools. Then he moves over to the sofa, where he sits with his arms crossed over his chest as he stares into the air.

"Sir?" I prompt.

He pulls himself out of his thoughts, looks up at me for a second, and then asks, "Have you had a hard-on all this time?"

"Yes. But that's not what's on your mind, is it?"

"No. Fact is...it's about Norm again. Three fingers up his butt hole's one thing, but a big fat sausage like Tony's pounding in and out of him, well, that's quite something else."

"You're really serious about your concern."

"Writing *is* serious. Even porn."

"I guess it is. Well, it seems to me...." I explain why I think it all makes perfectly logical sense, though my logic's probably swayed by the pleasantly annoying itch in my ass.

"Would *you* be able to manage a nine-incher, considering your virginal status?" The stress he puts on *your* sounds most skeptical. "I mean, if you could, then I would think *he* could."

"There's only one way to find out. But where do we find a big, fat nine-incher like Tony's?"

The slow, wicked smile that radiates his face encourages me to dare to hope.

Rising from the sofa, Mr. Slater plants his booted feet wide apart on the carpet and rests his hands on his hips. Staring at me, he says, "Where do you think?"

With this, he reaches into his crotch and gives its ample contents a good, hefty tug.

This is all the invitation I need. I drop to my knees and bury my face in his denim-enclosed crotch.

"Yeah, that's it, baby," he says, running his fingers through my hair. "Take all the time you want. I'm not going anywhere."

I inhale. The faint, heady aroma of crotch-sweat and worn Levis makes me feel light and buoyant and my hands seem to rise effortlessly upwards towards his metal belt buckle.

I have no difficulty undoing it, nor the waist-button of his Levis.

I grip his zipper tab and slowly lower it. His Levis part in a widening V, revealing white low-cut briefs.

As if he can read my mind, he says, "At work? Boxer shorts. The pleated pants I wear there's lot of room to hang loose."

I reach up and undo the lower three buttons of his shirt. The hard terrain of his chest comes into view, firm and muscular with a narrow descent of short, black hairs that make their way across his abdomen, below his navel and into his briefs.

I lower his jeans to his knees. His boots obstruct further progress.

As if reading my mind again, he sits down to allow me to pull off his boots. No small feat, this, but the feel of leather against my skin makes it well worth the effort. And when I'm done I take the chance he won't think I'm really twisted to kiss and caress them before neatly setting them aside.

He's wearing white cotton socks. I massage his unusually wide feet through them, sniffing at his insteps before peeling them off.

Then I pull off his jeans, neatly folding them and placing them next to his boots.

He stands up again, towering above me. I look up from between the double columns of his legs to admire his gym-disciplined, masterfully-proportioned body with that shock of white cotton fabric at his crotch.

I reach up and grip his briefs on either side. The moment is too good to be

true and I pause to savor it, taking a mental snapshot. Then I slowly pull down his shorts. His lower abdomen comes into view. Then his pubic bush, bristling out from behind his briefs. My hands move behind him, pulling my face near his crotch as I struggle to lower his briefs down the perfect contours of his firm butt. Then, returning to his crotch, I lower his briefs another inch, and the base of his rugged, light-brown dick comes into view. Is it really that thick - comparisons with California redwoods come into my mind - or am I just seeing what I want to see?

I continue to lower his briefs, unveiling a truly mighty dick networked with a riot of prominent blue veins. Inch after inch of it comes into view. Oh, how smug he must've felt when I teased him about where would we ever find a grand nine-incher like Tony's! I give his briefs one final tug. Liberated from its cotton constraints, his dick plops down heavily in front of my face long, thick and cut, with a perfectly formed cock head so outstanding in size and symmetry it strikes me as a king among cock heads.

I hear an admiring groan escape me as I gaze in admiration at this huge dick I've so often contemplated in the abstract at the office as I ogle his suited form like a detective, pulling together the suggestive clues of his body, his facial features, the breadth of his hands and the length of his fingers, conjuring up a mighty cock that would look like too much for even me to handle.

But this! No, not even in my wildest fantasies...!

And if this isn't enough, it responds to my mesmerized stare with a massive twitch, infused with a fresh flow of blood, his cock head slowly rising up as if as curious about me as I am about it.

"Go for it, kid. You've wanted it long enough," Mr. Slater prompts from above.

And I do, slowing moving towards it with open mouth until the tip of my outstretched tongue connects with his piss slit. The contact is electrifying. I run the tip of my tongue up and down the underside of his cock head, getting it to repeatedly jerk upwards, surprisingly responsive for its size, each time landing heavily against the flat of my tongue.

Finally, I capture his cock head between my lips, imprisoning its impressive circumference. I dig one hand into my jock-pouch to play with my own stiff rod. Cock in mouth and cock in hand, another irresistible wave of sensuality catches me in its undertow.

I slowly slide my stretched lips down the length of his rugged dick until his cock head presses against my throat. With a slight push and sheer force of will I achieve what would seem an impossibility I manage his cock head down my throat. I relax my gagging muscles and soon my nose is buried in the bristly forest of his pubic hairs.

When I finally dismount, his liberated cock springs up stiff, spit-shiny and up-curving in front of my face. And behind, two enormous balls hanging low in a reddish brown, clean-shaven ball sac. What I wouldn't give for the privilege of

razoring off his nut sac!

I go down on him again, taking the whole of his dick into my mouth and down my throat, and commence deep-throating him with even-paced suck strokes, losing myself in the rhythm of cock sucking this big-dicked Colossus of Rhodes standing tall above me, accepting my ministrations like homage due such a stunning specimen of manhood.

And while I continue to suck him off, I pull my jockstrap down mid-thigh to stroke my own big boner, paler and smoother than his, and perhaps a half inch shorter, but just as thick, I'm proud to say.

"Well, would you look at that," Mr. Slater says, pushing me off his dick and looking down at me just as I wrap my fist around my dick.

"No," he orders me. "Take your hand off so as I can see all of it."

I clasp my hands behind my back. In the excitement of this inspection I lose control of my dick, which incessantly jerks upwards as if begging for Mr. Slater's continued attention.

"You really do have an enormous dick, especially for someone your height. I thought so, the way it strained your jockstrap, but I didn't expect it to be that big and that fat. Get up."

And as I rise, hands still behind my back, he sits down on the sofa, scrutinizing my dick close up.

"And big balls," he comments as he inspects my hairy, furrowed nut sac, which clings to the base of my cock like a baseball lodged in my crotch.

"It's going to be a real pleasure watching you stroke that monster while I fuck you. Assuming," he says, clutching his own dick, "you think you can manage all of this up inside you."

I nod yes, and with his free hand he picks up the jar of Vaseline and hands it to me while he rises to his feet once again.

I take a step backwards and grease him up with my jack off hand, careful not to stroke the cum out of him before he can make his way up my butt hole. But I almost go too far.

"Hey, careful," he admonishes, jackknifing backwards so his dick slides out of my hand. "Besides, I think you've got it greased up enough. Now, sit down on the sofa. Yeah. And pull your legs up. That's it."

As he gets down onto his knees to slather some more lubricant into my butt hole he says, "Stroke your dick. Slower. Yeah. Like that. I don't want you to come too soon."

"Jesus, yes," he muses, continuing to grease up my hole. "Awfully big for a guy your size."

And then, after a pause of preoccupation with my hole, he asks, "Ready?" as he wipes the remaining lubricant off his hand.

"Yes sir," I whisper.

He takes my legs from me and pushes them farther back until my kneecaps reach my shoulders, and then presses against them as he rises into a vertical

pushup position, pressing his cock head against my butt hole.

I realize at that moment that given his body and my body and the dimensions of the sofa, this isn't going to be an easy fuck.

He immediately takes any potential awkwardness out of the situation with a good, hearty laugh as he lowers my legs and gets down on his knees again.

"Only in porn stories does everything go right. Actually, though, if this were a porn story we'd be doing it on my desk. But do you know how uncomfortable that would be?"

Truth to tell, I wouldn't mind finding out.

"No, the floor'll be better," he says grabbing two throw pillows from the corner of the sofa.

As I reposition myself on the plush-carpeted floor, he places one pillow under my head and tucks the other one under my butt.

"Comfortable?"

"Umm," I say, raising my legs and gripping my cock with my jack off hand, acutely aware of the heaviness of my ball sac and the expectant itch in my exposed butt hole.

As he lowers himself into position, confidently taking possession of me, I drape my bent knees over his shoulders and once again he presses his cock head against my butt hole.

"Ohh, yeah," he says. "This is much better. Much better."

I watch the collaboration of all his well-developed muscles working together like a finely tuned machine as he slowly sinks his dick into my hole. It slides in easily and I'm overwhelmed by the sensation of him entering me, filling me up and taking me over.

When he's fully inside me, he let his dick rest there as he looks deep into my eyes.

"Well," he says, "I guess Norm *could* take nine inches."

The intimacy of his cock up my hole and his intense gaze washes over me like too much of a good thing, and I can hardly believe my fortune when he lowers his lips to mine and gently kisses me.

"But could Norm sustain a full-fledged butt fuck, all the way to orgasm?" he asks with a wicked smile.

"I think I'm about to find out."

He slowly begins working his huge rod in and out my hole, his eyes never leaving mine.

I welcome each cock-thrust with a breathy, drawn-out "Ohh!" So I'm not at my most eloquent while getting the fuck of my life.

His mouth falls open and his eyes begin to blaze with ferocious lust. His heavy exhalations dramatically record his own progress towards orgasm, as does the thin film of sweat that begins to gleam on his forehead.

His plunges into me accelerate, growing more forceful. Each hip-thrust knocks against my butt with a slight shove. His face strains with the effort and

my "ohhs" grow louder as his breathing deepens and his entire body becomes a mass of sweaty, straining muscle. The dense aura of his masculinity wraps itself around me like a straitjacket and I savor him at his brutal best, welcoming the emergence of this beast I always hoped lurked within the folds of his impeccable suits and behind the curtain of civilized office deportment.

I abandon myself to him and he works his cock in and out of me with a force I can hardly believe while I furiously pound away at my own dick.

"Ah! Ahh! Ahhhhh!" our voices intertwine, intensifying, rising in pitch.

And then with the loudest wail yet, he plunges himself into me one final time with such force the aftershock of it jolts my entire body, and I feel his hot cum gushing out, making its way up my butt hole with all the power of a tidal wave.

He draws his dick out and plunges it into me second time, releasing a second gusher of cum.

This one sets off my own orgasm. "Ahhh! Ohhh! Ahhh, fuck!" Just then the cum starts to shoot out my dick in long, ropy strands that land all over me.

He continues shooting his cum up my ass while I quick-stroke my own abundant load onto my chest, the two of us losing ourselves in the bestial passion of this shared double orgasm.

And then when we're done, both of us drained, exhausted and panting, he falls on top of me, letting my feet slide off his shoulders and onto the floor. Despite his weight, the moment's too perfect to abandon with any sort of haste.

But eventually he lifts himself off, slowly pulling his softening cock out of me.

"So, Mr. Cardini," I ask, sitting up next to him, "are you convinced that Norm could take Tony's nine inches up his butt hole?"

"Yeah. But you've also convinced me of one other thing; that we should be seeing more of each other. Now, tomorrow afternoon if you'd care to help me and the real Tony work out the logistics of a threesome in the back of a UPS truck I'll be writing about...."

Beaming at the possibility, I dig my hands into his crotch to play with his balls, as I lean over and kiss him on the cheek, which I'm sure he takes as a yes. And then, as he pushes me back onto the floor again, crawling on top of me and plunging his tongue deep into my mouth, I think, shit, it's going to be awfully difficult going back to my regular job Monday morning!

THE BEST KIND OF COCK
by Jack Ricardo

I stopped at a local thrift shop hoping to pick up some good paperbacks. I ambled over to the wall of books. Another guy was also standing there perusing the volumes. I didn't pay much attention as I scanned the titles and selected three detective mysteries I hadn't read.

I sat on my haunches to check out the bottom stack. That's when I became very much aware of him. It was difficult not to. His crotch was face high. The creased pouch of his faded jeans was an instant aphrodisiac. My mind began flashing on what rested so comfortably inside those jeans. The symbolism was blatant. I was on my knees in front of this young hunk. I rose to my feet, pretending to scan more books, but actually sizing up my literate companion.

He was shorter than me. And *much* younger. I'm 52, and I guessed he was verging on twenty. He had short, curly, brown hair, a beard barely beginning to sprout, and a white T-shirt covering a smooth gut. He suddenly went down to his knees to look over the bottom stack.

The tables had turned. Again, the symbolism was obvious. Now I was standing and he was kneeling in front of my crotch. Not a bad crotch either, if I do say so myself, denim-stuffed, tingling, and attached to a thin body, a scraggly face, and a clipped head of dark hair sided with gray. He peered up at me cautiously, shyly glanced at my crotch, then eased his eyes back up to mine. I smiled. He rose to his feet, scratched his ass ineptly, nodded at my books, and said, "I see you like detective stories too."

I spied Hammett's *The Thin Man* in his hand and noted the avid look in his eye. "Yeah, I do."

"I have a slew of mysteries at my place. Wanna check 'em out?"

The interest was as mutual as the generated heat. "Sure."

In his tiny studio apartment near the campus, we sat at a breakfast counter and compared favorite authors. I was sure he was gay, but he didn't offer an opening and I guessed he was new at the game.

He gulped down his coffee and seemed to work up his nerve when he muttered, "Let me show you the books I have." He slid from his stool and opened a closet door. I joined him as he hauled a cardboard box from the shelf and set it on the floor.

"Take whatever you...you want...Da...Da...Dad," he stuttered.

I looked him in the eye and sensed a hopeful plea behind his thoughtful gaze. "You're generous..." I hesitated, then added, "...son."

"Well," he mumbled awkwardly, dropping his chin to his neck, stuffing his hands into his hip pockets. "You're my old man, aren't you?" He lifted his head with care. Apprehension mixed with cautious optimism seemed to ring his face, a hope.

"Of course, son," I assured him. Then suddenly, I became awkward, unsure how far to take this.

His face broke into a clumsy grin. Then he sensed my unease, shifted his weight from foot to foot, turned away, and went down to the floor, sitting on his heels at my feet, lumpishly fingering the books in the box. We were again at the shelves in the thrift shop. He on his knees, my pouch at his face. My chest grew hot, my nuts itched and, oddly, my heart warmed.

"This is my favorite," he mumbled, caressing *Parker's Early Autumn*, a tale of a gruff PI and a bungling boy yearning for a father.

"One of the best," I agreed. "I'd say we have some of the same things in common."

He sighed with anxious relief. "Think so, Dad?"

"I know so, son." My hips jutted out. A stuffed cock was growing fast inside my worn jeans. He saw it and looked up at me, as much fear in his eyes as desire. I nodded approval. He tentatively lifted a hand to pet the pouch. His touch was tender but charged. He leaned his face forward and licked, slowly, carefully draping his tongue over the coarse material and the heated clump inside. He swiped his tongue over the elongated outline and clamped his lips around a stiff shaft of pulsing blue denim.

"Oh, Daddy," he moaned, quietly, hoarsely, intimately.

I pressed the pouch of my balls into his chin. His chest was heaving. He was underfed and needful. He trailed his tongue over my shaft, brushed his tongue over my balls, paused to kiss them with a passion that was as subtle as it was erotic, then began gnawing his way back up to the vibrating rod of blue denim and dick.

When I unbuttoned the top of my jeans, he sat back on his heels, eyes wide open and guileless in their youthful excitement. I unzipped my fly and pushed my jeans to my knees. His mouth dropped open; he was gaping; his face was a picture of innocent adoration. A dark splotch of liquid slimed through the white cotton and topped the silhouetted head of the stiff dick crammed inside my briefs. "Will you clean those shorts for me," I suggested, "like the good son I know you are."

His words were buoyant, rapid-fire and respectful. "Oh, Daddy, sure, Daddy, sure, sure I will." He opened his mouth and smothered his lips over the cotton-covered dickhead. Warm, wet sensations eased through my body and engulfed my balls. His tongue swiping over the slime left me shivering and glowing. He swallowed loudly then slurped the entire bulbous cock head inside his mouth and trapped it between his lips, watered it with his spit, gnawed it, then spit it out, peering up at me, his face an open book of lust and devotion. He was as pleased as punch. His chest was heaving, his mouth was open and watering. He wiped the saliva from his lips with the back of his hand.

I was barely able to get the words out. "Get comfortable, son. Take off your jeans. Hell, take off your shorts, if you want. You don't have to be shy around your old man. You know that."

"Sure, Daddy, sure." His artless enthusiasm was genuine and for all that,

amusing. And amazingly erotic. The inflexible cock packed inside my shorts bounded against the mouth-sopped material.

He rose, toed his sneakers off, hopped from one leg to the next to pull off his jeans. He almost toppled over in the process. He pulled his T-shirt over his head and threw it aside. He pushed his shorts down and kicked them off. A proud cut cock speared the air, two remarkably large, scrumptious and hairless balls dangled below. He looked to me for approval; waiting, timid, trusting, ever hopeful.

My admiration and appreciation was obvious as I gulped down my spittle and stared. "That is one great set of knockers you got there, son." I licked the spit from my lips. I cupped the overflowing pouch of the balls bubbling inside my shorts and was rewarded with sparkles that lit my brain and flashed behind my eyes.

His face flushed. "The guys on the team tease me about my balls all the time," he muttered, hefting the bags hanging long and low underneath a solid cock that quivered with every word he spoke. The nuts were set neatly in his palm with the loose flesh lapping over his hand. "They say I don't have a hair on my ass." He laughed self-consciously. "But I have the biggest balls of anybody, they tell me too. The coach even says the same thing."

I smiled. "Chip off the old block."

His eyes widened, brightened, a childish glow filtered over his face. "Really?" he enthused.

"Yeah." I tugged off my boots, pulled off my jeans and tossed them aside. Before I could pull my shorts down, he said, "We even wear the same brand of underwear." He was more than pleased; he was ecstatic. "I thought so, Daddy, I thought so. I knew it, I just knew it."

His naive enthusiasm was contagious. "Of course," I told him, "after all, I'm your dad. Like father, like son." I lowered my briefs until they joined my jeans on the floor. My stiff cock snapped up, flapped against my belly hairs, then leveled off. It was longer than his, and wider, it's head rounder and leaking more freely. My balls hung low, slightly longer than his, heftier than his, hairier than his.

His chest expanded, contracted, loud and uncontrollably. He was panting. "Your balls are bigger than mine! Wow! You're cut too, just like me."

"The best kind of cock," I said. "Any son of mine would be the same way." The kid was as enthused by circumcised cocks as I was myself.

He inhaled, caught his breath and kept one hand clamped around his nuts. Bubbles of saliva were forming at the corner of his lips. I swallowed mine. He reached out to me, then hesitated. "Can I feel your balls, Daddy?" He looked up. "Please," he added hoarsely, a hushed appeal from an obedient son.

I nodded. "Of course, son." I spread my legs and clamped my hands over my biceps, the sizzling rush inside my chest coursing through my veins. "I'd be damn disappointed if you didn't."

"Gosh, they're great balls, and hairy too." His grateful sigh was loud, bursting from his lips in a swift gush of relief. He stepped forward. The shaft of his cock brushed mine and forced a bright pearl to ooze from my cock head. I clenched my toes. My jeans and shorts strained against my calves. He was staring intently at my cock, my balls. When his warm fingertips eased onto the underside of my nuts, I shivered. When his hand closed around my nuts, my insides quaked. A spasm rocked through my cock with an energy that slammed its head onto his. His cock head slammed back.

"Just like the old man," I said in a heated rush.

"Yeah," he said proudly, nobly. He lifted his gaze to mine, grinned, and gently nuzzled my balls in his fist, his fingers tracing the hairs that coated the prickly flesh.

"I wish I had hair on my balls," he said, more to himself than to me.

I answered him anyway. "Some day, son."

He lifted the other hand and held both our cocks together. The heat generated between them could have lit up the entire continent. They clamored and fought in his fist. He pulled the shafts of both cocks until my cock head was nudging his balls. My sigh was as loud and as intense as his. His thickly veined cock, his hefty nuts, lined the top of my cock. He fondled my balls slowly, measuring them, weighing them with a caress that was endearing. Another spurt leaked from my slit into his fine sparse cock hairs.

He gushed, "Can I suck your cock, Daddy? Can I?"

His mouth was trembling, his tongue was fluttering over his lips. This kid was one hungry cocksucker who wanted to eat his dad so badly he could already taste him. His passion was earnest, excitable, and infectious. The juice inside my balls was already brimming near the edge.

"If you don't blow my cock, son, and right now, the cum inside those balls you're holding is going to spit right in your fist." I sounded desperate, and the kid knew it.

"No, Daddy, no," he said, his voice edgy, verging on panic. "I want you come in my mouth. I want to feel your cum sliding down my throat. I want to swallow it. I need it. I do. Wait, wait," He released my balls and my cock. "Not yet, not yet. Don't come yet, Daddy."

He fell to the floor, his hands on his knees, his balls scraping the floor, his cock pointed at his stomach. No matter my will, my cock was on its own timetable and was twitching in front of his lips. His eyes were raised to my face and smiling when he stuck his tongue out and lapped the ooze from my cock head. My cock head slapped itself back on his lips. He swirled his tongue around the entire slippery crown while it bobbed and bounced in front of him like a helium balloon attached to a thick pole, bringing out sensations that thrilled me to the bone.

He lowered his head, slapping his tongue underneath the rubbery knob. The knob lifted. He lifted his head, again slobbering his tongue round and round. My

cock head weaved from side to side, up and down, while he played with it, using only his tongue, his mouth, his lips, slobbering over that dickhead like a boy with his favorite toy, until I was close to bursting at his playful, spirited, and oh so sensual efforts.

"Son, son, son, son...son...son..." I began sputtering. He knew what was happening. I couldn't stop, I didn't want to stop; I didn't want him to stop. He kept bobbing and gobbling my cock head, teasing it, slapping it with his tongue, licking it, while my balls became cramped in my sacs, while my asshole began clenching tightly. I was sweating and staring at my son who was bringing me to the brink by merely slapping my dickhead with his tongue, by worshipping his old man, his face a juvenile display of hunger and hope and need, his naked body literally bristling with the pleasure of the moment as I moaned loudly and the cum packed inside my nuts came spurting out. He quickly sucked the shooting dickhead between his lips, my cum splashing and coating the inside of his mouth, his tongue. He began swallowing, quivering, the cum leaking from his lips, his tongue lapping out to wipe it up and take it down into his stomach, until I was shimmering and shaking and empty. And weak in the knees.

I held on and looked down at one gorgeous sight of grateful worship. My cock was still impaled in his face, the cock head was still clamped between his lips; my nuts, my ball sacs were hanging low and empty. "My god," I sighed.

He pulled his face away, my cock flopped from his mouth. He handled the shaft gently as he licked the head clean then rested his butt back on his heels, hands by his side, his face a picture of pure worshipful love and appreciative contentment.

I leaned over him, shaky with the effort, took his face in my hands, and kissed my son.

A GARDENER'S HANDS
by Peter Rice

Jimmy Arthur heaved a sigh of relief as he waved to the fast receding Daimler. The driver returned the wave from his open window. Just before the vehicle turned out of sight round a bend in the road.

His mother's funeral was only two days behind him. There had been no time to think since she died. This was the first moment he had been alone since then. Everyone who felt they had some responsibility for him had done all they could. His aunt and uncle in Gloucester had insisted that he must not be alone in his bereavement. His uncle had gone with him to attend to all of the necessary details before the funeral and they had persuaded him to sleep the next two nights at their house as well.

He closed the tall wooden gates and looked up at the sky. Dark clouds were coming up and would soon cover the evening sun. He turned with relief up the drive towards the friendly house where he had lived all of his seventeen years, the first nine with his mother and father, until his father had been killed in a road accident. His mother had cared for him for the next two years and then she had developed multiple sclerosis. From then their roles gradually became reversed. For the next six years he had learned to run the house, wash and dress his mother and somehow to go to school and do his homework. There had been little time for any recreation and he had received scant help from the social services.

At first, he had tried to keep the garden tidy but it had proved to be too difficult and his mother had suggested they employ a gardener once a week. He had looked in the village shop window to see if any gardeners had advertised there. There had been just one. His name was Mark and he was much younger than Jimmy had expected. He was only twenty-one now. He came from a gardening family and his skill had been learned by experience. Lately he had decided to branch out on his own and was doing well.

Jimmy looked at the garden, thinking of him. It was just what a garden should be a mass of flowers in a riot of colors between richly flourishing shrubs, disguising the planning behind it. It had given his mother so much pleasure in those years since Mark had taken over. A feeling of regret passed over Jimmy as he reflected that he no longer had any excuse to employ a gardener.

He took out his keys as he walked up the drive. Unlocking the door he went in, closing it behind him as though to shut out the decisions he had to make. The hallway was quiet save for the deep ticking of the grandfather clock. The oak floor and paneled walls glowed in the mellow light shining through the frosted glass window panes.

This was home. Perhaps his feelings of the importance of that were heightened by his recent experiences. They had not been easy times but he had been even closer to his mother than most boys of his age because of the challenges he had faced. Perhaps, too, they were a reason for his deep love of

the house.

His aunt and uncle had been very kind but he knew that his mother would have liked to see more of her brother during her illness. It had particularly hurt her that her brother only occasionally came to see her, but she had known that his business occupied most of his time and his wife Gwen's, too.

Now they wanted Jimmy to go and live with them.

"You can't live in that big old place on your own at your age. Sell up and put some of the money towards an extension here. You'll have your own private rooms and yet you won't need to spend your time cooking or cleaning. You can get on with your studies undisturbed and we can keep an eye on you."

Uncle Ralph was a nice bloke but very much an ex-army officer: all right in small doses. The idea of his supervision was very unwelcome to a boy who had had so much responsibility and also some independence of a kind. Aunt Gwen was kind but constantly fussing about details and forever tidying up.

"I'll see to cleaning your room and I'll keep it straight for you."

"You aren't old enough to be alone, anyway, and you've no money coming in now your mum's gone," Uncle Ralph had added emphatically just before he had driven away. "I'll see the estate agents tomorrow about putting the house up for sale."

After living a life of total responsibility he suddenly felt as though he had no control over it any more. Tears of sorrow, mixed with frustration, crept down his cheeks almost unnoticed. Then he saw, for the first time, a scrap of paper lying near the wall, just inside the door. That hadn't been there when he'd last gone out, he was sure. Wondering who would have dropped it through the letter box he picked it up.

"*Dear Jimmy,*" it read. "*I know you'll be feeling low tonight. I thought a bit of company might help. I'll be round to see you about 8. If you'd rather be on your own instead I understand. In that case, give us a ring. Mark.*"

Jimmy smiled. Good old Mark. His spelling might be a bit cranky but of all the people who could have called to see him there was no one he wanted to see more at that moment. His depression eased. Mark was so uncomplicated. He had got to know him well over the years he had tended the garden. He had only been paid for one day's work each week but more and more he had come along in the evenings because, "I didn't finish pruning the apple trees," or "I thought, with the frost, your fuschias could do with some cover." There was always a plausible reason for his extra time but he would never take any money for it. "No, a' course not. Should've done it the other day." He would come in for a cup of cocoa in the evenings with Jimmy and his mother, increasingly as the months passed by.

"Of course I want you to come round," thought Jimmy as he went into the lounge and flicked on the gas fire. There was a bit of early frost in the air. It was only early September but the house felt cold. It was already six-thirty. He decided to rest in an armchair and read for a while. Choosing a book from the

shelves he sat down with it and began to read.

- - -

The doorbell was ringing as he felt the book slide from his knee and hit the floor with a bump. Mark, already!

Jimmy snatched up the fallen volume and put it on the coffee table, stumbling over the edge of the carpet in his sleep- numbed state. He hurried to open the front door, switching on the lounge and hall lights as he went.

It was Mark, as he had guessed. Jimmy was still not properly awake and he stood there looking at the young gardener for a moment as he thought how attractive he looked, his dark, curly hair framing an almost perpetually cheerful face. His features formed a half smile now but his eyes were without their usual sparkle. Jimmy became aware also that it was raining hard and that Mark was wet through. At last he roused himself from the last vestiges of sleep.

"Come in, Mark. God, you're soaked!"

"I'm sorry if it's not a good time, but you didn't phone. P'rhaps you didn't find my note. I'll come another time if you like?"

Mark was still standing on the door step, hesitant.

"Of course it's not inconvenient. Get yourself inside."

He stepped inside with the kind of deference that was born of the knowledge that someone much loved had recently died here. Water dripped from his clothes making tiny pools on the polished wood floor.

"I'm sorry, I'm making a bit of a mess. It wasn't raining when I left home."

It was a mile and a half to Jimmy's from Mark's dad's small holding and he had walked as he usually did.

"Come on in," said Jimmy. "I'll turn the gas fire up. You can take your wet things off and I'll dry them in the airing cupboard."

After turning on the fire he went upstairs to the cupboard and took out a king-sized woolen blanket. By the time he was downstairs again Mark had stripped off his supposedly waterproof anorak, his sweater, T-shirt, trainers and socks and they were lying in a soggy heap in the middle of the hearth rug. Mark was easing himself out of a pair of clinging jeans. Jimmy stood in the doorway absorbed in admiration for this lithe, athletic young man.

Jimmy knew his own inclinations but had never acted on them. There were lots of boys at school that he fancied but they all seemed to be unshakably hetero. The time had never seemed right to "come out" nor did he feel like being the only one to do it. He had never pretended to be other than he was, never had a girlfriend in any serious sense. Girls couldn't understand why he never came on to them but he had never explained himself.

He felt an emptiness inside himself as he looked at Mark, an emptiness left by his recent bereavement, by the prospect of having to leave his home and now magnified by his aching need for love. All of that need suddenly became focused on the bedraggled and beautiful young man before him. 'If, only ' he thought. Then he saw that the window curtains were still open. Even though

there were shrubs in the garden between the window and the road and a hedge along the bottom of the garden he hurried to draw the curtains across.

"I could charge for this." he said. "Male stripper reveals all!"

Mark turned and grinned as he finally won the fight with the reluctant trousers. He stood with them slung over his shoulder in the posture of the Michelangelo *David*. Jimmy was surprised to see that Mark had not been wearing under shorts of any kind.

"You think they'd pay to see me then?" he asked, his West Country accent giving his voice a sensuous inflection.

Jimmy looked him straight in the eyes as he answered, "I'm bloody sure they would."

Mark continued to hold his gaze.

"Would you?"

His eyes challenged and for a second Jimmy seemed about to acknowledge them but then he looked down.

"Would you expect me to?" he laughed, unconvincingly, as he bent to gather up the heap of wet clothes from the rug. As he stood upright with them Mark was right in front of him and his cock was more than half erect.

Mark took the wet clothes from him and dropped them again to the side.

"You'd never need to," he said, cupping Jimmy's chin in his hands. "If you want me, you can have me for free any time you like."

He kissed Jimmy gently on the lips.

"Tell me if you don't want me to do this," he whispered, kissing him again.

Jimmy was astonished, taken aback. Mark kissing him! Now Mark's arms were around his waist drawing them close. They were much of a height; there was no feeling of being overpowered. The initial tension subsided and his arms were around Mark without conscious movement. It was so natural that he and Mark should come together like this. Questions could come later. This was what he needed and Mark was the one he desired. That was enough for now.

"I do," breathed Jimmy softly. "I do want you to."

Mark kissed him more urgently, at the same time pulling Jimmy's shirt from the waistband of his trousers as the boy's hands followed the work muscled body that was offered for his enjoyment. He marveled, as one only does once in a lifetime, at the first electric sensations of the hands on another's warm skin. Mark's tongue was flickering against his lips, seeking entrance. He responded instinctively, lips parting, making the probing tongue welcome, touching it with the tip of his own before the two entwined in moist embrace.

Mark's hands fought to feel the contours of Jimmy's arse through the grey flannel trousers, frustrated. They battled with the belt about the trim waist, reaching beneath the waistband, finally slipping under the briefs Jimmy wore and tracing the crack of his arse to the anal bud, previously inviolate.

Jimmy quickly unfastened his belt and unbuttoned the trousers, slipping them from his hips together with the briefs. With that Mark gently pulled him to the

floor and rapidly unbuttoned the white cotton shirt, slipping it over his shoulders. He showered Jimmy's body with kisses, giving the nipples that extra attention and tonguing they needed. The kisses continued downwards about the abdomen and pelvis until they reached the pulsating cock head. He paused and looked up at Jimmy, smiling that lazy smile.

"My word, Jimmy boy, you've really been hiding something down here, haven't you?"

It was true. Jimmy's cock had been remarkable from the age of twelve. Boys made good-natured jokes in the showers at school about it.

"You'll make some lucky girl very happy," they would say. "Be careful how you turn round or you'll knock somebody over."

Once someone had said: "I reckon Jimmy's queer. Queers always have the biggest pricks."

Everyone had laughed, including Jimmy, who had retorted: "You'd better not turn your back on me then, had you?"

This time Jimmy felt very glad that he had a cock to be proud of. He smiled in return. "Not too much for you is it, Mark?"

Mark's response was to encase the blood engorged head in his mouth and savor it a moment before sliding it slowly and smoothly down his throat until his lips were buried deep in Jimmy's sandy blond bush. It was not achieved without a little gagging but achieved it was, not once, but then repeatedly and more quickly with such suction exerted on withdrawal that Jimmy felt his cock would burst. Abruptly, just as Jimmy was reaching the point of orgasm, Mark stopped and looked at him again.

"You were saying?"

Jimmy knew that this first time he was not going to be taking any initiatives. He was aware what men did together, and he was a bit scared. Perhaps he wouldn't be up to it. Somewhere Mark must have had a lot of experience. He might expect too much of him.

Then Mark was kissing him again and now Jimmy was no longer tentative. He kissed Mark, his tongue now invading Mark's mouth, eagerly jousting tongue against tongue. Mark rolled onto his back, pulling Jimmy onto him as Jimmy kicked the encumbering clothing from about his ankles. Mark's fingers again explored Jimmy's arse crack and now, on reaching his hole, began to investigate its tight virginity. Jimmy gasped and stiffened as a finger penetrated past the resistance. Mark paused.

"I'm sorry," he said. "I don't want to hurt you."

Jimmy nuzzled into his neck.

"It's okay, I'm not a baby. I've got to learn, haven't I?"

"Only if you want to."

"I do, Mark. Go on, it's all right."

The finger was joined by another after Mark had moistened them with a plentiful supply of saliva. As he massaged and manipulated the taut little

opening Jimmy began to respond to the sensation. He wanted to explore Mark's beautiful body with his hands, with his tongue, in any way that he could. He began to nibble and suck on a firm rosy nipple while making sure that Mark could continue with the good work on his arsehole. He ventured farther until his cheek encountered the swollen dick head. Then he took it in one hand raising it from its position tight against Mark's belly. He raised it against some resistance beyond a right angle then let it go. It sprang back with a slap against the firm abdominal muscles. Fascinated, he did the same again. As it happened a third time Mark thrust a third finger in beside the others. Jimmy no longer gasped with pain but the feeling that he could not be stretched any further without something tearing became total.

"I don't think I can take any more," he said.

Mark left the fingers inside Jimmy's arse while he drew him back on top of him.

"You can," he said. "And I know now that you will, for me."

He reached out to the bundle of clothes and felt with his free hand in a pocket from which he took a tube of lubricant.

"This'll make it easier."

"You planned this," accused Jimmy.

Manipulating the screw cap with one hand he opened it and squeezed some in the vicinity of Jimmy's hole.

"Yes, or rather, I hoped.... Well, I've waited a long time."

Laying the tube down he transferred the gel to the right place and now slid his three fingers easily in and out of the expanded opening.

"Tell me, if you want to stop."

In response Jimmy wriggled his moistened hole onto Mark's fingers.

"Will you let me fuck you?"

Jimmy had known all the while that this had been coming. He did want it, very much indeed, but his heart was thumping in reaction to the adrenalin coursing through his arteries. It was in reality a split second's hesitation. He would not say "no" to Mark in any case.

"Please, Mark. Yes, but I've never done it before."

"I didn't think you had, Jimmy. I'll be careful. It'll be okay, you'll see. It does hurt the first time but I'll make it as easy as I can."

"All right, go on."

Jimmy was tense as he felt the rigid cock against his arse and then against his partially eased anus. Mark was true to his promise. The tip pushed against the resistance, first very gently and then more insistently until finally the muscle's instinctive tension was overcome by the ample lubrication and the persistent pressure. The glans popped suddenly into Jimmy's rectum.

"Oh, God!" Jimmy gasped.

"Easy Jimmy, easy. Try to relax."

"I am trying, but it hurts like hell."

"I'll keep it still until you get used to it being there."

Jimmy wanted to get used to it. His sphincter was in a spasm of cramp more painful than anything he could remember. He'd never imagined it would be this bad. He was on the point of thinking he would have to ask Mark to stop, when the pain became slightly less sharp. Mark was kissing the back of his neck, nuzzling into his hair, whispering reassurance. He turned and kissed Mark.

"It's a bit better, now," Jimmy said. "Go on."

Mark began to move his dick slowly back and forth, at first only a little and then, still slowly, gradually penetrating farther. It must have been all of fifteen minutes later when he said: "Guess what?"

"What?"

"Feel round and see how far it's in."

Jimmy did, expecting that at least the first four inches or so might have made it. He was amazed to find that all eight plus inches of Mark's thick weapon were encased in the silky tube of his anal passage. He could not get his fingers between Mark's thick bush and his own backside.

He imagined his friend's superb penis inside himself as in an X-ray photograph. The thought overcame his remaining discomfort and made his own prick harder and firmer than he could ever recall. He took Mark's hand and placed it on his cock.

"Wow, Jimmy, boy. Seems to be working for you now all right."

Both were elated as Mark continued to fuck in longer and longer smooth strokes. Jimmy at last relaxed. He was feeling a bit sore but it was bearable, and the sensations as the cock pushed by his prostate were bringing him nearer and nearer his climax.

"Mark," he breathed. "You can do it harder if you want. It feels great now, really, really great. I'll be coming in a jiffy."

Mark responded by increasing the speed of the strokes. He was tempted to pull out and dive straight in again but he thought that might be too much for Jimmy's first time. He did not want to spoil things now. Anyway he was nearly past the point of no return himself. As he reached orgasm he turned onto his back, pulling Jimmy on top of him. Taking the lad's dick in his right hand, pushing Jimmy's away, he completed the masturbation and the thick white jism fired over the trim body and over his hand.

He put his hand to his lips and licked every trace from it.

"That's really sweet tasting, just like its maker."

"What's it taste like?" Jimmy was a bit surprised that anyone should want to taste it.

"Try some," said Mark, scooping some from Jimmy's chest on a forefinger and putting it to the boy's lips.

Tentatively he opened his mouth protruding his tongue. He licked a little from Mark's finger. It was sweet, but a bit salty as well. He opened his mouth and sucked the spunk-coated finger inside.

"Mmmm," he murmured as he savored the comforter.

Mark's prick had begun to slide from Jimmy's arse as they relaxed and it returned to a flaccid state. Now it abruptly escaped.

"Ow!" Jimmy complained.

"Sorry!" apologized Mark, though there was little he could have done to prevent it from happening.

Jimmy wriggled over and lay on top of the young gardener face down.

"That was really wonderful," he gushed..

"It was for me."

"And me."

"I was afraid you might not like it, in the end."

"Seems that's just where I do like it!"

They laughed.

Jimmy jumped up, feet astride his lover, looking down at him.

"I was going to make some hot cocoa to warm you up."

"This was much better."

"Mm, it was. Would you like some now, though."

"Well, p'rhaps." Mark reached up a hand and caught Jimmy's wrist. "But I don't want you to go."

"Come with me then," replied Jimmy, pulling him to his feet and leading him into the kitchen.

They soon had two hot drinks and took them back to the lounge.

Seeing the pile of now steaming wet clothes on the rug, Jimmy picked them up. "I'll hang these up to dry in the airing cupboard. I won't be a jiff."

While Jimmy went upstairs Mark pulled the woolen blanket around him and sat in front of the fire. He heard Jimmy padding down again a couple of minutes later and turned round. As Jimmy came into the room Mark was filled with warmth of a kind no drink nor food could provide. He said nothing. He only lifted the blanket for Jimmy to join him inside its folds.

After some moments of silence during which they sipped the cocoa and stared into the fire's rosy glow, savoring each other's nearness. Jimmy spoke first. "Why now?"

"How do you mean?"

"I mean, why did you wait all this time before saying anything, or doing anything?"

"Dunno, really. You were very young when I first knew you and I suppose I didn't expect you to be gay."

"Well, how *did* you guess that I'm gay?"

"I'm not sure. I suppose I didn't really, not for certain, I mean. A long time ago I began to think you could be, but there was nothing for sure, like there is with some."

"I'd never have thought you were."

"Why?"

"I just wouldn't. You don't act queer. I mean there's a boy at school. Everybody knows he is, you only have to see him."

"Oh, I suppose you think you act like him?"

"No, of course not."

"So, why should I? Any more than you?"

"Well then, that's what I mean. How did you guess I was?"

"I told you, I wasn't ever sure. It was just: well, for one thing you have no girlfriends."

"I haven't many friends of any sort; not close friends. There was never time, Mum being ill."

"Yes, I know that, but somehow I thought that I'd have seen you with a girl sometimes. I never did. I saw you with groups of boys and girls. That's different. And then there's the way you looked at me. If I had my shirt off working in the garden I'd see you watching, and if I saw you you'd nearly always pretend you were looking at something else. I'd take it off on purpose when you were there."

Jimmy smiled. He remembered Mark doing that lots of times.

"You always wanted me to stay around after I'd done work. You always tried to find a reason, if only because your mum enjoyed a chat with me. But mostly it was the way you looked at me."

"You took a risk this evening then, didn't you?"

"It was worth it though, wasn't it? And it might have been I put my arms round you just to comfort you, which I did, partly, anyway. When I did, that was when I somehow knew I could kiss you, that it would be right."

"I'm glad you did."

"Anyway, its different now. Your mum was alive before. It was her house. It wouldn't have been right, not under her roof. It's yours now."

Jimmy felt his stomach turn over. His house. Not for much longer it wasn't. The tears began to appear at the corner of his eyes. It was worse than ever, now. He had found his lover, only to lose him again. He would never see him if he moved in with Aunt Gwen and Uncle Ralph. He would no longer have his own house.

Mark looked at him, curious. Jimmy had suddenly begun to sob.

"Hey, Jimmy, boy. I've been a fool, haven't I? I've not forgotten how you must be feeling, though."

He put his arm round him and drew him close, while Jimmy's tears subsided.

Jimmy began to explain about his aunt and uncle and their plans, and what they had said about his living on his own.

Mark turned to him, putting a hand on each of Jimmy's shoulders, and looked into his eyes.

"They've got a point. You'll have no money coming in to live on if you're going to study. Banks won't lend a boy of your age any either. The thing is, do you want to leave here?

Jimmy shook his head, not trusting himself to hold back more tears if he spoke.

"Then perhaps there's a way out. That's if you think you won't upset your aunt and uncle too much. Can you stop your uncle going to the estate agent tomorrow?"

"I suppose I could, but I don't know what to tell him."

"Don't tell him anything much. Just ask him to leave it for a few days. You could say that you have heard of someone who's interested already."

"I suppose I could, but it wouldn't be true, would it?"

"All right. I've got an idea then. Why don't you take a lodger? That would bring in a bit to live on for now."

Jimmy looked at him, studying the half smile on Mark's lips, the gas fire lighting his features with a soft ruddy glow.

"I suppose you can suggest a suitable candidate?" he asked.

Mark leaned forward and kissed him.

"Who else?"

Jimmy wanted to say yes, at once. It would work out perfectly, he was sure. But it wouldn't be so easy to convince his aunt and uncle. The very idea of a seventeen-year-old taking a lodger would seem quite crazy to them. On the other hand, he wanted to say yes.

"I'll have to think carefully how to tell them," said Jimmy thoughtfully. "It won't be easy. They do care about me, but they wouldn't understand how I feel about you. Even if they did they'd say I'm too young to know what I want."

"Are you?" asked Mark, looking directly into his eyes.

"I don't think so," Jimmy asserted. "I'm not like kids who've never had any responsibility. I can do practical things like cooking and know how to look after a house and deal with money."

"Are you sure about *me*?"

"I'm sure how *I* feel, and I believe what you tell me and I *have* known you a good while now."

Mark drew Jimmy to him and kissed him.

"I always knew you were special," he whispered.

"Stay the night," appealed Jimmy.

"Are you sure?"

"Sure I'm sure. I want to get fucked again, anyway."

"Ah, that's it, is it? You're just after my body."

"Mmmm." Jimmy leaned down to take the end of Mark's well-exercised foreskin between his lips, inserting his tongue into the gathered rosebud of skin guarding the entrance to the sensitive glans within. At once the resting object of Jimmy's desire twitched in response to his ministration. Instinctively he tongued back the sheath of skin and swirled his tongue around the rapidly expanding head as it pulsed and strained towards the back of his throat. He loved the clean-showered yet wholly male smell as he experimentally took more of the cock in

his mouth and, for a moment, buried his nose in the curly bush at its root. He gagged and started to choke.

"Steady on, Jimmy, you have to learn to swallow it down until your throat doesn't react. Gently does it, mate."

Mark took Jimmy's head in his hands and lifted him a little, but Jimmy was becoming obsessed with the idea of taking that mighty meat as far down as it would go and plunged down again. He took the tip from Mark and swallowed and found that, although he did still gag a little it was much easier. His eyes were streaming with tears generated by the physical response to the unaccustomed bulk in his throat, but he relished every moment of this new experience and was becoming more skillful in a remarkably short time.

Mark groaned as his fully engorged cock was totally encased in Jimmy's young throat. It was as though none of his previous experiences had come close to this. He looked down at the slimly muscular young body of his friend and knew there was no one else anywhere who was ever likely to be his equal. If only he could hold on to him.

The thought that Jimmy might move right away at such a critical time for them both was hard to face.

None of these thoughts weakened the lust that consumed him as Jimmy worked his penis like an expert, or so he seemed, as his head bobbed up and down on Mark's rigid sex. He was inexorably building him towards orgasm and his head dropped back, his eyes closed, enraptured. Unbidden, his hips began to pump his dick upwards into the enthusiastic throat.

"I'm coming, I'm coming," he gasped in warning in case the inexperienced lad would not want the experience of jism spraying his mouth and throat.

He need not have worried. Jimmy worked his tongue around that pole and plunged his head down to receive it all. With an uncontrolled cry, Mark's body arched upwards and the spunk burst from his dick into the welcoming mouth in a spectacular series of ejaculations.

Jimmy gulped, repeatedly attempting to swallow every drop of the offering as it gushed forth. He had his first real taste of Mark's fluids and was swept into a state of bliss at the force and intimacy of what he was doing. As Mark's prick began to subside he continued to suck contentedly at this comforter, until it had reached its flaccid proportions.

"The well seems to have run dry," he said as he sat up, theatrically smacking his lips, "but, boy, was it good while it lasted?"

"Well was it?" smiled Mark.

"It has a subtle bouquet," Jimmy quipped. "And a sweet taste with undertones of the earthiness of its maker."

He rubbed his nose against Mark's.

"I guess you like it," Mark said. before placing his lips on Jimmy's.

The kiss was long and searching before Jimmy answered.

"I guess," he said, wrapping his arms about Mark's sinewy torso.

"Shall we go up to bed?" asked Mark.

Jimmy looked at him in the glow of the fire.

"You will stay over, then."

"I'll just have to let Mum and Dad know so they won't worry. Do you mind if I phone them? I don't make a habit of staying out. There's no reason, usually."

Jimmy felt quietly pleased at hearing that.

"Yes, 'course you can," he said. "The phone's in the hall."

- - -

When Mark left, the next morning, the sun glistened on rain-soaked paths and the crystal drops on the leaves, and Jimmy had a decidedly sore arse. He didn't mind. In fact he was glad, because it almost felt as though Mark were still there. But, in spite of his elation at the way things had suddenly turned out, he was no nearer to working out how he was going to explain to his aunt and uncle what he wanted to do. The scenarios he ran through in his head were ludicrous.

"Uncle Ralph, Aunty Gwen. I don't want to sell the house. Why not? Because I have a lover and I want to marry him," or, "I'm gay, and I want to live here with my man friend. I know you'll understand." Or, more deviously, "I think I'm grown up enough now to run my own home. I know I've no money coming in, but I'm going to take a lodger and the rent and the money Mum left will keep me going."

The last was all well and good, but even if they accepted that he was mature enough to cope, they wouldn't like the idea of his taking a lodger. It wouldn't be easy. Not only that, but he had a feeling that they had some ideas for the money from the sale of the house and the money in the bank that was now his. He knew the law was a bit of a mess. Eighteen was the legal age of maturity, and banks weren't too keen on you even then. At the same time relatives had no hold on you after the age of sixteen.

But there was now another dimension. There was Mark.

His mouth widened in a broad, silly grin as he thought of Mark, and last night.

Last night had turned his life around. It was as though his mother had arranged that he should not be alone. It was a good thing that his mother's funeral had been in the last week of school term. It was the only good thing apart from Mark. He was *the* good thing. Now there was at least time to think and arrange things.

Resolutely he turned from the kitchen breakfast bar and went to the phone in the hall and dialed the number in Gloucester. Almost on the first ring at the other end came Aunt Gwen's voice. Of course, she acted as Uncle Ralph's secretary.

"Arthur and Evans," she said in her efficient way, the voice electronically attenuated.

"Hello, Auntie it's James here." They had never called him Jimmy.

"It spoils the name to familiarize it!" Aunt Gwen's words, those.

Her voice immediately became more gentle.

"Oh, yes, dear. What can we do for you."

"Well, I wondered if I could ask Uncle Ralph not to go to the estate agent's yet."

"Oh, why ever not?"

"Well, you see, I've... well, I've been thinking that ...um ... perhaps I might decide... you see ... not to sell the house."

Silence for one . . two ...three... ...ten, or more, seconds.

Then, tentatively: "Why not, dear?"

"Well, you see, Aunty, I had a long think about it all last night and, well, the thing is, I don't want to leave."

Another silence.

"Well, I don't know, I'm sure. We wouldn't be doing our duty by you or your dear mother if we permitted you to live there all alone."

Permitted! That was a bit strong, even from Aunt Gwen. And *duty*. Is that what they were all about? He had thought that love came in somewhere. Pictures of Mark filled his mind, looking into his eyes, sucking his cock, fucking the guts out of him, and how he had felt at the time. That wasn't *duty*. Maybe in itself it wasn't love, either, but it as sure as hell beat duty.

When he spoke again he was more composed; more determined.

"Aunty Gwen, tell Uncle Ralph not to go to the estate agent's. I am not going to sell the house. I *am* going to stay here, but I won't be on my own. I'm taking a lodger."

"A lodger!" Aunt Gwen was incredulous.

"Yes."

She seemed to gather herself. "Some pretty girl, I've no doubt?"

"Aunty Gwen, what *are* you thinking?"

"You know very well what I'm thinking. Your mother would be horrified."

He didn't rise to that but it *was* below the belt.

"But, Aunty, I'm only a schoolboy. How could I possibly be planning anything like that," he protested with an air of injured innocence.

"You are a very mature boy for your age and a very handsome one. Some calculating floozie would think you a fine catch with your money and your house."

"As a matter of fact, Aunty Gwen, I'm not interested in floozies or any other members of the opposite sex. You see, I'm gay."

There. It was out. Why on earth had he said it? Because he wanted to do? It did seem the only thing left to say, but it fell like a lead balloon. The silence was prolonged.

Then: "James, you mustn't make jokes about things like that. It isn't funny."

"No, Aunty Gwen, it isn't funny not all the time anyway. But it is true. My lodger is gay as well."

There was a pause at the other end.

"No!"

"Yes, Aunty. I'm sorry."

Why had he apologized? For being gay?

"You have been perverted by this person. That's it, isn't it? It's some older man who has despoiled you."

Jimmy couldn't help laughing. Aunt Gwen's choice of words *in extremis* was hilarious.

"Hardly, Aunty. He's not that much older than me. He's the gardener boy, you know, you met him at the funeral. You said he was a charming boy."

Aunty Gwen ignored the last.

"The gardener! You propose to set up home with a gardener!?"

Jimmy was calm now. It was funny really. Aunty Gwen seemed to think that was far worse than his being gay.

"Yes, Aunty."

"Your uncle and I will be over to see you this evening. Don't go out."

There was an instant buzz on the line as Aunt Gwen banged down the receiver.

Jimmy looked for a moment at the device now dead in his hand and then calmly replaced it. It was done. Would Mark be there with him to face them? Whatever happened he would not give in now, no matter what.

Then there was a loud rapping on the door.

'Who the dickens can that be?' he wondered, taking the few steps to the door.

It was Mark.

"Hey, what are you doing here?" Jimmy asked in surprise. "Have you forgotten something?"

"Yeah, Jimmy boy, I'd forgotten what this feels like and I need a reminder."

With that he reached out to Jimmy and pulled him close and kissed him fervently and long, Jimmy responding with a hunger that would need constant assuaging.

When they finally parted and looked at each other it was Jimmy who spoke first.

"What about your work, Mark?"

"It can wait, just for one day, can't it?"

"I suppose so."

"Aren't you going to let me come in?"

With a laugh Jimmy stood aside. "Enter, O master," he said.

As Mark walked through he said, "Go through to the kitchen. I was just going to make some fresh coffee instant, I'm afraid."

When they reached the kitchen he added. "There's something we must talk about anyway."

"Oh, what's that."

"I phoned my Aunty and Uncle this morning."

"Oh, yes, and what did you say. Did you ask him not to go to the estate

- 258 -

agent?"

Jimmy nodded, as he switched on the refilled kettle. He proceeded to relate the conversation he'd had with his aunt. The story did not pass without a chuckle here and there from Mark, but he did not interrupt and, when Jimmy had finished, his face was serious.

"So, do you want me here?"

"Would you mind?"

Mark reached out a hand to hold Jimmy's.

"We face everything together now," he said.

Jimmy lifted Mark's hand to his lips and kissed his fingers. It would soon have progressed beyond that but the kettle came to the boil. Reluctantly, smiling into Mark's dark eyes, he released his hand and turned to switch off the wall switch. He took two clean mugs from the cupboard and after spooning in the coffee he poured on the hot water. The milk and sugar were on the breakfast bar beside Mark.

"I don't know what they are likely to say, but I've given them plenty of ammunition."

As he shoveled two heaped teaspoonfuls of sugar into his mug Mark said thoughtfully, "You did right, I think. Your uncle seems very practical, down to earth. I don't know about your aunt. She seemed very nice when you introduced me to her at the funeral."

"She can be, but she's very conventional. Uncle Ralph can go off the deep end as well."

"He's your mum's brother. If he's anything like her, he's got plenty of common sense."

He continued.

"There's something I've never told you that perhaps I should."

Jimmy looked at him sharply. He did not realize it but he heard the alarm bells of jealousy at Mark's last words. What should he have told him? Another boyfriend perhaps?

"It's something your mum said to me about six months ago."

Jimmy relaxed, but he was curious.

"What's that then?"

"She said I was the nearest you had to a brother and she knew I liked you a lot."

Jimmy blushed. Had his mother guessed everything?

"She asked me, as well," he went on, "to look after you when she was gone. That was one reason why I posted you the note."

Jimmy looked at him with the same piercing look as a few moments before.

"You thought it was your duty?" He thought of his aunt's words earlier.

Mark got up from the stool on which he had seated himself and put his arms around Jimmy again.

"I would have thought so, even if I didn't feel anything for you, but I think

I've proved I do...feel a lot, I mean. I've loved you for a couple of years now. I always liked you, right from the start, but you were only a kid then. I didn't know if you felt the same about me, though. Oh, I knew you fancied me, which was nice, but of more than that I had no idea, and I couldn't ask. You see that, don't you? I couldn't not when your mum was alive. I would have done so if you had been older, if the chance had come, but not with you still at school."

Jimmy nestled his forehead into Mark's shoulder.

"So, do you think Mum knew?"

"She may have, but I think it's more likely she only saw what good friends we could be."

"That's quite a lot. I was always too busy to think about any sort of relationship. In any case, I'd have thought I was much too young for you."

"At first you were, but that phase didn't last long. And you always had a beautiful body for your age. More important than that, though, I just liked you a lot."

"So, why are we letting valuable snogging time go by? If you aren't working today, let's get some practice in upstairs, okay? I haven't made the bed, though."

"Slut," Mark said lasciviously.

"I'll show you just how *much* of a slut I can be. C'mon."

- - -

Their clothes were shed and they were on the bed, snogging, in seconds. Never had Jimmy bounded up the stairs so fast. His inhibitions were dropped completely for the first time. Jimmy's body was his, he realized, and he could show Jimmy how he felt by his actions, not his words.

Kissing was wonderful: he could see that now, as his tongue explored Mark's mouth. What was ordinarily very private was now shared. He wasn't sure what was best; having his tongue in Mark's mouth or vice-versa. Both activities had driven his cock to full expansion. He lay on top of Mark, feeling his own hardness pressing into Mark's abdomen. He squirmed to feel his skin slide and rub over his friend's. All such sensations were still so new to him that he was driven near to orgasm in a very short time. Mark seemed to sense his imminent fulfillment and held him still.

"Don't hurry it, Jimmy," he whispered, as though someone might overhear them.

"Oh, Mark, I love you," moaned Jimmy, still squirming and trying to rub himself against Mark's body.

Mark realized that there was no delaying this first climax and he plunged his head down to engulf the already-pulsating penis with his mouth. Immediately he was gratified by the semen pouring in waves into his mouth. He swallowed as fast as he could until the flood subsided. He drew his head back, grasping the temporarily quiescent cock in his right hand and milking the last drops appearing at its tip. He looked at them each time as though delaying the grand moment when he might taste the precious flavor again, as though there might

never be any more, and then licked at them as a child might with an ice cream.

"That's vintage spunk, that is," he said appreciatively.

"You're a connoisseur, I take it?" asked Jimmy, grinning.

Mark looked up at him and winked slowly. "That'd be tellin' wouldn't it?"

"Let's see then," said Jimmy, reaching forward, and hauling him up towards him. He planted his lips on Mark's and drove his tongue into his mouth, swirling it around inside. Then he lay back smiling. "Hmm.... . it's sweeter than yours."

"Oh, is that so?"

"Yup. Definitely, much sweeter."

Supporting himself with hands on either side of Jimmy's chest, Mark brought his knees to his hands, sitting lightly on Jimmy's abdomen. He pressed his upright cock forward and down to within range of the boy's tongue.

"You don't want this any more, then?" he said.

Jimmy's eyes sparkled with humor as he said, "Why would I want an inferior brand?"

Thrusting his hips forward and gripping his rigid weapon firmly he repeatedly brushed it over Jimmy's closed lips.

"Sure?"

Jimmy was certain, that he did. There was no hope of resisting the delicious meat waving before him so enticingly. His tongue flickered between his lips, snakelike, of its own volition. Jimmy had almost no control over what he did. Mark pulled back his foreskin and Jimmy opened his mouth wide to encompass the shiny glans. Mark lifted it up.

"I don't think I'll let you have it," he said. "You don't deserve it now."

Jimmy strained his head up and towards Mark's dick, his tongue reaching out to reach the prize. Mark used his free hand on Jimmy's shoulder and firmly pressed him back to the pillows.

"Say please."

Jimmy's eyes locked with Mark's.

"Please."

"Say, please may I have your big prick filling my mouth and my throat."

Without hesitation Jimmy did as he was told, finding the situation so stirring that his so recently relieved sex began to twitch again into life.

He was fed the prime feast until Mark's pubic bush tickled his nose. He grunted with contentment. He had learned the technique so quickly that he had hardly any problems as the glans probed beyond his tonsils. He was smugly pleased with himself and he knew that Mark was very impressed.

"Hey, Jimmy, that's amazing. Suck on it, Jimmy boy, suck away."

He reached behind him and was surprised to find Jimmy fully aroused again.

"Wow, Jimmy, lad. That's terrific. Hang on a minute."

He took his dick from Jimmy's mouth. Jimmy was puzzled.

"What's up?" he asked.

"This is." Mark patted Jimmy's rigid cock. "And I'm going to make the most

Edited by John Patrick

of it."

He retrieved the tube of lubricant from his trouser pocket and applied it to the twitching cock. Positioning his anus above it he reached beneath him and lifted it so that its tip was touching his bud. He eased himself down until he had taken it past his prostate and he was sitting on Jimmy's pelvis. He took firm hold of Jimmy's shoulders and pulled him forward pressing the boy's mouth over his dick.

Jimmy was thrilled with this double experience. As he worked his mouth up and down Mark's pole, Mark began to raise and lower himself on Jimmy. Jimmy adapted his own movements to synchronize with him. Jimmy found it awkward to lift his own hips but each time Mark lowered himself he urged his cock upwards to achieve the maximum penetration of the hot, velvet interior of Mark's rectum.

Mark grunted with pleasure as he reached resistance and moaned with pleasure when his cock delved into the depths of Jimmy's throat. The rhythm was steady, not frantic, and their build to climax was the same. Jimmy felt totally consumed by the world of Mark's body and what it was doing to him. The tingling excitement in his balls and his prick mounted and he was trying his utmost to give Mark the same sensations. He knew now how wonderful the feeling of being fucked could be, but he had not fucked before, and though he was not doing much himself Mark was working on his cock with great expertise he realized that it was just as good, maybe better. Maybe. As he sucked hard on his massive mouthful and felt his cock, gripped by Mark's sphincter, massaged almost to its end and then down to its base, repeatedly, skillfully bringing him to the heights.

"Jimmy, Jimmy! I'm going to come! I'm going to come in your mouth. Get ready for it, mate."

At that moment Mark began to eject his thick cream into Jimmy's welcoming mouth. Jimmy tried to taste the sticky spunk around his tongue. The taste of it fired his own responses. He grabbed at Mark's slim hips and pulled him hard down as his dick erupted into Mark's colon. Dropping his head back onto the pillows he forced his cock up into Mark as far as he could, Mark's final convulsions spraying Jimmy's belly and chest with droplets of white.

Mark gripped Jimmy's dick tightly until its ejaculations had ceased. Then he fell forward on to Jimmy, kissing his face, Jimmy's now deflated penis slipping audibly from the cozy orifice.

"Oooh," Jimmy gasped. "My dick feels really tender."

"It'll recover quickly enough, I'm sure."

Jimmy returned Mark's kisses. He felt he was never going to get enough of him.

- - -

Later that afternoon they made themselves respectable for Jimmy's aunt and uncle. They had no idea, at that point, how they would tackle the situation. They

decided Jimmy's aunt and uncle should arrive to see Mark working in the garden. They already knew the situation as Jimmy had told it. Whether they believed it at that point was another matter. Jimmy thought they would arrive as early as they could. They would, no doubt be anxious, worried even. Jimmy thought it best if Mark was not involved directly. Certainly not at first.

The big car drew in through the already-opened gates. Jimmy opened the passenger door for Aunt Gwen. She got out, her anger of the phone conversation apparently forgotten. To his surprise she hugged and kissed him, bursting into tears.

"Oh, you poor boy!" she sobbed. "Oh, I am so sorry."

"Gwen, for pity's sake leave the boy alone. He doesn't want all that fuss, I'm sure." Uncle Ralph was not one for emotional display.

Gently but firmly Jimmy pushed his aunt to arms' length, smiled into her eyes. Then, putting an arm about her shoulders, he ushered her through the front door. His uncle caught sight of Mark, weeding the flower bed in front of the lounge window.

"I don't know bloody women!" he said to Mark, shaking his head, a gesture of shared understanding.

Mark began to feel more hopeful. This did not appear to be the same crusading aunt and uncle Jimmy had made them appear. Perhaps Jimmy's perspective had been wrong. Maybe he had been looking at them still with the eyes of a little boy.

And little boy he certainly was not. Mark could vouch for that. Jimmy had fucked him three times before they had come down from the bedroom, to say nothing of the couple of times his cock had found a home in Jimmy's pretty arse.

Jimmy sat his aunt and uncle in the lounge and went into the kitchen to make a cup of tea. He made it quite strong. He knew that was how they liked it. He knew also that they would be more relaxed with a cup of tea in their hands. Things would be more "everyday".

After he had seated himself he was aware that he would have to start the conversation.

"I want to stay here," he said. "I don't want to move away. For one thing I'll be taking my GCE's soon, and I don't want to change schools for a start."

Aunt Gwen pulled a richly embroidered handkerchief from her sleeve and wiped her eyes.

Uncle Ralph spoke, rather hesitantly for him, clearing his throat.

"That much you made plain earlier, young man... .But we'll get to that in a minute. It's this...this other business."

"Which, Uncle?" he asked innocently.

"Come, on, James, you know damn' well what I'm talking about."

"Oh, that I'm gay you mean?" He tried to sound as though that sort of revelation came to relations every day.

"Yes, dammit, that is what I mean. You were making a poor joke, weren't you.? You really upset your aunt."

"She upset me, rather," Jimmy said. "But it is true. I am gay."

He looked at his uncle unwaveringly.

"You're sure about it? I mean, well, um you know, you can't really know before you've tried, can you?"

"Ralph!" exclaimed Aunt Gwen. "He's only a boy. You shouldn't say things like that to him. You'll embarrass him."

Uncle Ralph smiled.

"I don't think I will, m'dear. He wasn't just a boy when he spoke to you on the phone. He says he already knows his inclinations, and he is old enough to know, particularly in this day and age. But that gardener boy. He's surely not a queer" He swallowed hard. "Not gay? He doesn't look it."

"Why should he? Do you think I look like a fairy? Do you think I look gay?"

"Of course not." He paused for a moment to marshal his thoughts. "Look here, James. If you are sure you want to live here on your own there is really nothing we could do to stop you if we wanted to, which we don't. We want you to be happy. We love you, you know, and we want for you only what you want yourself. We only wanted to support you after, well, you know, and we thought you would be happier with us. Your aunt and I talked it over all afternoon on the way here. We decided that the best thing we can do is to help you in whatever ways you want us to do."

"Then you don't mind that I'm gay?"

"Mind? If you are sure, what is there to mind? We can't change the way we're made, any of us. There are a lot of things worse than being gay, as you like to call it. Being mean and selfish for a start. We are really more worried about you living alone and being without an income. Your mother's money is yours now but for a few legacies. But if you have to live on it, it won't see you through university."

"Uncle Ralph. Mark is going to pay for the housekeeping, he said he would."

Aunt Gwen was still very concerned. "But how are you going to manage the house and with all the study you'll have to do?"

"I did it all on my own while I looked after Mum, with no help."

The words hit home.

"Yes, you did," said Uncle Ralph after a moment or two. "And a damn' fine job you made of it, too." There was a real respect in his voice now.

"When's this gardener moving in, then?"

"He has already as good as."

Uncle Ralph's right eyebrow shot up.

"Has he, b'jove? That was mighty fast work, wasn't it? What sort of chappie is he?"

"You met him at Mum's funeral."

"Oh, yes, of course I remember now, at the funeral yes. Dependable type I'd

say. Your mother spoke of him as well, a couple of years ago, and said how good he'd been."

He walked over to the window and looked out. Mark was still there, on the other side of the lawn now.

"Well there doesn't seem to be any more to discuss. Can we have a little something to eat, d'you think?"

"Of course you can. Would salad be all right?"

Aunt Gwen stepped in. "Salad will be fine dear. I'll give you a hand. Shall we go to the supermarket in Bodmin or have you got vegetables in?"

"We have everything in the back garden except the meat and we can cook some chicken pieces from the freezer."

"Show me where they are," said Aunt Gwen, getting up.

When Jimmy stood up, she put an arm round his waist and hugged him.

"You had me really worried, you silly boy. I can't say my mind is at all easy, even now."

He gave her a peck on the cheek. "No need to be worried, aunty. I promise if I have real problems I'll tell you."

"I'm going into the front garden," said Uncle Ralph, "to have word with your, err, that gardener. I want to know how he makes that *Tropoleum* thrive against that wall. It's a picture.

- - -

Once outside, Ralph crossed the lawn to Mark who was working crouched down with his back to the house.

"You do a grand job here, young feller."

Mark started. He had not heard Ralph come up behind him. He stood up brushing his hand on the green overalls he kept in the garden shed.

"I want to thank you for all the help you gave my sister and James."

"Oh, that's okay, sir."

"You'll not let young James down, will you?"

"You don't mind then about me and Jimmy, and me being older an' all."

Ralph chuckled.

"No. As a matter of fact, I'd have been more worried if you'd been his age."

"I'll not let him down, I promise you that, sir. It doesn't matter that I'm just a gardener then?"

"Matter? No b'jove salt of the earth, men who do real work. He couldn't find anyone better, I'm sure."

"Then, it's all sorted out, and it's all right?"

"Right as rain, dear boy, right as rain. Now, I want to pick your brains about growing this perennial *Tropoleum*. I've tried it and it won't grow for me. You have gardener's hands, hands that can make things grow."

Mark smiled. Jimmy would vouch for that.

DIFFERENT STROKES
by Daniel Miller

"Hey, Gerald? Remind me again why we're doing this."

My lover of five years and I were standing on the sidewalk in a long line of men. Some were rocking on the chunky heels of their artfully scuffed motorcycle boots, while others fiddled with studded black wrist straps. In front of us lay the shadowed entrance to the underground leather bar. I couldn't help thinking of it as a hungry maw waiting to suck us down inside its inky depths, but I couldn't deny that the tingle of fear in my crotch felt both oppressive and titillating.

"C'mon, Neil. You know these places are red-hot." I could only see the side of his face, but the muscles in his lightly bearded jaw were tense. Was he as jittery as I was, or just being stubborn? Even after so many years together, it was sometimes hard to tell.

I squirmed inside the stiff leather vest he'd bought me that morning. I was shirtless underneath it, and the lining blotted up my nervous sweat. "You know I'm all for living out a fantasy or two. But we're going to stick out like small dicks in mesh underpants."

Gerald smothered a grin. "Speak for yourself on that score. Besides, we'll be fine. Just remember those books we have at home. Meet people's eyes and don't say much."

"Okay, whatever you say." The line was moving forward now, and I shuffled along with it, practicing my most menacing stare. Somehow, I doubted that even a shelf full of John Rechy paperbacks and back issues of *Drummer* had prepared us to blend seamlessly with a bar full of experienced tops. Instead, I concentrated on the succulent swell between Gerald's thighs. Mentally, I released that powerful cock from its faded denim pouch and began to soothe its frustration with my fingers and tongue. I loved that big cock more than anything.

I was still daydreaming about Gerald's cock when the line lurched forward again, and Gerald and I found ourselves part of a mysterious underworld. For a moment, both of us froze in startled fascination.

The narrow space ahead of us was filled with men of all sizes and ages. Farther ahead in the tunnel, oval biceps and bare thighs flexed in murky red light. "Wow," I said, looking over at Gerald.

"Told you," he hissed through clenched teeth. "Let's get a drink."

We glided through a solid wall of half-bare, sweaty bodies. Just as Gerald reached the bar, I found myself pressed up against a broad chest, bare except for a studded harness that crisscrossed rocky pecs. Two rigid nipples pushed up against mine, and fierce heat penetrated my skin.

I looked up into the solid face of a tall, muscular man. His skull gleamed hairless except for his eyebrows and a sternly clipped goatee, and rippled torso muscles tapered into his tight leather chaps. A few exposed pubic hairs curled

over his waistband.

His white teeth flashed behind burnt-sienna lips. He arched his body, jabbing his bullet-shaped tits against mine. I swallowed hard, my prominent Adam's apple bobbing on my throat. With a wolfish grin, the man stuck out his thumb and pressed down on it hard. I flinched, startled by the brief choking sensation the slow pressure caused.

"Fucking amateur," he rumbled. "Let me guess, you're in town for a couple of days, and you wanted to see how you'd look in leather."

Before he'd finished speaking, Gerald had noticed what was going on and doubled back from the bar. "Excuse me"

"Ah, the other half of this enterprising duo. You think you're pretty hot in those shiny new duds, don't you? Fucking tourists, act like you're in some kind a zoo when you come here. Neither one of you would know a real leather man if he shoved his big dick up your pussy ass and pushed it out your fucking throat!"

Stunned by the man's savage tone, I turned to Gerald. His face was ashen underneath his beard, and the brim of the motorcycle cap barely hid the shock in his eyes.

"You're wrong," he blustered in a well-controlled stammer. "We know the score."

The big man found that the most amusing thing he'd heard, or said, all night. "The score? How can there be a score when the game hasn't even begun?" The muscles that framed his short beard suddenly relaxed. "Okay, assholes, here's the deal. The two of you want to learn how to wear that gear? Well, I'm the guy who can teach you, if you come with me right now. You do whatever I tell you to do when I tell you to do it, no questions asked. At the end of the night, if I'm satisfied with your performance, I'll let you back in here. Otherwise, both of you can get the hell out right now. And it's well within my power to make that happen, believe me."

Gerald expelled a long-held breath, then brought his hands to his hips and jauntily hooked his thumbs in his jeans.

"We'd love to," he announced. He fanned an almost belligerent gaze around the ring of onlookers. "But you might be surprised. We might end up teaching you a few things."

"Nice work, Gerald," I whispered under my breath.

Peals of laughter, not all of it good-natured, followed us as we made our way back up the steps to the street. Our new friend followed so closely behind us that I could feel his heat against my spine. Bolts of fear and excitement shot straight to my cock.

On the sidewalk, he faced us like a drill sergeant taking charge of his rawest recruits. He took no notice at all of the crush of nocturnal tourists, still milling around us in every direction.

"Folks around here call me Styx, but you two assholes will address me as 'Sir.' Walk single file up the street, and keep going until I tell you to stop. When

I tell you to face me again, I want to see both your flies open and those puny dicks ready for my inspection. If they're not, well, let's just say you won't want me to reach in and get them. Now move!"

We moved. Gerald and I marched past buildings, signs, and man-sized heaps of sand. We marched until the lights of Provincetown seemed miles behind us. My legs ached as much as my balls by the time Styx directed us to cut through the dunes.

He directed us down a sandy incline, beyond which dark waves lapped ominously. When he gave his next command, the two of us whirled around in perfect sync. Our hands flew to our crotches, unzipping and unsnapping in a sweaty blur. My cock bulged out a second before Gerald's. Our hard cocks curved up like two convenient fuck-handles.

His hands behind his back, his sooty nipples lifting the straps of his harness, our new master inspected us smugly.

"We won't be disturbed down here, so get the rest of that pussy-leather off those miserable chicken-skin bodies. I want to see both of you naked and down on your skinny knees before the count of ten. You got that?"

He paused for a moment, chewing a strand of his moustache. Then he sucked in a deep breath and bellowed, "One!"

Before he got to five, Gerald and I were naked, our new leather duds in a heap beside us. Styx had also stripped off everything except his studded body harness. Looped under his massive balls and fitted with an iron cock ring, it tilted his meat up at a jaunty, yet threatening, angle. Twin leather pouches dangled from his sides: the white cap of a K-Y jelly tube protruded from one, while small, telltale squares distorted the other.

"Can you believe this?" I mouthed to Gerald, who shook his head, riveted. We watched as Styx casually picked up the K-Y, squeezed a generous glob onto one hand, and began to slide it up and down his shaft. Soon his shaft heaved against the metal ring, standing at attention as if to salute the full moon.

"Crawl over here," Styx ordered, planting his feet in the sand. He undid the second pouch, pulled out a rubber, and shredded the wrapper. He used his right hand to pump his shaft while the left applied the condom. "Both of you."

The stirring of my own cock was so insistent that I barely noticed Gerald's warm hand on mine. "Let's go." He shuffled forward on his knees, his pale buttocks twinkling in the moonlight. The two of us left long, deep tracks like two waddling sea turtles as we took up our positions.

I wrapped my lips around Styx's shrink-wrapped tool. Powerfully aroused by the mixture of surf, moonlight, and my own naked servitude, I shoved my head down harder. While Styx shivered and moaned, I ran my lips over the curve of his meat and traced the web of pulsing veins with sharp, deliberate strokes.

Meanwhile, Gerald had wedged his face between those stony ass-cheeks. His tongue slithered along that broad, musky-smelling perineum until he was actually lapping Styx's nut sac from behind. I smiled around that mouth-filling

cock when I saw and felt what he was doing. That ball-licking trick was something I'd almost forgotten about, an unusual talent Gerald had shared with me in the earliest days of our relationship. From the way Styx was shuddering and twisting, he was enjoying it, too.

"Yes, that's it, you little fucker," Styx moaned, plugging my throat with his cock and sawing his ass against Gerald's face. Suddenly, I had a wicked idea. Without dislodging Styx's cock, I angled my head so that Gerald's tongue would just touch the tip of my chin on each down stroke. Realizing what I had in mind, Gerald pumped his head faster, purposely lapping Styx's ass and my face at the same time. It felt like I was kissing my lover through Styx's massive body, while Gerald's big tube of flesh pretended to fuck my throat.

Styx rode us both like a pumped-up naked cowboy, spearing my tonsils while he whacked Gerald's face with his balls. He came with a lurch that almost dislodged my skull from my neck, then flooded the rubber with a continuous, steaming volley. My fingers raked the globes of his firm ass while his soggy condom slid down my tongue. It moved in a zigzag pattern, pulled off center by the weight of his collected jizz.

"Enough!"

When he was done jizzing, Styx jerked his body away roughly. Gerald's mouth dropped open in surprise, his nose skidding through Styx's hot crack as he slumped face-down on the sand. I managed to catch myself and remained on my knees, my distended boner flogging my stomach.

Gerald lay on his stomach on the sand, but I could see by the flush on his butt that he was every bit as hard as I was. Arms folded, Styx loomed over us like a judgmental sea-god tossed up by the surf. His steely gaze lashed at my cock, then settled on Gerald's bare ass.

"You, on your hands and knees. Your friend here has something to give you." He stabbed a finger in my direction, then dipped back into his pouch and tossed me a fresh condom. "Ream his ass, just as hard as you can. And don't touch his cock until I say so."

Open-mouthed, Gerald scrambled into position. My fingers shook as I fitted the condom over myself, and my shaft rippled under my fingers. It wasn't that common for me to fuck Gerald's ass. He usually preferred to have me suck him, after which I'd scoot around and let him slide his moistened member into my back door. Somehow, it seemed like Styx had sensed that.

The hiss of the tide filled my head as I clambered onto Gerald's back. I hooked my feet around his bent knees and dug my heels into the pliant flesh of his calves.

A strange, heady feeling slowly overwhelmed me. If one of Styx's goals had been to challenge our usual hang-ups about fucking, he was sure as hell succeeding. Even on those rare occasions when I had screwed Gerald, his ass had felt tight and my strokes had never seemed very deep or very sure. Now, to my amazement, his butt-cheeks parted with a rasping sound, and I pushed

forward in a white-hot burst of strength. Enjoying his wails of surrender, I hammered his pucker while my nails clawed his sides.

Gerald was responding differently to me, too. At first, he just groaned and thrashed his rear end like a stubborn pony trying to unseat its rider. Pretty soon, even that token resistance faded. The clench of his sphincter grew more intense, and a moist, sucking sound filled the still air. I thought he'd split wide open as I drilled deeply into his tunnel, his hot flesh searing the rubber.

The pulse of the surf couldn't quite drown out the crinkle of another condom wrapper being torn open. Styx hunkered down behind me, his hot crotch flush with my ass. His rubber-covered cock head felt as big as a soda can in my chute, but his fingers cupped my nut sac with surprising gentleness. Electric jolts slithered through my heaving groin as I felt a single drop of hot sweat slide down the crease of my fully stuffed butt. Another dribbled into Gerald's crack.

The added stimulation hurtled me over the precipice. My long-withheld climax exploded into the latex sheath, which spiraled, in turn, into Gerald's hot rectum. With a gratified snarl, Styx hunched against me and released another fiery stream of his own juice.

Beneath me, Gerald gurgled and twisted his body with thinly veiled desperation. He wasn't used to being left out of things, I realized when the dark red haze finally faded from my head. When it was just the two of us, he'd be the first to unload his desire, either up my ass or down my throat. Now, Styx had relegated his pleasures to third place, if he allowed him to come at all. How ironic, I thought, that the whole expedition had been Gerald's idea.

Styx's fingers slid down my hips as he dislodged his prick with a jolt. I, too, cautiously extracted my softening organ from Gerald's hole. With a moan, Gerald flipped over and planted his bare butt in the sand, his thighs splayed open to flaunt a boner of breathtaking proportions. The domed tip had become a hard, crimson oval, his slit belching globules of pearly pre-cum. The long, bluish vein that bisected his shaft had swelled to nearly triple size.

Gerald's hand started toward his cock and then stopped. His eyes sought first mine, and then our master's.

"Please," he whispered.

Styx nodded once, curtly, and motioned me over to Gerald with his eyes.

I felt my cock throb into a fresh erection as I glided across the cool sand on my knees and elbows. I hunkered between his wide-open legs. The tip of his cock was on fire as it squirmed against my abdomen.

Gerald moaned, then bit down on my left nipple. It seemed like I could feel Styx's heavy glare resting on my back like a hand.

"All in good time," I whispered. I could feel his body shudder as my fist worked his meat in the alternately rough/ tender way he liked best.

Wheezing with lust, Gerald arched his back and urgently fucked my chest through my fist. To sweeten his torment, I made him wait just a few moments longer. Then, with an ear-splitting whoop, I vaulted myself onto his crotch.

I dropped onto his cock with my full weight, my fingers curling around my own cock. Gerald buried his face in my chest and practically inhaled my tit with a powerful suck. My ass-muscles clamped down on his hard cock, gnawing his bone with a will of their own. I couldn't remember a more vigorous coupling since the early days of our relationship.

"Yeah," Gerald moaned. "Make me come like I used to."

"I will." My entire torso pumped up and down as the familiar pleasure roared through my middle. Gerald's balls dilated against my crack, then released a flood of lava. My relentless asshole gripped the base of his shaft, eager to drain him to the roots.

I exploded at least as copiously as he had. The whole world pulsed to the rhythm of our lust, and the moment of pleasure lingered on and on. It was the most ecstatic fuck the two of us had ever shared.

We collapsed at almost the same instant. Gerald's head fell to the sand and mine rolled across his chest.

It took me a moment to find my voice. "Wow," I said, then suddenly remembered Styx. He hadn't given us permission to speak, wasn't that how it worked in those novels? I only hoped my next punishment would be as exciting as the first!

When I looked up again, Styx stood over us with his hands on his hips. A few telltale streamers of cum dotted his fingers.

"You can put on your clothes and come on back to the bar when you're ready," he said. Then he picked up his clothes, slung them over his shoulder, and sauntered off into the dunes.

"Well, that was anticlimactic," I commented when he had gone. "You really want to go back to that place?"

"Not really." The entire front of Gerald's body shone with K-Y and cum. "We'd be better off back at the guesthouse."

"Well, there's no hurry. I plan to stay in bed late tomorrow."

Gerald returned my smile. "Sounds good to me." Then he pointed at something behind me. "Hey, look over there."

I turned to see a small, upright object imbedded in the stirred-up sand. "The lube!" I exclaimed, then rushed over to retrieve it. "Styx left us something to remember him by."

When I turned, Gerald brushed his fingers over my temple. "Be a shame not to make use of it, don't you think?"

He slid onto his knees in front of me, wrapped both arms around my legs, and started to tickle my balls with the tip of his tongue. For once, in all the years we'd been together, I couldn't see a single reason not to agree with him completely.

SPECIAL BONUS REPORT

As a part of our salute to COCK WORSHIPPERS, we present, as a public service, some interesting takes on cock sucking by masters of the art.
Above, the magnificent international star Johan Paulik invites you to service him. Illustration courtesy Falcon Studios.

THE JOY OF BLOW-JOBS
by Ken Anderson

(Nice Work if You Can Get It)

There are countless reasons why anyone does anything, but the real reason why guys like to perform fellatio is, of course, sexual. The mouth is one of the two holes in a man into which to insert a cock, and the lips, the mouth, the throat, and the cock, to say the least, are all erogenous zones. Some men even have G-spots in their throats. But there are many other biological and psychological reasons as well why giving a good blowjob is very exciting and gratifying in and of itself, reasons which have to do with the womb, early infancy, and the idea of nurturing.

First of all, one of the reasons why guys like to perform fellatio is that it subconsciously reminds them of their prenatal state, which is naturally associated with security and pleasure. From its initial development, the mouth is an erogenous zone in order to insure that the fetus sucks its thumb as training for breast sucking. In other words, thumb sucking is nothing short of necessary for survival. Thumb sucking occurs, as well, in the context of, and therefore comes to be associated with, one of the first few phenomena which the fetus experiences, rhythm. In the womb, the fetus hears not only the beat of its own heart, but also the bigger, stronger, louder beat of its mother's. The same is also true not only for the mother's breathing, but also for the "breathing" of the fetus, the sibilant ingestion and expulsion of amniotic fluid into and from the lungs. The rhythmic nature of cock sucking, as well as that of any sexual act, for that matter, harkens back to the pleasant, assuring rhythms of the womb.

Another reason why guys like to perform fellatio is that it subconsciously reminds them of their infancy, which again is usually associated with security and pleasure. The thumb or anything like it, like the cock, is, in this light, a breast substitute, even though thumb sucking comes first chronologically, and to an infant, a nipple is as big as a cock is to an adult. Oral stimulation of the male nipple is reminiscent of latching on to Mom's, and sperm even looks like milk. Likewise, sucking sounds much the same whether someone is sucking a thumb, a breast, a bottle, or a cock. Of course, it is perfectly clear that in adulthood the cock is not a substitute for anything at all. It's the real thing.

The point is that everyone gets a whole lot of practice sucking other things first, things associated with a sense of well-being. A third reason why fellatio is fun is that it is psychologically nourishing. Since the cock replaces the breast and sperm milk, cock sucking, on one level, is a sort of nursing. The sperm is a

form of food which sustains a guy not so much physically as mentally and emotionally. Just as someone becomes hungry physically, he becomes starved for emotional sustenance as well. Without food, someone dies physically; without nourishment, he dies emotionally, too. A cock and sperm taste good, therefore, not only because of the erogenous zones involved, but also because of the mental and emotional satisfaction. From this standpoint, the recipient of the blowjob becomes the mother or provider of the emotional nourishment, and the one who sucks him off becomes the contented child. The physical climax of one is the emotional climax of the other.

In conclusion, other than the obvious erotic ones, some of the many reasons why cock sucking is a very exciting, indeed compelling end in itself include the following: (1) the sensitive mouth, thumb-like cock, and rhythmic sucking are associated with the sense of indescribable safety and, thus, pleasure of living in the womb, (2) the breast-like cock and milky sperm are likewise associated with the safety and pleasure of early infancy, and (3) the mother- and child-like roles played by participants, as well as the food-like character of sperm, are all psychologically, perhaps even spiritually nourishing.

In short, for a gay man, giving a good blowjob is, in most instances, not only an extremely pleasant experience, but also an act vitally necessary to his general health and growth.

COCKSUCKER'S SURVIVAL GUIDE
by Trunks

The first time I gave a guy a blowjob I was nervous, but as I got more comfortable with what I was doing, I started feeling like I was a pro. I remember thinking about all the porno movies I had watched and tried to act out what I had seen on the tapes. So, to the guy, it seemed like I knew what I was doing. Nowadays, I'm a hell of a lot better! Like my friend Lil' Kim says, "I used to be scared of the dick. Now I throw lips to the shit!"

The first thing you need to know is that you should suck on it, and suck on it hard! Just as you would suck on a lollipop, a straw in a soda, or a cigarette, for those who smoke. Suck it like it's going out of style. Many young fellas that are just starting out seem to be under the impression that all you have to do is just go up and down on it with your mouth. Nah, there's a lot more to it. The key to a good blowjob is to find the most sensitive areas on your partner's dick and then to get them off as much as you can.

Here are my helpful hints:

1. Look at it. Now don't be afraid to look at a dick before you start doing business on it. Play with it first. Get it hard. Then see if it curves, if it's straight, small, fat, or long. This is a good way of determining if you can go to town on this meat and have him begging for more. On the other hand, if you feel mad uncomfortable "inspecting" it and feel that your partner might ask, "Why are you starring at it?", sneak a peak. Sneaking a peek never hurt no body! Next, see how hard he gets and estimate. If you can get it all or at least halfway in your mouth that's good, because no one likes to choke. Now a good size to start off with could be around seven inches, then you can work your way up. Anything less would be uncivilized. Now for you daring types, if you wanna start off with the big guns, that's fine too, but don't forget: the bigger the dick, the bigger you're gonna have to open your mouth. Your jaw might be slightly larger afterwards.(Just kidding!) So if you don't wanna be called Jabber Jaw, please choose your sizes widely...uh, I mean wisely.

2. Have a wet mouth. This part is important. If you got a dry mouth, you are in for a uncomfortable experience. So, simply put, the wetter, the better. It's always good to have an excess amount of saliva present in your mouth. Having all this spit in your mouth feels slippery on the dick and yo it will drive them wild! Yo make him feel as good as possible. It'll give him a feeling like he's hitting it raw dog! He'll love it! Believe me he'll want it all the time. A good way of making your mouth wetter, and this is a little off da wall, but drink orange juice. The juice will intensify the amount of spit you have in your mouth, causing it to bundle and gather, all the while making him wanna fuck your mouth. Trust me it works! I've tried it myself. There are also flavored lubes that can help out if you have a dry mouth. Try the strawberry flavored kind. It's a good taste and it smells good too.

3. No teeth. This is very important. The less teeth you use, the more your

partner will be grateful. There is one problem that's the most common in bad blowjobs. Having a guy's teeth scrape on your dick as they're sucking you, is not only unpleasant, but it also hurts like crazy. The best way to get around this is to open your mouth wider, or even better yet, is to slightly curl your lips over your teeth. Here's a trick to make sure that no teeth is used. Take your lips and curl them over your teeth. This is good for fellas with full lips. This process cushions the hardness of your teeth. Be careful, you don't wanna curl your lips over too much. This is for those of you who have really rough stubble from not shaving, then having that can be equally painful. The trick is to avoid rubbing, or scraping your partner's dick with anything that might be unpleasant.

4. Work that tongue. The tongue is the most important part of your mouth. What you can do with your tongue can make or break you. Short ones, long ones, fat ones, whatever you got, you gotta work the tongue. Commonly, the most sensitive spots on a guy's dick are, the tip/head, the sides of the dick, and occasionally the bottom side of the shaft. A good way to stimulate your boy, is to form a tight ring around the dick with your lips, and to repeatedly let the tip of the dick, force it's way through that ring as you suck him. Another way is to swirl your tongue around the tip. You can tease him with your tongue by flicking it across the tip as you suck him, you can even tease the slit at the top of his dick.

Some guys, however, tend to be sensitive there, so it may not be too pleasurable for them to have their slit played with. You look for your partner's feedback. To stimulate the top side of the cock head during a blowjob, swirl your tongue around it on each top stroke. I do this trick very often and it does work. I got him calling out my name every time! I also strongly recommend getting a tongue piercing. Well, for those who have the stomach for getting one. I have one and, believe me, it was worth it! It helps out a lot with pleasing my boo. It adds a different feeling to the traditional blowjobs. It's almost like a second tongue.

5. Hands-on Training. This part is probably the most talked about, so bear with me. Now in every respect, hands are just as important as a mouth, tongue, or anything else that goes into blowjobs. Hands do certain tricks as well, if used correctly. A fun part of a blowjob can be having your balls played with. Be gentle though. Some guys love to have their balls played with, licked and sucked during a blowjob. Be careful with sucking on your partner's balls.

To some it's a very sensitive area, and it can hurt a little. When in doubt stick to licking, and gently nibbling on the ball sack. If he has balls of steel and can take anything, then by all means go to town on him. Hands can also change the course of how fast it takes for someone to come. If you can get that person to come from blowing them. So don't always expect your partner to cum from receiving a blowjob.

If I feel horny enough and have the energy to do so, I will suck on my man's dick 'til he comes. Sometimes this rarely happens. Sometimes it's gonna take

more to get a boy off. Since blowjobs feel really good already, getting off on them can be rare. This usually happens as a combination of a guy using his mouth and his hands. A good trick is to have the hand meet your mouth as you suck on the shaft. This way joining the spit with your hand, gives the "wet hole" effect.

What I recommend you can try, though, is occasionally turning your hand clockwise and counterclockwise as you suck him. That move is fly enough to do! That's a guaranteed cum spiller right there. In speaking of cum, to swallow or not to swallow? That is the question. That is entirely up to you, if you wanna swallow. I know I am not even comfortable with swallowing. Everyone knows the risk factors involved.

Some fellas have problems staying fully hard during a blowjob. It helps in this case to hold his dick firmly with one hand, make a ring around it with your index finger, and thumb and place your hand at the base of his dick squeezing the base of the shaft. This usually makes his dick a little harder. This method is cool, but if you really turn your man on, then he would be hard as hell already wouldn't he? So use this as a last ditch effort.

You can learn a lot by watching, of course. A good example would be to watch the ever-sexy porn star Kiko in action. In his scene in the popular new video *Off Dah Hook*, with newcomer Hector, Kiko uses his hands to slightly tug on Hector's balls. He massages Hector's sack and changes up a few times to pull on his shaft while he sucks on it. You don't always have to use your hands, though. You can let your hands roam over your partner's lower torso and chest, feel on his ass, on the legs and thighs, and even squeeze his chest or nipples. There are many places your hands can explore, and it's all good!

IN FRONT OF EVERYONE
by Antler

Tired, O tired of "cocksucker"
having a negative connotation,
Of persons demeaned and degraded
by being called cocksucker,
As if it was something awful to be,
something you should be
ashamed of,
loathsome, repugnant, sleazy,
When it turns out it's the reverse,
exactly the opposite.
Speak the word cocksucker clearly,
proudly, sweetly, kindly, warmly
the way a child says mommy, daddy, Jesus.
Let the word cocksucker replace the word God
for 2000 years to make up for 2000 years
Christianity believed
cocksucking a sin.
Let the word cocksucker replace the word America
to make up for all the years
cocksucking was a crime.
Let the word cocksucker replace the word soldier
to make up for all the cocksuckers
killed by soldiers screaming "cocksucker!"
Let the word cocksucker replace the word sucker
so that instead of a mother telling her son
"I'll give you a sucker if you're good"
a mother telling her boy
"I'll give you a cocksucker if you're good."
Bring babies to see a boy's cock being sucked off.
Bring old men and women in wheelchairs to see
a boy's cock being sucked off.
Bring the just-dead into a room
where passionate 69 is taking place
because hearing is the last sense to go
and you want to honor the just-dead
with the slurping sounds of cute boys
who are serious about each other.
Let a boy's cock being sucked off be the minister
who conducts the wedding service
and asks the questions
of the bride and groom

Edited by John Patrick

to which they reply "I do"
and then kiss each other
in front of everyone.

DELICIOUS
by Peter Gilbert

He was strange but harmless; that was the general opinion of Mr. Harvey. All I knew about him was that he was rich; much richer from the look of his car, than any of the other teachers at Morrison's Academy. He was tall, walked with a stoop and wore a wide-brimmed floppy hat which might once have been a Stetson but which looked more like a flower pot.

He was nothing whatever to do with me. Morrison's Academy was set up to help people like me with "learning difficulties." It's a boarding school and we each have our own personal tutor. Mr. Harvey wasn't my tutor or even one of my teachers. I didn't give him a thought until one day when I was coming out of the swimming pool with my towel wrapped under my arm and contemplating whether or not I should go to Janette's party. I didn't much like Janette but the other guests might make up for her empty chatter and high pitched giggling.

I was suddenly aware of this tall, gangling figure at my side.

"Swimmer eh?" he said.

"Sure," I said.

"Somebody told me you were a swimmer. Name?"

"Christian Schmidt. My father's German."

"Is he indeed? Do you speak the language?"

"Pretty well."

"Age?"

"Seventeen. Well, sixteen actually. I'll be seventeen next month."

"Weight?"

"A hundred and fifty one." I thought as I answered that it was an odd question. They got odder and more and more personal as we walked. He asked about my parents, my Dad's job. He even asked which bank I used. He wanted to know the names of my friends and whether they were all swimmers. By the time we reached the main school buildings he knew more about me than any Government agency.

That mystified me for some days. Then, one evening, I watched a TV play and it all fitted into place. This was about the second world war. A university professor in England recruited spies, using exactly the same technique. Same questioning followed by a background check. That was clever. The Prof called on the student's bank manager and asked if he would be wise to lend the student some money. "Of course I realize you can't discuss his account details," he said, but before long the bank manager was telling him everything he wanted to know. And that guy had asked about languages too.

I went to bed quite excited that night. I knew what would happen. I'd get a message asking me to report to some house in a back street in Washington D. C. for an interview. Well, there were worse jobs than Special Agent Schmidt (a.k.a. double oh nine). I was ready.

Nothing happened. I had told one or two people about meeting him. That's

when I learned that he was eccentric but harmless. After I cottoned on to his real purpose I kept my mouth shut.

My bank balance was okay. I led a pretty quiet life. No rave parties with glamorous female spies or anything like that. Morrison's Academy was pretty strict about mixing with the opposite sex. There had to be a teacher present if you gave a party. It was an attractive thought that I should soon be going to really wild affairs - and on an expense account.

Everything fitted together. I went to the doc. about a stomach bug which was going through the school at the time and the girl couldn't find my file. It was pretty obvious to me that it was on some bureaucrat's desk. *"Seems a healthy enough guy. Should be able to handle the training program."*

Then we met again. He was stepping out of some restaurant on the smarter side of town. I was on my way to have my watch repaired.

"Ah, Schmidt," he said.

"Hi, Mr. Harvey."

"Object of journey?"

"To get this fixed. It's stopped." I waved my wrist in front of his face.

"Why come all this way? There are cheaper places."

"It's genuine Swiss. The guys down town aren't so good as they are here."

"Rubbish! I'll take you somewhere where they'll do it cheaper than the places in this area."

I was quite amused. It was so obvious that the watch repairer was one of them. There was this guy bending over a table squinting through one of those special magnifiers and fiddling about in the innards of a watch with tweezers.

"Schmidt; Christian," said Mr. Harvey. "Watch Swiss. Make not stated. Stopped."

I took off the watch. The guy put down the tweezers and gazed at it through his magnifier. "Looks a good one," he said.

"It was an birthday present," I explained.

He grunted and flicked off the back. "Nice face. Nice movement," he said.

"Agreed," said Mr. Harvey who had seen neither. The guy sat down again, put the watch in a kind of vise and started to fiddle around inside it.

"Well made," he said.

"My impression too," said Mr. Harvey.

"Well worth looking after," said the watch-maker. "There!" He took the magnifier out of his eye and handed me the watch. It was going again.

"Thanks a lot," I said. "How much?"

The man frowned as if I had spoken in a foreign language. "You don't pay," said Mr. Harvey.

"But..."

"No charge," said the man. He smiled. I followed the Mr. Harvey out into the street.

"That was real decent of you, Mr. Harvey," I said, "but please let me pay

something."

He smiled and put both hands on my shoulders. "Think nothing of it," he said. You know, I suppose, why I'm taking such an interest in you?"

I smiled. "I've got a pretty good idea," I said.

"I thought so."

"I won't tell anybody we met today," I said.

"Probably as well. Got time to come back to my place?"

I looked at my now working watch and nodded.

"Good. The car should be ready. I left it in the car wash."

Clever stuff, I thought. Leave the car in the wash and there's no risk of enemy agents putting a bomb under it. I'd be doing that myself soon. I wondered what sort of car junior agents were issued.

One look at the area where he lived was enough to convince me that my new employers paid well. The houses were huge red - brick places; ivy climbing up the walls; big wrought iron gates separating them and the immaculate lawns in front of them from the road. I was glad I'd taken the bus that day and not gone into town on my bike.

He pulled up in front of one set of gates and drew a gadget out of the glove pocket. The gates swung open and we drove in.

The house was fantastic. I'd never been in a place like it. It was huge. From the glass doors at the back you could see a swimming pool glistening blue and looking very inviting indeed. It was a hot day.

I was impressed by the way he kept up the academic ruse. I guess it wasn't much of a ruse actually. He was a teacher after all. Hundreds of books lined the ground floor front room. There was a huge map of the world on the wall with colored pins stuck into it - most of them in Turkey and right up next to the old Russian border. Agents, I guessed. I'd be a pin in the map one day.

"Drink?" he asked.

"Please."

"Special requests?"

"Just something cool," I said. He left the room, leaving me in front of the map and dreaming about the future.

"How's double oh nine doing, Mr. Harvey?" (Actually, of course, he'd have a code name or number.)

"Very well. As far as the locals know he's doing archeological research on an old Greek settlement. He's fooled them completely but he's got all the details of the new rocket launcher. They've even let him dig in the new I. C. B. M. testing range. I knew he would be good that first day I met him."

"Coke okay?" said a voice behind me.

"Oh, sure. Thanks a lot!"

He sat down. I followed suit. "Do you live here alone?" I asked.

"Of course."

"Big place for one man."

"There's quite a lot of coming and going," he said with a broad smile. "If you know what I mean," he added.

I winked. "I've got a pretty good idea," I said.

"When we've drunk these, you might like to swim," he said. "I like to see all my new boys in the pool first."

"I was champion swimmer for my last school and swam for the county," said. I could tell he was impressed. It wouldn't be long before that piece of information was spinning, scrambled, along the lines to Virginia.

"How the hell are we going to get him out of there when he's done the job?"

"No worry with double oh nine, sir. He'll swim out to the sub."

We finished our drinks. He took my glass. "Ready?" he said.

"Sure. I, err... I don't have my swim things with me."

He laughed. "Well, of course not," he said. "This way."

The glass doors slid aside as if by magic and we stepped out. It really was some pool; as big, if not slightly bigger, than the one in the hotel Mom and Dad used to take me to when I was a kid. Mr. Harvey began to strip off his clothes. He didn't seem in the least embarrassed so I did the same. He had quite a good body. I guessed you had to have in that job.

He dove in straight away. I followed, managing to get right in the centre of the rapidly expanding circle of ripples he had left. It's an old trick of mine. He was a good swimmer too. I soon overtook him but he kept going. He wouldn't have been able to handle a real long distance swim but he was the sort of guy who could cross a pretty wide river fast and quietly. I wondered how often he'd done it and what it felt like to have bullets smacking into the water round your head as you swam. I guessed they'd teach that at training school but I was pretty good at underwater swimming. I decided to show him and put my head down. I glided down keeping my eyes open and focused on the tiled bottom. Forcing a bit more air out of my lungs, I lay on the tiles.

Suddenly I felt a hand on my leg. I was annoyed with myself. He obviously thought I was in trouble. I should have told him what I intended to do. I kicked out and shot to the surface. His head appeared a second or two later.

"I'm okay," I explained. "I often do that."

"Makes it a bit difficult for the other guy if he hasn't got an aqualung," he said. "Some things are better done on terra firma." I could see what he meant. Imagine giving a message or a roll of microfilm to a good swimmer like me to hand over to some other agent. He'd be hard pressed to keep up with me or down for long enough.

We clambered out of the water. I let him go first. He slung me a towel and I dried off as best as I could. He indicated for me to lie on one of the loungers.

"Right," he said. "Let's get down to it shall we? You do undertake never to breathe a word about what happens here? It really is important for both our sakes."

I nodded and the next minute had the shock of my life. His fingers tweaked

my nipples. For a split second I panicked. I'd heard of putting crocodile clips on them and giving the person the full mains voltage. But he had no crocodile clips; just his fingers.

"Absolutely massive!" he murmured.

I shut my eyes and felt his fingers circling. It actually felt quite nice, once you got used to the strangeness of it. I closed my eyes.

I blame Neil Anderson who lives three doors down from me for what happened next. I'd gotten into bed well after midnight and was just working out a real good story line for my nightly release of tension when there was a knock at the door. Both light bulbs in his room had blown. Could I do something to help? It's an odd phenomenon but if you are keen on computers, people automatically think you're an expert on electrics. He hadn't got a spare. Neither, for that matter, had I. He went out to get two from the janitor who wouldn't have been well pleased to be woken but Neil's one of those boys with rich parents who think that everyone is at their beck and call twenty four hours a day. Not knowing how long it would take him, I just sat on the bed and waited. He returned over an hour later. We screwed the bulbs in, using a flashlight to see what we were doing. No luck. It took another half an hour to find the correct circuit breakers. They were downstairs. His had flipped.

Mr. Harvey's hand moved down to my navel. I was tired and - more important - like a dog that's been deprived of exercise and hears its leash being rattled, my cock responded. I didn't know what to do. I felt like the guy who farted at a White House party. I opened my eyes. He was smiling! I was about to murmur some sort of apology when he spoke.

"Bigger than I thought," he said and actually touched it. It was more than a touch. I felt his fingers go round it. I closed my eyes again. Had I been trapped by a queer? It sure looked like it. Two seconds later I was certain of it. Very gently, he started to manipulate the foreskin, squeezing it.

I was tired but my brain went into overdrive. Kick him in the teeth and tell him to fuck off? No. Violence wasn't the answer.

Politely tell him to leave off and report him to the Principal? Suddenly, I understood. "You undertake not to breathe a word about what happens here." Very clever! It was a test. How do you find out if a guy can really keep quiet? You can tell him something in confidence and wait to see if the word spreads. Yes, but even better, get him in the nude and then toss him off.

"Mr. Harvey is queer! I went round to his place yesterday and he tried to wank me off." It would spread through the school like wildfire. He would deny it and the potential recruit would be dropped like a red hot cinder. You had to hand it to him. I did. I opened my legs.

It wasn't half as bad or as embarrassing after that. He said nothing; just carried on wanking me and occasionally playing with my balls. I kept my eyes closed.

"It would be worth while to store some of his semen, Olga. He is their best

man. We could produce agents of better quality."

"A good idea, Ivanovitch, but not this time. This time I shall drink it. I have never seen such a gorgeous cock. See how long it is. How hard and thick. And such balls!"

"It was a good idea to chain him up like that. See how he is squirming as Olga sucks him. He is very near. I think it will happen very soon. Yes... see how he is panting. There will be a lot of it I think. There! What did I tell you. How does it taste, Comrade Olga?"

"Delicious! I knew you wouldn't be a disappointment." I opened my eyes. Mr. Harvey was wiping his lips with the corner of a towel. Surely not? No. There was enough spattered over my belly and the cushions. I must have been mistaken. For some peculiar reason I was clutching the corners of the lounger above my head. I put my hands down and closed my eyes again.

"I guess you'd like another drink," he said.

"Mmm? Oh, yeah. Please. I think I must have dozed off." He laughed. I heard him get up and a few minutes later he returned.

"Wake up," he said.

I did. He'd put on a toweling robe. I took the drink.

"Mind if I talk business?" he asked. "I have to go out shortly."

"Sure."

"You'll find your bank balance has grown a bit tomorrow. Now then, how often can you come here without attracting too much attention?"

"Any time really. Friday afternoons is a good time. I don't have lessons then. It's our group's sports day."

"Good. Let's say every Friday at three o'clock."

"Fifteen hundred hours," I said. "I'll park the bike down the street and walk up to the house."

"Good thinking," he said. "I knew you were going to be an asset."

I "woke up" by taking another plunge in the water, got dressed and he took me to a place near the school.

"If anyone asks, I've been to the cinema," I said as I got out of the car.

"And it was a terrific film," he said. "Cheers, Chris. See you on Friday."

I watched as the car disappeared. He was obviously going to make his report. 'Schmidt - Christian. Test technique number three. Will keep under careful observation.'

He did. Several times in the next week we ran into each other 'by accident'. I was in a Wimpey when he walked past the window. He came into the library when I was there. I was playing tennis when I spotted him watching me from a small knoll near the court.

The hundred dollars in my bank account had been paid in cash. The cashier couldn't remember who had done it. I didn't press the point.

- - -

"You said you'd be free," said Mike. "I've booked the court."

"Sorry Mike," I said. "It's pretty important. I can't get out of it. I'll pay the court fee."

That made him happier. I set off. I parked the bike as I said I would at the end of the street and walked up to the house. I pressed the button.

"Who is it?"

"Christian." I didn't give my last name. It was on the tip of my tongue to say 'Double oh nine' but that, I thought, might reveal that I had guessed too much. The gate swung open. I crunched across the gravel forecourt. He was standing in the doorway waiting for me.

"Good lad!" he said. "We wondered if you'd come."

That 'we' was a dead giveaway, I thought. Headquarters obviously.

"On time too, thanks to your watch-maker buddy," I said. He laughed. "You can thank him personally," he said. "He's here." I followed him through the house to the pool. The watch-maker was sprawled, wearing a bath robe on one of the loungers. I said 'Hi'. He said his name was Lucas which certainly was not the name over his shop. Mr. Harvey went in to get me a drink.

"I kinda guessed you were in on it," I said, sitting down next to Lucas.

"That was sharp of you. We've been together for fifteen years. Not a word please."

"Don't worry," I said. "I know when to keep my mouth closed."

Mr. Harvey returned with my drink.

"Who's Olga?" said Lucas.

"Olga? I don't know anybody of that name."

"You mentioned it last time you were here," said Mr. Harvey. I think I must have blushed. "Oh! That was something I was thinking about. I guess I must have said the name without thinking."

"Let's hope you don't do that too often," said Lucas. "Do you have a girlfriend?"

"Not really, no."

"Good. They can be a hindrance in this game. John says you're very good."

"John? Oh! Mr. Harvey you mean? Good at what?"

"Er... swimming." Mr. Harvey said. "I was telling Lucas about how you can stay underwater for such a long time."

"Practice," I explained. "And you never know when it might come in useful."

"When you've finished your drink, show him."

"I can show him now. I've got swimming trunks on under my jeans this time."

That seemed to amuse them. I saw them exchange smiles. 'This guy's going to be a good agent. He's prepared for anything.'

I stripped off and plunged in. I gave them the full works. I could see them watching me. I did every stroke in the book and finished off with the longest underwater stay I could manage. I got to the surface with my lungs at bursting

point. They clapped and I clambered out.

"How do you do it?" asked Lucas.

"Lung capacity and practice," I said.

"Hmm. Come and lie down."

I did so. He stood up and bent over me. He put his hands on my still heaving chest. "See what you mean about capacity," he said, stroking my pecs. Then, just as Mr. Harvey had done, he started to play with my nipples.

What happened after that is still a bit confused in my mind. I remember Lucas asking if there was anything I would never do. I said I would never give away a secret.

"Even if you were subjected to torture?" he asked.

"Never," I said. "They'd have to kill me first."

And then they were both on me. It was like being attacked by an octopus. This time the conversation wasn't imaginary and between foreign agents. It was for real and they were both highly trained agents. I knew what they were waiting for. They were expecting me to react violently, to get away as soon as possible and denounce them.

"I always think legs feel nicer when they're wet," said Mr. Harvey. His hands were sliding up and down my thighs.

"The whole of him feels nice," said Lucas, rubbing my belly.

After that, I closed my eyes again.

One of them started kneading my cock through my trunks. It took longer to respond than it had the last time but the inevitable happened. My trunks were pulled down. I was aware of the wet smack they made as they hit the concrete.

"Nice pair of balls," said Lucas.

"Nice cock, too," Mr. Harvey added.

One of them lifted my legs. I felt fingers groping around down there and, for some reason, that turned me on. Lips and tongues went everywhere.

I remember wondering at what stage of the training, they showed you how to turn on potential agents. It was pretty effective.

"It's not just his lungs which are capacious," said Mr. Harvey. "Feel this."

I'd read somewhere about using that particular place for secreting rolls of film. I was determined to show them that, if necessary, I'd take a six reel epic and that time I really was the man who farted in the faces of the mighty.

"I can't wait," said Lucas.

"Take him to the west coast for a weekend. That would be the best thing," said Mr. Harvey. "Going to share the cream with me?"

"Sure. You go first. Oh gee! Just look at him go!"

I thought I would faint. I kept my eyes closed and tried to make it last as long as possible. Those guys had been really well trained. Lynette back home was said to be good at it but she was nothing compared to them for technique. It wasn't, I thought, a job I would relish but I guessed it was necessary. If they were to ask me to recruit Nicky Shemanovsky, I wouldn't mind that so much -

save that I doubted I could get my mouth over it. Nicky was only fifteen but hung like an elephant.

"I have to do this Nicky. I'm sure you understand."

"Sure Chris. Just get on with it. Gee! They certainly train you guys well. Oh, yeah! Lick my balls a bit. Get 'em nice 'n' wet...."

I don't know who got the first mouthful of mine. When I opened my eyes they were both licking my thighs like a couple of dogs.

"How did I do?" I asked when I'd got my breath back.

"Superbly!"

"Bloody marvelous!"

- - -

I'm due at Mr. Harvey's again tomorrow. There'll be another guy there.

"From Virginia?" I asked. I could see that they were embarrassed.

Lucas laughed. "Going to rather than from I think," he said.

And next month, we're all going to a smart hotel on the west coast. Flying there, of course. And somebody once said that being a spy was no fun!

PARTY BOYS

By

John Patrick

The Low-down on the High-life
A Series of Stories Edited by
STARbooks Press

"Nightlife has changed since the days I was doing Studio 54. It's not such a mindless experience, and people don't want to live in the past."
— Ian Schrager

- - -

"Live and let live, and party on!"
— Barry Goldwater's gay grandson Ty Ross, summing up his late grandfather's philosophy

CONTENTS

INTRODUCTION:
THE PIER SLUTS,
THE FLOATING PARTY,
AND OTHER TWISTED RITUALS

John Patrick

"Happiness will come...eventually.
Meanwhile, give a party."
— Lemke's Journals (translation)

In Manhattan, as the mayor remakes the city into a North Country Disneyland, "The erotic edge has gone so far underground that it can't be found without a guide," Richard Goldstein said in *Village Voice*. "...In Times Square, for instance, the Life has been replaced by the Tony award-winning musical of the same name.

"Maybe we do need a guided tour in order to grasp the richness and fragility of the city's interaction with sexual freedom. But most gays still keep the faith. The yearning to scope and score persists even though the culture of virtual virtue is turning us into zombies in a George Romero horror film, wandering through the mall with some vague memory of what a telephone is for. This is where the Pier Sluts come in.

"The name is a manifestation of Sex Panic!, the new queer group out to shatter the false consensus of public chastity, to celebrate a scene that represents everything the new Temperance League can't abide: the fabled sex piers off Christopher Street. Here, in the disco years, hundreds, maybe thousands, of men participated in a nightly saturnalia to the tumid lapping of polluted waves.

"Today, young gays gather in the strip that connects the few remaining piers. Signs warn against every imaginable quality-of-life infraction, even though this piece of misbegotten real estate (owned by New York State) fronts on one of the most noxious roads in town. Yet, for the kids who vogue and vamp there, Club Village, as they call the piers, is what it has long been for gays, a floating party and, sometimes literary, home. Those who gambol on the waterfront today know little about the disco era, when gay guides referred to this area as 'the Casbah.' Nor could the clones of yore hear, in their back rooms and trysting trucks, echoes of the waterfront where Walt Whitman saw 'two bronze-faced sailors' kissing fervently before they had to part.

"...Edmund White's description of the sex piers, in his 1978 novel *Nocturnes for the King of Naples*, captures the thrill of adventure and connection this place gave so many gay men. 'It was a funhouse, a free space,' White recalls today. 'It didn't belong to anyone.'

"On tour for *The Farewell Symphony*, White finds himself defending not just his past but his fight to honor it. His book has been bashed by Larry Kramer for its blunt appreciation of anonymous sex. 'His asshole was busier than his toilet,' hissed Kramer. White responds: 'Just as Women Against Pornography joined

forces with the Reaganites, I think Kramer has joined forces with the cops to close gay places down.'"

"Philip Gefter was 25 in the fall of 1976, a beautiful young man in New York City, where young men and women come to be beautiful," Charles Kaiser notes in *The Gay Metropolis*. Gefter remembers, "As a waiter at Berry's, I'd work from five to midnight. After my shift, I'd have several drinks at the bar, usually with Chuck, the chef, who became my cruising buddy. Chuck and I would go off into the night, often smoking a joint along the way, sometimes after taking drugs of every variety: cocaine, MDA, Quaaludes, and angel dust, which I rarely did because it numbed me, made me feel stupid, half-conscious, subhuman, unlike MDA, or THC, which made me feel alive, made everything seem to glisten, as if everything were outlined in electric pastels. I hated angel dust, but a lot of people used it. Chuck and I would begin our rounds at various bars. We'd arrive at the Ninth Circle to see who was there. We'd walk down Christopher Street, which was still lively at one o'dock in the morning. We'd hang out for a while at Keller's across the street from the Trucks, or the Cock Ring, where people would dance with handkerchiefs doused with ethyl chloride clenched between their teeth. Eventually, we'd wend our way up West Street to the Stud and to our inevitable destination, the Anvil."

(The Anvil was an extraordinary establishment in the meatpacking district of the West Village, located on the two lower floors of a building at the corner of 14th Street and Eleventh Avenue.) "I remember long lines to get in on Friday and Saturday nights," said Gefter, "and, sometimes, you'd see women on line masquerading as men...The Anvil was my favorite bar in the entire world. It was what I imagined Weimar Germany culture to be like, on acid. It seemed more like a club with a kind of festive, ersatz honky-tonk atmosphere than the dingy, seedy dive it appeared to be from the outside. Not that it wasn't seedy. It was. Dark, dank, dirty. Thank God the lights were out in the back room. I can't imagine what really lived and crawled on those floors in the vague light of day.

"When you entered the Anvil, you walked down a flight of stairs to the first level. What was so great was so much was going on at once. It was such a carnival, dancing men were parading around on top of the horseshoe bar, little red lights were strewn across the ceiling, as if it were always Christmas. There was always a pathetic little parody of a drag show on the little stage in the corner. And hundreds of men. It was always packed. The crowd ran the gamut from the most illustrious names in the press to the sleaziest people you would never want to meet. Of course, sometimes they're one and the same, but never mind. It was truly the most fabulous place.

"Sometimes I had sex in the back room at the Anvil, on the level below the first floor. I remember one evening that characterized a deep, dark level of my sexual activity, the ninth circle of my sexual experience. Looking back at my twenties, after all that has since transpired, I'm grateful that I experienced that sexual freedom."

Gefter felt he was representative of a time, "the beginning of homosexual identity in America. He said that this all made sense at the time: "Anyway, Chuck and I had been making our usual rounds. Our drink of choice then was the Wild Turkey Manhattan, and we must have had more than a few of those that night. I'm sure we had smoked a few joints, and, maybe, popped a Quaalude, and ended up at the Anvil at four or five in the morning. Not unusual. I was in the back room having a grand old time. There was a ledge that ran the length of the back room, which I never actually saw, but people would lie on the ledge and get fucked. I remember this particular night, there I was lying on the ledge, my underpants and my jeans cradled in my armpit beside me, being fucked randomly by several different men. I could feel them one at a time inside me, even though I never saw them. Either I was truly liberated or truly psychotic. Who knows? But you know what William Blake said: 'The road of excess leads to the palace of wisdom.' All I know is, I was in heaven, and I learned a few things while I was there.

"That may have been the darkest moment of my sexual experience, but I had experienced pure animal pleasure. I was having the time of my life."

"Why is it that when someone recounts a bit of history they never seem to get the facts straight?" Philip in New York asks. "Can it be they were too spaced out, for a good decade or two, on lord only knows what, and accept the psychedelics of that period as unshakable reality? Take, for instance, Gefter's description of what the Anvil was like in 'the fall of 1976.' Just the list of drugs Gefter consumed would have been enough to make a Chihuahua believe it was the incarnation of Hercules....

"Yes, I was at the Anvil, several times, thank you, in 1979. And being a country boy from upstate, with a head full of the wicked and dirty tales of what happened in that infamous place, I was scared shitless and begged my boyfriend to not leave me alone for a second, even to go use the bathroom!

"At any rate, I was never sloshed nor sleazy while at the Anvil and, in the three years between Gefter's outings and mine, I highly doubt the Anvil underwent massive renovations that would substantiate Gefter's claim of how the place was laid out. First of all, the two floors the Anvil occupied were the street level and basement and there were no stairs 'When you entered the first level'. You were then on the main floor of a rectangular building having entered its bowels from 14th Street; you had to turn right and walk a few paces before entering the bar. Upon which, turning left and facing the heart of the main floor; to the immediate right were the stairs leading down to the basement, then the horseshoe bar and then, the small stage. Along the left wall were, among other things, the toilet rooms. The left and right walls met at the far end, so why Gefter would claim that the stage was 'in the corner' is confounding.

"Downstairs, to the right there was a projection area, straight ahead there was an L-shaped (wet) bar, reversed, and to the left was an opening in the brick foundation (black draped) with one of several darkrooms beyond. At the time I

was there, the other entrances to the darkrooms were illuminated with low-watt, red lights from within, giving me the impression of them being yawning Devil's mouths and the mental thought of, 'Enter at one's own risk and hope to live through it all!' ...I got a good buzz while there but never had any sex."

If a place to rival those of the "golden age" of partying should open in Manhattan, it is quickly shut down. Consider the case of Cake, the bar that once brought a little excitement to Avenue B. Derek de Kiff of *On the Scene* remembers, "On any given night, stoppers-by had the chance to be carded by a 19-year-old girl, rock with their cocks out, or flit downstairs into the dark to be fondled in the shadows. While mingling, it wasn't unusual to hear such delightful epigrams as: 'This guy started sucking me off, and it was feeling really good, and then suddenly I realized he wasn't sucking me off at all. I was, like, totally doing him!' On one occasion, a drunken forty-something was reveling by the bar and suddenly dropped. Concerned rock 'n roll faggots gathered around and generally asserted that he was dead.

"On any given night, you could watch infamous go-go boy Joel have several fingers inserted in him, while still dancing in perfect sync to the Pixies' 'Tony's Theme.' It was generally unheard-of to go to the bathroom alone, or to actually go there to urinate. On any given night, you could spot such luminaries as John Waters, Marc Almond, or your boyfriend of two years making out with a go-go boy with whipped cream all over him. "The bar, to its credit, lasted over a year, but after 'inexplicable' pressure from Mayor Giuliani in the form of police raids and fire marshals, Cake ultimately closed down."

Meanwhile, out on Fire Island, the party scene is as exotic as ever, and all in the name of charity! A *Gay Times* of London reporter visited here and filed this report: "...Fire Island is an attractive weekend retreat no more than an hour away from the stifling summer heat in New York City. There are half a dozen self-contained season settlements along the island, two of which are gay, Cherry Grove (reasonably cheap, very cheerful, and on special weekends at least, decidedly dykey) and The Pines (decidedly expensive and very serious, serious about having a very nice time).

"In the Seventies, the place was a byword for weekend party heaven, all the sex, drugs, disco music, style and glamour that money and the post-gay liberation generation could possibly afford. Calvin Klein was at the top of the list of big time celebs who bought up the gorgeous cuboid all-wood dream homes on Millionaires Row with the ocean view (one lavishly furnished summer home I visited had specially sculpted walls to make the sound of the waves echo gently around the room).

"...If they're not the sort who want to relax, then invite them for the Morning Party, the drugfest beach party to end all drugfest beach parties, once a year on a Sunday morning in August. The event has been running for 15 years now and the 4,500 tickets sold raise nearly half a million dollars for the AIDS self-help organization Gay Men's Health Crisis. And the island homes are packed all

weekend with New York's gay finest, partying round the pool, partying in the Pavilion Club till the sun comes up, and then most importantly getting their tops off, getting in among the pumped-up men on the beach and partying till the sun goes down again."

Joseph Carman attended the same party and reported it in *New York Press*: "The party was in full swing on Fire Island, and, true to form, it was starting to look like Rome five minutes before the fall. The circuit-party queens had been warned by GMHC that mixing ecstasy and special K (ketamine, a horse tranquilizer) with their protease inhibitors was a serious health risk. But persuading these boys to stop taking designer drugs is like informing the citizens of Juarez that there is a border between Mexico and the U.S.

"Sheriffs, packing pistols, were patrolling the roped-off, tented area of the Pines beach, eager to pull any drug dealer off the floor and make a felony arrest for drug possession. The A-List fags with the steroided, nipple-ringed tits had outsmarted them, though; they took their drugs back at the beach house or on the ferry coming over from Sayville. Amyl nitrate bottles were discreetly pulled out deep in the middle of the jammed dance floor, impenetrable even by the ghosts of parties past. All that the men of law could do was admire the *faaaabulous* outfits.

"Homo muscle boys paraded their pumped-up bodies, which are now de rigueur for any serious AIDS fund-raising circuit party.

"...In addition to rampant recreational drug abuse, there are two other pillars of constancy in the American gay male community: fucking like rodents in the rites of spring and ultra-rotten disco music that too many queers mistake for high art.

"'My X just hit!' exclaimed one dancer. He was wearing a red plastic kilt and matching fireman's hat. His friend, bitching about his housemates, was identically dressed. This seemed to be a leitmotif in this year's fashion statements: a desire to dress like twins, and to escort each other, hand-in-hand, around the dance arena, like poodles in a dog show. Two more men flaunted their big baskets in fresh white '2xist' underwear, while another couple flounced in those fag-popular, nylon, rip-stop running pants (so comfortable in an August heat wave). There were more than a few pairs of red-velvet sailor's bellbottoms as well.

"'I just took my X,' giggled an L.A. import with a crew cut and tattoos covering his shoulders. An Australian hunk had 'Bondi' plastered across his ass. No one was allowed to dance on the speakers this year, and platforms were reserved 'for fan dancers only,' a grungy gang who looked as if they had kept alive the practice of fan dancing since their Studio 54 days in 1978. The over-hormoned crowd, sprinkled with a few die-hard fag hags (including one in a white taffeta prom dress who was having a red zit attack from the heat) screamed along the refrains, 'For the First Time In My Life,' 'Forever Young,' and, older lyrics like, 'Never Gonna Make It Without Your Love.'"

"'Should I take another hit of X?' whispered a queen in a grass skirt to his glazed-eyed, Spandex-clad companion, who sported an uncontrollable hard-on. The sweaty, unconscious throng boogied on, like one of those huge deep-sea jellyfish comprised of interconnected nerve centers that clumsily connect into an organism.

"A truly twisted ritual, the Morning Party is the silliest of events, an excuse for drug-enhanced, muscle-bound sissies to act like teenaged girls in a basement rec room. GMHC makes a shitload of money from it each year, while promoting safer sex practices, and then produces more parties so that gay men can fry their brains on ecstasy and have unsafe sex.

"'I need a butt-fuck *now*!' screamed an over-pierced male in fluorescent green Speedos. But there was no barebacking (fucking without a condom) at this year's Morning Party. That would be reserved for later at the private post-party parties and in the Meat Rack, behind the dunes in between the Pines and Cherry Grove."

Meanwhile, in Los Angeles, Robert Ellsworth of *Frontiers* magazine was visiting the annual Butt Boys Party, this year held at Hollywood Moguls. "Although the cover was a steep $30 bucks, I was told the money went to a good cause, it included such informative demonstrations as live penis pumping, nude flogging, candle wax burning and genital shaving, all under one roof! It was a veritable Who's Who of Tinseltown's leather studs. The butt contest, hosted by the Delta Burke of porn himself, Blue Blake, featured nubile butts jettisoning out from glory holes that were definitely larger than regulation size, greased up and shimmying for the title of L.A.'s best butt. The now-svelte Dino DiMarco used his riding crop to ruddy the contestants' cheeks, while Alex Stone splattered naughty slave boys with Cool Whip and maraschino cherries, you don't get that at Dairy Queen! Porn star Matt Bradshaw wandered around the halls in a chain link harness, cheering up the sometimes-lethargic partygoers.

"I spotted a few VIP studio execs in the inner bowels of the back room, which resembled sets from 'Caligula,' but due to the delicate nature of the event, I won't name names. So torture me. I won't even describe what went on there, but let's just say the Marquis de Sade himself would have felt right at home.
"Unfortunately, the homophobic fire department closed the place down early, causing back room patrons to scuttle out like roaches when the bright lights suddenly illuminated their salacious shenanigans. Even after a preponderance of pleasure-packed parties all summer, this is definitely one I won't soon forget."

My, how times have changed! Consider how it used to be at certain parties held by those on the A-list, as examined in the book about fabled film director George Cukor, *A Double Life*. Author Patrick McGilligan says, "The 1950s had been the heyday of Cukor's poolside parties. If anything, in the sanguine atmosphere of the Eisenhower era, the gatherings had grown larger and even more special, the invitations more coveted. It was still here, in safety and privacy, that the most handsome, available young men could meet illustrious

people over a cocktail and a sandwich, and exchange pleasantries and phone numbers. Cukor's own sex life was still active. Ingrained habits prevailed: He preferred the straight types and the no-names (no celebrities). The sex was still frequent and paid. The young men who entered his life stayed only for a few nights, or a few weeks. They were usually introduced, often 'passed on' by the friends who came to dinner. 'George and I shared a few tricks,' said one longtime friend. 'I remember a boy at a party once, a very handsome boy, a hustler. He talked a lot; they all talk a lot; they always talk. He said he knew George. He thought he was a poet.

"...Sometime in the late 1950s, two of the regulars of the Sunday group came to dinner. They brought with them, to show him off, a handsome, muscular newcomer. Cukor was not the only one of the Sunday group who thought the young man (younger than Cukor by some thirty years) a stunning beauty, a beachboy type, with rugged good looks, a vibrant smile, and sensuous mien. Everything about the young man seemed to be mysterious. He had no apparent connection to the motion-picture industry, and, unlike most of the regulars, he was neither prosperous nor well known. People knew only vaguely that he was from Canada and had been in the military. Because the two men were longtime Sunday participants, the last thing in the world they expected was to lose their young find to Cukor. Cukor himself was always respectful of other people's friends, and at his house there was a kind of unwritten rule that if a member of the group brought a 'girl' to those Sunday-night dinners, the person who brought 'her' was entitled to the last dance, at evening's end. But this time, as in one of those romantic screen stories that Cukor would have found difficult to believe, it was chemistry at first sight. Cukor was smitten, and for the first time that anyone could remember, he broke his own rules. 'It was a *Queen passional*,' in the words of Bob Wheaton. Furious, the two gentlemen never again returned to the Sunday gatherings. The young man, whose name was George Towers, became Cukor's frequent companion and friend.

"According to friends, Towers was the type Cukor had always fallen for a strapping 'real' man who kept his own sexual proclivities ambiguous. Towers seemed to play those ambiguities to the hilt, in front of others, copycatting the older man's quips and sayings, his mannerisms obvious, even in front of straight friends, in his warmth and affection for the Hollywood director. In the wholehearted way that he had always disdained, Cukor became attached to Towers, emotionally and psychologically. In turn, Towers seemed to latch on to Cukor, and to be at the house constantly.'"

A frequent guest at circuit parties, usually as a dancer, was the late, great Scott O'Hara. In his memoir, *Autopornography,* he recalled dancing at a Black Party and having fellow porn star Jon King in tow. Just the thought of it is arousing! He met Jon in 1986, when he went to see his performance at the Campus Theater, calling the man and the performance "hot stuff." "King recognized me in the audience," O'Hara related in his memoirs. "He sought me

out afterward, and made sure we got together. Nothing subtle about that boy: when he wanted something, he went for it. I like that in a man. We got together: I vividly remember meeting him at a motorcycle dealership to pick up his bike, which had been in for repairs, and riding home with him on the back of it. Jon enjoyed taking risks. But once home, this changed: it was Rubbertime. I'm not sure, at this point, whether or not to be happy about this. He claimed, at the time, that he was still negative, despite having been fucked, condomless, by a lot of men over the years. Well ... I gather that, sometime in the next nine years, his luck ran out. I could take satisfaction in knowing that it wasn't me who infected him; or I could, wistfully, wish that we'd fucked unprotected, since in the long run, it wouldn't have mattered. I guess I have a love/hate relationship with my virus; if someone like Jon King was determined to get himself infected, I kind of wish he'd chosen mine.

"Yes, our sex was truly stunning, right up there with the all-time best fucks of my life. That boy knew how to work his butt in a way that no one else could. He was hungry, and demanding. (It's nice to know that even a megabottom like Jon King can occasionally be manipulated into a top role, which he performed with great panache.) He only fucked me once, in all the times we played ... and I found myself wishing, as he shot inside me, that I could keep his cum up my butt as a souvenir.

"Then there were the times we ran into each other in New York. Jon spent a couple of nights with me at the Colonial House Inn, when I was performing at the Black Party. I think he was drugged out of his mind; I know he was impossible to wake."

I know one boy who didn't have *that* problem. Boytoy and porn star Kevin Kramer recalled making the video "The Biggest Piece I Ever Had" and being so entranced with his co-star, Jason Reddy, a beautifully hung stud, that he accompanied him to the White Party in Palm Springs. Kevin said, "We hit it off. He invited me to go back to Palm Springs with him for the White Party. I was in a discovery mode, and got a job dancing on the scaffolding at the Desert Palms. Jason was dancing also and he whipped his dick out and I started sucking it. The management climbed up and told us to stop. We wouldn't, the crowd loved it and we were being tipped very generously. People still talk about that! It was quite amateur, but it was gutsy."

Speaking of gutsy, one of the gutsiest people of recent times porn director and stage performer Chi Chi LaRue, also one of the great party people of our times: "I have to tell you," he said in his book *Making It Big*, "fame is everything it's cracked up to be and then some. For the most part I like my degree of fame. I'm known but I'm not *famous* famous. You certainly can get *too* famous; just ask Brad Pitt or Madonna or Dennis Rodman But I'm not there yet, so for me the benefits still outweigh the drawbacks.

"I get comped into clubs. I get flown around the country. I get to meet scads and scads of gorgeous men and see them naked. And sometimes, every so often,

I even get to have seen with them. It's well worth the demands on my time and the occasional fan who recognizes you even when you look like hell. The happenings of my life are major social events. Each November for my birthday, I fly to New York, where I have a wonderful, raucous celebration at some trendy club. Then I come home and have a separate party in L. A. for some 500 more of my closest friends. Then there are other people's parties, one or two virtually every weekend. This industry is one big, long party. And sometimes I feel like my life is that way too.

"It's not all roses and rim jobs, though. Sometimes it all gets to be too much. You're not always in the mood to party or to deal with a fawning public, and sometimes, quite frankly, it gets to be a real pain in the ass."

Speaking of pains in the ass, Peter Adam, in his biography of David Hockney, recounts how the artist established a pattern of going back and forth between London and California. It was in California that David found some of his most frustrating lovers, who were truly party boys of the highest order. Says Adam, "When David returned to London he brought with him a new friend from California called Bobby, the pretty all-American boy, blond, very sexy and rather dim. They had met in a Los Angeles gay bar, it was lust, sheer lust and David, in his often insanely generous way, had invited him to New York. Bobby was rather lost in the crowd and the boy from California hated everybody and everything, including New York. To cheer him up David brought Bobby with him to London, where David had a show at Kasmin's Gallery. They traveled on the revamped *France*. Most people thought David was mad, but he was proud to show off his new friend. He took him everywhere, 'once to a club where Ringo sat at a nearby table. But not even that impressed Bobby, all he wanted was sex,' David smilingly remembers. Then something must have gone wrong because a week later he announced that Bobby was gone. ...He became a go-go dancer."

MR. CHAMPDICK
AND THE STABLE BOY
Adapted by John Patrick
from the original folk tale

One unseasonably warm autumn, to take his mind off the grand party he was hosting that evening, Mr. Champdick went to where his magnificent thoroughbreds were housed. He had set his mind on a lively canter in the park to distract him from his apprehension about the success of the party. It was his first such occasion since his young wife had run off with a sailor boy over a year ago.

When he entered the sweet-smelling stable, a mare whinnied, whether from fright or nervousness he could not tell, but a suspicious scrambling sound of human footsteps gave him the clue, and opening the door of her stall he discovered the new stable boy, Pike, hurriedly buttoning his pants.

"Ho, ho," cried Mr. Champdick, catching the trembling youth by his collar, "what have we here? A fine piece of horse-play. So this is why Colleen has lost every race in the last six months!"

"No, Sire, it wasn't I, believe me. I just started here last week."

"Haven't I just now caught you buggering the poor beast with your common cock?"

"But Sire, this was the first time. I'll never do it again. I promise!"

Mr. Champdick let go of his collar and studied the long, wavy fronds of the animal's cunt. "This is ridiculous," he protested. "Fucking a horse! A man might as well put his cock in a vatful of cream."

Reassured that he would suffer no harm at the master's hand, the groom straightened but hesitated to answer his master. He watched him place his hand over the mare's sex, comparing its length and breadth and whistling in amazement. "Boy, tell me something. What possible pleasure can you get from her? You would do better to go after the cook. Stay away from horses. You will only ruin your chances with women." The groom did not answer him. He seemed to be turning something over in his mind and then, without warning, in a gesture full of pride, he boldly tore open his fly and dragged forth a prick that any stallion would envy.

The master ceased his remonstration, frankly overwhelmed at the evidence, amazed at the groom who stood with his legs apart to let the long and cumbersome cock dangle about his knees. Mr. Champdick, renowned for his own magnificent organ, felt somewhat humbled, even ridiculed, before the lad. "How did it happen?" he asked finally in a voice that was full of genuine concern.

"Sire, they say it's a disease. My father took me to all kinds of specialists, but they haven't been able to cure me." He went on to explain the shame he had felt and how he was afraid he would have to go through life deformed and banned from society. But the master was less interested in the boy's personal woes than in seeing that horrendous object in action. He interrupted the groom

and asked him if he could get it hard. He said he certainly could. "Then do so," ordered the master. The groom picked up the head of his club in both hands and began masturbating, beating it against the smooth flanks of the mare. She whinnied apprehensively. Bit by bit the cock began to stretch, filling out into its true proportions. When it came fully erect the master was no longer sure that even the mare was capable of containing such a cock.

"My god!" the master cried. "Well, son, you might as well put it into her just for curiosity," he added, remembering that he had chided the boy but a moment ago for that very thing. The groom needed no urging, now that he had himself back to his passionate state with official approbation to boot. He braced himself on the side of the stall, where a sort of shelving had been installed for this purpose, and swung himself into position before the twitching tail of the mare. He did not trouble to lift it out of his way but placed his violet-veined organ through the horsehair and, with one sudden shove that called for all his strength, he drove the ramrod through her cunt in one long, even movement, which nearly buckled the outspread legs of the animal. The crazed mare lifted her head skyward, emitted a penetrating squeal of pain and pleasure ending in a dying whinny that turned the stable into a clamor and racket of answering cries.

The master, his ears ringing in the bedlam, watched the prodigious penis slicing in and out of the mare like some greasy piston pumping a machine of flesh. It would have been an impressive sight in any case, but he was already so much in heat thinking about the party to come that he had all he could do to keep his hand from his fly.

The lubricious odor that emanated from the slobbering hole soon whipped the nostrils of the stallions into a frenzy of lust. Their own black-sheathed cocks pulsated with mounting passion. A ferocious stench filled the air, a biting odor that pinched the master's nostrils. "Do they always get so heated up when you fuck the mare?" shouted Mr. Champdick, trying to make himself heard above the din.

The boy did not answer his master. The long, churning prick delved in faster and faster, and the mare reared back, wobbling her dripping flanks from side to side as though there were not yet enough of that prick boring into her carcass. The groom, for his part, was rapidly working to orgasm, slamming his belly like a madman, oblivious of the ear-shattering chaos about him. He turned once in his labors, to give Mr. Champdick a fleeting grin, demonstrating his thrill of pride and power. It was inevitable that when the mare gave out the final cry of her orgasm that the sex-crazed stallions should no longer hold out, and in a demonic concert their flying hooves shattered the wooden stalls and they burst from the stable in a galloping mass of flaming nostrils, satanic eyeballs and huge erections.

"Oh, god!" Mr. Champdick cried as the groom obviously exploded in the mare's cunt, and he scurried from the stables, still shaken from the harrowing spectacle. "'Tis folly," he cursed, "pure folly!"

Late that night, Pike, curious about the party that had been going on for hours, walked by the front entrance of the chateau. Even before he came abreast of the steps he saw the door was open but not a soul was in sight. The golden chandelier that hung in the hallway dazzled him. Pike stood awhile at the foot of the steps but not even a stray butler came to the door, which would have been sufficient pretext for his entry. Shrugging his shoulders contemptuously, he went part way round the house and headed back to the stables. He had heard from a groundskeeper that, on occasion, the master would invite the help to participate in the revels, and he thought, after what the master had seen that afternoon, that perhaps he would, common as he was, be invited to join in.

As Pike neared the stables, in the dark he nearly ran into Cecil, who was coming from the direction of the stables.

"Where have you been?" the older, wiry man asked.

"I went for a walk," Pike replied. "What's it to you?"

"The master sent me to fetch you. He wants you to join the party. Why, I have no idea, but that's what he said."

Pike chuckled. He knew why the master wanted him, and his cock twitched in his pants. "Very well," Pike said, following Cecil to the chateau.

In moments, the youth was suddenly enjoying new sensations, things he had never even dreamed of. Aristocratic men and women had stripped themselves clean of every garment. Wide-eyed, he saw that a great circle was in progress, women rushing to be plowed by men with their cocks pointed straight out, dripping with lubrication. A man he recognized as a count was going cock head-first into the raging slit of a dancing baroness and came slipping out on the next step only to ram his steaming dick all the harder into a squealing duchess. It was like bathing in flesh, just pure warm, downy, vibrating, pulsating flesh.

In a far corner of the room, a score of Pekinese and other assorted lap dogs were clasped to the naked bellies of the maids and, knowing their work well, lapped the bushy cunts while the women squealed and shrieked. The women nearly tore the eyes of the animals from their sockets in the final lunges of their lust.

Upon stepping deeper into the cavernous room, Pike was seized and brought directly to the fray. They piled on him all together in a scrambling heap, bearing him down to the floor under their struggling bodies. How they sighed and moaned as they tore off his blouse. They wallowed and glutted like pigs in a trough, throwing out arms, legs, asses and elbows, anything that moved. They were getting as much of a thrill from themselves alone as rubbing Pike's body, for not many were actually able to reach him.

Soon there were erections coming at him from everywhere, sweeping over his cheeks; cocks that poked in his eyes, cocks that slid on his chest, on his thighs, on his arms. All of these pulsating penises sent new life into his heavy cock, which was still hidden in his pants.

It was inevitable that at last one of the mouths should stay, and beg for Pike,

and pull open his pants. He lay in a dream-like trance, succumbing to indefinable thrills as the huge, uncut cock was brought to Mr. Heath's eager lips. So far in had he pushed the monstrous thing that his tongue was shoved back in his throat, stopping his windpipe and he gasped and choked, but held onto the prick nevertheless.

Meanwhile, they licked with their tongues, caressed with their hands, and one, more hot-blooded than the others, came in a gush just as his cock rolled over Pike's face. The spicy stew ran into Pike's mouth, burning with an acid twang and firing his appetite so that he pumped vigorously at the mouth that was sucking on his penis. He screwed, blind-drunk, grabbing at buttocks, squeezing on thighs, biting on titties, smelling cunts. Nothing was spared in their lavish abuse, not an inch of flesh that didn't offer itself in the sacrificial heap, not a hole that went unscathed by a finger, a tongue or even a foot. Pike grabbed as many as he could hold when he felt he was coming and the force in his groin as he fired in Mr. Heath's mouth lifted them all high in the air and he blanked out in a wave of tumbling bodies and limbs.

However, not a minute's respite was given the strapping youth. They shoved over the fortunate Mr. Heath and a great fight ensued as they rushed to get on the astonishing prick! A duchess leaped on top, jabbing it in her cunt at first shot. She bounced on it for a few moments before being pushed off by an even drunker countess, leaving the duchess lying prostrate in ecstasy.

Finally, most of the revelers were petering out and dozing off into much-needed rest. Pike rolled away from the great mass, slipping in a puddle of sperm.

Meanwhile, upstairs, just outside Mr. Champdick's bedchamber, poor Miss Cramp was thwarted from having her hungry cunt satisfied by Mr. Champdick's boner. She had chased him all night and finally waylaid him in the hallway. He had insisted he was ready to retire, but Miss Cramp would have none of it. Mr. Champdick managed to get hard and stick her for a few minutes, but she was too old for him, and he could not keep an erection. Mr. Champdick excused himself to relieve his bladder. Just then, down the hallway came the bouncing ass of the frilly Mr. Heath, slightly drunk on wine and looking to relieve himself as well. He passed before the nearly nude Miss Cramp in a frigid manner, to enter the cabinet where Champdick was expelling the last drops of his bladder. It is no exaggeration to say that the effeminate Heath was profoundly moved by the sight of the cock before him. He forgot all about pissing as he reached out for it. But Mr. Champdick acted as if his virility was offended by this intrusion, and when Mr. Heath dropped to the floor and begged the gentleman to drive the "beautiful thing" in his mouth, Mr. Champdick shook the piss from it, then pulled the chain. As Mr. Champdick started to put the member back in his trousers, the stricken guest, turned desperate in the violence of his desire, clutched the ponderous handle in both hands and shoved his mouth over its head, filling his cheeks to bursting with the pulpy nub.

The annoyed Mr. Champdick told him to let go of the "God-damned thing,"

and then, seeing that Mr. Heath would never obey such a command, he began to pound the stubborn faggot angrily. Meanwhile, Miss Cramp, curious as to what was keeping Mr. Champdick, ripped open the door, only to stumble over the struggling men. The three of them fell into a struggle that promised to last a good while.

The chateau became alive with the running din upstairs, and the other guests came to see what was going on. They became engrossed with the scene that was unfolding in the toilet. The Duke of Porking, always up for a good fight, entered the cabinet, to find Mr. Champdick's resistance had crumbled, and the screams were ones of joy as Miss Cramp was sucking on Mr. Heath while Mr. Heath kept sucking on Mr. Champdick, who was feigning all the time a wish to have the faggot release him. Fairies, Mr. Champdick had observed on occasion, made up for their lack of numbers by the intensity of the passion they brought to their sexual activities. Mr. Champdick cried, "All the air I ever breathed was female perfumes, powders, colognes, like a hot-house flower. And now look at me, being sucked by a fairy!"

Seeing what Mr. Heath was doing to Mr. Champdick filled the Duke with a sudden jealousy, and he quickly entered the voluptuous ass of Mr. Heath. Mr. Heath was soon sighing in rapture as he felt this hot, eager cock begin to come and go in his ass, which sent thrill after thrill through his body until suddenly everything was too much to bear and he was shooting his juice deep into the throat of Miss Cramp.

The other guests were so ignited by this odd tableau in the cabinet that they paired off and began an orgy in the nearby hallways and winding staircase.

After all of his labors, the genial Duke was deprived of his climax by Mr. Champdick, who insisted on entering Mr. Heath himself. No sooner had Mr. Champdick left Mr. Heath's mouth than Miss Cramp was forcing Mr. Heath to eat her pussy. Mr. Heath pulled back in horror, but, just then, Mr. Champdick lustily invaded him, thrusting Mr. Heath deep into Miss Cramp's waiting lap. Mr. Champdick forced Mr. Heath to do something, anything, to Miss Cramp or he would remove his thrusting boner. Mr. Heath drew a deep breath and did his best to please the volatile Miss Cramp.

Mr. Champdick tried, but he could not achieve orgasm with his prick in Mr. Heath. He left the man to dally with Miss Cramp and staggered out into the corridor. Now he saw even the upstairs of the chateau was heaving and swaying in debauch and one needed but to turn to one side or the other to find Mr. Champdick a ready companion.

Mr. Champdick sought refuge downstairs. Descending the grand staircase, he was astonished to find Pike, who was headed upstairs when he met the Duke. The Duke made the mistake of patting the well-rounded ass of young Pike, and Pike took this as an invitation, since the Duke's prick was still semi-hard from being imbedded in Mr. Heath. Pike sat on the stairs and began sucking the Duke, intent on bringing him off.

The Duke's luck was running badly, however, because he was soon being assailed on the staircase by the butler, Cecil, who could never resist a good piece of ass. While all the fucking and hollering was going on around them, the three men formed a curious ménage a-trois on the staircase.

When the Duke saw Mr. Champdick, he feigned that he was being assaulted against his will, and he began trying to push Cecil away and remove his cock from the eager mouth of Pike. Champdick would have none of it. He laughed heartily and held the Duke in place so that the others could continue their attack. "Fucking is all in the mind," he said to the Duke. "You get a hard-on up here," and he pointed to his head, "before you get it down there." He stared at the Duke's cock sliding in and out of Pike's mouth, then at the sight of Cecil entering the Duke. Roaring with laughter, he looked down into the foyer and salon below to see dozens of spent, naked bodies. His party had been a success! So much so, that there hung in the air a heavy smell of aphrodisiacal pungency that could not be denied. He turned again to the sordid scene playing before his startled eyes. He could not believe that Pike, with his incredible endowment, though now hidden in his trousers, was sucking the Duke. It was at this thought that the great man stopped laughing. Everything, Mr. Champdick decided, had been warped, badly warped.

Just then, the Duke pulled his tool from Pike's mouth and was stroking it, close to an explosion. Pike held open his mouth, making a waiting receptacle to shut down on the gasping, spitting tool, swallowing the cum with great gulps.

At the same moment, Cecil came inside the Duke. Their lascivious movements provoked passionate discharges on the part of others near them. They cried into each other's ears, bit into the skin until blood flowed, and, with its scarlet drops falling from their lips, they collapsed like spinning drunkards.

Mr. Champdick stood spellbound watching the incredible sight. A beam of satisfaction began to spread from jowl to jowl. "This is something to see, by Jesus!" he exclaimed. "This is something few have ever enjoyed!" He stood there with his swelling erection poking out of his shirt-tails, and Pike, crazy with desire since he had not yet been relieved himself of his heavy build-up of spunk, hurriedly spat on Mr. Champdick's prick before he shoved it into his mouth. The wild-eyed boy tore at him with a viciousness far beyond his years. Mr. Champdick sighed, enjoying what he thought was one of the finer moments of his life.

As the boy continued to suck, Mr. Champdick realized the house had fallen silent, at last, and all he wished to do was take the new stable boy to his bedchamber. But he broke out into a cold sweat thinking of his reputation. Mr. Champdick, the world-renowned raconteur, the writer of ribald tales, the indomitable sportsman, the irresistible seducer, with a deformed groom! It was too ridiculous, yet he had been so terribly bored lately. Yet, he reasoned, he had experienced everything else on the face of the earth, why not this? Besides, he was widely revered for his unpredictable eccentricity. What he was about to do

was the most eccentric thing he had ever done, but he had never been confronted by the prospect of a bedmate with such a prodigious member before.

He leaned over and caressed the youth's smooth cheek and sank his bearded chin to his shoulder, sucking on it.

While he suckled the tender skin, he unbuttoned the youth's trousers and felt the massive pulp between his fingers. When he realized the youth was near to being fully hard, he stepped back to stare wild-eyed at the sight of the grotesque organ.

"Come," he said, "I want to get mine in my own bed."

Mr. Champdick tugged Pike by the penis all the way to the bedchamber. There, he again became fascinated by the member; it held him in evil fascination. He bent at the waist and kissed it, rolled its heftiness between his fingers. He became hypnotized by it, feeling a peculiar emotion, undefinable but overwhelming. He had laughed finally, and asked Pike to fuck him immediately.

Gleefully, Pike jumped upon the master in the huge bed and, imagining himself a ferocious stallion, he began attacking his master's ass. Mr. Champdick was sprawled helplessly on his back, gasping for air. Soon Pike was sweating abominably from his exertions to please his master.

Mr. Champdick lifted his head to watch the mammoth organ going in and out of his ass. So this is what we have come to, he thought, seeking the cause of his sudden conversion to homosexuality. The boy heaved and shoved with all the fire and heat of the stampeding stallions. One could only imagine the ripping and tearing of the sensitive walls of Mr. Champdick's ass as the boy pumped in him with all his might.

Mr. Champdick proceeded to begin playing with himself, finding a remnant of his sensuality still very much alive. Pike was gaining a certain vicious gratification in fucking such a splendid man of the world in a bed that doubtless had seen so many great moments of his amorous career. While he fucked, Pike gazed at the man's image and imagined how it must be to be such a man.

Mr. Champdick was enjoying this so much that he was astounded he had never had such thoughts before, that so late in life his dreams and fantasies had become those of an adolescent. Yet it was troubling the way the slamming of the incredible penis into his ass caused strange thrills to run up and down his spine. He was convinced at last that, however weird and preposterous it all seemed, this was his ultimate thrill.

After a while, the master was beside himself with the heady mix of pain and pleasure. Pike thought he would withdraw, but then he remembered one of his former patrons schooling him: "And remember, no matter how hard they yell or scream or bite, never, never pull out your cock. Don't be taken in by it." So he kept his place, ignoring Mr. Champdick's tearful pleas, pushing his pecker in deeper and deeper until his master grew weak and pale and his struggles subsided into soft moans. "Ohhh, at last. Ohh, what a thing! What an incredible thing! Push it all the way in!"

Edited by John Patrick

Pike wished to please his master, but there was no way he could do any such thing. Even with only about ten inches of his incredible cock inside the master, Pike was unquestionably the hero of the day and now this would add more to his prestige than anything he had ever done. They gave themselves over to new sensations entirely. Pike's cock was enjoying the close grip of the anus, and he erupted a great flow of cum deep within the master.

"Oh, god, hold it in me!" the master begged, clamping his hands on Pike's buttocks. While they lay glued together rubbing their bodies madly, Mr. Champdick finally came. They went crazy with their fierce cravings and the master nearly fainted with joy when he realized the stable hand was hard again and had returned to fucking him.

- - -

When Pike awoke some time later, the room was plunged in darkness and the door wide open. A faint glow of light illuminated somewhat the exterior hallway much in the manner of a stage setting. He was shivering from cold, and the noise of a rising wind could be heard blowing about the gothic towers of the house.

His stomach was aching with hunger and he left the bed and went out into the hallway. All about him lay the sprawled-out bodies of the sleeping lechers. Thighs were draped over thighs, arms flopped on breasts, torn fragments of dresses and corsets lay strewn all over in the dim light. So profoundly exhausted were the sleepers that even kicking one or two in the ribs had no effect at all.

Only tiny lamps at long intervals lighted the house, which threw long, eerie shadows down corridors and stairways. Windows rattled in their panes as the wind was reaching gale-force strength. Soon it began to rain, hard. A loud clap of thunder and a searing flash of lightning jolted Pike as he made his way through the chateau.

He climbed unfamiliar staircases and ran through dark, frightening halls. The doors he stopped to examine looked all the same. A door banged suddenly, somewhere in the house, and another roll of thunder boomed in his ears. His search was getting him nowhere. But at last he found the back stairs and made his way to the kitchen. He lit the lamp and found plenty of food left over from the feast. His noisy eating of it brought Cecil, clad in his full-length dressing gown, to the kitchen.

"You!" Cecil barked.

His mouth full of roasted hen, he mumbled, "Fuck you," or something to that effect, which infuriated Cecil. Stepping into the room, Cecil's eyes feasted for the first time on the appendage that hung between Pike's thighs as he sat on a stool next to the counter. His expression changed from one of anger to one of awe. "My god!" he cried.

Even though the light was dim, Pike could tell what Cecil was staring at. He was used to it by now and was even accepting that what may have been considered a curse was, in fact, a blessing. Pike spread his thighs and made his cock jump a bit. Cecil came closer, knelt on the floor beside the boy.

- 312 -

Pike kept stuffing himself with hen and helped himself to what wine was left in goblet after goblet. Meanwhile, he found it wasn't all disagreeable the way Cecil was toying with his cock. So while the wind blew and the storm crashed, Pike felt a sudden warmth, and soon they were both enjoying that sensual laziness of the late hours when the delights of sex are cast in a dream-like veil. Cecil's hand explored him once or twice all the way down his shaft and back, and then, unable to stand the titillating irritation he had caused, Pike thrust the head between Cecil's eager lips. Cecil began sucking in inch after inch of shaft, emitting a great sigh of contentment. Because his cock was raw from so much fucking, it burned all the way in, making Pike shudder and tremble. They were quiet for a while, drugging themselves with the endless sensations only cock sucking can provide. Then Pike began to move, slowly, back and forth, keeping only the head inside, allowing the lips to explore him and lap him relentlessly.

Cecil began fondling his own stiff prick, blindly satisfying his lust, and Pike knew he would never have been able to relinquish his prick until both of them had discharged. Lightning flashed and lit up the room, and in a groaning, drunken heave. Pike gushed on Cecil's head in a shower of cum. Cecil had never seen such a fierce discharge. Pike fell back like one dead, exhausted, unable to open his eyes. Cecil lay there quietly, still holding the huge member inside, warming it while he brought himself to a rapid orgasm of his own.

The incredible situation that had worked out so gratifying filled them both with a strange elation. Pike smiled at his fellow servant in the dim light, but knew it was time to go, to run no more risks. He kissed Cecil and slid noiselessly off the stool. Quickly he ran to the back stairway and climbed up to rejoin the master in his bed.

The storm had run its course and the wind was dying down; the sky was beginning to turn grey with the first streaks of dawn. And Pike was again lost in the maze of the endless corridors, naked, cold once more, and bleary-eyed.

Suddenly Mr. Champdick appeared, wrapped in a luxurious robe.

He smiled when he saw his stable boy in the corridor. "Ah, I thought I'd lost you!"

"Never, master," Pike answered.

It seemed Mr. Champdick had become aroused to the point of utter madness. As soon as they were back in the warm bed, he held the boy's stupendous cock; his eyes were again big with wonder, his breath held in adulation. He held the prick against his cheek, and soon he began to lick and suck on it. Then he drew back as if charmed, watching as it slowly pumped up, bigger and bigger, to its full Herculean proportions. Now he had Pike straddle his head and he began to suck in earnest. He ordered Pike to fuck his mouth as strenuously as he had fucked his ass. The youth rocked, wiggled, swayed and rocked over the master's head, and the rod was bent in a strained arc under the pressure. Now, just as the master thought he would surely choke to death, Pike came. Taking the youth's final orgasm of the long night deep down his throat, Mr. Champdick rejoiced.

Edited by John Patrick

Mr. Champdick would spend the rest of his life talking about the night of his miraculous conversion.

THE BOY WHO HATED PARTIES
John Patrick

He caught my eye immediately. Not only was he a tall, handsome stud, there was something arresting about the way he walked slowly, sexily, his back straight, with a calm, self-contained expression. He appeared to be above it all. Then I realized I had seen him before, not in person of course, but on film, porn films. I didn't know his name, and I barely recognized him with his clothes on, but I knew it was him.

I desperately wanted to speak to him, but there was so much adulation of him by all the guests that it had given him a chance to be selective, to explore the full realm of sexual possibility.

I followed him towards the bathroom. I was going to speak to him, introduce myself, find out his name, when a man came out of the bathroom and said, "Oh, Rex. Hi." The man leaned over and whispered something to him. Rex shook his head and moved on, to the bathroom.

Rex. Rex *Horner*. Of course. "New York Prime," "Meat Men." He could do *everything*, and he was hung beyond anything anyone had seen since John Holmes. My mind leaped ahead to the questions I'd ask him about himself, to the long conversations we'd have about what it was like, being in the business. I leaned against the wall, waiting. My first words couldn't be ordinary. All at once I heard a toilet flush and there he was, gliding right past me. He glanced at me. I half-raised my hand. His eyebrows went up thick dark eyebrows with all that blond hair. It was the perfect moment to speak, but I couldn't say a word.

But he saved me. "You havin' fun?" he asked.

"Oh, I suppose," I smiled, feeling suddenly light-headed.

"I hate parties, actually," Rex said.

"Me, too, usually."

"Usually?"

"Depends on who's there."

"You from New York?"

"No, just visiting."

"Me, too."

We made our way to the bar, where freshly poured glasses of white wine awaited.

He offered he was not originally from the city, or even the East. But he was living in New York, at an apartment owned by a man who was seldom in town. "He's married, you see."

"Oh, that's funny. So am I."

"I seem to attract them. I don't know why."

"Everyone's attracted to you, especially if they've seen your films."

"You've seen them?"

"Two. Just two."

He chuckled. "Ha! And I thought it was addicting."

"I might be. It's just that I have little opportunity."

"I understand," he said, squeezing my knee.

I was flattered that he had chosen to spend so much time with me. For me, it gave me a new lesson in the body's infinite capability to give and receive pleasure. I wanted to get to know him better, and he responded to my questions. He was no dummy. Still, he was a very sexual being. He told me he didn't want to settle down. His ambition was to find a hole in every port. He wasn't fussy about the precise location where he put his dick. He was the perfect vagabond, suitcase in one hand, waving with the other. He never stayed anywhere long, but he had stayed in Manhattan longer than anywhere else.

Rex believed that love had been invented to fool people. His theory was that there was sex and then there was friendship. And that was all there was. He said, "The only people who have ever fucked me over were the ones who said I was their lover." He warned me never to fall in love, although his words came too late because I was, of course, already married. But I had already fallen for him.

He asked, "Is she good in bed, your old lady?"

"Yes."

"You love her and she loves you?"

"Very much, yes."

He shook his head, as if he had lost patience with me. He frowned. "I hate parties."

"You said that."

"Let's go."

Before I could think further, we were in a cab heading uptown. In moments, it seemed, we had pulled in front of an apartment house on East Sixty-Sixth Street, just off Fifth Avenue, and I leaned over the seat and paid. The doorman, who with his brass buttons and epaulets looked like Napoleon Bonaparte, smiled at his familiarly and gave me a scowl. I followed Rex across the marble hallway. He took long strides, I noticed. We entered the small space of the brass and mahogany elevator.

"It's hot in here," Rex said, zipping open his leather jacket and unbuttoning his shirt to the navel. My eyes adored his hairless, sculpted chest. The elevator opened. Rex led me to a glossy black door. "Here we go," Rex said, turning the lock. We were soon in a small foyer. On the tiled floor stood a pair of Western boots; several umbrellas hung neatly from a brass hook. Inside the apartment, Persian rugs on the floor, white walls, a few pieces of art that did not interest me, a huge window that showed off the Manhattan skyline to the west. The place appeared to be professionally cleaned, I was looking at money, but not big money.

Suddenly, my lips had that buzzy drunken feeling about them, and I fell against the door frame.

Rex chuckled. "You okay?"

I nodded.

"I'll make some coffee," he said, and disappeared.

As I gazed at the view, he brought in mugs of coffee, set them on the coffee table. He turned on a floor lamp, the brightness of which made his white shirt even more translucent.

"You're shaking, married man," he said, taking me in his arms.

"Yes."

"You don't do this very often, right?"

"You could say that. At least not with someone famous."

"So you want me, eh?"

"From the moment I saw you."

This pleased him and he hugged me. I thought for a moment he was going to kiss me, and I wasn't sure how I would react to that, but he didn't. He just held me, rubbing my back, then kneading my buttocks.

"You want me to fuck it?"

"Yes. From the moment I saw you."

The bedroom was small, but the bed was enormous. His eyes looked downward as his fingers touched the buttons of his jeans. Never have I felt such guilt, never such excitement. I could feel the blood filling my penis heavily just looking at his, semi-hard, but longer and thicker than any cock I had ever seen. I sighed; it was far more beautiful than I had remembered from the films. As I slipped out of my shoes and shirt and pants and underwear, I couldn't take my eyes off him. He was magnificent in his youthful nakedness. He started for the bed.

"Please, just stand there a moment," I said.

"Why?"

"You know why."

He smiled as I got on my knees before him. "Yeah, I want you on your knees. It's time to see what you can do with that flapping mouth of yours." This was said as if it was dialogue, such as it was, from one of his movies.

Kneeling obediently, I gave him a preview of what I could do, licking and sucking the two fingers that he shoved in my mouth while I stroked his cock.

He removed his fingers when his cock was hard. Parting my lips, I found his cock head and began to kiss it, letting my tongue swirl around the tip and then moving down to pleasure the glans. Rex moaned softly as I licked it. Then I took his cock head hungrily into my mouth, suckling on it. I began to swallow his shaft. I felt the cock head pressing at the back of my throat; I fought against my gag reflex and pressed his cock into the tightness of my throat. I managed to get it down most of the way before my eyes started to water. I eased his cock back out and began to worship it with my tongue and lips, slurping it all over. I rubbed the spit-slick shaft over my face and nibbled playfully at Rex's firm, tight balls. I licked back up the shaft slowly, savoring every inch all ten of them, I guessed then licking around the head again before swallowing his whole prick into my mouth and pressing it down my throat. This time there was no hesitation; I didn't have to struggle to deep-throat the big thing. The shaft of his

cock glided easily down my throat, filling me. He pumped it in and I savored his hardness in my mouth, enjoying it more than I ever thought I would. Servicing him orally like this was turning me on and I began jacking off. I was soon in such a sexual frenzy that I was ready to explode. I left my cock alone, decided to take my time. My passion, my desire for him did not appear to embarrass him; indeed, he seemed to get off on it.

I left the cock momentarily and kissed his thighs, his belly, while my hands rubbed his ass, roamed over his pecs, then to the low-hanging balls, cupping them, amazed at their weight. I looked back up at Rex's face. He was breathing deeply, his eyes closed. This was not romance at all; this was pure carnality, and this was how I preferred it.

"Suck it!" he demanded.

I returned to the cock, finding it harder than before. I began sucking as much of it into my mouth as possible, suffocating on it, and the firm tumescence of it. It was the cock of my dreams, tantalizing me until I thought I might faint from the joy of it. Besides that, the aroma of him, a combination of a woodsy cologne, sweat and pre-cum, was also driving me crazy with desire. "I love your musky smell," I muttered, sucking on his balls. "Nothing sweeter." I tickled him with my lips and mouth while reaching around with one hand and grabbing my ready-to-explode shaft. "I'm so close," I warned.

"Okay," he said, lifting me up onto the bed. He rolled me over on my side, and I felt the head of his cock teasing the entrance to my anus. With pleasure, I rubbed my ass back and forth, feeling the porn stud's cock harden against my cheeks. And then his cock head was pushing in, opening me up, penetrating the tight hole. I gasped as his cock started to enter me, the head slipping past my entrance and the shaft sliding in. It was too much; I couldn't take it in this position.

"Please," I begged, "This way." I lifted myself up and slowly lowered myself down on it. Once the head was in, I pushed as hard and deep and as urgently as I could. Once I had most of it in me, I jumped up and down on it savagely, with all the meanness I was capable of. I couldn't stop myself from nuzzling back against him, impaling myself on his shaft. I let out a groan of pleasure as I felt Rex's cock entering me fully in one hard stroke.

I began to hump back against him as he thrust his hard cock into me with a slow rhythm that matched my own arousal perfectly. I whimpered and writhed and thrashed as Rex fucked me, and worked my hips in time with his.

Before I knew it, I was coming loudly and I felt Rex's cock spasming and heard his moans, and knew that he was coming inside me. When Rex was finished, I was overwhelmed with the exquisite feeling of being able to arouse him to this degree. Rex tugged his cock out of me and I gasped as it left me. As I relaxed back into the warmth of the bed, he began to stroke the sweat-slick globes of my ass. His fingertips toyed with me, teasing the now painfully sensitive ass lips. I felt his thumb sliding between my ass cheeks. Despite being

spent, it felt incredibly sensual to have my ass played with so soon after being fucked.

"You're so tight," he said.

"And you're so big."

"We were made for each other," he said, hugging me to him.

We dozed for a few moments. I woke with a start. Suddenly I heard music, rapid and faint above us somewhere. Outside it had started to snow.

He opened his eyes, stretched. He broke the silence. "Can I ask you something?" His voice was oddly bright and awake.

"No."

"Did you fuck her before you left Pittsburgh?"

"Yes." I remembered enjoying sex with Caroline, but now that pleasure seemed distant and theoretical.

"Tell me how is it different than with your wife."

"No."

"Your wife is attractive, right?"

I grunted. "You know the answer."

I rolled over so that I could look him directly in his face. He looked so young, so vulnerable, despite the hugeness of him. I suddenly felt the difference in our ages.

"My wife is a good person."

"I'm sure."

"You are a married man, too." I waved my hand, as if blessing the bedroom. "All this."

"Not really. It doesn't feel like that. It is always just a strange arrangement. He keeps trying to turn me inside out. I've never been married. I don't think I would want to be married and want what you want. I don't know." He rolled back toward me. "Did you think of her while we were doing it?"

"No."

"Do you think of other guys when you're fucking her?"

"Yes."

"You mean you think of guys and that helps you fuck her?"

"Yes."

"Me, too. When I have to fuck a bitch for the camera, you know, I think of another guy. The other guys, they fuck guys and they think of girls. I know one who thinks of transsexuals! It's all so nutty!"

The question of why all this had to be hung in the dark room, unanswered. I gazed upon him before I left. I cursed myself for being fascinated by him so. What an asshole I was. There was Caroline, at home with the kids, while I lay on a king-size bed in Manhattan, my dick wet and limp against my leg, with a hugely hung young porn star.

Still, I pressed my face into his warm, flat belly and felt glad, glad that life was still presenting me with such possibilities that, rightly or wrongly, I had

embraced, in the form of this strange youth.

I kissed his semi-hard cock. He groaned softly, and I knew with a little effort I could get him hard again. I began to suck him eagerly, using my lips and tongue to bring him off. He pumped into my mouth rapidly, and I felt the first spasms of his orgasm as my mouth filled with his cum. I swallowed eagerly and gulped more as some of his cum dribbled out of the corner of my mouth and splashed over my pecs. I sucked harder, feeling another stream fill my mouth. More semen dribbled out onto my pecs. I swallowed spurt after spurt of Rex's cum, licking his cock all over passionately as he finished. I felt his hands on my head, and I continued to bathe his softening cock with my tongue. The cock flopped from my mouth. I let my cheek rest against his hairy thigh, my lips kissing the softness of his spent cock. Rex was breathing very hard. I sighed and placed a wet kiss on the soft head of Rex's prick.

I felt a surge of regret, having to leave, but that was the lot of a married man in the Big Town.

In the mirrored brass of the elevator I gazed upon myself flushed, hair wet, lips slightly swollen. I felt less shame than I should have, I felt a dark little thrill, a faint pleasure in my balls, up my ass. I tightened my tie and buttoned my wool coat. The brass elevator door slid open, and I walked out of the lobby, past the front desk and Napoleon, the uniformed doorman. Now I saw him as a tiny, greasy man, and his eyes darted sideways as I went by. He gave me a slow, unctuous nod, tipped his finger to his cap, and indicated that a taxi was waiting outside. Only by the merest chance, after I had settled into the cab, after the doorman assumed I was looking elsewhere, did I see him glance at his watch, pull a pen and pad from his pocket, and make note of something make note, I realized, of me.

THE ANNIVERSARY PARTY
Daniel Miller

When Martin and I are out with our more mainstream gay friends, I refer to him only as my boyfriend or my partner. When we're with our more sexually adventurous associates, however, I openly call him "sir" or "master." In those dark bars filled with the smell of leather, cum, and naked flesh, he rules me completely, and I gladly surrender to his loving domination. Our favorite place to go and indulge this side of our relationship is The Cavern, a smoky leather bar in a neighboring city. Though we never elaborate to friends, it's where we met and where Martin first fucked my ass in front of a whole roomful of admiring spectators. Because of work and other commitments, we don't get to hang out there as much as we'd like but when we do, we push ourselves to the limit and get hot and humpy for each other all over again. When he's paddling my ass or making me suck him off in front of a bar full of other tops and their naked slaves, my urge to serve him completely sometimes becomes overpowering.

Last month was our third-year anniversary. Martin came home from work early and said he had a surprise for me. Knowing what he expected by the look on his face, I didn't say a word as I went to our downstairs playroom and came back with my studded dog collar in my mouth. When I came back, Martin had already changed into his jeans, boots, and leather jacket with no shirt underneath. He had left his belt and his button fly undone, however, which was a cue I'd learned to recognize.

I sank to my knees as he gently extracted the thick leather strap from between my teeth. While he stroked it across the palm of his hand, I nuzzled my nose and chin into the open "V" at the front of his pants. He wasn't wearing underwear, and the musky scent of his horny cock filled my nostrils until I was almost giddy from the aroma of our mutual lust.

I was longing to swallow his masterful tool down my hot throat in one powerful gulp. But I knew that Martin would expect me to make the delicious sensation on his swollen shaft last as long as I could. Shifting his hips, Martin eased back, sliding his cock upward along the roof of my mouth until only his fat, rubbery crown remained on my tongue. I took that as a sign that he wanted me to lick it first, to build up to a powerful climax that would please him on our anniversary.

"Yeah, I've been horny all day," he wheezed, as if reading my mind. "I want you to make this a good one,"

A pearl of pre-cum dripped onto my taste buds, sending a shiver of arousal straight down to my own cock and balls. I was dying to reach down and start jacking off, but I knew that my master would never permit that.

Martin moaned as I began thrashing the length of his burning organ with the flat of my tongue. I squeezed my own aching cock between my thighs as a torrent of cum billowed up inside my balls. I could feel my own pre-cum leaking fiercely from my flexing piss-slit, slicking the inside of my pants with the gooey fluids of need.

Soon Martin reached down to twist his fingers into the hair that fell over the nape of my neck, using his muscular forearm to guide my head up and down. It wasn't a gentle rocking motion, either, like he used on me when he was in the mood for a slow, leisurely fuck. In his excitement, Martin pushed my face down and then yanked me back up until his flange scraped hard against my tonsils. While I gasped for breath, he'd shove me down hard again so that his flaming serpent would slither all the way into the softer tunnel of my throat.

Every time he spiked my throat, the open flaps of his jeans would scrape against my flushed cheeks. The rough denim seared the tender flesh there, which was already stretched to its limit around his thick pole. Tears sprang to my eyes as I struggled for breath between every powerful thrust of his steel-hard pole. It almost felt like he was shoving a fireplace log down my gullet.

My windpipe was soon burning with his hard, quick lunges, and his hot, trickling cum left a searing trail all the way down to my stomach. Still, I stayed with him all the way as I felt his veins swell and pulse harder. As I grew more accustomed to his merciless pace, I started helping him out by rocking forward on my knees at every down stroke. Occasionally, I could push myself down far enough to take in part of his ball sac as well as his dick. I could feel those red-hot orbs expanding, too, filling with a torrent of jizz I longed to swallow into the depths of my completely yielding body.

When he finally shot, he shot as hard as I'd expected him to. He drew a loud, deep breath and then let out a growl of pleasure as the orgasm I'd given him raised his burly frame. His fingers seemed to be pulling my hair out by the roots as he jammed my face against his crotch, making sure his entire steaming blast would gush down my throat. The force of it nearly knocked me over, the musky liquid filling my guts and mouth until I imagined it would come bubbling out my nose at any moment. If I could have lifted my head long enough, I would have cried out with pleasure as his delicious seed washed through every fiber of my body.

When he was finished, my face was covered with sweat and his cum was running out of my mouth like frothy champagne. I closed my eyes as Martin slid out of me, my lips sucking hungrily at his retreating shaft as if I were trying to swallow it down once again. But it had gone soft, apparently drained to the core, and he stuffed it into his jeans with a grunt of satisfaction. I knew he didn't like it when I looked at his dick in anything but its most supremely erect state, so I leaned forward and used my mouth to button up his jeans, a trick I'd perfected in the course of our relationship.

Finally, when I was finished, my master pushed the neck of my polo shirt aside and locked the collar around my neck. Then he turned and went out to the car with me following. I didn't bother to wipe my face, leaving his cum to tingle inside my pores like some kind of horny aftershave.

We slid into the front seats, and Martin turned the key in the ignition. He turned to me with the intense expression he always assumes as soon as he

becomes "Master" instead of "my boyfriend."

"Take off your clothes," he ordered, and I immediately obeyed. A thin sheen of excited sweat covered my body, and my heart began to beat rapidly as I kicked off my shoes and socks, then peeled off my shirt, pants, and underwear and tossed them into the back seat in a ball. My underwear was drenched with sweat and pre-cum, and the car soon filled with the powerful aroma of male horniness both mine and his.

Soon I was sitting beside him in only my collar, my aroused cock slowly growing longer and harder against the plush fabric of the seat. The thought that we might get pulled over, or that someone driving past us would know from my collar that I wasn't just riding around shirtless, got me even more excited.

Martin eased into traffic with a smile. He knows how turned on I get when I fantasize about being naked out in public, and now I was actually doing it. I was longing for him to reach over and yank my cock, but knowing that he wouldn't made it swell to an almost unbelievably erect condition. My anniversary was turning out terrific so far!

It got even better when we got to the city and pulled into The Cavern's private parking area, where a chain link fence hid the patrons from the rest of the world. My whole body was blushing when he came around to my door and clipped a short leather lead onto my collar before having me step out, still completely nude, into the open. The leather-clad parking lot attendants watched with approval as I followed my master at respectful distance, my bright red hard-on swinging back and forth in front of me as we made our way to the entrance.

Inside, of course, I was no longer the only one who was naked. The guys waiting at the bar, and their own scantily covered slaves, turned to look at us as my master had me lick his finger. Then he stuck it right into my ass and left it there as he steered me toward the darkened center of the room. My sphincter clenched excitedly around his plump digit, my ass-cheeks already trembling in anticipation for whatever unknown delights he had in store for me.

As everyone crowded around to watch, my master held up a gold ring about the size of a quarter. He turned it around and around in front of my face without a word, and I saw that it had both our names engraved inside it. Then he clenched it in his fist and made me bend over a padded sawhorse. After tying the end of my leash to a stud on the crossbar, he circled around to stand in front of me.

"Suck me," he ordered. "Get me nice and wet so I can ream your ass good."

My pulse was hammering at fever pitch now. About 20 guys were watching intently as my master opened his thick belt and unbuttoned the fly of his 501s.

He parted his legs so that his blood-thickened cock stuck out like a steel bar. Struggling against the leash that kept my head down, I stretched my face forward and fastened my mouth on that appetizing tool. The thick shaft filled my mouth completely, and my master rocked forward to cram it all the way down

my throat.

Red-hot stabs of arousal shot through my body. Looking down, my master watched my cheeks redden and expand as his big pole stretched me out to the limit, thrashing my tongue with his burning length. My lips left a sticky snail-trail on his shaft every time he heaved himself away from me, then plunged forward to jab his cock in so deeply that I had to struggle not to gag.

The saliva was running from my jaws to form a puddle on the floor as I continued to suck boldly, even managing to take in part of his ball sac between gasps for air. He reached down to take my head between his hands roughly as a torrent of cum billowed up from his balls, expanding his piss-slit against the lapping tip of my tongue.

Somehow, incredibly, he managed to keep his orgasm under control, which was almost more than I could do! Abruptly, leaving my empty mouth chomping on air, he pulled out and circled around to my ass as it stuck up in the air. The crowd that had gathered murmured with approval as he began plugging my ass deeply with his spit-slickened ramrod.

Tears filled my eyes as he pushed forward with deep, guttural grunts. Each of his powerful thrusts threatened to split my quivering ass in half, from my straining asshole outward. At first, maybe because my rear was still clenching up with my own need to orgasm, he could only get about half of his cock into me. My fear of disappointing him and myself forced me to relax my ass and open my legs much wider. Finally, I both felt and heard the harsh slapping of his red-hot balls against the inside of my crack. His cock head slammed suddenly into the tender fibers of my prostate. He was all the way inside me now!

As he always did, he held his entire body as still as a statue while he spray-painted my inner ass-walls with hot jets of his seed. The crowd applauded as his spunk boiled out of my crack and down my legs. I bent my head down as far as my tether would allow and saw his white froth forming a second pool on the floor only inches away from the one formed by drool. The sight made my own cock lurch against the cross bar, and I fired my own stringy load onto his only seconds later.

My master pulled out of my ass, panting with satisfaction. He walked around in front of me and opened his fist to show me that he still held the engraved gold ring. I realized then that it wasn't intended for my finger. After we'd both had a few minutes to recover, a friend of ours who specializes in piercing came forward with his tools. I remained bent over the sawhorse as he went to work on my tender perineum. I was still so worked up that I barely felt any pain when he fastened the guiche halfway between my balls and my asshole, my master's name on the metal marking off that tender area as his territory alone.

It was the most incredible gift he'd ever given me, and I licked his boots for half an hour afterward to thank him. He promises that our fourth anniversary will be even more exciting, and I can't wait to find out for myself.

GOOD TIME CHARLIE
James Hosier

As parties go, it was a good one. Good music, plenty to drink and Janet was in a good mood. If her folks let her stay out I might have been lucky and this story would have had a very different ending. As it was, she had to be home by midnight. So did Suzanne. Ted drove us home. Janet and I were able to have a good time in the back seat while he said his lingering goodnight to Suzanne outside her house. Then it was his turn to wait not for long, unfortunately. Janet's folks were sitting up waiting for her and it was pouring rain. I returned to the car.

"Where to now?" said Ted.

"At midnight?"

"Why not? You're not on a curfew, are you?"

"Hell no. It's just that I don't have much cash on me right now."

"We could go to the gym," he said.

I couldn't believe my ears. There aren't an awful lot of night-spots in our town but there are some. Any of them would have been preferable to going to a gymnasium. Ted's a fitness freak; swimming, weight training and all that but at midnight?

"Fuck off!" I said. "It's a drink I need, not exercise."

He laughed so much that he had to stop the car. The 'Jim', he explained, was a private bar so called because of the huge number of empty Jim Beam bottles which had been used to decorate the place. I'd never heard of it but Ted has his own social circle and we usually only see each other at the swimming club.

When he'd gotten over his amusement, I'd set off. "You'll like Charlie," he said.

"Who's Charlie?"

"The guy we're going to see."

"Is he a regular there?"

"It's his place. He's a good guy."

We drove and drove. The rain got heavier, so heavy that the wipers could barely cope with it. Ted turned off the highway. We went down roads that got narrower and narrower. This was the farm belt on the outskirts of town. It sure was an odd area to have a bar. Ted obviously knew the place well. I peered out through the rain-and-mud-spattered windscreen. All I could see were trees and an occasional silo looming out of the darkness.

"Here we are!" said Ted at last. He swung the car into a sort of yard. The wheels squelched in thick mud. The headlights lit up a big house.

"This is a bar?" I said.

"A private bar. Come on. Watch where you put your feet."

I'd have been able to if there had been lights. We picked our way through a sea of mud, testing every footstep.

"Hasn't this guy Charlie ever heard of concrete?" I complained as my left foot sank. The drinks I'd had at the party were beginning to take effect and my

balance wasn't as good as usual.

"Quit moaning. Here we are. Watch the step."

He pressed the bell. Nothing happened. He rang it again, three times.

"Closed. They've all gone home," I said.

"This place never closes. He'll come. He knows my ring."

We heard a movement inside the house and then the door was opened.

"Hi, Ted!"

"Hi Charlie. Is the bar open?"

"Sure. Come on in."

Charlie was one of the biggest guys I have ever set eyes on. I don't just mean tall though he was certainly well over six feet he was huge in every respect. A bouncer there would have been redundant. I guessed him to be about thirty. He was wearing a pretty bright waistcoat and one of those floppy bow ties. Not exactly a leader of fashion if you know what I mean.

"Meet James. He's the guy in the swimming club I told you about."

"Oh yeah! Good to meet you, James." I was expecting a handshake like a steel vise but it was more like shaking hands with a frail old lady.

We followed him down the hallway, down some stairs into what had once been the cellar but was now a bar. Ted was right. I had never seen so many Jim Beam bottles put to such inventive uses. All the lamps were old Jim Beam bottles. The bar itself consisted of a wooden top supported on a stack of Jim Beam bottles and the walls were papered with Jim Beam labels. What struck me, because Janet collects them, were the miniature bottles on the shelves. There were hundreds of them. Unfortunately, Janet already has a miniature Jim Beam bottle or I'd have asked him for one. As it turned out, it's just as well I didn't!

"Welcome to the Jim," said Charlie. "What'll you have?"

There didn't seem to be much choice. He poured drinks for Ted and himself from a normal-sized bottle. For a moment I thought I wasn't going to get a drink and then he took a miniature and a glass and poured mine. I remember thinking it odd but didn't give it a lot of thought. I diluted mine. If he'd had Coke I think I would have asked for one. I don't know how much I had drunk at the party but it was a bit more difficult than usual to get on a bar stool.

"Why the miniature for me?" I asked.

Ted laughed. "Tradition of the place," he said.

"Oh yeah? What tradition?"

The question was ignored.

"So, what's the news, Ted?" Charlie asked.

"Not much. What's yours?"

"Oh, so so. Up and down. Usual."

"Yeah?"

"You're looking good," said Charlie.

"Thanks."

"And James too.

"What tradition?" I repeated.

Ted reached across to the side of the bar and produced a small sticky label. "Everybody who comes here has to sign a label and write a comment," he said.

For some reason this seemed to amuse them. They grinned at each other. They were having some sort of joke at my expense and I didn't like that. I guessed it was because of the way I'd nearly fallen off the stool. Determined to show them that I was a very long way from being pissed, I asked Charlie for a pen.

"What shall I write?" I asked.

"Oh, anything. 'Thanks for a good time' something like that." said Ted.

Very carefully I wrote 'Thanks for a good time' and signed it James Hosier.

"Date," said Ted.

"Oct. 28, 1996," I wrote, which should have proved I wasn't pissed. It had only been the twenty-eighth for an hour.

I looked up at rows of miniature bottles on the shelves. "Are those from people who've been here?" I asked.

"Yep! Every one."

I tried to count them but it was difficult to focus from that distance. I offered to put mine up there but Charlie said he would do it in the morning. That was just as well. I thought when I said it that I would have made a fool of myself trying to climb up there.

We had another drink this time mine came from a normal bottle and then another. Charlie and Ted chatted about people I'd never heard of. I guessed they were members of Ted's fitness club. You know the sort of thing....

"Do you still see David?"

"Yeah, I saw him the other day."

"How is he?"

"Oh he's fine. How about Mike?"

"He was here last week. What a body!"

I tried to count the miniatures again but gave up. We had another drink. "Is the toilet through there?" I asked, pointing to a door in the wall.

"No, it's upstairs. I'll show you," said Charlie.

It's just as well that he did. I'd have fallen down the stairs. I didn't realize how bad I was. I resolved not to have any more. Charlie hung around while I peed and helped me downstairs again.

"Another?" said Ted.

"No... If it's all right with you, I think we'd better be off," I said.

"Sure. What's the time, Charlie?"

It was three o'clock. We clambered up the stairs. Surprisingly, Ted seemed to be okay. I remember asking him if he was sure he could drive and him saying something about there being no cops around at that time.

We got into the car. Charlie stood to one side waving as Ted switched on the ignition. He got it into gear and let out the clutch. A fountain of liquid mud

spurted from the rear wheels but the car didn't move.

"Fuck!" said Ted.

"Stay there. James and I will give you a push," said Charlie.

The very last thing I felt like doing was pushing a car out of a quagmire. I managed to struggle out and joined Charlie at the trunk. "Should be easy enough," he said. "It's not too deep here."

It was deep enough to bury my shoe. I felt water seeping down my sock.

"Okay? Now!" said Charlie. He and I applied all our weight to the trunk. Ted revved the engine and the car shot forward. All I recall is seeing the taillight move away from me as I fell. There was nothing I could do to save myself; nothing to grab hold of. I landed face down in a sea of black, sticky mud.

Ted stopped the car and got out. Between them, they helped me to my feet. I was covered in slime. It was in my hair, on my face and my clothes were plastered with it.

"You can't go home like that," said Charlie. I said I was okay but Ted objected (and I could see the point) to having me in the car in that state. The car is actually the one his mom uses and she wouldn't have been too pleased.

"He'd better stay overnight," said Charlie. "I can get his clothes clean by the morning."

"Yeah. That'd be best," said Ted. "I can pick him up in the morning."

In normal circumstances I would have objected to being talked about like I was some sort of idiot unable to make my own decisions. Unfortunately, the circumstances were not normal. I had a desperate need for another pee and to be able to sit down. The ground was swaying and I sure didn't want to fall over again.

I dimly remember seeing the car pull away and Charlie helping me back into the house. Then I think I must have passed out. When I recovered I was lying on something and Charlie was taking my clothes off. I giggled. The lamp on the ceiling above my head seemed to revolve. I closed my eyes. What followed was like some weird dream. I was in a row boat, pulling hard against a raging sea. I felt the water on my face and my arms ached. There was someone behind me, chasing me. I felt his hands on my back and then on my ankles.

A brief period of semi-consciousness. What was I doing in a row boat without any clothes anyway? I had to get away from whoever it was but found I couldn't move my arms or legs. He was so close. I could hear him talking.

"There! That wasn't too difficult, was it? I won't ask if you're comfortable. Back in a moment."

I opened my eyes. Two Charlies, each carrying a bundle of clothes, opened two identical doors simultaneously and vanished. My arms were aching. Why? What was happening?

Slowly, reality returned. By concentrating hard I managed to stop the lamp revolving and resolved it into one lamp rather than two. I wanted to wipe my face, which still felt wet, but couldn't. It was ridiculous. Why couldn't I move

my arms?

....Because they were firmly secured above my head. I was suspended in a metal triangle. My ankles were secured to the bottom corners with elastic ropes and my wrists were fastened to the apex. I struggled. The ropes took all the strain. The frame didn't even creak. I summoned up all the energy I could, held my breath and made a supreme effort. The ropes bit into my skin and my arms ached even more. Apart from that I achieved nothing. I just hung there, panting for breath and cursing my bad luck.

Strangely enough, I can't recall being scared. I don't know why. I guess I was still hoping that it was all part of a nightmare and that I would wake up.

The door opened and Charlie just one Charlie this time returned, eating a sandwich.

"Thought I'd get myself a snack," he said. "You hungry?"

I shook my head.

"They never are," he observed, sitting in a chair opposite.

I don't remember exactly what I said to him. It was pretty well peppered with swear words and to the effect that unless he released me, pronto, I'd kill him. I would have too.

He smiled and continued to eat his sandwich. I swore at him again and struggled. I should have saved my breath.

"What do you think of my little toy?" he asked. "Rather clever, don't you think? I designed and made it myself. It takes all sizes. It's adjustable, you see, and admirable for its purpose. I can raise it or lower it; swing it round. Let me show you."

He picked up a remote control stick. A motor buzzed. I felt myself going upwards. It buzzed again and I descended. Another buzz and Charlie swung out of sight. I faced a white tiled wall and then he returned to view.

"Not making you dizzy, I hope?" he said. "I wouldn't want that."

I called him a few more choice names. He pulled a handkerchief out of his pocket and dusted the crumbs off his fingers.

"How do you feel?" he asked. The guy was amazing. A nut for sure. The way he asked, you'd think I was in a hospital bed, not strung up like an upside-down letter 'Y'.

"Well enough to sort you out, you bastard!" I growled. He laughed.

"Sobered up just enough," he said. "Just how I like them and I like seventeen year olds very much. Very much indeed. You could say that I am very partial to a seventeen-year-old, especially one as well built as you are."

He stood up and walked towards me. I couldn't resist the temptation to kick out and struggle. It was no use, of course. He stood behind me. I felt his hand on my shoulder blades.

"Your predecessor was nineteen. Only last night as a matter of fact," he said. "Now there's a lot to be said for nineteen- year-olds but seventeen-year-olds fuck better. I wonder why that is."

I guess you must think me stupid. Sure, I'd wondered why he'd strung me up but I hadn't even considered sex. Sex as far as I was concerned took place in beds or on couches. I'd been thinking in terms of way out medical experiments or whipping. Neither is my scene.

"It's a question of muscle tone, I think," he said. His hand dropped down to my butt. "Seventeen-year-olds are so delightfully tight. You're going to be good. I can tell."

I could have told him that. My four regular clients had a very high opinion of my ass and my ability to use it.

His voice became gentle and soothing again. "Don't be afraid. I won't hurt you," he said. "There's no way you can get out of the frame by yourself so you might as well relax and enjoy it as they say."

I heard him undressing. I couldn't see him. His shoes clumped onto the floor and I heard a zip fastener being undone. It was time, I decided, for a bit of play acting.

"Please don't do it," I pleaded. That delighted him.

"Don't worry," he said. "I won't hurt you. Not too much anyway."

I was on the right wave length. "Oh please, please!" I gasped, managing to get what sounded like a sob between the words. I struggled vainly.

"Don't worry," he said again. "You'll be all right. Your buddy Ted was just as frightened."

Ted? I could hardly believe my ears. He could only be talking about another Ted. Not the one I knew. Ted and Suzanne have been a couple for years. You hardly ever see one without the other. If you were to ask all the people who know Ted to name experiences that he had definitely never had they'd all name the same things: hard drugs and anything connected with the gay scene. But then, I thought, my buddies would say the same things about me. I am very, very careful.

"We have to get you ready first," he said. "I'm just going to put some oil in your ass. That'll make it easier for you."

I managed to overcome my usual instinct to open up for him with the result that his finger hurt like hell! I yelled out and that pleased him even more.

"It's always a bit uncomfortable for the first time," he said. The balance in my second, secret bank account could have testified that a good many fingers had been in there before his.

"You really are tight. Must be all that swimming. Ted was the same."

So it was the Ted I knew! They say life is full of surprises!

Not wanting to be torn apart, I managed, with appropriate difficulty, to slacken sufficiently to accommodate a second finger and yelled out. I wished, then, that I hadn't drunk so much. A good actor doesn't drink too much before he goes on the stage. For me to act the innocent virgin was like asking Tom and Jerry to change places.

His fingers wormed away inside me. I struggled and yelled out. Not too

much struggling but a hell of a lot of yelling! I was a bit afraid of my ability to keep acting if he touched my button. Amazingly, Charlie didn't go for it. I knew his finger tip was near it. I tensed up for the touch and it didn't come. An amateur? Someone with less experience than he claimed? It was possible.

It wasn't only possible. It was true. He put his free hand on my butt and pulled his fingers out like I was a glove. That hurt.

There was a tearing noise. Not, I am happy to say, from me. An empty packet dropped on the floor at my feet. That was a relief. The guy was probably loaded with viruses. He put his hand on my hips. The ropes took the strain. I felt his cock pushing in. All cocks feel a bit bigger at that moment than they really are. His felt big but not huge. The usual feeling like someone pushing a table-tennis ball between your cheeks. Big but not frighteningly so. I had no idea how long it was, of course. Naturally I had to react as if it were a gatepost. I sucked in as much air as I could and waited. I felt it shoving its way in and tightened up just slightly. Then I let out the loudest scream I could.

"Oh yeah!" he gasped. I screamed again.

"Yeah! Yeah! Oh yeah! Tighten up for me." He slapped my butt. I yelled again, like it was really hurting. To some extent it was. I don't need to tell you that there are techniques in fucking. Maybe it was because nobody had ever screwed me in that position. I don't think it was. He was just not good at it.

Michael does it nervously, like I'm made of porcelain and might break. Greg does it lovingly. Andy is... well, just sloppy but he fucks well. Charlie might just as well have been sticking his cock in a side of beef. His hips slapped against my butt; he was panting like a long distance runner. Me? I was totally unmoved in more senses than one. Several times I felt his hand reach round to my front and finger it. It stayed slack. The whisky probably but I was glad. It didn't do to let him know that I was enjoying it. I wasn't. It was slightly painful and my arms ached like hell. As he increased the pace, some of my yells were genuine. The problem was that his excitement increased every time I called out. A good thing as it happened. The ropes stretched and gripped my wrists and ankles so firmly that I lost all feeling in my hands and feet. I could feel his sweat on my back and his breath on my neck. Then, suddenly, he came. One minute he was hammering away at me and the next he'd stopped. Just like that.

The noise I made when he pulled it out was real. Anybody with any sense would wait for a minute or two. Not Charlie. He came round to face me. As I thought, it was nothing wonderful. In fact it was probably smaller than mine!

"You were good," he panted. "You liked it, didn't you?"

"No, I fucking didn't!"

"They all say that but I know different. Now we need to wait a bit to let you have a rest."

This was not good news. Was he thinking of doing it a second time? I waited till he'd peeled the rubber off and persuaded him to slacken the cords slightly. My feet felt like someone was sticking pins into them.

"I'll just have a look at the washing," he said. I don't know why but that was the weirdest part of the whole thing. A totally naked guy striding out of the room saying he was going to look at the washing. I waited and waited. No Charlie. I think I might even have fallen asleep though that seems unlikely. I couldn't get the thought of Ted out of my mind. Ted strung up like I was. Ted, the swimming team stud! What had Charlie said in the bar? "You're looking good." Ted would look even better strung up, I thought. I'd never actually seen Ted's equipment but Suzanne was obviously keen on it. I wondered how many other people were.

Common sense returned. Charlie had obviously been lying. There was no way Ted would have gotten himself tied up. For that you had to be drunk and Ted could hold his drink. And big as Charlie was, Ted would have flattened him if Charlie had as much as put a hand on his knee. It was a thought though.... My cock agreed.

It must have been at least an hour afterwards that I heard Charlie in the next room. The door opened and he came in, carrying the miniature bottle.

"Oh good! You're ready," he said.

"Ready for what?"

"Your little memento." He took my cock between his fingers. There was nothing I could do to stop it from rising. Charlie might have been inept at screwing but he sure knew how to handle a cock. Janet could have taken a few lessons from him. His hands felt like silk. One went under my balls and the other massaged the skin softly almost reverently. My heart started to thump. I felt my forehead sweating. I didn't look down but stared straight ahead.

"There, there," he whispered like he was talking to a baby. "There, there. Let's have the cream. Come on now. That's better..."

My balls ached. There was no point in holding back. I closed my eyes. Janet? No. Images of Janet at that moment seemed inappropriate. Who? Michael? No. Greg? Not really. Andy? I was fond of Andy but he didn't really fit the scenario. So who else? Well... Ted. Why not? It was only a fantasy after all.

Ted, but not tied up in a cellar. Ted in the changing room at the baths. "Go on James. Fuck me. I've never been fucked before. Oh! Gee! That feels so good!"

Ted would feel good too. Pushing gently between his ass cheeks, just like Michael did it to me. Then that warm, silky feeling. Holding on to him, pushing relentlessly, hearing him groan although I wasn't hurting him. "More. More! Oh gee, James does that feel good!"

Must go slowly. Mustn't hurt him. Slowly.... Mmmm. Right into him. A warm, tight feeling against my cock. If only the feeling would last but I knew it wouldn't. Just a few more strokes and....

"Aaaah!" Ted vanished. Charlie was holding the bottle against my cock, catching every last drop. He held it up to the light.

"Good!" he said, screwing the cap on. "Now you can rest. I don't think I shall need you again tonight."

He unclipped my legs first and then my wrists. There was no way I could kick out or hit him. My legs and arms didn't seem to belong to me and I fell out of the frame. He put some pillows on the floor and slung a blanket on them.

"Your clothes will be ready in the morning. Good night," he said - and he was gone.

He didn't lock the door. I waited for as long as I could and opened it. The bar was in darkness but I found the switch. The door leading out of the bar was locked. I thought for a moment of smashing it down but common sense returned. How the hell does a naked guy get home through pouring rain in the early hours of the morning? I was stuck there until Ted came for me. Charlie must have been lying about him, of course. Ted of all people! It was ludicrous! I turned off the light and went back into my cellar-prison.

Amazingly, I slept well. Again I guess it was the effect of the whisky.

"Hey! Wake up!"

"Uh? Who's that?"

"Ted. It's ten o'clock. I've got your clothes here."

"Where's Charlie?"

"In bed I guess. Charlie is strictly nocturnal."

"You can say that again! The bastard. I'll kill him!"

"Why? Charlie's okay."

"You don't know what he did. He's a pervert, man."

"Of course he is. Here, get dressed."

My clothes had been washed and beautifully ironed. Even my shoes had been polished.

"People like him should be in the pen and I'm just the guy to send him there," I said. "Your buddy Charlie screwed me and tossed me off. Tying up teenagers and sexually assaulting them is pretty serious."

I finished dressing, still seething with anger and followed Ted out through the bar, along the hall and, finally, into the open air. I took a deep breath.

"Let's get out of here as fast as possible," I said. "Where's the..... well, I'll be fucked!"

"You have been," said Ted. His car was parked on a large concrete raft to the left of the house. The mud patch was on the other side.

"You parked there deliberately!" I said.

"Guilty as charged."

"Did you fix it beforehand?"

"Guilty again."

"You... you...." I think I would have hit him but he dodged out of the way and it would have been difficult to get home from there. I got into the car.

"Don't forget the cops," I said. "I won't mention you but I sure as hell want to put that pervert behind bars."

"That would be foolish," said Ted. He started the car and we were off.

"Why?"

"Charlie has a miniature bottle of your spunk? Yes?"

"Yes."

"And what did you write on it?"

"I can't remember."

"I can. You wrote 'Thanks for a good time.' Not the sort of thing a guy would write if he didn't want to wank into the bottle, is it? He'll make out that you were willing and you'll be in the shit."

"The bastard."

"Oh, he's all right. Look in your pockets."

"Why?"

"Just look."

I did so and found a hundred dollar bill which had certainly not been there. Folded into it was a membership card saying that James Hosier was a member of the private drinking club known as the "Jim"..

"It was all set up, wasn't it?" I said.

"Oh sure."

"Some buddy you are!"

"Same thing happened to me."

"He said something about you but I didn't believe him."

"Oh it was true."

"But why bring me into it?"

I dunno, really. I mean, I'm sure as hell not gay. You're sure as hell not gay. But now that it's happened to someone else I feel better about it."

"It's happened to an awful lot of guys if those bottles are anything to go by," I said.

"Yeah, but I don't know any of them. I know you. We're buddies."

"Just as a matter of interest," I said, "what did you write on your bottle?"

He laughed. The first laugh of the day. "Thanks for letting me come," he said.

THE ORGY
James Hosier

"What you need," I said, "is an orgy. Like they had in ancient Rome. You know. Several guys; big guys of about my age with really big cocks and oiled assholes. Why, I know several guys at school who wouldn't mind."

I've said some pretty dumb things in my life but that was about the dumbest. None absolutely none of the guys I knew would give it a second thought. I'd have been beaten up pretty badly for even suggesting it.

"That's the very last thing I need," Greg replied. "Doctors do not participate in orgies especially when they live in a small town like this. Just imagine what the neighbors would say. One boy is enough for me. Your money's on the table downstairs."

"Not coming down to see me off?"

"Christ, James! Can't you find the way to the front door by yourself?"

That was the problem. When I first started going round to Greg, he'd offer me a drink, ask about school, my folks and my kid brother. If I'd done anything to my motor bike, he'd come outside with me and look at it. All that before he finally led me upstairs to his bedroom.

"Undress slowly," he used to say. "Let's have a long and lingering look at you. We're not in the hospital now."

That was how we first met. I got some sort of rash in my ass. That was nasty. Our doctor made an appointment for me to see the skin specialist at the hospital in town.

Dr. Gregory Turner M. D. (and I don't know what else) turned out to be a really nice guy. He was youngish (about thirty-five) and he very soon got the rash under control. It was on my third visit when he said, "I see we are neighbors. I live on Montpelier Avenue and you're on Ashgate Drive."

"If I'd known that, I could have saved myself a journey," I replied. I was lying, undressed and face-down on his couch at the time.

"I don't work from home," he said. "In fact, I try to keep quiet about what I do. Once people know there's a doctor in the street, the phone never stops ringing."

I knew what he meant and said so. I'm pretty good with bikes, and a cylinder only has to misfire once before the owner is on the phone wanting me to look at it.

"So, do me a favor and don't tell anybody," he said.

"Sure. You can trust me."

"Do you know anything about car engines?" he asked.

"A bit. What sort of car?"

"A BMW 850. It seems a bit sluggish, especially on long journeys."

"Timing probably. With twelve cylinders the timing is critical," I said.

"You wouldn't care to come round and look at it for me?"

"I could look but I doubt if I'd be able to do anything. Your best plan would be to take it to a BMW service depot."

- 335 -

Edited by John Patrick

"Which would charge me the earth and probably tell me there's nothing wrong with it. I wouldn't mind paying you. If you diagnose a fault I can take it in to them."

"Sure," I said. "When?"

"I'm at home most evenings. I'll give you my card before you leave."

He worked away on my back and my butt for a few minutes in silence. "There!" he said, finally. "That should do it. I don't need to do anything else but I would like to see it again in a few days."

"Could I make a suggestion," I said, thinking of the journey. Thirty miles is a long way to go just so some guy can look at your ass.

"Sure."

"I'll come and look at your car and you can look at my, err, rash."

He laughed. "Sounds like a good idea," he said, "but not a word to anyone. I do not tend kid brothers' bruised knees or mothers' headaches. I'm a dermatologist. I can't even put a bandage on straight."

"Agreed," I said. I got down and dressed. He gave me his card and I promised to call round.

There was something wrong with the car. We drove for miles. He used every possible gear and there was no doubt about it. Acceleration seemed to slacken off the farther we went. I was still taking notes of its performance when he suddenly pulled in.

"Time we had something to eat and drink," he said. I looked up from my notepad. You never saw a place like it! Well, maybe you have. I hadn't. It was called the "Silver Firs" and lay back from the road. One glimpse of the colored lights, the doorman and the guys in tuxedos and ladies in long dresses was enough for me.

"I can't go in there, Doctor Turner," I said.

"Why not?"

"In leather? You must be joking!" I had left the bike at his place.

"Some people would say that you're the smartest guy around tonight," he said. "Come on."

It was soon apparent that they knew him well. We sure got good service. I ate the biggest steak I had ever seen. He asked what I wanted to drink. I was only sixteen then and I didn't fancy asking for a Coke in a place like that.

"I know just the thing," he said. He ordered a "Turner Special". The waiter smiled and came back with the most extraordinary drink I had ever seen. As it's going to figure a lot in this story later on, I had better describe it. Imagine a long glass filled with a pink liquid. A slice of cucumber, a slice of orange and a slice of lemon floated on top, together with a mint leaf. The top of the glass was frosted with sugar. I sipped it. It was delicious but I knew, from the first drops on my tongue, that it was powerful stuff. If I drank it quickly, there was no way I would get home on the bike.

When we left the restaurant, my legs felt shaky and he had to fasten my seat

belt for me. I couldn't seem to find the slot.

We got back to his house. "I don't know what's in a Turner Special," I said, sinking into one of his chairs, "but it sure as hell is powerful stuff!"

He laughed. "We'd better have a look at you before you fall asleep then," he said.

There wasn't an examination couch in his home. I got undressed and lay on the sofa.

"Sorry it has to be hands," he said. "I don't keep any instruments at home."

I remember saying that his hands felt better. The gadget he used in the hospital to push my ass cheeks apart always made me shiver. It was so cold. I felt his finger probing around down there. He said something about everything going to plan and there being nothing to worry about.

Whether it was the drink or the soft feel of the cushions underneath me, I don't know, but I had a lot to worry about. I was concerned with about six inches of flesh, getting harder and harder by the minute. In a matter of minutes he was going to say, "Okay. Get dressed," and I was going to have to stand up. How the hell was I going to explain it away?

"Wait there. Don't move. I'm just going to get something," he said and left the room. For a second or two I wondered if I might have time to jerk off into a handkerchief but while I was thinking about it, I heard him coming down the stairs again. I just had time to shift slightly so that it was more comfortable.

"What are you going to do?" I asked, watching him pull on a rubber glove and smear one of the fingers with jelly of some sort.

"This'll make it more comfortable," he said. He touched the place between my balls and my ass. It felt cool. I just lay there while my problem got bigger and bigger.

"When will you take the car in?" I asked. I thought that talking about something else might make it go down.

"Tomorrow, I guess. I'm very grateful to you. Thanks a lot."

"But I didn't do anything," I protested. "There's something wrong but I don't know what it is."

"Your family doctor collected a hefty sum from your health insurance for saying just that," he said. "You're the car's family doctor. Now, on your recommendation, I'll take it to the specialist."

I hadn't thought of it like that. It was a good feeling. So was something else....

"This uncomfortable?" he asked.

"No." If I'd been truthful I would have said it felt good.

He didn't say anything else. Neither did I. My heart was going like an express train. I started to sweat and I was aware of shifting about on the cushions. Out of the corner of my eye I saw one of the cushions fall onto the floor. He was a doctor, I thought. He must know what's happening. I recall groaning. He still said nothing and the finger kept on moving down there,

finding a spot, tickling slightly and then moving on to another place where I was even more sensitive. Finally, it was right on my asshole. I felt it pushing very gently. There was no point in holding back. I couldn't have anyway. The first ejaculation felt warm, wet and sticky. It was followed, as always by several more. I lay there gasping for breath. He stopped doing whatever it was.

"Jeez! I'm sorry!" I panted.

"What for?"

Surely he couldn't be that dumb, I thought. Not a doctor.

"I've come all over your sofa."

"Great! Good for you! It doesn't take you long does it?"

I couldn't believe my ears. We're talking here about a solid leather sofa; not one like ours at home. If someone dares to spill a drop of anything on ours, my mother goes raving mad. God knows what she'd say about a teenager's full load!

"It'll wipe off," he said. "And who cares if it leaves a stain? Furniture is meant to be enjoyed, not worshipped. Do you want to clean yourself up?"

He showed me where the bathroom was. When I came downstairs, the sticky mess was gone and the cushions put back in order.

I apologized again. "That drink might have had something to do with it," I said. "That was powerful stuff. What was in it?"

He laughed. "A perfect example of psychogenesis," he said.

"A what?"

"Imagination," he said. "That drink was a mixture of lemonade and lime with a tiny dash of bitters. That's all, honestly."

I didn't believe him. "Next time we go, I'll get Peter to let you watch him make it," he said. "I wouldn't let you go home on a motorbike if you'd had any alcohol. You're as sober as a judge. Believe me."

"Next time?" I asked.

"Sure. You liked it, didn't you?"

It was a difficult question to answer. I didn't know if he meant the drive, the meal or what had happened on the sofa.

"Yeah. It was quite an experience," I said, which was true.

I picked up my helmet from the table in the hall, went to put it on and a fifty dollar bill fell out.

"For you," he said.

"What for?"

"Let's just say it's a fee for professional services and leave it at that," he said. I thanked him.

"It's for me to thank you," he said. "Err... I enjoyed it as much as you did. Come again soon, won't you?"

I had to laugh. "Sure but not on your sofa!" I said. He was still laughing as he closed the door behind me.

So that was how it started. At first I went round to Montpelier about every

two weeks. Then it was every week and sometimes twice a week. He always said he missed me and we went a bit further every time. Further in every sense. One Saturday we drove two hundred miles to a famous sea food restaurant he'd heard about. The sea food wasn't up to much but I remember that evening well because of what happened later.

"There's no taste in cockles," he said. "Not as much as in the first four letters. How would you feel about that?"

It took a few minutes for it to sink in. "You mean me? Me? Your place?" I said.

"Sure. What do you think?"

"Why not?" I said. We didn't finish that meal but he sure made a meal of me. There were no stains on the furniture that night. He swallowed the lot!

The nice thing about Greg was that he never came on strong outside the house. There were no phone calls or letters. He didn't wait for me outside school or insist that I visited. I'd just feel in the mood, sling my schoolbooks to one side and go and visit with Greg. I knew he was fond of me. I liked him too. We were real close buddies. I could make jokes with him and tease him and he did the same to me. The drink wasn't a joke though. I actually watched Peter at the Silver Firs make up a Turner Special and all Greg had said was right. The alcohol content was nil.

Of course it had to happen sooner or later. He made enough hints. I was getting on for seventeen and, to tell the truth, the prospect frightened me. We were lying on his bed. It was a Saturday afternoon and we'd been playing tennis.

"Your family doctor had a proctoscope up there. Did that hurt?" he asked.

"Well, no. But a cock is something else."

"You're dead right it is. Much nicer too, I can assure you."

"Some of the guys at school say it hurts like hell."

"Speaking from experience?"

I laughed. "Hell no!" I said. The thought of Tommy Tucker, Mike Blackmore and Walter Eames being cornholed was ludicrous.

"Well then, what say we give it a try? If you don't like it, just say and I'll stop."

It was good! Maybe because he was a doctor and knew all the right places and how to get to them. I just remember wriggling about and thinking how good it felt to have a cock in my ass and hoping that it would last for hours and hours.

After that I couldn't get enough of it. I spent every Saturday and Sunday afternoon round at Greg's place or maybe I should just say "round Greg."

Saturdays were the best. We could take time over it. I've told you how he liked me to undress slowly. Then he'd spend a long time stroking and tickling down there until I was just about beside myself, wriggling around and groaning, dying to feel it going in. When we'd finished we'd go out to a restaurant. Then, at the end of the meal, he'd pat his stomach and say "That filled a hole. Speaking of which.... " and I would nod and we got back to his place as fast as

possible for another session.

On Sundays I often had last minute school work to finish and my parents liked me to be home at a reasonable time. On Monday mornings I felt like I'd been skewered. I recall our school counselor stopping me in the corridor and telling me not to walk in a rolling, naval gait.

"It might have turned the dockyard girls on a few hundred years ago," he said, "but it doesn't work in twentieth century suburban America!"

It was on a Sunday afternoon that I first realized that things were going wrong. "Oh, it's you," said Greg as he opened the door. "You're early."

"My folks have gone out for the day," I said.

Normally he would have said, "How are they?" Not this time. "Come on in," he said and then, "Get up in the bedroom. I'll be with you in a minute."

I went upstairs, undressed and lay on the bed. Nothing happened. I waited. The minutes ticked by. I always got a hard on when I started to undress. I had to play with it a bit to keep it up. Finally, he came upstairs. He didn't say a word, just undressed, flinging things right left and center. There was none of the usual soft talk while he worked me up. I might just as well have been one of his patients. It was that thought that made me realize the cause of the trouble.

Here was a guy; a really nice guy who, in the course of his work; probably saw about a hundred naked young men in a day. A hundred different asses and cocks! Then he'd drive home and get me. It must have been like working in a five star restaurant and coming home to the same meal every day of the year. He needed a change. He went in, did the necessary (very satisfactorily!) and pulled out again. We cleaned up and that's when I made my dumb remark.

The more I thought about it, the more I thought I was right. He needed a change, a choice. He'd come back to me eventually but it was only fair. I kept thinking about it. Eleven o'clock in the morning. We were in a geography lesson. He was probably holding the huge cock of some great blond hunk and comparing it to my six inches. I looked over at Tommy Tucker. A great blond hunk. Star footballer. Not a lot up top but from what I'd seen in the changing room, his lack of brains was well compensated for down below.

Mike Blackmore too. Mike was intelligent and wanted to be a doctor. He and Greg could talk about medical matters. Not that Greg would want to talk shop when Mike was undressed and lying on his bed. The thought made my cock twitch. Mike was a real good looker with sleek black hair, a dark complexion and big brown eyes. The girls flocked round him like bees round a honey pot.

Or Walter Eames. Good old Walter. All he was interested in was electronics. He was good looking though and had one of those asses that seems to jut out. I'd never seen him undressed but I guessed that he would look pretty good spread out on Greg's bed. They all would. One after the other of course. It would be nice if Greg let me sit in the corner and watch....

I tried to shut the idea out of my mind and concentrate on the infrastructure of Ohio. The trouble is that everything Mrs. Evans said made me think of Greg

and my three classmates.

"There is definitely something wrong here." Greg in his consulting room. "Can you open your legs a bit wider for me?"

"The problem is, of course, that the tunnel is just too narrow." - Greg talking to Walter. "Don't worry. I'm just stretching it open a bit more. I won't hurt you."

"It's much bigger than it looks." That would be Mike Blackmore. Who could tell what that little three inches of flesh I'd seen in the changing room would be like after Greg had worked on it for a few minutes?

Then she said something that made everything click together. "The trouble is that people will believe anything and do anything providing the circumstances are right."

So I went to work. A place and a date. Place first.

None of my buddies liked to come to our house. They knew what my folks were like. Getting three visitors' passes to the Pentagon would be easier than getting permission to hold any sort of party at my place. I went to see Greg and explained the position or as much as he needed to know at that stage.

"I have a very big day on Friday," he said. "I won't be back till about nine. You'll make sure they behave properly won't you?"

"Sure. It's just to drink a beer and play cards. You won't even know they've been here."

Then for the participants. "Hey fellers. You know that guy I told you about? The one who lives on Montpelier Avenue?" They didn't remember, which is not surprising considering I had never mentioned him before.

"He has to be away all Friday night," I said, "and he wants me to look after his house. He said I could invite you. I thought we could play cards; have a beer or two you know."

"Who's paying for the beer?" asked Walter.

"Oh, he is. He's a real nice guy."

"Montpelier, eh?" said Mike. "How d'you get to know anyone living up there?"

"Oh, I've known him for some time. I'll tell you another thing. He's got a bottle of some foreign drink that is guaranteed to blow your head right off!"

"What's it called?" asked Tommy who, at eighteen, prided himself on his knowledge of such matters.

"I can't remember. Some foreign name."

I had chosen the bait well. They all played cards and the prospect of drink as well was enough. They agreed. I fixed the beer delivery and got the ingredients for several Turner Specials. I decanted it into empty wine bottles, spent a few hours on my computer doing some pretty impressive looking labels and, on the afternoon in question, ferried the stuff round to Montpelier Avenue. Greg had let me have the key. I put it all in the kitchen and spent half an hour slicing oranges and lemons and even did a few banana slices for good measure.

They arrived at six. "Some place!" said Tommy, looking round admiringly.

"You can see why he wants it looked after," I said. "We just have to be careful not to damage anything. He'd go through the roof. This furniture cost a hell of a lot."

"There's a stain on this sofa already," said Walter. "He can't blame us for that."

"No, he knows about it. Shall we start?"

I gave them a beer each and we started to play cards. They were pretty good but I have to say that I am as good. For once I was grateful to my dad, who had forced me into playing with him for years. It's his favorite form of relaxation.

Predictably, Tommy was the first to lose all his chips. We'd agreed not to play for money.

"Where's that drink you told us about?" he asked.

"Are you sure?" I asked.

"'Course I'm sure. Come on, let's sample it."

"I'm not at all sure I should. You have to drive home."

"It would take more than some foreign punk to affect me," he said. "Get it out."

I went into the kitchen, poured him a half pint of the mixture, decorated it beautifully and brought it back.

"I think there's something else you ought to know," I said, trying to look slightly sheepish. "It has an aphrodisiac side effect."

"A what?"

"He means it makes you horny," said Walter.

"Ha! We'll see. It looks good." He sipped it. "Mmm." he said slurping it around in his mouth. "That's good stuff."

Needless to say, his approval was enough for the others to want one. I poured out two more.

"What about yourself?" asked Mike.

"Hell no! Not after last time, Boy! Did I have a headache the morning after! I couldn't remember a thing!"

They sipped away and all agreed that it was the strongest stuff they had ever tasted. I showed them an empty bottle.

"The label's been done on a computer," said Tommy, showing a rare flash of intelligence. "That's a good sign. Means that the maker is a little guy. He probably makes not more than a thousand bottles a year. Wish I could read the language."

I was quite proud of the language. It had taken a long time to do. "I think it's Ukrainian or Mongolian," I said.

I refilled their glasses and suggested another game. "Count me out," said Tommy.

"What we could do," I said, "is play strip poker. You might not have any chips but you've got clothes."

To my surprise he agreed. So did Mike. Walter thought it would be a bit childish and wasn't keen.

"What happens if this guy comes back?" he asked.

"I told you before. He's away until tomorrow," I said. I glanced at my watch. It was eight o'clock. An hour to go. Walter was persuaded.

Predictably, Tommy lost everything except his briefs first. I made sure I wasn't too far behind him. Mike followed closely behind and soon sat with bare feet and bare torso. One look at that broad brown chest would send Greg into ecstasies. It was beginning to do things to me! I decided I would have a drink after all and poured myself a small one.

Walter suffered a devastating loss. I felt quite sorry for him as I watched him stepping out of his jeans.

"Don't worry," I said, pointing down to the bulge in my under shorts. It's the drink, not you." In fact the opposite was the truth. That ass of his was really something! I hiccupped.

"That's right," said Tommy. "It's beginning to get to me. Look."

Sure enough, his briefs were full to bursting point.

"It hasn't got to me yet," said Mike.

"Nor me," said Walter sitting down again.

"Last round to see who loses everything," I said. "Shall we have another drink first?"

They wondered whether they should. Walter asked if the owner would mind. I said he wouldn't. He had given me permission to use it up. Three and half more glasses were filled and we played the last round. I couldn't help staring at Tommy and not at his face. It was enormous.

Luck was with him that night. Amazingly, it was Walter who had to concede defeat first.

"Okay, I lose," he said.

"Well, come on, get them off!" said Mike, beating me to it.

"Oh hell. I don't actually have to...."

"Of course you do," I said. "Come on."

Reluctantly, he stood up and pulled down the brightest pair of boxers I had ever seen. Mind you, my attention was on what they had covered. A really nice looking cock, still limp but it was long and quite thick. Greg would go out of his mind when he saw it and, as for Walter's ass! Wow!

I made sure to be the next. "That drink's amazing!" said Mike, looking at my rampant cock with rather more interest than one would expect from the school stud. "I'm in the same state." Which was proved in the next few minutes. Another nice one and boy, was he hairy!

Soon, all four of us were as naked as the day we were born. Three cocks pointed up to the ceiling. Only Walter seemed unaffected. It was ten to nine. Greg was due at nine. Maybe he'd like to start with a limp cock, I thought. It would last longer.

"What now?" said Walter. "I vote we get dressed and start again."

"One more round," I said.

"What for, for Chrissake? None of us has anything more to lose."

"Forfeits," said Mike.

"Like what?" I asked. He'd taken the word right out of my mouth.

"You know. The loser has to do something."

"Such as?" said Walter.

"I dunno. Let's make them up as we go along."

Tommy lost to me. I made him clear up the bottles in the kitchen and put the empties back in the box. I let him have a good slug of the stuffCjust to empty the bottle.

Mike lost to Walter and had to get down on the floor and kiss Walter's bare feet. We were getting nearer and it was after nine o'clock. I was on tenterhooks listening for the car engine and the click of the garage door.

I lost to Walter. "What do you want me to do?" I asked.

"I dunno."

"I'll do anything. I have to."

"Wank," said Tommy.

"Eh?"

"Make him jerk off in front of you."

"Do you want me to?" I asked.

"If you like," said Walter.

"You'd better have something ready to catch it in," I said. "There's a handkerchief in my jeans pocket. Use that."

He stood up and bent over, enabling me to really appreciate the nicest ass in the school. Greg had to come back soon. The clock on the wall said nine-thirty!

I took it as slowly as I could, standing with legs apart in front of Walter, who sat there looking dazed, with a handkerchief in his hand. The others played a round.

"You can do the same," said Tommy. I watched as Mike stood up.

"In fact," said Tommy, "you can do it to me. That stuff's made me as horny as a tomcat."

"Shit man!" said Mike. "No way!" Tommy reminded him about the rules of the game. Not wanting to come, I looked away but I sure envied Mike. I'd have given a lot for a feel of Tommy's monster!

"Why don't we all do it in turns?" I said, leaving off for what I hoped might be a lengthy break. Greg, I thought, must have been held up. I thought of finding some excuse to get to the phone and calling the hospital to see if he had left.

"After all," I said. "Walter's the only guy not doing anything. That doesn't seem fair."

Walter protested of course, but he was over-ruled. Now we were getting there. If only Greg was!

Walter would have made a good barman. I had to remind him that it wasn't a

cocktail but a cock he was shaking. A few seconds of that treatment and I would have spattered it all round the room. He stopped and I showed him how it should be done. It took a few seconds to get his cock to react but he was soon panting like a long distance runner and it was standing up proudly. It wasn't quite so long as mine after all but it made up for that in thickness.

I looked at the clock. Nine-forty. I waited for the second hand to hit the twelve and called for a change of partners. Tommy moved to Walter. I got Mike. There was, and is, no doubt at all that Mike is one hundred percent hetero but you wouldn't have thought so at that moment. He was all over me. Grabbing me, pulling me towards him and breathing like an angry bull. Tommy had left him on the point of coming and there was no time to waste. I wondered for a few seconds. How would he react? To hell with it. He sure wouldn't say anything at school. I got down on my knees and took it into my mouth. I had never done it before. I could only try to remember how Greg had done it to me. I can't have been too bad. His hands grabbed my ears and I thought for a moment that he was going to push me away. Quite the contrary. He tried to get even more in and I choked. "Sorry!" he gasped, and then he let me get on with it.

It couldn't have lasted more than a few seconds. The first lot took me by surprise. I swallowed it. It wasn't as nice as a Turner Special but it wasn't as sour as I had feared. When the next few spurts were in my mouth I had time to taste it properly. Not bad at all.

"When do we change partners?" asked Walter in a very matter-of-fact voice. I looked round to see him wiping his cock with my handkerchief.

"After two minutes," I said.

"Which is up," said Tommy. "That leaves just you and me. Want to try some of that mouth stuff on me?"

Hell, man!" I said. "I want to get my own rocks off." My balls had started to ache and my cock was beginning to weep sticky tears.

"I'll tell you what," said once-shy Walter, "I'll wank yours while you suck Tommy's."

It was an excellent suggestion immediately vetoed by Mike! "What about me?" he asked. "What am I supposed to do? Just sit here and watch?" This was the school stud, remember? The guy who had laid more girls than I had had hot dinners! People are amazing!

"What we could do...." I said hesitantly.

"Yes?"

"If you two were to lie on the floor, Tommy and I could screw you. Not going in," I added hastily. "Just between your legs. That feels good."

"How do you know?" asked Walter.

"Happened to me years ago," I said. "Boy Scout camp. It's good, honestly. Come on. Try it out. We can always stop."

"Seems bloody weird to me," said Mike but he got to his feet.

"And me," said Walter, who staggered as he stood up. "Providing you keep it

away from my asshole."

It was difficult to arrange them in the right position without revealing that I wasn't a complete newcomer to this scene.

"That should be okay, I think," I said. The two of them lay on the floor over piles of Greg's cushions I'd been that way enough times in the past, once or twice in that very room.

Mike's ass was hairy. I wasn't keen. Walter's was even more of a picture than it had been when he had kindly recovered my handkerchief. It was firm looking but plump; smooth and a sort of creamy color.

"I'll take Walter," I said. "You can have Mike." I think Tommy was in such as state of randiness and imaginary drunkenness that, if Mike hadn't been there, he would have got down and fucked the cushions!

I looked at the clock as I got down on Walter. Ten-forty! "You sure missed out, old buddy," I said, thinking of Greg.

"What?" asked Walter.

"Nothing. Just open your legs a bit. There! That feel good?"

I need not have asked. He wriggled a bit and sighed as my cock head touched him. Two minutes later I was having to hold him still. Inwardly thanking Greg for the anatomy lessons he'd given me and for not coming home as planned, I really worked hard. After all, once Walter got the taste for it, I could bring him round to Greg's. It was only fair to let Greg be the first actually to screw him. My job was just to get him ready. Teach him that the area round his asshole was....what was the word? Erogenous. That was it and Walter was learning fast, squirming away as I pushed gently and rhythmically against the smooth skin.

Next to us, Mike groaned and Tommy panted. Once or twice Mike yelled out and Tommy apologized. I just hoped and prayed that Tommy wouldn't try to go too far. An asshole would need a lot of Greg's careful manipulation and preparation before it was ready to take a cock of that size.

I heard Tommy gasp and sigh. Then, at exactly ten-forty-five, I came. I know that because I looked at the clock as I lay on Walter feeling it spurting out of me, filling the space between his cheeks and running down onto the cushions.

It was nearly midnight when they left the house. They helped me to clean up. I arranged the two stained cushions back on the sofa with the stains underneath. I put the empty bottles in the trash can outside, burying them under the other stuff and disposed of the bits of fruit in the same way. I waited for a bit, just in case Greg should come home. He didn't, so I left at one o'clock and managed to get into my bedroom without waking the folks.

I managed to survive the inevitable cross-questioning the following morning. Dad said that someone had called just before eleven and I hadn't been there. He didn't know who it was. I said I must have gotten home very soon afterwards. At two-thirty, I fastened my leathers, put the helmet on and drove round to Montpelier Avenue. There was actually, I thought, as I negotiated the traffic, no real reason for regular sessions with Greg. I had Walter trained. Mike was pretty

keen too and so was Tommy. I decided that if Greg moaned about anything, I'd tell him to get lost. He could find another easily enough. I wondered how long the next one would last before Greg lost interest in him.

I pulled up. Greg was in the garden. "I've been dying for you to come," he said. "I called you at home late last night but you weren't in."

"I was here, cleaning up," I said.

"Oh. I thought you'd have left by then. I said I would be back at nine."

"I know you did. Where did you get to?"

"That's what I wanted to tell you. I went out with some friends. I've got a new job!"

"Congratulations," I said. "What is it?"

He stood up very straight and bowed.

"Meet Professor Gregory Turner, occupying the Chair of Dermatology at the Medical School," he said. "And I have you to thank."

"Me? Why me."

"For providing material for my thesis. That condition of yours was very rare, but more than anything else for your support. I must have been a real drag in the last few months. I'm sorry about that but getting the thesis done and worrying about it was a strain."

"I thought something was wrong," I said.

"There you go again, Doctor. But you didn't pack me off to see a specialist. How did your card party go?"

"Oh fine. They're three nice guys."

"You all left the place in good condition. I'd like to meet them sometime."

"Unlikely. They're all dating," I said. "What's the plan for today?"

He smiled. "How many buttons and fastenings on those leathers?" he asked.

"Ask me another. A lot."

"I'm going to undo every one individually," he said, "and then...."

I smiled. "And then?" I asked.

"I could use medical terminology as befits my new status. Let's make it simple and say I'm going to fuck your ass like it was never fucked before. Then we shall go to the Silver Firs for a meal and then..."

"A repeat prescription?"

"Yes, a repeat prescription. A case like yours needs repeated injections!"

WHEN IN ROME...
Peter Gilbert

Robert has just left. I can see him from the window, walking slowly towards his car. Robert is just nineteen and in training as a telephone engineer. More important and relevant: he has a very nice ass. It's one of those slowly tapering butts that seems to flow from thickening thighs. It's the color of a freshly peeled potato and just about as firm. Tight and apparently impregnable at first, yet his ass opens like a flower before closing down again when he's taken the lot. There must be something in this magic business after all. There has to be. Robert's the seventy third since we found it in the muddy English soil.

He won't look up at this window. He won't wave as he gets into the car. Robert is embarrassed. He's embarrassed because he enjoyed it and now he's worried about his sexuality. I wonder what he dreamt about. I must ask him next time. There will be a next time. There always is. Not for a few weeks maybe, but he'll be back and there might be a good book in his dreams. One day, I'm going to write a history book that will be a world best-seller.

Two interests occupy my life: archaeology and boy's asses. You could say that I work with pick and prick. Strangely, the two go together very well. A dig of any size employs student labor. Sure, you get a smattering of weedy creatures with thick pebble glasses who don't appeal to me at all. You also get superbly built hunks with muscles in all the right places. I've never had a great deal of luck with my pick but I've never come away from a dig without success of another kind.

Some are better than others. The Alexandria dig exhausted me, not so much because of the amount of sand that had to be shoveled out of the trenches as for Abdullah and Aziz. They were both twenty-one and post-graduate students. I'd swear that one of Abdullah's ancestors was the model for the Colossus of Rhodes! I'd never seen a cock like his. They both had really attractive milk chocolate butts that contrasted beautifully with their dark brown skins. Watching them kneeling with their heads on the ground to say their prayers was a delight. Screwing them was an even greater one.

You wouldn't, perhaps, put Greenland high on your list but Olaf, whom I met on that dig, couldn't get enough cock. He was amazing. He worked like a stevedore all day and still had enough energy to take two thorough screwings at night.

The discovery of a previously unknown Roman town in England hit the archaeological world like a streak of lightning. I wanted to apply to work on it but I had a number of commitments here in the States: lectures to prepare and a book to finish. Then I heard that the dig was to be led by Professor Reade. The lectures were cancelled, the book delayed and I was on the plane to England.

I'd worked with John before. He's good. One of the best archaeologists in the world. I've known him and his wife and their three daughters for years.

My hopes of another successful "dig" were dashed when I arrived. The main town site was being excavated by John and a huge team of attractive youngsters.

Edited by John Patrick

I was set to work on a small temple site about half a mile away, helped by two amiable half-wits, both in their thirties.

But gossip began to spread. Like many British academics, John has a slightly effeminate manner. He doesn't dangle painted fingernails in front of people but he uses words like "lovely" and "pretty" and when someone unearths something spectacular he's apt to say, "How absolutely super!"

Which is why Willem and David joined me and Bert and Fred were transferred to the main site. "We thought we needed a change," David growled. David was twenty. He was British. He was delightfully slim and walked gracefully, almost like a cat, save that where a cat has a tail, David had the sort of butt that makes my mouth water. Two neat, well-rounded buns set off to advantage by the old soccer shorts he wore. I also liked his dark, Celtish good looks, his thick-lipped mouth and his long legs.

Willem was Dutch. He was twenty-one years old, fair haired and built like a battleship. A colleague of mine often goes to Amsterdam. He'd told me about Dutch butts. If Willem was typical, the guy had been right. I'd rarely seen one like it. It jutted out from the hollow of his back so far that I'd swear that if you were to lay a pencil on top of those cheeks, it would stay there.

I hardly spoke to them for the first two days. They hacked and dug, uncovering the foundation walls and talking to each other, mostly about John. My prospects seemed to diminish with every sentence.

John, they mutually decided, was a raving queer and ought, for the betterment of society, be confined in some sort of establishment for such people.

Now, John always brings a star student to a dig. In the arcane world of British universities, to be selected as Professor Reade's star student is the first step on the ladder to fame. That year, the fortunate young man was Harry Groom, a postgraduate student. He happened to be very good looking and had a habit of tossing his long, fair hair back when he looked up at you from a trench.

"Just look at the way he's walking!" said David one day as Harry made his way from one trench to another. "I'll bet Professor. Reade fucked him silly last night."

Willem stopped work to look. "Bloody disgusting!" he said. "They say he always brings his latest fancy boy to a dig."

I said nothing. In fact, on the last two digs I'd worked on with John, the star student had been female.

"I hate queers," said David.

"Me too," said Willem and he hacked at the soft earth with more violence than usual. A lump of clay detached itself from the side of the trench, fell down and broke open.

"Hallo! What's this?" asked Willem, paying something white out of the soft clay.

He handed it to me. It was about the same shape and size as half a tennis ball, assuming it were possible to break a tennis ball in half. The outer, curved

surface was crinkled like a walnut.

"A fossilized brain?" David suggested.

"No. It's marble for sure," I said.

"Part of a small statue of someone. The marks are meant to be hair," said David. I weighed it in my hand and, as I did so, the most extraordinary thing happened. Up to that moment I'd managed to keep my imagination under control. Willem could bend down to look at something or David could sit out on the grass with his long brown legs splayed out in front of him and I never turned a hair, let alone anything else. But at that moment, my cock started inexorably to rise. I felt my face redden.

"Shall I get Professor Reade?" asked David. I put the piece of stone down and returned to reality.

"Perhaps you'd better," I replied. "If you don't mind, that is."

"Just let the bastard try anything on me," said David, We watched him lope over the field in the direction of the main dig. I put the piece of marble on the grass. My cock sank down. I was back under control.

"Do you know what it reminds me of?" said Willem with a grin.

"What?"

"A ball. A testicle."

I laughed, mostly with relief. My cock had shriveled completely. David and John were coming towards us, accompanied by Harry. A hard-on isn't really compatible with an archaeological discussion.

Willem picked it up. "That's what I think it is," he said. "Off a more than life-size statue. Unless he was a really big guy. There are people with balls as big as this."

"Sufferers from elephantiasis," I said.

"No. There's a guy at college. He's really big."

I found myself looking, not at Willem's face but at his midriff. Something was stirring under his cutaways. Something big. At first I'd have assumed it to be the folding pruning knife he carried to scrape mud off the tools. But pruning knives don't open automatically. Neither do they swell. By the time John was at our trench Willem looked as if he'd got a cucumber in his pants. Awkwardly, he clambered out of the trench. I followed him.

"You've found something?" John asked.

"Yes, this." Willem handed it to him as if it were red hot. John peered at it closely over the top of his semi-lunar glasses.

"How exciting!" he said. "A lovely find!"

"What do you reckon it is, John?" The question came from Harry.

"A piece of a scrotum," said John.

"That's what I said it was," said Willem triumphantly.

"Super! You were right. It's either Bacchus or Mithras. This temple must have been dedicated to one or the other. It would have had an ithyphallic statue of the god."

"A what?" said Willem.

"Oh dear! How dreadfully embarrassing! A statue of the god with an erection. It's unlikely that you'll find the rest unfortunately," he continued. "We know this place was Christianized in the second or third century. The early Christians would have smashed the statue but you might find some other fragments."

After they had gone, David said an extraordinary thing. "Did you notice he got an erection?" he asked.

Now, if there is one person I do not associate with an erect penis it's John Reade. One has to assume that it happens in the privacy of the nuptial bed but certainly not in a field in England. I laughed.

"Honestly, he did," said David.

"Probably thinking about what he's going to do with Harry tonight," said Willem. "It's odd though. The same thing happened to me when I held it. Peter noticed, didn't you Peter?"

I said something reassuring about it being a pretty normal thing to happen to virile young men who were missing their girlfriends. Nothing about thirty-seven-year-old gay archaeologists.

"I reckon it's got some sort of magic in it. It was a weird feeling," said Willem. "You never know how much truth there was in those old religions."

"Balls," said David, appropriately. "It would take more than a bit of marble to turn me on. Too much digging and not enough sex. That's your trouble."

The afternoon continued. Foot by foot we uncovered the foundations. The marble testicle lay on the ground by the side of the trench. At five o'clock, the "stop-work" whistle sounded. Painfully, we climbed out of the trench and cleaned the tools.

"Coming back to my tent?" I asked. The primitive showers were packed at the end of a day's work so I'd laid in a stock of soft drinks so that we could have a drink while waiting. John disapproved strongly of alcohol being consumed on the site and was unaware of the whisky bottle under my mattress. A tot of that in a Coke loosens tongues wonderfully and I had hopes that it might have a similar effect on other parts of Willem and David.

"Not me. I must write to my girlfriend," said Willem. "If I do it straightaway I can catch the last post."

"I'll come," said David. I spread my handkerchief on the ground, rapidly dropped the marble onto it and picked it up by the corners.

"Don't say that you believe it too," said David as we set off towards my tent.

"You can't be too careful," I said.

Inside the tent I gave him a Coke and he took up his usual place squatting on my mattress. I sat on the one and only folding chair.

"Let's have a look at that thing," he said.

"You sure?"

"'Course I am. Give it here."

I passed over the handkerchief and its contents. He spilt it out onto the palm of his hand. "No wonder he was a god if he had balls that size," he said. He was about to put it down again.

"I dare you to hold it for five minutes," I said.

"No problem. Willem misses his girl friend. That's why it happened to him."

"It happened to me too," I said but David didn't answer. He sat there staring at the tent roof. For a moment I thought a bird might have got trapped but there was no bird there. I lowered my gaze. Sure enough it was rising. In the position he was in, with his knees raised I could actually see it inching its purple head along his thigh like a snake testing the air before emerging from its burrow.

He spoke. I thought he said "Valerie."

"Your girlfriend?" I asked. He didn't answer.

He wasn't making any sense to me. In fact I was becoming a bit scared. He hadn't had a drop of alcohol but he sounded as if he'd been on the bottle all the afternoon. His speech was slurred and, all the time, his cock was swelling and moving along his leg. He said something else but I couldn't make out what it was.

The glass fell from his hand. Fortunately, it didn't break. David, still staring at me, collapsed or rather sank onto the mattress. He fell sideways, lay there for a moment or two in an embryonic position with his knees still tucked up to his chest and then straightened out and lay on his back. By this time I was panic stricken. The piece of marble was still in his hand. I tried to pry it out of his clenched fingers but he wouldn't let go. He just lay there, staring fixedly at the tent roof. I slapped his face.

"Sylvianus," he said, which made no sense to me at all. And then he said "Valeria," which did. The Twentieth (Valeria) Legion was Rome's crack regiment.

"The Roman equivalent to the Marine Corps," I said. He didn't answer and I think it was then that I realized that David was, if not unconscious, certainly not with me in spirit. 'Sylvianus' was somebody's name.

He put his hands to his sides and, with some difficulty, pulled down his shorts and kicked them away. Released like a Jack-in-the-box, eight inches of solid flesh sprang out. It was every bit as beautiful as I had imagined it to be. His cock head was a perfect pink. I remember noticing how wide-open the slit was. It grew out of a triangular black mat of pubic hair.

"Sylvianus," he said again. I reached down. Dare I? Would touching it bring him back to consciousness? There was only one way to find out. I got off my chair and sat next to him on the mattress.

It was as hard as the piece of stone gripped in his hand but warmer and very definitely alive. He groaned slightly. I was about to take my hand away when he grasped my wrist and moved it up and down. There was no mistaking that gesture or the way he said "Oh, Sylvianus!" He parted his legs and I caught my first glimpse of his balls, low hanging and large. I put my left hand under them

and continued to wank him with my right. There was no doubt at all in my mind that he was enjoying it. I bent over him and kissed the tip. The scent of perspiration filled my nostrils. I licked it. Then, slowly, I took it in, savoring the myriad tastes of an aroused young man who'd spent the day in manual labor. Abdullah and Aziz had been good. David was even better.

Then, suddenly, he pushed me away. For a moment I thought he'd realized what was happening but he hadn't. He turned over, spread his legs again and, reaching behind him, parted his ass cheeks. The invitation was unmistakable and I never was one to turn down an offer, especially an offer like his. His ass cheeks felt soft and smooth against my face as my tongue worked it's way between them. He shivered slightly as I slavered.

David, I thought when I stood up to undress, was going to be the fuck of a lifetime. I watched the pool of saliva I had deposited gradually vanish into him.

I was right. The others had been good but David was perfect. I loved the way he loosened up and then tightened again. It was if he was trying to coax as much of my cock into him as possible. "Syl...vi...an...us!" he gasped. It wasn't my name but the last two syllables were appropriate and it was a pleasantly melodious word, a much better accompaniment to screwing an almost certainly virgin ass than Aziz and Abdullah's guttural grunts or Olaf's instructions. "Push harder. That's right. Harder."

"Syl..." I lunged into him.

"Vi..." I gave another thrust.

"Oh! ...us!" I was away and so, I am glad to say, was he. I'd never fucked a boy as keen as he was. With the stone still in his fingers, he grasped the corners of the mattress and muttered something. I kept going, relishing the feel of him, the smell of him and his sinuous movements.

He came a split second before I did. I felt him tighten up. He gasped, shuddered and then, just as my own load filled the condom, he lay still.

"Oh, Sylvianus!" he whispered. I kissed the back of his head. For some moments we lay there. All too rapidly, my cock lost interest as I pondered upon the name Sylvianus. Who the hell was Sylvianus? I withdrew, threw the condom out of the tent, wiped myself dry and dressed. David still lay there, clutching the stone. I sat down. He didn't stir.

I was halfway through writing the dig log when the stone fell from his fingers. I wouldn't have known but it fell on the discarded glass and broke it.

He shook his head from side to side.

"Where the hell...?" he said,

"You fell asleep," I replied. "I didn't want to wake you."

"Where are my shorts? What's been going on?"

"I think you've been having a dream," I replied. "Who's Sylvianus? You kept on mentioning his name."

He turned over and blinked. "Oh Christ!" he said and his face reddened. His pubes were soaked. It was all over his thighs and, when he sat up, there was a

wet patch in the middle of the mattress.

"Don't worry," I said. "It'll soon dry out."

"God! I'm really sorry," he said. "I couldn't help it. It was weird!"

"Want to tell me about it?" I said.

"No. It was only a dream but I've never had one like it. It was so real I swear I can still feel the after-effects."

"What after effects? Tell me."

Reluctantly at first, but with increasing fluency and attention to detail as I confirmed the various points of his story, he told me about it.

He was British. Romano-British to be exact. He described the town in detail. For a young man who had only rarely been over to the main site, he gave a perfect description of the forum, the mansion, the public baths and the beer shop where he first met Sylvianus, a Tribune of the Twentieth Legion. He told me how Sylvianus had taken him to the Mithraic temple; how they had participated together in the bull-bleeding ceremony and thereby become partners and how Sylvianus had taken him to his tent.

"And then he ... well he...."

"He what?"

"He had sex with me. That's the weird part. My ass aches as if it really happened."

"Psychological. Must be," I said. "You're in the twentieth century now. If you care to retrieve your shorts we can go and have a shower. We'll be late for dinner otherwise."

"You won't tell anyone?" he said as we stood under a trickle of water.

"I think John might be interested in the buildings you described. But we won't mention the other matter."

"Christ no! He'll think I'm like his gay helper."

David was excused from his duties the following day. My idea. I knew his ass must be aching and I wanted him to draw a sketch map of the town as he had "seen" it.

"Odd kind of dream," said Willem as we hacked away at the English clay. "It's happened before though. I read about it in a book. You say he fell asleep holding that ball?"

"Yes."

"Maybe David's got second sight or psychic powers," said Willem. "I wonder if it would happen to me."

"Worth trying," I replied, glancing at his legs. "Everything is worth a try."

Two days later, he took a lot of persuading, it was Willem's turn on the mattress. He left the twentieth century almost immediately. If I hadn't undone the cut offs for him, I swear they would have burst. He made it very clear which role I was going to play by pulling my head down on to it.

Willem, or the character who took over his body, was only a boy when he met Marcus. Marcus was a Prefect, a high rank in the Roman army. His appetite

for Willem's spunk was insatiable. Twice a day, while Marcus was based in the town, he took Willem's cock in his mouth and sucked him dry. Marcus, as I can testify, was a connoisseur of cocks and youthful semen.

"Marcus didn't do anything else? Just sucked it?" I asked when he had woken up.

Like David before him, Willem blushed. "No. Just that. He wanted me to be a temple boy but my parents wouldn't agree."

"A temple boy?" I asked. My jaw was still aching. As I'd anticipated, Willem was huge. It had been like trying to get a beer can into my mouth. Not a bad simile. He came like a well- shaken beer can.

"Sure. There was another building near where we're working. That's where the temple boys lived. They had a good life. I wanted to be one. They had their own bath house and they were taught how to read and write, besides ... er ... other things."

"What other things?"

"Oh, you know. How to do it when their great day came round. They bent them over an altar. Loads of incense and chanting and then they got buggered. Anyway, I'd better get back. I've got today's installment of my girlfriend's letter to write. Thanks a lot for taking my shorts off. I'd sure have made a mess of them. It's really weird what that stone can do."

Why didn't I try it myself? Well, I have since then of course. At the time I think I was frightened of what might happen to me and I was getting a terrific kick out of its effects on the two lads.

Sooner or later, they began to discuss its more personal effects. That amused me. At such times I put myself out of sight but within earshot. According to David I must have been as embarrassed as hell watching him.

"He said I kicked my shorts off and turned over! God! Me! It's unbelievable!" he said.

"What about me?" said Willem. "Regular girlfriend. Three times a week when I'm at home and what do I dream about? Being sucked off by some randy Roman. Peter said I just lay there wanking in my sleep. He had to take my shorts right off or I'd have come all over them."

"It's bloody Professor Reade. That's what caused it. Not the stone I'm sure," said David. "Having a pooftah like him around together with his bum-boy. It's like a disease. It spreads. I reckon we ought to spend more time together."

"Wouldn't that be worse?" Willem asked.

"Of course not. You're normal. I'm normal. Peter's certainly normal. We can back each other up. You know. Sort of give each other moral support."

It was a suggestion that met with my total approval. From that afternoon, we worked together, we drank together after work, we showered together and we ate at a separate table from the rest. And, after dinner, we went down to the local pub together before returning to my tent for a night-cap. We talked about archaeology and girlfriends and the stone stayed hidden away in a box in the

corner of my tent.

Then came the time when John had to go and make his report to the dig sponsors. We'd uncovered most of our temple by then. Interestingly, Willem was absolutely right. We excavated the foundations of the boys' house and the walkway he described along which the boys processed and that led straight into the interior secret shrine. We also found a sizeable chunk of the altar over which they had been spread-eagle to receive some of the most famous cocks in the ancient world. Surprisingly, it did nothing to any of us. John described it as a "beautiful find", which dropped him several more points in their estimation.

"Thank Christ he's gone to London," said David on the first evening of his absence. "I see he's taken his fancy boy with him. Can't get enough of it, I guess. Bloody disgusting!"

"Yeah. The atmosphere in the camp is completely different," Willem agreed. "That stone wouldn't work now. Where is it by the way? Did you give it to the conservation people?"

"No. They wouldn't be interested," I said. "It's still here."

"Really? Get it out. Let's have another look at it."

I opened the box and proffered it as if it were a box of chocolates. David reached in and retrieved the stone.

"I'll tell you what," I said. "Why don't you both hold it at the same time? See if that theory about providing moral back up is right."

"Don't need it now that the queer isn't here," said Willem but David seemed to think it a good idea. I could see why. It had already started to show under his jeans.

So Willem reached over. David held it in the palm of his hand. Willem laid his hand over it and they clasped their fingers round it. For about a minute there was silence. Then Willem spoke.

"I think maybe..." he said, and that was all. He sank down onto the mattress rather like a punctured inflatable doll. His legs gave way first and then the rest of him. I think David was still conscious when his collapse started but, dragged down by Willem's weight, he hadn't a chance to relinquish his grip. With their hands still linked they lay side by side. Their eyes were open and staring up at the tent roof.

With his free hand, Willem started to grope in the region of David's shoulder. That had me puzzled at first until I realized that Roman tunics and togas were fastened there. I was only too ready to help. I unbuttoned both of their shirts and undid their belts and flies. I pulled off their shoes and socks. David started to suck on Willem's nipples.

The stone worried me. I knew that as soon as one of them let go of it, he would come out of the trance rapidly. I need not have worried. There were occasions when one of them had to release his grip but he always went back to it afterwards like a kid laying claim to a favorite toy.

Jeans came off. Then the shorts. I sat in my chair ogling as two bodies

merged into one. They were pressed against each other so tightly that I couldn't see their cocks. The powerful spasms in their ass muscles were enough to tell me what was happening. In a few minutes, they'd both come on each other's belly....

How wrong can you be? I saw David's free hand reach round to Willem's ass and a finger vanish between the Dutch boy's massive globes. Willem got the message. Letting go of the stone momentarily, he rolled over on to his front. David clambered into a kneeling position between his legs. Putting the hand with the stone in it on top of Willem's hand, he spat lengthily and noisily into his palm and transferred the saliva to Willem's virgin orifice. Whoever David was at that moment, I reflected, had done this before many times.

The impression was confirmed a few minutes later. Willem groaned softly as all eight inches of David's cock slid into him. I watched fascinated as it vanished from view at about the same pace as the second hand of a clock. First the junction of two veins was clearly visible above the soft mounds of Willem's ass. Then the junction wasn't there. Just the two veins, which seemed to move farther and farther apart until they had vanished from sight and David's groin was pressed hard against Willem's butt.

Great depressions formed in the sides of his buttocks as he gave the first thrust. Willem groaned again. His mouth opened. I thought he was going to cry out or say something but he didn't. He just grunted and grunted again as David shoved into him again. He must have got Willem's button then. Willem shuddered violently and then wriggled slightly. David grinned and lunged again.

"Eh! Ah! Ah! Eh!" Willem grunted. David joined in. I hoped that no one was walking by the tent at that time.

Willem came first. There was no mistaking that triumphant yell or the way he suddenly seemed to go limp. David's behind continued to heave for a few minutes and then he came. Pretty dramatically too. His ass tensed up four times. Four creamy shots. My mouth watered at the thought. The first lot had been wasted on the mattress. Now Willem's ass had been filled and I'd never even tasted it. The dig was due to fold in a few days and I knew I hadn't a chance. It was better forgotten.

I scribbled a note on a page of the dig log, left it on the mattress by Willem's sweating face and left the tent.

"Where have you been?" David asked when I returned about an hour later. They were both fully dressed.

"As I wrote in the note, John rang through to the pub wanting to talk to me so I had to go down there and call him," I said. "You were both asleep. Pleasant dreams this time?"

David leaned back on the mattress and placed an outspread hand over the wet stain in the middle.

"Of course not," he said. "We were both a bit tired I suppose. It's been a pretty strenuous vacation."

"Sure has," said Willem. "I ache all over. All that business about a bit of marble. It's all balls."

"Or half of one," said David as I retrieved it. It felt warm and sweaty. I put it in its box for the last time in England and, three days later, saw them off in the bus that came to collect them.

"What will you be doing this time next year?" David asked as they clambered aboard.

"God knows. Digging somewhere I guess."

"Providing Professor Reade isn't there I wouldn't mind helping you again. The thought of that man leaves a nasty taste in my mouth."

"But you wouldn't. You certainly wouldn't!" I said, addressing the parting bus.

THE BOUNCER
Dan Veen

The bouncer at Club UpTown seemed like a big easygoing hunk. A big body with big hands to match.

"You know what *that* means." My friend in line snickered.

Yeah...a *big* dick! But you didn't have to look at the bouncer's hands to see that. The big bulge in his green denim crotch told everything.

Bono had one of those Saturday-afternoon-TV-wrestler's bodies. He would've looked perfect in a Captain Colossal cape, smashing folding chairs over the heads of referees. His name, BONO, was emblazoned on his T-shirt in case he forgot, I guess.

I always liked the strong violent type, so I considered getting fresh with Bono. But when I got to the club door, he frowned: "Where *you* going, pretty boy?" Timber-sized arms fell across my chest.

"Where d'you think?" *Asshole.* I gave him my celebrity-sneer. "Hey, Bozo, why're you giving me such a hard time? My buddies are already in there." I crowded his space.

"Nunh huh," Bono shoved back, tearing my carefully-torn shirt. "We're already wall-to-wall pretty boys tonight. We're looking for dudes with character or credentials. And you ain't got neither."

"Get fucked, musclehead." I dared poke my finger into his chest.

That was all it took.

Bono charged like a rottweiler. I tried to dodge. Hydraulic biceps hurled me to the sidewalk. A fist grenaded my solar plexus. New York night crowds gathered round to enjoy the curbside entertainment no cover charge.

My ego lay bruised on the sidewalk. My confidence rolled into the gutter like a dropped quarter.

"Later, Chris!" my friend taa-taa'ed. He disappeared into Club UpTown.

"Yeah, Chris," Bono razzed me. "See ya later."

"Maybe I will, Bozo, maybe I will!" I shot him the finger, scurrying to a safe distance. Bono fired back an iron cannon of a finger. Italian cusswords graffittied the air.

A clubkid like me can't be brushed off that easy. This wasn't the first rave I'd crashed. I knew this dive back when it was HopScotch. Before that it was SpitFire. The delivery door behind the alley dumpsters was still the best entrance one could make.

Things haven't changed much since HopScotch had it last summer.

Halfway down the dim hall, couples huddle. Weenie roasts are already in progress. Guys rub their sticks together. The hog trough noises of guys fucking in darkness. Young studs batter each other's ass.

Happy hour.

A trio with their pants down around their knees swap sloppy tongues and greedy gropes. A black light phosphorizes their three dicks like luminous aquarium creatures. Just like the good old days.

In the corner a strawberry blond kid is already getting a workout from a Sicilian model. The model's hand reaches into the strawberry kid's zipper, fishing out an enormous cock, bigger than anything you'd expect to see on such a baby. He is one hung youngster.

As I'm about to join them, a familiar hand grips my shoulder.

"Shit! *Bozo!*" I squirm against the wall.

"Y'er coming with me, asswipe!" Bono hauls me bodily down the hallway. My boot heels spark across the corridor. He yanks me through a steel doorway. Slams it shut like a vault.

This had been the "point of no return" chamber during the infamous SpitFire days. Some of the leather boys' paraphernalia still clutters the room.

"Don't move, twink." Bono's hands frisk my body.

"Not even gonna kiss me first? Getting your jollies, closet case?"

"Shut up, pretty boy!" Bono yanks my short ponytail.

I see more stars than a weekend at Planet Hollywood. My entire nightlife passes before my eyes. Bono knots my arms behind my back.

"Oh shit, man!" My shoulders and triceps wrench in his grip. Things pop. *You stupid motherfucker! You bastard!*"

Bono's hand frisks my ass-crack. His finger rips a hole into the rear of my jeans.

"No underwear!" He filches my condoms from my back pocket. "Hey, you came ready for this fuck!" He rummages the crevice of my ass, clamps down hard on my gluteus to the maximus.

I squeal. Is he really going to do me?

Bono pastes his face to mine and hisses: "Yell as much as you want, pretty boy! These walls are four feet of solid brick. With that party going on outside, nobody's coming to save your pretty pink ass! Bend over!"

My head touches my knees. Bono's powerful legs straddle behind me.

"Let's see that ass, asshole!" He rips more into the inseam of my jeans. My bare butt sticks out, my ass and balls totally naked for his abuse.

"Now that's what I like to see easy access! You're gonna be my fuck hole tonight!"

Bono's hands squeeze my ass cheeks. Tremors ripple around my butt hole. They burn and quiver. He works my ass cheeks well apart. He tweaks a few of my ass hairs like he's plucking eyebrows.

"Ow!" My legs splay out to escape his sadistic fingers. My balls dangle down.

"That's it, spread those boy buns wide!" He backhands my nuts. "I like lots of room to maneuver when I fuck my pretty boys!"

His fingers burrow up to my shithole. A fat finger ruffles the olive indentation of my ass.

"I love turning pretty gym twinkboys like you into fuck-mush! I could fingerfuck dozens of you dick-ditzy blond studs before happy hour!" Bono

clutches my crotch. My fly-buttons near-melt with the heat of my engorged hard-on. "You're all crazy for this finger once I get you down and work you over. After this, you'll want to suck my hand every time you see me. And you *will* suck it if I tell you to. You guys work so hard to look so good, so hot, so sexy. You spend hours in the gym, and for what? So you can get fucked by guys like me, *right*?"

He has a point.

"Uh-huh." I pant total absolute submissive willing abject agreement.

Bono's finger taunts my hole, tickles my rectum rim. "Now pretend this finger is my cock."

Bono overpowers me, but lust for him comes from inside out. My concrete crotch balls up. His tickling finger gets me harder, hornier. Sperm surges in my hurting balls with every poke.

"Please!" I yell out for Bono's cock. Scream like a cock-crazy cheerleader. "Fuck me! Give me your cock! My ass really needs it! Dick me! Dick my ass!"

"Nun hunh. You'll take what I give you." He hisses in my ear. His finger dilates the pucker of my ass. "And here it is."

"*Give it to me.*"

"It's right here. Come get it, little asshole. I want to see you do it. It's waiting for you, fucker. It's all yours. Just fuck yourself. You want to finger fuck, don't you?"

"Yes I want you to fuck me. Let me put it in my ass. Please!" I prance impatiently on all fours now.

"That's a good asshole boy." Bono thumps my ass lips like he's testing a melon for ripeness. "Go ahead. Here it is. Come and get it. Put my finger up you."

I crouch back. My exposed rump wags high in the air.

"You're real hot around that pussy hole." He coos in my ear. His finger twirls and diddles me maddeningly back there. His phallic finger seems to grow up me. I arch and roll my rump around on that teasing finger. The whorls of his fingerprint feel like corduroy brushing my ass lips.

I slip his beefy fingertip into my shit chute. It plugs me. It stuffs up my asshole like a cork. I *have* to have the rest of it. I want his entire finger all the way up my butt!

"Ohhhhh!" My butt cheeks clamp together like a Venus flytrap trying to hold Bono's finger-dick in place. "Put it *in* me!" I rock back on it.

"Grab for it, finger-fucker, go ahead! Squirm on it!" The bastard laughs. He laughs at me and my butt hole lunging for his hand. "I do love watching pretty boys like you get fuck-crazy. I like to make 'em crawl. I love to tease them till they're wallowing, groveling dick pigs. You are a dick pig aren't you, twink-hole? You're nothing but pure pussy hole hot to make me cum. That's exactly what you are right now, huh? Huh?"

"Yeah, yeah, I'm all ass for you!" I buck. My hole spreads wider. "Let me be

your hole, please, *I want to be your hole!*"

"One hundred percent fuck hole! Go ahead, then. You like this finger so much. Stick your ass back on it! Open your hole!"

Swear to god, this stud has me scooting around the room backward on my hands and knees! Has me begging him to jam his finger farther up between my buns.

I raise myself on my haunches to get at it.

But Bono teases me with it.

He holds his finger at a hard-to-reach level. I can't get at it on my hands and knees. In order for me to get it in me he forces me to crouch. He has me holding my ass apart in a low, helpless, excruciating, knee-breaking squat. When I do what he says, he laughs at my discomfort and humiliation. He makes me sweat for it, plugging my pucker over his upright finger. He loves watching my horny legs shaking, my whole body spitted onto his finger.

Soon as I work his finger partway up into my ass, just to the first joint, barely kissing the crescent of his fingernail, I wiggle my ass like a hula dancer.

"Yeah, work out on my finger, pretty-boy! Slurp it up into your ass. Put on a show for me with that hot twinky-ass. I like to make my fuck toys sweat. All that work at the gym has got to be good for something, pretty boy. Flex those muscles. Work out! Feel the burn! No pain, no gain, right, finger puppet?

"Ahhhhhh!" I squat there, luxuriating in his welcome insertion of my asshole. His digit corkscrews up inside me; it crooks the finger a little; it makes me jump.

"You like that, huh?" His finger flicks some more. I feel it worming and squirming and fingering deep in my insides. He twists and bends it up into my butt hole. "Just like it wuz my dick! Make it feel good. See if you can make it *cum*."

Make his *finger* orgasm? Is he nuts? Well, I'd sure as shit try!

"I wanna watch you fuck yourself on it!" Bono slaps my straining backside. "Get my finger up in you! Move that ass around on it! I want to watch it sticking in you! Come on, pretty boy! Let's feel that ass wrap itself around my finger! Tighter. Reach for it!"

His finger penetrates in ways a dick never did. Bono is right. I am a ditzy blond dizzy for his finger fuck. I would suck his hand in public if he asked me. I would spread my legs every time he shows me his finger. I would....

Bono pulls his finger out of my asshole.

"Unh, please-!" My concrete cock strains against the fabric of my jeans. I ache to paw my cock, to jerk it, anything to free it from its tight box. I'm so close to coming!

Damn! I'd chase Bono all over New York to get that magic fuck-finger of his back up in my ass! "Please put it up me!"

He wipes his finger off on my shirt. He ignores my imploring hole.

Dammit! Bono lets me simmer there, bawling for a fuck. My emptied asshole

Play Hard, Score Big

aches with vacancy.

"Put it in me some more!" My ass cheeks squeeze together, reflexively feeling for something to fuck it. But nothing feels as good as Bono's six-inch finger-drill. I must've been a sight, angling my sloppy fuck hole up in the air. I roll on the floor. My button-down fly mashed against the concrete. My poor cock needs some relief. I could fuck a hole in the goddamn floor, Bono has me so fuck-crazy.

Bono eases his big body down into the chair. Casually he unrolls his green denims down to his ankles.

Naked, Bono's entire body expands. He is a big mastodon of nude muscle. His thighs splay open, baring the cavern of his ass pocket. Bono's balls hang down, fat and pink and suckable.

Sprouting up from his seed sack is Bono's fist-thick boner.

Bono's cock throbs above his abdomen. His cock is a firm, glistening fuck stalk. Its cock head forms a perfect round button of hotdog meat. A pink acorn drooling to drill my fuckhole. His mushroom-capped hard-on pulses. The meat stick beckons me between his legs, like Bono's obscene middle finger I've just fucked myself on.

"Give it some tongue!" Bono commands.

I snuggle my face between his legs. I inhale Bono's sweating hairy crevices. My sucking lips rub the stubble of his shaved pubic patch. I mouth the root of his cock.

I ladle Bono's spunk-plump balls onto my lips. My tongue polishes each ball. His hot ball sac is long and stretchy, like pizza cheese. I deep throat those balls, massaging each one against the soft back of my throat.

Bono lets me continue. His heavings tell me I'm sucking his cock the way he likes it sucked. I graze my own beard stubble on his cock. His ass cheeks squeeze together at this; his monster thighs vise my face into his ball sacking. I suck while he calls me every name in the book: "Cocksucker" "Twink-hole" "Cum-Catcher" "Cunt-Face", "Dicklicker" "Pussyboy."

"Turn around, fuck head." he finally says.

I turn around.

Bono is done getting his dick and balls sucked on, he says, He is going to fuck me now.

"Show me your hole!" he commands.

Eagerly, I kiss the floor. I show Bono my hole.

My knees burn. My shoulders ache. My fuck-sensitized ears detect a foil pouch torn open, then the peel of latex unrolling wetly down the entire length of Bono's stiff jizz-stick. It slides down his cock like a long, wet kiss, a tongue licking an envelope.

"Now I'm really gonna give you a hard time." He give his dick a shake, and shucks the rubber roll back like he's cocking a shotgun. "I'm gonna ball yer butt through the brick wall!"

He grips my shoulders, using my arms like reins to ride me with.

His digging dick slices into me like a knife into a watermelon. A satisfying sluice of fuck jam coats the tunnel of my ready hole. My butt welcomes the sharp sloshing darts of his cock.

"Mmm, boy, you got a lotta juice in you, kid. That's gonna make this ride nice and smooooooth!"

His mountain of muscles hammers me into the wall. My body shudders to grip the intruding penis. Bono's stiff prick enters me. The meaty piece seals my fresh-punched hole with his fleshy, moist ball sac.

His whipping cock blisters my backside. He balls me right into the wall. His industrial pelvis throws a round of haymaker punches into my ass.

I bounce against the wall and blubber like a baby. Every shove drives his thrusts deeper. My slick hole welcomes every wedged inch of his dick.

"Juicy...hot...asshole, you pretty boy cocksucker!" Bono raps above me.

He flattens my hole against the floor, fucking it hard. I'm a no-obligation party doll opened for my brutal fucker. My hole is getting used for what it's made for: getting rammed full of Bono's hot man cock. He sticks his gorilla prick in me till he's satisfied and my dicked-out butt brims with his cock cream.

"It's cuming! Here's that load you've been waiting for! I'm cuming up your tight ass!" Bono jiggles his dick one last time in my hole. His sloppy balls bounce with the rush of cum spurting out his prick tip.

"Watch it shoot, asshole! Watch me cum!"

Bono's vicious dick yanks out of me. It looms in front of my face again. He slaps it into my face for me to see it blast. The taut, cum-throbbing length of the meat quivers before my eyes. It spasms inside its bagging. His thrashing cock fills the receptacle tip of his gooey rubber. Creamy-white swirls of his man-milk balloon the end. It bulges into a sagging bulb of jizz. Stud-seed spews out like a milkshake. I lick the shaft, welcoming his semen.

I mouth those thrashing balls, popping each in and out of my mouth, I cover them with spittle, mashing my lips into his butt-crevice.

I could've parked my face between Bono's legs for the rest of the night.

But he stands up.

Shucking his rubber off, Bono hikes up his jeans. "I guess you can let yourself out." Buckling his belt: "And get yourself off."

But I have other plans for my leftover lust.

I'll find some dumb stud and I'll tell him my story. I'll tell him everything that just happened.

He'll want to know the details. *Dirty* details. All the nasty parts.

And I will tell him everything that just happened.

My finger itches to be inside some squirming stud's hot dancing asshole.

That's one party I *will* get into tonight!

A PARTY AT THE BEACH
Jesse Monteagudo

In 1973, Miami was a candy store for a young gay guy just out of the closet. There were just so many, many places for a gay boy to party in those days. Some of our favorite places to party were the bars. They ranged from out-of-the-way dives like the Nook in Coral Gables, which thought that Stonewall never happened, to swinging discos like the Warehouse VIII in Little Habana, which had a huge dance floor, a levi-leather bar in the back, a cruise bar upstairs, and a rooftop where anything could happen. There was Bachelors II, a neighborhood bar on Coral Way, and her sister, Bachelor's West, where I met my first boyfriend. For those of us who liked them butch, there was the Ramrod and the Rack, two Levi-leather joints located within walking distance of each other, in Downtown Miami.

I did not have a car, but that did not cramp my style. Thanks to the kindness of friends, boyfriends and tricks, I was able to get around as well as I would if I had my own wheels. Thanks to my friend Frenchy I cruised Broward's hot spots on a regular basis, from the Marlin Beach Hotel in Fort Lauderdale to Tee Jay's in Hollywood to Keith's Cruise Room in Hallandale. Keith's Cruise Room, named after the club's portly owner, was a disco that stayed open till six in the morning, at which time Keith would personally serve breakfast to "his boys." Since making money was not one of my talents, I learned how to make a drink last for hours, unlike my pal Frenchy, who would be totally smashed by the time breakfast came around.

Though Frenchy was a year younger than I, he's been on his own since he was fourteen when, in a drunken state, he told his conservative Cuban parents about his preference for dick. Thrown out of the home by his outraged parents, Frenchy made do by selling his ass on Biscayne Boulevard before he was taken up by the first of a series of sugar daddies. Frenchy was wild and outrageous, and totally uninhibited. Though I did not care much for the effeminate style affected by many gay *Cubanos* at that time, I learned to accept Frenchy's flamboyance and his friendship, his platform shoes and his constant use of feminine pronouns when talking about himself, me and everyone else. Besides, Frenchy was a good friend, one who was always willing to share his car and his drugs with a "sister" who was working his way through college. Besides, I needed to loosen up now and then, and there was no better one for that than Frenchy.

"*Ay*, Joe, don't be so serious!" Frenchy would shriek, three sheets to the wind. "Let's go over to the Warehouse and get us a couple of guys!" Cute and short, Frenchy always got his man. But then again, so did I. It was 1973, and the world was our playground. Though both Frenchy and I had our share of boyfriends at that time, they never cramped our style, or stopped our cruising. An abortive affair with a thirty-year-old man, who left me for the Pentecostal Church, convinced me once and for all that monogamy was not for me.

In fact, the hardest thing about cruising during the Golden Age was not

finding a man to fuck but finding a place to fuck in. Like most young *Cubanos*, I lived with my parents, while Frenchy lived in the back seat of his car whenever he was between sugar daddies. Though the rooftop at the Warehouse could be fun at times, we generally could not have sex in the bars, and backrooms were a thing of the future. Sometimes, if we could afford it, we rented a room at a *posada*, a Little Havana or Hialeah motel that rented by the hour. Once we had to make do with the front and back seats of Frenchy's car, where we were fucked by a pair of "straight" Puerto Ricans we picked up in a bisexual dive on Calle Ocho.

But the bars weren't the only places for a hot young Cuban to cruise in Miami in those days. Though the Regency Baths closed that year, we had the Club Miami, Jack Campbell's spanking-new sex emporium on Coral Way. There were adult cinemas, adult bookstores, Bayfront Park, and even the second floor library bathroom at my *alma mater*, Miami College. But my favorite place for tricking and cruising and being gay at was the beach. Not the tired old 23rd Street Beach, where tired old queens carried on under the eye of tired old vice cops. Dania Beach was inconvenient, 14th Street Beach was still the province of "straight" Cuban families, and Haulover Beach's heyday as a nude beach was in the future.

Those of us who went to the "gay beach" in the '70s usually went to Virginia Beach; not the former segregated "colored" that faced Rickenbacker Causeway but the then-undeveloped seashore that lined the Southern coast of Virginia Key beyond the public beach. This wild, unkempt area attracted people who for obvious reasons wanted a seashore that wasn't supervised by the authorities, first nudists and then gays. Being both gay and a nudist, Virginia Beach was the place for me.

By 1973 Virginia Beach was a popular place for young gay boys who wanted to spend a campy, sexy Sunday afternoon, away from the madding crowds and the trolls who thronged 23rd Street Beach. By noon the beach area was full of friendly guys in tight bathing suits, laughing and drinking and cruising and only occasionally getting into the water (they didn't want to get their suits wet). The more daring among us would remove our shorts, smoke a joint, or wander into the bushes for a quickie. This scene was too good to be true, and it wasn't. By the end of the seventies the powers-that-be caught on, staged a few highly-publicized raids, and closed Virginia Beach "for development."

But in 1973 police raids were few and far between, and the worst that a guy could get from the Beach was sunburn or the clap. On a typical Sunday afternoon we would park our cars by the access road that paralleled the shore and work our way through the brush to the Beach. We were a festive group. There was Frenchy, of course, as gay as ever. There was "Rosanna," a hairdresser and part-time drag queen who hated me for "stealing" his boyfriend away from him. (Actually I didn't Freddie and Rosanna had been exes for weeks when I met Freddie and, besides, none of us could compete with the Pentecostal

Church for Freddie's affection.) There was Olga, a tough Puerto Rican dyke who could out-run, out-drink and out-swear the rest of us. And there was Raul, a thirty-five-year-old Colombian drug dealer who was at that time Frenchy's main "sugar daddy."

We made our usual grand entrance, dropping our towels, umbrellas, ice cooler and "boom box" on the sand before an appreciative crowd. Rosanna, already drunk, played to "her" audience, sashaying and lip-synching through whatever song was hot at the time. Olga began to show who's boss, daring us to get into the water with her, bragging that we were not "woman enough" to follow her into the surf. Frenchy and Raul ignored everything, as they proceeded to make a scene with their loud and open necking. I just lay on my stomach on my beach towel, taking in the scenery, trusting that a young *Anglo* hot for a Cuban teenager would soon make his move.

"*Ay*, Joe, watch my radio!" shrieked Frenchy, as he and Raul made their way into the bushes. "We're going to take a walk." Knowing that Frenchy and Raul would be gone a long time, I changed the radio station, which was playing loud *salsa*, to one that played soul. Aretha's voice began to sing the soundtrack of my life.

"Look who's here!" boomed an all-too-familiar voice. I turned my head around to see my next door neighbors, Aristide and Hector Arquiaga, stand in amazement, wearing identical baggy shorts, sandals and sunglasses. Before I could say anything, the two boys were all over me.

"It's Joe," laughed Aristide, as he and Hector crouched around me. "What are *you* doing at a queer beach?"

"The same thing *you* are doing. And this is not just a 'queer beach'. All kinds of people come here."

"Sure, and I'm Dick Nixon. But that's not what Hector and I heard. We heard that fags come here all the time to suck cock and take it up the ass." He smiled. "So we figured that since you are here you gotta suck cock and take it up the ass, right?" Actually, I was and I did, but I wasn't about to admit it.

"But that's okay, Joe. We're cool," Hector smiled. I liked Hector. Only 18, he was nice and quiet, unlike his boisterous 20-year-old brother. "We knew you were gay since we saw you staring out the window at us, while we were mowing the lawn with our shirts off." I blushed, hoping that the brothers did not see my hard-on. Fortunately, I was lying on my stomach at the time.

"So what are you guys doing here?" After all, I figured, Aristide and Hector were straight dudes, with girlfriends around them all the time. Come to think of it, it was Ari who had the girlfriends around him all the time; Hector just went along for the ride. Was Hector gay? I began to wonder.

"We're kind of horny," said Ari, as he set his hands on my firm, round buns. Though I wouldn't admit it to them, I was kind of horny myself, and the Arquiaga boys were two hot *papis*. Both Ari and Hector were handsome, muscular, swarthy young *mulatos*, with chocolate milk skin, dark, curly hair,

and sensuous lips. Ari was tall and lean while Hector was short and stocky like me. Their smooth torsos were muscular from hours of high school football and wrestling and hard work at their dad's construction site. Though I was pretty muscular myself after years of soccer practice, swimming and karate I could not compete with the hot Arquiaga boys. "Can't you get any?"

"You know I can get all I want," boasted Ari, as he continued to play with my buns. "But Hector is hot as hell, and kind of shy, and he can't get a girl to put out. The *hebas* just shriek when they see what he's got. And he's horny something powerful!"

Aristide continued: "So I said to him, 'Hector, Br', what you need is a guy who'll give you a blowjob.' And Hector hemmed and hawed but I said, 'Don't worry, man! Just because you let a *maricon* swing on your dick doesn't mean you're one!' So we came over to Virginia Beach, looking for a guy who will suck off Hector's *pinga*. A guy like you." Ari pulled down my shorts, revealing my tasty, round orbs. "Did anyone ever tell you that you have a nice ass?"

"All the time," I said, truthfully. "But why don't you let Hector speak for himself?" Though I would have given Hector a blowjob under any circumstances, I wasn't going admit it. As if he were reading my mind, Hector bent over, taking my chin in his hand as he kissed me passionately. Our mustaches touched as our tongues explored each other's lips.

"I never told Ari about it, but I'm kind of "bi" myself. I wanted to make it with a guy for a long time now, especially with my cute next-door neighbor." If Ari was shocked by the news, he did not show it. Instead, he spread my cheeks apart, opening my asshole with his finger. Though basically "straight," Ari knew a good *culo* when he saw one.

"You know, Hec," said Ari, as he continue to finger-fuck my ass. "I betcha Joe don't know what he's got waiting for him. Why don't you show him." I gaped with amazement as Hector pulled down his shorts, revealing the biggest cock I had ever seen. Hector's sausage was big and thick, at least a foot long and almost as wide, covered by a thick, dark foreskin. Pleased with himself, Hector began to stroke his dick, filling the air with the pungent odor of young manhood. All resistance dissolved. I *wanted* that cock.

"You like it, don't you," whispered Aristide, leaning over me while continuing to play with my firm round buns. "So do my little 'bro a favor. You'll like it too." Though I was ready to suck Hector's cock right then and there, a crowd was beginning to gather. "Let's go into the bushes," I said, as we got on our feet. Without another word we took our towels into the brush, setting them down on a clearing by an old palm tree.

We stripped. All three of us were handsome, muscular, mustachioed young Cubans, with thick, uncut cocks and low-hanging balls. Though Ari could not compete with his brother's thick prick, his own massive *pinga* would put most men to shame. Ari smiled as I got on my knees, pulling back Hector's magnificent foreskin with my hand to reveal the treasure within. I licked the

thick, hard cock head, intoxicated by the pungent man-smell that surrounded me.

Without a warning, Hector shoved his cock deep inside my mouth. Though I was already an experienced cocksucker, I almost choked as Hector's massive prick filled my mouth and throat. Steadying myself, I began to suck, slowly at first, but then with rising determination. Hector groaned softly, surrendering himself to my oral pleasure. My teenage lover was at the height of his potent young manhood, and he wanted and needed the pleasure that only a man could give him.

"Suck my cock, Joe," begged Hector. "*Mamame la pinga!*" While I continued to swing on Hector's cock, his brother worked his way through my firm round ass. Spreading my cheeks, Ari dove in, sinking his tongue in and around my tender rectum. I moaned as Ari rimmed my sensitive young asshole. Straight or not, here was a guy who appreciated a good *culo*! Though we did not know it, a crowd gathered around, attracted by the sight of three hot young *Cubanos* in the throes of uninhibited man-sex. I winced as Ari shoved three fingers into my ass.

"Keep sucking his dick, cocksucker!" Ari ordered, as he took possession of my tender young bunghole. "A guy like you can take both of us at once!" As I continued to suck Hector's cock, his brother set me down on my back, lifting my legs up in the air and spreading them apart. I almost screamed as Ari's thick prick entered my rectum with a savage thrust. With the fury of a young animal, Ari held my legs apart as his cock impaled my sensitive boyhole. Soon the pain turned to pleasure, as Ari massaged my prostate with his rock-hard power tool.

I was in cock heaven. I was a boy toy for two young *mulato* musclemen, who used my mouth and my ass to give and receive man pleasure. I began to play with myself, stimulated by the ecstasy Ari and Hector's massive *pingas* were giving me. As I stroked my cock and pulled my balls, Hector added to my pleasure by pulling my hard, sensitive young tits.

Never had Virginia Beach seen such a sight. It seemed that every guy on the beach was watching. We were three muscular young animals, with thick, uncut cocks and low-hanging balls, and nothing on our mind but the force of our sex and the savage pleasure we were getting from one another. My lovers held on to each other as they fucked my mouth and my ass. Sweat poured down our bodies as we sent our partners to the point of no return.

After what seemed to be forever, Ari and Hector began to increase their thrust, indicating that they were ready to blast. Almost in unison, the brothers reached a savage climax, shooting their semen down my throat and up my rectum. Hector immediately bent over, taking my cock in his mouth as I reached my own orgasm. My hard young *pinga* took on a life of its own, shooting semen into Hector's hungry mouth. Totally satisfied, Hector and Ari fell over me, holding me tight as they held each other.

The crowd applauded. Though we could have been arrested, there were no cops in sight, and our "audience" made sure that none would be around to

interrupt our "performance." Frenchy, as usual, broke the ice, bringing us clean towels and a drink. "You were great, Joe. I didn't know you had it in you."

"I didn't know I had it in me either," I exclaimed, "but these guys brought it out of me."

Aristide and Hector Arquiaga soon got married, though Hector continues to play around with other guys, myself included. Virginia Beach soon became a thing of the past, as the City decided to close the beach and "redevelop" the area. But I will never forget that day in 1973 when time stood still, and three young men found perfect happiness in the pleasure of one another's body, without inhibition, without shame.

THE WATCHER ON THE SHORE
Peter Burton

Plop went the sun, plop. And disappeared below the horizon. Suddenly it was a lot less warm, though it seemed impossible that the fading sun had really warmed him any. The gentle breeze became cooler, took strength from the fact that it had no sun to warm it, chilled him to the bone. He shivered. Harsh squawkings. From the gulls circling above him. Screaming like souls in torment, longing, though never able to get rest. Boom, boom, boom, the waves breaking on the shingle beach. A shuffling, dragging sound as the shingle was pulled back into the sea by the receding water and then... boom, boom, boom, as it was thrown back and down again. He stood looking out at the sea, watching the waves, and waiting for the moon. His feet planted firmly in the damp, dirty, litter-strewn sand, his hands entrenched deeply in his greatcoat pockets, his eyes, remote and far, looking out to sea, but distant, thinking of those things that he could not see.

And behind him he could hear the sounds of the town. Drifting on the stiffening wind these sounds, and smells, the cries of the holiday-makers at play, the cries of the townsfolk who hated them but who, parasite like, fed off them and their fifty-week-fatted flesh. Smells burning sugar from the candy floss vendor, grease from the hot dog stalls, onions, vinegar, fish and chips, salt from the sea catching at his nostrils. He sniffed, dug his hands deeper, nestled them into the warmth of his crotch, and let his eyes travel along the beach. A couple, impossible, in this light to tell of what sex or sexes, sat farther along the beach smoking; he watched the tips of their cigarettes light up as they dragged and sucked in the smoke, then watched the glow momentarily dim again. He could almost smell the smoke, pungent, strong, delicious, French, he felt, *Disque Bleu* probably. He wondered if they were French, if it were a boy and a girl, two girls, or if it were two boys. Wondered what they would be like. He tried to distinguish them more clearly, peered and strained his eyes to see, but the darkness was falling faster and all he could see was the shadow on the black, two figures huddled together. He tried to imagine what they would be like. Thought, out of his own preference, they would be boys.

He watched. The two French boys dressed in faded jeans and warm, bright sweaters. Not the kind of French that you got in London, the terribly grand, haughty, these would be friendly and willing to be friendly with him. Maybe, though, only one was from France. The other probably lived down here and they'd just met, in one of the pubs, The Royal Flush or The Grey Wolf, shared a table perhaps. Got talking, the English boy would have offered to buy the other a drink, shyly they would have conversed, knowing so well that all the other men around them would be listening, listening to every word and, because they were both so beautiful, envying them and feeling sharp and bitchy, jealous.

Of course, he knew. How difficult it was to make conversation in any of the pubs or meeting places. Always feeling that same embarrassment and constraint. Knowing that everyone would be watching the moves, the careful courtship,

- 373 -

waiting to see the outcome. Feeling triumphant if it failed. Feeling let down, hurt, if it succeeded and these two creatures went away together. Buying a further drink. This one gulped down. Cold, almost tasteless pints of bitter. Then the suggestion. From the English boy? To leave. Rising, feeling the eyes, even without seeing them, all those little green eyes. The awkward exit. Exits with pickups always were difficult. Knowing that people knew you'd been there, in that bar, for a pickup.

Down the stairs. Out onto the busy evening street. The lights, the crowds. The call of the sea. Carried on the wind the call of the sea.

One of them would say: Let's walk a bit, okay?

And the other would nod, maybe yes: Yes, let's go down to the beach.

They'd cross the road, leave the hotels and boarding houses behind them, staring at their retreating backs and drift slowly, laughing, past the Palace Pier. The Palace Pier, with its illuminated name and cluster of people by the turnstile, slipping in, slipping out. Maybe they'd stop at the automatic photographing booth and have some photographs done. Even, perhaps, if they'd come out well, spend a little extra and have an enlarged print each. A summer night souvenir of a lust that has yet to be consummated. Walking away. Stuffing the photographs into pockets. Looking at each other and smiling.

Oh, yes, he could see it all. Sparks in the sky, like a firework. They'd thrown their cigarettes away. He almost heard the shingle rustle as they moved, closer together. Arms about each other.

As they walked down the steps to the beach the noise of the town would have disappeared. Magically. Not completely, of course, but enough for it to remain a dim, pleasing hum in the background. The sounds they heard most strongly now would have been of the roaring sea, crashing, crashing down, and, mingling with it, the boom, boom, boom, of their hearts. They'd already have tinglings, shiverings in the spine, sensations that were a prelude to excitement.

Oh, yes, he knew so well how it would all have been with them. That's the way it would have been, right down to the last detail. People: always, always, always, so predictable. A grating sound, a flare, two burning points, faces half seen in the match's flame as they light up further cigarettes. Even now, after that brief glimpse, he cannot be sure. Are they, are they? The shingle crunches, the two figures rise. Pull clothes, tug clothes straight. Shake out aching, tired, longing limbs. One makes a sharp, birdlike move, peck, peck, peck. Kisses the other.

"Hush, people will see."

A quick laugh from the birdboy.

"Oh, 'oo cares, what zey see?"

They suddenly, surprisingly fall together and dance about. Muffled laughter. They stop and look towards him. He feels their eyes upon him.

"Look, someone's watching us."

"Him."

A snort of contempt.

"Just ignore him. These beaches are littered with queens like that. Watching. Voyeurs, that's the name for them. Get their kicks out of watching other people at it. Go home and have a..."

The other boy laughed, a little nervously.

"You're not worried about him are you? Come on," snatching up the boy's hand, "let's give him a show."

He pulls the French boy towards him.

Oh, no, no, no. His breath catches. He can hardly breathe. A sharp pain beneath his heart. How can they? He feels a prickle of tears and the wetness as they trickle down his lined face. They're laughing at me, at me. They think I don't know what it's like. Think I've never experienced love. What do they know about it. They're too young.

The French boy pulls away, shakes his head. He's saying no, let's go away from here. The other boy laughs again. Everything seems funny to him. Even human weakness.

The tears catch against his lips. Salty. He licks his lips. Licks away the tears. The tracks of his tears dry on his face. He knows what these boys will do. Knows how they'll walk home together. Because of him, quieter. But excited still. Probably call into a fish and chip shop, share a bag of chips and a roll as they walk back through the town, oblivious to the people drifting along. Walk back to the bedsit the English boy lives in up near the station. Maybe not quite oblivious. The English boy is probably the type who looks at every pretty boy that passes, talking in the face, the crotch, the possibility.

The beach is still. He stands alone, hurt and shy. They stand, as if time has held them poised for a moment, watching him. He shuffles his feet. He stares back at them. Draws in his breath. Yes, they are beautiful. He cannot rid his mind of them. Of what they will do in bed. Their tugging off of clothes. The starting sex before they're even undressed. Falling on each other as the door closes. Rolling over the room. Sex that encompasses the entire room. Young, animal, sharply smelling of sweat and bitter, boyish cologne. Ripping the coverings away. Savage, savage sharp, biting each other's flesh, scratching, kissing, hard, burning passion, rising in each other's hands. Piercing each other's flesh. Panting and groaning, dying for release and holding it off....

He pants, gasps, he feels it, feels it in himself.

The two boys walk slowly towards him. He cannot look away. The boys are hard-faced. The French boy averts his eyes. The English boy stares straight at him. Scornfully, hatingly. They are almost on him now. Almost, almost, he pants and gasps. Almost....

They pass him.

"You filthy old bastard, you filthy old bastard...."

It echoes inside his head. Seems shouted in the wind. His stomach contracts with nervousness. Will they say anything? Will they shout back, draw attention

from up above? The promenade. Draw attention to him. Cause him trouble. He gasps and pants and cries, hoarse sounds escape from his throat. Tears fall from his eyes. Hot, stinging tears. His hand tears at his flesh. Tears and pulls as the tears flow down his face. His old, lined, unshaven face. The wind catches at the tail of his coat and it flaps about him. He stands an incongruous figure on that beach. Old, unshaven, military coat flying in the rising wind, legs apart, crying, gasping hoarsely into the wind, hand pumping away. Thinking of the two beautiful boys. Sobbing now. His whole being breaking apart. Pain, in his body, pain in his eyes, aching in his arm. Unable to stop. On and on, almost, almost, almost ... unable to stop, unable to come ... sobbing because he knows he's too old, too poor, too unloved. Alone.

AFTER THE PARTY
Rick Jackson

I live in a conservative building where the average age is probably 60, so it's no surprise that my neighbors are home in bed early. Since I like to think of myself as something of a slut, however, it's not at all unusual for me to drive up the entrance to our parking garage during the wee hours. There's always an attendant on duty to raise the little wooden barrier that guards us against intruders, but lately he has taken longer and longer to snap into action.

I figured that he was doubtless some minimum-wage college kid and stuck with the midnight-to-eight shift to boot, so I never exactly minded his being slow. People get what they pay for, after all. Still, while I waited for him to press the button to lift the barrier, I did begin noticing him more than one usually does garage attendants. He's good looking, for starters. Even after an evening of spewing three or four loads where they belonged, I always gave him a third glance.

I later discovered his name was Jimmy and that I was right on target when I guessed he was on the college wrestling team. He had that compact, muscular build most wrestlers and gymnasts do the kind that makes a man imagine being held down by all that muscle and ravaged hard. In addition to a cute neo-Brad-Pitt face (only with bigger dimples and blue eyes), Jimmy showed off broad shoulders and a wide chest, narrow hips and a gloriously hard ass. His smile was more seductive than any narcotic, and he used it a lot because he was always apologizing for reading on duty or sleeping on duty or just plain zoning out when he should have been doing his job.

The other night, I drove in around 3:30 after a 15-hour party at a local frat house. I needed salve and a bed in that order. What I didn't need was for Jimmy to be AWOL. I waited for about 30 seconds and then went over to his little booth to see if I could find the button that would let me in.

What I found was Jimmy lying on the floor his feet spread wide up on his bench, and his hand sliding along his thick college-boy dick. He'd slipped out of his trou, which he'd rolled up for a pillow. He was lying on the shirt he had stripped off. All Jimmy wore were his shoes and socks and the distant look of a man communing with the infinite. Because his eyes were closed, I could see his long, thick lashes not to mention stare at the thick dick he was so using to advantage.

He had more to offer than just a dick, of course: his swollen nipples that bagged unawares for my teeth, the full lower lip I yearned to suck, and his cute little button nose that would have felt so fine sliding along my asshole while he sucked and chewed on my hairy, aching nuts. His pecs were broad and hairless and his thighs were solid enough to crack marble to chips.

As I stood there watching him lash his lizard, I felt my own nine inches of abused bone miraculously rise from the dead. I knew what I had to do, even before Jimmy's hips began humping upwards against his hand and that fuckable mouth drifted into moans and that little whining noise men make that sounds for

all the world like a Chihuahua stuffed into a drawer.

I couldn't reach his dick without making noise, so I settled for leaning over and grabbing his calf. I'd expected him to catch a thrill, but the poor bastard leapt halfway to Burma. I pushed the button to raise the barrier and told him to get his ass into my car. I was taking him home for his own good.

He blushed and sputtered and fought hard to form a thought as he reached for his trou. I snatched them away from him and tossed them into my car. When I promised he wouldn't need clothes, I think he was confused because he pictured going to *his* home naked. I'll admit he looked unusual standing beside me in the elevator, but he looked damned good. Besides, feeling a little goofy with me might keep him from being caught later by someone who would have his ass fired.

When we hit my apartment and Jimmy followed me in with the body of a Greek god and the expression of a bloodhound caught shitting on the new shag carpet neither one of us had a clue what we were doing. Jimmy was savory beyond belief and I wanted his ass in the worst way, but I knew my shank couldn't take being slammed up another college jock anytime soon. I also knew myself well enough to know I was going to get Jimmy off whatever it took. In this case, loath though I normally am to let big dicks up my butt, I knew what duty and destiny demanded.

He had no sooner turned my offer of a beer down, than I grabbed his thang and pulled it on into the bedroom. Without a word, I shucked, lay back onto my bed, and lifted my legs. Jimmy blushed and stammered again as his synapses tried to fire. Then, finally, his mouth dropped and he said, "You mean CI can do you? Nobody's ever let me on top before!"

Bless his heart, with a dick as wicked as his, I'm not surprised. The thing was so evil it deserved to have a stake driven through its heart. I measured it later: it was only seven and a half inches long but was just a pubic hair under 3 inches wide and that was his shaft. The huge mushroom-shaped knob we won't talk about. Still, the radiant look on his face was almost worth all the pain I knew I would feel in the end. Almost.

For a long moment, he just stood there, beaming. Then he saw the fixings on my night stand and rubbered up. I made him use triple lube and pumped an Exxon *Valdez*-quality load up my ass, but I might have saved the trouble. When Jimmy climbed between my legs and parked his jism-slit against my hole, I thought for a second about asking him to finger me ready.

I didn't bother. For one thing, if this really was his first time in the saddle, I didn't want to shake his confidence. For another thing, I knew he could finger me like a Stradivarius cello and that dick would still split me open. Mainly, I didn't bother because the horny bastard slammed his overgrown dick up my ass before I could get my mouth open.

Once I was fucked, it wasn't only my mouth that wouldn't work. Sure, my jaws clenched tight so I wouldn't accidentally scream too loudly and draw the

police back to my apartment. I couldn't breathe. I'm sure my heart shut down until Jimmy's ravening butt-thrusts kick-started it again. Mostly, though, I was just plain hurting, and it didn't help that I had no one but myself to blame. I was probably 5 years older than Jimmy and knew how tight my ass was. What the fuck had I been thinking?

Well, clearly I'd been thinking the fuck about his bare, muscular body and the way his huge, cum-choked nuts swayed low between his thick thighs. His blue eyes and that kissable lower lip, his stiff tits and the way his pike was always up didn't help any. So, there I was, trying to shit that same monster dick in without popping my way into a stroke. I did my best to dodge the waves of agony rushing upwards from my ruptured hole, but that was like trying to avoid corn in Iowa.

Jimmy obviously knew enough about being fucked hard to pause for a moment and give my guts a chance to see reason, but there was no way a guy his age could control the primal urges that drove him relentlessly towards his destiny any more than I could or he wouldn't have been beating off on duty to begin with. He lingered deep within me for a moment and then heaved his ass towards the ceiling.

My guts collapsed around his retreating head, stroking him happy and giving me more to think of than my shattered shit hole. Just as his brutal corona slammed into my sphincter and bounced back into my blazing depths, I let slip a gasp that seemed to fuel his frenzy. He picked up speed right away, slamming me harder with every stroke and grinding his pubes into my ass when the impossible base of his dick had me nailed down tight.

I tried taking my mind off my troubles by worshiping his body the way it deserved. I looked down between us and saw his thick dick slamming in and out of my hole and had to admit the view was one righteous rush. My guts churned all the harder at his swollen nipples, almost forcing me to tweak them hard with my fingers. When his tits just poured plutonium on the pile of his passion, I moved my hands gently down his flanks, relishing the way his hard muscle knotted and clenched under my fingertips. His ass drew my hands like a magnet to that huge, hard didymous set of muscles, covered with the softest skin imaginable, yet clenching and writhing and bucking with the power of twin coils of carbon steel.

His heavy nuts crashed into my ass every time he dicked me deep, which seemed the only way he knew. I felt my own nine inches rubbing between our rutting bodies as his torso lowered itself almost onto me and his teeth found the hard muscle of my shoulder. Only his hot ass pumped up and down, powering his dick to drill through the bedrock of my soul until he struck enormous reserves of need and then overcame them all.

His breath jetted off my neck and into my ear while he used my ass and held tight. When he finally turned my neck loose, I shoved my mouth against his and let my tongue teach him how roughly men can kiss when they need to. My

hands had dropped his butt by that time to give my heels room to ride his ass, so I grabbed the back of his head and pulled him harder against my face.

His every motion was at once more savage because of his incredible build and yet more human because of the obvious excitement of his discovery. Every movement proved to him what a stud he really was, yet the way his massive muscles held me tight in his arms while he used me only emphasized how close a real man in the throes of fuck-frenzy is to a mindless ape.

Amazingly, I realized I liked being taken for a change and letting the other guy get his C especially when the creature who overpowers my every impulse is a cute-faced stud like Jimmy.

What's more, Mother Nature finally came to my rescue and played its ancient trick, turning the lead up my brutalized butt into the brightest, truest rapture of gold. Every inch of thrust and grind sent shivers rocketing up my spine; every time our hard, sweating bodies slammed together while Jimmy butted his head, he jolted me that much closer towards a mutual good time.

What I had up my ass wasn't the quick violence of a load sent blasting up to fill a butt; it was an even deeper satisfaction that a man's dick can caress into the tight hole around him. It begins with pain, but once the threshold of pleasure is breached, every twitch, every throb, every slam and taste and smell and touch all conspire to pull their victim one knowing, aware, inevitable step closer towards the abyss and I relished every single butt-busting, bone-crunching step.

Jimmy's face was a caricature of young love: his mouth set, his nostrils flared wide, his eyes locked on mine in mingled admiration and triumph.

Suddenly, I knew I had to reach out and pull him tight against me, hugging him to safety, even as his butt and dick rolled up and down and humped my way towards an ecstasy greater than any mortal should know. Each savage, growling thrust up my ass proved Jimmy's power and my own need and sealed us together forever, a Damocles and Dionysius for this new, more complicated age. Jimmy's sword was bone and flesh, but it bit more meaningfully than any antique hunk of iron.

As my arms held him tight, I tongue-fucked Jimmy's left ear and proved who was really boss.

Almost at once, seizures swept his body and racked his soul, and then, with a great bellow echoing down from the dawn of time, his body gave way. Those huge balls spewed their creamy cargo. My ass was wrapped so tight around his dick that I felt his cum-tube pulse with one blast after another as he clung to me, fucked into helplessness at last.

By the time his convulsions had passed away and he was mortal again, young Jimmy had learned all my ass could teach him and reminded me of more than a few home truths. He gave himself wholly up to my arms and caresses as he gulped for air, his thick dick still stuffed within me. I let him recover, because he would need his strength.

Almost from the first second I saw him above me, hunky and humping my

hole the way nature intended, I knew he was too good to pass up. Sure, I had enjoyed being of service, but now it was my duty to teach him the theory of turn-about and fair play.

As I finally rolled him over onto his back and carefully lifted my ass off our thick bone of contention, Jimmy's legs spread and lifted, proving he was eager to see how good I could be when I tried.

My dick was still sore, and all the swelling and throbbing didn't help any. Once I lubed it up and rubbered it down, I felt a little better.

When I slammed everything I had down Jimmy's ass and popped those blue eyes in six different directions at once, I felt a whole lot better.

I kept feeling better for the next couple hours.

By 5:45, Jimmy couldn't take any more and I certainly had nothing more to give. I returned his clothes and let him go back down to his booth before the early risers found him missing.

Now that I know what I have waiting for me alone, bored, and tight I might be coming home earlier from now on. Sure I'll be taking him away from his booth, but nobody goes in or out but me at that time of night anyway. If I'm going to be going in and out all night long, I can't think of a better way to do it than up Jimmy's incredible ass.

Besides, we're already paying his ass, even if it is only minimum-wage.

A CAPITOL NIGHT
Edmund Miller

Dancer

So glad to get out of the office where nobody appreciates me, I'm off to moonlight as a go-go boy. I know just how to milk admiration from a bar crowd.

Visitor

In Washington over night, I'm determined to check out the scene. I figure Tuesday will be slow, but a quirk in the liquor law allows nude dancing in bars. Dancers have to wear two pieces of clothing, but there's no rule about what body parts these two pieces cover up. Feet are the body parts of choice.

I find my way to what looks like a warehouse on Half Street and step inside. The place is empty! Well, empty by New York standards. But there are nude go-go boys who look almost like real people, not all pumped up the way one comes to expect in New York. After a general appraisal, I start tipping. They're friendly enough, squatting down right in my face. But they have no small talk and don't understand just how much tipping I am prepared to do. So I order a drink and sit to watch the passing scene such as it is for a while.

Dancer

Dan comes off and starts doing his Spanish homework, so I'm up. He tells me there's a live one here tonight. Oh, there he is. He's seen the changeover, and he's pulling out a big wad of bills. A real gentleman! I love the tie.

Visitor

Hey, that big one in the cowboy hat is throwing me a kiss! I go over to start tipping, and he assumes the position. He plays with himself a little and starts explaining the rules. "We aren't allowed to touch ourselves, and of course the patrons aren't allowed to touch us here either," he says, using my hand to illustrate. His bosses don't care this week anyway. But it always depends on the police. They had to stop serving liquor for two weeks once because a dancer was caught touching himself. It shot tips to hell.

The cowboy tells me all about his life and loves, his family, his dream of making a name as a photographer. He tells me all about the other dancers who have made porn films and what their real names are. I'm tipping him the whole time, of course, and feeling up his ass where there's just a little damp fur. This will make a book some day.

Dancer

So I barely say anything to him, and right away he starts putting dollar bill after dollar bill in my sox. He's just my type, all serious and soft-spoken. When I can get him to say a few words I find out he's a novelist. I've read one of his books!

Visitor

Then he takes a breath and asks about me. When he finds out I'm a writer, he gets all excited.

Dancer

"I'm an artist. You're an artist," I say. And he's feeling up my ass the whole

time, so he knows how to take charge of a big guy.

Visitor

I give him my card. When he says he comes to New York a couple of times a year, I invite him to stay with me, carefully pointing out that he can dictate the terms.

Dancer

He invites me to visit him in New York! I'm so excited I go limp. So I ask if he can help me out of my little predicament. And he doesn't even hesitate but is all prepared with rubber gloves, which he makes a show of putting on.

Visitor

Then I reach between his legs with one hand and slip a finger into his ass. I slide right in down to the hand no first-date jitters on this cowboy. In short order I have three fingers inside. I ask if it's O.K. to turn my hand. As I do, his cock springs to life.

Dancer

He's so gentle I hardly notice he's inside.

Visitor

I take a leather cock ring out of my pocket and strap him in. Then I step back and let the other patrons enjoy the view. There seem to be quite a few cock hounds in the room. As they converge on him, he goes crazy whacking himself off. After he comes all over his thighs, I check to see he gets respectable tips.

Dancer

I lose sight of my gentleman for a moment. Then he shows up bringing over napkins to help me clean up. The lights come up. Bartenders are urging people to leave. "Meet me outside," I say.

Visitor

He tells me to wait outside. There I find several others apparently also waiting for bar staff. There's a fey young couple from San Francisco and a hot sailor just demobilized after six months at sea. As one of the other go-go boys comes out and gets into his car, I call this fact to the attention of the sailor. From the corner of my eye I'd seen them talking while my cowboy was doing his thing. "Isn't that your date?" I ask. But he says, "No, I'm waiting for the cowboy who put on the big show."

Dancer

Outside the bar, I find a little group chatting. The two kids from San Francisco are saying, "That's who we're waiting for!" As I come up to him my gentleman says, "We're your date." Well, of course, I don't know what he's talking about, but somehow the kids and the sailor think I asked them to wait for me.

Visitor

"Have fun with the sailor," I say, whispering in his ear. "But I mean it about visiting me in New York."

Dancer

And then all of a sudden he gets into a taxi. At least I have his phone number. Now all I have to do is get rid of the kids. I tell the sailor he can crash at my place. He's just my roommate's type.

When you live on the edge, you risk falling off ...

Play Hard

by

JOHN PATRICK

An Erotic Novella

STARbooks Press

"If you cannot trust your teacher, you cannot trust anyone."

PROLOGUE

It all happened so fast. One moment Jeremy was standing near the boat ramp, waiting for a trick, and then the next he was in Nathan's new silver Toyota Camry coupe, on his way to a destiny he could never have imagined.

At first, Jeremy thought Nathan would just want a blowjob and he would be back at the ramp in less than a half an hour. Jeremy knew a secluded place where he often gave his johns oral service and he directed Nathan there. By the time Nathan had turned off the Toyota's engine, Jeremy was already sucking on his cock. After less than five minutes, Nathan was shaking himself mightily and a shudder ran through his wiry body. Jeremy had Nathan's cock in all the way now and Nathan twisted his hips, screwing into Jeremy to get that final inch in his mouth when the burst of pure pleasure shot through Nathan. He threw his head back and came, flooding Jeremy's innards with his cum.

"Wow," Nathan sighed as Jeremy lifted himself off, "you're very good."

Jeremy smiled and wiped the excess cum from his mouth with the back of his hand.

Jeremy sat quietly for a few moments waiting for Nathan to recover and pay him. But Nathan, even though he had come, was still excited. He stroked his cock, which would not go soft, and said, "Come home with me."

"Well, that'd be a hundred, you know. Plus the fifty."

"Yes, yes. But I want to get you in bed."

Jeremy reached over and stroked Nathan's cock. "I'd like that." Nathan's cut cock was a bit longer than average, but it was very thick and had a lovely head. Jeremy thought it would feel great deep in his ass.

On the way to Nathan's house, Jeremy continued stroking Nathan and fondling his balls.

At Nathan's house near the college where he taught art, the professor excused himself to pee, leaving Jeremy in the cluttered living room. Jeremy sat quietly looking about. One painting on a far wall intrigued him enough for him to get up from his chair and scrutinize the picture of the naked boy closely. He turned to find Nathan's fierce little eyes upon him, with an expression in them he could not quite make out, though certainly astonishment was part of it.

"You are interested in art?" Nathan asked, in a slightly annoying tone of incredulity.

"I don't know much about art, but I like him."

"It's a rather deplorable artistic effort really, but I agree with you, he is a beauty."

"Who painted it?"

"It was painted by one of my students, a long time ago." Nathan explained he had been teaching art for ten years. Jeremy sat back down. "I'm not educated, you know. I don't know anything about the things you'd think important," he said at last, in a small voice.

Nathan went over to him. "What's important to me is that mouth of yours.

May I kiss it?"

Jeremy looked into Nathan's eyes. "Yes," Jeremy said ruefully.

And so they kissed; kissing would not come easily to either of them for some time yet, but at least a start had been made.

Nathan pulled away and Jeremy took his hand. "I like you," Jeremy said.

Nathan was not as sure of the boy as he had been a few minutes earlier. That was always a problem for him: the more he found out about his tricks, the less he liked them. And yet, the sweetness of having this boy tell him he liked him got Nathan soaring, as if he had never in his life received a greater compliment. He basked in it until Jeremy's quiet words and tone of slight uncertainty recalled him to the complexities of the situation: "Will you fuck me now?"

Jeremy let Nathan take him by the hand and lead him to the bed. They climbed on and lay side by side on top of the sheets. Nathan's small, soft hands were all over Jeremy, exploring his naked flanks, stroking his loins, tracing his shoulder blades as he wrapped his arms around Jeremy. He inhaled his exciting smell, a mix of cologne and sweat. Jeremy's passions flared and he squirmed with great urgency against Nathan, whose hands found their way to Jeremy's ass, which he cupped and held, curving his hands to fit the meaty firmness of those pleasing twin contours that he had yearned to grab ever since he had first seen them in his headlights. Suddenly a seeking hand slithered down between their bodies and Nathan's prick was being manipulated once again by Jeremy's adept fingers. Jeremy's warm hand squeezed the shaft, then cupped his balls. Nathan tossed his head back and heard himself groan. Kissing Jeremy gratefully so he would know he appreciated the gesture, Nathan begged Jeremy to let him fuck him.

When they broke apart, Jeremy rolled over on his back, spread his thighs. He lay with his eyes closed, loose-limbed and acquiescent. Nathan's eager hands were all over that supple torso, molding the subtle curves along Jeremy's flanks, easily spanning his narrow waist, clamping on those compact, hairless hips while the passionate prostitute quivered and wiggled uncontrollably. Nathan moved down lower on the bed, till his face was only inches from Jeremy's rigid sex. And then, very deliberately, he brought his hand to it, admiring its shape, its length. Jeremy began making tiny whimpering noises, which grew higher in pitch and urgency. Nathan's hot breath created a cool, tingly feeling as he suckled on Jeremy's cock. Wild with excitement, Nathan was strong and aggressive, as he straddled Jeremy's body, sucking the cock, but he could only think in anxious anticipation of fucking the boy. On his knees, he rose up, his tongue sliding up and down from Jeremy's stomach to his chest, and he heard the pleasure Jeremy was feeling. Jeremy's body rose to meet Nathan's, and at impulse a finger entered Jeremy's tight ass, gently massaging the opening. Nathan slowly pushed him open. The deeper Nathan went, the more he could feel a pulling sensation beckoning him to come in. He watched this boy melt in his hands. He greased his fingers and then two fingers were sliding in and out,

slow and steady, going deeper with every thrust. Nathan's heart was racing at the sight and sound of Jeremy's loving it, his face all aglow. Jeremy's feet were waving in the air as Nathan folded back Jeremy's boyishly slim body, raising his ass upward, easily accessible now to Nathan's throbbing, erect prick.

Kneeling between Jeremy's legs, Nathan placed a hand on Jeremy's cock, already oozing pre-cum. Jeremy whimpered through tightly pressed lips as he arched his back and tossed back his head mindlessly from side to side. "Ooooooh! Fuck me! Fuck me," and he spread his legs even farther apart in lewd invitation.

"Oh, yes," Nathan whispered feverishly as he greased the hole. Then he eased himself forward, pressing his erection into Jeremy, moving his hips gently to let Jeremy get used to it. Once Nathan was all the way in, Jeremy tightened his butt muscles, clamping on Nathan, slackening and tightening in rapid spasms that excited Nathan in a way that nothing else had in a long time. Jeremy gave out a long, satisfied groan and arched back, twisting upward at the intensity of the deep penetration. Nathan was in to the hilt, grinding his hips against those smooth, hard mounds. Nathan allowed himself several moments to revel in the intense pleasure but Jeremy soon was stroking himself and wiggling his bottom impatiently, urging Nathan on. Nathan grabbed the boy's slim hips and began fucking him to orgasm.

While his cock was still lodged deep in Jeremy, Nathan asked the boy to stay overnight. He wanted more, and he was willing to pay. Jeremy thought about this news, not sure how he was to react. It didn't shock him, it intrigued him, and he agreed to stay.

In the morning, the older man explained that he worked hard and he played hard. He looked into Jeremy's eyes as he told him how hard he worked and how it was now time for him to play, and he intended to play hard. Jeremy remained still as Nathan spoke to him. Like the inquisitive child he had been years ago, Nathan wondered about how much his new friend could take. But he didn't just wonder; he intended to test the boy's capabilities and expand his limits. That morning, Nathan fucked Jeremy three times. And they were wonderful fucks; Jeremy was the first hustler in Nathan's experience who seemed to actually enjoy anal sex. What Jeremy lacked in finesse, he made up for in enthusiasm. And he couldn't get enough of Nathan's prick.

After that first full day together, Nathan was in love. He asked Jeremy to stay for the rest of the weekend. Then it was the rest of the week. And Jeremy never left.

Nathan called Jeremy "a clean slate," ready for the learned professor to teach in the most complete, intimate way. Nathan had never been presented with an opportunity like this and he was not about to let it go. Jeremy seemed content in Nathan's shadow, in his embrace, being a model for his paintbrush, a still life for his charcoal.

In the beginning, Nathan painted the boy every weekend. He had a

sketchbook in hand wherever they went. Up on the walls of Nathan's studio were charcoal sketches of the boy's eyes, his pouty mouth, the senuous lines of his coltish body.

Jeremy was an eager model and an even more earnest student and, before long, Nathan had convinced the boy to get his GED. Nathan also pulled some strings to get his protege in some classes at the college where he had taught so many students over the last ten years.

Physically, there was a striking similarity about them. Both were trim, Nathan hardly a head taller. Both were dark-haired, with a rough handsomeness to their features. To many they appeared to be brothers. In fact, in mixed company, Nathan encouraged people to accept them as brothers, which amused Jeremy.

One morning about six months into the relationship, after Nathan had fucked him, Jeremy begged Nathan to stay in bed and cuddle a little while before he left for class. Nathan said he would love to but he couldn't, he was already late.

"I only want to be with you," Jeremy told him.

Nathan smiled, taking his hand in his. "Sure, it's the same for me." But Nathan knew, despite what Jeremy said, he would never be enough for the boy. Nathan had begun to suspect Jeremy had been seeing some of his old clients, men he called his "regulars." Nathan would call the house when Jeremy was supposed to be home and get no answer. And Jeremy was tired a lot of the time, so their sex, which used to be a daily ritual, became sporadic. Nathan quietly accepted his fate, at the same time calculating how he would exact his revenge on the boy he loved more than anyone he had ever known.

ONE

Jeremy got into the passenger seat of Carl's pick-up truck, with Larry in between. Jeremy could feel Larry's thigh pushed up against his own. The rest of the guys piled into Greg's old Cadillac. They drove down Ocean Boulevard. The streets were deserted; there wasn't another vehicle in sight. Jeremy was happy to be with his old fuck buddies. They partied hard and played hard, and Jeremy needed to relax and to momentarily escape from the tension at home with Nathan. He was looking forward to getting to Carl's place and "fucking his brains out," as he liked to say. He wasn't worried about who would be having sex with him. At this point he didn't care; he just wanted to fuck without any problems.

Carl was driving slowly and with deliberation so that he wouldn't start weaving. They had left the Showbar early because Carl was feeling his booze. Still, he insisted on driving. They eased under the overpass and stopped as the light was changing from yellow to red.

Jeremy heard the motorcycle pull up beside the truck before he looked to see who it was. He turned his head and locked eyes with the stud, who had dark hair and wore a black leather jacket. The stud idled beside them, his legs straddling a big red Harley. Jeremy could feel his prick jump at the sight. The stud returned

the gleam of excitement in Jeremy's eyes.

"Where you going?" the apparition in leather yelled up to Jeremy.

"A party. You want to come?"

The stud said, "Yeah, I'd love to *come*," putting lewd emphasis on the last word.

"Okay, then, follow us," Jeremy shouted back. Carl was laughing and Larry was rubbing Jeremy's thigh. "Now you've done it," Larry said.

"I hope so," Jeremy chuckled.

Jeremy watched the stud dismount and approach. They eyed each other openly. The stud was taller and even more studly than Jeremy had imagined. The stranger followed Jeremy to Carl's house. Greg had beaten Carl to the house by several minutes, but there was no sign of him and his four friends. But candles were already lit and music came through the speakers as Jeremy and the stud settled onto the couch and started kissing and feeling each other all over. Carl was having an intimate conversation with Larry. They had been lovers for three years, but enjoyed entertaining, in every way. One of their roommates in the huge house, Patty, who managed Carl's florist shop in South Beach, emerged from the back, all wired from a long day at the shop. She and Carl and Larry disappeared into the kitchen, presumably to prepare some food for the group, and get caught up on the business of the day. Carl hadn't felt well enough to go in to the shop at all, which was happening with greater regularity these days.

Jeremy and the stud were staring at each other. Under the jacket that the stud removed, he was wearing a tight black T-shirt. He had incredible pecs, and Jeremy's eyes were riveted to them. The stud chuckled, sensing Jeremy's intense desire for him. "My name's Joe," he said, lifting his hand to Jeremy's flushed cheek. Jeremy's face was pretty, with dark eyes and high cheekbones. Joe was not handsome, but he wasn't ugly either. And Jeremy thought he had the hottest body he'd seen in months. Joe stood and allowed the boy's eyes to rove over his body while he undid his jeans. He left the jeans gaping open, stopping because he heard Carl enter the room. Jeremy ignored Carl and reached up to tug on Joe's pants. Joe held Jeremy's hands, still watching Carl, who by now was moving slowly, unsteadily up the stairs.

Joe shrugged and let Jeremy continue. Joe had been a little wary about what this was all about, but he soon relaxed enough to open himself to the excitement of Jeremy sucking his cock.

He watched as Jeremy sensually caressed the length of his enormous prick. Jeremy could sense that Joe would have preferred to stay right there, fuck him, and be gone, but the knowledge that there were others in the house excited Jeremy and he wanted to share his fantastic find with his pals, whose knowledge of each other's desires, tastes, and needs could be teased, flirted with, and exploited for incredible passion. Jeremy enjoyed playing with desire more than succumbing to expectation. And his sexuality differed from lover to lover,

bottoming for one, topping for another.

Upstairs, in Carl's "playroom," they were all rather coupled up, and everyone was making love. Jeremy could hear all the moans all around and everyone was happy. It was all overwhelming for Joe, who thought he was just going to fuck Jeremy, without an audience. But Jeremy lured him deeper into the room. Near total darkness. Quiet sounds. Breathing. Sucking sounds. Quiet moans. Lovemaking sounds. Bodies were coming into focus. Couples pressing against each other, one barely discernible from the next. Gingerly, Joe stepped farther into the room, allowing his eyes to grow accustomed to the darkness. Jeremy dragged Joe onto the bed. Once on the huge bed, which was really two double beds pushed together with a plastic cover, it was easy for all of them to touch one another. The men were excited by Joe's arrival. Most of them had already been lovers with each other at one time or another. They all knew one another's body very well. With all this caressing and licking and kissing going on, Jeremy and Joe became aroused and joined in, getting a daisy chain going. Soon everyone was licking and sucking and being licked and sucked at the same time.

Before long, everyone was coming in waves and waves going around the circle. It was like thunder rolling through the mountains, with the sound of orgasms building and subsiding, and echoing from one guy to another along the chain. Joe quickly picked up on Jeremy's attitude, that of latecomers, only playing for stimulation, as a prelude to harder stuff. Jeremy began to pay his complete attention to Joe, and everyone was completely caught up in Jeremy's sexual current, swept up in the utter decadence Jeremy always emitted. Joe watched in fascination as Jeremy sucked cock after cock, before swiftly returning to Joe's, then Joe's body began moving with Jeremy's, flesh pressed to flesh, surging towards ecstasy. Even while Jeremy sucked other guy's cocks, he gazed into Joe's eyes, and Joe began pressing and rubbing Jeremy's thighs, finally to part them. Jeremy was letting himself relax beneath Joe's commanding attention, and finally Jeremy let the others' cocks go.

Jeremy's skin was flawlessly smooth and tanned, obviously exciting Joe. Joe kissed and licked the skin, starting at the navel, working his way down to Jeremy's erection, then to the ass. First lightly and then more insistently, Joe opened Jeremy up, first with his tongue, then with his fingers. Someone handed him the lube and Joe leaned back, applied it, and then Jeremy took Joe deep and hard into him. Jeremy held onto two guy's cocks while Joe fucked him, squeezing the cocks as Joe's assault got going.

After a few moments of this, Jeremy changed his mind and got on top. He pushed his hips into Joe and kissed him roughly, drawing deeper and deeper breaths from the stud beneath him. Being on top, Jeremy had the power to grind in even harder, and as he began to suck the others again, he picked up more speed, with more steam and intensity.

Joe followed his movements, dancing wildly with the boy above him. They lifted and thrusted against each other. It was an incredible show: slapping and

bumping and grinding. Jeremy couldn't stand it, he wanted desperately to come, and he jumped up and down in a frenzied rush for his own release. He fucked and pumped and fucked and pumped until Joe was moaning and Jeremy finally came with a scream of pleasure.

The others stood over them jerking off, coming one after the other on Jeremy's back as Jeremy lowered himself on top of Joe, who was finishing inside Jeremy. They kissed as they others left the room.

Jeremy and Joe lay side by side regaining their breath. They kissed again, perfunctorily, then rolled to opposite sides of the bed. Finally they fell asleep, relaxed and satisfied.

TWO

Jeremy woke up first, with a glorious hard-on. Joe was just surfacing. Joe spread out on his back. Jeremy was turned on and very pleased to have such a stud in his bed, to do with as he wanted. Jeremy mounted Joe and started rubbing the stud's cock against his ass, trying to stimulate him into more sex. Jeremy was insatiable, and from the way Joe's cock was swelling he would soon be ready to comply. While Jeremy sucked his nipples, Joe plunged his fingers up Jeremy's ass, and then out to the tip and then back in again, and out again, and in again.

Joe was breathing heavily as Jeremy sucked his nipples harder and harder. Joe began to moan, and Jeremy could feel him arching up beneath, ready to start the fuck. Jeremy pulled up and applied lube to the now erect cock. As he mounted it and impaled himself with it, he shook and shuddered in tremor after tremor. When it finally was all the way in, Joe's delight was signaled by a long, deep sigh. But now it was Joe who controlled the rhythm. He held Jeremy's ass as he lowered the boy's body up and down on his cock. Jeremy let his excitement build up until he was almost verging on pain; he concentrated on jerking himself off, and then, with a final exquisite jolt, he came ecstatically on Joe's pecs.

They lay side by side, regaining some composure. Joe, who had not come, pulled his cock from Jeremy's ass. He excused himself and left for the bathroom. Jeremy, dazzled, watched his new lover in retreat and smiled.

Joe walked into the bathroom stark naked with his cock dripping with lube. Larry was brushing his teeth. Joe ignored Larry and stood over the toilet. He pissed like a racehorse, without skipping a beat. Larry could not believe this, the huge, beefy, leather-clad stud Jeremy had cruised the night before and brought into his house was relieving himself in his bathroom, without even a "good mornin'"! Having taken the horny bitch Patty to her room and fucked her, Larry had missed Jeremy and Joe's fuckfest, but he had heard all about it from the other guys as they left the house. Carl had missed it too, having passed out in his bedroom. So over breakfast Carl and Larry had conspired as to how they were going to get the lovers to do an encore just for them. Now Larry was staring at the monster, lube-coated dick as the piss streamed from it. No wonder everyone

was talking, Larry thought. Each of the others had only sampled it while they were in the daisy chain, before the cock disappeared up Jeremy's ass and they couldn't stop talking about it. Damn, Larry said, they were probably *still* talking about it!

Larry wiped the toothpaste from his mouth and moved closer to Joe. Joe gave Larry a sidelong glance, then looked back down at his cock as he finished his business. He shook the last of the piss from it and stood back, in effect inviting Larry to move closer. Larry dropped the seat of the toilet and sat down. "Now I know what everyone was talking about," he said, tentatively running his fingers along the shaft.

"Oh?"

"Yeah, you're the talk of the town by now."

"Is that what you're gonna do, talk?"

Joe's directness tickled Larry and he chuckled while he inspected the formidable equipment. His fingers toyed with the mammoth ball sac, while his other hand began stroking the shaft.

Larry took a washcloth from the rack and wiped the cock clean. Then he began licking the cock. As the cock-licking was gaining momentum, Joe began panting erratically with short, quick intakes of breath. His abdomen was rolling in wave after visible wave. He was moaning as his cock was being serviced with diligence and relish. Larry considered himself sexually "open," and he seemed to be drawn toward guys who claimed they were straight. His favorite saying was, "Mix a straight guy with a little alcohol and you get a bisexual."

Soon the straight-appearing stud's cock was glistening and swollen with anticipation, and Joe held Larry back and began slapping the thick member against Larry's hungry lips. This was just the kind of thing that got Larry going big time. Joe started using the thick head of his dick to tease Larry, whose mouth strained to suck more of it in. Finally, Joe held Larry's head with both hands and began face-fucking him.

After the cock plunged into Larry's throat, with one deep thrust and groan, Joe began pumping his dick in and out of the man's wide-open, wet hole, thrusting the shaft all the way in and then all the way out. The shaft was becoming juicier and more delicious with every retraction. Joe's hard ass cheeks tensed and then shook each time he was all the way in.

As Joe began a furious rhythm of in and out, in and out, in and out, suddenly Jeremy appeared in the doorway. He watched for a few moments, delighted to catch Larry in the act in the broad daylight, then entered the bathroom. Sexual fire was flashing. In a frenzy of movement, Jeremy was on his knees and he and Larry were sharing the cock. Joe was beyond caring who did or was doing what. This was sex and they were sex machines, pure and simple. Joe gave in to the luxury of being catered to. He didn't have to do anything but feel, submit to the ecstasy. Joe felt incredibly worshipped. He was riding the sexual waves, remembering Jeremy's tight ass, and he came. It was such an astounding

explosion that it caught both Larry and Jeremy off-guard. They each stroked the cock, finally to squeeze the last of the cum from it onto Jeremy's cheek.

Slowly and with deliberation, Jeremy led Joe back to the bedroom. Larry was in hot pursuit. Joe lay back on the bed, ready to accept more adulation from his new young lovers. He seemed to be amused by Larry, who seemed to be even more enamored with his cock than Jeremy was.

Larry's charm was well-rehearsed. He knew exactly how to attract other people's sexual interest, and he was incomparably seductive, a dark-haired, brown-eyed beauty. He would flash glints of passion, but then retreat. He wasn't easy, but he was incredibly alluring. Jeremy was immediately hooked the first time they met at a party. They had sex together right away. It was all-out surrender, unbridled give-and-take pleasure on Jeremy's part, and it wasn't like any other one-night stand Jeremy had ever experienced. There were no boundaries, no hesitations, no holding back. It wasn't piecemeal sex, it was a banquet. The idea that Larry was fucking everything in sight, male, female, transsexual, only added to his allure.

Jeremy gave Larry everything he wanted and Larry did the same. They were involved in pure passion, Larry fucking Jeremy all night, all morning, and half the next day. Larry let Jeremy bring him to orgasm after orgasm. His sensitivity was ultra high. They were completely attuned to each other, and their sex was incredible.

When they finally finished, they both looked at each other with amazement and embarrassment. They both had lovers and it would never do that they fall in love.

Jeremy left that day feeling fabulously well fucked but also a little bewildered. He had found the right sexual match in the wrong person. Destiny had thrown him a boomerang. Through the course of a year, Jeremy had come to own Larry sexually. He could do whatever he wanted, as long as Larry agreed. This made Jeremy very happy for a while, even though the "relationship" was clandestine. After all, Larry was Carl's lover and Jeremy had Nathan. But the secrecy was in itself a kind of kick, leaving room for pursuing others. For Jeremy, the ideal situation would be that he could do whatever he wanted but that Larry would be his and his alone. This, of course, was absurd. Larry, like Jeremy, was young and adventuresome, incapable of fidelity. But as the months progressed, they fucked occasionally and Jeremy thought he was getting what he wanted. He thought he was calling the shots, but he was actually playing out the role that Larry had assigned him, and the entire affair was being directed by Larry's dark needs.

So for months they carried on discreetly, Larry pleasing Carl, in exchange for a place to stay, Jeremy pleasing Nathan for the same reason, and more.

But now Jeremy was seeing a new Larry, a Larry he didn't know existed. Larry, the bisexual, was actually on his knees, begging Joe to fuck him! Jeremy had never seen Larry in this position; he thought he was an exclusive top. But,

apparently, confronted by a cock the size of Joe's, all bets were off. Jeremy fell in line, getting down shoulder to shoulder with Larry and inviting Joe to have his fun with both of them.

Over the next few minutes, it seemed Joe was flaunting his prowess, fucking one ass, then the other, with equal vigor. But Jeremy wanted more and he scrambled under Larry so that Larry could fuck him while Joe continued to screw his ass. It was so rare an occurrence that Larry found himself in the middle of such a fuck sandwich, he came almost immediately, but he was so turned on that he kept his cock in Jeremy and was able to resume after several moments.

The games they played had seldom been as successful as this one had obviously become. Earlier, Larry cursed himself for leaving the party and screwing Patty, but now at least he didn't have to share Joe with anyone but Jeremy.

THREE

Early in the morning several days later, Jeremy jumped out of bed. He felt terribly excited. He felt that some radical break in his life would soon take place. But then, perhaps because so few really significant things actually happened to him, he was always inclined to expect some radical break in his existence when something really did happen. He went to classes as usual, but cut the economics class late in the afternoon. He had made up his mind to pay Joe a visit.

When he was fucked by Larry he would occasionally feel pangs of guilt, but he tried to submerge them. He thought he could get used to anything that is, he resigned himself, accepting things rather than really getting used to them. Sex was his escape, making everything bearable. He took refuge in the adulterous affair he was having with Larry, and occasional sex with others.

Of course, it would have been best not to meet Larry at all. But that was out of the question. When something drew Jeremy, it really drew him, cock hard and pointing.

Sex with Nathan was rare now, accompanied by remorse, tears, cursing but, occasionally, even ecstasy.

Jeremy experienced moments of intoxication, when he would hit the rock-bottom of abjection, but these thoughts came few and far between, and he continued to pursue Larry. He began to enjoy the soiled feeling sex with Larry left. The sex was raw, sometimes filthy. There was none of the talk, the curious professor/pupil talk, that occupied his sex with Nathan. They would have a discussion of the beautiful lives of artists and poets and adapt this to the demands of the moment, whatever they might be. When Jeremy was fucked by Nathan, it was always leisurely, ending safely in a rapturous embrace.

On Saturday nights, the orgies became a ritual. On those nights, Jeremy might or might not participate. He would let Larry enjoy himself with the others, and he would sit and visit with Carl, who had pretty much stopped participating in the orgies. Jeremy had spent some pleasant moments with Carl but they had

never lasted, somehow or other always becoming overcast with gloom. Jeremy knew Carl suspected that he was abhorrent to him. To dispel this, if Jeremy had had enough to drink, and was especially horny, he would allow Carl to give him a blowjob. Then, when everyone else had gone, Jeremy would climb in bed with Larry.

In fact, although his sensuality was heightened by his affair with Larry, Jeremy had to admit he never really came when he was with Larry. It was Larry who came and Jeremy who kept control. Later, out of Larry's presence, Jeremy came.

With Joe, however, Jeremy was desperate to come.

Joe was a house painter and Jeremy found out where he was working and over the past week he would pass the house he was painting. He would not stop; he did not want to bother Joe before his crew, but he would slow down and sit in his car at the curb hoping to get a glimpse of his new infatuation. Occasionally, Joe would spot him and wave. Jeremy would wave back, but immediately leave.

But now Jeremy was not going to leave. And he was prepared to wait all evening if necessary, until Joe arrived home. Joe pulled in the driveway, parking behind Jeremy's car. "I happened to be in the neighborhood," Jeremy said.

Joe grunted an unintelligible response, but it seemed he was leading the way to the front door.

"Can I get you a beer?" Joe said once they were inside the house. It was an austere but clean place, with cheap furniture and no pictures on the walls. Jeremy smiled, thinking how different it was from Nathan's house, where every square inch of wall was decorated with a work of art.

"Yeah, sure," Jeremy answered, following Joe into the kitchen.

"You spend a lot of time in this neighborhood, don't you?"

"I do."

"I've seen you, you know. I wave, but you don't stop, you just keep on going."

"I'm sorry. I wasn't sure."

"C'mon," Joe said, sweeping Jeremy into his arms.

They kissed, passionately, but briefly. Jeremy's hands moved to Joe's crotch, and he began struggling with the zipper. Joe helped him, and Jeremy was on his knees as the huge cock sprang out.

"You have too much energy for me," Joe said, leaning back submissively, letting Jeremy suck.

"Okay then," Jeremy said, stroking the insides of Joe's thighs. All he wanted to do now was to satisfy his own hunger, the hunger between his legs, by jerking off while he sucked Joe. Joe was fine with that. He let Jeremy remove his pants and get to work. Jeremy was good, enthusiastic, and soon Joe was close to coming, but he held back. "Let's go to bed," Joe said.

On his stomach on Joe's bed, Jeremy felt as though his body were being split at the seams and his insides ripped apart as the indomitable dick began to plough

on relentlessly. One thing, however, Jeremy knew, he would never be the same again. Gradually the pain turned to pleasure and he began to enjoy once again the feel of this mighty cock deep within him.

- - -

Now, occasionally, when Nathan was teaching a night class, Jeremy went to Joe's and got fucked by candlelight, and with the rays of the moon filtering through the bamboo shades. It was accompanied by music, hard-driving disco that Jeremy loved.

As the affair progressed, they got to know each other better. Joe was certainly not Nathan Jeremy could never have a long-term relationship with someone so common. But their affair seemed to calm Jeremy, to make him want to heal his relationship with Nathan. Jeremy did not want to give Nathan up, and the fact that he had a lover on the side and a house where he could retreat to indulge himself with Larry and the others seemed to satisfy him. What Nathan did not know would never hurt him. And Jeremy did want to hurt Nathan.

Joe lived alone and said he liked it that way. He rented a small bungalow on the outskirts of town. Jeremy would drive by and if the truck Joe drove for work was outside, he would stop. This seemed to be okay with Joe; he always seemed pleased to see Jeremy, to let Jeremy suck his cock. The routine never varied: Jeremy would nuzzle his nose into Joe's crotch and then use his tongue to lick the length and breadth of the mighty cock. Before long, the pre-cum was flowing and Jeremy was swallowing the nectar. His tongue was working its way around Joe's prick. He flicked the sensitive head with the tip of his tongue and Joe's body jerked. Jeremy kept flicking as Joe was beginning to buck more and more wildly, until Joe was shaking out of control. Jeremy removed his mouth as Joe came in a rage of uncontrolled lust.

Jeremy left Joe in his puddle of cum, promising to come back when he had more time and let Joe fuck him.

But as the weeks went on, Jeremy sensed Joe was losing interest in him. Then he saw why Larry's old white Mustang was parked in the driveway late one afternoon.

Jeremy could almost taste Joe's cum as he sat in his car, imagining his ex-lover Larry giving Joe head. He jerked off in the car, then headed for home.

When he arrived home, the phone was ringing. It was Joe. "Why didn't you come in?" Joe asked.

"I didn't think you'd want any more company."

"Shit," was all Joe said. And then he hung up.

Later that night, Carl called. He was worried; he hadn't heard from Larry. Jeremy told him not to fuss, that he had seen Larry at the bar and that everything was okay. He made a lunch date with Carl for the next day.

Nathan entered the bedroom. Jeremy was still awake, watching the news. Nathan stood beside the bed, looking at Jeremy the way he did when he sketched the boy. He liked to sketch Jeremy while the boy was reading in his

overstuffed armchair. They had fun together for a time, and Jeremy thought Nathan was beautiful in his way. An exotic beauty. But Nathan's beauty was literally impenetrable. He liked to be adored and caressed, but he didn't like to be fucked. But Jeremy never stopped trying. "I'm just a fuck for you," Jeremy said.

"Do you really think being fucked by you would change my life?"

"It would make it better between us," Jeremy kept saying. He wanted variety. He enjoyed the guys he got to fuck at Carl and Larry's orgies, especially Greg, and he wanted to try it with Nathan. But Nathan had had a bad experience years before and anal sex was painful for him.

"No," Nathan said. "I don't think *anything* would make it better between us. Besides, I'm just another detour for you."

"You think I'm nothing but a little whore," Jeremy replied disgustedly. At first Jeremy's whoring had not affected their relationship, but eventually Nathan seemed to lose interest.

Jeremy grew tired of playing games with Nathan. Nathan had too many sexual hang-ups, and ultimately Jeremy thought Nathan was just like everyone else; he just wanted to fuck him.

But tonight Nathan did not even want to do that. When Jeremy reached up to pull him down on the bed, Nathan backed off. "Please don't. I'm tired," Nathan said.

The next morning, Nathan stood over the bed, fully dressed. The same look was on his face as the night before, but by now it seemed entirely out of character. He was actually staring at Jeremy with sexual interest. From total repression to seduction, like the click of a light switch. Nathan leaned across the bed and caressed Jeremy's shoulder. Jeremy moved his cheek against Nathan's hand, looking for affection, like a cat. Nathan pinched his earlobe and slipped his forefinger into Jeremy's ear canal. It was a suggestive penetration, one that was not lost on Jeremy. It was a little thing Nathan did when they were first together.

"Oh, Nathan," Jeremy sighed encouragingly. On his lips was a very coy smile.

Nathan took the boy's hand and brought it to the bulge in his trousers. He put his hand under Jeremy's chin and lifted. He looked for Jeremy's reaction, but Jeremy's eyes were closed. But his hands were busy unzipping his lover's pants.

"I'm sorry about last night," Nathan said.

It was his standard line, and Jeremy ignored it. Besides, he had his mouth full.

FOUR

With the taste of Nathan's cum still in his mouth, Jeremy drove down to Siesta Beach to meet Carl for a late lunch. They met at Carl's florist shop and then strolled to The Pelican, an expensive seafood restaurant perched on pilings over the bay. The restaurant was romantic and it was Carl's favorite; he was also

picking up the tab. They each had grouper, blackened, and shared a bottle of the white house wine, not that Carl needed anything more to drink. He admitted to Jeremy he now started to drink when he first got up in the morning: "Just a Screwdriver." Jeremy knew if it weren't for Patty, there would be no business at all any more.

"I'm so envious of your relationship with Nathan," Carl said.

"Nathan's special."

"You love him, don't you?"

"In my way, I guess. He's my rock. I owe everything to Nathan, you know. He got off me off drugs, out of hustling, into college."

"He's a good teacher, too, eh?" Carl asked, a lewd smile on his face.

Jeremy chuckled. "No, not in that way. I've taught him about sex; he's taught me about art, about history..." Jeremy paused, choosing his words carefully. Finally, he finished, "...about life."

Carl nodded, and looked out the window. "I know Larry's sneaking around. I never mind it when he does it at the house, with his pals, but now he's going out and not coming back until he's good and ready."

"Oh?" Jeremy could act stupid when he had to.

"Honey, I'm worried."

"I wouldn't be. I think I know who he's seeing and it won't last. You just have to give him time, time to wear it out."

"Who is it?"

"I think it's that house painter I picked up a month ago."

"The red Harley?"

"Yeah."

"The big cock?"

"Yeah."

Carl shook his head sadly. Jeremy thought about going on, trying to explain the incomprehensible to Carl, but he knew it was useless. He was happy to have a nice lunch and to listen while Carl raged on about the injustice of it all.

"I'll be okay," Carl said later, with seeming resolve, but Jeremy still accompanied him to the door of the restaurant. Carl tottered in a remarkably straight line outside to his car.

Jeremy returned to the table, sipping coffee and watching the daylight thin out toward dusk. He was feeling relaxed and very horny.

All during their lunch, Jeremy had flirted outrageously with the waiter, a cute blond boy Jeremy's age. After Carl left, Jeremy wanted to stay on. He was giddy from the wine and from the knowledge that he had shared his secret about Larry and Joe. He wondered just where all this would lead. He felt a perverse satisfaction from having revealed to Carl what he knew. Larry deserved to get into trouble for this one, Jeremy reasoned. If it hadn't been for Larry, Joe would still be fucking him. He was hot, he felt sexy, and he wanted to be serviced, and who better to do that than the waiter, whose name was Gary. He asked Gary if

he was going off his shift.

Gary said he was, but that he lived with his parents. Jeremy smiled and told the boy to follow him. Nathan had a late class again and what he wanted to do with Gary wouldn't take long.

In the car on the way to the house, Jeremy played with his cock. His cock seemed to be throbbing all the time these days. He loved that feeling of being alive and excited and always on the edge of desire. He loved the feeling of being turned on all the time.

They clung to each other as they entered the house. "You live alone?" Gary asked hesitantly.

"Hell, no, man. I'm just a student for chrissakes."

They went directly to the bedroom. Jeremy moved his thigh between Gary's legs and started rubbing his slender body against the boy's. Jeremy was getting himself ready for sex. He was like a bitch in heat. They kissed. Gary went to the bathroom while Jeremy pulled off his sneakers and jeans, and tossed them in a corner of the bedroom.

Rarely did he have sex with anyone in Nathan's house, but tonight he felt safe. When Gary emerged from the bathroom, Jeremy was on the bed, nude, playing with himself. Gary was also naked, and when he dropped the towel from his hand, Jeremy smiled at the size and quality of his erection.

Jeremy maneuvered his body to the edge of the bed and Gary rubbed the head of his cock over Jeremy's lips. The smell and taste of this freshly scrubbed youth was turning Jeremy on. Gary kept on rubbing, and Jeremy was responding by kissing and licking the boy's cock head.

"Oh, man, that's nice. Suck me for a while," Gary murmured. Jeremy began to suck and to kneading the tender flesh, pulling it, nibbling it, squeezing it with his lips. Jeremy's own cock was filling with sensation, swelling with warmth, but Gary's cock was on fire. Soon Gary was breathing fast. He lunged his cock into Jeremy's mouth. Jeremy let his mouth be fucked. Gary retracted and then plunged in again. He picked up speed, jabbing quickly into the tight hole. Jeremy held onto the tight buns, squeezed the muscles. Gary humped Jeremy's mouth, wildly screaming, "I'm coming," as Jeremy sucked, and Gary's cock discharged its load.

"Oh, fuck," Gary sighed as his cock slipped from Jeremy's mouth. "I wanted to come while you were fucking me." Gary stroked Jeremy's cock.

"You still can."

Gary dropped to the bed next to Jeremy. Jeremy rolled over, his heart pounding like mad. He straddled Gary and began licking his asshole. He licked and lapped and swirled his tongue all the way up and around. Jeremy felt delicious satisfaction; Gary's asshole felt so good. Gary lifted up and looked back at Jeremy. He had a twinkle in his eye. "I want to suck it before you stick it in there."

"Okay," said Jeremy, scrambling around to put his erection in Gary's face.

He didn't need any more stimulation, but he wanted to please. It was odd how much fun this was, having sex with a stranger in his lover's bed, taking a stranger's load in the exact spot where he had taken Nathan's just hours before.

Now the cute blond wanted to be fucked! It was all so unexpected, and therefore all the more thrilling.

Gary was an adequate cocksucker, but Jeremy was impatient anxious to fuck the youthful waiter. Jeremy went back to the ass, sucking on the lad's nuts, licking them, kissing them, then sliding his tongue between them while running his fingers along the crack of Gary's ass.

"That feels so good," Gary moaned, gliding his cum-slicked boner along Jeremy's cheek as he rocked back and forth . Jeremy shot a glance up at his face and saw his eyes were closed, the expression on his face rapturous. "Fuck me now, Jeremy."

Jeremy was at last ready. Gary had gotten the cock slick with saliva and Jeremy added some more, then some lube from the jar on the nightstand. His cock now slid into Gary's hungry ass easily, all the way down to Jeremy's pubic hairs. Jeremy slipped into an easy rhythm. In and out. Inch after inch. Gary's fist slid up and down his shaft as Jeremy fell into him and he messed the bed. "Jesus!" Gary groaned.

His forehead beaded with sweat, Jeremy was getting close. His thrusts grew shorter and shorter until only a little more than an inch of his generous eight-incher was sliding between Gary's ass lips with each lunge. Jeremy shuddered and his bush stayed glued to Gary's ass as he came. Gary sighed as he felt Jeremy's load coat his insides.

Suddenly, Nathan came into the room, his eyes scanning like a hawk, coming to rest on the bed. He made a kind of coughing splutter, but failed to apologize for his untimely entrance.

Jeremy's cock went soft and he rolled off Gary.

"Don't let me stop you," said the professor, his voice a few octaves higher than normal. He moved closer. It was obvious he had no intention of leaving.

Gary rolled over; his embarrassment was as obvious as Jeremy's, but his cock remained hard. So gloriously hard, in fact, that Nathan could not ignore it. He leaned across Jeremy to stroke it. Jeremy turned to Gary and their eyes met; Jeremy could see the bewilderment in the young waiter's eyes. Nathan's free hand now groped for Jeremy's shrunken cock. Jeremy shuddered as his cold fingers teased his groin.

Nathan chuckled. "Whoever said that 'A bird in the hand is worth two in the bush' obviously never had the privilege of holding two such prime cocks at one time."

Nathan's mood stunned Jeremy. This was the first time he had involved himself in any extra-marital activities; but then this was the first time Jeremy had entertained a trick in their own bed.

"And did you find this one at the boat ramp?"

"No, he's a waiter at the Pelican."

"And he came home to get his tip?"

"Something like that," Jeremy said, clinging to Gary, still not sure what Nathan had in mind.

Nathan let go of the cocks and stood up. Slowly, he began removing his clothes, but he said nothing more. Jeremy took Gary in his arms and began to kiss him. Gary was reluctant at first, but Jeremy began stroking his cock and the waiter succumbed. Jeremy continued to ignore his lover as he forced Gary to lean back against the headboard and he attended to the waiter's lovely hard-on.

In the silence of the room, the grating sound of Nathan's zipper being released seemed almost deafening to Jeremy. Nathan's body was trembling and his eyes were starting to mist over. His trousers dropped unceremoniously to the floor.

Now Nathan's slim, artistic fingers coursed over his lover's body, sending shivers of excitement racing from Jeremy's groin to his brain. Jeremy felt the heat of his body as Nathan leaned over him. Nathan straddled Jeremy's inert body and crouched on all fours, like a cheetah ready to spring. Jeremy got into position, his head in Gary's lap, his ass high in the air.

Nathan climbed on the bed and began to stroke his lover's smooth skin. But soon he was beginning to tire of playful pets and sensuous caresses. He took the grease from the nightstand and started to lubricate Jeremy's asshole. The sighs of ecstasy that emanated from Jeremy's lips soon turned to howls of frenzied pain as the fingers were replaced by Nathan's thick, throbbing prick. Gary's eyes were wide open, obviously enjoying the sight of Nathan's cock entering Jeremy. Finally Jeremy's squeals of agony changed to sobs of satisfaction as Nathan's formidable dick reached its full thrust. Jeremy went back to sucking Gary and Gary's eyes began turning hazy and contented sighs began escaping from his lips.

"Okay, kid, I've warmed it up for you," Nathan said suddenly to Gary, lifting off his lover.

Surprised, Gary grinned and took over. His first lunge made Jeremy bite hard into the pillow, which was wet with his sweat and saliva. The waiter's thrusting was brutal and Jeremy cried out in agony. Nathan watched the initial entry with great interest, then somehow managed to squeeze his head between the mattress and Jeremy's hips, and he was soon sucking on Jeremy's prick as though it were something out of a candy shop, all the while working his own dick with his hand. It became a tripartite explosion as they climaxed together. Jeremy's cum was being hungrily devoured by Nathan in his confined quarters.

Sweating profusely, Gary pulled out roughly and went to the bathroom, followed closely by Nathan. Jeremy lay in the tangled sheets, stunned by what had just transpired. He heard Nathan showing Gary out and then his lover locking up for the night. By the time Nathan came back to bed, Jeremy was asleep.

Jeremy slept fitfully spending most of the night on his stomach. In the morning, he had an ache in his ass. Gary had not been gentle. And his head ached as well. Jeremy wasn't looking forward to breakfast, but Nathan had already left the house without saying goodbye.

- - -

Jeremy did not go to class; he spent the day soaking in the Jacuzzi Nathan had installed off the sundeck behind the house.

Nathan called shortly after noon and told Jeremy they were going out for dinner.

"Where are we going?" Jeremy asked when Nathan got on the freeway.

"Your favorite place," Nathan said. He had been quiet, distant. Jeremy knew he was upset about the previous night, but he refused to open the discussion.

"I don't have a favorite place," Jeremy countered.

"Couldn't prove it by me."

Nathan had called ahead and found out Gary was waiting on tables that night. Nathan booked a table in his station.

When they neared the Pelican, Jeremy turned to his lover and begged, "Please, don't do this."

"You sure?"

"Yes. I'm sorry it happened."

"Will it ever happen again?"

"No."

"Okay," Nathan said, driving past the Pelican without stopping.

Instead, they dined at the Texas Longhorn. It had been months since Nathan had enjoyed a steak as much. He raved about the service, the low prices. He even liked the cheap house wine.

But Jeremy really knew why Nathan was so happy: Jeremy had again been shamed into submission.

On the way home, they stopped to see Nathan's mother at the rest home. Nathan had been a "bonus" baby and his mother was nearly forty when he was born. His father, who was also an artist, was even older and had passed away when Nathan was only twelve. Suffering from Alzheimer's, Rose rarely remembered Jeremy, so it was a surprise to her to see him. Rose reminded Jeremy of his own grandmother, the only person in the family he had any feelings for, so visits to Rose were always happy times. Jeremy didn't mind the repetitious discussions of Rose's prized shell collection, part of which remained with her at the home. She had been president of the Shell Club and old friends would bring her new finds so there was always something new to talk about. "The variety in shells is one of the things that make it fascinating," Nathan said. At one point Nathan even took some shells to one of his beginner classes and related them to studies of symmetry, shapes and life cycles.

It was one of Rose's better nights and she gave Jeremy one of her prized shells and a kiss on the cheek. "Shells were the first good luck charms," the old

lady told the boy. "This is for luck."

Nathan beamed as Jeremy kissed his mother goodbye. It was at times like this that Nathan was proud the boy had responded so well to him, wanted to stay with him. But Nathan knew he had to leave Jeremy a lot of slack.

Still, bringing strangers into their bed was a new twist that Nathan did not want to deal with again. But he was proud of himself tonight; he thought he had handled it well, and the fact that Jeremy's ass ached after it was over was, in Nathan's view, poetic justice.

Now, as they went to bed, Nathan asked Jeremy how he was feeling. Jeremy had been dreading this moment all night. With Nathan feeling happy, Jeremy knew sex would be on the menu, and the thought of a fuck distressed him. But Nathan respected Jeremy and his pain. He only wanted Jeremy to service him orally. In the darkness, he stood before the boy nude, running his fingers through Jeremy's soft hair, murmuring to him as Jeremy sucked. Jeremy was concentrating hard on bringing Nathan off as quickly as possible, and he did not hear Nathan tell him, over and over, just how much, how very much, he loved him, and how he knew Jeremy would always do the right thing in the end.

The quality of the oral service was superb; Nathan came in a few moments, holding Jeremy's head deep into his crotch as he ejaculated. "Oh, man, you're good," Nathan told the boy as he pulled away and rushed to the bathroom.

Jeremy lay back, exhausted. In minutes, with Nathan's cum still coating his lips and spread across his cheek, Jeremy fell fast asleep in Nathan's warm embrace and dreamt of Joe fucking Larry.

FIVE

A week later, Jeremy was shocked when the radical break in his life that he had felt was coming finally arrived. It was over the long Thanksgiving weekend that Larry drowned in the Gulf. He had been sailing with Carl. It was reported that the catastrophe was caused by a freak wave, which had flung Larry overboard; the theory was that he had hit his head and lost consciousness before he even entered the water, for he had apparently made no attempt to swim for survival.

"One moment he was standing there," Carl told Jeremy over the phone. "The next he was gone. God, it was awful! It was all so horribly suddenCand so final. I screamed and then there was just silence. He was dead when they found him. Can you think of a more dreadful, pointless accident?"

Jeremy could not, of course. But it took time to absorb the shocking news.

"Are you still there?" Carl asked.

That jerked Jeremy back to reality. "Of course. Now, Carl, I hope you aren't taking it too hard. Blaming yourself, that is. It was obviously just one of those ghastly accidents. No one's to blame."

"Thanks, Jeremy. You've always been so kind to me."

And Jeremy had. Many times he wished he hadn't: hadn't met Carl when he first arrived in town and was hustling, continued seeing Carl a couple of times a

month. Carl wasn't with Larry then. At least Larry hadn't moved in.

Jeremy remembered that first time as if it were yesterday. Carl's living room was cluttered, almost Victorian, though spotlessly clean. And not nearly as large as he would have guessed by the size of the house as they drove in the driveway. Overstuffed chairs were placed in front of what looked like a working fireplace. Heavy maroon curtains. Bric-a-brac and vases filled with long-stem roses. The room was dark. Deep reds. Mahogany furniture. Even the paintings, of storms at sea, were dark. Carl gave Jeremy a blowjob right there in the living room that first time. They never left the living room. Jeremy was back downtown in less than an hour. Carl took Jeremy, who was underage at the time, to the bar, introduced him around. Then Carl showed up with Larry, whom he had met on a trip to Key West and brought back with him. Everyone wanted Larry, and Larry wanted to fuck everybody, so the Saturday night orgies began.

- - -

The flow of people past Larry's coffin continued. A lot of people were crying, Jeremy more than anyone. The chapel was filled with flowers; Carl had seen to that. A great horseshoe made of white mums was the centerpeiece, something someone might see at the Kentucky Derby, hung around the neck of the champion stud, which seemed a fitting tribute to Larry, thought Jeremy.

The wake was filled with laughter, however, as people told stories they wouldn't tell in church. How when Larry and Carl went on vacation to Key West, a naked Larry, confused in the middle of the night, ended up in the hotel hallway instead of the bathroom. It could have happened to anyone except that because it was Larry, he tapped on a door, just any door, and ended up spending the night with a salesman from Milwaukee. Even Carl laughed at that one and everyone thought he had no sense of humor. Carl seemed to be sober, relaxed all through the ordeal of the funeral and the wake. At one point, he got misty eyed and said to Jeremy, "There was something about Larry that had let him screw over a number of men over the years and yet they still loved him. And they are all here today."

One mourner that wasn't there was Nathan. He would have come, he told Jeremy, if Carl would have stayed away.

There were many men Jeremy knew, some intimately, and he wondered if any of them still felt the way he did sometimes when he remembered how incredibly thorough Larry was in bed. Greg said, "Well, he's with the angels now."

Joe leaned over and said, "And I'll bet he seduces all the other angels before he's done."

"And they'll thank him for it," Jeremy replied. They clinked their Tanquerays and tonics Larry's favorite drink and shared a similar smile.

Jeremy was delighted Joe had come to the service and to the wake.

"How are you, really?" Joe asked.

"Coping."

Joe raised an eyebrow skeptically and after a moment he said, "I hope you don't think I stole him from you."

"I have a lover, remember?"

"How could I forget."

Jeremy swallowed hard when Joe said, "I don't feel much like drinking all night, do you?"

Jeremy shook his head and they stepped out into the warm late afternoon air together.

Joe had driven his truck and Jeremy followed him to his house.

How could Joe have known how badly Jeremy wanted him, especially now, on this night. After all this time. When finally they were alone together, when finally Jeremy could put his mouth on Joe's skin, he had to be honest with himself and admit just how much he had missed the stud and the way he made love.

Jeremy attacked Joe's erection with such vigor that Joe started stroking the back of his head because he sensed it would calm him. It had an almost immediate effect.

And soon Joe was so close. He looked down on Jeremy with a sensuous smile. Jeremy's heart hammered in his ears. He hadn't meant to start this up again, and he didn't know where it was going now that Larry was gone. Joe's fingers stroked Jeremy's hair as he came in an explosive gasp, arching under Jeremy.

Jeremy's head was pounding and he felt a cold shiver in his spine. He was frantically rising against Joe. Joe pulled him up and Jeremy's breath was coming in short whimpers. Joe's heat was intoxicating to Jeremy as the stud positioned him on the sofa in the living room. As Joe entered him, Jeremy cried out, then quieted when Joe's mouth found his. Jeremy's breathing grew taut and he wrapped his legs around Joe, rocking him as Joe rocked him. Jeremy's tongue reveled in the salty sweetness of Joe's saliva and cum. Joe knew the rhythm that would bring Jeremy's hips arching up, the pressure that would push them down into the sofa again. Then Jeremy froze under him and soon he was coming, crooning with pleasure, gasping for air, making all the noises Joe had heard before from the boys he'd fucked.

Jeremy collapsed under Joe. Joe continued to fuck and Jeremy began to cry softly. Not from distress, but from the cascade of emotions he was feeling. In his tiniest voice, quavering as a wave of longing swept over him, the sound muffled by Joe's thrusting body, he cried, "God, I love it, Joe. I've never loved getting fucked so much!"

- - -

Larry's drowning was reported, then dropped. But not by Nathan. "There's only one sure-fire murder method," Nathan contended. "A planned accident. The cops can never prove murder in an accident case, even if they suspect it."

Jeremy asked, "You mean something such as running over him in a car?"

"I mean something such as his falling out of a boat and drowning. While they were sailing."

Jeremy frowned.

They had decided to go away for the weekend, to get out of town, away after the funeral. Nathan was worried about Jeremy and told him a little vacation would do him good. Jeremy felt like telling Nathan that what he needed to do him good he's gotten on the evening of the wake, namely a furious fuck from Joe, but he played along.

The longer they drove, the more Jeremy began to relax into the carefree mood, the lack of purpose. As they drove, Nathan was speaking randomly, coming up with chilly images, disjointed observations. Jeremy started to tune into Nathan's strange imagination, and he, too, began to see the things that Nathan was conjuring up. Their thoughts were beginning to merge. After a time, Jeremy became hungry and horny.

They had dinner and rented a cabin by the lake. While Nathan showered, Jeremy got ready, greasing himself. Then he joined Nathan in the shower. They lathered each other all over, using the soap to slide their hands effortlessly along the contours and in every nook and cranny of each others' body. As they kissed, locked in embrace, the warm water cascaded over them. Nathan reached down and stuck his finger into Jeremy's anus. He moved his finger round and round. The muscles were relaxed and Nathan used his finger to fuck Jeremy anally until Jeremy had enough. Jeremy went into the bedroom first, to await Nathan.

Their day together was a success, Jeremy decided. He remembered how it was when he first met Nathan. Nathan's knowledge came from observation and interaction. He was artistically inclined, visually oriented, and he loved to watch people. He liked to pick up on people's gestures, and also their emotions. Jeremy was mesmerized by his intellect. Nathan's intelligence was different. It was more ambitious and drove Jeremy toward figuring things out, straightening out his life. He owed Nathan so much, and he repaid him with sex.

Freshly scrubbed and relaxed, Nathan stood before his lover, who sat on the edge of bed, his mouth open, eager. The suck began. Nathan gazed down at his lover, into his eyes that looked back with desire. "You suck it good." That's what had turned Nathan on from the start, that Jeremy gave better head than anybody he'd ever known.

And then Nathan fucked Jeremy in his gentle, vanilla way, carefully considerate, careful not to hurt Jeremy with his penis. When Nathan had come, he rolled off Jeremy and lay on his back staring at the ceiling. "It's funny, isn't it, how important sex is one minute and how meaningless the next? It goes from being everything to nothing in a flash. Then back to everything again. Then all of a sudden it's nothing."

Nathan had a way of putting things that demoralized Jeremy. He now felt empty, without desire. He covered his eyes with his arm. With Larry, with Joe, with dozens of others, even though he had come, even though he had been

fucked until he bled, he still wanted more. But with Nathan, it was simply over.

"You know, since all this started going wrong, I've been thinking a lot about the difference between us. It's got nothing to do with sex, has it? It's control. That's the difference between us. I'm in control; you're out of control."

"Do you get a charge out of stopping yourself? Of not letting yourself go? Does that make you feel good?"

"I think you always have to be in control of yourself. Otherwise it's chaos."

Jeremy rolled over and tried to fall asleep. Jeremy thought that they had nothing more to say.

The next day, when Nathan awoke his back was bothering him. "Sleeping in a strange bed," he said, and Jeremy gave him a massage. This lead to a blowjob, the morning blowjob Nathan never really asked for but sometimes received. It became one of the many reasons Nathan could not live without his Jeremy.

In the kitchenette of the cabin, Jeremy made some buttered toast and strong coffee.

Nathan began to feel better. By the time he emerged from the bathroom Nathan was reciting bright-eyed from *Henry V:* "'Once more unto the breach, dear friends, once more....'"

Once again Jeremy had healed someone in distress with his mouth and hands.

The thought of the murder seemed to appeal to Nathan's theatrical nature. He refused to let it drop: "Consider the background for a moment. I suspect that the heavy emotional side-effects of the affair with Patty made Larry feel bisexuality was not a way of life he wanted to pursue.

"No matter how many experiments he tried, Larry was sure he'd always revert eventually to his special preference and even his experiments would be limited by his personal taste," Nathan theorized. "But then he met Joe, and that changed everything. So as the weeks passed, a very tense situation built up and eventually reached dangerous proportions."

"But you weren't there."

"Thank God!"

"So how would you know?"

"You, sweet beautiful child, so often can't see the forest for the trees. But you do so delight in keeping me informed, thinking you are making me suffer, but instead."

"Instead you revel in it, like a pig in shit."

"Yes, if you like."

"So you imagine all this."

"It doesn't take much imagining, my love. Remember, I need to meet these people only once or twice and I can read 'em like a book."

"Yeah, sure."

"Sure." Unflappable, Nathan went on. "There was an explosion. My guess is that Carl's patience snapped. He was rejected and it finally drove him right out

of his mind. Someone as self-controlled as he is wouldn't go over the edge unless he was experiencing provocation on a grand scale. I think Larry told him that afternoon on the sailboat that he was going to leave him."

"You don't actually know he was crazy," Jeremy said. "Like, put him away kinda crazy." Nathan's explanation struck Jeremy as being impressively plausible but he felt more confused than ever by the issue of Carl's sanity. "He's not crazy. He's still functioning, still going out and about, still working and enjoying his sailing."

"Yes," Nathan agreed, "but for that moment he ceased to function normally, he who swung so far out of control that he committed murder."

Jeremy still wasn't buying it. "And now?" he asked.

Nathan smirked. He was finally getting through to Jeremy. "Well, now we can say that he's possessed, possessed by his grief, his guilt, his shame that he had killed the man he loved."

"What a way to live," Jeremy said.

"A living hell," Nathan agreed. At last they agreed on something.

SIX

As Jeremy eased off his worn, damp jockstrap, he knew that he would not could not leave the gym until he had sucked off the stranger he had been cruising as nature had clearly intended him to be sucked. It had been a slow day at the gym, and Jeremy and the man, who reminded him of Nathan in many ways, were alone in the shower room. They had cruised each other for the better part of two hours, and the man even spotted Jeremy for a time. The man's earthy smell intoxicated Jeremy. The man told Jeremy he was going to take a shower. Jeremy took this as an invitation.

Now Jeremy watched the man enter the shower room. His solid, husky body was naked and he had a thick, cut cock. Jeremy stepped into the shower next to the man. The water surged around the man's strong shoulders. He leaned backward for a second, showing off his swelling penis. Jeremy's mouth watered. He faded in and out of focus through the steam. Jeremy dropped to his knees and took the hefty cock in his hands.

Deftly, Jeremy maneuvered himself onto his back, pulling the man over him as he did so. Now the man was sitting on Jeremy's face, his knees anchored firmly on either side of Jeremy's face. His muscular thighs cushioned Jeremy's head. Jeremy tried to catch a glimpse of the man's face, to read his desire and excitement, but the man leaned over him, crushing him. Jeremy resigned himself to reaching up and, grabbing the man by his vigorously pumping hips, pulled his warm fullness even closer into his face. Suddenly aware of the throbbing in his own cock, Jeremy thought of reaching down to touch himself. Before he could, however, he felt his hips rise into the air, and his cock erupting. All he could do was press his face even more deeply into the man's crotch and take the load.

In his post-orgasmic stupor, Jeremy observed that the man, while excited, was nowhere near climax. Briefly, Jeremy was tempted to succumb to his own

satiation and exhaustion, to shove the man away, leaving him breathless and wanting on the tile floor as he walked out of the steam room and got dressed. No lovely reciprocity, no awkward attempts at politeness how liberating that would be. The only thing that held him there was the insistence of the man. Gripping the man's hips even more firmly, he forced the man to hurry his orgasm.

Standing, he looked down at the man, resting on the floor, the water splashing over him. The man's eyes were shut; his face, turned to one side, impassive but for the faintly creased forehead, the slightly flared nostrils and the dry lips, which he sought to moisten with the pink tip of his tongue. His body rocked slightly.

Jeremy marveled anew at the abandon with which he could suck off a stranger, especially in a rather public place. In places such as this, Jeremy felt both curiosity and terror, anxious to see the promise fulfilled and yet knowing there was to be nothing afterward.

Now, with a twinge of regret, Jeremy made his way over to the bench in the locker room, which was somehow reassuring in its hardness. He sat there for a while, not thinking, not moving. Opening his eyes, he felt himself in a dream. Focusing, his eyes blinked at the sight of the body that had just given him such amazing pleasure. The man's face remained passive. Then he looked at Jeremy's face. Jeremy smiled.

"Can I buy you a drink?" the man asked.

"Yeah, I think I need one."

In the parking lot, the man introduced himself as David. Jeremy checked his watch; Nathan had classes; he wouldn't be home until late. David agreed to go follow Jeremy home.

Jeremy unzipped David's zipper and clenched his pubic hair. Tangled and wet. He didn't want to see his face. Their bodies, not their identities, were what mattered. He stuck his tongue into opened trousers. David unbuttoned Jeremy's shirt and slid it off his shoulders. He sucked his nipples as his hands roamed down Jeremy's belly.

Jeremy stood, dropped his shorts, and fell on the bed on his stomach. When David's fingers had slid into Jeremy's asshole, Jeremy clenched them. He tried to draw David deeper into him. "I want to feel that thick dick inside me," Jeremy begged.

David shed his pants and climbed on the bed, his hard-on raging. Then Jeremy rolled over, grabbed his shoulders and hoisted himself up and pressed their bodies together. And they kissed until Jeremy's head buzzed. Still kissing Jeremy, David tugged his fingers out of him and put his arms around Jeremy. He caressed Jeremy's neck and ears and rubbed his back. He pulled out of their kiss and leaned back and pinched Jeremy's nipples, then looked at them and smiled, then kissed them, then nibbled, then bit his nipples. Jeremy locked his legs around his back and ran his hands down and up his thighs. They rolled and wrestled on the bed, fighting each other to top. They licked and sucked and

writhed until Jeremy got on top and arched his back and pumped himself up and down on the thick cock while Jeremy rubbed his belly.

David began to travel Jeremy's sweaty body with his mouth, teasing him into wildness with a pause at a nipple, a suck, a bite, a nibble of an earlobe, a tongue-flick in an ear. His hands held and squeezed and rubbed Jeremy's buttocks, thighs, and belly. Fingers seemed to stray toward Jeremy's erection, but avoided it, over and over until Jeremy was ready to beg. Before long, Jeremy totally lost control of himself, he needed it that bad. David moaned softly and rocked his hips toward Jeremy, all the while working Jeremy's body into a frenzy with his hands. Jeremy could stand no more. He gasped for air. His body shook. A release that he never imagined possible washed over him. His body was both expanding and contracting at the same time.

David encircled him in his arms until Jeremy's shaking subsided. Jeremy held one of his hands in both of his. He took the fingers that had been inside his ass into his mouth and licked and sucked. David rubbed Jeremy's ass as Jeremy got down on his stomach. Jeremy opened to him and he slid inside his asshole once more. He raised his hips to meet his thrusts and bucked against him. Jeremy climbed to all fours and David leaned over him, his hot chest resting on Jeremy's back, his beautiful cock penetrating the now-sloppy asshole. Jeremy ground myself against him. All too soon David was panting, twitching, howling. Jeremy's ears began to ring. His face and his whole body flushed. Convulsing, he collapsed to the bed in a puddle of his own cum. The exhaustion that he had expected to overtake him did not come. Despite, or perhaps because of such an illicit fuck, Jeremy was filled with strength. But David had to go. His wife was waiting dinner for him. "See you at the gym?" David asked.

Jeremy chuckled. "Sure."

Jeremy watched him drive away and wondered how it was that so often he found men who wanted this, how long it would be before he'd do it again with some guy, how many times he had to convince himself he really wasn't homosexual, he was just having fun. And it was fun, he couldn't take that away from it.

Jeremy had had experience with straight boys, or at least boys who thought they were straight. As a kid, his best friend George liked girls as much as Jeremy did, but for different reasons. While Jeremy confided in girls and became their pal, George wanted their pussies. George was crazy and charming and spoiled. And Jeremy was captivated. And they were constantly talking about sex.

One night they were just lying around, leafing through George's father's collection of *Playboy* magazines, when a girl George was dating, Marcia, called. Jeremy flopped down on his belly and kept reading the magazines while George rolled on his back, talking softly to Marcia. Very softly. After a while Jeremy was incapable of concentrating on the magazines. George's voice was like warm breath on his neck, seducing him, caressing him. George was talking dirty to

her.

Jeremy rolled over to his right side to face George and found him on his left side, facing Jeremy. Their eyes met and locked, and as his voice continued, smooth as honey silk, Jeremy found himself looking at the bulge in George's boxer shorts, and back up at his eyes again. Jeremy could feel his heart pounding. He was getting warm and very aware of George's body, his breath. He glanced at George's naked chest; his nipples stood up, waiting, aching to be touched. George saw him looking, heard his breath get faster. Their eyes met again. Jeremy realized Marcia was not the only one George was seducing. Jeremy couldn't help himself. Trembling, he reached out, so slowly his hand seemed to hang there, weightless, until finally his fingers brushed lightly over the bulge in the boxers. A shiver ran through him, knowing that now that he had touched him, their friendship was either over, or it was just beginning.

Jeremy moved closer, gripped the erection. George sighed and said quietly, "Marcia, I have to get off the phone now."

He set the receiver down in its cradle. "Well," he said, "this is different."

Their lips met, shyly, chastely, gently. This was a kiss like no other; this was perfection, this was power. A huge roar of lust swept through them both, full of desire and fear and uncertainty and finally a knowledge that yes, Jeremy wanted George, and yes, George would let him. It began as only a blowjob, Jeremy experimenting with George, with George guiding Jeremy, telling him what felt good. But soon they were anxious to try each other out, see how it all fit, taste everything, feel it all. And they did. It was a magical night. Again and again they pleasured one another with hands and tongues, stroking and tasting, briefly resting, only to dive again. Jeremy marveled at his orgasms; they were so full, so rich and creamy, like nothing he'd ever experienced before. George seemed to know what felt good, and he taught Jeremy so much that night. Jeremy didn't know what time it was when they finally dropped off to sleep, but he remembered the smell of sex in the room, and thinking, *I will always want this again.*

An hour later, five minutes into what felt like the sweetest, hungriest kiss Jeremy had ever been lost in, Jeremy was in bed with Nathan, and had forgotten everything except his lover, who was sweeping him away from everything. Jeremy pulled the rest of his clothes from him, got into position and, as Nathan entered him, where just moments before it seemed David had lodged, thicker, harder, even more eager, Jeremy was wanting to show him he was there, hot for him, there because he wanted to be. He spread his legs wide as he could, wanting to let him get at him as deeply as possible. When Jeremy felt his body tighten up in an imminent orgasm, Jeremy orgasmed from his pumping hand alone, coming until he was curled up practically sobbing.

"You're so good," Nathan gasped when he was finally done with Jeremy and his cock slipped from the opening.

And Jeremy laughed, and it was a laugh without shame.

SEVEN

As the days passed, Jeremy became convinced Nathan was right, that Carl was guilty of murder. He recalled many incidents, many occasions....

Marco, the hunky Showbar bartender, told him about the time Carl had, after a long night of drinking, asked the Italian stallion if he had any hit men as relatives. Marco laughed, "Who do you know worth bumpin' off?"

And then he mentioned, again, a week later. Marco told Jeremy it bothered him, but he just didn't take Carl seriously.

Carl was, when he thought about it, a man who was perpetually angry, who consistently hovered on violence, and he was trapped in his own private world. A person can become a world, Nathan told Jeremy, and Larry had become Carl's world.

Jeremy knew Carl was a Scorpio, vindictive, vengeful, with a memory of past injuries as long as life. Nathan had told him that most Scorpios are murderers or remarkably victims of murder. It was the same identity, Nathan said. What would a madman do next? Would he come after Larry's lovers next? Nathan filled Jeremy's mind with questions.

Jeremy began to wonder, even to worry, about Joe, about Joe's safety.

Jeremy went to see Joe on Sunday afternoon, and found Joe was cleaning his bike. He acknowledged Jeremy's presence, but went right on working. They exchanged pleasantries. Finally Joe told Jeremy, "My bike is a Way instead of a Means of gettin' around."

With true zeal Joe applied the bristles of the toothbrush to the spokes. Jeremy was intrigued by the bike, by Joe's love for it.

"I'll take you for a ride one day," Joe said.

"I want to go now."

"I haven't got a helmet for you."

"That doesn't matter. I won't come off."

"No, it's dangerous. If there were an accident I'd be responsible."

But Jeremy persisted. They set off, Jeremy without a helmet.

To begin with Joe was very cautious. He didn't want to break the speed limit. This was not the moment to get pulled over by the cops. He was cautious too because of his precious passenger, his arms around him, his pretty young head behind him. A motorcycle weaves through traffic, Joe explained. "It's the nature of the beast to overtake, accelerate, and go where automobiles can't. My Harley is more animal than machine. It's an extension of me. No, not just an extension; it's an expression of something inside me, to keep charging forward. See, kid, you can't reverse a bike. It's all forward rush."

And what a rush! At one point, on the freeway heading north, Joe really let rip. He couldn't help himself. Jeremy clutched the stud tighter for a while, but as Jeremy got used to the speed, he gradually relaxed his grip until he seemed almost comfortable.

Joe drove for about twenty minutes and suggested they stop somewhere off

the freeway for a cup of coffee. Jeremy wouldn't hear of it. He didn't want Joe to stop; he was hooked. Joe kept well within the speed limit on the way back. Just as they entered North Port, a raccoon ran across the road. Joe avoided him easily.

"That was close," Jeremy called out.

"Hardly."

Jeremy realized he was thinking like the driver of a car.

"Did you take Larry for rides?" Jeremy asked when they returned to the house.

"Once or twice. He liked to go down to Myakka Park. We'd make a day of it."

Jeremy understood. He could see Larry, on his knees back in the brush, sucking Joe's cock. "He was a lot of fun."

Joe nodded. "Sex is freedom," Joe said. "Larry never had any freedom."

Jeremy was high from his ride and wanted to fuck immediately. He didn't give Joe the time to get completely undressed, just kneeling in the living room and sucking his cock. After Joe came he went to the bathroom. Jeremy pulled himself together, got ready to leave, changed his mind, undressed, stayed. Hours passed, and still Jeremy didn't want to go back. They looked deep down into each other's eyes and knew they wanted to come together. To use each other; together. Motion of their bodies and what they did, to work out their desire. To have sex in a sweaty embrace, intimately aware of their partner's needs; timing it right, one waiting, loving the other, building him up, timing it right so they could both burst loose together in a wild, brief, joyous moment of ecstasy. This was the kind of sex Jeremy had had with Larry. He wondered if sex with Larry had taught Joe a thing or two. It was extraordinary.

As he was dressing, Jeremy asked Joe about Carl. Had he seen him?

"I wouldn't know him."

"The pick-up from the night we met."

"Don't remember it."

But Jeremy kept on, and Joe did recall being followed a couple of times, but it was by a panel truck.

"Beach Florist?"

"Yeah," Joe said. "I think. In fact, I saw it parked down the street a couple of times, but I didn't think much about it."

"Just be careful," Jeremy said. "Carl has been a bit crazy since the accident."

Finally, a well-fucked Jeremy was leaving Joe's house.

"Next time we'll drive at night," Joe said. "It's different."

EIGHT

Joe wanted to go to a gay bar.

"But I thought you were there," Jeremy said, "the night we picked you up."

"No, I've ridden my bike by there...often...but I never went in."

Jeremy agreed to take Joe inside Showbar, and in fifteen minutes they were

there. Jeremy guided the stud gallantly through the front bar, past the tables and piano, and past the men seated on barstools watching them in the blue-tinted mirror. They entered the back room where the music was blaring and the men were dirty dancing under flashing lights. Seeing them dancing reminded Jeremy of the movie and how much Joe reminded him of Patrick Swayze. Except Joe said he didn't dance.

Marco was tending bar, filling in that week in the back room of Showbar. He poured them a couple of hefty shots of tequila, on the house. Marco winked at Jeremy with a smile of complicity behind Joe's back.

They downed their shots and teetered onto the dance floor for part of a dance. Joe was agreeable now, a bit tipsy, and they soon moved back to the sidelines. Joe was staring at Jeremy again with unmistakable longing in his eyes. Jeremy took Joe's head in his hands and gave him a tender and passionate kiss on the lips. Joe surprised Jeremy by responding with equal passion and then he put his tongue into Jeremy's mouth. They were breathing deeply, studying the rising energy between them. Their kissing was getting fervent. Jeremy moved his arms around Joe's waist as he brought his pelvis underneath Joe's. He started to rock him from side to side with his hips. Joe responded by putting his thigh between Jeremy's legs, pressing into Jeremy's crotch.

Jeremy was thoroughly aroused. Joe seemed oblivious. But when he took Jeremy's fingers into his mouth and started sucking them, Jeremy exclaimed, "Not here. Follow me."

Joe followed him into the bathroom. Jeremy closed the door and reached up to disconnect the light bulb. Soon they were kissing in the dark. Jeremy was biting Joe's neck as Joe was leaning back and taking it with his mouth open, breathing heavily. Jeremy began rubbing Joe's erection quickly, stimulating him through his pants.

Jeremy was hot. He threw off his shirt, then pulled off Joe's. He pushed his nipples strongly against the other man's. They were rubbing and grinding their chests against each other, as Jeremy reached down into Joe's pants, sliding over his moist pubic hair, straining toward his trapped, steaming prick. He went up again, sucking hard on each of his hot, swollen nipples, one after the other.

Joe was hard and he nudged Jeremy's hand to his prick.

Suddenly, someone entered the john. Jeremy went to his knees, took out the prick. Someone else came in, stood next to the other guy in the dark, moving close to see what they could see. This unnerved Joe, who pulled Jeremy off his cock and up into his arms.

Joe switched moods again, as off as he had been on. "I have to go to work early. I'm going home."

"Do you want me to call you?" Jeremy asked.

"Yeah, do that."

When Jeremy called him on Saturday, Joe told him the whole bar thing "weirded him out." Jeremy said he was sorry that Joe felt that way. Jeremy

Edited by John Patrick

thought it was just too bad that Joe was as alienated from his fantasies as he was from his life.

A few nights later, back at Showbar, Jeremy hit the back bar again. He wanted to talk to Marco. Marco greeted him with a big smile. Damn, Jeremy thought, Marco looked cuter than ever, wearing a tight, striped muscle shirt and incredibly tight shorts. Marco had that swarthy Mediterranean complexion, which naturally enhanced the image. Jeremy was warming to the stud and wondered why Larry had never invited him to one of their orgies.

Marco was guzzling down a Coke. He smiled when he saw Jeremy. "That was a good-lookin' guy you were with the other night. How did it work out?"

"It didn't. He's straight."

"What?"

"A strange bird. A long story. Anyway, how have you been?"

"Still clean and sober. It's been two months already. I'm a regular at AA now."

"A bartender in AA. That's a laugh!"

"Works for me."

It was a slow night and Marco went on and on talking about twelve-stepping. He was doing AA, ACA, Cokenders. He was obsessed, Jeremy thought. But his enthusiasm was passionate, and Jeremy got the notion that maybe Marco would take Carl to a meeting.

"I don't think so. Not Carl. Carl would never admit he had a problem. Never. Besides he is one of our best customers, or rather he was. Now I think he drinks at home."

It was then that Jeremy laid on Marco Nathan's theory about Larry's untimely demise. Marco said he'd believe anything when it came to Carl.

As the night wore on, Jeremy was roaming freely, but he always returned to the back bar and Marco. Upon the last such return trip, Marco said one of his friends from his schooldays in upstate New York was visiting him. Marco winked, "He's been working out a lot while he's been here. He says he could use a good massage."

"I don't do that any more, you know that. I'm a student now."

Suddenly, Marco's friend was back from a journey to the john. His name was Kurt and he was absolutely stunning. A vision of divine muscle-bound beauty. Jeremy normally wasn't attracted to this type but Kurt was radiant. Golden shining hair cascaded over his shoulders. And his emerald eyes were reflecting Jeremy's interest. Kurt resembled that kind of idealized Celtic beauty that artists would carve into figures for mastheads on the most glorious prows of the finest ships. Jeremy was speechless. Marco introduced them and Jeremy tried to detach from the immediate infatuation. He answered Kurt's questions about his school, maintaining a politeness. But something was shifting beneath the surface, and underneath his words. Kurt was something out of a dream. Jeremy watched Kurt speaking to Marco. His eyes wandered from the delicate features

- 418 -

of his face, down the golden strands of hair to the pecs that were straining the seams of his tank top. Jeremy imagined his nipples were large and honey-rose as well. He imagined rolling his tongue around them. Yes, Kurt had the stuff of dreams.

By the time they finished the drinks Marco had delivered to them, Jeremy and Kurt had locked into a conversation. Kurt was telling Jeremy about what a wonderful lover Marco had turned out to be. It would seem Kurt was entirely unavailable. So Jeremy told Kurt about Nathan. Not about the fact that Nathan was a professor at the college and twenty years his senior. No, just about what a wonderful lover Nathan was. But while he was telling these fairy tales, it was hard for Jeremy not to stare into his eyes, and to keep a civilized distance. He was hot for this stud.

As the crowd began to thin, Jeremy watched Kurt, trying hard not to be too obvious. Kurt would throw out a thought and Jeremy caught it, ran it through his own mind and into his own personal territory. Sometimes he responded and sometimes he didn't, according to how much he did or didn't want to reveal. He was only as responsive as he pleased. He let Kurt lead the conversation, which Jeremy always enjoyed. Essentially, Jeremy became the good listener he learned to be during his hustling days.

Kurt also seemed comfortable with Jeremy's openness. Unlike most men, Jeremy knew how to really feel what Kurt needed him to feel. Kurt felt safe talking about what had happened to him at school during the year. Neither of them had made up his mind as to what to do with their life; both were majoring in business, feeling their way.

As Kurt related the tale of his lustful awakening, Jeremy felt himself getting hotter and hotter. Kurt was so ripe for someone to give him what he needed. Marco, Jeremy decided, was a lousy lay if Kurt was here, looking for a good massage. Jeremy wanted to take Kurt in his arms right there and go back to Marco's, or wherever he was staying, and fuck all night.

Finally Kurt agreed to let Jeremy drive him back to Marco's. They both hugged Marco goodnight.

As they left Jeremy was tingling all over. Oh, how he wanted to have sex with this man. He wanted to show Kurt where he could go with these kinds of feelings. Jeremy knew he would take such pleasure in watching Kurt open up.

At Marco's little apartment, Jeremy was full of Kurt. But Kurt disappeared into the bathroom. Jeremy stripped naked and lay in bed, waiting for Kurt to come out of the bathroom. While Kurt took a shower, Jeremy sat in the bedroom stroking his own cock thinking of making love to Kurt. His own body felt incredibly responsive under his practiced hands. He caressed himself like a lover, kneading the cheeks of his ass. He greased his fingers and slid them down his furry crack and slipped them into his ass. He slid them inside and fucked himself rhythmically. He saw Kurt's eyes and his smile in his mind. Jeremy came, lying on his back, his cock throbbing before him in a truly voluptuous

orgasm.

Just then, Kurt entered the bedroom. He was ravishing. His vivacious emerald eyes focused directly on Jeremy's steaming cock. The golden swirls of his long hair were a breathtaking sight hovering over Jeremy's cock, bringing on a new rush of sexual energy. Kurt's body was even more spectacular than Jeremy had imagined. The perfection of his body matched the beauty of his face. He had the kind of body any lover, male or female, would love to worship. But it was Kurt who was loving Jeremy, licking his spent cum, lapping at his cock. Jeremy couldn't hold back; he reached over and caressed his body delicately. The stud was delicious. Jeremy pulled Kurt on top of him. They rubbed against each other.

"Oh," Jeremy exclaimed, feeling Kurt's own excitement pressing hard against Jeremy's renewed erection.

They moved against each other for several moments until, with a stifled moan, Kurt came profusely against Jeremy's thigh. He ejaculated so fast it caught Jeremy by surprise. Both of them were shocked at how little it took to get off. The ice had been broken.

Now Jeremy could take his time. He used the flat of his tongue to lick the large, velvety-soft aureoles. He licked Kurt's breasts until the nipples were at full attention. Then he nibbled and sucked as Kurt moaned beneath him. Jeremy reached down and felt Kurt's cock swelling again. Jeremy moved down his body while licking him all over. Kurt lay back in a swoon. When Jeremy went back up to kiss him, Kurt closed his eyes and let himself feel Jeremy ravaging his lips, his nipples, his flat, tight belly. He could feel Jeremy's mouth on his crotch, sucking and swirling his tongue through his pubic hair. He nudged Kurt's legs apart. He studied the magnificence of Kurt's groin. He nuzzled into it. Kurt was breathing harder. Jeremy teased him by coming close, breathing heat on his erection, and then coming up again.

"Do it," Kurt implored, "fuck me!"

Jeremy had him on the edge. He rolled Kurt over and plunged his tongue deep into Kurt's asshole.

Jeremy moved his body all the way up on top of Kurt. He sucked on his neck and then went for his lips. Kurt let himself be kissed and plundered by Jeremy's tongue. He was digging his fingers into Kurt's buttocks and thighs. Jeremy moved his leg and opened Kurt again.

He placed his cock in Kurt's ass crack. Jeremy was getting himself harder and more and more excited. He stabbed at it with his cock and kept on stabbing. The energy between them was sharp and intense. Jeremy kept on stabbing. They came together on the edge of a knife at the same time.

When Jeremy recouped, he slid his fingers, three and then four, into Kurt's ass. This time Kurt opened wide on his own. He bent his knees to give Jeremy the opportunity to fuck him deeply. He gave himself the freedom to lift and respond to Jeremy's heated momentum. Jeremy fucked him wildly as the bed

shook and moved on the parquet floor. Kurt was thrashing his head from side to side, lifting and pumping his hips with every penetration. He shuddered deliriously and came in rippling waves, giving himself to the currents of pleasure. Jeremy kept his fingers inside, riding him all the way. When the orgasm subsided, Jeremy removed his fingers slowly and deliberately, and then rushed them out quickly at the end, so that Kurt would feel their absence. He wanted Kurt to want them inside him again.

Jeremy moved up to lick the sweat off his eyebrows. "Oh, God," Kurt begged, "no more. I need to rest." Jeremy moved off and was laughing. Kurt began to sob. There were tears rolling down his cheeks.

Jeremy asked anxiously, "Did I hurt you?"

Kurt opened his eyes, which were full of feeling. "Oh, no. It's joy not pain." Then he laughed at himself because he was laughing and crying at the same time.

Jeremy stroked Kurt's hair and caressed his head. They had reached a remarkable intimacy in so short at a time.

The head of the remarkable cock was revealed, begging to come. Jeremy sucked the head between his pursed lips. Kurt came, gritting his teeth and then groaning in a wail of ecstasy. When Jeremy looked up, Kurt's face was radiant and glowing; he was blissfully satisfied.

When Kurt left for the bathroom, he told Jeremy he was hungry. Jeremy said he'd see if he could find something in the kitchen. Jeremy got out of the bed all weak-kneed. He went to the kitchen to find some sweet rolls in a bakery bag on the counter. He carried them back into the bedroom. They each ate, and fed the other little nibbles. When they hit the last roll, they both bit into it at the same time like wild animals devouring their prey. They bit and growled at the piece left between them. This turned into a sweaty wrestling match between two animals competing for dominance. Kurt was even stronger than Jeremy would have imagined. He pinned Jeremy down before Jeremy knew what was happening. Jeremy was laughing too hard to stop him.

As Kurt declared his victory and climbed off, Jeremy seized the opportunity to gain his position. He pushed Kurt onto his back and shoved his fingers into Kurt's ass. Kurt was gasping in short, excited breaths as Jeremy kept pumping him. He kept it up until Kurt couldn't take it any more. Jeremy sucked his cock, and Kurt came again.

"God, where did Marco find you?" he murmured distractedly as he lay there, limp and smiling.

Jeremy fingered the foreskin of Kurt's cock. He had become enamored of this curiosity. Even in the couple of years he hustled, he had encountered few uncut males. The exoticness of it delighted him. He asked Kurt to shower with him. Kurt was into it. It was one of the things he never liked to do with anyone. It was a private thing. But with Jeremy it was different.

In the shower, Jeremy used his mouth to worship Kurt's cock, bringing

Kurt's semi-flaccid organ all the way into his mouth. Kurt was moaning. Jeremy knew that Kurt was feeling.

"Oh, my God, it's delicious," Kurt whimpered as Jeremy worked him into another electrified frenzy. He held Jeremy's head discharged in a third walloping orgasm.

They both lay down naked on the bed. They studied each other's body with their eyes and hands, registering every curve and surface. Kurt traced Jeremy's collarbones and sternum, and he felt his arm muscles and strong shoulders. "You've got so much upper-body strength," he said.

"I really work out more on the top," Jeremy told him.

"You turn me on so much," Kurt whispered.

"You too," Jeremy whispered back as he was stroking Kurt's cock. "We're two sex fiends."

Kurt chuckled. "I'm not usually like this."

"I know," Jeremy said, going back down on his cock again. But, of course, Jeremy knew no such thing.

In a few minutes, Kurt asked if Jeremy could give him the massage he had promised him. Jeremy was happy to comply. It was one of his specialties. As a child he would often massage his friends, working them up to erections of Herculean proportions that always needed to be released.

As Jeremy massaged, he concentrated on all the pressure points. He had once made a study of the art of massage. He knew all the strokes and sequences for pleasuring. He had grown even more practiced when he started hustling.

Before long, Kurt was ready to come again. This was amazing to Jeremy. He had never been with someone so multi-orgasmic.

Jeremy found Kurt's feet especially exciting. He felt like worshipping them as he had Kurt's cock. Jeremy knew their secrets. He knew how the feet are the maps for the rest of the body; how soles contain tens of thousands of nerve endings whose opposite ends are wired to specific places and zones throughout the entire body. Jeremy spent a lot of extra time stimulating those sections on the soles of Kurt's feet that corresponded to his heart and to his genitals.

After he finished the massage, he went down between Kurt's legs, which spread automatically. He nibbled and sucked his cock with intense concentration. As Kurt was revving up towards another orgasm, Jeremy got up and straddled him. Jeremy spread the cheeks of his own ass and placed his anus around Kurt's extended cock. He squeezed Kurt's cock with his sphincter, tightening and releasing, tightening and releasing with his muscle ring of pleasure. Kurt pushed upwards, fucking upwards as Jeremy bore down. Kurt pumped Jeremy's tight little hole and screamed with ecstasy as he ejaculated once again.

Jeremy arched back on his elbows, with his cock standing free and erect, protruding and yearning for Kurt to jerk. Kurt reached over and yanked and vibrated Jeremy's cock. Jeremy spurted his cum all over Kurt's chest. Jeremy

held onto the intensity of his own orgasm for as long as he could, wishing it could be forever. It was the longest and highest peak he had ever reached. "Oh baby, baby," Kurt uttered in amazement.

For his part, Jeremy collapsed on top of him, shuddering in Kurt's arms.

When he calmed down into the deepest, sweetest state of relaxation, Jeremy finally told Kurt, "I wish you lived in my bed and I could have you every time I wanted."

Kurt laughed and responded, "So do I, babe." They kissed sweetly and gently.

"But I have to go," Jeremy said.

"You do?"

"I'm expected at home. And Marco will be here soon."

"Fuck Marco."

"No, you fuck Marco. I'm going home."

Jeremy hurriedly dressed and raced from the apartment. He wanted to flee, to just hold this fabulous night as if a dream.

But Kurt was not willing to spend his last night in Florida alone. Marco had to work so he invited Jeremy to dinner. Chinese, he said.

But Kurt hadn't cooked. He ordered it when he was sure Jeremy was there. While they waited, they drank a bottle of white wine.

When the food arrived, they ate it directly out of the containers. Kurt lay back and put a shrimp inside his foreskin. Jeremy laughed and used his chopsticks to remove and eat it. Kurt put another one in, with its tail sticking out. Jeremy got on his knees and sucked it into his mouth. Then Jeremy began sucking in earnest. He sucked more and more and harder and harder, and he used his tongue to lap up all the pre-cum Kurt was secreting.

Jeremy brought Kurt to an intense orgasm. Then Jeremy took the bottle of wine and shoved it between Kurt's legs. He fucked him carefully and slowly, and then removed it and put his mouth to the task. Kurt's cum tasted so good, so salty and warm. Then Jeremy fucked Kurt from behind, ramming him as hard as he could. With his hand underneath, he jerked Kurt off before coming himself.

The next afternoon, Jeremy drove Kurt to the airport. They were trying not to be sad. In the parking garage, Jeremy and Kurt were kissing good-bye in the front seat. The kissing turned passionate right away. Kurt leaned his head back and Jeremy was ravishing his neck. He gave him a souvenir to remember in the form of a hickey. Jeremy had his hands under Kurt's T-shirt. He caressed Kurt's big nipples. Jeremy felt like a teenager in a drive-in, aware of the public space but compelled to move on his desire. As he squeezed Kurt's nipples, he humped himself against Kurt's thigh. Kurt unzipped Jeremy's fly, stuck his hand inside his underwear, and stroked him. Jeremy came hot and heavy around Kurt's knuckles. Kurt removed his fingers and sucked them seductively in front of Jeremy's gaze. This was too much. Jeremy was dying to lay him down and fuck him in the back seat. Fuck him 'til he screamed. He wished that they were both

teenagers and that they could give each other what neither of them had ever had before. God, they would have been awesome together. Kurt promised to write.

NINE

Jeremy didn't crash until the weekend when he awoke alone in his bed, missing Kurt. For Jeremy, Kurt's absence was more like paradise lost, where he still remembered paradise even though it was shrouded by clouds. Kurt wrote, saying he looked forward to another meeting. Jeremy sent Kurt a love note. He wrote that his time with Kurt was great for him as well. But it was like a dream shattered by an alarm clock. It had very little to do with his everyday life. Jeremy wrote Kurt that he hated the fact that reality was dominating his life. There were so many complications. Nathan. Carl. The loss of Larry. Joe. It was overwhelming, but, with Kurt, he enjoyed some wonderful moments when life could be seen as the joy it could really be. The more you remember and reconnect to the moments, Jeremy wrote, the more you see why life is worth living.

The idea of Love never left Jeremy's heart. He replayed the moments with Kurt in his mind. By the third week, the tapes had lost their effectiveness. Jeremy's body had a mind of its own. It began craving more tangible satisfaction. He began to ache and long for Kurt. He couldn't seem to concentrate on anything else without feeling a gnawing need for sexual fulfillment. He was climbing the walls.

At college, Jeremy could not keep his mind on his studies. He was so horny, and then there was the mental anguish over the problem of Carl and how it all happened. By now he was trying to convince himself Nathan was wrong, that it was an accident, not murder the way Nathan believed. No, Jeremy did not want to believe it was murder. An accident, a horrible accident, was what it must have been.

Finally Jeremy resolved that Carl had been drunk out of his mind, hadn't meant a word he said et cetera, et cetera ... But then they fought and ...

But now Carl was following Joe. Perhaps Carl was crazy after all, a truly dangerous man...

And then Patty called. Jeremy was surprised to hear from her. The last time he had laid eyes on her, she was angry with Jeremy because he had brought Joe into the house and Larry couldn't let go of Joe. But now she was worried about Carl. She had moved out of the house. She couldn't stand being there without Larry, and with Carl acting so strangely.

Patty had usually ignored Jeremy, that's why he was so surprised to get her call. He agreed to meet her for lunch, at the Pelican.

"Tell me," Jeremy said, "is it awful to see me again? Are you still angry?"

Patty shook her head. "I wish you'd stop going on and on about me being angry. I was never angry. I don't get angry. I thought you knew that. Hurt perhaps. But never angry. However, if you don't shut up about it, I will get angry! You know, perhaps you're angry at me and that's why you keep accusing

me of being angry at you."

"Oh, no. I forgave you long ago."

"Very big of you."

They could have gone on like that for hours, but Patty didn't have the time. She told Jeremy that Greg and several of the others of the old crowd had called her telling her of Jeremy's suspicions.

Jeremy told her, "They aren't my suspicions. I was just telling them what Nathan thought."

"I don't know what to think, but I do know that he's crazy now, almost as if he'd been attacked by an evil spirit."

Jeremy shook his head. "I don't think so. What I'm trying to do is just forget about it."

"How can you?"

"That's what you do, you know, you screw around, stab each other in the back, but then you get drunk together and forget about it. I don't have the time to be worrying about what something means, or what something's supposed to mean."

"Forget, forget what he did?"

"What did he do?"

"I don't believe this! You're the one that started it and now you've changed your mind?"

"No, I'm not the one. It was Nathan. He's always disliked Carl."

"You know what happened as sure as I do. We all knew it but we didn't dare think it, until you brought it up."

"What makes you so sure?"

"I lived there, remember? I've watched him go from this giddy kid to the sickest man I've ever seen. Larry made him sick. Physically. Mentally. Drove him crazy."

Everyone had been in the grip of an uncontrollable passion for Larry.

"But I just don't buy it. Why not just throw him out?"

"Would *you* throw Larry out?"

Jeremy laughed. "Hell, no."

"Neither would I. And I probably slept with him more than anybody. But I'd never let him drive me crazy. He was just fun, that's all. I knew I could never have anything with him, anything permanent."

"Carl didn't seem to mind your sleeping with Larry."

"No, not as long as it was just fooling around, as long as it wasn't serious. But with Joe, I think Carl thought he actually would lose Larry. He just couldn't take it. I suppose you could say jealousy finally won."

My God, Jeremy thought, she was saying she agreed with Nathan, that Joe was the catalyst, the affair that finally pushed Carl over the edge. Now there was no escaping the truth.

When Jeremy returned home, the phone was ringing. It was Joe. Jeremy was

surprised to hear from him, but Joe wasn't interested in a blowjob. He was calling to complain: "That guy with the florist shop. He switched to the pick-up truck. He tailed me all day. Now he's sitting out front. I'm gonna call the cops."

"No, don't. I'll handle it."

"Okay, but be careful. This is gettin' weird."

But what was weird was going to Joe's, not to see Carl in his pick-up but to see Patty getting out of the panel truck and going into the house! How could this be? Jeremy asked himself. He just had lunch with Patty and she never mentioned she was seeing Joe. He took the long way home. He wanted to pass Carl's house, to see if the pick-up was parked in the drive. It was. And he also wanted to think about this latest revelation: Joe with Patty!

TEN

"Just tell me why," Jeremy demanded. He shifted his weight and started playing with the gold chain around his neck that Nathan had given him on their second anniversary.

"I don't know," Joe said. "I always considered myself straight. You know that."

He stared at this stranger sitting across the table from him, whom he thought he'd once known, as his whole world was crumbling. "Joe." His tone of voice said he meant business.

"Listen. I never lied to you."

Jeremy's heart raced. He wished he hadn't come here again.

God only knew who would be driving up next.

Joe shrugged. "Look kid, I know you're not going to like this, but something has happened to me. This business with Carl following me around. Well, I went to the florist shop and there she was again, that girl who lived with Carl and Larry. And...."

"Oh, come on."

Joe smiled, but somehow Jeremy failed to see the humor of the situation. The irony however wasn't lost on him. Things had come full circle in more ways than one.

Joe drained his can of beer and then went on. "Don't you see Jeremy, it works both ways. I'd forgotten what a woman was like. After my divorce, I'd sworn off. Now everything felt new, like I was being born all over again. I forgot what it felt like to be held by a woman, to...."

"Oh, spare me." Jeremy leaned back and crossed his arms. He couldn't stand seeing him look so...so goddamn dreamy about it.

"Kid, I know you're upset, but I wish you would try to understand. I'm not like you. I wasn't satisfied with a guy's this and guy's that and half the world hating me because of it and not even being able to walk down the street holding your hand."

"You wanted to hold my hand?"

"I'd like to...maybe. But I can't."

That was the last straw. Jeremy didn't give a shit what people thought, unless he was in some dangerous situation like walking by a bunch of Skinheads or Neo-Nazis or something, which wasn't too likely in this town. Joe, on the other hand, hated even the thought of people staring at him. "So, you walk around holding this girl's hand." Jeremy didn't wait for his acknowledgement. "And you kiss her hello when you meet her downtown and you put your arm around her at the movies and you're going to marry her and share health insurance and tax breaks and you expect me to be happy for you?" He unfolded his arms and leaned forward.

Joe swallowed hard, crushed his beer can with his hand. "To tell you the truth, it's a big relief."

"Excuse me, I'm about to be sick," Jeremy mumbled, and headed for the bathroom. But it was a false alarm, he just wanted to get away from Joe. His head was beginning to ache, so he stayed in the bathroom for a while, washing out his mouth and trying to get it together. If there had been a back door he would have exited then and there, but unfortunately this wasn't the movies. This was his life. Slowly, and against his better judgment, he made his way back to the kitchen, where Joe sat drinking another beer.

"Are you okay?"

"Better now. I did get sick though."

"Poor baby." He almost reached for Jeremy's hand. Out of habit, Jeremy supposed.

"I got sick this morning, too. Didn't go to work."

Now Jeremy, inexplicably, was touched. He was no longer thinking of his own discontent, he was moved by Joe's obvious discomfort. "Don't worry. I'll take care of Carl. You just take care of Patty. Be kind to her. I think she's a nice girl." He squeezed Joe's shoulder as he walked past him, out into the warm, still night.

He thought about going home, but Nathan was teaching a class and attending a discussion group afterward. He decided to stop at the bar for a drink.

It was a slow night and Marco was working the front bar. "Just the cocktail hour," he said. "I'm off at eight. Maybe we could go to a movie or something?" Marco didn't wait for an answer; he seemed to be floating down the bar to attend to an old gentleman who had been drinking all afternoon. Maybe he didn't need an answer, Jeremy decided. Maybe it was a statement of fact, that Jeremy was leaving with him at eight o'clock.

Jeremy wasn't interested in seeing a movie. He wanted to have sex. Marco suggested they stop for dinner. He knew a good pizza place on the way to his apartment.

As they walked into the pizza place, Jeremy started to take Marco's hand. He was thinking about Joe and Patty, holding hands. But he only caressed Marco's hand. Marco smiled.

Jeremy's heart was beating as he sat across from Marco. He knew he'd never

wanted anybody the way he wanted Marco right that second, frankly, and he didn't care if the whole town knew. But he knew better than to make Marco uneasy with a public display of affection.

"Do you mind if I have some wine?" Jeremy asked.

"No, not at all. Just don't make me drink any."

"I don't think anyone could *make* you do anything."

"I don't know about that. I don't mind being forced every once in a while."

Jeremy was tempted to ask if Kurt forced him, but then decided Kurt would never have to force himself on anyone. Jeremy couldn't help it; Marco would forever be linked with Kurt in his mind. It was true he was looking at Marco in an entirely new light now, after Kurt.

Marco said he was having trouble with his lock and Jeremy, giddy from the wine, laughed, thinking he said "cock." Marco laughed himself as he toyed with his front door for what seemed like forever 'til it finally gave way and they stumbled inside. Or rather Jeremy stumbled. He didn't think Marco ever stumbled a day in his life, at least now that he was clean and sober.

Before Jeremy knew it, there he was, flat on his back on the sofa with Marco up above him, unbuttoning his shirt and sliding his jeans down. Marco started kissing Jeremy and Jeremy's whole body began to shake. His instincts told him just to lie back and enjoy this. Just thinking about Kurt and Marco together got him even more excited, and before he knew what was happening, his cock was exploding and he was gasping and moaning.

It didn't seem to upset Marco; he laughed and came up to kiss Jeremy. Jeremy smelled himself on his face and tasted himself on his lips, and that just got him going all over again.

Marco slid his fingers into Jeremy's ass, slow and easy, never taking his eyes away from Jeremy for a second. Then he started licking Jeremy clean, all over.

- - -

Nathan's voice floated in from the kitchen. "Breakfast, Jeremy. Come and get it."

"I'm coming." But still Jeremy didn't move himself off the bed, though he did shift onto his side and shut his eyes. "Just give me five minutes," he mumbled, as if five minutes could make his ass feel any better. He began rubbing the crease between his eyebrows, where his headache always started. Maybe he could ignore the whole thing. "Just pretend it never happened."

But it did. Jeremy walked in quietly, as usual, and joined Nathan at the kitchen table where Nathan was eating bagels and doing the *New York Times* crossword puzzle in pen, left over from Sunday. As Jeremy, naked, was slathering butter a bagel, Nathan looked up and asked, "Have a nice time?"

Jeremy nodded and his lover studied him. "You look beautiful after you've been fucked. I mean, you always look beautiful, but you have a special glow about you today. I don't know what it is."

Nathan never knew what it was, but he loved it after Jeremy had been out 'til

late and came home, his ass hurting.

But Jeremy knew what it was all right. He tried not to blush, but as the brand new memory of Marco's big dick inside his ass washed over him, he turned as red as the strawberry jelly he was now smoothing onto his bagel.

Jeremy ate the rest of his breakfast in blissful silence. Nathan got up, cleared the table, then wiped his hands on a dish towel dotted with miniature seagulls. "You okay?"

Jeremy lowered his eyes, then lifted 'em again. He nodded, and finished his coffee.

Nathan gave his nipples a tweak. "Hey!"

"Hey yourself." Nathan kissed the back of Jeremy's neck. "C'mon gorgeous. Give me the daily special."

"I need a hug first." Jeremy turned around and leaned against Nathan.

Nathan let himself be held for a long, peaceful moment and then sighed "You okay, baby?" he asked, stroking his hair.

"Yeah, I guess so." He pulled back just enough to unbutton Nathan's shorts and release his cock, which was swelling with anticipation. Morning sex was a ritual Jeremy could live with, endure, sometimes even enjoy. Occasionally Nathan would ask about where he'd been, what he'd done, but mostly he didn't. He probably fantasized about it, Jeremy reasoned, and to know the truth would destroy the fantasy.

Jeremy knew how much Nathan loved his blowjobs, but Jeremy took forever on his balls. He kneaded them, kissed them, licked at them, rubbed them together, pushed them. He knew Nathan's cock was begging to be touched, but he refused. Instead, he yanked Nathan's shorts all the way down and snaked his tongue down his body, licking the insides of Nathan's thighs, and stopped just inches away from the cock. He wouldn't allow Nathan to touch it either. Instead, he went back to sucking his balls.

Soon Nathan could stand it no longer and his cock was spurting cum without anyone touching it. Jeremy now brought his mouth to it, taking the load as it gushed from the head, and kissing the cock head when Nathan was finished.

"Oh, baby," Nathan said, running his fingers through Jeremy's hair. "Come on. I have something to show you."

Jeremy followed Nathan into the garage, which had been sealed off and was now Nathan's studio. He rarely went into the studio, which was always filled with a mishmash of completed paintings, works in progress, seashells, glue, paintbrushes and a photograph of him, taken after they first met, in a silver frame, on one wall. Jeremy was always moved by the prominence of his picture, but in his penchant for orderliness, he could never figure out how Nathan ever turned out anything from the mess of materials that were cluttered on the tables and floor.

Nathan had created a new picture, which he had titled, "Jeremy in the Morning." Nathan told Jeremy that sleeping with him and feeling his smooth,

warm body pressed against his was one of the joys he had with the boy, especially when, as they just had, they incorporated some sex into their morning coffee routine.

Jeremy admired the picture very much. So much in fact, that tears came to his eyes. He was tired, aching from Marco's assault, and he had just swallowed Nathan's load, so he had to admit his defenses were down, but to begin sobbing like a baby after a painting was a real stretch. Still, he was moved. Nathan had never painted his portrait before.

"So, you like it, eh?"

Jeremy nodded.

Nathan saw the look in Jeremy's eyes and smiled at him with a mischievous grin, lightly running his fingernails up and down his back. Jeremy could feel the heat rising between them. Nathan played Jeremy like an instrument, knowing just when to rub hard and when to pull back and gently caress. Nathan came up behind Jeremy and hugged him tightly. His hands reached for Jeremy's cock, which had started to swell. He planted delicate kisses on his neck while he began to finger him. Jeremy groaned, then reached behind and grabbed his ass cheeks, pulling him close to his body.

Nathan led Jeremy to the bed. He made him lie face down. He told Jeremy he was going to give him a massage. He started at his neck, rubbing gently, feeling his smooth skin move beneath his fingers. Gradually he worked his way down his spine, kneading the soft flesh around his shoulders. Every now and again he would bend down and trace the curve of Jeremy's spine with his tongue, burying deep in the indentation just above his ass. When he reached his ass, Nathan spent a long time kneading the firm, creamy cheeks. Then he leaned down and gently tongued the cleavage between them. Jeremy moaned and lifted his hips to meet Nathan's mouth. He licked and sucked at the ripe hole, then pushed his tongue inside. By now, Jeremy's cock was throbbing with a will of its own. As Nathan entered Jeremy, Jeremy came, soaking the sheet below him.

Nathan uttered a low growl and rolled Jeremy over. He moved his head back and forth, his chin and cheeks sliding in the wetness of his cum. Occasionally he would nibble and suck Jeremy's cock, at first gently, then with increasing force. His fingers wound tightly, almost painfully, around the cock and then he began licking at it with long, firm strokes that traveled from the opening of his ass to the tip of the prick. Finally his mouth released him and he rose to his hands and knees and moved up the bed to take him in his arms.

"I love you, Jeremy. I really do," Nathan said, and all Jeremy could do was whimper.

ELEVEN

Jeremy tried to distract himself by switching on the television, but he couldn't concentrate on anything. He decided to water the dying pot-plants. That took some time. Then he sat down and started to cry. He knew what he had to do; he just had to summon the courage to do it.

It had begun to drizzle as Jeremy made his way south on the Interstate. Traffic was heavy and he didn't get to Carl's house until nearly six.

Carl did not act surprised to see Jeremy. It was as if he had been expecting him.

Seeing Carl now shattered Jeremy. Carl had the look of someone who wanted to die. It wasn't desperate. It wasn't hopeless. It was just vacant. There was no memory behind it.

"Have a drink?" Carl asked. He had a nearly empty glass in his hand.

"No, thanks."

"Mind if I do?"

"Not at all."

Jeremy wondered how much he had had to drink while he was waiting for Jeremy to appear.

"I just don't understand you," Jeremy said.

"What do you believe in, Jeremy?" Carl asked.

"Nothing," Jeremy answered.

"People usually believe in something. Nature abhors a vacuum."

"I guess I believe in what Larry believed in: having a good time."

"Larry believed in himself. Getting on, going far, fucking everything in sight."

"Okay. But what's wrong with that? Why did he have to *die*?"

Carl's dark eyes widened. Then without a word he clawed his way to his feet and bolted to the bathroom, where he vomited.

When he staggered back to the living room Jeremy had a tall glass of cold water waiting for him.

"Thanks," he said. He was becoming steadily nicer as the effects of the alcohol waned.

"There's a rumor going around." Carl began to shudder. "And they tell me you started it."

"I don't know about any rumor, but I've always wondered how Larry could justC"

Carl snapped. "Look, you sonofabitch, if there was any way I could have saved him, I would have. It was just a freak accident. The police believed me. Why the hell won't you?" He groped for a cigarette but his hand was shaking so badly that he had trouble manipulating the lighter.

Jeremy began to feel increasingly uncomfortable. He wiped the sweat from his forehead.

Between puffs, Carl went on. "I don't know what happened to me. I thought I could take it, his fucking around. But I found I couldn't blot him out, I was too deeply connected to him, and I just couldn't get him out of my mind."

"So it was easier once he was dead?"

"No, harder. I began to feel as if his memory had become a corpse that was strapped to my back."

"But at least there was no more being tormented by jealousy."

"Oh, I've never been jealous. Not really. He had made me a part of it, you see."

"But what about Joe?"

"My God, you know about everything."

"No, not everything. But I guess I was a part of everything. Somehow. Now I'm part of nothing. There's nothing now, is there?"

Carl finished his glass of water. "No, nothing."

When confronted, Carl admitted that he had followed Joe, on several occasions. "There is a crazy excitement following someone in a car. With every turn in the road, wondering where they are going, guessing what they are thinking, imagining the place and the person they are on their way to," Carl said.

Jeremy could see now that Larry had driven him to the end of his tether. Carl had suffered a reaction from all these huge emotional dramas and decided he hated everyone, including himself. "Where sex is concerned, everyone's capable of anything," Nathan had said.

Finally, Carl sighed, put out his cigarette, and said, "It's a relief to talk to someone, actually. It's been bothering me for some time. But I never thought it would be you who would come here."

Jeremy shrugged, moved to the edge of his chair. He wanted to leave, yet he didn't. "Why *not* me?"

"Yes, I guess it *had* to be you," Carl snarled. "The boy-whore. The slut. The hustler."

Jeremy looked at his watch. "It's late. I think I should go and you should go to bed."

"Will you help me upstairs, boy-whore?"

Jeremy nodded. What was he doing? This was so perverse it was wild.

Jeremy followed Carl upstairs. He climbed the stairs slowly, dreading what he was about to do.

The bed was unmade. The crumpled sheets, the cover half-fallen on the floor, the dented pillows, and a pair of soiled white briefs at the foot of the bed, all gave the impression of the aftermath of sex.

Jeremy helped Carl to the bed. Carl hugged the boy to him. They stayed like that for several minutes. Carl's hands gave him away. Jeremy knew what Carl wanted. As Carl unzipped Jeremy's pants, Jeremy felt as if he was just a second act.

"You entertained someone last night?"

"Yeah, one of those guys who advertises a lot. He left his shorts for me." Carl picked up the soiled underpants. "Nice eh?"

"Was it nice, that is?"

"Not as nice as this," Carl said, taking Jeremy's semi-flaccid dick in his hand.

When Jeremy's cock entered Carl's mouth, they became, for a moment, what

they had been in the beginning, client and customer. "It's been so long," Carl said, slipping the cock from his mouth and holding it. "It's a beautiful cock," he said, and then slid it back in. He worked on it for several minutes, and finally Jeremy came.

Carl looked up at Jeremy. Carl's eyes were soft and wet and blue. He rubbed the messy cock all over his lips, his cheeks. "I want to tell you something," he said.

"Yeah?"

"I did kill Larry. Oh, not in the way you think. You see, I could have saved him. I really think I could have, but I didn't. I just sat there. I couldn't move. I just watched him. I'll never be able to forgive myself. I want you to know that now. You were right about everything. But can you forgive me?"

Everything slowed down. Jeremy backed away, leaned against the closet door. There was a pounding in his head, but slow, like another of his famous headaches coming on. When he blinked, his eyes seemed to close for several seconds at a time.

Carl leaned back on the bed and motioned to Jeremy to step toward the bed. Jeremy obeyed. Carl handed Jeremy the pillow. Carl said he was ready for it. And Jeremy, without knowing it, was also prepared.

"Help me to do it. Please," Carl begged.

As if guided by a force beyond himself, Jeremy took the pillow and moved over the man. Carl didn't struggle. There was no gasping or twitching. He just fell asleep. Jeremy had never felt such power, such control.

When Jeremy lifted the pillow from Carl's face he had no conscious idea whether Carl was dead or not. Carl's eyes were closed; there was no nightmare expression on his face. Jeremy's cum had dried on Carl's lips, on his cheek. It was as if Carl had simply fallen into a deep sleep.

In the car, Jeremy turned the radio off and drove home in silence. He began to rationalize to himself what had just happened. Carl hadn't murdered Larry exactly. And he hadn't murdered Carl. Maybe it was revenge on both their parts. These were certainly crimes of passion. Carl had let Larry perish. Now he himself was dead. Justice had been served. Life could begin again.

"What happened?" Nathan asked as Jeremy entered the house. Nathan was finishing a painting in his studio. "Did you find him?"

"Yes," Jeremy answered, collapsing in the old armchair beside Nathan's easel.

"And...?"

"And it's over," Jeremy said. "Nothing like that'll ever happen again."

"I'm glad," Nathan said, stepping back to admire his painting of a sailboat, ripped from its dock by hurricane-force winds. He had already titled it: "Lost at Sea".

EPILOGUE

Sergeant Scott walked into the interrogation room and skewered Charlie with

a look. His eyes told Charlie, a kid used to dealing with the law, everything: he would not be allowed to leave the room without confessing to something. After a few whispers from a second cop, Scott nodded and reached in his coat pocket for the small crib sheet he carried with him everywhere, just in case. It bore a shorthand version of a criminal suspect's constitutional rights, to be read before any formal questioning.

Charlie had the right to say nothing more until he had an attorney present. Further, if he waived that right, anything he said could be used against him in court. Those were the rules, and that's what Scott recited from his card. Still, the pale, thin youth who sat before them agreed to talk, attorney or not. He had nothing to hide. The police had already told him that they had found Charlie's ad at the scene of Carl's suffocation, with some scribbled notes in the margins of the gay magazine on the nightstand.

Granted, Charlie said he had been called by Carl around noon. He had agreed to visit him, to give him a massage. When he left the house at four, Carl was very much alive. In fact, he was fixing himself a drink.

"A massage?" Scott asked, skeptical as always.

"Yes."

"Do you give a massage in the nude?"

"Sometimes."

"Do you have an orgasm all over the client's face? Is that part of the deal?"

"I didn't do that."

"Then how did sperm end up all over the dead man's face?"

"I don't know."

Neither did the police. Tests showed the cum on Carl's face and in his stomach was not Charlie's. Further, Charlie had an alibi. He had stopped at the Showbar after he left Carl's and was there until nearly midnight. There were several witnesses, including the bartender, Marco.

To this day, the investigation into Carl's "mysterious" death remains open.

The Contributors
(Other than the Editor, John Patrick)

"The Joys of Blowjobs"
Ken Anderson

The author's first novel, the sensational *Someone Bought the House on the Island*, is now available from STARbooks Press, as is his collection of poems, *Intense Lover*.

"In Front of Everyone"
Antler

The poet lives in Milwaukee when not traveling to perform his poems or wildernessing. His epic poem *Factory* was published by City Lights. His collection of poems *Last Words* was published by Ballantine. Winner of the Whitman Award from the Walt Whitman Society of Camden, New Jersey, and the Witter Bynner prize from the Academy and Institute of Arts & Letters in New York, his poetry has appeared in many periodicals (including *Utne Reader, Whole Earth Review* and *American Poetry Review)* and anthologies (including *Gay Roots, Erotic by Nature,* and *Gay and Lesbian Poetry of Our Time).*

"Hot Reunion"
Kevin Bantan

The author lives in Ohio, where he is working on several new stories for STARbooks.

"Fantasyland"
David Patrick Beavers

A favorite of readers of our anthologies, the author's novel *Thresholds* was published last year to critical acclaim. He lives in L.A. and travels frequently.

"Nature Boy"
Frank Brooks

The author is a regular contributor to gay magazines. In addition to writing, his interests include figure drawing from the live model and mountain hiking.

"The Watcher on the Shore"
Peter Burton

The distinguished London-based author has just completed his exhaustive, long-awaited study of Somerset Maugham and he is currently working on a book about scandal.

"Secret Lusting"
Leo Cardini

The celebrated author of the best-selling *Mineshaft Nights*, Leo's short stories and theatre-related articles have appeared in numerous magazines. An enthusiastic nudist, he reports that, "A hundred and fifty thousand people have seen me naked, but I only had sex with half of them."

Edited by John Patrick

"Cherry No More"
Jason Carpenter
This Texas-based author is frequently published by gay erotic magazines under many aliases.

"Drilling Crew"
Corbin Chezner
A frequent contributor to gay erotic magazines under different pen names, the author lives in Tulsa, Oklahoma, but is a native of South Texas. Although he has a master's degree himself, he prefers blue-collar men for his fiction tales. Extensive "research" has taught him that "working-class men are simply sexier than academic typesCno doubt about it!"

"The Erection Crew"
Peter Eros
The author has contributed many tales to STARbooks Press.

"When in Rome..."
Peter Gilbert
"Semi-retired" after a long career with the British Armed Forces, the author now lives in Germany but is contemplating a return to England. A frequent contributor to various periodicals, he also writes for television. He enjoys walking, photography and reading. His stories have swiftly become favorites by readers of STARbooks' anthologies.

"Sussex College" and "Only Some Are Dangerous"
"The Orgy" and "Good Time Charlie"
James Hosier
The youthful author lives in a little town that is "definitely not sleepy." He says he is straight but admits that he lets guys do what they want: "I need the money and I happen to have a good body (thanks to the swimming club). Provided they're prepared to pay, I let them go ahead." Stay tuned.

"Lust Behind Glass"
Thomas C. Humphrey
The author, who resides in Florida, is working on his first novel, All the Difference, and has contributed stories to First Hand publications.
"My Antonio", "After the Party" and "A Wanton Craving" Rick Jackson, USMC
The oft-published author specializes in jarhead stories. When not traveling, he is based in Hawaii.

"Greenhorn"
David Laurents
More of David's stories appear in STARbooks's *Smooth 'N' Sassy*, *Juniors*, and *In the Boy Zone*. He keeps a high profile in Manhattan.

"The Little Devil"
James Lincoln
The author is new to the erotica scene. He has a number of supernatural tales slated for publication by various magazines and anthologies. Originally from New York, he says he currently resides in the deep south, "against my better judgment." More of his stories will appear in future STARbooks anthologies.

"Street Tough's Ball"
Bert McKenzie
Bert's earlier works for STARbooks appeared in *Secret Passions*, *In the Boy Zone*, *Barely Legal*, and *Mad About the Boys*.

"Different Strokes" and "The Anniversary Party"
Daniel Miller
The author, who lives in Massachusetts, is a frequent contributor to gay publications. His stories appear in STARbooks's *Intimate Strangers* and *Come Again*, among others.

"The Best Kind of Cock"
Jack Ricardo
The author, who lives in Florida, is a novelist and frequent contributor to various gay magazines. His latest novel is *Last Dance at Studio 54*.

"A Gardener's Hands"
Peter Rice
The author is a frequent contributor to STARbooks's anthologies, including *Naughty By Nature*, among others. He lives in England.

"The Big Bouncer" and "In the Mix"
Dan Veen
The popular New Orleans-based author's stories for STARbooks have appeared in, among others, *Intimate Strangers*, *Naughty By Nature*. He is working on a major work about sex during Mardi Gras.

"A Cheap Thrill"
Austin Wallace
The author is a 17 year veteran of the book business having worked at Lambda Rising, Obelisk, White Rabbit, Simply Books, SFMOMA and others.

Edited by John Patrick

He currently resides in San Francisco where he works at Chronicle Books and continues to mine the city for more stories

"I'll Do Anything"
James Wilton
James has had several stories appear in STARbooks's anthologies, including *In the Boy Zone* and *Beautiful Boys*. He resides in Connecticut.

ABOUT THE EDITOR

JOHN PATRICK was a prolific, prize winning author of fiction and non fiction. One of his short stories, "The Well," was honored by PEN American Center as one of the best of 1987. His novels and anthologies, as well as his non fiction works, including Legends and The Best of the Superstars series, continue to gain him new fans every day. One of his most famous short stories appears in the Badboy collection Southern Comfort and another appears in the collection The Mammoth Book of Gay Short Stories.

A divorced father of two, the author was a longtime member of the American Booksellers Association, the Publishing Triangle, the Florida Publishers' Association, American Civil Liberties Union, and the Adult Video Association. He lived in Florida, where he passed away on October 31, 2001.